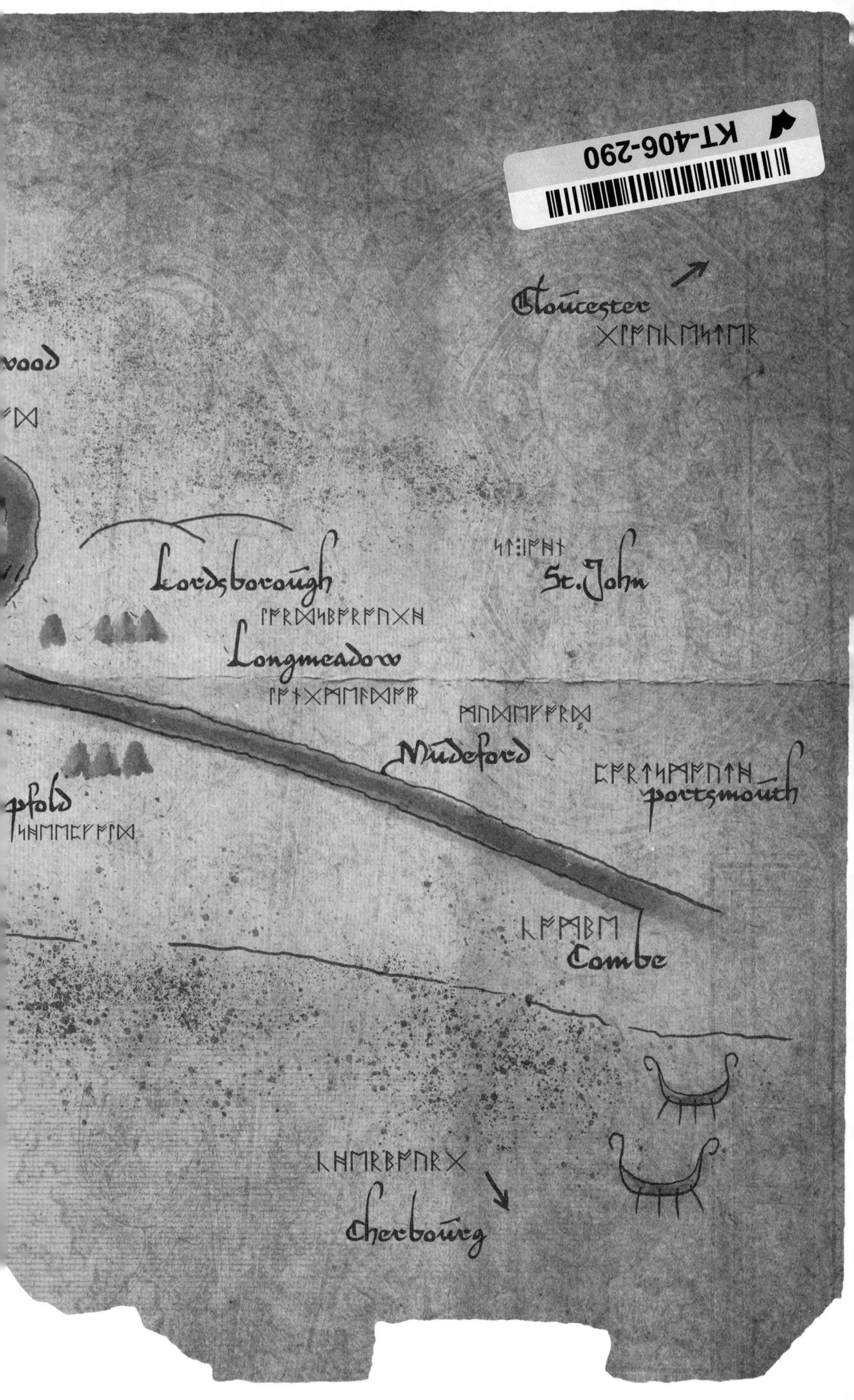

Gloucester
Lordsborough
St. John
Longmeadow
Mudeford
portsmouth
Combe
Cherbourg

THE
EVENING
AND THE
MORNING

KEN FOLLETT

THE EVENING AND THE MORNING

THE PREQUEL TO THE PILLARS OF THE EARTH

MACMILLAN

First published 2020 by Macmillan
an imprint of Pan Macmillan
The Smithson, 6 Briset Street, London ECIM 5NR
Associated companies throughout the world
www.panmacmillan.com

ISBN 978-1-4472-7878-8

1 3 5 7 9 8 6 4 2

A CIP catalogue record for this book is available from the British Library.

Map artwork by Daren Cook

Typeset in Celestia Antiqua by Palimpsest Book Production Ltd, Falkirk, Stirlingshire
Printed and bound by CPI Group (UK) Ltd, Croydon, CRO 4YY

Visit **www.panmacmillan.com** to read more about all our books
and to buy them. You will also find features, author interviews and
news of any author events, and you can sign up for e-newsletters
so that you're always first to hear about our new releases.

In memoriam,
E. F.

When the Roman Empire declined, Britain went backwards. As the Roman villas crumbled, the people built one-room wooden dwellings without chimneys. The technology of Roman pottery – important for storing food – was mostly lost. Literacy declined.

This period is sometimes called the Dark Ages, and progress was painfully slow for five hundred years.

Then, at last, things started to change . . .

PART ONE

THE WEDDING

997 CE

1

IT WAS HARD TO stay awake all night, Edgar found, even on the most important night of your life.

He had spread his cloak over the reeds on the floor and now he lay on it, dressed in the knee-length brown wool tunic that was all he wore in summer, day and night. In winter he would wrap the cloak around him and lie near the fire. But now the weather was warm: Midsummer Day was a week away.

Edgar always knew dates. Most people had to ask priests, who kept calendars. Edgar's elder brother Erman had once said to him: 'How come you know when Easter is?' and he had replied: 'Because it's the first Sunday after the first full moon after the twenty-first day of March, obviously.' It had been a mistake to add 'obviously', because Erman had punched him in the stomach for being sarcastic. That had been years ago, when Edgar was small. He was grown, now. He would be eighteen three days after Midsummer. His brothers no longer punched him.

He shook his head. Random thoughts sent him drifting off. He tried to make himself uncomfortable, lying on his fist to stay awake.

He wondered how much longer he had to wait.

He turned his head and looked around by firelight. His home was like almost every other house in the town of Combe: oak plank walls, a thatched roof, and an earth floor partly covered with reeds from the banks of the nearby river. It had no windows. In the middle of the single room was a square of stones surrounding the hearth. Over

3

the fire stood an iron tripod from which cooking pots could be hung, and its legs made spidery shadows on the underside of the roof. All around the walls were wooden pegs on which were hung clothes, cooking utensils and boat-building tools.

Edgar was not sure how much of the night had passed, because he might have dozed off, perhaps more than once. Earlier, he had listened to the sounds of the town settling for the night: a couple of drunks singing an obscene ditty, the bitter accusations of a marital quarrel in a neighbouring house, a door slamming and a dog barking and, somewhere nearby, a woman sobbing. But now there was nothing but the soft lullaby of waves on a sheltered beach. He stared in the direction of the door, looking for tell-tale lines of light around its edges, and saw only darkness. That meant either that the moon had set, so the night was well advanced, or that the sky was cloudy, which would tell him nothing.

The rest of his family lay around the room, close to the walls where there was less smoke. Pa and Ma were back to back. Sometimes they would wake in the middle of the night and embrace, whispering and moving together, until they fell back, panting; but they were fast asleep now, Pa snoring. Erman, the eldest brother at twenty, lay near Edgar, and Eadbald, the middle one, was in the corner. Edgar could hear their steady, untroubled breathing.

At last, the church bell struck.

There was a monastery on the far side of the town. The monks had a way of measuring the hours of the night: they made big graduated candles that told the time as they burned down. One hour before dawn they would ring the bell, then get up to chant their service of Matins.

Edgar lay still a little longer. The bell might have disturbed Ma, who woke easily. He gave her time to sink back into deep slumber. Then, at last, he got to his feet.

Silently he picked up his cloak, his shoes and his belt with its sheathed dagger attached. On bare feet he crossed the room, avoiding the furniture: a table, two stools and a bench. The door opened silently: Edgar had greased the wooden hinges yesterday with a generous smear of sheep's tallow.

If one of his family woke now, and spoke to him, he would say he was going outside to piss, and hope they did not spot that he was carrying his shoes.

Eadbald grunted. Edgar froze. Had Eadbald woken up, or just made a noise in his sleep? Edgar could not tell. But Eadbald was the passive one, always keen to avoid a fuss, like Pa. He would not make trouble.

Edgar stepped out and closed the door behind him carefully.

The moon had set, but the sky was clear and the beach was starlit. Between the house and the high-tide mark was a boatyard. Pa was a boatbuilder, and his three sons worked with him. Pa was a good craftsman and a poor businessman, so Ma made all the money decisions, especially the difficult calculation of what price to ask for something as complicated as a boat or ship. If a customer tried to bargain down the price, Pa would be willing to give in, but Ma would make him stand firm.

Edgar glanced at the yard as he laced his shoes and buckled his belt. There was only one vessel under construction, a small boat for rowing upriver. Beside it stood a large and valuable stockpile of timber, the trunks split into halves and quarters, ready to be shaped into the parts of a boat. About once a month, the whole family went into the forest and felled a mature oak tree. Pa and Edgar would begin, alternately swinging long-handled axes, cutting a precise wedge out of the trunk. Then they would rest while Erman and Eadbald took over. When the tree came down, they would trim it then float the wood downriver to Combe. They had to pay, of course: the forest belonged to Wigelm, the thane to whom most people in Combe paid their rent, and he demanded twelve silver pennies for each tree.

5

As well as the timber pile, the yard contained a barrel of tar, a coil of rope and a whetstone. All were guarded by a chained-up mastiff called Grendel, black with a grey muzzle, too old to do much harm to thieves but still able to bark an alarm. Grendel was quiet now, watching Edgar incuriously with his head resting on his front paws. Edgar knelt down and stroked his head. 'Goodbye, old dog,' he murmured, and Grendel wagged his tail without getting up.

Also in the yard was one finished vessel, and Edgar thought of it as his own. He had built it himself to an original design, based on a Viking ship. Edgar had never actually seen a Viking – they had not raided Combe in his lifetime – but two years ago a wreck had washed up on the beach, empty and fire-blackened, its dragon figurehead half smashed, presumably after some battle. Edgar had been awestruck by its mutilated beauty: the graceful curves, the long serpentine prow and the slender hull. He had been most impressed by the large out-jutting keel that ran the length of the ship, which – he had realized after some thought – gave the stability that allowed the Vikings to cross the seas. Edgar's boat was a lesser version, with two oars and a small, square sail.

Edgar knew he had a talent. He was already a better boatbuilder than his elder brothers, and before long he would overtake Pa. He had an intuitive sense of how forms fitted together to make a stable structure. Years ago he had overheard Pa say to Ma: 'Erman learns slowly and Eadbald learns fast, but Edgar seems to understand before the words are out of my mouth.' It was true. Some men could pick up a musical instrument they had never played, a pipe or a lyre, and get a tune out of it after a few minutes. Edgar had such instincts about boats, and houses too. He would say: 'That boat will list to starboard,' or: 'That roof will leak,' and he was always right.

Now he untied his boat and pushed it down the beach. The sound of the hull scraping on the sand was muffled by the shushing of the waves breaking on the shore.

He was startled by a girlish giggle. In the starlight he saw a naked woman lying on the sand, and a man on top of her. Edgar probably knew them, but their faces were not clearly visible and he looked away quickly, not wanting to recognize them. He had surprised them in an illicit tryst, he guessed. The woman seemed young and perhaps the man was married. The clergy preached against such affairs, but people did not always follow the rules. Edgar ignored the couple and pushed his boat into the water.

He glanced back at the house, feeling a pang of regret, wondering whether he would ever see it again. It was the only home he could remember. He knew, because he had been told, that he had been born in another town, Exeter, where his father had worked for a master boatbuilder; then the family had moved, while Edgar was still a baby, and had set up home in Combe, where Pa had started his own enterprise with one order for a rowboat; but Edgar could not remember any of that. This was the only home he knew, and he was leaving it for good.

He was lucky to have found employment elsewhere. Business had slowed since the renewal of Viking attacks on the south of England when Edgar was nine years old. Trading and fishing were dangerous while the marauders were near. Only the brave bought boats.

There were three ships in the harbour now, he saw by starlight: two herring fishers and a Frankish merchant ship. Dragged up on the beach were a handful of smaller craft, river and coastal vessels. He had helped to build one of the fishers. But he could remember a time when there had always been a dozen or more ships in port.

He felt a fresh breeze from the south-west, the prevailing wind here. His boat had a sail – small, because they were so costly: a full-size sail for a seagoing ship would take one woman four years to make. But it was hardly worthwhile unfurling it for the short trip across the bay. He began to row, something that hardly taxed him. Edgar was heavily muscled, like a blacksmith. His father and brothers were the same. All day, six days a week, they worked with axe, adze and auger, shaping the oak strakes that formed the hulls of boats. It was hard work and it made strong men.

His heart lifted. He had got away. And he was going to meet the woman he loved. The stars were brilliant; the beach glowed white; and, when his oars broke the surface of the water, the curling foam was like the fall of her hair on her shoulders.

Her name was Sungifu, which was usually shortened to Sunni, and she was exceptional in every way.

He could see the premises along the seafront, most of them workplaces of fishermen and traders: the forge of a tinsmith who made rustproof items for ships; the long yard in which a roper wove his lines; and the huge kiln of a tar maker who roasted pine logs to produce the sticky liquid with which boatbuilders waterproofed their vessels. The town always looked bigger from the water: it was home to several hundred people, most making their living, directly or indirectly, from the sea.

He looked across the bay to his destination. In the darkness he would not have been able to see Sunni even if she had been there, which he knew she was not, since they had arranged to meet at dawn. But he could not help staring at the place where she soon would be.

Sunni was twenty-one, older than Edgar by more than three years. She had caught his attention one day when he was sitting on the beach staring at the Viking wreck. He knew her by sight, of course – he knew everyone living in the small town – but he had not particularly noticed her before, and did not recall anything about her family. 'Were you washed up with the wreck?' she had said. 'You were sitting so still, I thought you were driftwood.' She had to be imaginative, he saw right away, to say something like that off the top of her head; and he had explained what fascinated him about the lines of the vessel, feeling that she would understand. They had talked for an hour and he had fallen in love.

Then she told him she was married, but it was already too late.

Her husband, Cyneric, was thirty. She had been fourteen when she married him. He had a small herd of milk cows, and Sunni managed the dairy. She was shrewd, and made plenty of money for her husband. They had no children.

Edgar had quickly learned that Sunni hated Cyneric. Every night, after the evening milking, he went to an alehouse called the Sailors and got drunk. While he was there, Sunni could slip into the woods and meet Edgar.

However, from now on there would be no more hiding. Today they would run away together; or, to be exact, sail away. Edgar had the offer of a job and a house in a fishing village fifty miles along the coast. He had been lucky to find a boatbuilder who was hiring. Edgar had no money – he never had money, Ma said he had no need of it – but his tools were in a locker built into the boat. They would start a new life.

As soon as everyone realized they had gone, Cyneric would consider himself free to marry again. A wife who ran away with another man was, in practice, divorcing herself: the Church might not like it, but that was the custom. Within a few weeks, Sunni said, Cyneric would go into the countryside and find a desperately poor family with a pretty fourteen-year-old daughter. Edgar wondered why the man wanted a wife: he had little interest in sex, according to Sunni. 'He likes to have someone to push around,' she had said. 'My problem was that I grew old enough to despise him.'

Cyneric would not come after them, even if he found out where they were, which was unlikely at least for some time to come. 'And if we're wrong about that, and Cyneric finds us, I'll beat the shit out of him,' Edgar had said. Sunni's expression had told him that she thought this was a foolish boast, and he knew she was right. Hastily, he had added: 'But it probably won't come to that.'

He reached the far side of the bay, then beached the boat and roped it to a boulder.

He could hear the chanting of the monks at their prayers. The monastery was nearby, and the home of Cyneric and Sunni a few hundred yards beyond that.

He sat on the sand, looking out at the dark sea and the night sky, thinking about her. Would she be able to slip away as easily as he had? What if Cyneric woke up and prevented her leaving? There might be a fight; she could be beaten. He was suddenly tempted to change the plan, get up from the beach and go to her house and fetch her.

He repressed the urge with an effort. She was better off on her own. Cyneric would be in a drunken slumber and Sunni would move like a cat. She had planned to go to bed wearing around her neck her only item of jewellery, an intricately carved silver roundel hanging from a leather thong. In her belt pouch she would have a useful needle and thread and the embroidered linen headband she wore on special occasions. Like Edgar, she could be out of the house in a few silent seconds.

Soon she would be here, her eyes glistening with excitement, her supple body eager for his. They would embrace, hugging each other hard, and kiss passionately; then she would step into the boat and he would push it into the water to freedom. He would row a little way out, then kiss her again, he thought. How soon could they make love? She would be as impatient as he. He could row around the point, then drop the roped rock he used as an anchor, and they could lie down in the boat, under the thwarts; it would be a little awkward, but what did that matter? The boat would rock gently on the waves, and they would feel the warmth of the rising sun on their naked skin.

But perhaps they would be wiser to unfurl the sail and put more distance between themselves and the town before they risked a halt.

He wanted to be well away by full day. It would be difficult to resist temptation with her so close, looking at him and smiling happily. But it was more important to secure their future.

When they got to their new home they would say they were already married, they had decided. Until now they had never spent a night in bed. From today they would eat supper together every evening, and lie in each other's arms all night, and smile knowingly at one another in the morning.

He saw a glimmer of light on the horizon. Dawn was about to break. She would be here at any moment.

He felt sad only when he thought about his family. He could happily live without his brothers, who still treated him as a foolish kid and tried to pretend that he had not grown up smarter than both of them. He would miss Pa, who all his life had told him things he would never forget, such as: 'No matter how well you scarf two planks together, the joint is always the weakest part.' And the thought of leaving Ma brought tears to his eyes. She was a strong woman. When things went wrong, she did not waste time bemoaning her fate, but set about putting matters right. Three years ago Pa had fallen sick of a fever and almost died, and Ma had taken charge of the yard – telling the three boys what to do, collecting debts, making sure customers did not cancel orders – until Pa had recovered. She was a leader, and not just of the family. Pa was one of the twelve elders of Combe, but it was Ma who had led the townspeople in protest when Wigelm, the thane, had tried to increase everyone's rents.

The thought of leaving would be unbearable but for the joyous prospect of a future full of Sunni.

In the faint light Edgar saw something odd out on the water. He had good eyesight, and he was used to making out ships at a distance, distinguishing the shape of a hull from that of a high wave or a low cloud, but now he was not sure what he was looking at. He strained to hear any distant sound, but all he picked up was the noise of the waves on the beach right in front of him.

After a few heartbeats he seemed to see the head of a monster, and he suffered a chill of dread. Against the faint glow in the sky he thought he saw pointed ears, great jaws and a long neck.

A moment later he realized he was looking at something even worse than a monster: it was a Viking ship, with a dragon head at the tip of its long curved prow.

Another came into view, then a third, then a fourth. Their sails were taut with the quickening south-westerly breeze, and the light vessels were moving fast through the waves. Edgar sprang to his feet.

The Vikings were thieves, rapists and murderers. They attacked along the coast and up rivers. They set fire to towns, stole everything they could carry, and murdered everyone except young men and women, whom they captured to sell as slaves.

Edgar hesitated a moment longer.

He could see ten ships now. That meant at least five hundred Vikings.

Were these definitely Viking ships? Other builders had adopted their innovations and copied their designs, as Edgar himself had. But he could tell the difference: there was a coiled menace in the Scandinavian vessels that no imitators had achieved.

Anyway, who else would be approaching in such numbers at dawn? No, there was no doubt.

Hell was coming to Combe.

He had to warn Sunni. If he could get to her in time, they might yet escape.

Guiltily he realized his first thought had been of her, rather than of his family. He must alert them, too. But they were on the far side of the town. He would find Sunni first.

He turned and ran along the beach, peering at the path ahead for half-hidden obstacles. After a minute he stopped and looked out at the bay. He was horrified to see how fast the Vikings had moved. There were already blazing torches approaching swiftly, some reflected in the shifting sea, others evidently being carried across the sand. They were landing already!

But they were silent. He could still hear the monks praying, all oblivious of their fate. He should warn them too. But he could not warn everyone!

Or perhaps he could. Looking at the tower of the monks' church silhouetted against the lightening sky, he saw a way to warn Sunni, his family, the monks and the whole town.

He swerved towards the monastery. A low fence loomed up out of the dark and he leaped over it without slowing his pace. Landing on the far side he stumbled, regained his balance, and ran on.

He came to the church door and glanced back. The monastery was on a slight rise, and he could view the whole town and the bay. Hundreds of Vikings were splashing through the shallows onto the beach and into the town. He saw the crisp, summer-dry straw of a thatched roof burst into flames; then another, and another. He knew all the houses in town and their owners but, in the dim light, he could not figure out which was which, and he wondered grimly whether his own home was alight.

He threw open the church door. The nave was lit by restless candlelight. The monks' chant became ragged as some of them saw him running to the base of the tower. He saw the dangling rope, seized it, and pulled down. To his dismay, the bell made no sound.

One of the monks broke away from the group and strode towards him. The shaved top of his head was surrounded by white curls, and Edgar recognized Prior Ulfric. 'Get out of here, you foolish boy,' the prior said indignantly.

Edgar could hardly trouble himself with explanations. 'I have to ring the bell!' he said frantically. 'What's wrong with it?'

The service had broken down and all the monks were now

watching. A second man approached: the kitchener, Maerwynn, a younger man, not as pompous as Ulfric. 'What's going on, Edgar?' he asked.

'The Vikings are here!' Edgar cried. He pulled again at the rope. He had never before tried to ring a church bell, and its weight surprised him.

'Oh, no!' cried Prior Ulfric. His expression changed from censorious to scared. 'God spare us!'

Maerwynn said: 'Are you sure, Edgar?'

'I saw them from the beach!'

Maerwynn ran to the door and looked out. He came back white-faced. 'It's true,' he said.

Ulfric screamed: 'Run, everyone!'

'Wait!' said Maerwynn. 'Edgar, keep pulling the rope. It takes a few tugs to get going. Lift your feet and hang on. Everyone else, we have a few minutes before they get here. Pick something up before you run: first the reliquaries with the remains of the saints, then the jewelled ornaments, and the books – and then run to the woods.'

Holding the rope, Edgar lifted his body off the floor, and a moment later he heard the boom of the great bell sound out.

Ulfric snatched up a silver cross and dashed out, and the other monks began to follow, some calmly collecting precious objects, others yelling and panicking.

The bell began to swing and it rang repeatedly. Edgar pulled the rope frantically, using the weight of his body. He wanted everyone to know right away that this was not merely a summons to sleeping monks but an alarm call to the whole town.

After a minute he felt sure he had done enough. He left the rope dangling and dashed out of the church.

The acrid smell of burning thatch pricked his nostrils: the brisk south-westerly breeze was spreading the flames with dreadful speed. At the same time, daylight was brightening. In the town, people were running out of their houses clutching babies and children and whatever else was precious to them, tools and chickens and leather bags of coins. The fastest were already crossing the fields towards the woods. Some would escape, Edgar thought, thanks to that bell.

He went against the flow, dodging his friends and neighbours, heading for Sunni's house. He saw the baker, who would have been at his oven early; now he was running from his house with a sack of flour on his back. The alehouse called the Sailors was still quiet, its occupants slow to rise even after the alarm. Wyn the jeweller went by on his horse, with a chest strapped to his back; the horse was charging in a panic and he had his arms around its neck, holding on desperately. A slave called Griff was carrying an old woman, his owner. Edgar scanned every face that passed him, just in case Sunni was among them, but he did not see her.

Then he met the Vikings.

The vanguard of the force was a dozen big men and two terrifying-looking women, all in leather jerkins, armed with spears and axes. They were not wearing helmets, Edgar saw, and as fear rose in his throat like vomit he realized they did not need much protection from the feeble townspeople. Some were already carrying booty: a sword with a jewelled hilt, clearly meant for display rather than battle; a money bag; a fur robe; a costly saddle with harness mounts in gilded bronze. One led a white horse that Edgar recognized as belonging to the owner of a herring ship; one had a girl over his shoulder, but Edgar saw gratefully that it was not Sunni.

He backed away, but the Vikings came on, and he could not flee because he had to find Sunni.

A few brave townsmen resisted. Their backs were to Edgar so he could not tell who they were. Some used axes and daggers, one a bow and arrows. For several heartbeats Edgar just stared, paralysed by the sight of sharp blades cutting into human flesh, the sound of wounded men howling like animals in pain, the smell of a town on fire. The only violence he had ever seen consisted of fistfights between aggressive boys or drunk men. This was new: gushing blood and spilling guts and screams of agony and terror. He was frozen with fear.

The traders and fishermen of Combe were no match for these attackers whose livelihood was violence. The locals were cut down in moments, and the Vikings advanced, more coming up behind the leaders.

Edgar recovered his senses and dodged behind a house. He had to get away from the Vikings, but he was not too scared to remember Sunni.

The attackers were moving along the main street, pursuing the townspeople who were fleeing along the same road; but there were no Vikings behind the houses. Each home had about half an acre of land: most people had fruit trees and a vegetable garden, and the wealthier ones a henhouse or a pigsty. Edgar ran from one backyard to the next, making for Sunni's place.

Sunni and Cyneric lived in a house like any other except for the dairy, a lean-to extension built of cob, a mixture of sand, stones, clay and straw, with a roof of thin stone tiles, all meant to keep the place cool. The building stood on the edge of a small field where the cows were pastured.

Edgar reached the house, flung open the door and dashed in.

He saw Cyneric on the floor, a short, heavy man with black hair. The rushes around him were soaked with blood and he lay perfectly still. A gaping wound between his neck and shoulder was no longer bleeding, and Edgar had no doubt he was dead.

Sunni's brown-and-white dog, Brindle, stood in the corner, trembling and panting as dogs do when terrified.

But where was she?

At the back of the house was a doorway that led to the dairy. The door stood open, and as Edgar moved towards it he heard Sunni cry out.

He stepped into the dairy. He saw the back of a tall Viking with yellow hair. Some kind of struggle was going on: a bucket of milk had spilt on the stone floor, and the long manger from which the cows fed had been knocked over.

A split-second later Edgar saw that the Viking's opponent was Sunni. Her suntanned face was grim with rage, her mouth wide open showing white teeth, her dark hair flying. The Viking had an axe in one hand but was not using it. With the other hand he was trying to wrestle Sunni to the ground while she lashed out at him with a big kitchen knife. Clearly he wanted to capture her rather than kill her, for a healthy young woman made a high-value slave.

Neither of them saw Edgar.

Before Edgar could move, Sunni caught the Viking across the face with a slash of her knife, and he roared with pain as blood spurted from his gashed cheek. Infuriated, he dropped the axe, grabbed her by both shoulders, and threw her to the ground. She fell heavily, and Edgar heard a sickening thud as her head hit the stone step on the threshold. To his horror she seemed to lose consciousness. The Viking dropped to one knee, reached into his jerkin and drew out a length of leather cord, evidently intending to tie her up.

With the slight turn of his head, he spotted Edgar.

His face registered alarm, and he reached for his dropped weapon; but he was too late. Edgar snatched up the axe a moment before the Viking could get his hand on it. It was a weapon very like the tool Edgar used to fell trees. He grasped the shaft, and in the dim back of his mind he noticed that handle and head were beautifully balanced. He stepped back, out of the Viking's reach. The man started to rise.

Edgar swung the axe in a big circle.

He took it back behind him, then lifted it over his head, and finally brought it down, fast and hard and accurately, in a perfect curve. The sharp blade landed precisely on top of the man's head. It sliced through hair, skin and skull, and cut deep, spilling brains.

To Edgar's horror the Viking did not immediately fall dead, but seemed for a moment to be struggling to remain standing; then the life went out of him like the light from a snuffed candle, and he fell to the ground in a bundle of slack limbs.

Edgar dropped the axe and knelt beside Sunni. Her eyes were open and staring. He murmured her name. 'Speak to me,' he said. He took her hand and lifted her arm. It was limp. He kissed her mouth and realized there was no breath. He felt her heart, just beneath the curve of the soft breast he adored. He kept his hand there, hoping desperately to feel a heartbeat; and he sobbed when he realized there was none. She was gone, and her heart would not beat again.

He stared unbelievingly for a long moment then, with boundless tenderness, he touched her eyelids with his fingertips – gently, as if fearing to hurt her – and closed her eyes.

Slowly he fell forward until his head rested on her chest, and his tears soaked into the brown wool of her homespun dress.

A moment later he was filled with mad rage at the man who had taken her life. He jumped to his feet, seized the axe, and began to hack at the Viking's dead face, smashing the forehead, slicing the eyes, splitting the chin.

The fit lasted only moments before he realized the gruesome hopelessness of what he was doing. When he stopped, he heard shouting outside in a language that was similar to the one he spoke but not quite the same. That brought him back abruptly to the danger he was in. He might be about to die.

I don't care, I'll die, he thought; but that mood lasted only seconds. If he met another Viking, his own head might be split just like that of the man at his feet. Stricken with grief as he was, he could still feel terror at the thought of being hacked to death.

But what was he to do? He was afraid of being found inside the dairy, with the corpse of his victim crying out for revenge; but if he went outside he would surely be captured and killed. He looked about him wildly: where could he hide? His eye fell on the overturned manger, a crude wooden construction. Upside-down, its trough looked big enough to conceal him.

He lay on the stone floor and pulled it over him. As an afterthought he lifted the edge, grabbed the axe and pulled it under with him.

Some light came through the cracks between the planks of the manger. He lay still and listened. The wood muffled sound somewhat, but he could hear a lot of shouting and screaming outside. He waited in fear: at any moment a Viking could come in and be curious enough to look under the manger. If that happened, Edgar decided, he would try to kill the man instantly with the axe; but he would be at a serious disadvantage, lying on the ground with his enemy standing over him.

He heard a dog whine, and understood that Brindle must be standing beside the inverted manger. 'Go away,' he hissed. The sound of his voice only encouraged the dog, and she whined louder.

Edgar cursed, then lifted the edge of the trough, reached out, and pulled the dog in with him. Brindle lay down and went silent.

Edgar waited, listening to the horrible sounds of slaughter and destruction.

Brindle began to lick the Viking's brains off the blade of the axe.

ÞÞÞ

HE DID NOT know how long he remained there. He began to feel warm, and guessed the sun must be high. Eventually the noise from outside became less, but he could not be sure the Vikings had gone and, every time he considered looking out, he decided not to risk his life yet. Then he would turn his mind to thoughts of Sunni, and he would weep all over again.

Brindle dozed beside him, but every now and again the dog would whimper and tremble in her sleep. Edgar wondered whether dogs had bad dreams.

Edgar sometimes had nightmares: he was on a sinking ship, or an oak tree was falling and he could not get out of the way, or he was fleeing from a forest fire. When he woke from such dreams he experienced a feeling of relief so powerful that he wanted to weep. Now he kept thinking that the Viking attack might be a nightmare from which he would awake at any moment to find Sunni still alive. But he did not wake.

At last he heard voices speaking plain Anglo-Saxon. Still he hesitated. The speakers sounded troubled but not panicked; grief-stricken, rather than in fear of their lives. That must surely mean the Vikings had gone, he reasoned.

How many of his friends had they taken with them to sell as slaves? How many corpses of his neighbours had they left behind? Did he still have a family?

Brindle made a hopeful noise in her throat and tried to stand up. She could not rise in the confined space, but clearly she felt it was now safe to move.

Edgar lifted the manger. Brindle immediately stepped out. Edgar rolled from under, holding the Viking axe, and lowered the trough back to the floor. He got to his feet, limbs aching from prolonged confinement. He hooked the axe to his belt.

Then he looked out of the dairy door.

The town had gone.

For a moment he was just bewildered. How could Combe have disappeared? But he knew how, of course. Almost every house had burned to nothing. A few were still smouldering. Here and there masonry structures remained standing, and he took a while to identify them. The monastery had two stone buildings, the church and a two-storey edifice with a refectory on the ground floor and a dormitory upstairs. There were two other stone churches. It took him longer to identify the home of Wyn the jeweller, who needed stonework to protect him from thieves.

Cyneric's cows had survived, clustering fearfully in the middle of their fenced pasture: cows were valuable but, Edgar reasoned, too bulky and cantankerous to take on board ship – like all thieves, the Vikings would prefer cash or small, high-priced items such as jewellery.

Townspeople stood in the ruins, dazed, hardly speaking, uttering monosyllables of grief and horror and bewilderment.

The same vessels were anchored in the bay, but the Viking ships had gone.

At last he allowed himself to look at the bodies in the dairy. The Viking was barely recognizable as a human being. Edgar felt strange, thinking that he had done that. It was hardly believable.

Sunni looked surprisingly peaceful. There was no visible sign of the head injury that had killed her. Her eyes were half open, and Edgar closed them again. He knelt down and again felt for a heartbeat, knowing it was foolish. Her body was already cool.

What should he do? Perhaps he could help her soul get to heaven. The monastery was still standing. He should take her to the monks' church.

He took her in his arms. Lifting her was more difficult than he expected. She was slender, and he was strong, but her inert body unbalanced him and, as he struggled to stand, he had to crush her to his chest harder than he would have wished. Holding her in such a rough embrace, knowing she felt no pain, harshly accentuated her lifelessness and made him cry again.

He walked through the house, past the body of Cyneric, and out through the door.

Brindle followed him.

It seemed to be mid-afternoon, though it was hard to tell: there were ashes in the air, along with the smoke from embers, and a disgusting odour of burned human flesh. The survivors looked around them perplexedly, as if they could not take in what had happened. More were making their way back from the woods, some driving livestock.

Edgar walked towards the monastery. Sunni's weight began to hurt his arms, but perversely he welcomed the pain. However, her eyes would not remain closed, and somehow this distressed him. He wanted her to look as if she were asleep.

No one paid him much attention: they all had their own individual tragedies. He reached the church and made his way inside.

He was not the only person to have this idea. There were bodies lying all along the nave, with people kneeling or standing beside them. Prior Ulfric approached Edgar, looking distraught, and said peremptorily: 'Dead or alive?'

'It's Sungifu, she's dead,' Edgar replied.

'Dead people at the east end,' said Ulfric, too frantically busy to be gentle. 'Wounded in the nave.'

'Will you pray for her soul, please?'

'She'll be treated like all the rest.'

'I gave the alarm,' Edgar protested. 'I may have saved your life. Please pray for her.'

Ulfric hurried away without answering.

Edgar saw that Brother Maerwynn was attending to a wounded man, bandaging a leg while the man whimpered in pain. When Maerwynn finally stood up, Edgar said to him: 'Will you pray for Sunni's soul, please?'

'Yes, of course,' said Maerwynn, and he made the sign of the cross on Sunni's forehead.

'Thank you.'

'For now, put her down at the east end of the church.'

Edgar walked along the nave and past the altar. At the far end of the church twenty or thirty bodies were laid in neat rows, with grieving relatives staring at them. Edgar lay Sunni down gently. He straightened her legs and crossed her arms on her chest, then tidied her hair with his fingers. He wished he were a priest so that he could take care of her soul himself.

He stayed kneeling for a long time, looking at her motionless face, struggling to understand that she would never again look back at him with a smile.

Eventually thoughts of the living intruded. Were his parents alive? Had his brothers been taken into slavery? Only a few hours ago he had been on the point of leaving them permanently. Now he needed them. Without them, he would be alone in the world.

He stayed with Sunni a minute longer, then left the church, followed by Brindle.

Outside, he wondered where to start. He decided to go to his home. The house would have gone, of course, but perhaps he might find the family there, or some clue as to what had happened to them.

The quickest way was along the beach. As he walked towards the sea he hoped he would find his boat on the shore. He had left it some distance from the nearest houses, so there was a good chance it had not burned.

Before he reached the sea he met his mother walking into town from the woods. At the sight of her strong, resolute features and her purposeful stride he felt so weak with relief that he almost fell down. She was carrying a bronze cooking pot, perhaps all she had rescued from the house. Her face was drawn with grief but her mouth was set in a line of grim determination.

When she saw Edgar her expression changed to joy. She threw her arms around him and pressed her face into his chest, sobbing: 'My boy, oh, my Eddie, thank God.'

He hugged her with his eyes closed, more grateful for her than he had ever been.

After a moment he looked over her shoulder and saw Erman, dark like Ma but mulish rather than determined; and Eadbald, who was fair and freckled; but not their father. 'Where's Pa?' he said.

Erman answered: 'He told us to run. He stayed behind to save the boatyard.'

Edgar wanted to say: *And you left him?* But this was no time for recriminations – and, in any case, Edgar too had left.

Ma released him. 'We're going back to the house,' she said. 'What's left of it.'

They headed for the shore. Ma strode quickly, impatient to know the truth, good or bad.

Erman said accusingly: 'You got away fast, little brother – why didn't you wake us?'

'I did wake you,' Edgar said. 'I rang the monastery bell.'

'You did not.'

It was like Erman to try to start a squabble at a time like this. Edgar looked away and said nothing. He did not care what Erman thought.

When they reached the beach, Edgar saw that his boat was gone. The Vikings had taken it, of course. They would recognize a good vessel. And it would have been easy to transport: they could simply have tied it to the stern of one of their ships and towed it.

It was a grave loss, but he felt no pain: it was trivial by comparison with the death of Sunni.

Walking along the shore they came across the mother of a boy of Edgar's age lying dead, and he wondered if she had been killed trying to stop the Vikings taking her son into slavery.

There was another corpse a few yards away, and more farther along. Edgar checked every face: they were all friends and neighbours, but Pa was not among them, and he began cautiously to hope that his father might have survived.

They reached their home. All that was left was the fireplace, with the iron tripod still standing over it.

To one side of the ruin was the body of Pa. Ma gave a cry of horror and grief, and fell to her knees. Edgar knelt beside her and put his arm around her shaking shoulders.

Pa's right arm had been severed near the shoulder, presumably by the blade of an axe, and he seemed to have bled to death. Edgar thought of the strength and skill that had been in that arm, and he wept angry tears at the waste and loss.

He heard Eadbald say: 'Look at the yard.'

Edgar stood up and wiped his eyes. At first he was not sure what he was seeing, and he rubbed his eyes again.

The yard had burned. The vessel under construction and the stock of timber had been reduced to piles of ash, along with the tar and rope. All that remained was the whetstone they had used to sharpen their tools. In among the cinders, Edgar made out charred bones too small to be human, and he guessed that poor old Grendel had burned to death at the end of his chain.

All the family's wealth had been in that yard.

Not only had they lost the yard, Edgar realized; they had lost their livelihood. Even if a customer had been willing to order a boat from three apprentices, they had no wood with which to build it, no tools to shape the timber, and no money to buy any of what they needed.

Ma probably had a few silver pennies in her purse, but the family had never had much to spare, and Pa had always used any surplus to buy timber. Good wood was better than silver, he had liked to say, because it was harder to steal.

'We've got nothing left, and no way to make a living,' Edgar said. 'What on earth are we going to do?'

2

BISHOP WYNSTAN OF SHIRING reined in his horse at the top of a rise and looked down over Combe. There was not much left of the town; the summer sun shone on a grey wilderness. 'It's worse than I expected,' he said. There were some ships and boats undamaged in the harbour, the only hopeful sign.

His brother Wigelm came alongside and said: 'Every Viking should be roasted alive.' He was a thane, a member of the landholding elite. Five years younger than Wynstan at thirty, he was quick to anger.

But this time Wynstan agreed with him. 'Over a slow fire,' he said.

Their elder half-brother heard them. As was the custom, the brothers had names that sounded alike, and the oldest was Wilwulf, forty, usually called Wilf. He was ealdorman of Shiring, ruler of a part of the west of England that included Combe. He said: 'You've never seen a town after a Viking raid. This is how it looks.'

They rode on into the devastated town, followed by a small entourage of armed men. They made an imposing sight, Wynstan knew: three tall men in costly clothes riding fine horses. Wilf had a blue knee-length tunic and leather boots; Wigelm a similar outfit but red. Wynstan had a plain black ankle-length robe, as appropriate to a priest, but the fabric was finely woven. He also wore a large silver cross on a leather thong around his neck. Each brother had a luxuriant fair moustache but no beard, in the style fashionable among wealthy Englishmen. Wilf and Wigelm had thick fair hair; Wynstan had the top of his head shaved in a tonsure, like all priests. They looked wealthy and important, which they were.

The townspeople were moving disconsolately among the ruins, sifting and digging and making pathetic piles of their recovered possessions: twisted pieces of iron kitchenware, bone combs blackened by fire, cracked cookpots and ruined tools. Chickens pecked and pigs snuffled, searching for anything edible. There was an unpleasant smell of dead fires, and Wynstan found himself taking shallow breaths.

As the brothers approached, the townspeople looked up at them, faces brightening with hope. Many knew the brothers by sight, and those who had never seen them could tell by their appearance that they were powerful men. Some called out greetings, others cheered and clapped. They all left what they were doing and followed. Surely, the people's expressions said, such mighty beings would be able to save them somehow?

The brothers reined in at a patch of open ground between the church and the monastery. Boys competed to hold their horses as they dismounted. Prior Ulfric appeared to greet them. There were black smuts in his white hair. 'My lords, the town stands in desperate need of your help,' he said. 'The people—'

'Wait!' said Wynstan, in a voice that carried to the crowd all around. His brothers were unsurprised: Wynstan had forewarned them of his intention.

The townspeople fell silent.

Wynstan took the cross from around his neck and held it high over his head, then turned and walked with slow ceremonial steps towards the church.

His brothers came after him, and everyone else followed.

He entered the church and slow-marched up the aisle, noticing the rows of wounded lying on the floor but not turning his head. Those who were able bowed or knelt as he passed, still holding the cross high. He could see more bodies at the far end of the church, but those were dead.

When he reached the altar he prostrated himself, lying completely still, face down on the earth floor, his right arm extended towards the altar, holding the cross upright.

He stayed there for a long moment, while the people watched in silence. Then he rose to his knees. He spread his arms in a beseeching gesture and said loudly: 'What have we done?'

There was a sound from the crowd like a collective sigh.

'Wherein did we sin?' he declaimed. 'Why do we deserve this? Can we be forgiven?'

He went on in the same vein. It was half prayer, half sermon. He needed to explain to the people how what had happened to them was God's will. The Viking raid had to be seen as punishment for sin.

However, there was practical work to do, and this was only the preliminary ceremony, so he was brief. 'As we begin the task of rebuilding our town,' he said in conclusion, 'we pledge to redouble our efforts to be devout, humble, God-fearing Christians, in the name of Jesus our Lord. Amen.'

The congregation said: 'Amen.'

He stood up and turned, showing his tear-stained face to the crowd. He hung the cross around his neck again. 'And now, in the sight of God, I call upon my brother, Ealdorman Wilwulf, to hold court.'

Wynstan and Wilf walked side by side down the nave, followed by Wigelm and Ulfric. They went outside and the townspeople followed.

Wilf looked around. 'I'll hold court right here.'

'Very good, my lord,' said Ulfric. He snapped his fingers at a monk. 'Bring the great chair.' He turned again to Wilf. 'Shall you want ink and parchment, ealdorman?'

Wilf could read but not write. Wynstan could read and write, like most senior clergy. Wigelm was illiterate.

Wilf said: 'I doubt we'll need to write anything down.'

Wynstan was distracted by a tall woman of about thirty wearing a torn red dress. She was attractive, despite the ash smeared on her cheek. She spoke in a low voice, but he could hear the desperation in her tone. 'You must help me, my lord bishop, I beg you,' she said.

Wynstan said: 'Don't talk to me, you stupid bitch.'

He knew her. She was Meagenswith, known as Mags. She lived in a large house with ten or twelve girls – some slaves, others volunteers – all of whom would have sex with men for money. Wynstan replied without looking at her. 'You can't be the first person in Combe I commiserate with,' he said, speaking quietly but urgently.

'But the Vikings took all my girls as well as my money!'

They were all slaves now, Wynstan thought. 'I'll discuss it with you later,' he muttered. Then he raised his voice for the benefit of people nearby. 'Get out of my sight, you filthy fornicator!'

She backed away immediately.

Two monks brought a big oak chair and set it in the middle of the open space. Wilf sat down, Wigelm stood on his left, Wynstan on his right.

While the townspeople gathered around, the brothers held a worried conversation in low tones. All three drew income from Combe. It was the second most important town in the ealdormanry, after the city of Shiring. Every house paid rent to Wigelm, who shared the proceeds with Wilf. The people also paid tithes to the churches, which shared them with Bishop Wynstan. Wilf collected customs duties on imports and exports passing through the harbour. Wynstan took an income from the monastery. Wigelm sold the timber in the forest. As of two days ago, all those streams of wealth had dried up.

Wynstan said grimly: 'It will be a long time before anyone here can pay anything.' He would have to reduce his spending. Shiring was not a rich diocese. Now, he thought, if I were archbishop of Canterbury, I would never need to worry: all the wealth of the Church in the south of England would be under my control. But as mere bishop of Shiring he was limited. He wondered what he could cut out. He hated to renounce a pleasure.

Wigelm was scornful. 'All these people have money. You find it when you slice their bellies open.'

Wilf shook his head. 'Don't be stupid.' It was something he said often to Wigelm. 'Most of them have lost everything,' he went on. 'They have no food, no money to buy any, and no means of earning anything. Come wintertime they'll be gathering acorns to make soup. Those who survived the Vikings will be enfeebled by hunger. The children will catch diseases and die; the old will fall over and break their bones; the young and strong will leave.'

Wigelm looked petulant. 'Then what can we do?'

'We will be wise to reduce our demands.'

'We can't let them live rent-free!'

'You fool, dead people pay no rent. If a few survivors can get back to fishing and making things and trading, they may be able to recommence payments next spring.'

Wynstan agreed. Wigelm did not, but he said no more: Wilf was the eldest and outranked him.

When everyone was ready, Wilf said: 'Now, Prior Ulfric, tell us what happened.'

The ealdorman was holding court.

Ulfric said: 'The Vikings came two days ago, at the glimmer of dawn, when all were asleep.'

Wigelm said: 'Why didn't you fight them off, you cowards?'

Wilf held up a hand for silence. 'One thing at a time,' he said. He turned to Ulfric. 'This is the first time Vikings have attacked Combe in my memory, Ulfric. Do you know where this particular group came from?'

'Not I, my lord. Perhaps one of the fishermen might have seen the Viking fleet on their voyages?'

A burly man with grey in his beard said: 'We've never seen them, lord.'

Wigelm, who knew the townspeople better than his brothers did, said: 'That's Maccus. He owns the biggest fishing boat in town.'

Maccus went on: 'We believe the Vikings make harbour on the other side of the Channel, in Normandy. It's said they take on supplies there, then raid across the water, and go back to sell their loot to the Normans, God curse their immortal souls.'

'That's plausible, but not very helpful,' Wilf said. 'Normandy has a long coastline. I suppose Cherbourg must be the nearest harbour?'

'I believe so,' Maccus said. 'I'm told it's on a long headland that sticks out into the Channel. I haven't been there myself.'

'Nor have I,' said Wilf. 'Has anyone from Combe been there?'

'In the old days, perhaps,' said Maccus. 'Nowadays we don't venture so far. We want to avoid the Vikings, not meet them.'

Wigelm was impatient with this kind of talk. He said: 'We should assemble a fleet and sail to Cherbourg and burn the place the way they burned Combe!' Some of the younger men in the crowd shouted approval.

Wilf said: 'Anyone who wants to attack the Normans doesn't know anything about them. They're descended from Vikings, remember. They may be civilized now but they're no less tough. Why do you think the Vikings raid us but not the Normans?'

Wigelm looked crushed.

Wilf said: 'I wish I knew more about Cherbourg.'

A young man in the crowd spoke up. 'I went to Cherbourg once.'

Wynstan looked at him with interest. 'Who are you?'

'Edgar, the boatbuilder's son, my lord bishop.'

Wynstan studied the lad. He was of medium height, but muscular, as boatbuilders generally were. He had light-brown hair and no more than a wisp of a beard. He spoke politely but fearlessly, evidently not intimidated by the high status of the men he was addressing.

Wynstan said: 'How did it happen that you went to Cherbourg?'

'My father took me. He was delivering a ship we had built. But that was five years ago. The place may have changed.'

Wilf said: 'Any information is better than none. What do you remember?'

'There's a good, big harbour with room for many ships and boats. It was ruled by Count Hubert – probably still is, he wasn't old.'

'Anything else?'

'I remember the count's daughter, Ragna. She had red hair.'

'A boy would remember that,' Wilf said.

Everyone laughed, and Edgar blushed.

The lad raised his voice over the laughter and said: 'And there was a stone tower.'

'What did I tell you?' Wilf said to Wigelm. 'It's not easy to attack a town with stone fortifications.'

Wynstan said: 'Perhaps I can make a suggestion.'

'Of course,' said his brother.

'Could we make friends with Count Hubert? He might be persuaded that Christian Normans and Christian Englishmen should work together to defeat murderous Odin-worshipping Vikings.' Those Vikings who had made their homes in the north and east of England had generally converted to Christianity, Wynstan knew, but the seafarers still clung to their heathen gods. 'You can be persuasive when you want something, Wilf,' he said with a grin. It was true: Wilf had charm.

'I'm not sure about that,' Wilf said.

'I know what you're thinking,' Wynstan said quickly. He lowered his voice, to speak of matters that were over the heads of the townspeople. 'You wonder how King Ethelred would feel about it. International diplomacy is a royal prerogative.'

'Exactly.'

'Leave that to me. I'll make it right with the king.'

'I have to do something before these Vikings ruin my ealdormanry,' Wilf said. 'And this is the first practical suggestion I've heard.'

The people shifted and muttered. Wynstan sensed that talk of befriending the Normans was too theoretical. They needed help today, and they were looking to the three brothers to provide it. The nobility had a duty to protect the people – it was the justification for their status and their riches – and the three brothers had failed to keep Combe safe. Now they were expected to do something about it.

Wilf picked up the same pulse. 'Now to practical matters,' he said. 'Prior Ulfric, how are the people being fed?'

'From the monastery's stores, which were not despoiled,' Ulfric answered. 'The Vikings disdained the monks' fish and beans, preferring to steal gold and silver.'

'And where do the people sleep?'

'In the nave of the church, where the wounded lie.'

'And the dead?'

'At the east end of the church.'

Wynstan said: 'If I may, Wilf?'

Wilf nodded.

'Thank you.' Wynstan raised his voice so that all could hear. 'Today before sundown I will hold a collective service for the souls of all the dead, and I will authorize a communal grave. In this warm weather there is a danger that the corpses will cause an outbreak of disease, so I want every dead body underground before the end of tomorrow.'

'Very good, my lord bishop,' said Ulfric.

Looking at the crowd, Wilf frowned and said: 'There must be a thousand people here. Half the population of the town has survived. How did so many manage to escape the Vikings?'

Ulfric answered: 'A boy who was up early saw them coming and ran to the monastery to warn us, and the bell was rung.'

'That was smart,' said Wilf. 'Which boy?'

'Edgar, who just spoke up about Cherbourg. He is the youngest of the three sons of the boatbuilder.'

A bright lad, Wynstan thought.

Wilf said: 'You did well, Edgar.'

'Thank you.'

'What are you going to do now?'

Edgar tried to look brave, but Wynstan could see he was fearful of the future. 'We don't know,' Edgar said. 'My father was killed, and we've lost our tools and our stock of timber.'

Wigelm said impatiently: 'We can't get into discussions about individual families. We need to decide what is going to happen to this whole town.'

Wilf nodded agreement and said: 'The people must try to rebuild their houses before winter comes. Wigelm, you will forgo rents due on Midsummer Day.' Rents were usually payable four times a year, on the quarter days: Midsummer, which was the twenty-fourth day of June; Michaelmas, the twenty-ninth of September; Christmas, the twenty-fifth of December; and Lady Day, the twenty-fifth of March.

Wynstan glanced at Wigelm. He looked disgruntled, but said nothing. He was stupid to be angry about this: the people had no means with which to pay their rents, so Wilf was giving away nothing.

A woman in the crowd called out: 'And the Michaelmas rents, please, lord.'

Wynstan looked at her. She was a small, tough-looking woman of about forty.

'When Michaelmas comes, we'll see how you're getting on,' Wilf said cannily.

The same woman said: 'We'll need timber to rebuild our houses – but we can't pay for it.'

Wilf spoke aside to Wigelm: 'Who's she?'

'Mildred, the boatbuilder's wife,' Wigelm answered. 'She's a troublemaker.'

Wynstan was struck by a thought. 'I may be able to rid you of her, brother,' he murmured.

Wilf said quietly: 'She may be a troublemaker, but she's right. Wigelm is going to have to let them have free timber.'

'Very well,' said Wigelm reluctantly. Raising his voice, he said to the crowd: 'Free timber, but only for Combe townspeople, only for houses, and only until Michaelmas.'

Wilf stood up. 'That's all we can do, for now,' he said. He turned to Wigelm. 'Speak to that man Maccus. Find out if he's willing to take me to Cherbourg, and what he might want by way of payment, and how long the voyage is likely to take, and so on.'

The crowd were muttering discontentedly. They were disappointed. That was the disadvantage of power, Wynstan thought: people expected miracles. Several people surged forward to demand some kind of special treatment. The men-at-arms moved to keep order.

Wynstan stepped away. At the church door he ran into Mags again. She had decided to change her tone, and instead of desperate she was wheedling. 'Would you like me to suck your cock around the back of the church?' she said. 'You always say I do it better than the young girls.'

'Don't be foolish,' Wynstan said. A sailor or a fisherman might not care who saw him being sucked off, but a bishop had to be discreet. 'Get to the point,' he said. 'How much do you need?'

'What do you mean?'

'To replace the girls,' Wynstan said. He had had good times at Mags's house, and he hoped to do so again. 'How much money do you need to borrow from me?'

35

Mags was practised at responding quickly to men's changes of mood, and she adjusted her demeanour again, becoming businesslike. 'If they're young and fresh, slave girls cost about a pound each at Bristol market.'

Wynstan nodded. There was a big slave market at Bristol, several days' journey from here. He made up his mind quickly, as always. 'If I lend you ten pounds today, can you pay me back twenty a year from now?'

Her eyes lit up, but she pretended to be doubtful. 'I don't know whether custom will come back that fast.'

'There will always be visiting sailors. And fresh girls will attract more men. You're in a profession that never lacks for clients.'

'Give me eighteen months.'

'Pay me twenty-five pounds at Christmas next year.'

Mags looked worried but she said: 'All right.'

Wynstan summoned Cnebba, a big man in an iron helmet who was custodian of the bishop's money. 'Give her ten pounds,' he said.

'The chest is in the monastery,' Cnebba said to her. 'Come with me.'

'And don't cheat her,' Wynstan said. 'You can fuck her if you like, but give her the full ten pounds.'

Mags said: 'God bless you, my lord bishop.'

Wynstan touched her lips with a finger. 'You can thank me later, when it gets dark.'

She took his hand and licked his finger lasciviously. 'I can't wait.'

Wynstan stepped away before anyone noticed.

He scanned the crowd. They were disconsolate and resentful, but nothing could be done about that. The boatbuilder's son met his eye, and Wynstan beckoned him. Edgar came to the church door with a brown-and-white dog at his heel. 'Fetch your mother,' Wynstan said. 'And your brothers. I may be able to help you.'

'Thank you, lord!' said Edgar with eager enthusiasm. 'Do you want us to build you a ship?'

'No.'

Edgar's face fell. 'What, then?'

'Fetch your mother and I'll tell you.'

'Yes, lord.'

Edgar went away and came back with Mildred, who looked warily at Wynstan, and two young men who were evidently his brothers, both bigger than Edgar but lacking his look of inquiring intelligence. Three strong boys and a tough mother: it was a good combination for what Wynstan had in mind.

He said: 'I know of a vacant farm.' Wynstan would be doing Wigelm a favour by ridding him of the seditious Mildred.

Edgar looked dismayed. 'We're boatbuilders, not farmers!'

Mildred said: 'Shut your mouth, Edgar.'

Wynstan said: 'Can you manage a farm, widow?'

'I was born on a farm.'

'This one is beside a river.'

'But how much land is there?'

'Thirty acres. That's generally considered enough to feed a family.'

'That depends on the soil.'

'And on the family.'

She was not to be fobbed off. 'What's the soil like?'

'Much as you'd expect: a bit swampy beside the river, light and loamy farther up the slope. And there's a crop of oats in the ground, just shooting green. All you'll have to do is reap it, and you'll be set for the winter.'

'Any oxen?'

'No, but you won't need them. A heavy plough is unnecessary on that light soil.'

She narrowed her eyes. 'Why is it vacant?'

It was a shrewd question. The truth was that the last tenant had been unable to grow enough on the poor soil to feed his family. The wife and three small children had died, and the tenant had fled. But this family was different, with three good workers and only four mouths to feed. It would still be a challenge, but Wynstan had a feeling they would manage. However, he was not going to tell them the truth. 'The tenant died of a fever and his wife went back to her mother,' he lied.

'The place is unhealthy, then.'

'Not in the least. It's by a small hamlet with a minster. A minster is a church served by a community of priests living together, and—'

'I know what a minster is. It's like a monastery but not as strict.'

'My cousin Degbert is the dean, and also landlord of the hamlet, including the farm.'

'What buildings does the farm have?'

'A house and a barn. And the previous tenant left his tools.'

'What's the rent?'

'You'll have to give Degbert four fat piglets at Michaelmas, for the priests' bacon. That's all!'

'Why is the rent so low?'

Wynstan smiled. She was a suspicious cow. 'Because my cousin is a kindly man.'

Mildred snorted sceptically.

There was a silence. Wynstan watched her. She did not want the farm, he could see; she did not trust him. But there was desperation in her eyes, for she had nothing else. She would take it. She had to.

She said: 'Where is this place?'

'A day and a half's journey up the river.'

'What's it called?'

'Dreng's Ferry.'

3

THEY WALKED FOR A day and a half, following a barely visible footpath beside the meandering river: three young men, their mother and a brown-and-white dog.

Edgar felt disoriented, bewildered and anxious. He had planned a new life for himself, but not this one. Destiny had taken a turn that was completely unexpected, and he had had no time to prepare for it. In any case, he and his family still had little idea of what was ahead of them. They knew almost nothing of the place called Dreng's Ferry. What would it be like? Would the people be suspicious of newcomers, or welcome them? How about the farm? Would the ground be light soil, easy to cultivate, or recalcitrant, heavy clay? Were there pear trees or honking wild geese or wary deer? Edgar's family believed in plans. His father had often said that you had to build the entire boat in your imagination before picking up the first piece of timber.

There would be a lot of work to do, to reinvigorate an abandoned farm, and Edgar found it difficult to summon up enthusiasm. This was the funeral of his hopes. He was never going to have his own boatyard, never build ships. He felt sure he would never marry.

He tried to interest himself in his surroundings. He had never walked this far before. He had once sailed many miles, to Cherbourg and back, but in between he had looked at nothing but water. Now for the first time he was discovering England.

There was a lot of forest, just like the one in which the family had

39

been felling trees for as long as he could remember. The woodland was broken up by villages and a few large estates. The landscape became more undulating as they trudged farther inland. The woods grew thicker but there were still habitations: a hunting lodge, a lime pit, a tin mine, a horse-catcher's hut, a small family of charcoal burners, a vineyard on a south-facing slope, a flock of sheep grazing on a hilltop.

They met a few travellers: a fat priest on a skinny pony, a well-dressed silversmith with four grim-faced bodyguards, a burly farmer driving a big black sow to market, and a bent old woman with brown eggs to sell. They stopped and talked to each one, exchanging news and information about the road ahead.

Everyone they met had to be told about the Viking raid on Combe: this was how people got their news, from travellers. Ma gave most people a short version, but in affluent settlements she sat down and told the whole story, and the four of them got food and drink in return.

They waved at passing boats. There were no bridges, and just one ford, at a place called Mudeford Crossing. They could have spent the night in the alehouse there, but the weather was fine and Ma decided they would sleep outside and save money. However, they made their beds within shouting distance of the building.

The forest could be dangerous, Ma said, and she warned the boys to be alert, increasing Edgar's sense of a world suddenly without rules. Lawless men lived rough here and stole from travellers. At this time of year such men could easily hide in the summer foliage and spring out unexpectedly.

Edgar and his brothers could fight back, he told himself. He still carried the axe he had taken from the Viking who killed Sunni. And they had a dog. Brindle was no use in a fight, as she had shown during the Viking raid, but she might sniff out a robber in a bush, and bark a warning. More importantly, the four of them evidently had little worth stealing: no livestock, no fancy swords, no ironbound chest that might contain money. Nobody robs a pauper, Edgar thought. But he was not really sure even of that.

Ma set the walking pace. She was tough. Few women lived to her age, which was forty; most died in the prime childbearing years between marriage and mid-thirties. It was different for men. Pa had been forty-five, and there were plenty of men even older.

Ma was herself when dealing with practical problems, making decisions and giving advice; but in the long miles of silent walking Edgar could see that she was possessed by grief. When she thought no one was looking she let down her guard and her face became drawn with sorrow. She had been with Pa more than half her life. Edgar found it hard to imagine that they had once experienced the storm of passion that he and Sunni had had for one another, but he supposed it must be so. They had produced three sons and raised them together. And after all those years they had still woken up to embrace one another in the middle of the night.

He would never know such a relationship with Sunni. While Ma mourned for what she had lost, Edgar grieved for what he would never have. He would never marry Sunni, nor raise children with her, nor wake up in the night for middle-aged sex; there would never be time for him and Sunni to grow accustomed to one another, to fall into routines, to take one another for granted; and he felt so sad he could hardly bear it. He had found buried treasure, something worth more than all the gold in the world, and then he had lost it. Life stretched ahead of him empty.

On the long walk, when Ma sank into bereavement, Edgar was assaulted by flashes of remembered violence. The lush abundance of oak and hornbeam leaves around him seemed to vanish. Instead he saw the opening in Cyneric's neck, like something on a butcher's block; he felt Sunni's soft body cooling in death; and he was appalled all over again to look at what he had done to the Viking, the blond-bearded

Nordic face a bloody mess, disfigured by Edgar himself in a fit of uncontrollable insane hatred. He saw the field of ash where there had been a town, the scorched bones of the old mastiff Grendel, and his father's severed arm on the beach like jetsam. He thought of Sunni now lying in a mass grave in Combe cemetery. Although he knew her soul was with God, still he found it horrible to think that the body he loved was buried in the cold ground, tumbled with hundreds of others.

On the second day, when by chance Edgar and Ma were walking fifty yards or so ahead, she said thoughtfully: 'Obviously you were some distance away from home when you saw the Viking ships.'

He had been waiting for this. Erman had asked puzzled questions, and Eadbald had guessed that something clandestine had been going on, but Edgar did not have to explain himself to them. However, Ma was different.

All the same, he was not sure where to begin, so he just said: 'Yes.'

'I suppose you were meeting some girl.'

He felt embarrassed.

She went on: 'No other reason for you to sneak out of the house in the middle of the night.'

He shrugged. It had always been hard to hide things from her.

'But why were you secretive about it?' she asked, following the chain of logic. 'You're old enough to woo a girl. There's nothing to be ashamed of.' She paused. 'Unless she was already married.'

He said nothing, but he felt his cheeks flame red.

'Go ahead, blush,' she said. 'You deserve to feel ashamed.'

Ma was strict, and Pa had been the same. They believed in obeying the rules of the Church and the king. Edgar believed in it too, but he had told himself that his affair with Sunni had been exceptional. 'She hated Cyneric,' he said.

Ma was not going to buy that. She said sarcastically: 'So you think the commandment says: "Thou shalt not commit adultery, unless the woman hates her husband".'

'I know what the commandment says. I broke it.'

Ma did not acknowledge his confession. Her thoughts moved on. 'The woman must have died in the raid,' she said. 'Otherwise you wouldn't have come with us.'

Edgar nodded.

'I suppose it was the dairyman's wife. What was her name? Sungifu.'

She had guessed it all. Edgar felt foolish, like a child caught in a lie.

Ma said: 'Were you planning to run away that night?'

'Yes.'

Ma took Edgar's arm, and her voice became softer. 'Well, you chose well, I'll give you that. I liked Sunni. She was intelligent and hard-working. I'm sorry she's dead.'

'Thank you, Ma.'

'She was a good woman.' Ma released his arm, and her voice changed again. 'But she was someone else's woman.'

'I know.'

Ma said no more. Edgar's conscience would judge him, and she knew that.

They stopped by a stream to drink the cold water and rest. It was hours since they had eaten, but they had no food.

Erman, the eldest brother, was as depressed as Edgar but did not have the sense to shut up about it. 'I'm a craftsman, not an ignorant peasant,' he grumbled as they resumed walking. 'I don't know why I'm going to this farm.'

Ma had little patience for whining. 'What was your alternative, then?' she snapped, interrupting his lament. 'What would you have done if I had not made you take this journey?'

Erman had no answer to that, of course. He mumbled that he would have waited to see what might turn up.

'I'll tell you what would have turned up,' said Ma. 'Slavery. That's your alternative. That's what happens to people when they're starving to death.'

Her words were directed at Erman, but Edgar was the more shocked. It had not occurred to him that he might face the prospect of becoming a slave. The thought was unnerving. Was that the fate that awaited the family if they could not make the farm viable?

Erman said petulantly: 'No one's going to enslave me.'

'No,' said Ma. 'You'd volunteer for it.'

Edgar had heard of people enslaving themselves, though he did not know anyone who had actually done it. He had met plenty of slaves in Combe, of course: about one person in ten was a slave. Young and good-looking girls and boys became the playthings of rich men. The others pulled a plough, were flogged when they got tired, and spent their nights chained up like dogs. Most of them were Britons, people from the wild western fringes of civilization, Wales and Cornwall and Ireland. Every now and again they raided the wealthier English, stealing cattle and chickens and weapons; and the English would punish them by raiding back, burning their villages and taking slaves.

Voluntary slavery was different. There was a prescribed ritual, and Ma now depicted it scornfully to Erman. 'You'd kneel down in front of a nobleman or woman with your head bowed low in supplication,' she said. 'The noble might reject you, of course; but if the person put hands on your head, you would be a slave for life.'

'I'd rather starve,' Erman said in an attempt at defiance.

'No, you wouldn't,' Ma said. 'You've never gone hungry for as much as a day. Your father made sure of that, even when he and I had to do without to feed you boys. You don't know what it's like to eat nothing for a week. You'll bow your head in no time, just for the sake of that first plate of food. But then you'll have to work the rest of your life for no more than sustenance.'

Edgar was not sure he believed Ma. He felt he might rather starve.

Erman spoke with sulky defiance. 'People can get out of slavery.'

'Yes, but do you realize how difficult it is? You can buy your freedom, true, but where would you get the money? People sometimes give slaves tips, but not often, and not much. As a slave, your only real hope is that a kindly owner may make a will that frees you. And then you're back where you started, homeless and destitute, but twenty years older. That's the alternative, you stupid boy. Now tell me you don't want to be a farmer.'

Eadbald, the middle brother, stopped suddenly, wrinkled his freckled brow, and said: 'I think we might be there.'

Edgar looked across the river. On the north bank was a building that looked like an alehouse: longer than a regular home, with a table and benches outside, and a large patch of green where a cow and two goats grazed. A crude boat was tied up nearby. A foot-worn track ran up the slope from the alehouse. To the left of the road were five more timber houses. To the right was a small stone church, another large house, and a couple of outhouses that might have been stables or barns. Beyond that, the road disappeared into woodland.

'A ferry, an alehouse and a church,' Edgar said with rising excitement. 'I think Eadbald is right.'

'Let's find out,' said Ma. 'Give them a yell.'

Eadbald had a big voice. He cupped his hands around his mouth, and his shout boomed across the water. 'Hey! Hey! Anybody there? Hello? Hello?'

They waited for a response.

Edgar glanced downstream and noticed that the river divided around an island that seemed to be about a quarter of a mile long. It was heavily wooded but he could see, through the trees, what looked like part of a stone building. He wondered with eager curiosity what it could be.

'Shout again,' Ma said.

Eadbald repeated his cries.

The alehouse door opened and a woman came out. Peering across the river, Edgar made her out to be little more than a girl, probably four or five years younger than he. She looked across the water at the newcomers but made no acknowledgement. She was carrying a wooden bucket, and she walked unhurriedly to the water's edge, emptied the bucket into the river, rinsed it out, then went back into the tavern.

Erman said: 'We'll have to swim across.'

'I can't swim,' said Ma.

Edgar said: 'That girl is making a point. She wants us to know that she's a superior person, not a servant. She'll bring the boat over when she's good and ready, and she'll expect us to be grateful.'

Edgar was right. The girl emerged from the tavern again. This time she walked at the same leisurely pace to where the boat was moored. She untied the rope, picked up a single paddle, got into the boat and pushed off. Using the paddle on alternate sides, she rowed out into the river. Her movements were practised and apparently effortless.

Edgar studied the boat with consternation. It was a hollowed-out tree trunk, highly unstable, though the girl was evidently used to it.

He studied her as she came closer. She was ordinary-looking, with mid-brown hair and spotty skin, but he could not help noticing that she had a plump figure, and he revised his estimate of her age to fifteen.

She rowed to the south bank and expertly halted the canoe a few yards from the shore. 'What do you want?' she said.

Ma answered with a question. 'What place is this?'

'People call it Dreng's Ferry.'

So, Edgar thought, this is our new home.

Ma said to the girl: 'Are you Dreng?'

'That's my father. I'm Cwenburg.' She looked with interest at the three boys. 'Who are you?'

'We're the new tenants of the farm,' Ma told her. 'The bishop of Shiring sent us here.'

Cwenburg refused to be impressed. 'Is that so?'

'Will you take us across?'

'It's a farthing each and no haggling.'

The only coin issued by the king was a silver penny. Edgar knew, because he was interested in such things, that a penny weighed one-twentieth of an ounce. There were twelve ounces in a pound, so a pound was two hundred and forty pennies. The metal was not pure: thirty-seven parts in forty were silver, the rest copper. A penny would buy half a dozen chickens or a quarter of a sheep. For cheaper items, a penny had to be cut into two halfpennies or four farthings. The exact division caused constant quarrels.

Ma said: 'Here's a penny.'

Cwenburg ignored the proffered coin. 'There's five of you, with the dog.'

'The dog can swim across.'

'Some dogs can't swim.'

Ma became exasperated. 'In that case she can either stand on the bank and starve or jump in the river and drown. I'm not paying for a dog to ride in a ferry.'

Cwenburg shrugged, brought the boat to the water's edge, and took the coin.

Edgar boarded first, kneeling down and holding both sides to stabilize the boat. He noticed that the old tree trunk had tiny cracks, and there was a puddle in the bottom.

Cwenburg said to him: 'Where did you get that axe? It looks expensive.'

'I took it from a Viking.'

'Did you? What did he say about that?'

'He couldn't say much, because I split his head in half with it.' Edgar took some satisfaction in saying that.

The others boarded and Cwenburg pushed off. Brindle jumped into the river without hesitation and swam after the boat. Away from the shade of the forest, the sun was hot on Edgar's head.

He asked Cwenburg: 'What's on the island?'

'A nunnery.'

Edgar nodded. That would be the stone building he had glimpsed.

Cwenburg added: 'There's a gang of lepers, too. They live in shelters they make out of branches. The nuns feed them. We call the place Leper Island.'

Edgar shuddered. He wondered how the nuns survived. People said that if you touched a leper you could catch the disease – though he had never heard of anyone who had actually done that.

They reached the north bank, and Edgar helped Ma out of the boat. He smelt the strong brown odour of fermenting ale. 'Someone's brewing,' he said.

Cwenburg said: 'My mother makes very good ale. You should come into the house and refresh yourselves.'

'No, thanks,' Ma said immediately.

Cwenburg persisted. 'You may want to sleep here while you fix up the farm buildings. My father will give you dinner and breakfast for a halfpenny each. That's cheap.'

Ma said: 'Are the farm buildings in bad condition, then?'

'There were holes in the roof of the house last time I walked past.'

'And the barn?'

'Pigsty, you mean.'

Edgar frowned. This did not sound good. Still, they had thirty acres: they would be able to make something of that.

'We'll see,' said Ma. 'Which house does the dean live in?'

'Degbert Baldhead? He's my uncle.' Cwenburg pointed. 'The big one next to the church. All the clergy live there together.'

'We'll go and see him.'

They left Cwenburg and walked a short distance up the slope. Ma said: 'This dean is our new landlord. Act nice and friendly. I'll be firm with him if necessary, but we don't want him to take against us for any reason.'

The little church looked almost derelict, Edgar thought. The entrance arch was crumbling, and was prevented from collapse only by the support of a stout tree trunk standing in the middle of the doorway. Next to the church was a timber house, double the normal size like the alehouse. They stood outside politely, and Ma called: 'Anyone home?'

The woman who came to the door carried a baby on her hip and was pregnant with another, and a toddler hid behind her skirts. She had dirty hair and heavy breasts. She might have been beautiful once, with high cheekbones and a straight nose, but now she looked as if she was so tired she could barely stand. It was how many women looked in their twenties. No wonder they died young, Edgar thought.

Ma said: 'Is Dean Degbert here?'

'What do you want with my husband?' said the woman.

Clearly, Edgar thought, this was not the stricter kind of religious community. In principle the Church preferred priests to be celibate, but the rule was broken more often than it was kept, and even married bishops were not unheard of.

Ma said: 'The bishop of Shiring sent us.'

The woman shouted over her shoulder: 'Degsy? Visitors.' She stared at them a moment longer, then disappeared inside.

The man who took her place was about thirty-five, but had a head like an egg, without even a monkish fringe. Perhaps his baldness was due to some illness. 'I'm the dean,' he said with his mouth full of food. 'What do you want?'

Ma explained again.

'You'll have to wait,' Degbert said. 'I'm in the middle of my dinner.'

Ma smiled and said nothing, and the three brothers followed her example.

Degbert seemed to realize he was being inhospitable. All the same he did not offer to share his meal. 'Go to Dreng's alehouse,' he said. 'Have a drink.'

Ma said: 'We can't afford to buy ale. We're destitute. The Vikings raided Combe, where we lived.'

'Wait there, then.'

'Why don't you just tell me where the farm is?' Ma said pleasantly. 'I'm sure I can find it.'

Degbert hesitated, then said in a tone of irritation: 'I suppose I'll have to take you.' He looked back. 'Edith! Put my dinner by the fire. I'll be an hour.' He came out. 'Follow me,' he said.

They walked down the hill. 'What did you do in Combe?' Degbert asked. 'You can't have been farmers there.'

'My husband was a boatbuilder,' Ma said. 'The Vikings killed him.'

Degbert crossed himself perfunctorily. 'Well, we don't need boats here. My brother Dreng has the ferry and there's no room for two.'

Edgar said: 'Dreng needs a new vessel. That canoe is cracking. One day soon it will sink.'

'Maybe.'

Ma said: 'We're farmers now.'

'Well, your land begins here.' Degbert stopped on the far side of the tavern. 'From the water's edge to the tree line is yours.'

The farm was a strip about two hundred yards wide beside the river. Edgar studied the ground. Bishop Wynstan had not told them how narrow it was, so Edgar had not imagined that such a large proportion of the land would be waterlogged. As the ground rose away from the river it improved, becoming a sandy loam, with green shoots growing.

Degbert said: 'It goes west for about seven hundred yards, then there's forest again.'

Ma set off to walk between the marsh and the rising ground, and the others followed.

Degbert said: 'As you see, there's a nice crop of oats coming up.'

Edgar did not know oats from any other grain, and he had thought the shoots were plain grass.

Ma said: 'There's as much weed as there is oats.'

They walked for less than half a mile and came to a pair of buildings at the crest of a rise. Beyond the buildings, the cleared land came to an end and the woods went down to the bank of the river.

Degbert said: 'There's a useful little orchard.'

It was not really an orchard. There were a few small apple trees and a cluster of medlar shrubs. The medlar was a winter-ripening fruit that was hardly palatable to humans, and was sometimes fed to pigs. The flesh was tart and hard, though it could be softened either by frost or by overripening.

'The rent is four fat piglets, payable at Michaelmas,' Degbert said.

That was it, Edgar realized; they had seen the whole farm.

'It's thirty acres, all right,' said Ma, 'but they're very poor acres.'

'That's why the rent is low.'

Ma was negotiating, Edgar knew. He had seen her do this many times with customers and suppliers. She was good at it, but this was a challenge. What did she have to offer? Degbert would prefer the farm to be tenanted, of course, and he might want to please his cousin the bishop; but on the other hand he was clearly not much in need of the small rent, and he could easily tell Wynstan that Ma had refused to take on such an unpromising prospect. Ma was bargaining from a weak position.

They inspected the house. Edgar noted that it had earth-set timber posts with wattle-and-daub walls between the posts. The reeds on the floor were mouldy and smelt bad. Cwenburg had been right, there were holes in the thatched roof, but they could be patched.

Ma said: 'The place is a dump.'

'A few simple repairs.'

'It looks like a lot of work to me. We'll have to take timber from the forest.'

'Yes, yes,' said Degbert impatiently.

Despite the peevish tone Degbert had made an important concession. They could fell trees, and there was no mention of payment. Free timber was worth a lot.

The smaller building was in worse condition than the house. Ma said: 'The barn is practically falling down.'

Degbert said: 'At the moment you have no need of a barn. You have nothing to store there.'

'You're right, we're broke,' Ma said. 'So we won't be able to pay the rent come Michaelmas.'

Degbert looked foolish. He could hardly argue. 'You can owe me,' he said. 'Five piglets at Michaelmas next year.'

'How can I buy a sow? These oats will be barely enough to feed my sons this winter. I won't have anything left over to trade.'

'Are you refusing to take the farm?'

'No, I'm saying that if the farm is to be viable you have to give me more help. I need a rent holiday, and I need a sow. And I need a sack of flour on credit – we have no food.'

It was a bold set of demands. Landlords expected to be paid, not to pay out. But sometimes they had to help tenants get started, and Degbert had to know that.

Degbert looked frustrated, but he gave in. 'All right,' he said. 'I'll lend you flour. No rent this year. I'll get you a female piglet, but you'll have to owe me one from your first litter, and that's on top of the rent.'

'I suppose I'll have to accept that,' said Ma. She spoke with apparent reluctance, but Edgar was pretty sure she had made a good bargain.

'And I'll have to get back to my dinner,' Degbert said grumpily, sensing that he had been defeated. He left, heading back towards the hamlet.

Ma called after him: 'When do we get the piglet?'

He answered without looking back. 'Soon.'

Edgar surveyed his new home. It was dismal, but he felt surprisingly good. They had a challenge to meet, and that was a lot better than the despair he had felt earlier.

Ma said: 'Erman, go into the forest and gather firewood. Eadbald, go to that alehouse and beg a burning stick from their fireplace – use your charm on that ferry girl. Edgar, see if you can make temporary patches for the holes in the roof – we've no time now to repair the thatch properly. Snap to it, boys. And tomorrow we'll start weeding the field.'

ÞÞÞ

DEGBERT DID NOT bring a piglet to the farmhouse in the next few days.

Ma did not mention it. She weeded the oats with Erman and Eadbald, the three of them bending double in the long, narrow field, while Edgar repaired the house and barn with timber from the forest, using the Viking axe and a few rusty tools left behind by the previous tenant.

But Edgar worried. Degbert was no more trustworthy than his cousin Bishop Wynstan. Edgar feared that Degbert would see them settling in, decide that they were now committed, and go back on his word. Then the family would struggle to pay the rent – and once they defaulted it would be desperately difficult to catch up, as Edgar knew from observing the fate of improvident neighbours in Combe.

'Don't fret,' Ma said when Edgar voiced his concern. 'Degbert can't escape me. The worst of priests has to go to church sooner or later.'

Edgar hoped she was right.

When they heard the church bell on Sunday morning they walked the length of their farm to the hamlet. Edgar guessed they were the last to arrive, having the farthest to come.

The church was nothing more than a square tower attached to a one-storey building to the east. Edgar could see that the entire structure was leaning downhill: one day it would fall over.

To enter they had to step sideways through an entrance that was partly blocked by the tree trunk supporting the round arch. Edgar could see why the arch was collapsing. The mortared joints between the stones of a round arch formed lines that should all point to the centre of one imaginary circle, like the spokes of a well-made cart wheel, but in this arch they were random. That made the structure weaker, and it looked ugly too.

The nave was the ground floor of the tower. Its high ceiling made the place seem even more cramped. A dozen or so adults and a few small children stood waiting for the service to begin. Edgar nodded to Cwenburg and Edith, the only two he had met before.

One of the stones making up the wall was carved with an inscription. Edgar could not read, but he guessed that someone was buried here, perhaps a nobleman who had built the church to be his last resting place.

A narrow archway in the east wall led into the chancel. Edgar peered through the gap to see an altar bearing a wooden cross with a wall painting of Jesus behind it. Degbert was there with several more clergymen.

The members of the congregation were more interested in the newcomers than in the clergy. The children stared openly at Edgar and his family, while their parents sneaked furtive glances then turned away to talk in low voices about what they had observed.

Degbert went through the service rapidly. It seemed hasty to the point of irreverence, Edgar thought, and he was not a particularly devout person. Perhaps it did not matter, for the congregation did not understand the Latin words anyway; but Edgar had been used to a more measured pace in Combe. In any event it was not his problem, so long as his sins were forgiven.

Edgar was not much troubled by religious feelings. When people discussed how the dead spent their time in heaven, or whether the devil had a tail, Edgar became impatient, believing that no one would ever know the truth of such things in this life. He liked questions that had definite answers, such as how high the mast of a ship should be.

Cwenburg stood near him and smiled. Evidently she had decided to be nice. 'You should come to my house one evening,' she said.

'I've no money for ale.'

'You can still visit your neighbours.'

'Maybe.' Edgar did not want to be unfriendly, but he had no desire to spend an evening in Cwenburg's company.

At the end of the service Ma determinedly followed the clergy out of the building. Edgar went with her, and Cwenburg followed. Ma accosted Degbert before he could get away. 'I need that sow you promised me,' she said.

Edgar was proud of his mother. She was determined and fearless. And she had picked her moment perfectly. Degbert would not want to be accused of reneging on a promise in front of the entire village.

'Speak to Fat Bebbe,' he said curtly, and walked on.

Edgar turned to Cwenburg. 'Who's Bebbe?'

Cwenburg pointed to a fat woman squeezing herself around the tree trunk. 'She supplies the minster with eggs and meat and other produce from her smallholding.'

Edgar identified the woman to Ma, who approached her. 'The dean told me to speak to you about a piglet,' she said.

Bebbe was red-faced and friendly. 'Oh, yes,' she said. 'You're to be given a weaned female piglet. Come with me and you can take your pick.'

Ma went with Bebbe, and the three boys followed.

'How are you getting on?' Bebbe asked kindly. 'I hope that farmhouse isn't too ruinous.'

'It's bad, but we're repairing it,' Ma said.

The two women were about the same age, Edgar thought. It looked as if they might get along. He hoped so: Ma needed a friend.

Bebbe had a small house on a large lot. At the back of the building was a duck pond, a henhouse and a tethered cow with a new calf. Attached to the house was a fenced enclosure where a big sow had a litter of eight. Bebbe was well-off, though probably dependent on the minster.

Ma studied the piglets intently for several minutes then pointed to a small, energetic one. 'Good choice,' said Bebbe, and she picked up the little animal with a swift, practised movement. It squealed with fright. She drew a handful of leather thongs from the pouch at her belt and tied its feet together. 'Who's going to carry it?'

'I will,' said Edgar.

'Put your arm under its belly, and take care it doesn't bite you.'

Edgar did as instructed. The piglet was filthy, of course.

Ma thanked Bebbe.

'I'll need those thongs back as soon as is convenient,' Bebbe said. All kinds of string were valuable, whether hide, sinew or thread.

'Of course,' said Ma.

They moved away. The piglet squealed and wriggled frantically as it was taken away from its mother. Edgar closed its jaws with his hand to stop the noise. As if in retaliation, the piglet did a stinking liquid shit all down the front of his tunic.

They stopped at the tavern and begged Cwenburg to give them some scraps to feed the piglet. She brought an armful of cheese rinds, fish tails, apple cores and other leftovers. 'You stink,' she said to Edgar.

He knew that. 'I'll have to jump in the river,' he said.

They walked back to the farmhouse. Edgar put the piglet in the barn. He had already repaired the hole in the wall, so the little animal could not escape. He would put Brindle in the barn at night to guard it.

Ma heated water on the fire and threw in the scraps to make a mash. Edgar was glad they had a pig, but it was another hungry mouth. They could not eat it: they had to feed it until it was mature then breed from it. For a while it would be just another drain on their scarce resources.

'She'll soon feed herself from the forest floor, especially when the acorns begin to fall,' Ma said. 'But we have to train her to come home at night, otherwise she'll be stolen by outlaws or eaten by wolves.'

Edgar said: 'How did you train your pigs when you were growing up on the farm?'

'I don't know – they always came to my mother's call. I suppose they knew she might give them something to eat. They wouldn't come to us children.'

'Our piglet could learn to respond to your voice, but then she might not come to anyone else. We need a bell.'

Ma gave a sceptical snort. Bells were costly. 'I need a golden brooch and a white pony,' she said. 'But I'm not going to get them.'

'You never know what you might get,' said Edgar.

He went to the barn. He had remembered something he had seen there: an old sickle, its handle rotted and its curved blade rusted and broken in two. He had thrown it into a corner with other odds and ends. Now he retrieved the broken-off end of the blade, a foot-long crescent of iron that was no apparent use for anything.

He found a smooth stone, sat down in the morning sunshine, and started to rub the rust off the blade. It was a strenuous and tedious task, but he was used to hard work, and he kept going until the metal was clean enough for the sun to glint off it. He did not sharpen the edge: he was not going to cut anything with it.

Using a pliant twig as a rope, he suspended the blade from a branch, then struck it with the stone. It rang out, not with a bell-like tone but with an unmusical clang that was nevertheless quite loud.

He showed it to Ma. 'If you bang that before you feed the piglet every day, she will learn to come at the sound,' he said.

'Very good,' Ma said. 'How long will it take you to make the golden brooch?' Her tone was bantering, but there was a touch of pride in it. She thought Edgar had inherited her brains, and she was probably right.

The midday meal was ready, but it was only flat bread with wild onions, and Edgar wanted to wash before he ate. He walked along the river until he came to a little mud beach. He took off his tunic and washed it in the shallows, rubbing and squeezing the woollen cloth to get rid of the stink. Then he spread it on a rock to dry in the sun.

He immersed himself in the water, ducking his head to wash his hair. People said that bathing was bad for your health, and Edgar never bathed in winter, but those who never bathed at all stank all their lives. Ma and Pa had taught their sons to keep themselves fresh by bathing at least once a year.

Edgar had been brought up by the sea, and he had been able to swim for as long as he could walk. Now he decided to cross the river, just for the fun of it.

The current was moderate and the swim was easy. He enjoyed the sensation of the cool water on his bare skin. When he reached the far side he turned and came back. Near the shore he found his footing and stood up. The surface was at the level of his knees, and the water dripped from his body. The sun would soon dry him.

At that moment he realized he was not alone.

Cwenburg was sitting on the bank, watching him. 'You look nice,' she said.

Edgar felt foolish. Embarrassed, he said: 'Would you please go away?'

'Why should I? Anyone can walk along the bank of a river.'

'Please.'

She stood up and turned around.

'Thank you,' Edgar said.

But he had misunderstood her intention. Instead of walking away, she pulled her dress over her head with a swift movement. Her naked skin was pale.

Edgar said: 'No, no!'

She turned around.

Edgar stared in horror. There was nothing wrong with her appearance – in fact, some part of his mind noted that she had a nice round figure – but she was the wrong woman. His heart was full of Sunni, and no one else's body could move him.

Cwenburg stepped into the river.

'Your hair's a different colour down there,' she said, with a smile of uninvited intimacy. 'Sort of gingery.'

'Keep away from me,' he said.

'Your thing is all shrivelled up with the cold water – shall I warm it up?' She reached for him.

Edgar pushed her away. Because he was tense and embarrassed he shoved her harder than he needed to. She lost her balance and fell over in the water. While she was recovering he went past her and onto the beach.

Behind him, she said: 'What's the matter with you? Are you a girlie-boy who likes men?'

He picked up his tunic. It was still damp, but he put it on anyway. Feeling less vulnerable, he turned to her. 'Yes, that's right,' he said. 'I'm a girlie-boy.'

She was glaring angrily at him. 'No, you're not,' she said. 'You're making that up.'

'Yes, I'm making it up.' Edgar's self-control began to slip. 'The truth is that I don't like you. Now will you leave me alone?'

She came out of the water. 'You pig,' she said. 'I hope you starve to death on this barren farm.' She pulled her dress on over her head. 'Then I hope you go to hell,' she said, and she walked off.

Edgar was relieved to be rid of her. Then, a moment later, he felt sorry that he had been unkind. It was partly her fault for being insistent, but he could have been gentler. He often regretted his impulses, and wished he had more self-discipline.

Sometimes, he thought, it was difficult to do the right thing.

ÞÞÞ

THE COUNTRYSIDE WAS quiet.

At Combe there was always noise: herring gulls' raucous laughter, the ring of hammers on nails, a crowd's murmur and the cry of a lone voice. Even at night there was the creaking of boats as they rose and fell on the restless water. But the countryside was often completely silent. If there was a wind, the trees would whisper discontentedly, but if not, it could be as quiet as the tomb.

So when Brindle barked in the middle of the night, Edgar came awake fast.

He stood up immediately and took his axe from its peg on the wall. His heart was beating hard and his breath was shallow.

Ma's voice came out of the gloom. 'Be careful.'

Brindle was in the barn, and her bark was distant but alarmed. Edgar had put her there to guard the piglet, and something had alerted her to danger.

Edgar went to the door, but Ma was there ahead of him. He saw the firelight glint ominously on the knife in her hand. He had cleaned and sharpened it himself, to save her the effort, so he knew it was deadly keen.

She hissed: 'Step back from the door. One of them may be lying in wait.'

Edgar did as he was told. His brothers were behind him. He hoped that they, too, had picked up weapons of some kind.

Ma lifted the bar carefully, making almost no noise. Then she threw the door wide.

Right away a figure stepped into the doorway. Ma had been right to warn Edgar: the thieves had anticipated that the family would wake, and one thief had stood ready to ambush them if they came incautiously running out of the house. There was a bright moon, and Edgar clearly saw the long dagger in the thief's right hand. The man thrust blindly into the darkness of the house, stabbing nothing but air.

Edgar hefted his axe, but Ma was quicker. Her knife gleamed and the thief roared in pain and fell to his knees. She stepped closer and her blade flashed across the man's throat.

Edgar pushed past them both. As he emerged into the moonlight he heard the piglet squeal. A moment later he saw two more figures coming out of the barn. One of them wore some kind of headgear that partly covered his face. In his arms he held the wriggling piglet.

They saw Edgar and ran.

Edgar was outraged. That pig was precious. If they lost it, they would not get another one: people would say they could not look after their livestock. In a moment of piercing anxiety Edgar acted without thinking. He swung the axe back over his head then hurled it at the back of the thief with the pig.

He thought it was going to miss, and he groaned in despair; but the sharp blade bit into the fugitive's upper arm. He gave a high-pitched scream, dropped the pig, and fell to his knees, clutching the wound.

The second man helped him up.

Edgar dashed towards them.

They ran on, leaving the pig behind.

Edgar hesitated for a heartbeat. He wanted to catch the thieves. But if he let the pig go, it might run a long way in its terror, and he might never find it. He abandoned pursuit of the men and went after the animal. It was young and its legs were short, and after a minute he caught up, threw himself on top of it, and got hold of a leg with both hands. The pig struggled but could not escape his grip.

He got the little beast securely in his arms, stood up, and walked back to the farmhouse.

He put the pig in the barn. He took a moment to congratulate Brindle, who wagged her tail proudly. He retrieved his axe from where it had fallen and wiped the blade on the grass to clean off the thief's blood. Finally he rejoined his family.

They were standing over the other thief. 'He's dead,' said Eadbald.

Erman said: 'Let's throw him in the river.'

'No,' said Ma. 'I want other thieves to know we killed him.' She was in no danger from the law: it was well established that a thief caught red-handed could be killed on the spot. 'Follow me, boys. Bring the corpse.'

Erman and Eadbald picked it up. Ma led them into the woods and went a hundred yards along a just-visible path through the undergrowth until she came to a place where it crossed another almost imperceptible track. Anyone coming to the farm through the forest would have to pass this junction.

She looked at the surrounding trees in the moonlight and pointed to one with low spreading branches. 'I want to hang the body up in that tree,' she said.

Erman said: 'What for?'

'To show people what happens to men who try to rob us.'

Edgar was impressed. He had never known his mother to be so harsh. But circumstances had changed.

Erman said: 'We haven't got any rope.'

Ma said: 'Edgar will think of something.'

Edgar nodded. He pointed to a forked branch at a height of about eight feet. 'Wedge him in there, with one bough under each armpit,' he said.

While his brothers were manhandling the corpse up into the tree, Edgar found a stick a foot long and an inch in diameter and sharpened one end with his axe blade.

The brothers got the body into position. 'Now pull his arms together until his hands are crossed in front.'

When the brothers were holding the arms in position, Edgar held one dead hand and stuck the stick into the wrist. He had to tap it with the head of the axe to push it through the flesh. Very little blood flowed: the man's heart had stopped some time ago.

Edgar lined up the other wrist and hammered the stick through that, too. Now the hands were riveted together and the body was firmly hung from the tree.

It would remain there until it rotted away, he thought.

But the other thieves must have returned, for the corpse was gone in the morning.

ÞÞÞ

A FEW DAYS later Ma sent Edgar to the village to borrow a length of stout cord to tie up her shoes, which had broken. Borrowing was common among neighbours, but no one ever had enough string. However, Ma had told the story of the Viking raid twice, first in the priests' house and then at the alehouse; and although peasants were never quick to accept newcomers, the inhabitants of Dreng's Ferry had warmed to Ma on hearing of her tragedy.

It was early evening. A small group sat on the benches outside Dreng's alehouse, drinking from wooden cups as the sun went down. Edgar still had not tasted the ale, but the customers seemed to like it.

He had met all the villagers now, and he recognized the members of the group. Dean Degbert was talking to his brother, Dreng. Cwenburg and red-faced Bebbe were listening. There were three other women present. Leofgifu, called Leaf, was Cwenburg's mother; Ethel, a younger woman, was Dreng's other wife or perhaps concubine; and Blod, who was filling the cups from a jug, was a slave.

As Edgar approached, the slave looked up and said to him in broken Anglo-Saxon: 'You want ale?'

Edgar shook his head. 'I've no money.'

The others looked at him. Cwenburg said with a sneer: 'Why have you come to an alehouse if you can't afford a cup of ale?'

Clearly she was still smarting from Edgar's rejection of her advances. He had made an enemy. He groaned inwardly.

Addressing the group, rather than Cwenburg herself, he said humbly: 'My mother asks to borrow a length of stout cord to mend her shoe.'

Cwenburg said: 'Tell her to make her own cord.'

The others were silent, watching.

Edgar was embarrassed, but he stood his ground. 'The loan would be a kindness,' he said through gritted teeth. 'We will repay it when we get back on our feet.'

'If that ever happens,' Cwenburg said.

Leaf made an impatient noise. She looked about thirty, so she must have been fifteen when she gave birth to Cwenburg. She had once been pretty, Edgar guessed, but now she looked as if she drank too much of her own strong brew. However, she was sober enough to be embarrassed by her daughter's rudeness. 'Don't be so unneighbourly, girl,' she said.

Dreng said angrily: 'Leave her alone. She's all right.'

He was an indulgent father, Edgar noted; that might account for his daughter's behaviour.

Leaf stood up. 'Come inside,' she said to Edgar in a kindly tone. 'I'll see what I can find.'

He followed her into the house. She drew a cup of ale from a barrel and handed it to him. 'Free of charge,' she said.

'Thank you.' He took a mouthful. It lived up to its reputation: it was tasty, and it instantly lifted his spirits. He drained the cup and said: 'That's very good.'

She smiled.

It crossed Edgar's mind that Leaf might have the same kind of designs on him as her daughter. He was not vain, and did not believe that all women must be attracted to him; but he guessed that in a small place every new man must be of interest to the women.

However, Leaf turned away and rummaged in a chest. A moment later she came up with a yard of string. 'Here you are.'

She was just being kind, he realized. 'It's most neighbourly of you,' he said.

She took his empty cup. 'My best wishes to your mother. She's a brave woman.'

Edgar went out. Degbert, evidently having been relaxed by what he was drinking, was holding forth. 'According to the calendars, we are in the nine hundred and ninety-seventh year of our Lord,' he said. 'Jesus is nine hundred and ninety-seven years old. In three years' time it will be the millennium.'

Edgar understood numbers, and he could not let that pass. 'Wasn't Jesus born in the year one?' he said.

'He was,' said Degbert. He added snootily: 'Every educated man knows that.'

'Then he must have had his first birthday in year two.'

Degbert began to look unsure.

Edgar went on: 'In year three, he became two years old, and so on. So this year, nine hundred and ninety-seven, he becomes nine hundred and ninety-six.'

Degbert blustered. 'You don't know what you're talking about, you arrogant young pup.'

A quiet voice in the back of Edgar's mind told him not to argue, but the voice was overwhelmed by his wish to correct an arithmetical error. 'No, no,' he said. 'In fact, Jesus's birthday will be on Christmas Day, so as of now he's still only nine hundred and ninety-five and a half.'

Leaf, watching from the doorway, grinned and said: 'He's got you there, Degsy.'

Degbert was livid. 'How dare you speak like that to a priest?' he said to Edgar. 'Who do you think you are? You can't even read!'

'No, but I can count,' Edgar said stubbornly.

Dreng said: 'Take your string and be off with you, and don't come back until you've learned to respect your elders and betters.'

'It's just numbers,' Edgar said, backtracking when it was too late. 'I didn't mean to be disrespectful.'

Degbert said: 'Get out of my sight.'

Dreng added: 'Go on, get lost.'

Edgar turned and walked away, heading back along the river bank, despondent. His family needed all the help it could get, but he had now made two enemies.

Why had he opened his fool mouth?

4

THE LADY RAGNHILD, DAUGHTER of Count Hubert of Cherbourg, was sitting between an English monk and a French priest. Ragna, as she was called, found the monk interesting and the priest pompous – but the priest was the one she was supposed to charm.

It was the time of the midday meal at Cherbourg Castle. The imposing stone fort stood at the top of the hill overlooking the harbour. Ragna's father was proud of the building. It was innovative and unusual.

Count Hubert was proud of many things. He cherished his warlike Viking heritage, but he was more gratified by the way the Vikings had become Normans, with their own version of the French language. Most of all, he valued the way they had adopted Christianity, restoring the churches and monasteries that had been sacked by their ancestors. In a hundred years the former pirates had created a law-abiding civilization the equal of anything in Europe.

The long trestle table stood in the great hall, on the upstairs floor of the castle. It was covered with white linen cloths that reached to the floor. Ragna's parents sat at the head. Her mother's name was Ginnlaug, but she had changed it to the more French-sounding Genevieve to please her husband.

The count and countess and their more important guests ate from bronze bowls, drank from cherry-wood cups with silver rims, and held parcel-gilt knives and spoons; costly tableware, though not extravagant.

The English monk, Brother Aldred, was miraculously handsome. He reminded Ragna of an ancient Roman marble sculpture she had seen at Rouen, the head of a man with short curly hair, stained with age and lacking the tip of the nose, but clearly part of what had once been a statue of a god.

Aldred had arrived the previous afternoon, clutching to his chest a box of books he had bought at the great Norman abbey of Jumièges. 'It has a scriptorium as good as any in the world!' Aldred enthused. 'An army of monks copying and decorating manuscripts for the enlightenment of mankind.' Books, and the wisdom they could bring, clearly constituted Aldred's great passion.

Ragna had a notion that this passion had taken the place, in his life, that might otherwise have been held by a kind of romantic love that was forbidden by his faith. He was charming to her, but a different, hungrier expression came over his face when he looked at her brother, Richard, who was a tall boy of fourteen with lips like a girl's.

Now Aldred was waiting for a favourable wind to take him back across the Channel to England. 'I can't wait to get home to Shiring and show my brethren how the Jumièges monks illuminate their letters,' he said. He spoke French with some Latin and Anglo-Saxon words thrown in. Ragna knew Latin, and she had picked up some Anglo-Saxon from an English nursemaid who had married a Norman sailor and come to live in Cherbourg. 'And two of the books I bought are works that I've never previously heard of!' Aldred went on.

'Are you prior of Shiring?' Ragna asked. 'You seem quite young.'

'I'm thirty-three, and no, I'm not the prior,' he said with a smile. 'I'm the armarius, in charge of the scriptorium and the library.'

'Is it a big library?'

'We have eight books, but when I get home we'll have sixteen. And the scriptorium consists of me and an assistant, Brother Tatwine. He colours the capital letters. I do the plain writing – I'm more interested in words than colours.'

The priest interrupted their conversation, reminding Ragna of her duty to make a good impression. Father Louis said: 'Tell me, Lady Ragnhild, do you read?'

'Of course I do.'

He raised an eyebrow in faint surprise. There was no 'of course' about it: by no means all noblewomen could read.

Ragna realized she had just made the kind of remark that gave her a reputation for haughtiness. Trying to be more amiable, she added: 'My father taught me to read when I was small, before my brother was born.'

When Father Louis had arrived a week ago, Ragna's mother had drawn her into the private quarters of the count and countess and said: 'Why do you think he's here?'

Ragna had frowned. 'I don't know.'

'He's an important man, secretary to the count of Reims and a canon of the cathedral.' Genevieve was statuesque but, despite her imposing appearance, she was easily overawed.

'So what brings him to Cherbourg?'

'You,' Genevieve had said.

Ragna had begun to see.

Her mother went on: 'The count of Reims has a son, Guillaume, who is your age and unmarried. The count is looking for a wife for his son. And Father Louis is here to see whether you might be suitable.'

Ragna felt a twinge of resentment. This kind of thing was normal, but all the same it made her feel like a cow being appraised by a prospective purchaser. She suppressed her indignation. 'What's Guillaume like?'

'He's a nephew of King Robert.' Robert II, twenty-five years old, was King of France. For Genevieve the greatest asset a man could have was a royal connection.

Ragna had other priorities. She was impatient to know what he

69

was like, regardless of his social status. 'Anything else?' she said, in a tone of voice which, she realized immediately, was rather arch.

'Don't be sarcastic. It's just the kind of thing that puts men off you.'

That shot went home. Ragna had already discouraged several perfectly appropriate suitors. Somehow she scared them. Being so tall did not help – she had her mother's figure – but there was more to it than that.

Genevieve went on: 'Guillaume is not diseased, or mad, or depraved.'

'He sounds like every girl's dream.'

'There you go again.'

'Sorry. I'll be nice to Father Louis, I promise.'

Ragna was twenty years old, and she could not remain single indefinitely. She did not want to end up in a nunnery.

Her mother was getting anxious. 'You want a grand passion, a lifelong romance, but those exist only in poems,' Genevieve had said. 'In real life we women settle for what we can get.'

Ragna knew she was right.

She would probably marry Guillaume, provided he was not completely repugnant; but she wanted to do it on her own terms. She wanted Louis to approve of her, but she also needed him to understand what sort of wife she would be. She did not plan to be purely decorative, like a gorgeous tapestry her husband would be proud to show to guests; nor would she be merely a hostess, organizing banquets and entertaining distinguished visitors. She would be her husband's partner in the management of his estate. It was not unusual for wives to play such a role: every time a nobleman went off to war he had to leave someone in charge of his lands and his fortune. Sometimes his deputy would be a brother or a grown-up son, but often it was his wife.

Now, over a dish of bass fresh from the sea cooked in cider, Louis started to probe her intellectual abilities. With a distinct touch of scepticism he asked: 'And what kind of thing do you read, my lady?' His tone said he could hardly believe that an attractive young woman would understand literature.

If she had liked him better, she would have found it easier to impress him.

'I like poems that tell stories,' she said.

'For example . . . ?'

He obviously thought she would be unable to name a work of literature, but he was wrong. 'The story of St Eulalie is very moving,' she said. 'In the end she goes up to heaven in the form of a dove.'

'She does indeed,' said Louis, in a voice that suggested she could not tell him anything about saints that he did not already know.

'And there's an English poem called "The Wife's Lament".' She turned to Aldred. 'Do you know it?'

'I do, although I don't know whether it was English originally. Poets travel. They amuse a nobleman's court for a year or two, then move on when their poems become stale. Or they may win the esteem of a richer patron and be lured away. As they go from place to place, admirers translate their works into other tongues.'

Ragna was fascinated. She liked Aldred. He knew such a lot, and he was able to share his knowledge without using it to prove his superiority.

She turned to Louis again, mindful of her mission. 'Don't you find that fascinating, Father Louis? You're from Reims, that's near the German-speaking lands.'

'It is,' he said. 'You're well educated, my lady.'

Ragna felt she had passed a test. She wondered whether Louis' condescending attitude had been a deliberate attempt to provoke her. She was glad she had not risen to the bait. 'You're very kind,' she said insincerely. 'My brother has a tutor, and I'm allowed to sit in on the lessons as long as I remain silent.'

'Very good. Not many girls know so much. But as for me, I mainly read the holy scriptures.'

'Naturally.'

Ragna had won a measure of approval. Guillaume's wife would have to be cultured, and able to hold her own in conversation, and Ragna had proved herself in that respect. She hoped that made up for her earlier hauteur.

A man-at-arms called Bern the Giant came and spoke quietly to Count Hubert. Bern had a red beard and a fat belly.

After a short discussion the count got up from the table. Ragna's father was a small man and seemed even smaller beside Bern. He had the look of a mischievous boy, despite his forty-five years. The back of his head was shaved in the style fashionable among the Normans. He came to Ragna's side. 'I have to go to Valognes unexpectedly,' he said. 'I'd planned to investigate a dispute in the village of Saint-Martin today, but now I can't go. Will you take my place?'

'With pleasure,' Ragna said.

'There's a serf called Gaston who won't pay his rent, apparently as some kind of protest.'

'I'll deal with it, don't worry.'

'Thank you.' The count left the room with Bern.

Louis said: 'Your father is fond of you.'

Ragna smiled. 'As I am of him.'

'Do you often deputize for him?'

'The village of Saint-Martin is special to me. All that district is part of my marriage portion. But yes, I often stand in for my father, there and elsewhere.'

'It would be more usual for his wife to be his deputy.'

'True.'

'Your father likes to do things differently.' He spread his arms to indicate the castle. 'This building, for example.'

Ragna could not tell whether Louis was disapproving or just intrigued. 'My mother dislikes the work of governing, but I'm fascinated by it.'

Aldred put in: 'Women sometimes do it well. King Alfred of England had a daughter called Ethelfled who ruled the great region of Mercia after her husband died. She fortified towns and won battles.'

It occurred to Ragna that she had an opportunity to impress Louis. She could invite him to see how she dealt with the ordinary folk. It was part of the duty of a noblewoman, and she knew she did it well. 'Would you care to come with me to Saint-Martin, Father?'

'I would be pleased,' he said immediately.

'On the way, perhaps you can tell me about the household of the count of Reims. I believe he has a son my age.'

'He does indeed.'

Now that her invitation had been accepted, she found she was not looking forward to a day talking to Louis, so she turned to Aldred. 'Will you come, too?' she said. 'You'll be back by the evening tide, so if the wind should change during the day you could still leave tonight.'

'I'd be delighted.'

They all got up from the table.

Ragna's personal maid was a black-haired girl her own age called Cat. She had a tip-tilted nose with a sharp point. Her nostrils looked like the nibs of two quill pens laid side by side. Despite that she was attractive, with a lively look and a sparkle of mischief in her eyes.

Cat helped Ragna take off her silk slippers, then stored them in the chest. The maid then got out linen leggings to protect the skin of Ragna's calves while riding, and replaced her slippers with leather boots. Finally she handed her a riding whip.

Ragna's mother came to her. 'Be sweet to Father Louis,' she said. 'Don't try to outsmart him – men hate that.'

'Yes, Mother,' Ragna said meekly. Ragna knew perfectly well that women should not try to be clever, but she had broken the rule so often that her mother was entitled to remind her.

She left the keep and made her way to the stables. Four men-at-arms, led by Bern the Giant, were waiting to escort her: the count must have forewarned them. Stable hands had already saddled her favourite horse, a grey mare called Astrid.

Brother Aldred, strapping a leather pad to his pony, looked admiringly at her brass-studded wooden saddle. 'It's nice-looking, but doesn't it hurt the horse?'

'No,' Ragna said firmly. 'The wood spreads the load, whereas a soft saddle gives the horse a sore back.'

'Look at that, Dismas,' said Aldred to his pony. 'Wouldn't you like something so grand?'

Ragna noticed that Dismas had a white marking on his forehead that was more or less cross-shaped. That seemed appropriate for a monk's mount.

Louis said: 'Dismas?'

Ragna said: 'That was the name of one of the thieves crucified with Jesus.'

'I know that,' said Louis heavily; and Ragna told herself not to be so clever.

Aldred said: 'This Dismas also steals, especially food.'

'Huh.' Louis clearly did not think such a name should be used in a jokey way, but he said no more, and turned away to saddle his gelding.

They rode out of the castle compound. As they made their way down the hill, Ragna cast an expert eye over the ships in the harbour. She had been raised in a port and she could identify different styles of vessel. Fishing boats and coastal craft predominated today, but at the dockside she noticed an English trader that must be the one Aldred planned to sail in; and no one could mistake the menacing profile of the Viking warships anchored offshore.

They turned south, and a few minutes later were leaving the houses of the small town behind. The flat landscape was swept by sea breezes. Ragna followed a familiar path beside cow pastures and apple orchards. She said: 'Now that you've got to know our country, Brother Aldred, how do you like it?'

'I notice that noblemen here seem to have one wife and no concubines, at least officially. In England, concubinage and even polygamy are tolerated, despite the clear teaching of the Church.'

'Such things may be hidden,' Ragna said. 'Norman noblemen aren't saints.'

'I'm sure, but at least people here know what's sinful and what's not. The other thing is that I've seen no slaves anywhere in Normandy.'

'There's a slave market in Rouen, but the buyers are foreigners. Slavery has been almost completely abolished here. Our clergy condemn it, mainly because so many slaves are used for fornication and sodomy.'

Louis made a startled noise. Perhaps he was not used to young women talking about fornication and sodomy. Ragna realized with a sinking heart that she had made another mistake.

Aldred was not shocked. He continued the discussion without pause. 'On the other hand,' he said, 'your peasants are serfs, who need the permission of their lord to marry, change their way of making a living, or move to another village. By contrast, English peasants are free.'

Ragna reflected on this. She had not realized that the Norman system was not universal.

They came to a hamlet called Les Chênes. The grass was growing tall in the meadows, Ragna saw. The villagers would reap it in a week or two, she guessed, and make hay to feed livestock in the winter.

The men and women working in the fields stopped what they were doing and waved. 'Deborah!' they called. 'Deborah!' Ragna waved back.

Louis said: 'Did I hear them call you Deborah?'

'Yes. It's a nickname.'

'Where does it come from?'

Ragna grinned. 'You'll see.'

The sound of seven horses brought people out of their houses. Ragna saw a woman she recognized, and reined in. 'You're Ellen, the baker.'

'Yes, my lady. I pray I see you well and happy.'

'What happened to that little boy of yours who fell out of a tree?'

'He died, my lady.'

'I'm so sorry.'

'They say I shouldn't mourn, for I've got three more sons.'

'Then they're fools, whoever they are,' said Ragna. 'The loss of a child is a terrible grief to a mother, and it makes no difference how many more you may have.'

Tears fell on Ellen's wind-reddened cheeks, and she reached out a hand. Ragna took it and squeezed gently. Ellen kissed Ragna's hand and said: 'You understand.'

'Perhaps I do, a little,' said Ragna. 'Goodbye, Ellen.'

They rode on. Aldred said: 'Poor woman.'

Louis said: 'I give you credit, Lady Ragna. That woman will worship you for the rest of her life.'

Ragna felt slighted. Louis obviously thought she had been kind merely as a way of making herself popular. She wanted to ask him whether he thought no one ever felt genuine compassion. But she remembered her duty and kept silent.

Louis said: 'But I still don't know why they call you Deborah.'

Ragna gave him an enigmatic smile. Let him figure it out for himself, she thought.

Aldred said: 'I notice that a lot of people around here have the wonderful red hair that you have, Lady Ragna.'

Ragna was aware that she had a glorious head of red-gold curls.

'That's the Viking blood,' she said. 'Around here, some people still speak Norse.'

Louis commented: 'The Normans are different from the rest of us in the Frankish lands.'

That might have been a compliment, but Ragna thought not.

After an hour they came to Saint-Martin. Ragna halted on the outskirts. Several men and women were busy in a leafy orchard, and among them she spotted Gerbert, the reeve, or village headman. She dismounted and crossed a pasture to talk to him, and her companions followed.

Gerbert bowed to her. He was an odd-looking character, with a crooked nose and teeth so misshapen that he could not close his mouth completely. Count Hubert had made him headman because he was intelligent, but Ragna was not sure she trusted him.

Everyone stopped what they were doing and clustered around Ragna and Gerbert. 'What work are you doing here today, Gerbert?'

'Picking off some of the little apples, my lady, so the others will grow fatter and juicier,' he said.

'So you can make good cider.'

'Cider from Saint-Martin is stronger than most, by the grace of God and good husbandry.'

Half the villages in Normandy claimed to make the strongest cider, but Ragna did not say that. 'What do you do with the unripe apples?'

'Feed them to the goats, to make their cheese sweet.'

'Who's the best cheesewright in the village?'

'Renée,' said Gerbert immediately. 'She uses ewes' milk.'

Some of the others shook their heads. Ragna turned to them. 'What do the rest of you think?'

Two or three people said: 'Torquil.'

'Come with me, then, all of you, and I'll taste them both.'

The serfs followed happily. They generally welcomed any change in the tedium of their days, and they were rarely reluctant to stop work.

Louis said with a touch of irritation: 'You didn't ride all this way to taste cheese, did you? Aren't you here to settle a dispute?'

'Yes. This is my way. Be patient.'

Louis grunted crabbily.

Ragna did not get back on her horse, but walked into the village, following a dusty track between fields golden with grain. On foot she could more easily talk to people on the way. She paid particular attention to the women, who would give her gossipy information that a man might not bother with. On the walk she learned that Renée was the wife of Gerbert; that Renée's brother Bernard had a herd of sheep; and that Bernard was involved in a dispute with Gaston, the one who was refusing to pay his rent.

She always tried hard to remember names. It made them feel cared for. Every time she heard a name in casual conversation she would make a mental note.

As they walked, more people joined them. When they reached the village they found more waiting. There was some mystical communication across fields, Ragna knew: she could never understand it, but men and women working a mile or more away seemed to find out that visitors were arriving.

There was a small, elegant stone church with round-arched windows in neat rows. Ragna knew that the priest, Odo, served this and three other villages, visiting a different one every Sunday; but he was here in Saint-Martin today – that magical rural communication again.

Aldred went immediately to talk to Father Odo. Louis did not: perhaps he felt it was beneath his dignity to converse with a village priest.

Ragna tasted Renée's cheese and Torquil's, pronouncing them both so good that she could not pick a winner; and she bought a wheel of each, pleasing everyone.

She walked around the village, going into every house and barn, making sure she spoke a few words to each adult and many of the children; then, when she felt she had assured them all of her goodwill, she was ready to hold court.

Much of Ragna's strategy came from her father. He enjoyed meeting people and was good at making them his friends. Later, perhaps, some would become enemies – no ruler could please everyone all the time – but they would oppose him reluctantly. He had taught Ragna a lot and she had learned more just by watching him.

Gerbert brought a chair and placed it outside the west front of the church, and Ragna sat while everyone else stood around. Gerbert then presented Gaston, a big, strong peasant of about thirty with a shock of black hair. His face showed indignation but she guessed he was normally an amiable type.

'Now, Gaston,' she said, 'the time has come for you to tell me and your neighbours why you will not pay your rent.'

'My lady, I stand before you—'

'Wait.' Ragna held up a hand to stop him. 'Remember that this is not the court of the King of the Franks.' The villagers tittered. 'We don't need a formal speech with high-flown phrases.' There was not much chance of Gaston making such a speech, but he would probably try if he was not given a clear lead. 'Imagine that you're drinking cider with a group of friends and they've asked you why you're so riled up.'

'Yes, my lady. My lady, I haven't paid the rent because I can't.'

Gerbert said: 'Rubbish.'

Ragna frowned at Gerbert. 'Wait your turn,' she said sharply.

'Yes, my lady.'

'Gaston, what is your rent?'

'I raise beef cattle, my lady, and I owe your noble father two year-old beasts every Midsummer Day.'

'And you say you don't have the beasts?'

Gerbert interrupted again. 'Yes, he does.'

'Gerbert!'

'Sorry, my lady.'

Gaston said: 'My pasture was invaded. All the grass was eaten by Bernard's sheep. My cows had to eat old hay, so their milk dried up and two of my calves died.'

Ragna looked around, trying to remember which one was Bernard. Her eye lit on a small, thin man with hair like straw. Not being sure, she looked up and said: 'Let's hear from Bernard.'

She had been right. The thin man coughed and said: 'Gaston owes me a calf.'

Ragna saw that this was going to be a convoluted argument with a long history. 'Wait a moment,' she said. 'Is it true that your sheep cropped Gaston's pasture?'

'Yes, but he owed me.'

'We'll get to that. You let your sheep into his field.'

'I had good reason.'

'But that's why Gaston's calves died.'

Gerbert, the reeve, put in: 'Only this year's newborn calves died. He still has *last* year's. He's got two one-year-olds he can give to the count for his rent.'

Gaston said: 'But then I'll have no one-year-olds next year.'

Ragna began to get the dizzy feeling that always came when she tried to grasp a peasant squabble. 'Quiet, everyone,' she said. 'So far we've established that Bernard invaded Gaston's pasture – perhaps with reason, we shall see about that – and as a result Gaston feels – rightly or wrongly – that he is too poor to pay any rent this year. Now, Gaston, is it true that you owe Bernard a calf? Answer yes or no.'

'Yes.'

'And why have you not paid him?'

'I will pay him. I just haven't been able to yet.'

Gerbert said indignantly: 'Repayment can't be postponed for ever!'

Ragna listened patiently while Gaston explained why he had borrowed from Bernard and what difficulties he had paying back. Along the way, a variety of barely relevant issues were raised: perceived insults to one another, wives' insults to other wives, disputes about which words had been uttered and in what tone of voice. Ragna let it run. They needed to vent their anger. But finally she called a halt.

'I've heard enough,' she said. 'This is my decision. First, Gaston owes my father, the count, two year-old calves. No excuses. He was wrong to withhold them. He will not be punished for his transgression, because he was provoked; but what he owes, he owes.'

They received this with mixed reactions. Some muttered disapprovingly, others nodded agreement. Gaston's face was a mask of injured innocence.

'Second, Bernard is responsible for the deaths of two of Gaston's calves. Gaston's unpaid debt does not excuse Bernard's transgression. So Bernard owes Gaston two calves. However, Gaston already owed one calf to Bernard, so that leaves only one calf to pay.'

Now Bernard looked shocked. Ragna was being tougher than the people had expected. But they did not protest: her decisions were lawful.

'Finally, this dispute should not have been allowed to fester, and the blame for that lies with Gerbert.'

Gerbert said indignantly: 'My lady, may I speak?'

'Certainly not,' said Ragna. 'You've had your chance. It's my turn now. Be silent.'

Gerbert clammed up.

Ragna said: 'Gerbert is the reeve and should have resolved it long ago. I believe he was persuaded not to do so by his wife, Renée, who wanted him to favour her brother, Bernard.'

Renée looked abashed.

Ragna went on: 'Because all this is partly Gerbert's fault, he will forfeit a calf. I know he's got one, I saw it in his yard. He will give the calf to Bernard, who will give it to Gaston. And so debts are settled and wrongdoers are punished.'

She could tell instantly that the villagers approved of her judgement. She had insisted on obedience to the rules, but she had done it in a clever way. She saw them nodding to each other, some smiling, none objecting.

'And now,' she said, standing up, 'you can give me a cup of your famous cider, and Gaston and Bernard can drink together and make friends.'

The buzz of conversation grew as everyone discussed what had happened. Father Louis came to Ragna and said: 'Deborah was one of the judges of Israel. That's how you got your nickname.'

'Correct.'

'She is the only female judge.'

'So far.'

He nodded. 'You did that well.'

I've impressed him at last, Ragna thought.

They drank their cider and took their leave. Riding back to Cherbourg, Ragna asked Louis about Guillaume.

'He's tall,' Louis said.

That might help, she thought. 'What makes him angry?'

Louis' glance told Ragna that he recognized the shrewdness of her question. 'Nothing much,' he said. 'Guillaume takes life phlegmatically, in general. He may get irritated when a servant is careless: food badly cooked, a saddle loosely strapped, rumpled bed linen.'

He sounded pernickety, Ragna thought.

'He's very well thought of at Orléans,' Louis went on. Orléans was the main seat of the French court. 'His uncle, the king, is fond of him.'

'Is Guillaume ambitious?'

'No more than is usual in a young nobleman.'

A wary response, Ragna thought. Either Guillaume was ambitious to a fault, or the reverse. She said: 'What is he interested in? Hunting? Breeding horses? Music?'

'He loves beautiful things. He collects enamelled brooches and embellished strap ends. He has good taste. But you haven't asked me what I thought might have been a girl's first question.'

'What's that?'

'Whether he's handsome.'

'Ah,' said Ragna, 'on that matter I must make my own judgement.'

As they rode into Cherbourg, Ragna noticed that the wind had changed. 'Your ship will sail this evening,' she said to Aldred. 'You have an hour before the tide turns, but you'd better get on board.'

They returned to the castle. Aldred retrieved his box of books. Louis and Ragna went with him as he walked Dismas down to the waterfront. Aldred said: 'It's been a delight meeting you, Lady Ragna. If I'd known there were girls like you, perhaps I wouldn't have become a monk.'

It was the first flirtatious remark he had made to her, and she knew right away that he was merely being polite. 'Thank you for the compliment,' she said. 'But you would have become a monk anyway.'

He smiled ruefully, clearly understanding what she was thinking.

Ragna would probably never see him again, which was a shame, she thought.

A ship was coming in on the tail of the tide. It looked like an English fishing vessel, she pondered. The crew furled the sail and the ship drifted towards the shore.

Aldred went on board his chosen vessel with his horse. The crew were already untying the ropes and raising the anchor. Meanwhile the English fishing boat was doing the reverse.

Aldred waved to Ragna and Louis as the ship began to float away from land on the turning tide. At the same time, a small group of men disembarked from the newly arrived vessel. Ragna looked at them with idle curiosity. They had big moustaches but no beards, which marked them as English.

Ragna's eye was drawn to the tallest of them. Aged about forty, he had a thick mane of blond hair. A blue cloak, ruffled now by the breeze, was fastened across his broad shoulders by an elaborate silver pin; his belt had a highly decorated silver buckle and strap end; and the hilt of his sword was encrusted with precious stones. English jewellers were the best in Christendom, Ragna had been told.

The Englishman walked with a confident stride, and his companions hurried to keep up. He came straight towards Ragna and Louis, no doubt guessing from their clothes that they were people of importance.

Ragna said: 'Welcome to Cherbourg, Englishman. What brings you here?'

The man ignored her. He bowed to Louis. 'Good day, Father,' he said in poor French. 'I have come to speak with Count Hubert. I am Wilwulf, ealdorman of Shiring.'

ÞÞÞ

WILWULF WAS NOT handsome in the way Aldred was handsome. The ealdorman had a big nose and a jaw like a shovel, and his hands and arms were disfigured by scars. But all the maids in the castle blushed and giggled when he strode past. A foreigner was always intriguing, but Wilwulf's attraction was more than that. It had to do with his size and the loose-limbed way he walked and the intensity of his gaze. Most of all, he had a self-confidence that seemed ready for anything. A girl felt that at any moment he might effortlessly pick her up and carry her off.

Ragna was intrigued by him, but he seemed supremely unaware of her or any of the women. He spoke to her father and to visiting Norman noblemen, and he chatted to his men-at-arms in fast guttural Anglo-Saxon that Ragna could not understand; but he hardly ever spoke to women. Ragna felt slighted: she was not used to being ignored. His indifference was a challenge. She felt she had to get under his skin.

Her father was less enchanted. He was not inclined to take the side of the English against the Vikings, who were his uncivilized kinsmen. Wilwulf was wasting his time here.

Ragna wanted to help Wilwulf. She felt little affinity with Vikings and sympathized with their victims. And if she helped him perhaps he would stop ignoring her.

Although Count Hubert had little interest in Wilwulf, a Norman nobleman had a duty to show hospitality, so he organized a boar hunt. Ragna was thrilled. She loved the hunt, and perhaps this would prove a chance to get to know Wilwulf better.

The party assembled by the stables at first light and took a standing breakfast of lamb cutlets and strong cider. They chose their weapons; any could be used, but the most favoured was a special heavy spear with a long blade and a handle of equal length, and between the two a crossbar. They mounted up, Ragna on Astrid, and set off on horseback with a pack of hysterically excited dogs.

Her father led the way. Count Hubert resisted the temptation of many small men to compensate by riding a big horse. His favourite hunting mount was a sturdy black pony called Thor. In the woods it was just as fast as a larger beast, but more nimble.

Wilwulf rode well, Ragna noticed. The count had given the Englishman a spirited dappled stallion called Goliath. Wilwulf had mastered the horse effortlessly, and sat as easily as if in a chair.

A packhorse followed the hunt with panniers full of bread and cider from the castle kitchen.

They rode to Les Chênes then turned into the Bois des Chênes, the largest remaining area of woodland in the peninsula, where the most wildlife could be found. They followed a track through the trees while the dogs quartered the ground frantically, snuffling in the undergrowth for the pungent scent of wild pig.

Astrid stepped lightly, enjoying the feeling of trotting through the woods in the morning air. Ragna felt mounting anticipation. The exhilaration was intensified by the danger. Boars were mighty, with big teeth and powerful jaws. A full-grown boar could bring down a horse and kill a man. They would attack even when wounded, especially if cornered. The reason that a boar spear had a crossbar was that without it an impaled boar might run up the spear and attack the hunter despite being fatally wounded. Hunting boar required a cool head and strong nerves.

One of the dogs picked up a scent, barked triumphantly, and headed off. The others followed in a pack, and the horsemen went after them. Astrid dodged between the thickets sure-footedly. Ragna's young brother, Richard, passed her, riding overconfidently, as teenage boys did.

Ragna heard the *gu-gu-gu* screech of an alarmed boar. The dogs went wild and the horses picked up their pace. The chase was on, and Ragna's heart beat faster.

Boars could run. They were not as fast as horses on cleared ground, but in the woods, zig-zagging through the vegetation, they were hard to catch.

Ragna glimpsed the prey crossing a clearing in a group: a big female, five feet long from snout to tail tip, probably weighing more than Ragna herself; plus two or three smaller females and a clutch of little striped piglets that could go surprisingly fast on their short legs. Boar family groups were matriarchal; males lived separately except in the winter rutting season.

The horses loved the thrill of the chase, especially when riding at speed in a pack with the dogs. They crashed through the undergrowth, flattening shrubs and saplings. Ragna rode one-handed, holding the reins in her left while keeping her spear ready in her right. She lowered her head to Astrid's neck to avoid overhanging branches, which could be more deadly than the boar to a careless rider. But although she rode prudently she felt reckless, like Skadi, the Norse goddess of hunting, all-powerful and invulnerable, as if nothing bad could happen to her in this state of elation.

The hunt burst out of the woods into a pasture. Cows scattered, lowing, terrified. The horses caught up with the boar in moments. Count Hubert speared one of the lesser females, killing it. Ragna chased a dodging piglet, caught up, leaned down, and speared its hindquarters.

The old female turned dangerously, ready to fight back. Young Richard charged at her fearlessly, but his thrust was wild, and he stuck his spear into the heavily muscled hump. It penetrated only an inch or two then broke. Richard lost his balance and came off his horse, hitting the ground with a thump. The old female charged at him, and Ragna screamed in fear for her brother's life.

Then Wilwulf came from behind, riding fast, spear raised. He jumped his horse over Richard then leaned perilously low and impaled the boar. The iron went through the beast's throat into its chest. The point must have reached the heart, for the boar instantly fell dead.

The hunters reined in and dismounted, breathless and happy, congratulating one another. Richard was at first white-faced from his narrow escape, but the young men praised his bravery, and soon he was acting like the hero of the hour. The servants disembowelled the carcases, and the dogs fell greedily on the guts that spilled onto the ground. There was a strong smell of blood and shit. A peasant appeared, silently furious, and herded his distressed cows into a neighbouring field.

The packhorse with its panniers caught up, and the hunters drank thirstily and tore into the loaves.

Wilwulf sat on the ground with a wooden cup in one hand and

a chunk of bread in the other. Ragna saw an opportunity to talk, and sat beside him.

He did not look particularly pleased.

She was accustomed to men being impressed with her, and his lack of interest pricked her pride. Who did he think he was? But she had a contrary streak, and now she wanted all the more to bring him under her spell.

She spoke in hesitant Anglo-Saxon. 'You saved my brother. Thank you.'

He replied amiably enough. 'Boys of his age need to take risks. Plenty of time to be cautious when he's an old man.'

'If he lives that long.'

Wilwulf shrugged. 'A timid nobleman gains no respect.'

Ragna decided not to argue. 'Were you rash in your youth?'

His mouth twitched, as if his recollections amused him. 'Utterly foolhardy,' he said, but it was more of a boast than a confession.

'Now you're wiser, of course.'

He grinned. 'Opinions differ.'

She felt she was breaking through his reserve. She moved to another topic. 'How are you getting on with my father?'

His face changed. 'He is a generous host, but he's not inclined to give me what I came here for.'

'Which is . . . ?'

'I want him to stop sheltering Vikings in his harbour.'

She nodded. Her father had told her as much. But she wanted Wilwulf to talk. 'How does that affect you?'

'They sail from here across the Channel to raid my towns and villages.'

'They haven't troubled this coast for a century. And that's not because we're descended from Vikings. They no longer attack Brittany or the Frankish lands or the Low Countries. Why do they pick on England?'

He looked startled, as if he had not expected a strategic question from a girl. However, she had clearly raised a subject close to his heart, for he responded with heat. 'We're wealthy, especially our churches and monasteries, but we're not good at defending ourselves. I've talked to learned men, bishops and abbots, about our history. The great King Alfred chased the Vikings off, but he was the only monarch to fight back effectively. England is a rich old lady with a box full of money and no one to guard it. Of course we get robbed.'

'What does my father say to your request?'

'I imagined that, as a Christian, he would readily agree to such a demand – but he has not.'

She knew that, and she had thought about it. 'My father doesn't want to take sides in a quarrel that doesn't concern him,' she said.

'So I gathered.'

'Do you want to know what I would do?'

He hesitated, looking at her with an expression between scepticism and hope. Taking advice from a woman clearly did not sit easily with him. But his mind was not completely closed to the notion, she was glad to see. She waited, unwilling to force her views on him. Eventually he said: 'What would you do?'

She had her answer ready. 'I'd offer him something in return.'

'Is he so mercenary? I thought he would help us from fellow-feeling.'

She shrugged. 'You're in a negotiation. Most treaties involve an exchange of benefits.'

His interest was heightened. 'Perhaps I should think about that – giving your father some incentive for doing what I ask.'

'It's worth a try.'

'I wonder what he might want.'

'I could make a suggestion.'

'Go on.'

89

'Merchants here in Cherbourg sell goods to Combe, especially barrels of cider, wheels of cheese and fine linen cloth.'

He nodded. 'Often of high quality.'

'But we're constantly obstructed by the authorities at Combe.'

He frowned in annoyance. 'I am the authority at Combe.'

Ragna pressed on. 'But your officials seem to be able to do anything they like. There are always delays. Men demand bribes. And there's no knowing how much duty will be charged. In consequence, merchants avoid sending goods to Combe if they can.'

'Duty must be charged. I'm entitled to it.'

'But it should be the same every time. And there should be no delays and no bribes.'

'That would create difficulties.'

'More than a Viking raid?'

'Good point.' Wilwulf looked thoughtful. 'Are you telling me this is what your father wants?'

'No. I haven't asked him, and I'm not representing him. He'll speak for himself. I'm just offering you advice based on my close knowledge of him.'

The hunters were getting ready to depart. Count Hubert called: 'We'll go back past the quarry – there are sure to be more boar around there.'

Wilwulf said to Ragna: 'I'll think about this.'

They mounted up and headed off. Wilwulf rode next to Ragna, not speaking, lost in thought. She was pleased with the conversation. She had got him interested at last.

The weather warmed up. The horses went faster, knowing they were on the way home. Ragna was beginning to think the hunt was over when she saw a patch of churned-up ground where the boar had been digging for roots and moles, both of which they liked to eat. Sure enough, the dogs picked up the scent.

They charged off again, horses following the dogs, and soon Ragna spotted the prey: a group of males this time, three or perhaps four. They ran through a copse of oak and beech and then divided, three heading along a narrow path and the fourth crashing through a thicket. The hunt followed the three, but Wilwulf went after the fourth, and Ragna did the same.

It was a mature beast with long canine teeth curving out of its mouth and, despite its peril, it cannily uttered no sound. Wilwulf and Ragna rode around the thicket and sighted the boar ahead. Wilwulf jumped his horse over a large fallen tree. Ragna, determined not to be left behind, went after him, and Astrid made the jump, just.

The boar was strong. The horses kept pace but could not close with it. Every time Ragna thought she or Wilwulf was almost near enough to strike, the beast would suddenly change direction.

Ragna was vaguely aware that she could no longer hear the rest of the hunt.

The boar crashed into a clearing with no cover, and the horses put on a burst of speed. Wilwulf came up on the beast's left, Ragna on its right.

Wilwulf drew level and stabbed. The boar dodged at the last moment. The blade of the spear entered its hump, wounding it but not slowing it down. It swerved and charged directly at Ragna. She leaned left and jerked at the reins, and Astrid turned towards the boar, sure-footed despite her speed. Ragna rode straight at the boar with her spear pointing down. The beast tried to dodge again, but too late, and Ragna's weapon went straight into its open mouth. She gripped the handle tightly, pushing until the resistance threatened to dislodge her from her saddle; then she let go. Wilwulf wheeled his horse and struck again, penetrating the boar's thick neck; and it fell.

They dismounted, flushed and panting. Ragna said: 'Well done!'

'Well done to you!' said Wilwulf, and then he kissed her.

The kiss began as an exuberant congratulatory peck on the lips, but quickly changed. Ragna sensed his sudden desire. She felt his moustache as his mouth moved hungrily on her lips. She was more than willing, and opened her mouth eagerly to his tongue. Then they both heard the hunt coming towards them, and they broke apart.

A moment later they were surrounded by the other hunters. They had to explain how the kill had been a joint effort. The boar was the biggest of the day, and they were congratulated again and again.

Ragna felt dazed by the excitement of the kill and, even more, by the kiss. She was glad when everyone mounted up and headed home. She rode a little apart from the rest so that she could think. What did Wilwulf mean by the kiss, if anything?

Ragna did not know much about men, but she realized that they were happy to grab a random kiss with a beautiful woman more or less any time. They were also capable of forgetting it quite soon. She had sensed his quickening interest in her, but perhaps he had enjoyed her the way he might have enjoyed a plum, thinking no more about it afterwards. And how did she feel about the kiss? Although it had not lasted long, it had shaken her. She had kissed boys before, but not often, and it had never been like that.

She remembered bathing in the sea as a child. She had always loved the water, and was now a strong swimmer, but once when little she had been bowled over by a huge breaking wave. She had squealed, then found her feet, and finally rushed right back into the surf. Now she remembered that feeling of being completely helpless to resist something both delightful and a little bit frightening.

Why had the kiss been so intense? Perhaps because of what had happened before it. They had discussed Wilwulf's problem like equals, and he had listened to her. This despite the outward impression he gave of being a typical aggressively masculine nobleman who had no time for women. And then they had killed a boar together, collaborating as if they had been a hunting team for years. All that, she thought on reflection, had given her a degree of trust in him that meant she could kiss him and enjoy it.

She wanted to do it again; she had no doubt about that. She wanted to kiss him for longer next time. But did she want anything else from him? She did not know. She would wait and see.

She resolved not to change her attitude to him in public. She would be cool and dignified. Anything else would be noticed. Women picked up that sort of thing the way dogs scented boar. She did not want the castle maids gossiping about her.

But it would be different in private – and she was determined to get him alone at least one more time before he left. Unfortunately, no one had any privacy except the count and countess. It was difficult to do anything in secret at a castle. Peasants were luckier, she thought; they could sneak off into the woods, or lie down unseen in a big field of ripe wheat. How was she going to arrange a clandestine meeting with Wilwulf?

She arrived back at Cherbourg Castle without finding an answer.

She left Astrid to the stable hands and went into the keep. Her mother beckoned her to the private quarters. Genevieve was not interested in hearing about the hunt. 'Good news!' she said, her eyes gleaming. 'I've been talking to Father Louis. He starts for Reims tomorrow. But he told me he approves of you!'

'I'm very glad,' said Ragna, not sure she meant it.

'He says you're a bit forward – as if we didn't know – but he believes you'll become less so with maturity. And he thinks you'll be a strong support for Guillaume when he becomes the count of Reims. Apparently, you resolved the problem at Saint-Martin skilfully.'

'Does Louis feel that Guillaume is in need of support?' Ragna asked suspiciously. 'Is he weak?'

'Oh, don't be so negative,' her mother said. 'You may have won a husband – be happy!'

'I am happy,' said Ragna.

ÞÞÞ

SHE FOUND A place where they could kiss.

As well as the castle there were many other buildings within the wooden stockade: stables and livestock barns; a bakery, a brewery and a cookhouse; houses for families; and storerooms for smoked meat and fish, flour, cider, cheese and hay. The hay store was out of use in July, when there was plenty of new grass for the livestock to graze.

The first time, Ragna took him there under the pretext of showing him a place where his men could temporarily store their weapons and armour. He kissed her as soon as she closed the door, and the kiss was even more exciting than the first time. The building quickly became a place of regular assignation. As night fell – late in the evening at this time of year – they would leave the keep, as most people did in the hour before bedtime, and go separately to the hay store. The room smelled mouldy, but they did not care. They caressed one another more intimately with each passing day. Then Ragna would call a halt, panting, and leave quickly.

They were scrupulously discreet, but they did not completely fool Genevieve. The countess did not know about the hay store but she could sense the passion between her daughter and the visitor. However, she spoke indirectly, as was always her preference. 'England is an uncomfortable place,' she said one day, as if making small talk.

'When were you there?' Ragna asked. It was a sly question, for she already knew the answer.

'I've never been,' Genevieve admitted. 'But I've heard that it's cold and it rains all the time.'

'Then I'm glad I don't have to go there.'

Ragna's mother could not be shut down that easily. 'Englishmen are untrustworthy,' she went on.

'Are they?' Wilwulf was intelligent and surprisingly romantic. When they met in the hay store he was gently tender. He was not domineering, but he was irresistibly sexy. He had dreamed one night of being tied up with a rope made of Ragna's red hair, he told her, and he had woken up with an erection. She found that thought powerfully arousing. Was he trustworthy? She thought he was, but evidently her mother disagreed. 'Why do you say that?' Ragna asked.

'Englishmen keep their promises when it suits their convenience, and not otherwise.'

'And you believe that Norman men never do that?'

Genevieve sighed. 'You're clever, Ragna, but not as clever as you think you are.'

That's true of a lot of people, Ragna thought, from Father Louis all the way down to my seamstress Agnes; why shouldn't it be true of me? 'Perhaps you're right,' she said.

Genevieve pushed her advantage. 'Your father has spoiled you by teaching you about government. But a woman can never be a ruler.'

'That's not so,' Ragna said, speaking more heatedly than she had intended. 'A woman can be a queen, a countess, an abbess or a prioress.'

'Always under the authority of a man.'

'Theoretically, yes, but a lot depends on the character of the individual woman.'

'So you're going to be a queen, are you?'

'I don't know what I'm going to be, but I'd like to rule side by side with my husband, talking to him as he talks to me about what we need to do to make our domain happy and prosperous.'

Genevieve shook her head sadly. 'Dreams,' she said. 'We all had them.' She said no more.

Meanwhile, Wilwulf's negotiations with Count Hubert progressed. Hubert liked the idea of smoothing the passage of Norman exports through the port of Combe, since he profited by levies on all ships entering and leaving Cherbourg. The discussions were detailed: Wilwulf was reluctant to reduce customs duties and Hubert would have preferred none at all, but both agreed that consistency was important.

Hubert questioned Wilwulf about getting the approval of King Ethelred of England for the agreement they were negotiating. Wilwulf admitted that he had not sought prior permission, and said rather airily that he would certainly ask the king to ratify the deal but he felt sure that would be a mere formality. Hubert confessed privately to Ragna that he was not really satisfied with this, but he thought he had little to lose.

Ragna wondered why Wilwulf had not brought one of his senior counsellors with him to help, but eventually she realized that Wilwulf did not have counsellors. He made many decisions at the shire court, with his thanes in attendance, and he sometimes took advice from a brother who was a bishop, but much of the time he ruled alone.

Eventually Hubert and Wilwulf came to an agreement and Hubert's clerk drew up a treaty. It was witnessed by the bishop of Bayeux and several Norman knights and clergymen who were in the castle at the time.

Then Wilwulf was ready to go home.

Ragna waited for him to speak about the future. She wanted to see him again, but how was that possible? They lived in different countries.

Did he see their romance as merely a passing thing? Surely not. The world was full of peasant girls who would not hesitate to spend a night with a nobleman, not to mention slave girls who had no choice about the matter. Wilwulf must have seen something special in Ragna, to contrive to meet her in secret every day only to kiss and caress her.

She could have asked him outright what his intentions were, but she hesitated. It did a girl no good to seem needy. Besides, she was too proud. If he wanted her, he would ask; and if he did not ask, then he did not want her enough.

His ship awaited him, the wind was favourable, and he was planning to leave the next morning, when they met at the hay store for the last time.

The fact that he was leaving, and that she did not know whether she would ever see him again, might have dampened her ardour, but in the event it did the opposite. She clung to him as if she could keep him in Cherbourg by holding on tightly. When he touched her breasts she was so aroused that she felt moisture trickle down the inside of her thigh.

She pressed her body to his so that she could feel his erection through their clothes, and they moved together as if in intercourse. She lifted the long skirt of her dress up around her waist, to feel him better. That only made her desire stronger. In some deep cellar of her mind she knew that she was losing control, but she could not make herself care.

He was dressed like her except that his tunic was knee length, and somehow it got lifted up and pushed aside. Neither of them was wearing underwear – they donned it only for special reasons, such as comfort when riding – and with a thrill she felt his bare flesh against her own.

A moment later he was inside her.

She vaguely heard him say something like: 'Are you sure . . . ?'

She replied: 'Push, push!'

She felt a sudden sharp pain, but it lasted only seconds, and then all was pleasure. She wanted the feeling to go on for ever, but he moved faster, and suddenly they were both shaking with delight, and she felt his hot fluid inside her, and it seemed like the end of the world.

She held on to him, feeling that her legs might give way at any moment. He kept her close for a long time, then at last drew back a little to look at her. 'My word,' he said. He looked as if something had surprised him.

When at last she could speak, she said: 'Is it always like that?'

'Oh, no,' he said. 'Hardly ever.'

ÞÞÞ

THE SERVANTS SLEPT on the floor, but Ragna and her brother Richard and a few of the senior staff had beds, wide benches up against the wall with linen mattresses stuffed with straw. Ragna had a linen sheet in summer and a wool blanket when it was cold. Tonight after the candles had been snuffed she curled up under her sheet and remembered.

She had lost her virginity to the man she loved, and it felt wonderful. Furtively, she pushed a finger inside herself and brought it out sticky with his fluid. She smelled its fishy smell, then tasted it and found it salty.

She had done something that would change her life, she knew. A priest would say she was now married in the eyes of God, and she felt the truth of that. And she was glad. The thrill that had overwhelmed her in the hay store was the physical expression of the togetherness that had grown so fast between them. He was the right man for her, she knew that for certain.

She was also committed to Wilwulf in a more practical way. A noblewoman had to be a virgin for her husband. Ragna could certainly never wed anyone other than Wilwulf now, not without a deception that could blight the marriage.

And she might be pregnant.

She wondered what would happen in the morning. What would Wilwulf do? He would have to say something: he knew as well as she did that everything was changed now that they had done what they had done. He must speak to her father about their marriage.

There would be an agreement about money. Both Wilwulf and Ragna were nobility, and there might be political consequences to discuss. Wilwulf might need King Ethelred's permission.

He needed to discuss it with Ragna, too. They had to talk about when they would marry, and where, and what the ceremony would be like. She looked forward eagerly to that.

She was happy, and all these issues could be dealt with. She loved him and he loved her, and they would be partners together throughout their lives.

She thought she would not close her eyes all night, but she soon fell into a heavy sleep, and did not wake until it was full daylight and the servants were clattering bowls on the table and bringing in huge loaves from the bakery.

She leaped up and looked around. Wilwulf's men-at-arms were packing their few possessions into boxes and leather bags, ready to depart. Wilwulf himself was not in the hall: he must have gone out to wash.

Ragna's parents came out of their quarters and sat at the head of the table. Genevieve was not going to be happy about this morning's news. Hubert would be less dogmatic, but nevertheless his permission would not be readily given. They both had other plans for Ragna. But if necessary she would tell them she had already lost her virginity to Wilwulf, and they would have to give in.

She took some bread, spread it with a paste made of crushed berries and wine, and ate hungrily.

Wilwulf came in and took his place at the table. 'I've spoken to the captain,' he said to everyone. 'We leave in an hour.'

Now, Ragna thought, he will tell them; but he drew his knife, cut a thick slice of ham from a joint, and began to eat. He'll speak after breakfast, she thought.

Suddenly she was too tense to eat. The bread seemed to stick in her throat, and she had to take a mouthful of cider to help her swallow. Wilwulf was talking to her father about the weather in the Channel and how long it would take to reach Combe, and it was like a speech in a dream, words that made no sense. Too quickly the meal came to an end.

The count and countess decided to walk down to the waterfront and see Wilwulf off, and Ragna joined them, feeling like an invisible spirit, saying nothing and following the crowd, ignored by all. The mayor's daughter, a girl of her own age, saw her and said: 'Lovely day!' Ragna did not reply.

At the water's edge Wilwulf's men hitched up their tunics and prepared to wade out to their vessel. Wilwulf turned and smiled at the family group. Now, surely, he would say: 'I want to marry Ragna.'

He bowed formally to Hubert, Genevieve, Richard and finally Ragna. He took both her hands in his and said in halting French: 'Thank you for your kindness.' Then, incredibly, he turned away, splashed through the shallows, and climbed aboard the ship.

Ragna could not speak.

The sailors untied the ropes. Ragna could not believe what she was seeing. Surely this was a nightmare from which she would soon wake up? The crew unfurled the sail. It flapped for a moment, then caught the wind and swelled. The ship picked up pace.

Leaning on the rail, Wilwulf waved once, then turned away.

5

RIDING THROUGH THE WOODS on a summer afternoon, watching the shifting patterns of dappled sunlight on the beaten track ahead, Brother Aldred sang hymns at the top of his voice. In between he talked to his pony, Dismas, asking the beast whether he had enjoyed the last hymn, and what he might like to hear next.

Aldred was a couple of days away from Shiring, and he felt he was returning home in triumph. His mission in life was to bring learning and understanding where before there was blind ignorance. The eight new books in the box strapped to Dismas's rump, written on parchment and beautifully illustrated, would be the modest foundation of a grand project. Aldred's dream was to turn Shiring Abbey into a great centre of learning and scholarship, with a scriptorium to rival that of Jumièges, a large library, and a school that would teach the sons of noblemen to read, count and fear God.

The abbey today was a long way from that ideal. Aldred's superiors did not share his ambitions. Abbot Osmund was amiable and lazy. He had been good to Aldred, promoting him young, but that was mainly because he knew that once he had given Aldred a job, he could consider it done, and need exert himself no farther. Osmund would go along with any proposal that did not require him to do any work. More stubborn opposition would come from the treasurer, Hildred, who was against any proposal that required spending, as if the mission of the monastery was saving up money, rather than bringing enlightenment to the world.

Perhaps Osmund and Hildred had been sent by God to teach Aldred patience.

Aldred was not completely alone in his hopes. Among monks generally there was a long-standing movement for reform of old institutions that had slipped into idleness and self-indulgence. Many beautiful new manuscript books were being produced in Winchester, Worcester and Canterbury. But the drive for improvement had not yet reached Shiring Abbey.

Aldred sang:

'Now we must honour the guardian of heaven,
The work of the father of glory—'

He stopped suddenly, seeing a man appear on the path in front of him.

Aldred had not even observed where he came from. He wore no shoes on his filthy feet, he was clad in rags, and he wore a rusty iron battle helmet that hid most of his face. A bloody rag tied around his upper arm evidenced a recent wound. He stood in the middle of the path, blocking Aldred's way. He might have been a poor homeless beggar, but he looked more like an outlaw.

Aldred's heart sank. He should not have taken the risk of travelling alone. But this morning, in the alehouse at Mudeford Crossing, there had been no one going his way, and he had yielded to impatience and set off, instead of waiting a day or more until he could proceed with others in a group.

Now he reined in. It was important not to appear afraid, as with a dangerous dog. Trying to keep his voice calm, he said: 'God bless you, my son.'

The man replied in a hoarse tone, and the thought crossed Aldred's mind that he might be disguising his voice. 'What kind of priest are you?'

Aldred's haircut, with a shaved patch at the top of his head, indicated a man of God, but that might mean anything from a lowly acolyte up. 'I'm a monk of Shiring Abbey.'

'Travelling alone? Aren't you afraid of being robbed?'

Aldred was afraid of being murdered. 'No one can rob me,' he said with false confidence. 'I have nothing.'

'Except for that box.'

'The box isn't mine. It belongs to God. A fool might rob God, of course, and condemn his soul to eternal damnation.' Aldred spotted another man half hidden by a bush. Even if he had been inclined to make a fight of it, he could not take on two of them.

The ruffian said: 'What's in the box?'

'Eight holy books.'

'Valuable, then.'

Aldred imagined the man knocking at the door of a monastery and offering to sell a book. He would be flogged for his cheek, and the book would be confiscated. 'Valuable perhaps to someone who could sell them without arousing suspicion,' Aldred said. 'Are you hungry, my son? Do you want some bread?'

The man seemed to hesitate, then said defiantly: 'I don't need bread, I need money.'

The hesitation told Aldred that the man was hungry. Food might satisfy him. 'I have no money to give you.' This was true, technically: the money in Aldred's purse belonged to Shiring Abbey.

The man seemed lost for words, not sure how to respond to the unexpected turn the conversation had taken. After a pause he said: 'A man could sell a horse easier than a box of books.'

'He could,' said Aldred. 'But someone might say: "Brother Aldred had a pony with a white cross on its forehead, just like that – so where did you get this beast, friend?" And what would the thief say to that?'

'You're a clever one.'

'And you're a bold one. But you're not stupid, are you? You're not going to murder a monk for the sake of eight books and a pony, none of which you can sell.' Aldred decided this was the moment to end the interchange. With his heart in his mouth he urged Dismas forward.

The outlaw stood his ground for a moment or two then stepped aside, faltering with indecision. Aldred rode past him, pretending indifference.

Once past, he was tempted to kick Dismas into a trot, but that would have betrayed his fear, so he forced himself to let the pony walk slowly away. He was shaking, he realized.

Then the man said: 'I would like some bread.'

That was a plea that a monk could not ignore. It was Aldred's holy duty to give food to the hungry. Jesus himself had said: 'Feed my lambs.' Aldred had to obey, even at the risk of his life. He reined in.

He had half a loaf and a wedge of cheese in his saddlebag. He took out the bread and gave it to the outlaw, who immediately tore off a piece and crammed it into his mouth, stuffing it through the hole in his decrepit helmet. Clearly he was starving.

'Share it with your friend,' Aldred said.

The other man came out of the bushes, hood pulled half over his face so that Aldred could hardly see him.

The first man looked reluctant, but broke the loaf and shared it.

The other muttered from behind his hand: 'Thank you.'

'Don't thank me, thank God who sent me.'

'Amen.'

Aldred gave him the cheese. 'Share that, too.'

While they were dividing the cheese, Aldred rode away.

A minute later he looked behind and saw no sign of the outlaws. He was safe, it seemed. He sent up a prayer of thanks.

He might have to go hungry tonight, but he could put up with that, grateful that today God had asked him to sacrifice his dinner but not his life.

The afternoon softened into evening. Eventually he saw, across the water, a hamlet of half a dozen houses and a church. To the west of the houses was a cultivated field that stretched along the north bank of the river.

Some kind of boat was tied up on the other side. Aldred had never been to Dreng's Ferry – he had taken a different route on his outward journey – but he guessed this was the place. He dismounted and shouted over the water.

Presently a girl appeared. She untied the boat, got in, and began to paddle across. She was well-fed but plain-looking, Aldred saw as she came closer, and she wore a grumpy expression. When she was within earshot he said: 'I am Brother Aldred of Shiring Abbey.'

'My name is Cwenburg,' she responded. 'This ferry belongs to my father, Dreng. So does the alehouse.'

So Aldred was in the right place.

'It's a farthing to cross,' she said. 'But I can't take a horse.'

Aldred could see that. The crude boat would capsize easily. He said: 'Don't worry, Dismas will swim.'

He paid his farthing. He unloaded the pony and put the box of books and the saddle in the boat. He held the reins as he boarded and sat down, then tugged gently to encourage Dismas into the water. For a moment the horse hesitated, as if he might resist. 'Come on,' Aldred said reassuringly, and at the same moment Cwenburg pushed away from the bank; then Dismas walked into the water. As soon as it got deep he began to swim. Aldred kept hold of the reins. He did not think Dismas would try to escape, but there was no point in taking the chance.

As they crossed the river Aldred said to Cwenburg: 'How far is it from here to Shiring?'

'Two days.'

Aldred looked at the sky. The sun was low. There was a long evening ahead, but he might not find another place to stay before dark. He had better spend the night here.

They reached the other side, and Aldred picked up the distinctive smell of brewing.

Dismas found his feet. Aldred released the reins and the pony climbed the river bank, shook himself vigorously to get rid of the water soaking his coat, and then began to crop the summer grass.

Another girl came out of the alehouse. She was about fourteen, with black hair and blue eyes, and despite her youth she was pregnant. She might have been pretty but she did not smile. Aldred was shocked to see that she wore no headdress of any kind. A woman showing her hair was normally a prostitute.

'This is Blod,' said Cwenburg. 'Our slave.' Blod said nothing. 'She speaks Welsh,' Cwenburg added.

Aldred unloaded his box from the ferry and set it down on the river bank, then did the same with his saddle.

Blod picked up his box helpfully. He watched her uneasily, but she just carried it into the alehouse.

A man's voice said: 'You can fuck her for a farthing.'

Aldred turned. The newcomer had emerged from a small building that was probably a brewhouse, and the source of the strong smell. In his thirties, he was the right age to be Cwenburg's father. He was tall and broad-shouldered, reminding Aldred vaguely of Wynstan, the bishop of Shiring, and Aldred seemed to remember hearing that Dreng was Wynstan's cousin. However, Dreng walked with a limp.

He looked speculatively at Aldred, through eyes set narrowly either side of a long nose. He smiled insincerely. 'A farthing is cheap,' he added. 'She was a penny when she was fresh.'

'No,' said Aldred.

'No one wants her. It's because she's pregnant, the stupid cow.'

Aldred could not let that pass. 'I expect she's pregnant because you prostitute her, in defiance of God's laws.'

'She enjoys it, that's her trouble. Women only get pregnant when they enjoy it.'

'Do they?'

'Everyone knows that.'

'I don't know it.'

'You don't know anything about that sort of thing, do you? You're a monk.'

Aldred tried to swallow the insult in a Christ-like way. 'That's true,' he said, and bowed his head.

Showing humility in the face of insults sometimes had the effect of making the insulter too ashamed to go on, but Dreng seemed immune to shame. 'I used to have a boy – he might have interested you,' he said. 'But he died.'

Aldred looked away. He was sensitive to this accusation because in his youth he had suffered from just that kind of temptation. As a novice, at Glastonbury Abbey, he had been passionately fond of a young monk called Brother Leofric. What they did was only boyish fooling around, Aldred felt, but they had been caught in flagrante delicto, and there had been a tremendous row. Aldred had been transferred, to separate him from his lover, and that was how he had ended up at Shiring.

There had been no repetition: Aldred still had troubling thoughts, but he was able to resist them.

Blod came back out of the tavern, and Dreng told her, with hand gestures, to pick up Aldred's saddle. 'I can't carry heavy weights, I've got a bad back,' Dreng said. 'A Viking knocked me off my horse at the battle of Watchet.'

Aldred checked on Dismas, who seemed settled in the pasture, then went into the alehouse. It was much like a regular house except for its size. It had a lot of furniture, tables and stools and chests and wall hangings. There were other signs of affluence: a large salmon hanging from the ceiling, being cured in the smoke from the fire; a barrel with a bung standing on a bench; hens pecking in the reeds on the floor; a pot bubbling on the fire and giving off a tantalizing fragrance of spring lamb.

Dreng pointed to a thin young woman stirring the pot. Aldred noticed that she wore an engraved silver disc on a leather thong around her neck. 'That's my wife Ethel,' said Dreng. The woman glanced at Aldred without speaking. Dreng was surrounded by young women, Aldred thought, all of them appearing unhappy.

He said: 'Do you get many travellers passing through this place?' The level of prosperity was surprising for such a little settlement, and the thought crossed his mind that it might be funded by robbery.

'Enough,' Dreng said shortly.

'Not far from here I encountered two men who looked like outlaws.' He watched Dreng's face and added: 'One of them wore an old iron helmet.'

'We call him Ironface,' said Dreng. 'He's a liar and a murderer. He robs travellers on the south side of the river, where the track runs mostly through forest.'

'Why hasn't someone arrested him?'

'We've tried, believe me. Offa, the reeve of Mudeford, has offered two pounds of silver to anyone who can catch Ironface. Obviously he's got a hideout somewhere in the woods, but we can't find it. We've had the sheriff's men down here and everything.'

It was plausible enough, Aldred thought, but he remained suspicious. Dreng with his limp could not be Ironface – unless the limp was faked – but he might benefit in some way from the robberies. Perhaps he knew where the hideout was and got paid for silence.

'His voice is odd,' Aldred said, probing.

'He's probably Irish or Viking or something. No one knows.' Dreng changed the subject. 'You'd better have a flagon of ale, to refresh you after your journey. My wife makes very good ale.'

'Later, perhaps,' Aldred said. He did not spend the monastery's money in alehouses if he could help it. He spoke to Ethel. 'What's the secret of making good ale?' he asked.

'Not her,' said Dreng. 'My other wife, Leaf, makes the ale. She's in the brewhouse now.'

The Church struggled with this. Most men who could afford it had more than one wife, or a wife and one or more concubines, and slave girls too. The Church did not have jurisdiction over marriage. If two people exchanged vows in front of witnesses, they were married. A priest might offer a blessing, but he was not essential. Nothing was written down unless the couple were wealthy, in which case there might be a contract about any exchange of property.

Aldred's objection to this was not just moral. When a man like Dreng died there was often a rancorous quarrel over inheritance that turned on which of his children were legitimate. The informality of weddings left room for disputes that could fracture families.

So Dreng's household was not exceptional. However, it was surprising to find this in a little hamlet adjacent to a minster. 'The clergy at the church would be troubled if they knew about your domestic arrangements,' he said severely.

Dreng laughed. 'Would they?'

'I'm sure of it.'

'Well, you're wrong. They know all about it. The dean, Degbert, is my brother.'

'That should make no difference!'

'That's what you think.'

Aldred was too angry to continue the discussion. He found Dreng loathsome. To avoid losing his temper he went outside. He headed along the river bank, trying to walk off his mood.

Where the cultivated land came to an end there was a farmhouse and barn, both old and much-repaired. Aldred saw a group sitting outside the house: three young men and an older woman – a family with no father, he guessed. He hesitated to approach them for fear that all the residents of Dreng's Ferry might be like Dreng. He was about to turn and walk back when one of them gave a cheery wave.

If they waved to strangers, perhaps they were all right.

Aldred walked up a slope to the house. The family evidently had no furniture, for they were sitting on the ground to eat their evening meal. The three boys were not tall, but broad-shouldered and deep-chested. The mother was a tired woman with a resolute look. The faces of all four were lean, as if they did not eat much. A brown-and-white dog sat with them; it, too, was thin.

The woman spoke first. 'Sit with us and rest your legs, if you're so inclined,' she said. 'I am Mildred.' She pointed out the boys, eldest to youngest. 'My sons are Erman, Eadbald and Edgar. Our supper isn't fancy, but you're welcome to share it.'

Their meal certainly was not fancy. They had a loaf of bread and a large pot containing lightly boiled forest vegetables, probably lettuce, onions, parsley and wild garlic. No meat was visible. It was no wonder they did not get fat. Aldred was hungry, but he could not take food from people who were so desperately poor. He refused politely. 'It smells tempting, but I'm not hungry, and monks must avoid the sin of gluttony. However, I will sit with you, and thank you for your welcome.'

He sat on the ground, something monks did not often do, despite their vows. There was poverty, Aldred thought, and then there was real poverty.

Making conversation, he said: 'The grass looks almost ready to reap. You'll have a good harvest of hay in a few days' time.'

Mildred answered. 'I wasn't sure we'd be able to make hay, because the riverside land is almost too marshy, but it dried up in the hot weather. I hope it does the same every year.'

'Are you new here, then?' Aldred asked.

'Yes,' she said. 'We came from Combe.'

Aldred could guess why they had left. 'You must have suffered in the Viking raid. I saw the devastation when I passed through the town the day before yesterday.'

Edgar, the youngest of the brothers, spoke. He looked about eighteen, with only the pale soft hair of an adolescent on his chin. 'We lost everything,' he said. 'My father was a boatbuilder – they killed him. Our stock of timber was burned and our tools were ruined. So we've had to make a completely new start.'

Aldred studied the young man with interest. Perhaps he was not handsome, but there was something appealing about his looks. Although the conversation was informal his sentences were clear and logical. Aldred found himself drawn to Edgar. Get a grip on yourself, he thought. The sin of lust was more difficult to avoid than the sin of gluttony, for Aldred.

He asked Edgar: 'And how are you getting on, in your new life?'

'We'll be able to sell the hay, provided it doesn't rain in the next few days, and then we'll have some money at last. We've got oats ripening on the higher ground. And we have a piglet and a lamb. We should get through the winter.'

All peasants lived in such insecurity, never sure that this year's harvest would be enough to keep them alive until next year's. Mildred's family were better off than some. 'Perhaps you were lucky to get this place.'

Mildred said crisply: 'We'll see.'

Aldred said: 'How did it happen that you came to Dreng's Ferry?'

'We were offered this farm by the bishop of Shiring.'

'Wynstan?' Aldred knew the bishop, of course, and had a low opinion of him.

'Our landlord is Degbert Baldhead, the dean at the minster, who is the bishop's cousin.'

'Fascinating.' Aldred was beginning to understand Dreng's Ferry.

Degbert and Dreng were brothers, and Wynstan was their cousin. They made a sinister little trio. 'Does Wynstan ever come here?'

'He visited soon after Midsummer.'

Edgar put in: 'Two weeks after Midsummer Day.'

Mildred went on: 'He gave a lamb to every house in the village. That's how we got ours.'

'The bountiful bishop,' Aldred mused.

Mildred was quick to pick up his undertone. 'You sound sceptical,' she said. 'You don't believe in his kindness?'

'I've never known him to do good without an ulterior motive. You're not looking at one of Wynstan's admirers.'

Mildred smiled. 'No argument here.'

Another of the boys spoke. It was Eadbald, the middle son, with the freckled face. His voice was deep and resonant. 'Edgar killed a Viking,' he said.

The eldest, Erman, put in: 'He says he did.'

Aldred said to Edgar: 'Did you kill a Viking?'

'I went up behind him,' Edgar said. 'He was struggling with . . . a woman. He didn't see me until it was too late.'

'And the woman?' Aldred had noticed the hesitation, and guessed she was someone special.

'The Viking threw her to the ground just before I struck him. She hit her head on a stone step. I was too late to save her. She died.' Edgar's rather lovely hazel eyes filled with tears.

'What was her name?'

'Sungifu.' It came in a whisper.

'I will pray for her soul.'

'Thank you.'

It was clear Edgar had loved her. Aldred pitied him. He also felt relieved: a boy who could love a woman that much was unlikely to sin with another man. Aldred might be tempted, but Edgar would not. Aldred could stop worrying.

Eadbald, the freckled one, spoke again. 'The dean hates Edgar,' he said.

Aldred said: 'Why?'

Edgar said: 'I argued with him.'

'And you won the argument, I suppose, thereby annoying him.'

'He said that we are in the year nine hundred and ninety-seven, so that means Jesus is nine hundred and ninety-seven years old. I pointed out that if Jesus was born in the year one, his first birthday would fall in the year two, and he would be nine hundred and ninety-six next Christmas. It's simple. But Degbert said I was an arrogant young pup.'

Aldred laughed. 'Degbert was wrong, though it's a mistake others have made.'

Mildred said disapprovingly: 'You don't argue with priests, even when they're wrong.'

'Especially when they're wrong.' Aldred got to his feet. 'It's getting dark. I'd better return to the minster while there's still some light, or I might fall in the river on my way. I've enjoyed meeting you all.'

He took his leave and headed back along the river bank. He felt relieved to have met some likeable people in this unlovable place.

He was going to spend the night at the minster. He went into the alehouse and picked up his box and his saddlebag. He spoke politely to Dreng but did not stay to chat. He led Dismas up the hill.

The first house he came to was a small building on a large lot. Its door stood open, as doors generally did at this time of year, and Aldred looked in. A fat woman of about forty was sitting near the entrance with a square of leather in her lap, sewing a shoe in the light from the window. She looked up and said: 'Who are you?'

'Aldred, a monk of Shiring Abbey, looking for Dean Degbert.'

'Degbert Baldhead lives the other side of the church.'

'What's your name?'

'I'm Bebbe.'

Like the alehouse, this place showed signs of prosperity. Bebbe had a cheese safe, a box with muslin sides to let air in and keep mice out. On a table beside her was a wooden cup and a small pottery jug that looked as if it might contain wine. A heavy wool blanket hung from a hook. 'This hamlet seems well-off,' Aldred said.

'Not very,' Bebbe said quickly. After a moment's reflection she added: 'Though the minster spreads its wealth a little.'

'And where does the minster's wealth come from?'

'You're a curious one, aren't you? Who sent you to spy on us?'

'Spy?' he said in surprise. 'Who would trouble to spy on a little hamlet in the middle of nowhere?'

'Well, then, you shouldn't be so nosey.'

'I'll bear that in mind.' Aldred left her.

He walked up the hill to the church and saw, on its east side, a large house that must be the residence of the clergy. He noticed that some kind of workshop had been built at the back, up against the end wall. Its door was open and there was a fire blazing inside. It looked like a smithy, but it was too small: a blacksmith needed more space.

Curious, he went to the door and looked in. He saw a charcoal fire on a raised hearth, with a pair of bellows beside it for making the heat fiercer. A block of iron firmly stuck into a massive section of a tree trunk formed an anvil about waist high. A clergyman was bent over it, working with a hammer and a narrow chisel, carving a disc of what looked like silver. A lamp stood on the anvil, lighting his work. He had a bucket of water, undoubtedly for quenching hot metal, and a heavyweight pair of shears, probably for cutting sheet metal. Behind him was a door that presumably led into the main house.

The man was a jeweller, Aldred guessed. He had a rack of neat, precise tools: awls, pliers, heavy trimming knives, and clippers with small blades and long handles. He looked about thirty, a plump little man with double chins, concentrating hard.

Not wanting to startle him, Aldred coughed.

The precaution was ineffective. The man jumped, dropped his tools, and said: 'Oh, my God!'

'I didn't mean to disturb you,' Aldred said. 'I beg your pardon.'

The man looked frightened. 'What do you want?'

'Nothing at all,' said Aldred in his most reassuring voice. 'I saw the light and worried that something might be on fire.' He was improvising, not wanting to seem nosey. 'I'm Brother Aldred, from Shiring Abbey.'

'I'm Cuthbert, a priest here at the minster. But visitors aren't allowed in my workshop.'

Aldred frowned. 'What are you so anxious about?'

Cuthbert hesitated. 'I thought you were a thief.'

'I suppose you have precious metals here.'

Involuntarily Cuthbert looked over his shoulder. Aldred followed his gaze to an ironbound chest by the door into the house. That would be Cuthbert's treasury, where he kept the gold, silver and copper he used, Aldred guessed.

Many priests practised different arts: music, poetry, wall painting. There was nothing strange about Cuthbert being a jeweller. He would make ornaments for the church, probably, and might have a profitable sideline in jewellery for sale; there was no shame in a clergyman making money. So why did he act guilty?

'You must have good eyes, to do such precise work.' Aldred looked at what was on the workbench. Cuthbert seemed to be engraving an intricate picture of strange animals into the silver disc. 'What are you making?'

'A brooch.'

A new voice said: 'What the devil are you doing, poking your nose in here?'

The man addressing Aldred was not partially bald in the usual way, but completely hairless. He must be Degbert Baldhead, the dean.

Aldred said calmly: 'My word, you folks are touchy. The door was open and I looked in. What on earth is the matter with you? It almost seems as if you might have something to hide.'

'Don't be ridiculous,' Degbert said. 'Cuthbert needs quiet and privacy to do highly delicate work, that's all. Please leave him alone.'

'That's not the story Cuthbert told. He said he was worried about thieves.'

'Both.' Degbert reached past Aldred and pulled the door so that it slammed, shutting himself and Aldred out of the workshop. 'Who are you?'

'I'm the armarius at Shiring Abbey. My name is Aldred.'

'A monk,' said Degbert. 'I suppose you expect us to give you supper.'

'And a place to sleep tonight. I'm on a long journey.'

Degbert was clearly reluctant, but he could not refuse hospitality to a fellow clergyman, not without some strong reason. 'Well, just try to keep your questions to yourself,' he said, and he walked away and entered the house by the main door.

Aldred stood thinking for a few moments, but he could not imagine the reason for the hostility he had experienced.

He gave up puzzling and followed Degbert into the house.

It was not what he expected.

There should have been a large crucifix on prominent display, to indicate that the building was dedicated to the service of God. A minster should always have a lectern bearing a holy book so that passages could be read to the clergy while they ate their frugal meals. Any wall hangings should feature biblical scenes that would remind them of God's laws.

This place had no crucifix or lectern, and a tapestry on the wall showed a hunting scene. Most of the men present had the shaved patch on top of the head called a tonsure, but there were also women and children who looked as if they were at home. It had the air of a large, affluent family house. 'This is a minster?' he said incredulously.

Degbert heard him. 'Who do you think you are, to come in here with that attitude?' he said.

Aldred was not surprised at his reaction. Lax priests were often hostile to the stricter monks, suspecting them of a holier-than-thou attitude – sometimes with reason. This minster was beginning to look like the kind of place that the reform movement was directed at. However, Aldred suspended judgement. Degbert and his team might be carrying out all the required services impeccably, and that was the most important thing.

Aldred put his box and his saddlebag up against the wall. From the saddlebag he took some grain. He went outside and fed it to Dismas, then hobbled the pony's hind legs so that it could not wander far in the night. Then he returned inside.

He had hoped that the minster might be an oasis of calm contemplation in a bustling world. He had imagined spending the evening talking to men with interests similar to his own. They might discuss some question of biblical scholarship, such as the authenticity of *The Epistle of Barnabas*. They could talk about the troubles of the beleaguered English king, Ethelred the Misled, or even about issues in international politics, such as the war between Muslim Iberia and the Christian north of Spain. He had hoped they would be keen to hear all about Normandy, and in particular Jumièges Abbey.

But these men were not leading that kind of life. They were talking to their wives and playing with their children, drinking ale and cider. One man was attaching an iron buckle to a leather belt; another cutting the hair of a little boy. No one was reading or praying.

There was nothing wrong with domestic life, of course; a man should take care of his wife and children. But a clergyman had other duties too.

The church bell rang. The men unhurriedly stopped what they were doing and prepared themselves for the evening service. After a few minutes they ambled out, and Aldred followed. The women and children stayed behind, and no one came from the village.

The church was in a state of disrepair that shocked Aldred. The entrance arch was propped up by a tree trunk, and the whole building seemed not quite straight. Degbert should have spent his money maintaining it. But of course a married man put his family first. That was why priests should be single.

They went inside.

Aldred noticed an inscription carved into the wall. The letters were time-worn, but he could make out the message. Lord Begmund of Northwood had built the church and was buried here, the inscription said, and he had left money in his will to pay for priests to say prayers for his soul.

Aldred had been dismayed by the lifestyle at the house, but the service shocked him. The hymns were a toneless chant, the prayers were gabbled, and two deacons argued throughout the ceremony about whether a wild cat could kill a hunting dog. By the final amen, Aldred was fuming.

It was no wonder that Dreng showed no shame about his two wives and his slave prostitute. There was no moral leadership in this hamlet. How could Dean Degbert reprove a man for defying the Church's teaching on marriage when he himself was just as bad?

Dreng had disgusted Aldred, but Degbert enraged him. These men were serving neither God nor their community. Clergymen took money from poor peasants and lived in comfort; the least they could do in return was to perform the services conscientiously and pray for the souls of the people who supported them. But these men were simply taking the Church's money and using it to support an idle life. They were worse than thieves. It was blasphemy.

But there was nothing to be gained, he told himself, by giving Degbert a piece of his mind and having a row.

He was now highly curious. Degbert was fearless in his

transgression, probably because he had the protection of a powerful bishop – but that was not all. Normally, villagers were quick to complain about lazy or sinful priests; they liked moral leaders to have the credibility that came from obeying their own rules. But no one Aldred had spoken to today had criticized Degbert or the minster. In fact, most people had been reluctant to answer questions. Only Mildred and her sons had been friendly and open. Aldred knew he did not have the common touch – he wished he could be like Lady Ragna of Cherbourg, and make everyone his friend – but he did not think his manner was bad enough to explain the taciturnity of Dreng's Ferry residents. Something else was going on.

He was determined to find out what it was.

6

EARLY AUGUST 997

THE RUSTY OLD TOOLS left behind by the previous tenant of the farm included a scythe, the long-handled reaping tool that enabled a person to cut the crop without stooping. Edgar cleaned the iron, sharpened the blade and affixed a new wooden handle. The brothers took turns to reap the grass. The rain held off and the grass turned to hay, which Ma sold to Bebbe for a fat pig, a barrel of eels, a rooster and six hens.

Next they reaped the oats, then came the threshing. Edgar made a flail from two sticks, a long handle and a short swipple, joined by a strip of leather that he had failed to return to Bebbe. On a breezy day he tried it out, watched by the dog, Brindle. He spread some ears of oats on a flat patch of dry ground and began to flog them. He was no farmer, and he was making this up as he went along, with Ma's help. But the flail seemed to be doing what it should: the nutritious seeds became separated from the worthless husks, which blew away in the wind.

The grains left behind looked small and dry.

Edgar rested a moment. The sun was shining and he felt good. The eel meat in the family stew had made him stronger. Ma would smoke most of the creatures in the rafters of the house. When the smoked eel ran out they might have to kill the pig and make bacon. And they should get some eggs from the chickens before they had to eat them. It was not much to last four adults through a winter, but with the oats they probably would not die of starvation.

The house was habitable now. Edgar had mended all the holes in the walls and roof. There were fresh rushes on the ground, a stone hearth, and a pile of deadfalls from the forest for firewood. Edgar did not want to spend his life like this, but he was beginning to feel that he and his family had survived the emergency.

Ma appeared. 'I saw Cwenburg a few minutes ago,' she said. 'Was she looking for you?'

Edgar felt embarrassed. 'Certainly not.'

'You seem very sure. I had the idea she was, well, interested in you.'

'She was, and I had to tell her frankly that I didn't feel that way about her. Unfortunately, she took offence.'

'I'm glad. I was afraid you might do something foolish after losing Sungifu.'

'I wasn't even tempted. Cwenburg is neither pretty nor good-natured, but even if she were an angel I wouldn't fall for her.'

Ma nodded sympathetically. 'Your father was the same – a one-woman man,' she said. 'His mother told me he never showed interest in any girl except me. He was the same after we were married, which is even more unusual. But you're young. You can't stay in love with a dead girl for the rest of your life.'

Edgar thought he might, but he did not want to argue the point with his mother. 'Maybe,' he said.

'There will be someone else, one day,' she insisted. 'It will probably take you by surprise. You'll believe you're still in love with the old one, and suddenly you'll realize that all the time you're thinking about a different girl.'

Edgar turned the tables on her. 'Will you marry again?'

'Ah,' she said. 'Clever you. No, I shan't.'

'Why not?'

She was silent for a long moment. Edgar wondered whether he had offended her. But no, she was just thinking. At last she said:

'Your father was a rock. He meant what he said and he did what he promised. He loved me, and he loved you three, and that didn't change in more than twenty years. He wasn't handsome, and sometimes he wasn't even good-tempered, but I trusted him utterly, and he never let me down.' Tears came to her eyes as she said: 'I don't want a second husband but, even if I did, I know I wouldn't find another like him.' She had been speaking in a careful, considered way, but at the end her feelings broke through. She looked up at the summer sky and said: 'I miss you so much, my beloved.'

Edgar felt like crying. They stood together for a minute, saying nothing. At last Ma swallowed, wiped her eyes, and said: 'Enough of that.'

Edgar took her cue and changed the subject. 'Am I doing this threshing right?'

'Oh, yes. And the flail works fine. But I see the grains are a bit stunted. We're going to have a hungry winter.'

'Did we do something wrong?'

'No, it's the soil.'

'But you think we'll survive.'

'Yes, though I'm relieved that you're not in love with Cwenburg. That girl looks as if she eats heartily. This farm couldn't feed a fifth adult – let alone any children that might come along. We'd all starve.'

'Perhaps next year will be better.'

'We'll manure the field before we plough again, and that should help, but in the end there's no way to get rich crops out of poor earth.'

Ma was as shrewd and forceful as ever, but Edgar worried about her. She had changed since the death of Pa. For all her spirit, she no longer seemed invulnerable. She had always been strong, but now he found himself hastening to help her lift a big log for the fire or a full pail of water from the river. He did not speak to her about his worries: she would resent the imputation of weakness. In that way she was more like a man. But he could not help thinking about the dismal prospect of life without her.

Brindle barked suddenly and anxiously. Edgar frowned: the dog often sounded the alarm before the humans knew anything was wrong. A moment later he heard shouting – not just noisy speech but furious, aggressive yelling and snarling. It was his brothers, and he could hear both voices: they must be fighting each other.

He ran towards the noise, which seemed to be coming from near the barn on the other side of the house. Brindle ran with him, barking. Out of the corner of his eye Edgar saw Ma bend to pick up the threshed oats, frugally saving them from the birds.

Erman and Eadbald were rolling on the ground outside the barn, punching and biting one another, screaming with rage. Eadbald's freckled nose was bleeding and Erman had a bloody abrasion on his forehead.

Edgar yelled: 'Stop it, you two!' They ignored him. What fools, Edgar thought; we need all our strength for this damn farm.

The reason for the fight was instantly visible. Cwenburg stood in the barn doorway, watching them, laughing with delight. She was naked. Seeing her, Edgar was filled with loathing.

Erman rolled on top of Eadbald and drew back a big fist to punch his face. Seizing the chance, Edgar grabbed Erman from behind, gripping both arms, and pulled him backwards. Off balance, Erman could not resist, and he toppled to the ground, releasing Eadbald.

Eadbald leaped to his feet and kicked Erman. Edgar grabbed Eadbald's foot and lifted, throwing him backwards to the ground. Then Erman was up again, shoving Edgar aside to get at Eadbald. Cwenburg clapped her hands enthusiastically.

Then the voice of authority was heard. 'Stop that at once, you stupid boys,' said Ma, coming around the corner of the house. Erman and Eadbald immediately stood still.

Cwenburg protested: 'You spoiled the fun!'

Ma said: 'Put your dress back on, you shameless child.'

For a moment Cwenburg looked as if she might be tempted to defy Ma, and tell her to go to the devil, but she did not have the nerve. She turned around, took a step into the barn, and bent down to pick up her dress. She did so slowly, making sure they all got a good view of her rear. Then she turned around and lifted the dress over her head, raising her arms so that her breasts stuck out. Edgar could not help looking, and he noticed that she had put on weight since he saw her naked in the river.

At last she lowered the garment over her body. For a final touch she wriggled inside it until she was comfortable.

Ma murmured: 'Heaven spare us.'

Edgar spoke to his brothers. 'I suppose one of you was shagging her and the other objected.'

Eadbald said indignantly: 'Erman forced her!'

'I did not force her,' said Erman.

'You must have – she loves me!'

'I did not force her,' Erman repeated. 'She wanted me.'

'She did not.'

Edgar said: 'Cwenburg, did Erman force you?'

She looked coy. 'He was very masterful.' She was enjoying this.

Edgar said: 'Well, Eadbald says you love him. Is that true?'

'Oh, yes.' She paused. 'I love Eadbald. And Erman.'

Ma made a disgusted noise. 'Are you telling us you've lain with both of them?'

'Yes.' Cwenburg looked pleased with herself.

'Many times?'

'Yes.'

'For how long?'

'Since you arrived here.'

Ma shook her head in revulsion. 'Thank God I never had daughters.'

Cwenburg protested: 'I didn't do it on my own!'

Ma sighed. 'No, it takes two.'

Erman said: 'I'm the eldest, I should marry first.'

Eadbald gave a scornful laugh. 'Who told you that was a rule? I'll marry when I want, not when you say.'

'But I can afford a wife and you can't. You've got nothing. I'm going to inherit the farm one day.'

Eadbald was outraged. 'Ma has three sons. The farm will be divided among us when Ma dies, which I hope will not happen for many years.'

Edgar said: 'Don't be stupid, Eadbald. This farm can barely support our family now. If the three of us each tried to raise a family on one third of the land, we'd all starve.'

Ma said: 'Edgar is the only one of you talking sense, as usual.'

Eadbald looked genuinely hurt. 'So, Ma, does that mean you're going to throw me out?'

'I would never do such a thing. You know that.'

'Do the three of us have to be celibate, like a convent of monks?'

'I hope not.'

'What are we going to do, then?'

Ma's answer caught Edgar by surprise. 'We're going to talk to Cwenburg's parents. Come on.'

Edgar was not sure this would help. Dreng had little common sense, and might just try to throw his weight around. Leaf was smarter, and kinder, too. But Ma had something up her sleeve, and Edgar could not guess what.

They tramped along the river bank. The grass was already growing again where they had reaped the hay. The hamlet basked in the August sun, quiet but for the ever-present shush of the river.

They found Ethel, the younger wife, and Blod, the slave, in the alehouse. Ethel smiled at Edgar; she seemed to like him. She said that Dreng was at his brother's minster, and Cwenburg went to fetch him. Edgar found Leaf in the brewhouse, stirring her mash with a rake. She was happy to break off from her work. She filled a jug with ale and carried it to the bench in front of the alehouse. Cwenburg returned with her father.

They all sat in the sun, enjoying the breeze off the water. Blod poured everyone a cup of ale, and Ma set out the problem in a few words.

Edgar studied the faces around him. Erman and Eadbald were beginning to realize what fools they looked, each thinking he had deceived the other, each having been deceived. Cwenburg was simply proud of the power she had over them. Her parents did not seem surprised by what she had done: perhaps there had been previous incidents. Dreng bristled at any hint of criticism of his daughter. Leaf just looked weary. Ma was in command, confident; in the end, Edgar thought, she would decide what was going to be done.

When Ma had finished, Leaf said: 'Cwenburg must be married soon. Otherwise she will fall pregnant by some random ferry passenger who will disappear, leaving us with his bastard to raise.'

Edgar wanted to say: That bastard would be your grandchild! But he kept the thought to himself.

Dreng said: 'Don't speak of my daughter like that.'

'She's my daughter too.'

'You're too hard on her. She may have her faults—'

Ma interrupted. 'We all want her to marry, but how is she to live? My farm will not feed another mouth – never mind two.'

Dreng said: 'I'm not going to marry her to a husband who can't support her. I'm a cousin of the ealdorman of Shiring. My daughter could marry a nobleman.'

Leaf laughed derisively.

Dreng went on: 'Besides, I can't let her go. There's too much work to do around here. I need someone young and strong to paddle the ferry. Blod is too pregnant and I can't do it myself – I've got a bad back. A Viking knocked me off my horse—'

'Yes, yes, at the battle of Watchet,' said Leaf impatiently. 'I've heard you were drunk, and you fell off a whore, not a horse.'

Ma said: 'As to that, Dreng, when Cwenburg leaves you can employ Edgar.'

Well, Edgar thought, I didn't see that coming.

'He's young and strong, and, what's more, he can build you a new boat to replace that old tree trunk, which is going to sink any day now.'

Edgar was not sure what he thought of that. He would love to build another boat, but he hated Dreng.

'Employ that cocky pup?' Dreng said scornfully. 'No one wants a dog that barks at its master, and I don't want Edgar.'

Ma ignored that. 'You can pay him half a penny per day. You'll never get a cheaper boat.'

A calculating look came over Dreng's face as he figured that Ma was right. But he said: 'No, I don't like it.'

Leaf said: 'We have to do something.'

Dreng looked obstinate. 'I'm her father, and I'll decide.'

'There is one other possibility,' said Ma.

Here it comes, Edgar thought. What scheme has she dreamed up?

'Come on, spit it out,' said Dreng. He was trying to be in charge, but no one else believed it.

Ma was silent for a long moment, then said: 'Cwenburg must marry Erman and Eadbald.'

Edgar had not seen that coming, either.

Dreng was outraged. 'And she would have two husbands?'

Leaf said pointedly: 'Well, plenty of men have two wives.'

Dreng looked indignant but could not, for the moment, find words to express just where Leaf was wrong.

'I've heard of such marriages,' Ma said calmly. 'It happens when two or three brothers inherit a farm that is too small for more than one family.'

Eadbald said: 'But how does it work? I mean . . . at night?'

Ma said: 'The brothers take it in turn to lie with their wife.'

Edgar was sure he wanted no part of this, but he kept quiet for the moment, not wanting to undermine Ma. He would state his position later. Come to think of it, Ma must already have guessed how he felt.

Leaf said: 'I knew such a family, once. When I was a child I sometimes played with a girl who had one mama and two daddies.' Edgar wondered whether to believe her. He looked hard at her face and saw an expression of genuine reminiscence. She added: 'Margaret, her name was.'

'That's how it should be,' said Ma. 'When a child is born, no one knows which brother is the father, which the uncle. And, if they're sensible, no one cares. They just raise all the children as their own.'

Eadbald said: 'What about the wedding?'

'You will make all the usual vows, in front of a few witnesses – just the members of the two families, I suggest.'

Erman said: 'No priest would bless such a marriage.'

'Fortunately,' said Ma, 'we don't need a priest.'

Leaf said scathingly: 'But if we did, Dreng's brother would surely oblige us. Degbert has two women.'

Dreng said defensively: 'A wife and a concubine.'

'Though no one knows which is which.'

'Very well,' said Ma. 'Cwenburg, do you have something to tell your father?'

Cwenburg was puzzled. 'I don't think so.'

'I think you do.'

Edgar thought: What now?

Cwenburg frowned. 'No.'

'You haven't had your monthly blood since we arrived in Dreng's Ferry, have you?'

Edgar thought: That's the third time Ma has surprised me.

Cwenburg said to Ma: 'How did you know that?'

'I know because your shape has changed. You've put on a little weight around your middle, and your breasts are bigger. I expect your nipples hurt.'

Cwenburg was frightened and looked pale. 'How do you know all this? You must be a witch!'

Leaf understood what Ma was getting at. 'Oh, dear,' she said. 'I should have seen the signs.'

Edgar thought: Your eyesight was blurred by ale.

Cwenburg said: 'What are you all talking about?'

Ma spoke gently. 'You're going to have a baby. When you stop getting the monthly blood, that's how you know you're pregnant.'

'Is it?'

Edgar wondered how a girl could reach the age of fifteen without knowing that.

Dreng was infuriated. 'You mean she's already with child?'

'Yes,' said Ma. 'I knew it when I saw her naked. And she doesn't know whether the father is Erman or Eadbald.'

Dreng stared malevolently at Ma. 'You're saying she's no better than a whore!'

Leaf said: 'Calm down, Dreng. You shag two women – does that make you a male whore?'

'I haven't shagged you for a while.'

'A mercy for which I thank heaven daily.'

Ma said: 'Someone has to help Cwenburg raise the baby, Dreng. And there are only two possibilities. She can stay here with you, and you can help her raise the grandchild.'

'A child needs its father.' Dreng was being unusually decent. Edgar had noticed that he softened when Cwenburg was around.

Ma said: 'The alternative is that Erman and Eadbald will marry Cwenburg and they will raise the child together. And if that happens,

Edgar must come here to live, and be paid half a penny a day on top of his food.'

'I don't like either choice.'

'Then suggest another.'

Dreng opened his mouth, but no words came out.

Leaf said: 'What do you think, Cwenburg? Do you want to marry Erman and Eadbald?'

'Yes,' Cwenburg said. 'I like them both.'

Leaf said: 'When shall we have the wedding?'

'Tomorrow,' Ma said. 'At noon.'

'Where? Here?'

'Everyone in the hamlet will show up.'

Dreng said grumpily: 'I don't want to give them all free beer.'

Ma said: 'And I don't want to explain the marriage ten times over to every fool in Dreng's Ferry.'

Edgar said: 'At the farm, then. They can all find out about it later.'

Leaf said: 'I'll provide a small barrel of ale.'

Ma looked inquiringly at Ethel, who had not spoken.

Ethel said: 'I'll make honey cakes.'

'Oh, good,' said Cwenburg. 'I love honey cakes.'

Edgar stared at her in disbelief. She had just agreed to marry two men, and she was able to get excited about cakes.

Ma said: 'Well, Dreng?'

'I'll pay Edgar a farthing a day.'

'Done,' said Ma. She stood up. 'We'll expect you all tomorrow at noon, then.'

Her three sons stood and followed her as she walked away from the alehouse.

Edgar thought: I'm not a farmer any more.

7

RAGNA WAS NOT PREGNANT.

She had suffered agonies of apprehension for two weeks after Wilwulf left Cherbourg. To be impregnated and deserted was the ultimate humiliation, especially for a noble maiden. A peasant's daughter who suffered the same fate would be equally mocked and scorned, but might eventually find someone to marry her and take on the raising of another man's child, but a lady would be shunned by every man of her class.

However, she had escaped that fate. The arrival of the monthly blood had been as welcome as sunrise.

After that she should have hated Wilwulf, but she found she could not. He had betrayed her, but she still yearned for him. She was a fool, she knew. Anyway it hardly mattered, for she would probably never see him again.

Father Louis had gone home to Reims without spotting the early signs of Ragna's romance with Wilwulf, and it seemed he had reported that Ragna would make a suitable wife for the young Viscount Guillaume, for Guillaume himself had arrived at Cherbourg to make the final decision.

Guillaume thought Ragna was perfect.

He kept telling her so. He studied her, sometimes touching her chin to move her face a little to one side or the other, up or down, to catch the light. 'Perfect,' he would say. 'The eyes, green like the sea, such a shade as I never saw before. The nose, so straight, so fine.

The cheekbones, perfectly matched. The pale skin. And most of all, the hair.' Ragna kept her hair mostly covered, as did all respectable women, but a few locks were artfully allowed to escape. 'Such a bright gold – angels' wings must be that colour.'

She was flattered, but she could not help feeling that he was looking at her as he might have admired an enamelled brooch, the most prized of his collection. Wilwulf had never told her she was perfect. He had said: 'By the gods, I can't keep my hands off you.'

Guillaume himself was very good-looking. As they stood on the high parapet of Cherbourg Castle, looking down at the ships in the bay, the breeze tousled his hair, which was long and glossy, dark brown with auburn lights. He had brown eyes and regular features. He was much more handsome than Wilwulf, but all the same the castle maids never blushed and giggled when he walked by. Wilwulf exerted a masculine magnetism that Guillaume just did not have.

He had just given Ragna a present, a silk shawl embroidered by his mother. Ragna unfolded it and studied the design, which featured intertwining foliage and monstrous birds. 'It's gorgeous,' she said. 'It must have taken her a year.'

'She has good taste.'

'What is she like?'

'She's absolutely wonderful.' Guillaume smiled. 'I suppose every boy thinks his mother is wonderful.'

Ragna was not sure that was true, but she kept the thought to herself.

'I believe a noblewoman should have complete authority over everything to do with fabrics,' he said, and Ragna sensed she was about to hear a prepared speech. 'Spinning, weaving, dyeing, stitching, embroidery, and of course laundry. A woman should rule that world the way her husband rules his domain.' He spoke as if he were making a generous concession.

Ragna said flatly: 'I hate all that.'

Guillaume was startled. 'Don't you do embroidery?'

Ragna resisted the temptation to prevaricate. She did not want him to suffer any misapprehensions. I am what I am, she thought. She said: 'Lord, no.'

He was baffled. 'Why not?'

'I love beautiful clothes, like most people, but I don't want to make them. It bores me.'

He looked disappointed. 'It bores you?'

Perhaps it was time to sound more positive. 'Don't you think a noblewoman has other duties too? What about when her husband goes to war? Someone has to make sure the rents are paid and justice is dispensed.'

'Well, yes, of course, in an emergency.'

Ragna decided she had made herself clear enough. She conceded a point in the hope of lowering the temperature. 'That's what I mean,' she said untruthfully. 'In an emergency.'

He looked relieved, and changed the subject. 'What a splendid view.'

The castle provided a lookout over the surrounding countryside, so that hostile armies could be seen from afar, in time for defensive preparations – or flight. Cherbourg Castle also looked out to sea, for the same reason. But Guillaume was studying the town. The river Divette meandered left and right through the timber-and-thatch houses before reaching the waterfront. The streets were busy with carts going to and from the harbour, their wooden wheels raising dust from the sun-dried roads. The Vikings no longer moored here, as Count Hubert had promised Wilwulf, but several ships of other nations were tied up and others were anchored farther out. An incoming French vessel was low in the water, perhaps bringing iron or stone. Behind it, in the distance, an English ship was approaching. 'A commercial city,' Guillaume commented.

Ragna detected a note of disapproval. She asked him: 'What kind of city is Reims?'

'A holy place,' he said immediately. 'Clovis, king of the Franks, was baptised there by Bishop Remi long ago. On that occasion, a white dove appeared with a bottle, called the Holy Ampulla, containing sacred oil that has been used since for many royal coronations.'

Ragna thought there must be some buying and selling in Reims, as well as miracles and coronations, but once again she held back. She seemed always to be holding back when she talked to Guillaume.

Her patience was running low. She told herself she had done her duty. 'Shall we go down?' she said. Insincerely she added: 'I can't wait to show this lovely shawl to my mother.'

They descended the wooden steps and entered the great hall. Genevieve was not in sight, which gave Ragna an excuse to leave Guillaume and enter the private apartment of the count and countess. She found her mother going through her jewel box, selecting a pin for her dress. 'Hello, dear,' said the countess. 'How are you getting on with Guillaume? He seems lovely.'

'He's very fond of his mother.'

'How nice.'

Ragna showed her the shawl. 'She embroidered this for me.'

Genevieve took the shawl and admired it. 'So kind of her.'

Ragna could hold out no longer. 'Oh, mother, I don't like him.'

Genevieve made an exasperated noise. 'Give him a chance, won't you?'

'I've tried, I really have.'

'What's wrong with him, for goodness' sake?'

'He wants me to be in charge of fabrics.'

'Well, naturally, when you're the countess. You don't think he should sew his own clothes, do you?'

'He's prissy.'

'No, he's not. You imagine things. He's perfectly all right.'

'I wish I were dead.'

'You've got to stop pining for that big Englishman. He was completely unsuitable, and anyway he's gone.'

'More's the pity.'

Genevieve turned around to face Ragna. 'Now listen to me. You can't remain unmarried much longer. It will begin to look permanent.'

'Perhaps it is.'

'Don't even say that. There's no place for a single noblewoman. She's no use, but she still requires gowns and jewels and horses and servants, and her father gets tired of paying out and getting nothing back. What's more, the married women hate her, because they think she wants to steal their husbands.'

'I could become a nun.'

'I doubt that. You've never been particularly devout.'

'Nuns sing and read and take care of sick people.'

'And sometimes they have loving relationships with other nuns, but I don't think that's your inclination. I remember that wicked girl from Paris, Constance, but you didn't really like her.'

Ragna blushed. She had had no idea that her mother knew about her and Constance. They had kissed and touched each other's breasts and watched each other masturbate, but Ragna's heart had not been in it, and eventually Constance had turned her attention to another girl. How much had Genevieve guessed?

Anyway, her mother's instinct was right: a love affair with a woman was never going to be what made Ragna happy.

'So,' Genevieve resumed, 'Guillaume is probably an advantageous choice at this point.'

An advantageous choice, thought Ragna; I wanted a romance that would make my heart sing, but what I've got is an advantageous choice.

All the same, she thought she would have to marry him.

In sombre mood she left her mother. She passed through the great hall and went out into the sunshine, hoping that might cheer her up.

At the gate of the compound was a small group of visitors, presumably off one of the two ships she had seen approaching earlier. At the centre of the group was a nobleman with a moustache but no beard, presumably an Englishman, and for a heart-stopping moment she thought it was Wilwulf. He was tall and fair, with a big nose and a strong jaw, and there flashed into her mind an entire fantasy in which Wilwulf had come back to marry her and take her away. But a moment later she realized that this man's head was tonsured, and he wore the long black robe of a clergyman; and as he drew nearer she saw that his eyes were closer together, his ears were huge, and although he might have been younger than Wilwulf his face was already lined. He walked differently, too: where Wilwulf was confident, this man was arrogant.

Ragna's father was not in sight, nor were any of his senior clerks, so it was up to Ragna to welcome the visitor. She went up to him and said: 'Good day to you, sir. Welcome to Cherbourg. I am Ragna, the daughter of Count Hubert.'

His reaction startled her. He stared at her keenly, and a mocking smile played under his moustache. 'Are you, now?' he said as if fascinated. 'Are you really?' He spoke good French with an accent.

She did not know what to say in reply, but her silence did not seem to bother the visitor. He looked her up and down as he might have studied a horse, checking all the key points. His gaze began to feel rude.

Then he spoke again. 'I am the bishop of Shiring,' he said. 'My name is Wynstan. I am the brother of Ealdorman Wilwulf.'

ÞÞÞ

RAGNA WAS UNBEARABLY agitated. Wynstan's mere presence was thrilling. He was Wilwulf's brother! Every time she looked at Wynstan she thought about how close he was to the man she loved. They had been raised together. Wynstan must know Wilwulf intimately; must admire his qualities, understand his weaknesses and recognize his moods so much better than Ragna could. And he even looked a bit like Wilwulf.

Ragna told her lively maid Cat to flirt with one of Wynstan's bodyguards, a big man called Cnebba. The bodyguards spoke nothing but English, so communication was difficult and unreliable, but Cat thought she had understood a little about the family. Bishop Wynstan was in fact the half-brother of Ealdorman Wilwulf. Wilwulf's mother had died, his father had remarried, and the second wife had borne Wynstan and a younger brother, Wigelm. The three formed a powerful triad in the west of England: one ealdorman, one bishop and one thane. They were wealthy, although their prosperity was under threat from Viking raids.

But what brought Wynstan to Cherbourg? If the bodyguards knew, they were not saying.

Most likely the visit had to do with the implementation of the treaty agreed between Wilwulf and Hubert. Perhaps Wynstan had come to check that Hubert was keeping his promise, and refusing to let Vikings moor in Cherbourg harbour. Or perhaps the visit had something to do with Ragna.

She learned the truth that night.

After supper, as Count Hubert was retiring, Wynstan cornered him and spoke in a low voice. Ragna strained to hear but could not make out the words. Hubert replied equally quietly, then nodded and continued on to the private quarters, followed by Genevieve.

Not long afterwards Genevieve summoned Ragna.

'What's happened?' Ragna said breathlessly as soon as she was in the room. 'What did Wynstan say?'

Her mother looked thunderously cross. 'Ask your father,' she said.

Hubert said: 'Bishop Wynstan has brought a proposal of marriage to you from Ealdorman Wilwulf.'

Ragna could not conceal her delight. 'I hardly dared hope for it!'

she said. She had to restrain herself from jumping up and down like a child. 'I thought he might have come about the Vikings!'

Genevieve said: 'Please don't think for one moment that we will consent to it.'

Ragna barely heard her. She could escape from Guillaume – and marry the man she loved. 'He does love me, after all!'

'Your father has agreed to listen to the ealdorman's offer, that's all.'

Hubert said: 'I must. To do otherwise would rudely suggest that the man is unacceptable on any terms.'

'Which he is!' said Genevieve.

'Probably,' said Hubert. 'However, that's the kind of thing one thinks but does not say. One has no wish to offend.'

Genevieve said: 'Having listened to the terms, your father will politely refuse.'

Ragna said: 'You'll tell me what the offer is, Father, before you turn it down, won't you?'

Hubert hesitated. He never liked to slam doors. 'Of course I will,' he said.

Genevieve made a disgusted noise.

Ragna pushed her luck. 'Will you let me attend your meeting with Wynstan?'

He said: 'Are you capable of remaining silent throughout?'

'Yes.'

'Promise?'

'I swear it.'

'Very well.'

'Go to bed,' Genevieve said to Ragna. 'We'll discuss this in the morning.'

Ragna left them and lay down in the hall, curled up on her bed by the wall. She found it difficult to keep still, she was so excited. He *did* love her!

As the rush lights were extinguished and the room became dark, so her heartbeat slowed and her body relaxed. At the same time she began to think more clearly. If he did love her, why had he fled without explanation? Would Wynstan offer a justification for that? If not, she would ask for one directly, she decided.

That sobering thought brought her down to earth, and she fell asleep.

She woke at first light, and Wilwulf was the first thought to come into her mind. What would his offer be? Normally an aristocratic bride had to be guaranteed enough income to keep her if her husband died and she became a widow. If the children were likely to be heirs to money or titles, they might have to be brought up in the father's country, even if he died. Sometimes the offer was conditional on the king's approval. An engagement could be dismayingly like a commercial contract.

Ragna's main concern was that Wilwulf's offer should contain nothing that would give her parents reason to object.

Once she was dressed, she wished she had slept later. The kitchen staff and the stable hands were always up early, but everyone else was still fast asleep, including Wynstan. She had to resist the temptation to grab him by the shoulder and shake him awake and question him.

She went to the kitchen, where she drank a cup of cider and ate a piece of pan bread dipped in honey. She took a half-ripe apple, went to the stables, and gave the apple to Astrid, her horse. Astrid nuzzled her gratefully. 'You've never known love,' Ragna murmured in the horse's ear. But it was not quite true: there were times, usually in summer, when Astrid carried her tail up and had to be roped in firmly to keep her away from the stallions.

The straw on the stable floor was damp and smelly. The hands were lazy about changing it. Ragna ordered them to bring fresh straw immediately.

The compound was coming awake. Men came to the well to drink, women to wash their faces. Servants carried bread and cider into the great hall. Dogs begged for scraps, and cats lay in wait for mice. The count and countess emerged from their quarters and sat at the table, and breakfast began.

As soon as the meal was over, the count invited Wynstan into the private apartment. Genevieve and Ragna followed, and they all sat in the outer chamber.

Wynstan's message was simple. 'When Ealdorman Wilwulf was here six weeks ago he fell in love with the Lady Ragna. Back at home, he feels that without her his life is incomplete. He begs your permission, count and countess, to ask her to marry him.'

Hubert said: 'What provision would he make for her financial security?'

'On their wedding day he will give her the Vale of Outhen. It's a fertile valley with five substantial villages containing altogether about a thousand people, all of whom will pay her rent in cash or kind. It also has a limestone quarry. May I ask, Count Hubert, what the Lady Ragna would bring to the marriage?'

'Something comparable: the village of Saint-Martin and eight smaller villages nearby amounting to a similar number of people, just over one thousand.'

Wynstan nodded but did not comment, and Ragna wondered if he wanted more.

Hubert said: 'The income from both properties will be hers?'

'Yes,' said Wynstan.

'And she will retain both properties until her death, whereupon she may bequeath them to whomever she will?'

'Yes,' said Wynstan again. 'But what about a cash dowry?'

'I had thought Saint-Martin would be sufficient.'

'May I suggest twenty pounds of silver?'

'I'll have to think about that. Will King Ethelred of England approve of the marriage?'

It was usual to ask royal permission for aristocratic nuptials. Wynstan said: 'I have taken the precaution of asking for his consent in advance.' He directed an oily smile at Ragna. 'I told him that she is a beautiful and well-brought-up girl who will bring great credit to my brother, to Shiring and to England. The king agreed readily.'

Genevieve spoke for the first time. 'Does your brother live in a home like this?' She raised her hands to indicate the stones of the castle.

'Madam, no one lives in a building like this in England, and I believe there are few like it even in Normandy and the Frankish lands.'

Hubert said proudly: 'That's true. There is only one building like this in Normandy, at Ivry.'

'There are none in England.'

Genevieve said: 'Perhaps that's why you English seem so unable to protect yourselves from the Vikings.'

'Not so, my lady. Shiring is a walled town, strongly defended.'

'But clearly it doesn't have a stone-built castle or keep.'

'No.'

'Tell me something else, if you will.'

'Anything, of course.'

'Your brother is somewhere in his thirties?'

'A young-looking forty, my lady.'

'How come he is unmarried, at that age?'

'He was married. In fact, that's why he did not propose marriage while he was here in Cherbourg. But sadly his wife is no longer with us.'

'Ah.'

So that was it, Ragna thought. He couldn't propose in July because he was married then.

Her head filled with speculation. Why had he been unfaithful to his wife? Perhaps she had already been ill, and her death anticipated.

She might have suffered a slow deterioration, and been unable for some time to perform her wifely duty – that would explain how come Wilwulf had been so hungry for love. Ragna had a dozen questions, but she had promised to remain silent, and she clenched her jaw in frustration.

Wynstan said: 'May I take home a positive answer?'

Hubert replied: 'We will let you know. We must consider what you've said very carefully.'

'Of course.'

Ragna tried to read Wynstan's face. She had the feeling he was not enthusiastic about his brother's choice. She wondered why he might be ambivalent. No doubt he wanted to succeed in the mission his high-ranking brother had given him. But perhaps there was something about it that he did not like. He could have a candidate of his own: aristocratic marriages were highly political. Or perhaps he just did not like Ragna – but that, she was aware, would be unusual in a normal red-blooded man. Whatever the reason, he did not seem unduly dismayed by Hubert's lack of enthusiasm.

Wynstan stood up and took his leave. As soon as the door closed behind him, Genevieve said: 'Outrageous! He wants to take her to live in a wooden house and be a prey to Vikings. She could end up in the slave market at Rouen!'

'I think that's perhaps a little exaggerated, my dear,' said the count.

'Well, there can be no doubt that Guillaume is superior.'

Ragna burst out: 'I don't love Guillaume!'

'You don't know what love is,' her mother said. 'You're too young.'

Her father said: 'And you've never been to England. It's not like here, you know. It's cold and wet.'

Ragna felt sure she could put up with rain for the sake of the man she loved. 'I want to marry Wilwulf!'

'You talk like a peasant girl,' said her mother. 'But you're the child of nobility, and you don't have the right to marry anyone you choose.'

'I will not marry Guillaume!'

'Yes, you will, if your father and I say so.'

Hubert said: 'In your twenty years you've never known what it's like to be freezing cold or starving hungry. But there's a price to be paid for your privileged existence.'

Ragna was silenced. Her father's logic was more effective than her mother's bluster. She had never thought of her life that way. She felt sobered.

But she still wanted Wilwulf.

Genevieve said: 'Wynstan needs something to do. Take him for a ride. Show him the district.'

Ragna suspected her mother was hoping Wynstan would say or do something to put her off going to England. She really wanted to be alone with her thoughts, but she would entertain Wynstan and learn more about Wilwulf and Shiring. 'I'll be glad to,' she said, and she went out.

Wynstan agreed readily to the idea and together they went to the stable, taking Cnebba and Cat with them. On the way Ragna said quietly to Wynstan: 'I love your brother. I hope he knows that.'

'He was anxious that the manner of his departure from Cherbourg may have soured any feelings you may have had for him.'

'I ought to have hated him, but I couldn't.'

'I'll reassure him of that as soon as I get home.'

She had a lot more to say to Wynstan, but she was interrupted by the noise of a small, excited crowd. Some yards beyond the stable two dogs were fighting, a short-legged black hound and a grey mastiff. The stable hands had come out to watch. They were yelling encouragement at the dogs and making bets on which would win.

Irritated, Ragna went into the stable to see if anyone was there to help saddle the horses. She saw that the hands had brought dry straw, as she had ordered, but all of them had abandoned their work for the dog fight, and most of the straw stood in a pile just inside the door.

She was about to go and drag one or two away from the excitement when her nostrils twitched. She sniffed and smelled burning. Her senses went on high alert. She spotted a wisp of smoke.

She guessed that someone had brought a brand from the kitchen to light a lamp in a dark corner, then had abandoned the project and put the brand down carelessly when the fight began. Whatever the explanation, some of the new straw was smouldering.

Ragna looked around and saw a water barrel that supplied the horses' needs, with a wooden bucket upside-down on the floor nearby. She grabbed the bucket, filled it, and threw the water on the smoking straw.

She saw immediately that this would not be enough. In the few seconds it had taken her the fire had grown, and now she saw flames licking up. She handed the bucket to Cat. 'Throw more water on it!' she ordered. 'We'll go to the well.'

She ran out of the stable. Wynstan and Cnebba followed her. As she ran she shouted: 'Fire in the stable – fetch buckets and pots!'

At the well she told Cnebba to operate the winch – he looked strong enough to do it tirelessly. Cnebba did not understand her, of course, but Wynstan rapidly translated into the guttural-sounding English language. Several people grabbed nearby containers and Cnebba started to fill them.

The hands were so wrapped up in the dog fight that none of them had yet become aware of the emergency. Ragna yelled at them, but failed to get their attention. She ran into the crowd, violently shoving men aside, and reached the fighting dogs. She grabbed the black dog by its back legs and lifted it off the ground. That stopped the fight. 'Fire in the stable!' she yelled. 'Form a line to the well and pass the water along.'

There was chaos for a few moments, but in commendably quick time the hands had formed a bucket chain.

Ragna went back inside the stable. The new straw was blazing fiercely and the fire had spread. The horses were neighing in fear, kicking out, and struggling to break the ropes that kept them in their places. She went to Astrid, tried to calm her, untied her and led her out.

She saw Guillaume watching the activity. 'Don't just stand there,' she said. 'Do something to help!'

He seemed surprised. 'I don't know what to do,' he said vaguely.

How could he be so useless? In exasperation she said: 'You idiot, if you can't think of anything else just piss on it!'

Guillaume looked insulted and stalked off.

Ragna gave Astrid's rope to a little girl and ran back inside. She untied all the horses and let them run out, hoping they would not injure anyone in their panic. For a few seconds they constrained the firefighters, but their departure left room to manoeuvre, and after a few more minutes the flames were extinguished.

The thatched roof had not caught fire, the stable had been saved, and numerous costly horses had been spared from death.

Ragna stopped the bucket chain. 'Well done, everyone,' she called. 'We caught the blaze in time. No great damage has been done, and no people or horses are hurt.'

One of the men shouted: 'Thanks to you, Lady Ragna!'

Several others agreed loudly, and then they all cheered.

She caught Wynstan's eye. He was looking at her with something like respect.

She looked around for Guillaume. He was nowhere to be seen.

ÞÞÞ

SOMEONE MUST HAVE heard what she had said to Guillaume, for by suppertime everyone in the compound seemed to know about it. Cat told her they were all talking about it, and after that she noticed that when people caught her eye they smiled at her, then murmured to one another and laughed, as if recalling the punch line of a joke.

Twice she overheard someone say: 'If you can't think of anything else just piss on it!'

Guillaume left for Reims the next morning. He had been insulted and now he was the butt of a joke. His dignity could not stand it. His departure was quiet and unceremonious. Ragna had not wanted to humiliate him, but she could not help rejoicing to see him ride away.

Ragna's parents' resistance crumbled. Wynstan was told that his brother's proposal was accepted, including the dowry of twenty pounds, and the wedding was fixed for All Saints' Day, the first of November. Wynstan went back to England with the good news. Ragna would take a few weeks to get ready, then she would follow.

'You get your way, as you so often do,' Genevieve said to Ragna. 'Guillaume doesn't want you, I don't have the energy to search for yet another French nobleman, and at least the English will take you off my hands.'

Hubert was more gracious. 'Love triumphs in the end,' he said. 'Just like in those old stories you love.'

'Quite,' said Genevieve. 'Except that the stories usually end in tragedy.'

EDGAR WAS DETERMINED TO build a boat that would please Dreng.

It was hard to like Dreng, and few people did. He was malevolent and miserly. Living at the alehouse, Edgar quickly became familiar with the family. The elder wife, Leaf, was coldly indifferent to Dreng most of the time. The younger woman, Ethel, seemed scared of her husband. She bought the food and cooked it, and cried when he complained about the cost. Edgar wondered whether either woman had ever loved Dreng, and decided not: both were from poor peasant families and had probably married for financial security.

Blod, the slave, hated Dreng. When she was not servicing passing strangers who wanted sex, Dreng kept her busy cleaning the house and outbuildings, tending the pigs and chickens, and changing the rushes on the floor. He always spoke harshly to her, and she in turn was permanently surly and resentful. She would have made more money for him if she had not been so miserable, but he seemed not to realize that.

The women liked Brindle, Edgar's dog. She won their affection by chasing foxes away from the henhouse. Dreng never patted the dog, and in response she acted as if Dreng did not exist.

However, Dreng seemed to love his daughter, Cwenburg, and she him. He smiled when he saw her, whereas he greeted most people with a sneer or, at best, a smirk. For Cwenburg Dreng would always drop what he was doing, and the two of them would sit and talk in low voices, sometimes for an hour.

That proved it was possible to have a normal human relationship with Dreng, and Edgar was determined to try. He was not aiming for affection: just a briskly practical liaison without rancour.

Edgar set up an open-air workshop on the river bank, and by good fortune the hot August sunshine continued into a warm September. He felt happy to be constructing something again, honing his blade, smelling the cut wood, imagining shapes and joins and then making them real.

When he had fashioned all the wooden parts he laid them out on the ground, and the outlines of the boat became discernible.

Dreng looked and said accusingly: 'In a boat, the planks usually overlap.'

Edgar had anticipated questions, and he had answers ready, but he was wary. He needed to convince Dreng without coming across as a know-it-all – always a danger for Edgar, he knew. 'That type of hull is called clinker-built. But this boat will be flat-bottomed, so it will be carvel-built, with the planks set edge-to-edge. By the way, we call them strakes, not planks.'

'Planks, strakes, I don't care, but why is it flat-bottomed?'

'Mainly so that people and cattle can stand upright, and baskets and sacks can be stacked securely. Also, the vessel won't roll side to side so much, which helps to keep the passengers calm.'

'If that's such a smart idea, why aren't all boats built that way?'

'Because most boats have to cut through the waves and currents at speed. That doesn't apply to the ferry. There are no waves here, the current is steady but not strong, and speed is not the main issue in a journey of fifty yards.'

Dreng grunted, then pointed at the strakes forming the sides of the boat. 'I assume the rails will be higher than that.'

'No. There are no waves, so the boat doesn't need high sides.'

'Boats are usually pointed at the front end. This one seems blunt at both ends.'

'Same reason – it doesn't need to cut through the water fast. And the square ends make it easier to get on and off. That's also the reason for the ramps. Even cattle can board this boat.'

'Does it need to be so wide?'

'To take a cart, yes.' Trying to win a word of approval, Edgar added: 'The ferry across the estuary at Combe charges a farthing per wheel: one farthing for a wheelbarrow, a halfpenny for a handcart, and a whole penny for an oxcart.'

A greedy look passed across Dreng's face, but he said: 'We don't get many carts.'

'They all go to Mudeford because your old boat couldn't manage them. You'll see more with this one, you wait.'

'I doubt it,' Dreng said. 'And it will be damnably heavy to paddle.'

'It won't have paddles.' Edgar pointed to two long poles. 'The river is never more than about six feet deep, so the ferry can be poled across. One strong man can do it.'

'I can't, I've got a bad back.'

'Two women could do it working together. That's why I made two poles.'

Some of the villagers had drifted down to the river to stare curiously. One of them was the clergyman-jeweller, Cuthbert. He was skilled and knowledgeable, but a timid and unsociable man who was bullied by his master, Degbert. Edgar often spoke to Cuthbert, but got monosyllabic replies except when discussing issues of craftsmanship. Now Cuthbert said: 'Did you do all this with a Viking axe?'

'It's all I've got,' said Edgar. 'The back of the head serves me as a hammer. And I keep the blade sharp, which is the main thing.'

Cuthbert looked impressed. He said: 'How will you fix the strakes to one another edge-to-edge?'

'I'll peg them to a timber skeleton.'

'With iron nails?'

Edgar shook his head. 'I'll use tree nails.' A tree nail was a wooden peg with split ends. The peg was inserted in a hole, then wedges were hammered into the split ends, widening the peg until it was a tight fit. After that the protruding ends of the peg were cut off flush with the strake to make a smooth surface.

'That will work,' said Cuthbert. 'But you'll need to waterproof the joins.'

'I'll have to go to Combe and buy a barrel of tar and a sack of raw wool.'

Dreng heard that and looked indignant. 'More money? You don't make boats out of wool.'

'The joins between the strakes have to be stuffed with tar-soaked wool to make them watertight.'

Dreng looked resentful. 'You've got your smart answers, I'll grant you that,' he said.

It was almost praise.

ᚦᚦᚦ

WHEN THE BOAT was ready, Edgar pushed it into the water.

It was always a special moment. While Pa had been alive the whole family had gathered to watch, and they had usually been joined by many of the townspeople. But now Edgar did it alone. He did not fear that the boat would sink, he just did not want to seem triumphal. As a newcomer here he was trying to fit in, not stand out.

With the vessel roped to a tree so that it could not float away, he eased it away from the bank and studied the way it lay in the water. It was straight and level, he saw with satisfaction. No water trickled through the joins. He undid the rope and stepped onto the ramp. His weight shifted the trim of the boat a fraction, as it should.

Brindle was watching him eagerly, but he did not want her on board for this trip. He wanted to see the boat perform without passengers. 'You stay here,' he said, and she lay down with her nose between her paws, watching him.

The two long poles rested in wooden crotchets, a row of three on each side. He drew a pole out, put the end in the water, made contact with the river bed, and pushed. It was easier than he expected, and the ferry moved smoothly off.

He walked to the forward end then put the pole in the water on the downstream side, heading the vessel slightly upstream, to counteract the current. He found it well within the capability of a strong woman or an average man – Blod or Cwenburg could do it, and Leaf and Ethel would easily manage it together, especially if he gave them a lesson.

As he was crossing the river he glanced at the luxuriant late-summer foliage on the far bank and saw a sheep. Several more emerged from the woods, herded by two dogs; and finally the shepherd appeared, a young man with long hair and a straggly beard.

Edgar had his first passengers.

Suddenly he was nervous. He had designed the vessel to be boarded by livestock, but he knew a lot about boats and nothing about sheep. Would they do what he expected? Or would they panic and stampede? Did sheep stampede? He did not even know that.

He might be about to find out.

Reaching the bank, he disembarked and tied the ferry to a tree.

The shepherd smelled as if he had not washed for years. He looked hard at Edgar for a long moment and then said: 'You're new here.' He appeared pleased with his own perspicacity.

'Yes. I'm Edgar.'

'Ah. And you've got a new boat.'

'Beautiful, isn't it?'

'Different from the old boat.' With each completed sentence the shepherd paused to enjoy the satisfaction of achievement, and Edgar wondered if that was because he normally had no one to talk to.

'Very different,' Edgar said.

'I'm Saemar, usually called Sam.'

'I hope you're well, Sam.'

'I'm driving these hoggets to market.'

'I guessed that.' Edgar knew that hoggets were one-year-old sheep. 'To cross by the ferry is a farthing for each man or beast.'

'I know.'

'For twenty sheep, two dogs and you, that will be five pence and three farthings.'

'I know.' Saemar opened a leather purse attached to his belt. 'If I give you six silver pennies, you'll owe me a farthing.'

Edgar was not prepared for financial transactions. He had nowhere to put the money, no change, and no shears to cut coins into halves and quarters. 'You can pay Dreng,' he said. 'We should be able to take the herd across in one trip.'

'In the old boat, we had to transport them two at a time. It took all morning. And even then, sure enough, one or two of the stupid buggers would fall in the water, or panic and jump in, and have to be rescued. Can you swim?'

'Yes.'

'Ah. I can't.'

'I don't think any of your sheep will fall off this boat.'

'If there's a way to do themselves harm, sheep'll usually find it.'

Sam picked up a sheep and carried it onto the ferry. His dogs followed him on board and explored excitedly, sniffing the new wood. Sam then gave a distinctive trilling whistle. The dogs responded instantly. They jumped off the ferry, rounded up the sheep, and herded them to the river bank.

This was the challenging moment.

The leading sheep hesitated, needlessly intimidated by the small watery gap between the ground and the end of the boat. It looked from side to side, searching for an alternative, but the dogs cut off its escape. The sheep looked ready to refuse the next step. Then one of the dogs growled softly, low in its throat, and the sheep jumped.

It landed surefootedly on the interior ramp and trotted happily down onto the flat bottom of the boat.

The rest of the flock followed, and Edgar smiled with satisfaction.

The dogs followed the sheep on board and stood like sentries either side. Sam came last. Edgar untied the rope, jumped aboard, and deployed the pole.

As they moved out into midstream, Sam said: 'This is better than the old boat.' He nodded sagely. Each banality was uttered like a pearl of wisdom.

'I'm glad you like it,' said Edgar. 'You're my first passenger.'

'Used to be a girl. Cwenburg.'

'She got married.'

'Ah. They do.'

The ferry reached the north bank, and Edgar jumped out. As he was tying the rope, the sheep began to disembark. They did so with more alacrity than they had shown boarding. 'They've seen the grass,' Sam said in explanation. Sure enough they began to graze beside the river.

Edgar and Sam went into the alehouse, leaving the dogs to mind the sheep. Ethel was preparing the midday dinner, watched by Leaf and Dreng. A moment later Blod came in with an armful of firewood.

Edgar said to Dreng: 'Sam hasn't paid yet. He owes five pence and three farthings, but I didn't have a farthing to give him in change.'

Dreng said to Sam: 'Make it a round six pence and you can fuck the slave girl.'

Sam looked eagerly at Blod.

Leaf spoke up. 'She's too far gone.' Blod was now close to nine months pregnant. No one had wanted sex with her for three or four weeks.

But Sam was keen. 'I don't mind that,' he said.

'I wasn't worrying about you,' Leaf said scathingly. The sarcasm went over Sam's head. 'This late, the baby could be harmed.'

Dreng said: 'Who cares? No one wants a slave bastard.' With a contemptuous gesture he motioned Blod to get down on the floor.

Edgar could not see how Sam could possibly lie on top of the bump of Blod's pregnancy. But she went down on her hands and knees, then threw up the back of her grubby dress. Sam promptly knelt behind her and pulled up his tunic.

Edgar went out.

He walked down to the water and pretended to check the mooring of the ferry, though he knew perfectly well that he had tied it tight. He felt disgusted. He had never understood the men who paid for sex at Mags's house in Combe. The whole idea seemed joyless. His brother Erman had said: 'When you got to have it, you got to have it,' but Edgar had never felt that way. With Sunni, the two of them had enjoyed it equally, and Edgar thought anything less was hardly worth having.

What Sam was doing was worse than joyless, of course.

Edgar sat on the river bank and looked across the calm grey water, hoping for more passengers to take his mind off what was going on in the alehouse. Brindle sat beside him, waiting patiently to see what he would do next. After a few minutes she went to sleep.

It was not long before the shepherd emerged from the alehouse and drove his flock up the hill between the houses onto the westbound road. Edgar did not wave.

Blod came down to the river.

Edgar said: 'I'm sorry that happened to you.'

Blod did not look at him. She stepped into the shallows and washed between her legs.

Edgar looked away. 'It's very cruel,' he said.

He suspected that Blod understood English. She pretended not to; when something went wrong she cursed in the liquid Welsh tongue. Dreng gave her orders with gestures and snarls. But sometimes Edgar had the feeling she was following the conversation in the alehouse, albeit furtively.

Now she confirmed his suspicion. 'It's nothing,' she said. Her English was accented but clear, her voice melodic.

'You're not nothing,' he said.

She finished washing and stepped onto the bank. He met her eye. She was looking suspicious and hostile. 'Why so nice?' she demanded. 'You think you'll get a free fuck?'

He looked away again, directing his gaze across the water to the far trees, and made no reply. He thought she would walk away, but she stayed where she was, waiting for an answer.

Eventually he said: 'This dog used to belong to a woman I loved.'

Brindle opened one eye. Strange, Edgar thought, how dogs know when you are talking about them.

'The woman was a little older than me, and married,' Edgar said to Blod. She showed no emotion, but seemed to be listening attentively. 'When her husband was drunk she would meet me in the woods and we would make love on the grass.'

'Make love,' she repeated, as if unsure what it meant.

'We decided to run away together.' To his surprise he found himself close to tears, and he realized it was the first time he had spoken about Sunni since talking to Ma on the journey from Combe. 'I had the promise of work and a house in another town.' He was telling Blod things even his family did not know. 'She was beautiful and clever and kind.' He began to feel choked up but, now that he had started the story, he wanted to go on. 'I think we would have been very happy,' he said.

'What happened?'

'On the day we planned to go, the Vikings came.'

'Did they take her?'

Edgar shook his head. 'She fought them, and they killed her.'

'She was lucky,' Blod said. 'Believe me.'

Thinking about what Blod had just done with Sam, Edgar almost agreed. 'Her name . . .' He found it hard to say. 'Her name was Sunni.'

'When?'

'A week before midsummer.'

'I am very sorry, Edgar.'

'Thank you.'

'You still love her.'

'Oh, yes,' said Edgar. 'I'll always love her.'

ÞÞÞ

THE WEATHER TURNED stormy. One night in the second week of September there was a terrific gale. Edgar thought the church tower might be blown down. However, all the buildings in the hamlet survived except one, the flimsiest – Leaf's brewhouse.

She lost more than the building. She had had a cauldron brewing on the fire, but the huge pot had been overturned, the fire extinguished and the ale lost. Worse than that, barrels of new ale had been smashed by falling timbers, and sacks of malted barley were soaked beyond rescue by torrential rain.

Next morning, in the calm after the storm, they went out to inspect the damage, and some of the villagers – curious as ever – gathered around the ruins.

Dreng was furious, and raged at Leaf. 'That shack was barely standing before the storm – you should have moved the ale and the barley somewhere safer!'

Leaf was not impressed by Dreng's tantrum. 'You could have moved it yourself, or told Edgar to do it,' she said. 'Don't blame me.'

He was impervious to her logic. 'Now I'm going to have to buy ale in Shiring and pay to have it carted here,' he went on.

'People will appreciate my ale more when they've had to drink Shiring ale for a few weeks,' Leaf said complacently.

Her unconcern drove Dreng wild. 'And this isn't the first time!' he raved. 'You've burned the brewhouse down twice. Last time you passed out dead drunk and nearly burned yourself to death.'

Edgar had a brainwave. He said: 'You should build a stone brewhouse.'

'Don't be daft,' Dreng said without looking at him. 'You don't put up a palace to make ale in.'

Cuthbert, the portly jeweller, was in the crowd, and Edgar now noticed that he was shaking his head in disagreement with Dreng. Edgar said: 'What do you think, Cuthbert?'

'Edgar's right,' Cuthbert said. 'This will be the third time in five years that you've rebuilt the brewhouse, Dreng. A stone building would withstand storms and wouldn't burn down. You'd save money in the long run.'

Dreng said scornfully: 'Who's going to build it, Cuthbert? You?'

'No, I'm a jeweller.'

'We can't make ale in a brooch.'

Edgar knew the answer. 'I can build it.'

Dreng gave a scornful grunt. 'What do you know about building in stone?'

Edgar knew nothing about building in stone, but he felt he could turn his hand to just about any type of construction. And he yearned for the opportunity to show what he could do. Displaying more confidence than he felt, he said: 'Stone is just like wood, only a bit harder.'

Dreng's default position was scorn, but now he hesitated. His gaze flickered to the riverside and the sturdy money-making ferryboat tied up there. He turned to Cuthbert. 'What would that cost?'

Edgar felt hopeful. Pa had always said: 'When the man asks the price, he's halfway to buying the boat.'

Cuthbert thought for a moment, then said: 'Last time repairs were done to the church, the stone came from the limestone quarry at Outhenham.'

Edgar said: 'Where's that?'

'A day's journey upriver.'

'Where did you get the sand?'

'There's a sandpit in the woods about a mile from here. You just have to dig it up and carry it.'

'And the lime for the mortar?'

'That's difficult to make, so we bought ours in Shiring.'

Dreng repeated: 'What would it cost?'

Cuthbert said: 'The standard rough stones cost a penny each at the quarry, if I remember rightly, and they charged us a penny per stone for delivery.'

Edgar said: 'I'll make a plan, and work it out exactly; but I would probably need about two hundred stones.'

Dreng pretended to be shocked. 'Why, that's almost two pounds of silver!'

'It would still be cheaper than rebuilding in wood and thatch again and again.' Edgar held his breath.

'Work it out exactly,' said Dreng.

ÞÞÞ

EDGAR SET OFF for Outhenham at sunrise on a cool morning, with a chill September breeze wafting along the river. Dreng had agreed to pay for a stone brewhouse. Now Edgar had to make good on his boasting, and build it well.

He took his axe with him on the journey. He would have preferred to go with one of his brothers, but both were busy on the farm, so he had to take the risk of travelling alone. On the other hand, he had already met the outlaw Ironface, who had gone away the worse for the encounter and might hesitate to attack him again. All the same, he carried the axe in his hand, for readiness, and he was glad to have Brindle to give him early warning of danger.

The trees and bushes along the bank were luxuriant after a fine summer, and it was often a struggle to make progress. Around mid-morning he came to a place where he had to detour inland. Fortunately, the sky was mostly clear, so he could usually see the sun, and this helped him to keep his bearings, so that eventually he was able to find his way back to the river.

Every few miles he passed through a large or small settlement, the same timber-and-thatch houses clustered on the river bank or inland around a crossroads, a pond or a church. He slung his axe in his belt as he approached, to make a peaceable impression, but drew it out as soon as he found himself alone again. He would have liked to stop and rest, drink a cup of ale and eat something, but he had no money, so he just exchanged a few words with the villagers, checked that he was on the right road, and walked on.

He had thought it a simple matter to follow the river. However, numerous streams flowed into it and he could not always be sure which was the main river and which the tributary. On one occasion he made the wrong choice, and learned at the next settlement he came to – a village called Bathford – that he needed to retrace his steps.

Along the way he thought about the brewhouse he would construct for Leaf. Perhaps it should have two rooms, like the nave and chancel of a church, so that valuable stores could be kept away from the fire. The hearth should be made of trimmed stones mortared together, so that it would easily bear the weight of the cauldron and be less likely to collapse.

He had hoped to reach Outhenham by mid-afternoon, but his detours had delayed him, so the sun was low in the western sky when he thought he might be approaching the end of his journey.

He was in a fertile valley of heavy clay soil which he thought must be the Vale of Outhen. In the surrounding fields peasants were harvesting barley, working late to make the most of dry weather. At a place where a tributary joined the river he came to a large village of more than a hundred houses.

He was on the wrong side of the water, and there was no bridge or ferry, but he swam across easily, holding his tunic above his head and using only one hand to propel himself. The water was cold and he shivered when he got out.

At the edge of the village was a small orchard where a grey-haired man was picking fruit. Edgar approached with some trepidation, fearing he might be told he was far from his destination. 'Good day, friend,' he said. 'Is this Outhenham?'

'It is,' the man said amiably. He was a bright-eyed fifty-year-old with a friendly smile and an intelligent look.

'Thank heaven,' said Edgar.

'Where have you come from?'

'Dreng's Ferry.'

'A godless place, I've heard.'

Edgar was surprised that Degbert's laxity was known about so far away. He was not sure how to respond to that, so he said: 'My name is Edgar.'

'And I'm Seric.'

'I've come here to buy stone.'

'If you go east to the edge of the village, you'll see a well-worn track. The quarry is about half a mile inland. There you'll find Gaberht, called Gab, and his family. He's the quarry master.'

'Thank you.'

'Are you hungry?'

'Starving.'

Seric gave him a handful of small pears. Edgar thanked him and went on. He ate the pears, cores and all, right away.

The village was relatively prosperous, with well-built houses and outbuildings. At its centre, a stone church faced an alehouse across a green where cows grazed.

A big man in his thirties came out of the alehouse, spotted Edgar, and took up a confrontational stance in the middle of the pathway.

'Who the hell are you?' he said as Edgar approached him. He was heavy and red-eyed, and his speech was slurred.

Edgar stopped and said: 'Good day to you, friend. I'm Edgar, from Dreng's Ferry.'

'And where do you think you're going?'

'To the quarry,' Edgar said mildly. He did not want a quarrel.

But the man was belligerent. 'Who said you could go there?'

Edgar's patience began to wear thin. 'I don't believe I need permission.'

'You need my permission to do anything in Outhenham, because I'm Dudda, the headman of the village. Why are you going to the quarry?'

'To buy fish.'

Dudda looked mystified, then it dawned on him that he was being mocked, and he reddened. Edgar realized he had been too clever for his own good – again – and regretted his wit. Dudda said: 'You cheeky dog.' Then he swung a big fist at Edgar's head.

Edgar stepped back nimbly.

Dudda's swing failed to connect, and he overbalanced, stumbled, and fell to the ground.

Edgar wondered what the hell to do next. He had no doubt he could beat Dudda in a fight, but what good would that do him? If he antagonized people here, they might refuse to sell stone to him, and his building project would be in trouble when it had hardly got started.

He was relieved to hear the calm voice of Seric behind him. 'Now, Dudda, let me help you home. You might want to lie down for an hour.' He took Dudda's arm and helped him to his feet.

Dudda said: 'That boy hit me!'

'No, he didn't, you fell down, because you drank too much ale with your dinner, again.' Seric jerked his head at Edgar, indicating that he should make himself scarce, and walked Dudda away. Edgar took the hint.

He found the quarry easily. Four people were working there: an older man who was evidently in charge and therefore must be Gab; two others who might have been his sons; and a boy who was either a late addition to the family or a slave. The quarry rang with the sound of hammers, punctuated at intervals by a dry cough that came from Gab. There was a timber house, presumably their home, and a woman standing in the doorway watching the sun go down. Stone dust hung in the air like a mist, the specks glittering golden in the rays of the evening light.

Another customer was ahead of Edgar. A sturdy four-wheeled cart stood in the middle of the clearing. Two men were carefully loading it with cut stones, while two oxen – presumably there to pull the cart – grazed nearby, their tails flicking at flies.

The boy was sweeping up stone chips, probably to be sold as gravel. He approached Edgar and spoke with a foreign accent, which made Edgar think he was a slave. 'Have you come to buy stone?'

'Yes. I need enough for a brewhouse. But there's no rush.'

Edgar sat on a flat stone, observed Gab for a few minutes, and quickly understood how he worked. He would insert an oak wedge into a small crack in the rock, then hammer the wedge in, widening the crack until it turned into a split and a section of rock fell away. Failing the convenience of a naturally formed crack, Gab would make one with his iron chisel. Edgar guessed that a quarryman would have learned from experience how to locate the weaknesses in the rock that would make the work easier.

Gab split the larger stones into two or sometimes three pieces, just to make them easier to transport.

Edgar turned his attention to the purchasers. They put ten stones on their cart then stopped. That was probably as much weight as the oxen could pull. They began to put the beasts into the shafts, ready to leave.

Gab finished what he was doing, coughed, looked at the sky, and appeared to decide it was time to stop work. He went to the ox cart and conferred with the two buyers for a few moments, then one of the men handed over money.

Then they cracked a whip over the oxen and left.

Edgar went to Gab. The quarryman had picked up a trimmed branch from a pile and was carefully marking it with a neat row of notches. This was how craftsmen and traders kept records: they could not afford parchment, and if they had any, they would not know how to write on it. Edgar guessed that Gab had to pay taxes to the lord of the manor, perhaps the price of one stone in five, and so needed a record of how many he had sold.

Edgar said: 'I'm Edgar from Dreng's Ferry. Ten years ago you sold us stones for the repair of the church.'

'I recollect,' said Gab, putting the tally stick in his pocket. Edgar noticed that he had cut only five notches, although he had sold ten stones; perhaps he was going to finish it later. 'I don't remember you, but then you would have been a small child.'

Edgar studied Gab. His hands were covered with old scars, no doubt from his work. He was probably wondering how he could exploit this ignorant youth. Edgar said firmly: 'The price was two pence per stone delivered.'

'Was it, now?' Gab said with pretended scepticism.

'If it's still the same, we want about two hundred more.'

'I'm not sure we can do it for the same price. Things have changed.'

'In that case, I have to return and speak with my master.' Edgar did not want to do this. He was determined to go back and report success. But he could not allow Gab to overcharge him. Edgar mistrusted Gab. Perhaps the man was only negotiating, but Edgar had a feeling he might be dishonest.

The quarryman coughed. 'Last time we dealt with Degbert Baldhead, the dean. He didn't like spending his money.'

'My master, Dreng, is the same. They're brothers.'

'What's the stone for?'

'I'm building a brewhouse for Dreng. His wife makes the ale and she keeps burning the wooden buildings down.'

'You're building it?'

Edgar lifted his chin. 'Yes.'

'You're very young. But Dreng wants a cheap builder, I suppose.'

'He wants cheap stone, too.'

'Did you bring the money?'

I may be young, Edgar thought, but I'm not stupid. 'Dreng will pay when the stones arrive.'

'He'd better.'

Edgar guessed the quarrymen would carry the stones, or transport them in a cart, as far as the river, then load them on a raft for the journey downstream to Dreng's Ferry. It would take them several trips, depending on the size of the raft.

Gab said: 'Where are you spending the night? In the tavern?'

'I told you, I've no money.'

'You'll have to sleep here, then.'

'Thank you,' said Edgar.

ÞÞÞ

GAB'S WIFE WAS Beaduhild but he called her Bee. She was more welcoming than her husband, and invited Edgar to share the evening meal. As soon as his bowl was empty he realized how tired he was after his long walk, and he lay down on the floor and fell asleep immediately.

In the morning he said to Gab: 'I'm going to need a hammer and chisel like yours, so that I can shape the stones to my needs.'

'So you are,' said Gab.

'May I look at your tools?'

Gab shrugged.

Edgar picked up the wooden hammer and hefted it. It was big

and heavy, but otherwise simple and crude, and he could easily make one like it. The smaller, iron-headed hammer was more carefully made, its handle firmly wedged to the head. Best of all was the iron chisel, with a wide, blunt blade and a spreading top that looked like a daisy. Edgar could forge a copy in Cuthbert's workshop. Cuthbert might not like sharing his space, but Dreng would get Degbert to insist, and Cuthbert would have no choice.

Hanging on pegs next to the tools were several sticks with notches. Edgar said: 'I suppose you keep a tally stick for each customer.'

'What business is that of yours?'

'Sorry.' Edgar did not want to appear nosey. However, he could not help noticing that the newest stick had only five notches. Could it be that Gab recorded only half the stones he sold? That would save him a lot in taxes.

But it was no business of Edgar's if Gab was cheating his lord. The Vale of Outhen was part of the ealdormanry of Shiring, and Ealdorman Wilwulf was rich enough already.

Edgar ate a hearty breakfast, thanked Bee, and set out to walk home.

From Outhenham he thought he could find his way easily, having already made the journey in the opposite direction, but to his dismay he got lost again. Because of the delay it was near dark when he arrived home, thirsty and hungry and weary.

In the alehouse they were getting ready to go to sleep. Ethel smiled at him, Leaf gave a slurred welcome, and Dreng ignored him. Blod was stacking firewood. She stopped what she was doing, straightened up, put her left hand on the back of her hip, and stretched her body as if easing an ache. When she turned around, Edgar saw that she had a black eye.

'What happened to you?' he said.

She did not answer, pretending not to understand. But Edgar could guess how she had got it. Dreng had been more and more angry with her in the last few weeks, as her time approached. There was nothing unusual about a man using violence on his family, of course, and Edgar had seen Dreng kick Leaf's backside and slap Ethel's face, but he had a special malice towards Blod.

'Is there any supper left?' Edgar asked.

Dreng said: 'No.'

'But I've been walking all day.'

'That'll teach you not to be late.'

'I was on an errand for you!'

'And you get paid, and there's nothing left, so shut your mouth.'

Edgar went to bed hungry.

Blod was up first in the morning. She went to the river for fresh water, always her first chore of the day. The bucket was made of wood with iron rivets, and it was heavy even when empty. Edgar was putting his shoes on when she came back. He saw that she was struggling, and he moved to take the bucket from her but, before he could do so, she stumbled over Dreng, lying half asleep, and water sloshed from the bucket onto his face.

'You dumb cunt!' he roared.

He jumped up. Blod cowered away. Dreng raised his fist. Then Edgar stepped between them, saying: 'Give me the bucket, Blod.'

There was fury in Dreng's eyes. For a moment Edgar thought the man was going to punch him instead of Blod. Dreng was strong, despite the bad back he mentioned so often: he was tall, with big shoulders. Nevertheless, Edgar made a split-second decision to hit back if attacked. He would undoubtedly be punished, but he would have the satisfaction of knocking Dreng to the ground.

However, like most bullies, Dreng was a coward when confronted by someone stronger. The anger gave way to fear, and he lowered his fist.

Blod made herself scarce.

Edgar handed the bucket to Ethel. She poured water into a cooking pot, hung the pot over the fire, added oats to the water, and stirred the mixture with a wooden stick.

Dreng stared at Edgar malevolently. Edgar guessed he would never be forgiven for coming between Dreng and his slave, but he could not find it in his heart to regret what he had done, even though he would probably suffer for it.

When the porridge was ready Ethel ladled it into five bowls. She chopped some ham and added it to one of the bowls, then gave that to Dreng. She handed the others around.

They ate in silence.

Edgar finished his in seconds. He looked over at the pot, then at Ethel. She said nothing but discreetly shook her head. There was no more.

It was Sunday, and after breakfast everyone went to church.

Ma was there with Erman and Eadbald and their shared wife, Cwenburg. The twenty-five or so residents of the hamlet all knew by now of the polyandrous marriage, but no one said much about it. Edgar had gathered, from overheard fragments of conversation, that it was considered unusual but not outrageous. He had heard Bebbe say the same as Leaf: 'If a man can have two wives, a woman can have two husbands.'

Seeing Cwenburg standing between Erman and Eadbald, Edgar was struck by the difference in their clothes. The homespun knee-length tunics of his brothers, the brownish colour of undyed wool, were old, worn and patched, just like his own; but Cwenburg had a dress of closely woven cloth, bleached and then dyed a pinkish red. Her father was miserly with everyone but her.

Edgar stood beside Ma. In the past she had never been noticeably devout, but nowadays she seemed to take the service more seriously, bowing her head and closing her eyes as Degbert and the other clergy went through their ritual, her reverence undiminished by their carelessness and haste.

'You've become more religious,' he said to her as the service came to an end.

She looked at him speculatively, as if wondering whether to confide in him, and seemed to decide he might understand. 'I think about your father,' she said. 'I believe he is with the angels above.'

Edgar did not really understand. 'You can think about him whenever you like.'

'But this seems the best place and time. I feel I'm not so far away from him. Then, during the week, when I miss him, I can look forward to Sunday.'

Edgar nodded. That made sense to him.

Ma said: 'How about you? Do you think of him?'

'When I'm working, and have a problem to solve, a joint that won't close or a blade that won't come sharp, I think: "I'll ask Pa." Then I remember that I can't. It happens almost every day.'

'What do you do then?'

Edgar hesitated. He was afraid of seeming to claim that he had miraculous experiences. People who saw visions were sometimes revered, but they might just as easily be stoned as agents of the devil. However, Ma would comprehend. 'I ask him anyway,' he said. 'I say: "Pa, what should I do about this?" – in my head.' He added hastily: 'I don't see an apparition, or anything like that.'

She nodded calmly, unsurprised. 'And then what?'

'Usually, the answer comes to me.'

She said nothing.

A bit nervously he said: 'Does that sound peculiar?'

'Not at all,' she said. 'That's how spirits work.' She turned away and spoke to Bebbe about eggs.

Edgar was intrigued. *That's how spirits work.* It would bear thinking about.

But his reflections were interrupted. Erman came to him and said: 'We're going to make a plough.'

'Today?'

'Yes.'

Edgar was jerked from mysticism back into everyday practicalities. He guessed they had chosen to do this on a Sunday so that he would be available. None of them had ever made a plough, but Edgar could build anything. 'Shall I come and help you?' he said.

'If you want.' Erman did not like to acknowledge that he needed assistance.

'Have you got the timber ready?'

'Yes.'

It seemed that anyone could take timber from the forest. At Combe the thane, Wigelm, had made Pa pay for felling an oak. But there, Edgar reflected, it was easier to police the woodcutters, for they had to bring the timber into the town in full view. Here it was not clear whether the forest belonged to Degbert Baldhead or the reeve of Mudeford, Offa, and neither of them claimed payment: no doubt it would involve much surveillance for little reward. In practice timber was free to anyone willing to chop down the trees.

Everyone was moving out of the little church. 'We'd better get on with it,' Erman said.

They walked to the farmhouse together: Ma, the three brothers and Cwenburg. Edgar noticed that the bond between Erman and Eadbald seemed unchanged: they were basically in harmony, despite a continuous low level of petty squabbling. Their uncommon marriage clearly worked.

Cwenburg kept giving Edgar triumphant looks. 'You turned me down,' her expression seemed to say, 'but see what I got instead!' Edgar did not mind. She was happy and so were his brothers.

Edgar himself was not unhappy, for that matter. He had built a ferry and was working on a brewhouse. His wages were so low they amounted to theft, but he had escaped from farming.

Well, almost.

He looked at the wood his brothers had piled up outside the barn and visualized a plough. Even town dwellers knew what one of those looked like. It would have an upright pointed stick to loosen the soil, and an angled mouldboard to undercut the furrow and turn the soil over. Both had to be attached to a frame that could be pulled from the front and guided from behind.

Erman said: 'Eadbald and I will draw the plough and Ma will steer it.'

Edgar nodded. The loamy soil here was soft enough to yield to a man-drawn plough. The clay soil of a place such as Outhenham required the strength of oxen.

Edgar drew his belt knife, knelt down, and began to mark the wood for Erman and Eadbald to shape. Although the youngest brother was taking charge, the other two made no protest. They recognized Edgar's superior skill, though they never admitted it aloud.

While they went to work on the timbers, Edgar began to make the ploughshare, a blade fixed to the front of the mouldboard to cut more easily through the soil. The others had found a rusting iron spade in the barn. Edgar heated it in the house fire, then beat it into shape with a rock. The result looked a bit rough. He could have done better with an iron hammer and an anvil.

He sharpened the blade with a stone.

When they got thirsty they went down to the river and drank from their cupped hands. They had no ale and no cups either.

They were almost ready to join the pieces together with pegs when Ma called them for the midday meal.

She had prepared smoked eel with wild onions and pan bread. Edgar's mouth watered so violently that he felt a sharp pain under his jawbone.

Cwenburg whispered something to Erman. Ma frowned – whispering in company was bad manners – but she said nothing.

When Edgar reached for a third piece of bread, Erman said: 'Go easy, will you?'

'I'm hungry!'

'We haven't got much food to spare.'

Edgar was outraged. 'I've given up my day of rest to help you build your plough – and you begrudge me a piece of bread!'

Anger flared quickly, as it always had between the brothers. Erman said hotly: 'You can't eat us out of house and home.'

'I had no supper yesterday, and only one small bowl of porridge this morning – I'm starved.'

'I can't help that.'

'Then don't ask me to help you, you ungrateful dog.'

'The plough is almost finished – you should have gone back to the alehouse for your dinner.'

'Precious little I get to eat there.'

Eadbald was more temperate than Erman. He said: 'The thing is, Edgar, Cwenburg needs more, being pregnant.'

Edgar saw Cwenburg smother a smirk, which annoyed him even more. He said: 'So eat less yourself, Eadbald, and leave me to my dinner. I'm not the one who made her pregnant.' He added in an undertone: 'Thank heaven.'

Erman, Eadbald and Cwenburg all began shouting at the same time. Ma clapped her hands, and they fell silent. She said: 'What did you mean, Edgar, when you said you get precious little to eat at the tavern? Surely Dreng can afford plenty of food.'

'Dreng may be rich, but he's mean.'

'But you had breakfast today.'

'A small bowl of porridge. He has meat with his, but the rest of us don't.'

'And supper last night?'

'Nothing. I walked here from Outhenham and arrived late. He said it was all gone.'

Ma looked angry. 'Then eat as much as you want here,' she said. 'As for the rest of you, shut up, and try to remember that my family will always be fed at my house.'

Edgar ate his third piece of bread.

Erman looked surly. Eadbald said: 'How often are we going to have to feed Edgar, then, if Dreng won't?'

'Don't you worry,' said Ma, tight-lipped. 'I'll deal with Dreng.'

ÞÞÞ

FOR THE REST of the day Edgar wondered how Ma was going to fulfil her promise and 'deal with' Dreng. She was resourceful and bold, but Dreng was powerful. Edgar had no physical fear of his master – Dreng punched women, not men – but he was the master of everyone in the house: husband of Leaf and Ethel, owner of Blod, and employer of Edgar. He was the second most important man in the little hamlet, and the number one was his brother. He could do more or less anything he liked. It was unwise to cross him.

Monday began like any other weekday. Blod went for water and Ethel made porridge. As Edgar was sitting down to his inadequate breakfast, Cwenburg came storming in, indignant and furious. Pointing an accusing finger at Edgar, she said: 'Your mother is an old witch!'

Edgar had a feeling this was going to be welcome news. 'I've often thought so myself,' he said good-humouredly. 'But what has she done to you?'

'She wants to starve me to death! She says I can have only one bowl of porridge!'

Edgar guessed where this was going, and he smothered a grin.

Dreng spoke in the confident tones of the powerful. 'She can't do that to my daughter.'

'She just did!'

'Did she give any reason for it?'

'She said she's not going to feed me any more than you feed Edgar.'

Dreng was startled. Clearly he had not anticipated anything like this. He looked baffled and said nothing for a moment. Then he turned on Edgar. 'So you went crying to your mother, did you?' he sneered.

It was a feeble attack, and Edgar was untroubled. 'That's what mothers are for, isn't it?'

'Right, that's it, I've heard enough,' said Dreng. 'You're out of here, go home.'

But Cwenburg was not having that. 'You can't send him back to us,' she said to Dreng. 'He's another mouth, and there's hardly enough to eat as it is.'

'Then you'll come here.' Dreng was pretending to be in full control, but he was looking a bit desperate.

'No,' said Cwenburg. 'I'm married, and I like it. And my baby needs a father.'

Dreng realized he was cornered, and he looked livid.

Cwenburg said: 'You have to give Edgar more to eat, that's all. You can afford it.'

Dreng turned to Edgar with a look loaded with malevolence. 'You're a sly little rat, aren't you?'

'This wasn't my idea,' Edgar said. 'Sometimes I wish I were as clever as my mother.'

'You're going to regret your mother's cleverness, I promise you that.'

Cwenburg said: 'I like something nice in my porridge.' She opened the chest where Ethel kept foodstuffs and took out a jar of butter. Using her belt knife she took a generous scoop and put it in Edgar's bowl.

Dreng looked on helplessly.

'Tell your mother I did that,' Cwenburg said to Edgar.

'All right,' Edgar said.

He ate the buttered porridge fast, before anyone could stop him. It made him feel good. But Dreng's sentence echoed in his mind: *You're going to regret your mother's cleverness, I promise you that.*

It was probably true.

9

RAGNA SET OFF FROM Cherbourg with a heart full of happy anticipation. She had triumphed over her parents, and she was going to England to marry the man she loved.

The whole town came to the waterfront to cheer her off. Her ship, the *Angel*, had a single mast with a large multi-coloured sail, plus sixteen pairs of oars. The figurehead was a carved angel blowing a trumpet, and at the stern a long tail curved up and forward to terminate in a lion's head. Its captain was a wiry greybeard called Guy, who had crossed the Channel to England many times before.

Ragna had sailed in a ship only once: three years ago she had gone with her father to Fécamp, ninety miles across the Bay of Seine, never far from land. The weather had been good, the sea had been calm, and the sailors had been charmed to have a beautiful young noblewoman aboard. The trip had been pleasantly uneventful.

So she had been looking forward eagerly to this journey, the first of many new adventures. She knew, in theory, that any sea voyage was hazardous, but she could not help feeling exhilarated: it was her nature. You could spoil anything by worrying too much.

She was accompanied by her maid Cat; Agnes, her best seamstress; three other maids; plus Bern the Giant and six more men-at-arms to protect her. She and Bern had horses – hers was her favourite, Astrid – and they took four ponies to carry the baggage. Ragna had packed four new dresses and six new pairs of shoes. She also had a small personal wedding gift for Wilwulf, a belt of soft leather with a silver buckle and strap end, packed in its own special box.

The horses were tethered on board with straw underfoot, for a measure of cushioning in case the motion of the sea should cause them to fall. With a crew of twenty the ship was crowded.

Genevieve cried when the ship raised its anchor.

They set off in warm sunshine, with a brisk south-westerly wind that promised to take them to Combe in a couple of days. Now for the first time Ragna became anxious. Wilwulf loved her, but he might have changed. She was eager to make friends with his family and his subjects, but would they like her? Would she be able to win their affection? Or would they disdain her foreign ways, and even resent her wealth and beauty? Would she like England?

To banish such worries Ragna and her maids practised speaking Anglo-Saxon. Ragna had been taking lessons every day from an Englishwoman married to a Cherbourg man. Now she made the others giggle by telling them the words for the different male and female parts of the body.

Then, with hardly any warning, the summer breeze turned into an autumn storm, and cold rain whipped the ship and all its passengers.

There was no shelter. Ragna had once seen a gaily painted river barge with a canopy to shade noble ladies from the heat of the sun, but apart from that she had never come across a ship with any kind of cabin or protective roof. When it rained, passengers and crew and cargo alike all got wet. Ragna and her maids huddled together, pulling the hoods of their cloaks over their heads, trying to keep their feet out of the pools that gathered in the bottom.

But that was only the beginning. They stopped smiling as the wind turned into a gale. Captain Guy seemed calm, but he lowered the sail for fear of capsizing. Now the ship went where the weather took it. The stars were hidden behind clouds, and even the crew did not know which way they were heading. Ragna began to be scared.

The crew dropped a sea-anchor off the stern. This was a big sack that filled with water and acted as a drag on the ship, moderating its motion and keeping the stern to the wind. But the swell grew. The ship pitched violently: the angel blew his trumpet up at the black sky then, a second later, down into the roiling deeps. The horses could not keep their footing, and fell to their knees, neighing in terror. The men-at-arms tried to calm them, without success. Water slopped over the sides. Some of the crew started to say prayers.

Ragna began to think she would never get to England. Perhaps she was not destined to marry Wilwulf and have his children. She might die, and go to hell to be punished for the sin she had committed in making love to him before they were husband and wife.

She made the mistake of picturing what it would be like to drown. She recalled a childhood game of holding her breath to see how long she could keep it up, and she felt the panic that had come over her after a minute or two. She imagined the terror of being so desperate to breathe that she inhaled lungfuls of water. How long did it take to die? The thought made her feel ill, and she threw up the dinner she had enjoyed in sunshine only a couple of hours earlier. Vomiting failed to quiet her stomach, but nausea took away her fear, for now she hardly cared whether she lived or died.

She felt as if it would go on for ever. When she could no longer see the rain falling she realized it was night. The temperature dropped and she shivered in her sodden clothing.

She had no idea how long the storm had continued when, at last, it eased. The downpour became a drizzle and the wind dropped. The ship drifted in the dark: it carried lamps and a jar of oil in a waterproof chest, but there was no fire with which to light them. Captain Guy said he might have raised the sail if he had known for sure that they were far from land, but with no knowledge of the ship's position and no light by which to see signs that land was near, it was too dangerous. They had to wait for day to restore their vision.

When dawn came Ragna saw that his caution had been wise: they were within sight of cliffs. The sky was clouded, but the clouds were brighter in one direction, which must therefore be east. The land to the north of them was England.

The crew went quickly to work despite the continuing rain: first they raised the sail, then they gave out cider and bread for breakfast, then they baled the water from the bottom of the ship.

Ragna was amazed that they could simply resume their duties. They had all nearly died; how could they act normally? She could hardly think of anything but the fact that she was still, miraculously, alive.

They sailed along the coast until they saw a small harbour with a few boats. The captain did not know the place, but he guessed they might be forty or fifty miles east of Combe. He turned the ship landward and sailed into the harbour.

Suddenly Ragna longed for the feeling of firm ground beneath her feet.

The ship was taken into shallow water, then Ragna was carried through the shallows to a pebble beach. With her maids and bodyguards she climbed the slope to the waterfront village and went into an alehouse. Ragna was hoping for a roaring fire and a hot breakfast, but it was early in the day. The fire was low and the hostess was tousled and grumpy, rubbing sleep from her eyes as she tossed sticks onto a feeble flame.

Ragna sat shivering, waiting for her luggage to be unloaded so that she could put on dry clothing. The hostess brought stale bread and weak ale. 'Welcome to England,' she said.

ÞÞÞ

RAGNA'S SELF-CONFIDENCE WAS rocked. In her whole life she had never been so frightened for so long. When Captain Guy said they should wait until the weather changed and then sail west along the English coast to Combe, she refused firmly. She wished never to step on board a ship again. There might be more rude shocks ahead for her, and if so she wanted to meet them on dry land.

Three days later she was not sure that had been the right decision. The rain had not stopped. Every road was a swamp. Wading through the mud exhausted the horses, and being perpetually cold and wet made everyone bad-tempered. The alehouses where they stopped for refreshment were dark and dismal, offering scant respite from the discomfort outdoors, and people hearing her foreign accent would shout at her, as if that would make it easier for her to understand their language. One night the group was welcomed into the comfortable home of a minor nobleman, Thurstan of Lordsborough, but on the other two they stayed overnight at monasteries, clean but cold and cheerless.

On the road Ragna huddled in her cloak, swaying as Astrid trudged wearily on, and reminded herself that waiting at the end of her journey was the most wonderful man in the world.

On the afternoon of the third day a baggage pony slipped on a slope. It fell to its knees, and its load slid to one side. It tried to rise, but the lopsided burden caused it to overbalance again. It skidded down a mud slide, neighing frantically, and fell into a stream. Ragna cried: 'Oh, the poor beast! Save it, you men!'

Several men-at-arms jumped into the water, which was about three feet deep. But they could not get the animal onto its feet. Ragna said: 'You'll have to take the bags off its back!'

That worked. One man held the horse's head in an attempt to stop it thrashing around, and two others undid the straps. They grabbed the bags and chests and passed them to others waiting. When the pony was unloaded it came upright without help.

Looking at the baggage stacked beside the stream, Ragna said: 'Where's the little box with Wilwulf's present?'

Everyone looked around but no one could see it.

Ragna was dismayed. 'We can't have lost it – it's his wedding gift!' English jewellery was famous, and Wilwulf probably had high standards, so Ragna had had the buckle and strap-end made by the best jeweller in Rouen.

The men who had got wet rescuing the pony now went back into the water and scrabbled around the bottom of the stream, searching for the package. But it was sharp-eyed Cat who spotted it. 'There!' she cried, pointing.

Ragna saw the box a hundred yards away, floating downstream.

Suddenly a figure appeared from the bushes. Ragna had a glimpse of a head wearing some kind of helmet as the man took one step into the water and snatched up the box. 'Oh, well done!' Ragna called.

For a split-second he turned and looked at her, and she got a full view of a rusty old battle helmet with holes for the eyes and mouth, then the man bounded back to dry land and vanished into the vegetation.

Ragna realized she had been robbed.

She yelled: 'Go after him!'

The men went in pursuit. Ragna heard them calling to one another in the woods, then their cries became muffled by the trees and the rain. After a while the riders returned one by one. The forest was too thickly overgrown for them to make any speed, they said. Ragna began to feel pessimistic. As the last man appeared, Bern said: 'He eluded us.'

Ragna tried to put a brave face on it. 'Let's move on,' she said briskly. 'What's gone is gone.' They trudged forward through the mire.

But the loss of the gift was too much for Ragna to bear, on top of the storm at sea and three days of rain and dismal lodgings. Her parents had been right in their dire warnings: this was a horrible country and she had doomed herself to live in it. She could not hold back the tears. They ran hot down her face, mingling with the cold rain. She pulled her hood forward and turned her face down in the hope that others would not see.

An hour after the loss of the gift, the group came to the bank of a river and saw a hamlet on the far side. Peering through the weather, Ragna made out a few houses and a stone church. A sizeable boat was moored on the opposite bank. According to the inhabitants of the last village they had passed through, the hamlet with the ferry was two days' journey from Shiring. Two more days of misery, she thought woefully.

The men shouted over the water, and quite promptly a young man appeared and untied the ferry boat. A brown-and-white dog followed him and jumped into the boat, but the man spoke a word and the dog jumped out again.

Seeming not to care about the rain, he stood in the prow of the vessel and poled across the water. Ragna heard Agnes, the seamstress, murmur, 'Strong boy.'

The boat bumped into the near bank. 'Wait for me to tie up before you board,' said the young ferryman. 'It's safer that way.' He was pleasant and polite, but unintimidated by the arrival of a noblewoman with a large escort. He looked directly at Ragna and smiled, as if recognizing her, but she had no recollection of seeing him before.

When he had secured the boat he said: 'It's a farthing for each person and animal. I see thirteen people and six horses, so that makes four pence and three farthings, if you please.'

Ragna nodded to Cat, who kept a purse on her belt with a small amount of money for incidental expenses. One of the ponies was carrying a locked ironbound chest with most of Ragna's money in it, but that was opened only in private. Cat gave the ferryman five English pennies, small and light, and he gave her back a tiny quarter-disc of silver in change.

'You can ride straight on board, if you're careful,' he said. 'But if you feel nervous, dismount and lead your horse. I'm Edgar, by the way.'

Cat said: 'And this is the Lady Ragna, from Cherbourg.'

'I know,' he said. He bowed to Ragna. 'I'm honoured, my lady.'

She rode onto the boat, and the others followed.

The vessel was remarkably steady on the river, and seemed well made, with close-fitting strakes. There was no water in the bottom. 'Fine boat,' Ragna said. She did not add *for a dump like this* but it was implied, and for a moment she wondered whether she might have given offence.

But Edgar showed no sign that he had noticed. 'You're very kind,' he said. 'I built this boat.'

'On your own?' she said sceptically.

Once again he might have felt slighted. Ragna realized she was forgetting her resolution to befriend the English. This was not like her: normally she was quick to bond with strangers. The wretchedness of the journey and the strangeness of the new country had made her short-tempered. She resolved to be nice.

But Edgar apparently did not feel put down. He smiled and said: 'There aren't two boatbuilders in this little place.'

'I'm astonished there's one.'

'I'm a bit startled myself.'

Ragna laughed. This boy was quick-witted and did not take himself too seriously. She liked that.

Edgar saw the people and animals onto the vessel then untied it and began to pole across. Ragna was amused to see Agnes the seamstress begin a conversation with him in halting Anglo-Saxon. 'My lady is to marry the ealdorman of Shiring.'

'Wilwulf?' said Edgar. 'I thought he was already married.'

'He was, but his wife died.'

'So your mistress is going to be everyone's mistress.'

'Unless we all drown in the rain on the way to Shiring.'

'Doesn't it rain in Cherbourg?'

'Not like this.'

Ragna smiled. Agnes was single and eager to marry. She could do worse than this resourceful young Englishman. It would be no great surprise if one or more of Ragna's maids found a husband here: among small groups of women, marriage was infectious.

She looked ahead. The church on the hill was built of stone but was nevertheless small and mean-looking. Its tiny windows, all different shapes, were placed haphazardly in its thick walls. In a Norman church the windows were no bigger, but they were generally all the same shape and set in regular rows. Such consistency spoke more eloquently of the orderly God who had created the hierarchical world of plants, fish, animals and people.

The boat reached the north bank. Once again Edgar jumped out and tied it up, then invited the passengers to disembark. Again Ragna went first, and her horse gave confidence to the rest.

She dismounted outside the alehouse door. The man who came out reminded her momentarily of Wilwulf. He was the same size and build, but his face was different. 'I can't accommodate all these people,' he said in a tone of resentment. 'How am I going to feed them?'

Ragna said: 'How far is it to the next village?'

'Foreigner, are you?' he said, noticing her accent. 'The place is called Wigleigh, and you won't get there today.'

He was probably just working up to asking outrageous prices. Ragna became exasperated. 'Well, then, what do you suggest?'

Edgar intervened. 'Dreng, this is the Lady Ragna from Cherbourg. She's going to marry Ealdorman Wilwulf.'

Dreng immediately became obsequious. 'Forgive me, my lady, I had no idea,' he said. 'Please step inside, and welcome. You're going to be my cousin-in-law, you may not know.'

Ragna was disconcerted to hear that she was to be related to this alehouse keeper. She did not immediately accept his invitation to go inside. 'No, I did not know,' she said.

'Oh, yes. Ealdorman Wilwulf is my cousin. You'll be family to me after the wedding.'

Ragna was not pleased.

He went on: 'My brother and I run this little village, under Wilwulf's authority, of course. My brother, Degbert, is dean of the minster up the hill.'

'That little church is a minster?'

'Just half a dozen clergy, quite small. But come inside, please.' Dreng put his arm around Ragna's shoulders.

This was going too far. Even if she had liked Dreng she would not have allowed him to paw her. With a deliberate movement she took his arm off her shoulders. 'My husband would not like me to be caressed by his cousin,' she said coolly. Then she walked ahead of him into the house.

Dreng followed her in saying: 'Oh, our Wilf wouldn't mind.' But he did not touch her again.

Ragna looked around the inside of the building with a feeling that was becoming familiar. Like most English alehouses it was dark, smelly and smoky. There were two tables and a scatter of benches and stools.

Cat was close behind her. She moved a stool nearer to the fire for Ragna, then helped her take off her sodden cloak. Ragna sat by the fire and held out her hands to warm them.

There were three women in the tavern, she saw. The eldest was presumably Dreng's wife. The youngest, a pregnant girl with a pinched face, wore no headdress of any kind, usually the sign of a prostitute; Ragna guessed she might be a slave. The third woman was about Ragna's age, and might be Dreng's concubine.

Ragna's maids and bodyguards crowded into the house. Ragna said to Dreng: 'Would you please give my servants some ale?'

'My wife shall attend to it at once, my lady.' He spoke to the two women. 'Leaf, give them some ale. Ethel, get the supper started.'

Leaf opened a chest full of wooden bowls and cups, and began to fill them from a barrel on a stand in the corner. Ethel hung an iron cauldron over the fire and poured water into it, then produced a large leg of mutton and added it to the pot.

The pregnant girl brought in an armful of firewood. Ragna was surprised to see her doing heavy work when her time was evidently so near. It was no wonder she looked tired and morose.

Edgar knelt by the hearth and built up the fire twig by twig. Soon it was a cheerful blaze that warmed Ragna and dried her clothes.

She said to him: 'On the ferry, when my maid Cat told you who I was, you said: "I know." How did you know me?'

Edgar smiled. 'You won't remember, but we've met before.'

Ragna did not apologize for not recognizing him. A noblewoman met hundreds of people and could not be expected to recall them all. She said: 'When was that?'

'Five years ago. I was only thirteen.' Edgar drew his knife from his belt and set it on the hearth stones so that the blade was in the flames.

'So I was fifteen. I've never been to England before now, so you must have come to Normandy.'

'My late father was a boatbuilder at Combe. We went to Cherbourg to deliver a ship. That's when I met you.'

'Did we speak?'

'Yes.' He looked embarrassed.

'Wait a minute.' Ragna smiled. 'I vaguely remember a cheeky little English boy who came into the castle uninvited.'

'That sounds like me.'

'He told me I was beautiful, in bad French.'

Edgar had the grace to blush. 'I apologize for my insolence. And for my French.' Then he grinned. 'But not for my taste.'

'Did I reply? I don't remember.'

'You spoke to me in quite good Anglo-Saxon.'

'What did I say?'

'You told me I was charming.'

'Ah, yes! Then you said you were going to marry someone like me.'

'I don't know how I could have been so disrespectful.'

'I didn't mind, really. But I think I may have decided the joke had gone far enough.'

'Yes, indeed. You told me to go back to England before I got into real trouble.' He stood up, perhaps thinking that he was teetering on the edge of impertinence, as he had five years earlier. 'Would you like some warm ale?'

'I'd love it.'

Edgar got a cup of ale from the woman called Leaf. Using his sleeve as a glove he picked up his knife from the fire and plunged the blade into the cup. The liquid fizzed and foamed. He stirred it then handed it to her. 'I don't think it will be too hot,' he said.

She touched the cup to her lips and took a sip. 'Perfect,' she said, and drank a long swallow. It warmed her belly.

She was feeling more cheerful.

'I should leave you,' Edgar said. 'I expect my master wants to talk to you.'

'Oh, no, please,' Ragna said hastily. 'I can't bear him. Stay here. Sit down. Talk.'

He drew up a stool, thought for a moment, then said: 'It must be difficult to start a new life in a strange country.'

You have no idea, she thought. But she did not want to appear glum. 'It's an adventure,' she said brightly.

'But everything is different. I felt bewildered that day in Cherbourg: a different language, strange clothes, even buildings that looked queer. And I was only there for a day.'

'It's a challenge,' she admitted.

'I've noticed that people aren't always kind to foreigners. When I lived at Combe we saw a lot of strangers. Some of the townspeople enjoyed laughing at the mistakes made by French or Flemish visitors.'

Ragna nodded. 'An ignorant man thinks foreigners are stupid – not realizing that he himself would appear just as foolish if he went abroad.'

'It must be hard to bear. I admire your courage.'

He was the first English person to sympathize with what she was going through. Ironically, his compassion undermined her facade of determined stoicism. To her own dismay she began to cry.

'I'm so sorry!' he said. 'What have I done?'

'You've been kind,' she managed to say. 'No one else has, not since I landed in this country.'

He was embarrassed again. 'I didn't mean to upset you.'

'It's not you, really.' She did not want to complain about how awful England was. She fastened on the outlaw. 'I lost something precious today.'

'I'm sorry. What was it?'

'A gift for my husband-to-be, a belt with a silver buckle. I was so looking forward to giving it to him.'

'What a shame.'

'It was stolen by a man wearing a helmet.'

'That sounds like Ironface. He's an outlaw. He tried to steal my family's piglet, but my dog gave warning.'

A man with a bald head came into the house and approached Ragna. Like Dreng, he bore a faint resemblance to Wilwulf. 'Welcome to Dreng's Ferry, my lady,' he said. 'I'm Degbert, dean of the minster and landlord of the village.' In a lower voice he said to Edgar: 'Push off, lad.'

Edgar got up and left.

Degbert sat down uninvited on the stool vacated by Edgar. 'Your fiancé is my cousin,' he said.

Ragna said politely: 'I'm glad to meet you.'

'We're honoured to receive you here.'

'It's a pleasure,' she lied. She wondered how long it would be before she could go to sleep.

She made small talk with Degbert for a few dull minutes, then Edgar returned, accompanied by a stout little man in clerical dress carrying a chest. Degbert looked up at them and said irritably: 'What's this?'

Edgar said: 'I asked Cuthbert to bring some of his jewellery to show the Lady Ragna. She lost something precious today – Ironface robbed her – and she may like to replace it.'

Degbert hesitated. He was clearly enjoying his monopoly of the high-ranking visitor. However, he decided to yield gracefully. 'We at the minster are proud of Cuthbert's skill,' he said. 'I hope you'll find something to your liking, my lady.'

Ragna was sceptical. The best English jewellery was splendid, and was prized all over Europe, but that did not mean that everything produced by Englishmen would be good; and it seemed unlikely that fine things would be made in this little settlement. But she was glad to get rid of Degbert.

Cuthbert had a timid air. He said nervously: 'May I open the box, my lady? I don't want to intrude, but Edgar said you might be interested.'

'By all means,' said Ragna. 'I'd love to see.'

'You don't have to buy anything, don't worry.' Cuthbert spread a blue cloth on the floor and opened the chest. It was full of objects wrapped in woollen cloth. He brought items out one by one, carefully unwrapped them, and laid them in front of Ragna, glancing anxiously at her all the time. She was pleased to see that the quality of the workmanship was high. He had made brooches, buckles, clasps, arm rings and finger rings, mostly silver, all engraved with elaborate patterns, often inlaid with a black substance that Ragna assumed was niello, a mixture of metals.

Her eye lit on a chunky arm ring with a masculine look. She picked it up and found it satisfyingly heavy. It was silver with an engraved pattern of intertwining serpents, and she could picture it on Wilwulf's muscular arm.

Cuthbert said slyly: 'You've picked my best piece, my lady.'

She studied it. She felt sure Wilwulf would like it, and wear it with pride. She said: 'What's the price?'

'There's a lot of silver in it.'

'Is the silver pure?'

'One part in twenty is copper, for strength,' he said. 'Same as our silver coins.'

'Very good. How much?'

'Would it be for Ealdorman Wilwulf?'

Ragna smiled. He was not going to name a price until he had to. He was trying to figure out how much she would be willing to pay. Cuthbert might be timid, she thought, but he was sly, too. 'Yes,' she replied. 'A wedding gift.'

'In that case, I must let you have it for no more than it cost me, as my way of honouring your nuptial celebrations.'

'You're very kind. How much?'

Cuthbert sighed. 'A pound,' he said.

It was a lot of money: two hundred and forty silver pennies. But there was about half a pound of silver in the arm ring: the price was reasonable. And the more she looked at it, the more she wanted it. She imagined herself slipping it over Wilwulf's hand and up his arm, then looking at his face to see him smile.

She decided not to haggle: it was undignified. She was not a peasant woman buying a ladle. But she pretended to hesitate, just for the sake of appearances.

Cuthbert said: 'Don't make me sell it for less than it cost me, dear lady.'

'Very well,' she said. 'A pound.'

'The ealdorman will be delighted. This will look wonderful on his mighty arm.'

Cat had been watching the interchange, and now Ragna saw her quietly move to where their luggage was stowed and unobtrusively unlock an ironbound chest.

Ragna put the ring on her own arm. It was far too big, of course, but she liked the engraving.

Cuthbert wrapped up his remaining ornaments and lovingly stowed them away.

Cat came back with a small leather bag. Meticulously she counted out pennies in multiples of twelve. Cuthbert recounted each twelve. Finally Cuthbert put the money in his chest, closed the box, and left, wishing Ragna a splendid wedding day and many years of happy marriage.

Supper was served at the two tables. The visitors ate first. There were no plates; instead, thick slices of bread were placed on the table and Ethel's mutton with onions was ladled onto the bread. They all waited for Ragna to begin. She speared a piece of meat with her knife and put it in her mouth, then they all tucked in. The stew was simple but tasty.

Ragna felt cheered by food, ale, and the pleasure of buying a gift for the man she loved.

Night fell while they were eating, and lamps around the room were lit by the pregnant slave.

As soon as Ragna had finished eating she said: 'Now I'm tired. Where do I sleep?'

Dreng said cheerfully: 'Anywhere you like, my lady.'

'But where is my bed?'

'I'm afraid we don't have beds, my lady.'

'No beds?'

'I'm sorry.'

Did they really expect her to wrap herself in her cloak and lie down in the straw with everyone else? The creepy Dreng would probably try to lie next to her. At the English monasteries she had been given a simple wooden bed with a mattress, and Thurstan of Lordsborough had provided a sort of box with leaves in the bottom. 'Not even a box bed?' she said.

'No one in Dreng's Ferry has a bed of any kind.'

Edgar spoke up. 'Except the nuns.'

Ragna was surprised. 'Nobody told me about any nuns.'

'On the island,' said Edgar. 'There's a small convent.'

Dreng looked cross. 'You can't go there, my lady. They look after lepers and all sorts. That's why it's called Leper Island.'

Ragna was sceptical. Many nuns cared for the sick, and they rarely caught the infections of their patients. Dreng just wanted the prestige of hosting Ragna overnight.

Edgar said: 'The lepers aren't allowed into the convent.'

Dreng said crossly: 'You know nothing, you've only lived here a quarter of a year, keep your mouth shut.' He smiled unctuously at Ragna. 'I couldn't let you risk your life, my lady.'

'I'm not asking your permission,' Ragna said coldly. 'I shall make up my own mind.' She turned to Edgar. 'What are the sleeping arrangements at the nunnery?'

'I've only been there once, to repair the roof, but I think there are two bedrooms, one for the mother superior and her deputy, and a large room for the other five or six nuns. They all have wooden bedsteads with mattresses and blankets.'

'That sounds perfect. Will you take me there?'

'Of course, my lady.'

'Cat and Agnes will come with me. The rest of my servants will remain here. If the nunnery turns out to be unsuitable for any reason, I'll come straight back.'

Cat picked up the leather bag that contained the few items Ragna needed at night, such as a comb and a piece of Spanish soap. She had discovered that England had only liquid soap.

Edgar took a lamp from the wall and Cat another. If Dreng objected, he did not dare say so.

Ragna caught Bern's eye and gave him a hard look. He nodded, understanding her. He was in charge of the chest containing the money.

She followed Edgar out, and Cat and Agnes came behind. They made their way to the waterside and boarded the boat while Edgar untied the rope. His dog jumped aboard. Edgar picked up a pole and the boat moved off.

Ragna hoped the nunnery was as advertised. She was badly in need of a clean room and a soft bed and a warm blanket. She felt like a thirsty person whose throat burns with desire on seeing a flagon of cold cider.

She said: 'Is the nunnery wealthy, Edgar?'

'Moderately,' he said. He poled the boat effortlessly and had no shortage of breath for talking. 'They own land at Northwood and St-John-in-the-Forest.'

Agnes said: 'Are you married to one of the ladies in the tavern, Edgar?'

Ragna smiled. Clearly Agnes was attracted to Edgar.

He laughed. 'No. Two of them are Dreng's wives, and the pregnant girl is a slave.'

'Are men allowed to have two wives in England?'

'Not really, but the priests can't stop it.'

'Are you the father of the slave's baby?'

Another pointed question, Ragna thought.

Edgar was mildly offended. 'Certainly not.'

'Who is?'

'No one knows.'

Cat said: 'We don't have slaves in Normandy.'

It was still raining. No moon or stars were visible. Ragna could see very little. But Edgar knew his way, and in a short time the ferry nudged a sandy bank. By the light of the lamps Ragna made out a little rowboat tied to a post. Edgar moored the ferry.

'The bank drops off steeply,' he said to the women. 'Shall I carry you? It's only two steps, but you will get your dresses wet.'

Cat answered. 'Carry my lady, please,' she said briskly. 'Agnes and I will manage.'

Agnes made a disappointed sound, but did not dare to argue with Cat.

Edgar stood in the water beside the boat. It came up to his thighs. Ragna sat on the edge of the boat with her back to him, then turned her body and put an arm around his neck, and finally swung her legs over the side. He took her weight on both arms, supporting her effortlessly.

She found herself enjoying his embrace. She felt a little ashamed: she was in love with another man, and about to marry him – she had no business snuggling up to someone else! But she had a good excuse and it was over in no time. Edgar took two steps through the water then set her down on the bank.

They followed a footpath up a slope. At its end was a large stone building. Its outlines were not clear in the lamplight, but Ragna thought she saw twin gables, and guessed that one marked the church and the other the convent. To the side of the convent was a little tower.

Edgar knocked on the wooden door.

After a while they heard a voice. 'Who's knocking at this time of night?'

Nuns went to bed early, Ragna recalled.

Edgar said: 'This is Edgar the builder. I've brought the Lady Ragna from Cherbourg, who commands your hospitality.'

The door was opened by a thin woman of about forty with pale blue eyes. A few strands of grey hair had escaped from her cap. She held a lantern up and looked at the visitors. When she saw Ragna her eyes widened and her mouth opened. It happened a lot; Ragna was used to it.

The nun stood back and let the three women in. Ragna said to Edgar: 'Wait a few minutes, please, just in case.'

The nun closed the door.

Ragna saw a pillared room, dark and empty now, but probably the place where the nuns lived when they were not praying in the church. She made out the shadowy silhouettes of two writing-desks, and concluded that these nuns copied and perhaps illuminated manuscripts as well as caring for lepers.

The nun who had let them in said: 'I'm Mother Agatha, the abbess here.'

Ragna said amiably: 'Named after the patron saint of nurses, I assume?'

'And of rape victims.'

Ragna guessed there was a story there, but she did not want to hear it tonight. 'These are my maids, Cat and Agnes.'

'I'm glad to welcome you all here. Have you had supper?'

'Yes, thank you, and we're very tired. Can you give us beds?'

'Of course. Please come with me.'

She led them up a wooden staircase. This was the first building Ragna had seen in England that had an upstairs floor. At the top Agatha turned into a small room lit by a single rush light. There were two beds. One was empty, and in the other was a nun about the same age as Agatha but more rounded, sitting up and looking surprised.

Agatha said: 'This is Sister Frith, my deputy.'

Frith stared at Ragna as if she could hardly believe her eyes. There was something in her look that made Ragna think of the way men gazed at her sometimes.

Agatha said: 'Get up, Frith. We're giving up our beds to the guests.'

Frith got out of bed hurriedly.

Agatha said: 'Lady Ragna, please take my bed, and your maids can share Frith's.'

Ragna said: 'You're very kind.'

'God is love,' said Agatha.

'But where will you two sleep?'

'In the dormitory next door, with the other nuns. There's plenty of room.'

To Ragna's profound satisfaction the room was pristine. The floor was of bare boards, swept clean. On a table stood a jug of water and a bowl, no doubt for washing: nuns washed their hands a lot. There was also a lectern on which rested an open book. This was clearly a highly literate nunnery. There were no chests: nuns had no possessions.

Ragna said: 'This is heavenly. Tell me, Mother Agatha, how did there come to be a convent here on this island?'

'It's a love story,' said Agatha. 'The nunnery was built by Nothgyth, the widow of Lord Begmund. After he died and was buried in the minster, Nothgyth did not wish to remarry, for he was the love of her life. She wanted to become a nun and live near his remains for the rest of her days, so that they would rise together at the Last Judgement.'

'How romantic,' Ragna said.

'Isn't it?'

'Will you tell young Edgar that he may return to the mainland?'

'Of course. Please make yourselves comfortable. I'll come back and see if there's anything else you need.'

The two nuns went out. Ragna threw off her cloak and climbed into Agatha's bed. Cat hung Ragna's cloak on a peg in the wall. From the leather bag she had brought, she took a small vial of olive oil. Ragna held out her hands and Cat poured a drop of oil on each. Ragna rubbed her hands together.

She made herself comfortable. The mattress was made of linen and stuffed with straw. The only sound was the wash of the river as it bathed the shores of the island. 'I'm so glad we discovered this place,' she said.

Agnes said: 'Edgar the builder has been a godsend – building up the fire, bringing you hot ale, fetching that little jeweller, and finally bringing us here.'

'You like Edgar, don't you?'

'He's lovely. I'd marry him in a heartbeat.'

The three women giggled.

Cat and Agnes got into their shared bed.

Mother Agatha returned. 'Is everything all right?' she said.

Ragna stretched luxuriously. 'Everything is perfect,' she said. 'You're so kind.'

Agatha bent over Ragna and kissed her softly on the lips. It was more than a mere peck, but did not last long enough to merit an objection. She stood upright, went to the door, and turned back.

'God is love,' said Mother Agatha.

10

THE ONLY MASTER EDGAR had known for the first eighteen years of his life had been his father, who could be harsh but was never cruel. After that, Dreng had come as a shock. Edgar had never before suffered sheer malice for its own sake.

However, Sunni had, from her husband. Edgar thought a lot about how Sunni had handled Cyneric. She let him have his own way most of the time but, on the rare occasions that she went against him, she was bold and stubborn. Edgar tried to deal with Dreng in a similar way. He avoided confrontations, and put up with petty persecution and minor injustices, but when he could not avoid a quarrel he fought to win.

He had prevented Dreng from punching Blod on at least one occasion. He had steered Ragna to the nunnery against the will of Dreng, who had clearly wanted her to spend the night at the alehouse. And with his mother's help he had forced Dreng to feed him decently.

Dreng would have liked to get rid of Edgar, undoubtedly. But there were two snags. One was his daughter, Cwenburg, who was now part of Edgar's family. Dreng had been taught a firm lesson by Ma: he could not hurt Edgar without bringing repercussions onto Cwenburg. The other problem was that Dreng would never find another competent builder for only a farthing a day. A good craftsman would demand three or four times as much in payment. And, Edgar reflected, Dreng's parsimony outweighed his malice.

Edgar knew he was walking on the edge of a cliff. At heart Dreng was not completely rational, and one day he might lash out regardless of the consequences. But there was no safe way to deal with him – other than to lie down under his heel like the rushes on the floor, and Edgar could not bring himself to do that.

So he went on alternately pleasing and defying Dreng, while watching carefully for signs of a coming storm.

The day after Ragna left, Blod came to him and said: 'Do you want a free go? I'm too big to fuck, but I can give you a lovely suck.'

'No!' he said; and then, feeling embarrassed, he added: 'Thank you.'

'Why not? Am I ugly?'

'I told you about my girl Sunni, who died.'

'Then why are you so nice to me?'

'I'm not nice to you. But I'm different from Dreng.'

'You are nice to me.'

He changed the subject. 'Do you have names for your baby?'

'I don't know that I'll be allowed to name him or her.'

'You should give it a Welsh name. What are your parents called?'

'My father is Brioc.'

'I like that, it sounds strong.'

'It's the name of a Celtic saint.'

'What about your mother?'

'Eleri.'

'Pretty name.'

Tears came to her eyes. 'I miss them so much.'

'I've made you sad. I'm sorry.'

'You're the only English person who ever asked me about my family.'

A shout came from inside the alehouse. 'Blod! Get in here.'

Blod left, and Edgar resumed work.

The first consignment of stones had come downstream from Outhenham on a raft steered by one of Gab's sons, and had been unloaded and stacked near the ruins of the old brewhouse. Edgar had prepared the foundations of the new building, digging a trench and half filling it with loose stones.

He had to guess how deep the foundations should go. He had checked those of the church, digging a small hole alongside the wall of the chancel, and found that there were almost no foundations at all; that would explain why it was falling down.

He poured mortar over the stones, and here he came across another problem: how to make sure the surface of the mortar was level? He had a good eye, but that was not enough. He had seen builders at work, and now he wished he had watched them more carefully. In the end he invented a device. He made a thin, flat stick a yard long and carved out the inside to form a smooth channel. The result was a miniature version of the log canoe Dreng had used as a ferry. Edgar got Cuthbert in his forge to make a small, polished iron ball. He laid the stick on the mortar, put the ball in the channel, and tapped the stick. If the ball rolled to one end that showed that the mortar was not level, and the surface had to be adjusted.

It was a lengthy process, and Dreng was impatient. He came out of the alehouse and stood with his hands on his hips, watching Edgar, for a few minutes. Eventually he said: 'You've been working on this a week, and I don't see any wall rising.'

'I have to get the foundations level,' Edgar explained.

'I don't care if it's level,' Dreng said. 'It's a brewhouse, not a cathedral.'

'If it's not level, it will fall down.'

Dreng looked at Edgar, not sure whether to believe him but unwilling to reveal his ignorance. He walked away saying: 'I need Leaf to make ale as soon as possible. I'm losing money buying it from Shiring. Work faster!'

While Edgar was working, his mind often went back to Ragna. She had appeared in Dreng's Ferry like a visitor from paradise. She was so tall, and poised, and beautiful that when you looked at her it was hard to believe she was a member of the human race. But as soon as she spoke she revealed herself to be charmingly human: down-to-earth and warmly sympathetic and capable of weeping over a lost belt. Ealdorman Wilwulf was a lucky man. The two of them would make a remarkable couple. Wherever they went, all eyes would follow them, the handsome ruler and his lovely bride.

Edgar was flattered that she had talked to him, even though she had told him frankly that her motive was to keep Dreng away. He was inordinately pleased that he had been able to find her a place to sleep that suited her better than the tavern. He sympathized with her wish not to lie down on the floor with everyone else. Even quite plain-looking women were liable to be pestered by men in alehouses.

On the following morning he had poled the ferry across to Leper Island to pick her up. Mother Agatha had walked Ragna with Cat and Agnes down to the waterside, and in that short distance Edgar had seen clearly that Agatha, too, was enchanted by Ragna, hanging on her words and hardly able to take her eyes off her. The nun had stayed at the water's edge, waving, until the boat reached the other side and Ragna went into the alehouse.

Before they left, Agnes had told Edgar that she hoped she would see him again soon. The thought had crossed his mind that her interest in him might be romantic. If that were so, he would have to confess to her that he was not able to fall in love, and explain about Sunni. He wondered how many times he was going to have to tell that story.

Towards evening he was startled by a cry of pain from within the tavern. It sounded like Blod, and Edgar thought Dreng might be beating her. He dropped his tools and ran inside.

But there was no beating. Dreng was sitting at the table looking irritated. Blod was slumped on the floor with her back to the wall. Her black hair was wet with sweat. Leaf and Ethel were standing up, watching her. As Edgar arrived she gave another shriek of pain.

'God save us,' said Edgar. 'Did something terrible happen?'

'What's the matter with you, you stupid boy?' Dreng jeered. 'Haven't you ever seen a woman giving birth?'

Edgar had not. He had seen animals giving birth, but that was different. He was the youngest in the family and had not been alive when his brothers were born. He knew about human childbirth in theory, so he was aware that it might hurt, and – now that he came to think about it – he had sometimes heard cries of pain from neighbouring houses, and he recalled his mother saying: 'Her time has come.' But he had never experienced it close up.

The only thing he knew for sure was that the mother often died.

He found it harrowing to look at a girl in pain and be unable to help her. 'Should we give her a sip of ale?' he said in desperation. Strong drink was usually good for people in pain.

Leaf said: 'We can try.' She half filled a cup and handed it to Edgar.

He knelt beside Blod and held the cup to her mouth. She gulped the ale then grimaced with pain again.

Dreng said: 'It was original sin that caused this. In the garden of Eden.'

Leaf said sarcastically: 'My husband, the priest.'

'It's true,' Dreng said. 'Eve disobeyed. That's why God punishes all women.'

Leaf said: 'I expect Eve was driven mad by her husband.'

Edgar did not see what more he could do, and the others seemed to feel the same. Perhaps it was all in the hands of God. Edgar went back outside and resumed his work.

He wondered what childbirth would have been like for Sunni. Obviously their lovemaking was likely to lead to pregnancy, but Edgar had never thought very hard about that. He realized now that he would have found it unbearable to see her in such pain. It was bad enough watching Blod, who was no more than an acquaintance.

He finished mortaring the foundation as it began to get dark. He would double-check the level in the morning, but all being well he would lay the first course of stones tomorrow.

He went into the alehouse. Blod was lying on the floor and seemed to be dozing. Ethel served supper, a stew of pork and carrots. This was the time of year when everyone had to decide which animals would live through the winter and which should be slaughtered now. Some of the meat was eaten fresh, the rest smoked or salted for the winter.

Edgar ate heartily. Dreng threw bad-tempered looks his way but said nothing. Leaf drank more ale. She was getting tipsy.

As they finished the meal Blod began to moan again, and the pains seemed to come more frequently. Leaf said: 'It won't be long now.' Her words were slurred, as often happened by this time in the evening, but she was still making sense. 'Edgar, go to the river and get fresh water to wash the baby with.'

Edgar was surprised. 'Do you have to wash a baby?'

Leaf laughed. 'Of course – you wait and see.'

He picked up the bucket and made his way to the river. It was dark, but the sky was clear and there was a bright half-moon. Brindle followed him, hoping for a boat ride. Edgar dipped the bucket in the river and carried it to the alehouse. Back inside he saw that Leaf had laid out clean rags. 'Put the bucket near the fire, so that the water can warm up a bit,' she said.

Blod's cries were more anguished now. Edgar saw that the rushes under her hips were soaked with some kind of fluid. Surely this could not be normal? He said: 'Shall I ask Mother Agatha to come?' The nun was usually called upon in medical emergencies.

Dreng said: 'I can't afford to pay her.'

'She doesn't charge a fee!' Edgar said indignantly.

'Not officially, but she expects a donation, unless you're poor. She'd want money from me. People think I'm a rich man.'

Leaf said: 'Don't worry, Edgar. Blod is going to be all right.'

'Do you mean to say this is normal?'

'Yes, it is.'

Blod tried to get up. Ethel helped her. Edgar said: 'Shouldn't she lie down?'

'Not now,' Leaf said.

She opened a chest. She took out two thin strips of leather. Then she threw a bunch of dried rye on the fire. Burning rye was supposed to drive away evil spirits. Finally she picked up a large clean rag and draped it over her shoulder.

Edgar realized there was a ritual here that he knew nothing about.

Blod stood with her legs apart and bent forwards. Ethel stood at her head, and Blod put her arms around Ethel's thin waist for support. Leaf knelt behind Blod and lifted her dress. 'The baby's coming,' she said.

Dreng said: 'Oh, disgusting.' He stood, pulled on his cloak, picked up his tankard, and limped outside.

Blod made heaving noises, as if she were lifting a weight so heavy that she was in agony. Edgar stared, fascinated and horrified at the same time: how could something as big as a baby come out of there? But the opening got larger. Some object seemed to be pushing through. 'What's that?' said Edgar.

'The baby's head,' said Leaf.

Edgar was aghast. 'God help Blod.'

The baby did not come out in one smooth motion. Rather, the skull seemed to push outwards for a few moments, widening the opening, then stop, as if to rest. Blod cried in pain with every surge.

Edgar said: 'It's got hair.'

Leaf said: 'They generally do.'

Then, like a marvel, the baby's entire head came into the world.

Edgar was possessed by a powerful emotion he could not name. He was awed by what he was seeing. His throat constricted as if he was about to weep, yet he was not sad; in fact, he felt joyous.

Leaf took the rag from her shoulder and held it between Blod's thighs, supporting the baby's head with her hands. The shoulders appeared, then its belly with something attached which, he realized immediately, was the cord. The whole body was covered with some slimy fluid. At last the legs appeared. It was a boy, he saw.

Ethel said: 'I feel strange.'

Leaf looked at her and said: 'She's going to faint – catch her, Edgar.'

Ethel's eyes rolled up and she went limp. Just in time, Edgar caught her under the arms and laid her carefully on the floor.

The boy opened his mouth and cried.

Blod slowly lowered herself to her hands and knees. Leaf wrapped the rag around the tiny baby and laid him gently in the rushes on the floor. Then she deployed the mysterious thin strips of leather. She tied both tightly around the cord, one close to the baby's belly and the other a couple of inches away. Finally she drew her belt knife and cut the cord.

She dipped a clean rag in the bucket and washed the baby, gently cleaning blood and mucus from his face and head, then the rest of his body. He cried again at the feel of the water. She patted him dry then wrapped him up again.

Blod groaned with effort, as if she were giving birth again, and the thought of twins crossed Edgar's mind briefly; but what came out was a shapeless lump, and when he frowned in puzzlement Leaf said: 'The afterbirth.'

Blod rolled over and sat with her back to the wall. Her normal expression of guarded hostility had been wiped away, and she just looked pale and exhausted. Leaf gave her the baby, and Blod's face changed again, softening and brightening at the same time. She looked with love at the tiny body in her arms. The baby's head turned towards her, so that his face pressed against her chest. She pulled down the front of her dress and put the baby to her breast. He seemed to know what to do: his mouth closed eagerly around the nipple and he began to suck.

Blod closed her eyes and looked contented. Edgar had never seen her like that before.

Leaf helped herself to another cup of ale and drained it in a gulp.

Brindle stared at the baby, fascinated. A tiny foot stuck out from the bundle and Brindle licked it.

Getting rid of spoiled straw was normally Blod's job, and Edgar decided that now he had better do it. He picked up the mess where Blod had stood, including the afterbirth, and took it outside.

Dreng was sitting on a bench in the moonlight. Edgar said: 'The baby is born.'

Dreng put his cup to his mouth and drank.

Edgar said: 'It's a boy.'

Dreng said nothing.

Edgar dumped the straw next to the dunghill. When it was dry he would burn it.

Back inside, both Blod and the baby seemed to be sleeping. Leaf was lying down with her eyes closed, exhausted or drunk or both. Ethel was still out cold.

Dreng came in. Blod opened her eyes and looked warily at him, but he only went to the barrel and refilled his tankard. Blod closed her eyes again.

Dreng took a long draught of ale then put his tankard on the table. In a swift, confident move he bent over Blod and picked up the baby. The rag fell to the floor and he said: 'A boy it is, the little bastard.'

Blod said: 'Give him to me!'

'Oh, so you can speak English!' said Dreng.

'Give me my baby.'

Ethel did not stir, but Leaf said: 'Give her the baby, Dreng.'

'I think he needs fresh air,' Dreng said. 'Too smoky in here for a baby.'

'Please,' said Blod.

Dreng took the baby outside.

Leaf went after him. Blod tried to get up but fell back. Edgar followed Leaf. 'Dreng, what are you doing?' Leaf cried fearfully.

'There,' Dreng said to the baby. 'Taste the clean air from the river. Isn't that better?' He moved down the slope to the water's edge.

The fresh air probably was better for the baby, Edgar thought, but was that really what was on Dreng's mind? Edgar had never seen him do a kindness for anyone other than Cwenburg. Had the drama of childbirth reminded him of when Cwenburg came into the world? Edgar followed Dreng at a distance, watching.

Dreng turned to face Edgar and Leaf. The moonlight shone white on the baby's tiny body. Summer had turned to autumn, and the cold air on bare skin woke the baby and made him cry.

Leaf cried: 'Keep him warm!'

Dreng grasped the baby by the ankle and held him upside down. The crying became urgent. Edgar did not know what was happening but he felt sure it was bad, and in sudden fear he dashed at Dreng.

With a rapid, vigorous motion Dreng swung the baby, windmilling his arm, and hurled him out across the water.

Leaf screamed.

The baby's crying was abruptly silenced as he splashed into the river.

Edgar crashed into Dreng and they both fell into the shallows.

Edgar sprang up immediately. He jerked off his shoes and pulled his tunic over his head.

Dreng, spluttering, said: 'You tried to drown me, you madman!'

Edgar dived naked into the water.

The little body had gone far out into midstream: Dreng was a big man, and the bad back of which he constantly complained did not much affect his throwing ability. Edgar swam strongly, heading for the place where he thought the baby had splashed down. There was no cloud and the moon was bright, but as he looked ahead he saw, with dismay, that there was nothing on the surface. Surely the baby would float? Human bodies did not normally sink to the bottom, did they? All the same, people drowned.

He reached and passed what he thought was the spot without seeing anything. He waved his arms around under water, hoping to touch something, but he felt nothing.

The urge to save the child was overpowering. He felt desperate. It had something to do with Sunni, he was not sure how – and he did not let the thought distract him. He trod water and turned in a circle, staring hard, wishing the light was brighter.

The current always took flotsam downstream. He swam in that direction, going as fast as he could while scanning the surface left and right. Brindle came alongside him, paddling hard to keep up. Perhaps she would smell the baby before Edgar saw him.

The current moved him towards the north side of Leper Island, and he had to assume it had done the same with the baby. Debris from the hamlet sometimes washed up opposite the island, and Edgar decided his best hope was to look there for the baby. He swam to the edge. Here the bank was not clearly defined; instead there was puddled swampy ground, part of the farm though not productive. He swam along, peering in the moonlight. He saw plenty of litter: bits of wood, nutshells, animal bones, and a dead cat. If the baby was there, Edgar would surely see his white body. But he was disappointed.

Feeling increasingly frantic, he gave up on that stretch and swam across the river to Leper Island. Here the bank was overgrown, and he could not easily see the ground. He came up out of the water and walked along, going towards the nunnery, scanning the water's edge as best he could in the moonlight. Brindle growled, and Edgar heard movement nearby. He guessed the lepers were watching him: they were known to be shy, perhaps reluctant to let people see their deformities. But he decided to speak. 'Hey, anybody,' he said loudly.

The shuffling stopped abruptly. 'A baby fell into the river,' he said. 'Have you seen anything?'

The silence continued some moments, then a figure appeared from behind a tree. The man was dressed in rags but did not appear misshapen; perhaps the rumours were exaggerated. 'No one saw a baby,' the man said.

Edgar said: 'Will you help me look?'

The man hesitated, then nodded.

Edgar said: 'He may have been washed up somewhere along the shore.'

There was no response to this so Edgar just turned and resumed searching. Gradually he became aware that he was accompanied. Someone was moving through the bushes alongside him, and another was treading the shallows behind him. He thought he saw movement farther ahead, too. He was grateful for the extra eyes: it would be easy to miss something small.

But as he moved back in the direction of the alehouse, closing the circle, he found it hard to maintain hope. He was exhausted and shivering: what state would a naked baby be in? If it had not drowned, it might now have died of the cold.

He drew level with the convent building. There were lights in its windows and outside, and he saw hurried movement. A nun approached him, and he recognized Mother Agatha. He remembered that he was stark naked, but she seemed not to notice.

She carried a bundle in her arms. Edgar's hopes leaped. Had the nuns found the baby?

Agatha must have seen the eagerness in his face, for she shook her head sadly, and Edgar was filled with alarm.

She came close and showed him what she held in her arms. Wrapped in a white wool blanket was Blod's baby. His eyes were closed and he was not breathing.

'We found him on the shore,' Agatha said.

'Was he . . . ?'

'Dead or alive? I don't know. We took him into the warm, but we were too late. We baptised him, though, so he's with the angels now.'

Edgar was overwhelmed by grief. He cried and shivered at the same time, and his eyes blurred with tears. 'I saw him born,' he said between sobs. 'It was like a miracle.'

'I know,' said Agatha.

'And then I saw him murdered.'

Agatha unwrapped the blanket and gave the tiny baby to Edgar. He held the cold body to his bare chest and wept.

11

EARLY OCTOBER 997

As RAGNA DREW NEARER to Shiring, her heart filled with apprehension.

She had embarked on this adventure eagerly, impatient for the pleasures of marriage with the man she loved, careless of perils. Bad-weather delays had been frustrating. Now she was more aware, with every mile she travelled, that she did not really know what she had let herself in for. All of the short time she and Wilwulf had spent together had been at her home, where he was a stranger trying to fit in. She had never seen him in his own place, never watched him move among his own people, never heard him talk to his family, his neighbours, his subjects. She hardly knew him.

When at last she came in sight of his city, she stopped and took a good look.

It was a big place, several hundred homes clustered at the foot of a hill, with a damp mist drifting over the thatched roofs. It was surrounded by an earth rampart, no doubt for defence against Vikings. Two large churches stood out, pale stone and wet shingles against the mass of brown timber. One appeared to be part of a group of monastic buildings enclosed by a ditch and a fence, and was undoubtedly the abbey where the handsome Brother Aldred was in charge of the scriptorium. She looked forward to seeing Aldred again.

The other church would be the cathedral, for alongside it was a two-storey house that must be the home of the bishop, Wilwulf's brother Wynstan, soon to be Ragna's brother-in-law. She hoped he would act like a kind of older brother to her.

A stone building with no bell tower was probably the home of a moneyer, containing a stock of silver metal that had to be guarded from thieves. England's currency was trusted, she had learned: the purity of its silver pennies was carefully regulated by the king, who imposed brutal punishments for forgery.

There would be more churches in a town of this size, but they were probably built of timber, just like houses.

On top of the hill, dominating the town, was a stockaded compound, twenty or thirty assorted buildings enclosed by a stout fence. That must be the seat of government, the residence of the ealdorman, the home of Wilwulf.

And my home too now, Ragna thought nervously.

It had no stone buildings. That did not surprise her: it was only recently that the Normans had begun to build stone keeps and gatehouses, and most of them were simpler and cruder than her father's castle at Cherbourg. Undoubtedly she would be a little less safe here.

She had known in advance that the English were weak. The Vikings had first raided this country two centuries ago and the English still had not been able to put a permanent stop to it. People here were better at jewellery and embroidery than at fighting.

She sent Cat and Bern ahead to warn of her arrival. She followed slowly, to give Wilwulf time to prepare a welcome. She had to suppress the urge to kick Astrid into a canter. She was desperately keen to hold Wilwulf in her arms, and she resented every moment's delay, but she was eager to make a dignified entrance.

Despite the drizzle of cold rain, the town was busy with commerce: people buying bread and ale, horses and carts delivering sacks and barrels, pedlars and prostitutes walking the mud streets. But business stopped as Ragna and her entourage approached. They formed a large group, richly dressed, and her men-at-arms all sported the severe haircut that marked them distinctively as Norman. People stared and pointed. They probably guessed who Ragna was: the forthcoming wedding was surely general knowledge in the town, and the people must have long anticipated her arrival.

Their looks were wary, and she guessed they were not certain how to respond to her. Was she a foreign usurper, come to steal the most eligible man in the west of England away from more deserving local girls?

She noticed that her men had instinctively formed a protective ring around her. That was a mistake, she realized. The people of Shiring needed to see their princess. 'We look too defensive,' she said to one of her men-at-arms. 'This won't do. You and Odo ride ten paces ahead, just to clear the way. Tell the rest to fall back. Let the townsfolk see me.'

He looked worried, but he changed the formation as instructed.

Ragna began to interact with the people. She met the eyes of individuals and smiled at them. Most people found it hard not to return a smile, but here she sensed a reluctance. One woman gave a tentative wave, and Ragna waved back. A group of thatchers putting a roof on a house stopped work and called out to her; they spoke English with a broad accent that she could not understand, so she was not sure whether their shouted comments represented enthusiasm or mockery, but she blew them a kiss. Some onlookers smiled in approval. A little crowd of men drinking outside an alehouse waved their caps in the air and cheered. Other bystanders followed suit. 'That's better,' said Ragna, her anxiety easing a little.

The noise drew people out of their houses and shops to see what was going on, and the crowd thickened ahead. Everyone followed behind the entourage, and as Ragna headed up the hill to the compound the buzz became a roar. She was infected by their enthusiasm. The more she smiled, the more they cheered; and the more they cheered, the happier she felt.

The wooden stockade had a big double gate, and both sides stood wide. Just inside, another crowd had gathered, presumably Wilwulf's servants and hangers-on. They applauded as Ragna came into view.

The compound was not very different from that at Cherbourg apart from the lack of a castle. There were houses, stables and storerooms. The kitchens were open-sided. One house was double-sized, and had small windows at both ends: that would be the great hall, where the ealdorman held meetings and hosted banquets. The other houses would be homes for important men and their families.

The crowd formed two lines and clearly expected Ragna to ride between them to the great hall. She went slowly, taking time to look at the faces and smile at individuals. Almost every expression was welcoming and happy; just a handful were stonily non-committal, as if warily withholding judgement, waiting for further evidence that she was all right.

Outside the door of the long house stood Wilwulf.

He was just as she remembered him, tall and loose-limbed, with a mane of fair hair and a moustache but no beard. He wore a red cloak with an enamelled brooch. His smile was broad but relaxed, as if they had parted company only yesterday, rather than two months ago. He stood in the rain without a hat, not caring about getting wet. He spread his arms wide in a gesture of welcome.

Ragna could restrain herself no longer. She leaped off her horse and ran to him. The onlookers cheered at this display of uncontained enthusiasm. His smile became wider. She threw herself into his arms and kissed him passionately. The cheering became thunderous. She put her arms around his neck and jumped up with her legs around his waist, and the crowd went wild.

She kissed him hard, but not too long, then put her feet on the ground again. A little vulgarity went a long way.

They stood grinning at each other. Ragna was thinking about making love with him, and she felt he knew what was in her mind.

They let the people cheer for a minute, then Wilwulf took her hand and they walked side by side into the great hall.

A smaller crowd waited there, and there was more applause. As Ragna's eyes grew accustomed to the dimmer light she saw a group of a dozen or so people, more richly dressed than those outside, and she guessed these were Wilwulf's family.

One stepped forward, and she recognized the large ears and the close-set eyes. 'Bishop Wynstan,' she said. 'I'm pleased to see you again.'

He kissed her hand. 'I'm glad that you're here, and proud of the modest part I played in making the arrangements.'

'For which I thank you.'

'You've had a long journey.'

'I've certainly got to know my new country.'

'And what do you think of it?'

'It's a bit wet.'

Everyone laughed, which pleased Ragna, but she knew this was not the moment for candid honesty, and she added an outright lie. 'The English people have been friendly and kind. I love them.'

'I'm so glad,' said Wynstan, apparently believing her.

Ragna almost blushed. She had been miserable ever since she set foot in England. The alehouses were dirty, the people were unfriendly, ale was a poor substitute for cider, and she had been robbed. But no, she thought, that was not the whole truth. Mother Agatha had welcomed her, and that ferry boy had been zealously helpful. No doubt the English were a mixture of good and bad, as were the Normans.

And the Normans had no one like Wilwulf. As she made small talk with the family, pausing often to search her memory for the right Anglo-Saxon word, she glanced at him every chance she got, feeling a jolt of pleasure each time she recognized a familiar feature: his strong jaw, his blue-green eyes, the blond moustache she was longing to kiss again. Each time she looked she found he was staring at her, wearing a proud smile with a hint behind it of impatient lust. That made her feel good.

Wilwulf introduced another tall man with a bushy blond moustache. 'Allow me to present my younger half-brother, Wigelm, the lord of Combe.'

Wigelm looked her up and down. 'My word, you are very welcome,' he said. His words were kind but his grin made Ragna uneasy, even though she was accustomed to men staring at her body. Wigelm confirmed her instinctive dislike by saying: 'I'm sure Wilf explained to you that we three brothers share everything, including our women.'

This joke caused the men to laugh uproariously. The women present did not find it so hilarious. Ragna decided to ignore it.

Wilwulf said: 'And this is my stepmother, Gytha.'

Ragna saw a formidable woman of about fifty. She was short – her sons must have inherited the build of their late father, Ragna guessed. Her long grey hair framed a handsome face, with strongly marked eyebrows. Ragna imagined shrewdness and a sturdy will. She sensed that this woman was going to be a force in her life, for good or ill. She offered a fulsome compliment: 'How proud you must be, to have given England these three remarkable men.'

'You're very kind,' said Gytha, but she did not smile, and Ragna foresaw that Gytha would be slow to succumb to her charm.

Wilwulf said: 'Gytha will show you around the compound, then we'll have dinner.'

'Splendid,' said Ragna.

Gytha led the way. Ragna's maids were waiting outside. Ragna said: 'Cat, come with me. The rest of you, wait.'

Gytha said: 'Don't worry, we'll take care of everything.'

Ragna was not ready to surrender control. She asked Cat: 'Where are the men?'

'In the stables, seeing to the horses.'

'Tell Bern to stay with the baggage until I send for him.'

'Yes, my lady.'

Gytha led Ragna around. It was clear, from the deference shown to Gytha, that she was the boss, in charge of Wilwulf's domestic life. That would have to change, Ragna thought. She was not going to be told what to do by her stepmother-in-law.

They walked past the slave quarters and entered the stable. The place was crowded, but Ragna noticed that the English stable hands were not talking to the Normans. That would not do. She put her arm around Bern. Raising her voice, she said: 'You Englishmen, this is my friend Bern the Giant. He's very gentle with horses –' She took his hand and held it up – 'and with women.' There was a low chuckle from the men. They always bantered about penis size, which was said to be correlated with hand size, and Bern's hands were huge. 'He's gentle with women,' she repeated, and now they were smiling, for they knew the gag was coming. She gave an arch look and said: 'He needs to be.'

They all laughed, and the ice was broken.

Ragna said: 'When my men make mistakes speaking your language, be nice to them, and maybe they'll teach you some words of Norman French. Then you'll know what to say to any French girls you may meet . . .'

They laughed again, and she knew she had bonded with them. She went out before the laughter died away.

Gytha showed her a double-sized building that was barracks for the men-at-arms. 'I won't go in,' Ragna said. It was a male dormitory, and for her to enter might be too forward. There was a narrow line between a delightfully flirtatious woman and a contemptible tart, and a foreigner had to be especially careful not to cross it.

However, she noticed a lot of men milling around outside, and recalled that the stables had been crowded. 'So many men,' she said to Gytha. 'Is something going on?'

'Yes. Wilf is mustering an army.' That was the second time Ragna had heard someone call him 'Wilf'. It was obviously the familiar short form of his name. 'The South Welsh have raided across the border,' Gytha went on. 'They sometimes do at this time of year – after the harvest, when our barns are full. But don't worry, Wilf won't go until after the wedding.'

Ragna felt a chill of fear. Her husband was going into battle right after they got married. It was normal, of course; she had seen her father ride off many times, armed to the teeth, to kill or be killed. But she never got used to it. It scared her when Count Hubert went to war, and it would scare her when Wilwulf did the same. She tried to put it out of her mind. She had other things to think about.

The great hall was in the centre of the compound. To one side was an assortment of domestic buildings: the kitchen, the bakery, the brewhouse and several stores. On the other side were individual residences.

Ragna went into the kitchen. As was usual, the cooks were men, but they were assisted by half a dozen women and girls. She greeted the men politely, but she was more interested in the females. A big, good-looking woman of about thirty struck her as the type who might be a leader. Ragna said to her: 'Dinner smells good!'

The woman gave her a friendly smile.

Ragna asked: 'What's your name?'

'Gildathryth, my lady, called Gilda for short.'

Next to Gilda was a girl washing mud off a huge stack of small purplish carrots. She looked a bit like Gilda, and Ragna said: 'Is this pretty child related to you?' It was a fairly safe guess: in a small community most people were related somehow.

'My daughter Winthryth,' Gilda said proudly. 'Twelve years old.'

'Hello, Winthryth. When you grow up, will you make lovely dinners, like Mummy?'

Winthryth was too shy to speak, but she nodded.

'Well, thank you for washing the carrots,' Ragna said. 'When I eat one, I will think of you.'

Winthryth beamed with pleasure.

Ragna left the kitchen.

Over the next few days she would speak to everyone who lived or worked in the compound. It would be hard to remember all the names, but she would do her best. She would ask about their children and grandchildren, their ailments and their superstitions, their homes and their clothes. She would not need to pretend interest: she had always been curious about the everyday lives of the people around her.

Cat would find out more, especially as her English became more confident. Like Ragna, she befriended people quickly, and soon the maids would share gossip with her: which laundress had a lover, which stable hand liked to lie with men rather than women, who was stealing from the kitchen, which man-at-arms was afraid of the dark.

Ragna and Gytha moved towards the houses. Most of them were half the length of the great hall, but they were not all of the same quality. All had stout corner posts and thatched roofs. Most had walls of wattle-and-daub, upright branches interwoven with horizontal twigs and covered with a mixture of mud and straw. The three best houses were immediately behind the great hall. They had walls of upright planks neatly joined edge-to-edge and footed in a heavy timber sill-beam.

Ragna said: 'Which one is Wilwulf's?'

Gytha pointed to the central building. Ragna walked to the entrance. Gytha said: 'Perhaps you should wait for an invitation.'

Ragna smiled and walked in.

Cat followed her, and Gytha was the reluctant last.

Ragna was pleased to see a low bed, plenty wide enough for two, with a big mattress and an inviting pile of bright-dyed blankets.

Otherwise the place had a military air, with sharpened weapons and gleaming armour hanging from pegs around the walls – perhaps ready for Wilwulf's coming conflict with the South Welsh. His other possessions were stored in a few large wooden chests. A wall tapestry showed a hunting scene, well executed. There appeared to be no materials for writing or reading.

Ragna walked out again and turned towards the back of Wilwulf's home. Another fine house stood behind it. As Ragna headed that way, Gytha said: 'Perhaps I should show you your house.'

Ragna was not willing to be told what to do by Gytha, and she felt the need to make that clear sooner rather than later. Without stopping she said: 'Whose house is this one?'

'That's mine. You can't go in.'

Ragna turned. 'No building in this compound is closed to me,' she said quietly but firmly. 'I am about to marry the ealdorman. Only he tells me what to do. I will be the mistress here.'

She went into the house.

Gytha followed her.

The place was richly furnished. There was a comfortable cushioned chair like those used by kings. On a table was a basket of pears and a small barrel of the type that usually contained wine. Costly wool dresses and cloaks hung from pegs.

Ragna said: 'Very nice. Your stepson is good to you.'

'And why shouldn't he be?' Gytha said defensively.

'Quite.' Ragna went out.

Gytha had said *Perhaps I should show you your house*, and that suggested that Ragna would have a home separate from Wilwulf's. This was not an unusual arrangement, but somehow she had not anticipated it. The wife of a wealthy nobleman often had a nearby second house for babies and children and their nursemaids; she would spend some nights there and others with her husband. However, Ragna did not expect to spend any nights apart from

Wilwulf before a baby made it necessary. The separate house seemed premature. She wished Wilwulf had talked to her about it. But they had had no chance to talk about anything.

She was uncomfortable, the more so because it was Gytha who was telling her about it. Ragna knew that mothers could be irrationally hostile to their sons' women, and that probably applied to stepmothers too. Ragna recalled an incident in which her brother, Richard, had been caught embracing a laundress on the ramparts of the castle at Cherbourg. Their mother, Genevieve, had wanted to have the girl flogged. It was natural that she should not want a servant to be impregnated with her son's child, but Richard had only been stroking the girl between her legs, and Ragna was pretty sure all adolescent boys did that whenever they got the chance. Clearly there had been more to Genevieve's rage than simple prudence. Could a mother, or even a stepmother, be jealous of her son's lovers? Was Gytha unfriendly to Ragna because they were rivals for Wilwulf's affection?

Ragna was wary about this but, in the end, not deeply anxious. She knew how Wilwulf felt about her and she was confident she could hold and keep his love. If she wanted to spend every night in his bed, she would do so, and she would make sure he was happy about it.

She turned her steps towards the last of the three houses.

'That's Wigelm's place,' Gytha said, but this time she did not try to stop Ragna entering.

The interior of Wigelm's home had a temporary look, and Ragna supposed he spent a lot of time at Combe, the town of which he was lord. But he was here now, sitting with three other young men around a jug of ale, throwing dice and betting silver pennies. He stood up when he saw Ragna. 'Come in, come in,' he said. 'The house suddenly seems warmer.'

She immediately regretted entering, but she was not willing to retreat hastily, as if scared. She was making a point of her right to go anywhere. She ignored Wigelm's banter and said: 'Aren't you married?'

'My wife is at Combe, supervising the rebuilding of our home there after the Viking raid. But she will be here for your wedding.'

'What's her name?'

'Mildburg, called Milly for short.'

'I look forward to meeting her.'

Wigelm came closer and lowered his voice to a more intimate tone. 'Will you sit down and share a cup of ale with me? We'll teach you to play at dice if you like.'

'Not today.'

Casually, he put his hands on her breasts and squeezed. 'My, they really are big, aren't they?'

Cat made an indignant noise.

Ragna stepped back and pushed his hands away. 'But they're not for you,' she said.

'I'm just checking the goods before my brother buys them.' He shot an arch look at his pals and, on cue, they burst out laughing.

Ragna glanced at Gytha and saw the trace of a smirk on her lips.

Ragna said: 'Next time the Vikings raid, I hope you brave men will be there to meet them.'

Wigelm was silenced, unable to work out whether that was a compliment or a curse.

Ragna took the opportunity to make her exit.

A man could be fined for touching the breast of a woman, but Ragna was not going to make a court case out of the incident. However, she vowed to find a way to punish Wigelm.

Outside, she turned to Gytha and said: 'So, Wilf has prepared a house for me?'

Her phrasing was deliberate. It was Wilwulf's responsibility to make sure she was comfortable. He had probably left it to Gytha to make the arrangements, but Ragna would complain to him if dissatisfied, not Gytha, and she wanted Gytha to understand that from the start.

'This way,' said Gytha.

Next to Wigelm's home was a cheaper house with draughty wattle-and-daub walls. Gytha walked in and Ragna followed.

It was adequately furnished, with a bed, a table with benches, several chests, and plenty of wooden cups and bowls. There was a stack of firewood by the hearth and a barrel that presumably contained ale. The place lacked any touch of luxury.

It was a poor welcome, Ragna felt.

Gytha sensed Ragna's reaction and said hesitantly: 'No doubt you have brought your own personal choice of wall hangings and so on.'

Ragna had not. She had expected everything to be provided. She had money to buy whatever she needed, but that was not the point. 'Blankets?' she said.

Gytha shrugged. 'Why do you need blankets? Most people sleep in their cloaks.'

'I noticed that Wilf has plenty of blankets in his house.'

Gytha did not reply.

Ragna looked around the walls. 'Not enough pegs,' she said. 'You didn't think a bride might have a lot of clothes to hang up?'

'You can put in more pegs.'

'I'll have to borrow a hammer.'

Gytha looked puzzled, then realized that Ragna was being sarcastic. 'I'll send you a carpenter.'

'The place is too small. I have five maids and seven men-at-arms.'

'The men can be lodged in the town.'

'I prefer them near me.'

'That may not be possible.'

'We'll see.' Ragna was angry and hurt. However, she needed to think and plan before taking action. She turned to Cat. 'Fetch the other maids, and tell the men to bring the baggage.' Cat went out.

Gytha tried to regain the initiative. She adopted an authoritative tone and said: 'You'll live here, and when Wilf wants to spend the night with you he will either come here or invite you to his house. You should never go to his bed uninvited.'

Ragna ignored that. She and Wilf would work things out without the help of his stepmother. She resisted the temptation to say so.

She had had enough of Gytha. 'Thank you for showing me around,' she said in a tone of dismissal.

Gytha hesitated. 'I hope everything is all right.'

Gytha had probably expected a frightened young foreign girl who could be pushed around. Now, Ragna guessed, she was anxiously revising her opinion.

'We'll see,' Ragna said tersely.

Gytha tried again. 'What will you say to Wilf about your accommodation?'

'We'll see,' Ragna repeated.

It must have been obvious that Ragna wanted Gytha to leave, but Gytha was ignoring her hints. She had been the senior female here for years, and perhaps she did not believe she could be given orders by another woman. Ragna had to be more forceful. 'I have no further need for you at present, Stepmother-in-law,' she said; and when Gytha still did not go out she raised her voice and added: 'You may go.'

Gytha flushed with embarrassment and anger, but she went out at last.

Cat returned with the others, the men toting chests and bags. They stacked the luggage up against the wall. Cat said: 'This place is crowded, with all of us in here.'

'The men must sleep elsewhere.'

'Where?'

'Somewhere in the town. But don't unpack. Just what we need for one night.'

Bishop Wynstan came through the open door. 'Well, well,' he said, looking around. 'So this is your new house.'

'So it seems,' Ragna said.

'Is it not satisfactory?'

'I'll discuss it with Wilf.'

'Good idea. He wishes for nothing more than your happiness.'

'I'm glad.'

'I've come for your dowry.'

'Really?'

Wynstan frowned severely. 'You did bring it?'

'Of course.'

'Twenty pounds of silver. That was what I agreed with your father.'

'Yes.'

'Then perhaps you would let me have it.'

Ragna did not trust Wynstan, and this request sharpened her misgivings. 'I shall give it to Wilf when we are married. *That* was what you agreed with my father.'

'But I must count it.'

Ragna did not want Wynstan to know even which box it was in. 'You may count it on the morning of the wedding. Then, after the vows have been taken, it will be handed over – to my husband.'

Wynstan gave her a look that mingled dislike with respect. 'As you wish, of course,' he said, and he went out.

ÞÞÞ

RAGNA GOT UP before dawn the next day.

She thought carefully about what to wear. Yesterday she had arrived in a fawn dress and a red cloak, a fetching outfit, but the clothes had been damp and muddy, and she had not looked her best. Today she wanted to be like a flower that had bloomed at daybreak. She chose a yellow silk dress with embroidery at the neck, cuffs and hem. Cat washed the corners of her eyes and brushed her thick red hair, then tied a green scarf over her head.

While it was still dark Ragna ate some bread dipped in weak ale and concentrated on what she was about to do. She had spent much of the night thinking over her strategy. Wigelm must be punished, but that was a secondary matter. Her big task was to prove that she, not Gytha, was now in charge of Wilf's home life. Ragna did not want a quarrel but she could not let Gytha's rule continue even for a day, because every moment that she seemed to accept it left her weaker. She had to take immediate action.

It was risky, though. She might displease her husband-to-be, and that would be bad enough; but, worse, she might lose the battle, and a victory for Gytha at this stage could be permanent.

Cat handed her the arm band she had bought from Cuthbert in Dreng's Ferry, and Ragna slipped it into the leather purse attached to her belt.

She stepped outside. There was a faint silvery glow on the eastern horizon. It had rained in the night, and the ground was muddy underfoot, but the day promised to be bright. Down in the dark town, the monastery bell tolled for the morning office of prime. The compound was just beginning to come alive: she saw a boy slave in a threadbare tunic carrying a pile of firewood, then a strong-armed maid with a pail of fresh milk that steamed in the morning air. Everyone else was out of sight, probably still warm in bed, eyes shut tight, pretending it was not yet day.

Ragna crossed the compound to Wilf's house.

There was one other person in view. A young woman stood outside Gytha's door, leaning against the wall, yawning. She caught sight of Ragna and stood upright.

Ragna smiled. Gytha was keeping her under surveillance, not taking any chances. As it happened, that suited Ragna's purpose today.

She went to Wilf's door, watched by the maid.

It suddenly occurred to her that Wilf might bar his door at night: some people did. That could spoil her plan.

But when she lifted the latch the door opened, and she relaxed. Perhaps Wilf thought that to lock his door at night might make him seem timorous in the eyes of his men.

Out of the corner of her eye she saw the watching maid scurry inside Gytha's house.

Wilf had another reason for feeling confident. As Ragna stepped inside, she heard a deep growl. Wilf had a dog to warn him of intruders.

Ragna looked towards where she knew the bed to be. There was a glow from the embers of the fire, and a faint light coming through the small windows. She saw a figure sit upright in the bed and reach for a weapon.

Wilf's voice said: 'Who's there?'

Ragna said quietly: 'Good morning, my lord.'

She heard him chuckle. 'It's a good morning now that you're here.' He lay down again.

There was a movement on the floor, and she saw a big mastiff resume his position lying by the fire.

She sat on the edge of the bed. This was a delicate moment. Her mother had urged her not to lie with Wilf until after the ceremony. He would want it, Genevieve had said, and Ragna had known that she would want it too. But she was determined to resist the temptation. She could not say exactly why this was so important, especially as they had already done it once. Her feelings had to do with how happy they both would feel about their marriage when at last they were able to yield to their desires without guilt or fear.

All the same, she kissed him.

She leaned over his broad chest. She grasped the hem of his blanket in both hands, keeping it in place as an additional barrier between their bodies. Then she slowly lowered her head until their lips met.

He made a low sound of satisfaction.

She ran her tongue around his mouth, feeling his soft lips and the bristle of his moustache. He buried one big hand in the thickness of her hair, dislodging her scarf. But when his other hand reached for her breast she pulled away. 'I have a gift for you,' she said.

'You have several,' he said in a voice thick with desire.

'I brought you a belt from Rouen with a lovely silver buckle, but it was stolen from me on the journey.'

'Where?' he said. 'Where were you robbed?' He was responsible for law and order, she knew, and any theft reflected on him.

'Between Mudeford and Dreng's Ferry. The thief wore an old helmet.'

'Ironface,' he said angrily. 'The reeve of Mudeford has searched the forest but can't find his hideout. I'm going to tell him to search again.'

She had not meant to complain, and she was sorry she had angered him. She moved quickly to rescue the romantic atmosphere. 'I got you something else, something better,' she said. She got up, looked around, and spotted the whiteness of a candle. She lit it at the fire and stood it on a bench near the head of the bed. Then she took out the arm band she had bought from Cuthbert.

'What's this?' he said.

She brought the candle closer so that he could examine it. He ran a finger over the incised lines of the complex pattern, engraved in the silver and picked out with niello. 'It's exquisite work,' he said, 'but it still has a bold, manly look about it.' He slipped it up his left arm, over the elbow. It fitted closely to the muscles of his upper arm. 'You have such good taste!' he said.

Ragna was thrilled. 'It looks magnificent.'

'I shall be the envy of all England.'

That was not quite what Ragna wanted to hear. She did not want to be a symbol of greatness, like a white horse, or an expensive sword.

He said: 'I want to spend all day kissing you.'

That was more like it, and she leaned towards him again. Now he was more assertive, and when he grasped her breast and she tried to pull away he prevented her, and drew her towards him. She became a little anxious. She still had the physical advantage while he was lying down, but if it came to a real struggle she could not resist him.

Then came the interruption she was expecting. The dog growled, the door creaked, and Gytha's voice said: 'Good morning, my son.'

Ragna took her time breaking the clinch: she wanted Gytha to see how much Wilf wanted her.

Gytha said: 'Oh! Ragna! I didn't know you were here.'

Liar, thought Ragna. The maid had told Gytha that Ragna had gone into Wilf's house, and Gytha had dressed hastily and come to see what was going on.

Ragna turned slowly. She was entitled to kiss her fiancé, and she took pains not to look guilty. 'Mother-in-law,' she said. 'Good morning.' She was polite, but she allowed a hint of irritation into her voice. Gytha was the intruder here, the one who had ventured where she had no right to go.

Gytha said: 'Shall I send the barber to shave your chin, Wilf?'

'Not today,' he said with a touch of impatience. 'I'll shave on the morning of the wedding.' He spoke as if she should have known this, and it was obvious that she had asked only because she needed a pretext for being there.

Ragna rearranged her headdress, taking more time than she needed, underlining the fact that Gytha had intruded upon a moment of intimacy. While tying the scarf she said: 'Show Gytha your gift, Wilf.'

Wilf pointed to the band on his arm. It glinted in the firelight.

'Very attractive,' said Gytha without warmth. 'Silver is always good value.' It was cheaper than gold, she was implying.

Ragna ignored the jibe. 'And now, Wilf, I must ask you for something.'

'Anything, my beloved.'

'You've put me in a very poor house.'

He was startled. 'Have I?'

His surprise confirmed Ragna's suspicion that he had left this to Gytha. Ragna said: 'It has no window, and the walls let in the cold air at night.'

Wilf looked at Gytha. 'Is this true?'

She said: 'It's not that bad.'

That answer angered Wilf. 'My fiancée deserves the best of everything!' he said.

'It's the only house available,' Gytha protested.

Ragna said: 'Not quite.'

'There is no other empty house,' Gytha insisted.

'But Wigelm doesn't really need a house for himself and his men-at-arms,' Ragna said in a tone of gentle rationality. 'His wife isn't even here. Their home is at Combe.'

Gytha said: 'Wigelm is the ealdorman's brother!'

'And I am the ealdorman's bride.' Ragna was working hard to suppress her anger. 'Wigelm is a man, with a man's simple needs, but I am a bride preparing for my wedding day.' She turned her gaze to Wilf. 'Which of us do you wish to favour?'

There was only one possible answer a bridegroom could make. 'You, of course,' he said.

'And after the wedding,' she said, holding Wilf's gaze, 'I will be closer to you at night, for Wigelm's house is right next door.'

He smiled. 'That clinches it.'

Wilf had made up his mind, and Gytha gave in. She was too wise to argue when she had already lost. 'Very well,' she said. 'I'll swap

Ragna and Wigelm.' She could not resist adding: 'Wigelm won't like it.'

Wilf said crisply: 'If he complains, just remind him which brother is the ealdorman.'

Gytha bowed her head. 'Of course.'

Ragna had won, and Wilf was displeased with Gytha. Ragna decided to push her luck. 'Forgive me, Wilf, but I need both houses.'

Gytha said: 'What on earth for? No one has two houses.'

'I want my men nearby. At present they're lodged in the town.'

Gytha said: 'Why do you need men-at-arms?'

Ragna gave her a haughty look. 'It is my preference,' she said. 'And I am about to be the ealdorman's wife.' She turned her face to Wilf.

Now he was losing patience. 'Gytha, give her what she wants, and no more argument.'

'Very well,' said Gytha.

'Thank you, my love,' said Ragna, and she kissed him again.

12

ON THE DAY OF the hundred court, Edgar was nervous but determined.

The Hundred of Dreng's Ferry consisted of five small settlements, widely scattered. Bathford was the largest village, but Dreng's Ferry was the administrative centre, and the dean of the minster traditionally presided over the court.

Court was held every four weeks. It took place out-of-doors, regardless of the weather, but today happened to be bright, though cold. The big wooden chair was positioned outside the west end of the church, and a small table was set beside it. Father Deorwin, the oldest priest, brought from underneath the altar the pyx. Made by Cuthbert, this was a round silver container with a hinged lid, its sides engraved with images of the crucifixion. It held a consecrated wafer from the Mass, and it would be used today for administering oaths.

Men and women from all five villages came, including children and slaves, some on horseback but most on foot. Everyone showed up if they possibly could, because the court made decisions that affected their everyday lives. Even Mother Agatha was there, though not any of the other nuns. Women were not allowed to testify, at least in theory, but strong characters such as Edgar's ma often spoke their minds.

Edgar had attended court many times in Combe. On several occasions his father had been obliged to bring suit against people who were slow to pay their bills. His brother Eadbald had gone through a phase of minor delinquency and had twice been charged with fighting in the street. So Edgar was not unfamiliar with the law and legal proceedings.

Today there was more excitement than usual, because an accusation of murder was to be heard.

Edgar's brothers had tried to talk him out of bringing the charge. They did not want trouble. 'Dreng is our father-in-law,' Eadbald had said, watching Edgar trimming a rough-hewn stone into a neat oblong shape, using his new hammer and chisel.

Anger made Edgar's arm strong as he struck flakes off the stone. 'That doesn't mean he can break the law.'

'No, but it means my brother can't be his accuser.' Eadbald was the more intelligent of Edgar's two brothers, capable of a persuasive rational argument.

Edgar had put down his tools to give Eadbald his full attention. 'How can I keep silent?' he had replied. 'A murder has been done, here in our village. We can't pretend it never happened.'

'I don't see why not,' Eadbald had said. 'We're just getting settled here. People are accepting us. Why do you have to make trouble?'

'Murder is wrong!' Edgar had said. 'What other reason should I need?'

Eadbald had made a frustrated noise and walked away.

The other brother, Erman, had accosted Edgar that evening outside the tavern. He had taken a different tack. 'Degbert Baldhead presides over the hundred court,' he had said. 'He will make sure the court doesn't convict his brother.'

'He may not be able to do that,' Edgar had replied. 'The law is the law.'

'And Degbert is the dean, and our landlord.'

Edgar knew that Erman was right, but it made no difference. 'Degbert may do what he wants, and answer for it on the Day of Judgement, but I won't condone the killing of a child.'

'Aren't you scared? Degbert is the power here.'

'Yes,' said Edgar. 'I'm scared.'

Cuthbert had also tried to dissuade him. Edgar had made his new tools in Cuthbert's workshop, which was the only forge in Dreng's Ferry. There was more sharing here than there had been in the town of Combe, Edgar had learned: a small place had limited facilities and everyone needed help sooner or later. As Edgar was shaping his new tools on Cuthbert's anvil, the clergyman had said: 'Degbert is furious with you.'

Edgar guessed that Cuthbert had been told to say this. The man was too timid ever to venture a criticism on his own initiative.

'I can't help that,' Edgar had said.

'He's a bad man to have as an enemy.' Genuine fear was audible in Cuthbert's tone: clearly he was terrified of the dean.

'I don't doubt it.'

'And he comes from a powerful family. Ealdorman Wilwulf is his cousin.'

Edgar knew all that. Exasperated, he said: 'You're a man of God, Cuthbert. Can you stand silently by when murder is done?'

Cuthbert could, of course; he was weak. But he took offence at Edgar's question. 'I didn't see any murder,' he had said peevishly, and he had walked away.

As the people were assembling, Father Deorwin spoke to the most important of them, especially the headmen of each village. Edgar knew, from having attended previous hundred courts, that Deorwin was asking whether they had issues they needed to bring before the court, and making a mental list to communicate to Degbert.

Finally Degbert emerged from the priests' house and sat in the chair.

In principle, what happened at a hundred court was that the people of the neighbourhood reached a collective decision. In practice, the court was often presided over by a rich nobleman or a senior clergyman who might dominate proceedings. However, some degree of consensus was needed, because it was difficult for one side to compel the other. A nobleman could make life difficult for the peasants in a dozen different ways, but the peasants could simply refuse to obey him. There was no machinery for enforcing court decisions other than general consent. So court often involved a power struggle between two more or less equal forces, as when a sailor found that the wind was blowing his boat one way while the tide took it another.

Degbert announced that the court would first discuss the sharing of the ox team.

There was no rule that said he had the right to set the agenda. In some places the headman of the largest village would take that role. But Degbert had long ago seized the privilege.

The sharing of the ox team was a perennial issue. Dreng's Ferry had no heavy plough land, but the other four settlements had clay soil and shared a team of eight oxen, which had to be driven from one place to another during the winter ploughing season. The ideal time was when it got cold enough to stop the weeds growing and wet enough for the ground to have softened after the dryness of summer. But everyone wanted the ox team first, because villages that ploughed later might have to contend with drenched and slimy soil.

On this occasion the headman of Bathford, a wise old greybeard called Nothelm, had worked out a reasonable compromise, and Degbert, who had no interest in ploughing, made no objection.

Next Degbert invited Offa, the reeve of Mudeford, to speak. He had been ordered by Ealdorman Wilwulf to search – again – for the hideout of Ironface, who had had the temerity to rob Wilwulf's bride-to-be. Offa was a big man of about thirty with a twisted nose, probably from some battle. He said: 'I searched the south bank between here and Mudeford, and questioned everyone I met, even Saemar the smelly shepherd.' There was a chuckle from the crowd:

everyone knew Sam. 'We think Ironface must live on the south bank, because he always robs there, but I searched the north bank anyway. Same as always, there's no trace of him.'

No one was surprised. Ironface had been evading justice for years.

At last it was time to hear Edgar. First Degbert called on him to swear an oath. Edgar put his hand on the silver pyx and said: 'By Almighty God I say that Dreng the ferryman murdered an unnamed boy born to Blod the slave by throwing the newborn baby into the river twelve days ago. I saw this with my own eyes and heard it with my own ears. Amen.'

There was a murmur of revulsion from the crowd. They had known in advance what the charge was, but perhaps they had been unaware of the details; or maybe they knew but were horrified to hear them spoken out loud in Edgar's clear voice. Whatever the reason, Edgar was glad they were shocked. They should be. And perhaps their indignation would shame Degbert into agreeing to some kind of justice.

Now, before the case went farther, Edgar said: 'Dean Degbert, you cannot preside over this trial. The accused man is your brother.'

Degbert pretended to be affronted. 'Are you suggesting that I might judge corruptly? You may be punished for that.'

Edgar had anticipated this reaction, and he had his answer ready. 'No, dean, but a man should not be asked to condemn his own brother.' He saw some among the crowd nod approvingly. Villagers were jealous of their rights and resentful of the tendency of noblemen to domineer over local courts.

Degbert said: 'I am a priest, the dean of the minster, and the lord of the village. I shall continue to preside over this hundred court.'

Edgar persisted, not because he thought he could win the argument, but to emphasize Degbert's bias more strongly to the villagers. 'The headman of Bathford, Nothelm, could perfectly well preside.'

'Quite unnecessary.'

Edgar conceded defeat with a nod. He had made his point.

Degbert said: 'Do you wish to call any oath-helpers?'

An oath-helper was someone who would swear that someone else was telling the truth, or simply that he was an honest man. The weight of the oath was greater if the swearer was someone of high status.

Edgar said: 'I call Blod.'

'A slave can't testify,' said Degbert.

Edgar had seen slaves testify in Combe, though not often, and he said: 'That's not the law.'

'I'll tell you what the law is and is not,' said Degbert. 'You can't even read.'

He was right, and Edgar had to give in. He said: 'In that case I call Mildred, my mother.'

Mildred put her hand on the pyx and said: 'By the Lord, the oath is pure and not false that Edgar swore.'

Degbert said: 'Any more?'

Edgar shook his head. He had asked Erman and Eadbald, but they had refused to swear against their father-in-law. He had not even bothered to ask Leaf or Ethel, who could not testify against their husband.

Degbert said: 'What does Dreng say to the accusation?'

Dreng stepped forward and put his hand on the pyx.

Now, Edgar thought, will he risk his immortal soul?

Dreng said: 'By the Lord, I am guiltless both of deed and instigation of the crime with which Edgar charges me.'

Edgar gasped. It was perjury, and his hand was on the holy object. But Dreng seemed oblivious of the damnation he was risking.

'Any oath-helpers?'

Dreng called Leaf, Ethel, Cwenburg, Edith, and all the clergy of the minster. They formed an impressively high-status group, but they were all dependent in some way on either Dreng or Degbert. How would the villagers of the hundred weigh their oaths? Edgar could not guess.

Degbert asked him: 'Anything else to say?'

Edgar realized that he did. 'Three months ago the Vikings killed my father and the girl I loved,' he said. The crowd had not been expecting this, and they went quiet, wondering what was coming. 'There was no justice, because the Vikings are savages. They worship false gods, and their gods laugh to see them murder men and rape women and steal from honest families.'

There was a hum of agreement. Some of the crowd had direct experience of the Vikings, and most of the others probably knew people who had suffered. They all hated the Vikings.

Edgar went on: 'But we're not like that, are we? We know the true God and we obey his laws. And he tells us: Thou shalt not kill. I ask the court to punish this murderer, in accordance with God's will, and prove that we are not savages.'

Degbert said quickly: 'That's the first time I've been lectured on God's will by an eighteen-year-old boatbuilder.'

It was a clever put-down, but the onlookers had been rendered solemn by the horror of the case, and they were in no mood to laugh at witticisms. Edgar felt he had won their support. People were looking at him with approval in their eyes.

But would they defy Degbert?

Degbert invited Dreng to speak. 'I'm not guilty,' Dreng said. 'The baby was stillborn. It was dead when I picked it up. That's why I threw it in the river.'

Edgar was outraged by this blatant lie. 'He wasn't dead!'

'Yes, it was. I tried to say that at the time, but no one was listening: Leaf was screaming her head off and you jumped straight into the river.'

Dreng's confident tone made Edgar even angrier. 'He cried when you threw him – I heard it! And then the crying stopped when he fell naked into the cold water.'

A woman in the crowd murmured: 'Oh, the poor mite!' It was Ebba, who did laundry for the minster, Edgar saw. Even those who depended on Degbert for their living were shocked. But would that be enough?

Dreng continued in the same sneering tone: 'How could you hear him cry, with Leaf screaming?'

For a moment Edgar was floored by the question. How could he have heard? Then the answer came to him. 'The same way you can hear two people talking. Their voices are different.'

'No, lad.' Dreng shook his head. 'You made a mistake. You thought you saw a murder when you didn't. Now you're too proud to admit that you were wrong.'

Dreng's voice was unattractive and his attitude arrogant, but his story was infuriatingly plausible, and Edgar feared that the people might believe him.

Degbert said: 'Sister Agatha, when you found the baby on the beach, was it alive or dead?'

'He was near death, but still alive,' said the nun.

A voice in the crowd spoke up, and Edgar recognized Theodberht Clubfoot, a sheep farmer with pastures a couple of miles downriver. He said: 'Did Dreng touch the body? Afterwards, I mean?'

Edgar knew why he was asking the question. People believed that if the murderer touched the corpse it would bleed afresh. Edgar had no idea whether that was true.

Blod shouted out: 'No he did not! I kept my baby's body away from that monster.'

Degbert said: 'What do you say, Dreng?'

'I'm not sure whether I did or not,' Dreng said. 'I would have, if necessary, but I don't believe I had any reason to.'

It was inconclusive.

Degbert turned to Leaf. 'You were the only one there, other than Dreng and his accuser, when Dreng threw the baby.' That was true: Ethel had passed out in the alehouse. 'You screamed, but are you now sure it was alive? Could you have made a mistake?'

All Edgar wanted was for Leaf to tell the truth. But would she have the courage?

She said defiantly: 'The baby was born alive.'

'But it died before Dreng threw the body into the river,' Degbert persisted. 'However, at the time, you imagined it was still alive. That was your mistake, wasn't it?'

Degbert was bullying Leaf outrageously, but no one could stop him.

Leaf looked from Degbert to Edgar to Dreng, with panic in her eyes. Then she looked at the floor. She was silent for a long moment, and then when she spoke it was almost a whisper. 'I think . . .' The crowd went quiet as everyone strained to hear her words. 'I might have made a mistake,' she said.

Edgar despaired. She was obviously a terrified woman giving false evidence under pressure. But she had said what Dreng needed her to say.

Degbert looked at the crowd. 'The evidence is clear,' he announced. 'The baby was dead. Edgar's accusation is not proved.'

Edgar stared at the villagers. They looked unhappy, but he saw at once that they were not angry enough to go against the two most powerful men in the neighbourhood. He felt sick. Dreng was going to get away with it. Justice had been refused.

Degbert went on: 'Dreng is guilty of the crime of improper burial.'

That was clever, Edgar saw bitterly. The baby had now been buried in the churchyard, but at the time Dreng had, by his own account, disposed of a body illicitly. More importantly, he would now be punished for a minor offence, and that would make it a bit easier for the villagers to accept that he had got away with the greater crime.

Degbert said: 'He is fined six pence.'

It was too little, and the villagers muttered, but they were discontented rather than rebellious.

Then Blod cried out: 'Six pence?'

The crowd went silent. Everyone looked at Blod.

Tears were streaming down her face. 'Six pence, for my baby?' she said.

She turned her back on Degbert eloquently. She strode away, but after half a dozen paces she stopped, turned, and spoke again. 'You English,' she said, her voice choked with grief and rage.

She spat on the ground.

Then she walked away.

ÞÞÞ

DRENG HAD WON, but something shifted in the hamlet. Attitudes to Dreng had changed, Edgar mused as he ate his midday meal in the alehouse. People such as Edith, the wife of Degbert, and Bebbe, who supplied the minster with food, would in the past have stopped to talk to Dreng when their paths crossed, but now they just spoke a brief word and hurried on. Most evenings the alehouse was empty, or nearly so: Degbert sometimes came to drink Leaf's strong ale, but others stayed away. People were polite to Degbert and Dreng, to the point of deference, but there was no warmth. It was as if the inhabitants were trying to make amends for their failure to insist on justice. Edgar did not think God would consider that sufficient.

When those who had testified for Dreng walked past Edgar, as he worked on building the new brewhouse, they looked shamefaced and avoided his eye. One day on Leper Island, as he was delivering a barrel of ale to the nuns, Mother Agatha went out of her way to speak to him and tell him he had done the right thing. 'Justice will be done in the next life,' she had said. Edgar had felt grateful for her support, but he wanted justice in this life too.

In the alehouse Dreng was more bad-tempered than ever. He slapped Leaf for giving him a cup of ale with dregs in it, punched Ethel in the stomach when his porridge was cold, and knocked Blod to the ground with a blow to the head for no reason at all. Each time he acted quickly, giving Edgar no chance to intervene; and then, after the blow was struck, he directed a challenging look at Edgar, defying him to do something about it. Unable to prevent what had already been done, Edgar would just look away.

Dreng never hit Edgar. Edgar was glad. He had within him such a build-up of rage that if a fight started it might not stop until Dreng was dead. And Dreng seemed to sense that, and held back.

Blod was oddly calm. She did her work and obeyed orders without protest. Dreng continued to treat her with contempt. However, when she looked at him her eyes blazed with hatred, and as the days went by Edgar could see that Dreng was scared of her. Perhaps he feared she would kill him. Perhaps she would.

While Edgar was eating, Brindle barked a warning. A stranger was approaching. As it was probably a ferry passenger, Edgar got up from the table and went outside. Two poorly dressed men with a packhorse were approaching from the north. Tanned hides were piled high on the back of the horse.

Edgar greeted them and said: 'Do you want to cross the river?'

'Yes,' said the older of the two. 'We're going to Combe to sell our leather to an exporter.'

Edgar nodded. The English killed many cows, and their hides were often sold to France. But something about the men made Edgar wonder whether they had acquired the leather honestly. 'The fare is a farthing per person or animal,' he said, not sure they could afford it.

'All right, but we'll take a bite to eat and a pot of ale first, if this is an alehouse.'

'It is.'

They unloaded the beast, to give it a rest, and put it to graze while they went inside. Edgar returned to his dinner, and Leaf gave the travellers ale while Ethel served them from the stew pot. Dreng asked them what was the news.

'The ealdorman's bride has arrived from Normandy,' said the older visitor.

'We knew that – the Lady Ragna spent a night here on the way,' Dreng said proudly.

Edgar said: 'When's the wedding?'

'All Saints' Day.'

'So soon!'

'Wilwulf is impatient.'

Dreng sniggered. 'I'm not surprised. She's a beauty.'

'That, too, but he needs to ride against the Welsh raiders, and he won't go until he's married.'

'I don't blame him,' Dreng said. 'It would be a shame to die and leave her a virgin.'

'The Welsh have taken advantage of his delay.'

'I'm sure they have, the barbarians.'

Edgar almost laughed. He wanted to ask whether the Welsh were so barbaric as to murder newborn babies, but he held his tongue. He shot a look at Blod, but she seemed oblivious to the slur on her people.

The older traveller continued: 'They've already penetrated farther than anyone can remember. There's a lot of discontent about it. Some say it's the ealdorman's duty to protect people first, and get married after.'

'None of their damn business,' Dreng said. He did not like to hear people criticize the nobility. 'I don't know who these people think they are.'

'We hear the Welsh have reached Trench.'

Edgar was startled, as was Dreng. 'That's only a couple of days from here!' said Dreng.

'I know. I'm glad we're headed in the opposite direction, with our valuable load.'

Edgar finished his food and went back to work. The brewhouse was rising quickly, one course of stones on top of another. Soon he would have to shape timbers for the roof.

Dreng's Ferry had no defences of any kind against a Welsh incursion, he reflected; nor, for that matter, against a Viking raid should the Vikings ever get this far upriver. On the other hand, raiders might think there was not much for them in a little place such as this – unless they knew about Cuthbert and his jewellery workshop. England was a dangerous place, Edgar thought, with the Vikings in the east and the Welsh in the west, and men such as Dreng in the middle.

After an hour the travellers reloaded their horse and Edgar poled them across the river.

When he got back he found Blod hiding inside the half-built brewhouse. She was crying, and there was blood on her dress. 'What happened?' he said.

'Those two men paid to fuck me,' she said.

Edgar was shocked. 'But it's not two weeks since you had the baby!' He was not sure how long women were supposed to abstain, but surely it would take a month or two to recover from what he had seen Blod go through.

'That's why it hurt so much,' she said. 'Then the second one wouldn't pay the full amount because he said I spoiled it by crying. So now Dreng is going to beat me.'

'Oh, merciful Jesus,' Edgar said. 'What are you going to do?'

'I'm going to kill him before he kills me.'

Edgar did not think she should do that, but he asked a practical question. 'How?' Blod had a knife, as did everyone over the age of about five, but hers was small, like a child's, and she was not allowed to keep it too sharp. She could not kill anyone with that.

She said: 'I'm going to get up in the night, take your axe off its hook, and sink the blade into Dreng's heart.'

'They'll execute you.'

'But I'll die satisfied.'

'I've got a better idea,' said Edgar. 'Why don't you run away? You could sneak out when they go to sleep – they're usually drunk by nightfall, they won't wake. This is a good time: the Welsh raiders are only two days away. Travel by night and hide by day. You could join up with your own people.'

'What about the hue and cry?'

Edgar nodded. The hue and cry was the means by which offenders were arrested. All men were obliged, by law, to chase after anyone who committed a crime within the hundred. If they refused, they were liable for the cost of the damage caused by the crime, usually the value of the goods stolen. Men rarely refused: it was in their interest to capture criminals, and anyway the chase was exciting. If Blod ran away, Dreng would start a hue and cry, and in all probability Blod would be recaptured.

But Edgar had thought of that. 'After you've gone, I'll take the ferry boat downstream and beach it somewhere, then walk back. When they see that it's gone, they'll think you must have used it to escape, and they'll assume you will have gone downstream, to travel faster and put the maximum distance between yourself and them. So they'll search for you along the river to the east. Meanwhile you'll be headed the opposite way.'

Blod's pinched face lit up with hope. 'Do you really believe I could escape?'

'I don't know,' said Edgar.

ÞÞÞ

IT WAS NOT until later that Edgar realized what he had done.

If he helped Blod escape, he would be committing a crime. Just days ago he had stood up in the hundred court and insisted that the law must be obeyed. Now he was about to break it. If he was found out, his neighbours would have little mercy on him; they would call him a hypocrite. He would be sentenced to pay Dreng the price of a new slave. He would be in debt for years. He might even have to become a slave himself.

But he could not go back on his word. He did not even want to. He was sickened by Dreng's treatment of Blod and he felt he could not let it continue. Perhaps there were principles more important than the rule of law.

He would just have to make sure he did not get caught.

Dreng had been drinking more than usual since the hundred court, and that evening was no exception. By dusk he was slurring his speech. His wives encouraged him, for when he was drunk his punches often missed their target. At nightfall he just about managed to undo his belt and wrap himself in his cloak before passing out in the rushes on the floor.

Leaf always drank a lot. Edgar suspected she did it to make herself unattractive to Dreng. Edgar had never seen the two of them embrace. Ethel was Dreng's choice for sex, when he was sober enough, but that was not often.

Ethel was not as quick as the others to fall asleep, and Edgar listened to her breathing, waiting for it to fall into the steady rhythm of slumber. He was reminded of the night four months ago when he had lain awake in his family's house at Combe. He felt the pain of grief as he remembered how exciting the future had seemed with Sunni, and how bleak it turned out to be without her.

Both Leaf and Dreng were snoring, Leaf in a steady drone, Dreng in great snorts followed by gasps. At last Ethel's breathing became regular. Edgar looked across the room at Blod. He could see her face in the firelight. Her eyes were open, and she was waiting for a signal from him.

This was the moment of final decision.

Edgar sat upright, and Dreng moved.

Edgar lay back down.

Dreng stopped snoring, turned over, breathed normally for a minute, then scrambled to his feet. He picked up a cup, filled it from the water bucket, drank, and went back to his place on the floor.

After a while he resumed snoring.

There will never be a better time, Edgar thought. He sat up. Blod did the same.

They both stood up. Edgar's hearing was alert for any change in the sound made by the sleepers. He lifted his axe off its hook, stepped softly to the door, and glanced back.

Blod had not followed him. She was bending over Dreng. Edgar felt a flash of panic: was she going to kill her tormentor? Did she think she could silently slit his throat and walk away? That would make Edgar a murderer's accomplice.

In the rushes beside Dreng lay his belt with its attached sheath containing his dagger. It was what he used for general purposes, including to cut up his meat, but it was longer and sharper than Blod's. Edgar stopped breathing. Blod quietly slid the blade out of the sheath, and Edgar felt sure she was about to stab the killer of her child. She straightened up with the knife in her hand. Then she twisted the hilt of the dagger into the cord she used as a belt and turned towards the door.

Edgar suppressed a grunt of relief.

He guessed that Blod had stolen Dreng's dagger as a precaution in case she should meet dangerous men during her night-time travels – a situation in which her own little knife would be of little use.

He opened the door slowly. It creaked, but not loudly.

He held it for Blod and she passed through, followed by Brindle. Fortunately the dog was intelligent enough to know when to be quiet.

Edgar glanced at the sleepers one last time. To his horror, he saw that Ethel's eyes were wide open and she was watching him. His heart seemed to stop.

He stared at her. What would she do? For a long moment both were frozen. Perhaps she was working up the courage to yell a warning and wake Dreng.

But she did nothing.

Edgar stepped out and closed the door softly behind him.

He stood still and quiet outside, waiting for the shout of alarm, but all he heard was the quiet flow of the river. Ethel had decided to let them go. Once again Edgar slumped with relief.

He slung his axe from his belt.

The sky was partly overcast, and the moon peeped from behind a cloud. The river gleamed, but the hamlet was sunk in gloom. Edgar and Blod walked up the hill between the houses. Edgar feared that a dog would hear them and bark, but nothing happened: the village hounds probably recognized their steps, or smelled Brindle, or both. For whatever reason, they decided that no alarm was necessary.

As Edgar and Blod passed the church, Blod turned into the churchyard. Edgar was alarmed. What was she up to?

The grass had not yet grown over the grave of her child. On the turned earth, a pattern of smooth stones formed a cross, something Blod must have done herself. She knelt at the foot of the cross with her hands folded in prayer, and Edgar did the same.

Out of the corner of his eye, Edgar saw someone step out of the priest's house.

He touched Blod's arm to warn her. It was Father Deorwin, he saw. The old man stumbled a few yards then lifted the skirt of his robe. He and Blod froze in position. They were not invisible by any means, but he had to hope that they faded sufficiently into the darkness to elude an old man's eyesight.

Like all children, Edgar had been taught that it was bad manners to stare at someone relieving himself, but now he watched Deorwin warily, praying that the old man would not raise his gaze. However, Deorwin was intent on what he was doing, and had no interest in looking around the hamlet as it slept in darkness. Finally he dropped his robe and slowly turned. For a moment his face was towards Edgar and Blod, and Edgar tensed, waiting for a reaction; but Deorwin seemed not to see them, and went back inside.

They went on, grateful for an old man's poor eyesight.

They continued to the top of the rise. On the ridge the road forked. Blod was heading north-west, towards Trench.

Blod said: 'Goodbye, Edgar.' She looked sad. She should have been happy: she was running away to freedom.

'Good luck,' said Edgar.

'I will never see you again.'

I hope not, Edgar thought; if we meet again, it will mean you have been caught. He said: 'Give my regards to Brioc and Eleri.'

'You remembered my parents' names!'

He shrugged. 'I liked the sound of them.'

'They're going to hear all about you.' She kissed his cheek. 'You've been a friend to me,' she said. 'The only one.'

All he had done was treat her like a human being. 'It wasn't much.'

'It was everything.' She put her arms around him, laid her head on his shoulder, and hugged him hard. She rarely showed emotion, and the passion in her hug surprised him.

She released him and, without speaking again, she walked away along the road. She did not look back.

He watched her until she was out of sight.

He returned down the hill, still treading softly. It seemed no one else was awake. That was good: if he were seen now he could offer no possible excuse. A slave had escaped, and Edgar was up and walking around in the middle of the night: his complicity was undeniable. The consequences of that hardly bore thinking about.

He was tempted to re-enter the alehouse and lie down in cosy safety, but he had promised to lay a false trail for Blod.

He went to the river bank and untied the ferry. Brindle jumped in. Edgar boarded and quietly picked up the pole.

It needed only one thrust to push the ferry out into the current. The flow of water took the vessel around the north side of Leper Island. Edgar deployed the pole to keep away from the banks on both sides.

He floated past the farm. Erman and Eadbald had ploughed the field, and the moon shone on damp furrows. No light showed from the house, not even firelight, for there was no window.

The current was fastest a little to the right of midstream. Brindle stood to attention in the bow, sniffing the air, ears cocked for any sound. They passed through thick woodland interspersed with villages and single-family settlements. An owl hooted, and Brindle growled.

After an hour Edgar began to study the left bank, looking for a suitable place to leave the ferry. He needed a location where the boat might have got tangled in riverside vegetation so badly that a small, thin girl could not extricate it. He had to fake evidence that would tell a plain, clear story. If there was the least flaw, then suspicion would immediately fall on him. There must be no room for doubt.

The place he chose was a small patch of shingle overhung by drooping trees and bushes. He poled to the bank and jumped. With an effort he hauled the heavy boat partly out of the water and pushed it into the vegetation.

He stepped back to study the picture he had created. It looked exactly as if an inexperienced person had lost control and allowed the boat to become entangled and beach itself.

His work was done. Now he had to walk back.

First he needed to cross the river. He took off his tunic and shoes and made a bundle of them. He stepped into the river, holding his clothes above his head with one hand to keep them dry, and swam across. On the other side he dressed quickly, shivering, while Brindle energetically shook herself dry.

Side by side, Edgar and his dog started to walk home.

The forest was not empty of people. However, even Ironface should be asleep now. If anyone was awake and moving nearby, Brindle would give warning. All the same, Edgar drew his axe from his belt, to be ready for anything.

Would his ruse work? Would Dreng and the other residents of the hamlet make the false deduction Edgar was trying to lead them to? Suddenly he could not judge how plausible the whole deception was. Doubts tortured him: he could hardly bear the thought of Blod being recaptured, after all she had been through.

He passed Theodberht Clubfoot's sheepfold, and Theodberht's dog barked. He suffered a moment of anxiety: if Theodberht saw him, the deception would lose all credibility. He hurried on, and the dog quieted. No one came out of the house.

Walking along the bank, occasionally having to fight through vegetation, he found that progress was slower than when on the ferry, and it took him almost two hours to get back. The moon set as he was passing the farm, and the stars were obscured by cloud, so he did the last stretch in thick darkness.

He made his way to the alehouse by memory and feel. Now came the final moment of danger. He paused outside the door, listening. The only sounds from inside were snores. He lifted the latch gently and pulled the door open. The snoring continued undisturbed. He stepped inside. In the firelight he could see three sleeping forms: Dreng, Leaf and Ethel.

He hung his axe on its hook and lowered himself carefully into the straw. Brindle stretched out beside the fire.

Edgar took off his shoes and belt, closed his eyes, and lay down.

After so much tension he thought he would lie awake a long time, but he fell asleep in seconds.

Þ Þ Þ

HE WOKE UP when someone shook his shoulder. He opened his eyes to daylight. It was Ethel rousing him. A quick look around showed him that Dreng and Leaf were still asleep.

With a jerk of her head Ethel beckoned him, then stepped outside. He followed.

He shut the door behind him and spoke in a low voice. 'Thank you for not giving us away.' It was too late for her to do so, because she would have to reveal that she had seen them go and had done nothing. Now she, too, was complicit.

'What happened?' she whispered.

'Blod's gone.'

'I thought you had run away together!'

'Together? Why would I run away?'

'Aren't you in love with Blod?'

'Certainly not.'

'Oh.' Ethel looked thoughtful, readjusting assumptions. 'Then why did you go out with her in the middle of the night?'

'Just to see her on her way.' Edgar did not like lying but, he was beginning to realize, one deception led to another.

Ethel noticed something. 'The boat has gone.'

'I'll tell you the whole story another time,' Edgar said. 'Meanwhile we have to act normally. We say we don't know where Blod is, we don't understand her disappearance, but we're not worried, she's sure to turn up.'

'All right.'

'For a start, I'll get you some wood for the fire.'

Ethel went inside. When Edgar re-entered with the wood, Dreng and Leaf were awake. Dreng said: 'Where's my dagger?'

251

'Where you left it last night,' Leaf said tetchily. She was never cheerful in the morning.

'I left it here, in its sheath, attached to my belt. The belt is in my hand, now, and the sheath, but there's no knife.'

'Well, I haven't got it.'

Edgar dumped the wood and Ethel started to build up the fire.

Dreng looked around. 'Where's that slave?'

No one answered.

Dreng focused on Edgar. 'Why are you fetching wood? That's her job.'

Edgar said: 'I expect she went to the churchyard, to visit the grave of her child. She sometimes does that first thing in the morning, when you're still dead to the world.'

Dreng said indignantly: 'She should be here!'

Edgar picked up the bucket. 'Don't worry, I'll get the water.'

'Fetching the water is her job, not yours.'

Edgar was about to make another conciliatory remark when he realized it would be suspicious if he seemed too emollient, so he let his real feelings show. 'You know something, Dreng? Life makes you so unhappy that I wonder you don't just jump in the godforsaken river and drown your miserable self.'

That got to Dreng. 'You insolent puppy!' he shouted.

Edgar went out.

As soon as he was outside he realized he needed to show surprise at the disappearance of the ferry.

He opened the door again. 'Where's the boat?' he said.

Dreng answered. 'Where it usually is, you foolish boy.'

'No, it's not.'

Dreng came to the door and looked out. 'Then where has it gone?'

'That's what I asked you.'

'Well, you should know.'

'It's your boat.'

'It's floated off. You didn't tie it up properly.'

'I tied it up tight. I always do.'

'I suppose the fairies must have untied it,' Dreng sneered. 'Is that what you're saying?'

'Them, or Ironface.'

'Why would Ironface want a boat?'

'Why would the fairies?'

A suspicion began to dawn on Dreng. 'Where's that slave?'

'You already said that.'

Dreng was malign, but he was not stupid. 'The boat has gone, my dagger has gone, and the slave has gone,' he said.

'What are you saying, Dreng?'

'The slave has escaped on the ferry, you fool. It's obvious.'

For once Edgar did not mind Dreng's abuse. He was glad that Dreng had immediately jumped to the conclusion Edgar had planned. He said: 'I'll go and look in the churchyard.'

'Call at every house – it won't take you long. Tell everyone we have to start the hue and cry unless she's found in the next few minutes.'

Edgar went through the motions. He walked to the graveyard, looked into the church, then entered the priests' house. The mothers were feeding the children. He told the men there was probably going to be a hue and cry – unless Blod suddenly turned up. The younger clergy began to lace up their shoes and put on their cloaks. Edgar looked hard at Deorwin, but the old man ignored him, and appeared unaware of anything untoward in the night.

Edgar went to the home of Fat Bebbe, just so that he could say he had looked for Blod there. Bebbe was asleep, and he did not wake her. Women were not obliged to join the hue and cry, and anyway she would be too slow.

The other residents were small families of servants who worked for the minster, doing cooking, cleaning, laundry and other household chores. He roused Cerdic, who supplied them with firewood from the forest, and Hadwine, called Had, who changed the rushes on their floor.

When he got back to the alehouse the group was already gathering. Degbert and Dreng were on horseback. All the dogs in the hamlet were there, too: they could sniff out a fugitive in hiding. Degbert pointed out that it would be useful to give them some old clothing of Blod's to sniff, so that they would know what smell they were searching for; but Dreng said Blod was wearing all the clothes she had.

Dreng said: 'Edgar, fetch a length of cord from the chest in the house, in case we need to tie the slave up.'

Edgar did as he was told.

When he came out of the alehouse, Dreng raised his voice to address them all. 'She stole the ferry, and it's a heavy vessel for a girl to pole upstream, so it's certain she went downstream.'

Edgar was glad to see that Dreng was set on following the false trail. However, Degbert was not so credulous. 'Might she have untied the boat and let it drift away to set us on the wrong track while she went in a different direction?'

Dreng said: 'She's not that clever.'

There was another flaw in Degbert's scenario, but Edgar did not dare to point it out, for he was fearful of seeming suspiciously keen on the downstream search. However, Cuthbert said it for him. 'The boat wouldn't go far on its own. The current would have taken it to the beach opposite Leper Island.'

Others nodded: that was where most debris fetched up.

Cerdic said: 'There is another boat – the one belonging to the nuns. We could borrow that.'

Cuthbert said: 'Mother Agatha wouldn't lend it willingly. She's angry with us over the death of the baby. She probably thinks Blod should be let go.'

Cerdic shrugged. 'We could just take it.'

Edgar pointed out: 'It's a tiny vessel, with room for only two people. It wouldn't be much help.'

Dreng said decisively: 'I don't want trouble with Agatha, I've got enough to worry about. Let's move. The slave is getting farther away every minute.'

In fact, Edgar thought, she was probably now hiding somewhere in the forest to the north-west, between here and Trench. She would be in the middle of a dense thicket, out of sight, trying to catch some sleep on the cold ground. Most forest creatures were timid, and would stay away from her. Even an aggressive boar or wolf would not attack a human unprovoked, unless the person was evidently wounded or otherwise incapable of defence. The main danger was outlaws such as Ironface, and Edgar had to hope that no one of that type would spot her.

The men of Dreng's Ferry set out, heading downstream on the right bank of the river, and Edgar began to feel that his scheme was working. They stopped at the farmhouse, and Erman and Eadbald joined the group. At the last minute Cwenburg decided to come too. She was almost four months pregnant, but it hardly showed, and she was strong.

The horses turned out to be a hindrance. They were fine where the bank was grassy, but often there was dense forest, and they had to be led through closely entangled shrubs and saplings. Zeal and excitement diminished among men and dogs as the going became more strenuous.

Degbert said: 'Are we sure she came this way? Her homeland lies in the opposite direction.'

This made Edgar anxious.

Fortunately Dreng disagreed with his brother. 'She's headed for Combe,' he said. 'She thinks she won't draw attention there. A big town always has strangers. It's not like a village, where every traveller has to explain himself.'

'I don't know,' said Degbert.

Nobody knew, fortunately, Edgar thought, so they had to go with their best guess, and this was it.

Soon they came to Theodberht Clubfoot's place. A slave was minding the sheep with the help of a dog. The dog barked, and Edgar recognized its voice as the one he had heard in the middle of the night. It was a good thing dogs could not talk.

Theodberht came limping out of the house, followed by his wife. He said: 'What's the hue and cry for?'

'My slave escaped last night,' Dreng said.

'I know her,' said Theodberht. 'I've noticed her in the alehouse. A girl about fourteen.' He seemed about to say more, then glanced at his wife and changed his mind. Edgar guessed he had done more than just notice Blod.

'You haven't seen her in the last twelve hours?' Dreng asked.

'No, but someone passed here in the night. The dog barked.'

'That will have been her,' Dreng said decisively.

The others agreed enthusiastically, and spirits were lifted. Edgar was pleased. Theodberht's dog had done him an unexpected favour.

Dreng said: 'When your dog barked, was it early in the night, or approaching dawn?'

'No idea.'

Theodberht's wife said: 'It was about the middle of the night. I woke too.'

Theodberht said: 'She could be a long way from here by now.'

'Never mind,' said Dreng. 'We'll catch the little bitch.'

'I'd join you,' said Theodberht, 'but I'd only slow you down.'

Dreng grunted, and the group moved on.

Soon afterwards they came to a place Edgar had not seen in the dark. A few yards inland from the river was a fenced corral with three ponies. By the gate of the corral was the biggest mastiff Edgar had ever seen, lying under a crude shelter. He was tied up by a rope just long enough to permit him to attack anyone trying to get at the horses. Alongside the corral was a house in poor condition.

'The horse-catchers,' Degbert said. 'Ulf and Gwen.' There were wild ponies in the forest, shy and nimble, difficult to spot, hard to catch, and highly resistant to being tamed. It was a specialized way of life and the people who followed it were rough-and-ready types, violent to the animals and unsociable with humans.

Two people came out of the house: a small, wiry man and his somewhat larger wife, both wearing dirty clothes and stout leather boots. Ulf said: 'What do you want?'

Dreng said: 'Have you seen my slave? A Welsh girl about fourteen.'

'No.'

'Did anyone pass here in the night? Did your dog bark?'

'He's not meant to bark. He's meant to bite.'

'Would you give us a cup of ale? We'll pay for it.'

'Haven't got no ale.'

Edgar hid a smile. Dreng had met someone even more disagreeable than himself.

Dreng said: 'You ought to join the hue and cry, and help us find her.'

'Not me.'

'It's the law.'

'I don't live in your hundred.'

In all probability, Edgar guessed, no one knew which hundred Ulf and Gwen lived in. That would exempt them from rents and tithes. Given how little wealth they appeared to have, it would not be worth anyone's while to try to pin them down.

Dreng said to Gwen: 'Where's your brother? I thought he lived here with you.'

'Begstan died,' she said.

'Where's his body, then? You didn't bury him at the minster.'

'We took him to Combe.'

'Liar.'

'It's the truth.'

Edgar guessed that they had buried Begstan in the woods to save the price of a priest. But it hardly mattered, and Dreng said impatiently: 'Let's move on.'

The group soon drew near the place where Edgar had beached the ferry. Edgar saw it before anyone else, but he decided he could not be the one who spotted it first: that might arouse suspicion. He waited for someone else to notice it. They were focused on the way ahead, through the forest, and he began to think no one would see it.

At last his brother Erman said: 'Look – isn't that Edgar's boat, on the other side of the river?'

Dreng said sourly: 'It's not his boat, it's mine.'

'But what's it doing there?'

Degbert said: 'It looks as if she sailed this far then, for some reason, she decided to continue on foot on the far side.' He had abandoned the theory of the alternative route, Edgar noted with satisfaction.

Cuthbert was sweating and panting: he was too fat for this kind of work. He said: 'How are we going to get across? The boat is on the other side.'

Dreng said: 'Edgar will go and get it. He can swim.'

Edgar did not mind, but he pretended to be reluctant. He took off his shoes and tunic slowly and then, naked, he slipped shivering into the cold water. He swam across, got into the ferry, and poled it back.

He put his clothes back on while the group boarded. He ferried them across then tied up the boat. Degbert said: 'She's on this side of the river, somewhere between here and Combe.'

Combe was two days from Dreng's Ferry. The hue and cry would not get that far.

At midday they stopped at a village called Longmede, which

marked the south-east boundary of the hundred. No one there had seen a runaway slave, as Edgar already knew. They bought ale and bread from the villagers and sat down to rest.

When they had eaten Degbert said: 'There's been no trace of her since Theodberht's sheepfold.'

Cuthbert said: 'I'm afraid we've lost the scent.'

He just wanted to give up and go home, Edgar guessed.

Dreng protested: 'She's a valuable slave! I can't afford another. I'm not a rich man.'

'It's long past noon,' Degbert said. 'If we want to be home by dark, we have to turn back now.'

Cuthbert said: 'We can go back to the ferry and return in that.'

Dreng said: 'Edgar can pole us.'

'No,' said Edgar. 'We'll be going against the current. It will take two men poling at the same time, and they'll tire after an hour. We'll have to take turns.'

Dreng said: 'I can't do it, I've got a bad back.'

Degbert said decisively: 'We've got enough young men to manage it easily.' He glanced up at the sun. 'But we'd better get started.' He got to his feet.

The group began its return journey.

Blod had escaped, Edgar thought jubilantly. His ruse had worked. The hue and cry had wasted its energy in a futile journey. She was halfway to Trench by now.

He looked down as he walked, hiding the smile of triumph that kept rising to his lips.

13

BISHOP WYNSTAN WAS GOING to be furious, Aldred knew.

The storm broke the day before the wedding. That morning Aldred was summoned by the abbot. The novice who brought the message added that Brother Wigferth of Canterbury had arrived, and Aldred knew right away what this must mean.

The novice found him in the covered walkway that joined the main building of Shiring Abbey to the monks' church. It was there that Aldred had set up his scriptorium, which was nothing more than three stools and a chest of writing materials. One day, he dreamed, the scriptorium would be a dedicated room, warmed by a fire, where a dozen monks would labour all day at copying and illuminating. Right now he had one assistant, Tatwine, recently augmented by a pimply novice called Eadgar, and the three of them sat on stools and wrote on angled boards that rested on their knees.

Aldred set his work aside to dry, then washed the nib of his quill in a bowl of water and wiped it on the sleeve of his robe. He went to the main building and climbed the exterior staircase to the upstairs level. This was the dormitory, and the abbey servants were shaking mattresses and sweeping the floor. He walked the length of the room and entered the private quarters of Abbot Osmund.

The room managed to combine a bare, utilitarian look with a good deal of discreet comfort. A narrow bed up against the wall had a thick mattress and heavy blankets. There was a plain silver cross on the east wall with a prayer stool facing it, and a velvet cushion on the floor, worn and faded but well stuffed to protect Osmund's old knees. The stone jug on the table contained red wine, not ale, and there was a wedge of cheese beside it.

Osmund was not an enthusiast for the mortification of the flesh, as anyone could tell by looking at him. Although he wore the coarse black robe of the monastery, and his head was shaved in the approved monkish tonsure, nevertheless, he was pink-faced and rotund, and his shoes were made of furry squirrel skins.

Treasurer Hildred was beside Osmund. This set-up was familiar to Aldred. Previously it had signified that Hildred disapproved of something Aldred was doing – usually because it cost money – and had persuaded Osmund to issue a reproof. Now Aldred looked keenly at Hildred's thin face, with the sunken cheeks that looked dark even when freshly shaved, and noted that Hildred was not wearing the smug look that would have suggested he was about to spring a trap. In fact, he looked almost benign.

The third monk in the room wore a robe soiled with the mud of a long journey in an English October. 'Brother Wigferth!' said Aldred. 'I'm glad to see you.' They had been novices together at Glastonbury, though Wigferth had looked different then: over the years the face had rounded out, the chin stubble had thickened, and the lean body had grown stout. Wigferth was a frequent visitor to the region, and it was rumoured that he had a mistress in the village of Trench. He was the archbishop's messenger, and collected rents due to the Canterbury monks.

Osmund said: 'Wigferth brings us a letter from Elfric.'

'Good!' said Aldred, though he also felt a shiver of trepidation.

Elfric was the archbishop of Canterbury, the leader of the Christian Church in the southern half of England. He had formerly been the bishop of Ramsbury, not far from Shiring, and Osmund knew him well.

Osmund picked up a sheet of parchment from the table and read aloud. 'Thank you for your report on the distressing situation at Dreng's Ferry.'

Aldred had written that report, though Osmund had signed it. Aldred had detailed the crumbling church, the perfunctory services, and the luxurious home of the married priests. Aldred had also written privately to Wigferth about Dreng, whose two wives and slave prostitute were condoned by his brother, Dean Degbert.

It was this letter that was going to infuriate Bishop Wynstan, when he heard about it, for Wynstan had appointed Degbert, who was his cousin. That was why Osmund had decided to complain directly to Archbishop Elfric: there was no point in talking to Wynstan.

Osmund read on: 'You say the problem can best be remedied by dismissing Degbert and his clergy and replacing them with monks.'

This, too, had been Aldred's suggestion, but it was not an original idea. Elfric himself had done something similar when he arrived at Canterbury, expelling indolent priests and bringing in disciplined monks. Aldred had high hopes that Elfric would agree to do the same at Dreng's Ferry.

'I agree with your proposal,' Osmund read.

'Excellent news!' Aldred said.

'The new monastery will be a cell of Shiring Abbey, with a prior under the authority of the abbot of Shiring.'

That had also been suggested by Aldred. He was pleased. The minster at Dreng's Ferry was an abomination and now it had been condemned.

'Brother Wigferth also carries a letter to our brother in Christ Wynstan, telling him of my decision, as Dreng's Ferry comes within his bishopric.'

Aldred said: 'Wynstan's reaction is going to be interesting.'

Hildred said: 'He will be displeased.'

'To say the least.'

'But Elfric is the archbishop, and Wynstan must bow to his

authority.' For Hildred, a rule was a rule, and that was the end of the matter.

Aldred said: 'Wynstan thinks everyone should follow the rules – except himself.'

'True, but he also has a keen sense of Church politics,' said Osmund comfortably. 'I can't imagine he'll pick a quarrel with his archbishop over a hole in the wall like Dreng's Ferry. If there were more at stake, it might be a different matter.'

Aldred hoped he was right.

He said to Wigferth: 'I'll walk you over to the bishop's palace.'

They went down the outside staircase. 'Thank you for this news!' said Aldred as they crossed the square that formed the centre of the town. 'That dreadful minster made me angry.'

'The archbishop felt the same way when he heard about it.'

They passed Shiring Cathedral, a typical large English church with small windows set high in its thick walls. Next to it was Bishop Wynstan's residence; this and the monastery were the only two-storey edifices in Shiring. Aldred knocked at the door and a young clergyman appeared. Aldred said: 'This is Brother Wigferth, come from Canterbury with a letter from Archbishop Elfric to Bishop Wynstan.'

The clergyman said: 'The bishop is out, but you can give the letter to me.'

Aldred remembered the young man's name: Ithamar. He was a deacon, and served as a secretary to Wynstan. He had a baby face and ash-blond hair, but Aldred felt sure he was no innocent. He said severely: 'Ithamar, this man is a messenger from your master's master. You must welcome him, invite him in, offer him food and drink, and ask if there is any other service you can do for him.'

Ithamar shot him a look of poisonous resentment, but he knew Aldred was right, and after a pause he said: 'Please come in, Brother Wigferth.'

Wigferth remained where he stood and said: 'How long do you think Bishop Wynstan will be away from home?'

'An hour or two.'

'I'll wait.' Wigferth turned to Aldred. 'I'll return as soon as I've delivered the letter. I prefer to sleep at the abbey.'

Good decision, Aldred thought; life at a bishop's residence might offer temptations that a monk would prefer not to struggle with.

They parted. Aldred turned back towards the abbey, then hesitated. It was past time he paid a call on Ealdorman Wilwulf's bride-to-be. The Lady Ragna had been welcoming to Aldred at Cherbourg and he wanted to do the same for her in Shiring. If he went now, he could wish her well for the wedding.

He headed on through the stores and workshops of the town centre.

The rapidly growing town of Shiring existed to serve three establishments: the ealdorman's compound, with its men-at-arms and hangers-on; the cathedral and bishop's palace, with priests and servants; and the abbey, with monks and lay brothers. The tradesmen included makers of pots, buckets, table knives and other domestic hardware; weavers and tailors; saddlers and harness makers; woodcutters and carpenters; armourers making mail, swords, and helmets; bowyers and fletchers; dairymaids, bakers, brewers and slaughterers who provided everyone else with meat.

But the most lucrative industry was embroidery. A dozen women in the town spent their days interlacing designs in coloured wool on sheets of pale linen. Their work usually depicted Bible stories and scenes from the lives of the saints, often decorated with strange birds and abstract borders. The linen, or sometimes pale wool, was eventually incorporated into priestly vestments and royal robes, and sold all over Europe.

Aldred was well known, and folk greeted him on the street. He was obliged to stop and talk to several individuals on his way: a weaver who leased his house from the abbey and was behind with his rent; Abbot Osmund's wine supplier, who had trouble getting money out of Treasurer Hildred; and a woman who wanted the monks to pray for her sick daughter, because everyone knew that the prayers of celibate monks were more efficacious than those of regular priests.

When finally he reached the compound, he found it busy with preparations for the wedding. The gateway was jammed with carts delivering barrels of ale and sacks of flour. Servants were setting up long lines of trestle tables outside: clearly there would be too many guests for them all to dine in the great hall. A butcher was slaughtering animals ready for the spit, and an ox hung by its hind legs from a stout oak tree, hot blood from its mighty neck splashing into a barrel.

Aldred found Ragna in the house that had formerly been occupied by the youngest of the three brothers, Wigelm. The door was open. Ragna was there with three of her servants from Cherbourg: the pretty maid Cat, the seamstress Agnes, and the red-bearded bodyguard called Bern. Also present was Offa, the reeve of Mudeford, and Aldred wondered briefly what he was doing there, but quickly turned his attention to Ragna. With her two maids she was examining silk slippers of different colours, but she looked up and smiled broadly as she recognized Aldred.

'Welcome to England,' he said. 'I've come to see if you're settling in to your new home.'

'There's so much to do!' she said. 'But it's all exciting.'

He studied her animated face. He recalled thinking that she was beautiful, but the memory was a pale imitation of the real thing. His mind had not retained the unique sea-green colour of her eyes, the graceful curve of her high cheekbones, or the luxuriant thickness of her red-gold hair, peeping out now from beneath a brown silk headscarf. Unlike most men he was not led to the sin of lust by the allure of women's breasts, but even he could see that she had a marvellous figure.

He said: 'And how do you feel about the wedding?'

'Impatient!' she said, and then she blushed.

Aldred thought: So that's all right, then. 'I expect Wilf is impatient too,' he said.

'He wants a son,' Ragna said.

Aldred changed the subject to save her blushes. 'I imagine Wigelm was displeased to be ousted from his house.'

'He could hardly claim priority over the ealdorman's bride,' Ragna said. 'Besides, he's on his own – his wife is still at Combe – so he doesn't really need it.'

Aldred looked around. The house was a high-quality timber construction, but not as comfortable as it might have been. Wooden houses needed major repairs after about twenty years and fell apart completely after fifty. He could see a misaligned shutter at the window, a bench with a broken leg, and a leak in the roof. 'You need a carpenter in here,' he said.

She sighed. 'They're all busy making benches and tables for the wedding. And the head carpenter, Dunnere, is usually drunk by afternoon.'

Aldred frowned. The ealdorman's bride ought surely to have priority. 'Can't you get rid of Dunnere?'

'He's Gytha's nephew. But yes, shaking up the maintenance crew here is high on my list.'

'There was a boy at Dreng's Ferry who seemed to be a good craftsman: Edgar.'

'I remember him. Could I ask him to fix up this house?'

'You don't need to ask when you can command. Edgar's master is Dreng, Wilwulf's cousin. Just order Dreng to send his servant to you.'

She smiled. 'I'm still not sure what I'm entitled to here. But I'll take your advice.'

A vague thought was nagging at Aldred. He had the sense that Ragna had said something important, but he had missed its significance. Now he could not recall it.

He said: 'How do you like Wilwulf's family?'

'I've talked to Gytha, and she has accepted that I'm to be mistress here; but I have a lot to learn and I wish I could depend on her help.'

'I feel sure you'll win everyone's affection. I've seen you do it.'

'I hope you're right.'

She was wary, but nevertheless Aldred was not sure she fully understood what she had let herself in for. He said: 'It's unusual for two brothers to be bishop and ealdorman in the same territory. It gives a great deal of power to one family.'

'It makes sense. Wilf needs someone he can trust as bishop.'

Aldred hesitated. 'I wouldn't say he exactly trusts Wynstan.'

Ragna looked interested.

Aldred had to be careful of his words. To him, Wilwulf and his family were wild cats in a cage, always on the brink of attacking one another, kept from violence only by self-interest; but he did not want to say so bluntly to Ragna, for fear of demoralizing her. He needed to warn her without scaring her. 'I'd say his brothers are less likely to surprise him, that's all.'

'The king must like the family, to have given them such power.'

'Perhaps he did, once.'

'What do you mean?'

She did not know, Aldred realized. 'Wilwulf is out of favour with King Ethelred because of the treaty with your father. He should have asked the king's permission.'

'He told us that permission would be readily forthcoming.'

'It wasn't.'

'My father was worried about that. Was Wilf punished?'

'He was fined by the king. But he hasn't paid the fine. He thinks Ethelred is being unreasonable.'

'What will happen?'

'Nothing much, in the short term. If a nobleman boldly defies the royal court, there's not much a king can do immediately. In the long run, who knows?'

'Is there anyone who acts as a counterbalance to the family's power? Any post Wilf was unable to fill with his own appointee?'

It was the key question, and Ragna went up in Aldred's estimation for asking it. She had learned everything her father had to teach her, Aldred guessed, and perhaps she had even added wisdom of her own. 'Yes,' he said. 'The sheriff, Den.'

'Sheriff? We don't have such a thing in Normandy.'

'He's the shire reeve, the king's representative in the locality. Wilwulf wanted Wigelm to have the job, but King Ethelred refused and put in his own man. They may call him Ethelred the Misled, but he's not completely stupid.'

'Is it an important role?'

'Sheriffs have recently grown more powerful.'

'How come?'

'It has to do with the Vikings. Twice in the last six years Ethelred has bought off a Viking invasion with a cash payment – but it's hugely expensive. Six years ago he paid ten thousand pounds; three years ago it was sixteen thousand.'

'We heard about that in Normandy. My father said it was like feeding a lion in the hope that it would stop him eating you.'

'Many people here said something similar.'

'But how did it make sheriffs powerful?'

'They had to collect the money. That meant they had to have the power of enforcement. A sheriff now has his own military force, small but well paid and well armed.'

'And that makes him a countervailing power to Wilf.'

'Exactly.'

'Doesn't the sheriff's role clash with that of the ealdorman?'

'All the time. The ealdorman is responsible for justice, but the sheriff must deal with offences against the king, which includes not paying tax. Obviously there are borderline cases that cause friction.'

'How interesting.'

She was like a musician putting her fingers on the strings of a lyre, Aldred thought, trying it out before playing it. She was going to be a force in the region. She might do a lot of good. On the other hand, she might be destroyed.

If Aldred could help her, he would. 'Let me know if there's anything I can do for you,' he said. 'Come to the abbey.' It occurred to him that the sight of a woman like Ragna might be more than some of the young monks could bear. 'Or just send a message.'

'Thank you.'

As he turned to the door, his eye was again caught by the large frame and busted nose of Offa. As a minor servant of the ealdorman, the reeve had a house in the town, but as far as Aldred knew he had no business with Ragna.

She saw his glance and said: 'Do you know Offa, the reeve of Mudeford?'

'Yes, of course.' Aldred saw Ragna glance at Agnes, who dropped her eyes shyly, and he saw immediately that Offa was there to court Agnes, evidently with Ragna's approval. Perhaps Ragna was keen for some of her servants to put down roots in England.

He took his leave and walked out of the compound. In the centre of the town, crossing the square between the cathedral and the abbey church, he ran into Wigferth emerging from the bishop's residence. 'Did you deliver the letter to Wynstan?' he said.

'Yes, a few moments ago.'

'Did he boil over?'

'He took the letter and said he would read it later.'

'Hmm.' Aldred almost wished Wynstan had raged: the suspense was becoming unbearable.

The two monks returned to the abbey. The kitchener was serving the midday meal: eel boiled with onions and beans. While they were eating, Brother Godleof read the prologue to the Rule of St Benedict: '*Obsculta, o fili, praecepta magistri, et incline aurem cordis tui.*' Listen, son, and turn the ear of your heart to the precepts of your master. Aldred loved the phrase *aurem cordis*, the ear of the heart. It suggested a way of listening more intense and thoughtful than the norm.

Afterwards the monks filed along the covered walkway to the church for the afternoon service of Nones. It was larger than the church at Dreng's Ferry, but smaller than Shiring Cathedral. It consisted of two rooms, a nave about twelve yards long and a smaller chancel, separated by a narrow arch. The monks entered by a side door. The senior men went into the chancel and took their places around the altar, while the rest stood in three neat rows in the nave, where the congregation would also stand, though there was rarely much of a congregation.

As Aldred stood alongside his brethren, chanting the prayers, he began to feel at peace with himself, with the world and with God. On his travels he had missed this.

However, today the peace did not last long.

A few minutes into the service he heard the opening creak of the west door, the main entrance that was rarely used. All the younger monks turned to see who was coming in. Aldred recognized the pale-blond hair of Bishop Wynstan's young secretary, Deacon Ithamar.

The older monks determinedly carried on with the prayer. Aldred decided that someone had to find out what Ithamar wanted. He stepped out of the line and spoke to Ithamar in a whisper. 'What is it?'

The deacon looked nervous but spoke loudly. 'Bishop Wynstan summons Wigferth of Canterbury.'

Aldred involuntarily glanced at Wigferth, who looked back with a frightened expression on his chubby face. Aldred was scared himself, but decided he was not going to let Wigferth go alone to confront an angry Wynstan: there were still men who responded to an unwelcome message by sending back the messenger's head in a sack. For Wynstan to do such a thing was unlikely, but not impossible.

Aldred faked a confident tone. 'Be so good as to apologize to the bishop and say that Brother Wigferth is at prayer.'

Ithamar clearly did not want to return with that reply. 'The bishop will not be pleased to be told to wait.'

Aldred knew that. He kept his voice calm and reasonable. 'I'm sure Wynstan would not want to interrupt a man of God at prayer.'

Ithamar's expression said clearly that Wynstan had no such scruples, but the young deacon hesitated to voice the thought.

Not all monks were priests, but Aldred was both, and he outranked Ithamar, who was merely a deacon, so Ithamar had to give in to him sooner or later. After a long moment of thought Ithamar came to the same conclusion, and reluctantly left the church.

First blood to the monks, Aldred thought giddily. But his feeling of triumph was muted by the thought that this was surely not over.

He returned to prayer, but his mind was elsewhere. What would happen after the service, when Wigferth would no longer have an excuse? Would Aldred and Wigferth go to the bishop's palace together? Aldred was not suited to the role of bodyguard, but perhaps he was better than nothing. Could he persuade Abbot Osmund to accompany them? Wynstan would surely hesitate to molest an abbot. On the other hand, Osmund was not a brave man. It would be typical of Osmund to say pusillanimously that Elfric of Canterbury had written the message and sent Wigferth, so it was up to Elfric to protect his messenger.

However, the explosion came sooner.

The main door opened again, this time with a bang. The chanting stopped instantly, and every monk turned to look behind. Bishop

Wynstan strode in, his cloak flying. He was followed by Cnebba, one of his men-at-arms. Wynstan was a big man, but Cnebba was bigger.

Aldred was terrified, but he managed to hide it.

Wynstan roared: 'Which one of you is Wigferth of Canterbury?'

Aldred could not have said why, but he was the one who stepped forward to confront Wynstan. 'My lord bishop,' he said, 'you are interrupting the monks at the service of Nones.'

'I'll interrupt whoever I like,' Wynstan shouted.

'Even God?' said Aldred.

Wynstan reddened with anger and his eyes seemed to bulge. Aldred almost stepped back a pace, but forced himself to stand his ground. He saw Cnebba's hand go to his sword.

Behind Aldred, Abbot Osmund spoke from the altar in a voice shaky but determined. 'You'd better not draw that sword in church, Cnebba, unless you want God's eternal curse on your mortal soul.'

Cnebba paled, and his hand flew up as if the sword hilt had burned him.

Perhaps Osmund was not completely without courage, Aldred thought.

Wynstan had lost a little of his momentum. His rage was formidable, but the monks had not succumbed.

Wynstan turned his furious gaze on the abbot. 'Osmund,' he said, 'how dare you complain to the archbishop about a minster that comes under my authority? You've never even been there!'

'But I have,' said Aldred. 'With my own eyes I witnessed the depravity and sin of the church at Dreng's Ferry. It was my duty to report what I had seen.'

'You shut your mouth, lad,' said Wynstan, although he was only a couple of years older. 'I'm talking to the sorcerer, not the sorcerer's cat. It's your abbot, not you, who is trying to seize my minster and add it to his empire.'

Osmund said: 'The minster belongs to God, not men.'

It was another brave riposte, and another blow to Wynstan. Aldred began to believe that Wynstan might have to go away with his tail between his legs.

But defeat in argument only made Wynstan more threatening. 'God has entrusted the minster to me,' he roared. He stepped towards Osmund, and Osmund flinched back. 'Now you listen to me, abbot. I will not permit you to take over the church at Dreng's Ferry.'

Osmund's reply was defiant, but his voice was shaky. 'The decision has been made.'

'But I will fight it in the shire court.'

Osmund quailed. 'That would be unseemly,' he said. 'A public dispute between the two leading men of God in Shiring.'

'You should have thought of that before you wrote a sneaky underhand letter to the archbishop of Canterbury.'

'You must submit to his authority.'

'But I won't. If necessary, I will go to Canterbury and report your sins there.'

'Archbishop Elfric already knows my sins, such as they are.'

'I bet I can think of a few he hasn't heard about.'

Osmund did not have any serious sins, Aldred knew; but Wynstan would probably invent some, and even get people to swear to them, if it suited his purpose.

Osmund said: 'It would be wrong of you to defy your archbishop's will.'

'It was wrong of you to force me to this extreme.'

And that was the puzzling thing, Aldred thought. Wynstan had not been forced into anything. Dreng's Ferry seemed unimportant. Aldred had felt sure it was not worth fighting about. But that had been a mistake: Wynstan was ready to go to war.

Why? The minster paid Wynstan some of its earnings, though that could not be much. It gave Degbert a job, but not a very prestigious one. Degbert was not even a close relative, and anyway Wynstan could easily find him another post.

So what was so important about Dreng's Ferry?

Wynstan was still raving. 'This struggle will go on for years – unless you do the sensible thing today, Osmund, and back down.'

'What do you mean?'

'Write a reply to Elfric.' Wynstan's tone become almost a parody of reasonableness. 'Say that, in a Christian spirit, you do not wish to quarrel with your brother in Christ the bishop of Shiring, who has sincerely promised to put matters right at Dreng's Ferry.'

Wynstan had made no such promise, Aldred noted.

Wynstan went on: 'Explain that Elfric's decision threatens to cause a scandal in the shire, and you do not think the little minster merits such upheaval.'

Osmund hesitated.

Aldred said indignantly: 'God's work always merits upheaval. Our Lord did not hesitate to cause a scandal when he threw the moneychangers out of the temple. The Gospel—'

This time it was Osmund who shut him up. 'Leave this to your elders,' he snapped.

Wynstan said: 'Yes, Aldred, keep your mouth shut. You've done enough damage.'

Aldred bowed his head, but inside he was boiling. Osmund had no need to back down – he had the archbishop on his side!

Osmund said to Wynstan: 'I will consider your complaint prayerfully.'

That was not enough for Wynstan. 'I'm going to write to Elfric today,' he said. 'I shall tell him that his suggestion – his *suggestion* – is not welcome; that you and I have discussed the matter; and that I believe you agree with me, on mature reflection, that the minster should not become a monastery at this moment in time.'

'I've told you,' Osmund said peevishly. 'I shall think about it.'

Wynstan ignored this, sensing that Osmund was weakening. 'Brother Wigferth can take my letter with him.' He stared at the rows of monks, not knowing which one was Wigferth. 'And by the way, if by any chance my letter should fail to reach the archbishop, I will personally take off Wigferth's balls with a rusty knife.'

The monks were shocked to hear such violent language.

Osmund said: 'Leave our church now, bishop, before you further besmear the House of God.'

'Write your letter, Osmund,' said Wynstan. 'Tell Archbishop Elfric that you've changed your mind. Otherwise you'll hear worse.' With that Wynstan turned and strode out of the church.

He thinks he's won, Aldred said to himself.

And I think so too.

14

RAGNA MARRIED WILF ON All Saints' Day, the first of November, a day of alternating sunshine and showers of rain.

The compound was familiar to Ragna now. It smelled of stables, unwashed men, and fish being boiled in the kitchen. It was noisy: dogs barked, children screeched, men yelled and women cackled; the blacksmith hammered out horseshoes and the carpenters split tree trunks with their axes. The west wind blew the clouds across the sky, and the shadows of clouds chased one another over the thatched roofs.

Ragna took breakfast in her house, with just her servants present. She needed a peaceful morning to prepare herself for the ceremony. She felt nervous about how she would look and whether she would play her part correctly. She wanted everything to be perfect for Wilf.

She had been desperately impatient for this day to come, and now she longed for it to be over. Pageantry and ritual were commonplace in her life; what she needed was to lie down with her husband at night. She had resisted the temptation to anticipate the wedding, but it had been a strain. However, she was glad now that she had been firm, for Wilf's desire for her had become stronger every day he waited. She saw it in his eyes, and the way his hand lingered on her arm, and the yearning in his goodnight kiss.

They had spent many hours together just talking. He had told her about his childhood, the death of his mother, the shock of his father's remarriage to Gytha, and the arrival in his life of two younger half-brothers.

However, he did not like to answer questions. She had discovered this when she asked him about his quarrel with King Ethelred. It was an offence to his pride to be interrogated like a prisoner-of-war.

Ragna and Wilf had hunted together once, in the forest between Shiring and Dreng's Ferry. They had stayed overnight in Wilf's hunting lodge, remote and isolated, with stables, kennels, stores and a large house where everyone slept in the rushes on the floor. That evening Wilf had talked at length about his father, who had also been ealdorman of Shiring. The position was not hereditary, and as Wilf recounted the power struggle that had followed his father's death, Ragna had learned a good deal about English politics.

Now, on the day of her wedding, she was glad she knew Wilf so much better than she had when she'd arrived in Shiring.

She had wanted a peaceful morning today, but she did not get it. Her first visitor was Bishop Wynstan, his cloak dripping with rain. He was followed in by Cnebba carrying a stilyard, a straight-beam balance, plus a small box probably containing weights.

Ragna was polite. 'Good morning, my lord bishop, I hope I see you in good health.'

Wynstan took the courtesies as read and got right down to business. 'I'm here to check your dowry.'

'Very well.' Ragna had been expecting this, and became alert for any tricks Wynstan might be up to.

Hanging from the rafters were several ropes, used for various purposes including keeping food out of the reach of mice. Cnebba now attached the stilyard to one such rope.

The iron bar of the balance had two unequal sides: the shorter side had a hanging tray in which to place the item to be weighed, and the longer bore a weight that could slide along a graduated scale. With nothing in the tray and the sliding weight at the innermost mark, the two sides balanced and the bar swung gently in the air.

Cnebba then placed his box on the table and opened it. The weights inside were squat lead cylinders, each with a silver coin embedded in its top to guarantee that it was officially verified. Wynstan said: 'I borrowed these from the Shiring mint.'

Cat moved to pick up a small chest which contained the dowry, but Ragna held up a hand to detain her. Ragna did not trust Wynstan. With Cnebba here to defend him, Wynstan might be tempted to just walk off with the chest under his arm. 'Cnebba can leave us now,' Ragna said.

'I prefer him to stay,' said Wynstan.

'Why?' said Ragna. 'Can he weigh coins better than you?'

'He's my bodyguard.'

'Of whom are you afraid? Me? My maid Cat?'

Wynstan looked at Bern but decided not to answer Ragna's question. 'Very well,' he said. 'Wait outside, Cnebba.'

The bodyguard left.

Ragna said: 'Let's check the balance.' She put a five-pound weight in the tray, causing the short arm of the stilyard to drop. Then she moved the slide on the opposite side outwards until the two arms were in balance. The slide stood at the five-pound mark. The balance was accurate.

Ragna nodded to Bern, who picked up the chest and put it on the table. Ragna unlocked it with a key she had around her neck on a thong.

The chest contained four small leather bags. Ragna put one on the stilyard in place of the five-pound weight. The two arms balanced almost perfectly: the bag was slightly heavier. 'The leather accounts for the insignificant extra weight,' Ragna said.

Wynstan waved a dismissive hand at that. He had a more important concern. He said: 'Show me the coins.'

Ragna emptied the bag onto the table. Hundreds of small silver coins poured out, all of them English, with a cross on one side and the head of King Ethelred on the other. The marriage contract specified English pennies, which contained more silver than French deniers.

Wynstan nodded in satisfaction.

Ragna returned the silver coins to the bag then repeated the entire exercise with the remaining three bags. Each weighed exactly five pounds. The dowry was as promised. She put the bags back in the chest.

Wynstan said: 'I'll take it now, then.'

Ragna gave the chest to Bern. 'When I'm married to Wilf.'

'But you'll be married by noon today!'

'Then the dowry will be handed over at twelve o'clock.'

'That means this check has been pointless. In the next two hours you could steal fifty coins out of each bag.'

Ragna locked the chest, then handed the key to Wynstan. 'There,' she said. 'Now I can't open it and you can't steal it.'

Wynstan pretended to think she was taking caution to ridiculous extremes. 'The guests are arriving already!' he said. 'The oxen and pigs have been roasting all night. The barrels of ale have been tapped. The bakers have a hundred loaves in the ovens. Do you seriously believe Wilf is going to grab your dowry now and cancel the wedding?'

Ragna smiled sweetly. 'I'm going to be your sister-in-law, Wynstan,' she said. 'You must learn to trust me.'

Wynstan grunted and left.

Cnebba came back in and took away the stilyard and the weights. As he went out, Wigelm arrived. He had the family big nose and chin, and the same fair hair and moustache, but there was a petulant cast to his face, as if he perpetually felt unfairly treated. He had on the clothes he had worn yesterday, a black tunic and a brown cloak, as if to tell the world that today was not a special day as far as he was concerned. 'So, my sister,' he said, 'today you lose your virginity.'

Ragna blushed, for she had lost it four months ago.

Fortunately Wigelm misunderstood the cause of her embarrassment. 'Ah, don't be shy,' he said with a lascivious chuckle. 'You'll enjoy it, I promise you.'

You have no idea, Ragna thought.

Wigelm was followed in by a short, voluptuous woman of about his own age, thirty. She was attractive in a plump way, and walked with the sway of a woman who knows she is sexy. She did not introduce herself, and Wigelm made no effort to explain her presence, so Ragna said to her: 'I don't think we've met.'

She did not reply, but Wigelm said: 'My wife, Milly.'

Ragna said: 'I'm glad to see you, Milly.' On impulse she stepped forward and kissed Milly's cheek. 'We are to be sisters,' she said.

Milly's response was cool. 'How strange that is,' she said, 'when we hardly speak one another's language.'

'Oh, anyone can learn a new language,' Ragna said. 'All it takes is a little patience.'

Milly looked around the interior of the house. 'I was told you had a carpenter in to transform the place,' she said.

'Edgar of Dreng's Ferry has been working here for the past week.'

'It looks much the same to me.'

It had been a bit decrepit when Milly had been in charge of it, and no doubt this explained Milly's unfriendliness: she must have felt slighted when Ragna insisted on improvements. Ragna shrugged and said: 'Just a few running repairs,' making light of it.

Gytha came in, and Wigelm said: 'Good day to you, Mother.' Gytha wore a new dress, dark grey with a red lining that showed in flashes, and her long grey hair was pinned up in an elaborate hat.

Ragna immediately felt wary. Gytha sometimes made the servants laugh by imitating Ragna's accent. Cat had reported this to her mistress. Ragna had vaguely noticed the women smiling occasionally when she said something not intended to be amusing, and she guessed that her way of speaking had become a joke in the compound. She could live with that, but she was disappointed in Gytha, whom she wanted as a friend.

However, Gytha now surprised her by saying something kind. 'Do you need any help with your dress and hair, Ragna? I'm ready, and I'll be happy to send you one or two of my maids, if you like.'

'I don't need extra help, but thank you for being so thoughtful,' Ragna said. She meant it: Gytha was the fourth in-law to call on her this morning, but the first to say something nice. Ragna had not yet succeeded in winning the affections of her husband's family, a project she had thought would be easier.

When Dreng limped in she almost groaned aloud.

The ferryman wore a cone-shaped hat that was so tall it looked comical. 'I just dropped by to pay my respects to the Lady Ragna on this auspicious morning,' he said, bowing low. 'We're already acquainted, aren't we, cousin-in-law to be? You honoured my humble alehouse with a visit on your journey here. Good morning, cousin Wigelm, I hope I see you well; and you, cousin Milly; and the Lady Gytha – I never know whether to call you cousin or aunt.'

'More distant than either,' said Gytha sourly.

Ragna noted that Dreng was not warmly received by the family, no doubt because he so obviously exaggerated his closeness to them as a way of enhancing his own status.

Dreng pretended to misunderstand Gytha. 'It *is* a long way to come, thank you for your concern, and of course I have a bad back – a Viking knocked me off my horse at the battle of Watchet, you know – but I couldn't possibly miss this great occasion.'

Wilf walked in, and suddenly Ragna felt that all was well. He took her in his arms and kissed her passionately in front of everyone. He adored her, and the unfriendliness of his family meant nothing.

She broke the embrace, panting, and tried not to look triumphant.

Wilf said: 'The clouds have blown away and the sky is blue. I was afraid we might have to move the banquet indoors, but now I think we can eat outside as planned.'

Dreng nearly burst with excitement. 'Cousin Wilf!' he said, his voice breaking into a falsetto bleat. 'I hope I see you well, such a pleasure to be here, I offer you a thousand congratulations, your bride is an angel, indeed an archangel!'

Wilf gave a nod of patient tolerance, as if to acknowledge that although Dreng was a fool he was family. 'I welcome you, Dreng, but I think this house is getting crowded. My bride needs time to herself as she prepares for the wedding. Out, all of you, come on!'

It was exactly what Ragna wanted him to say, and she smiled in gratitude.

The family trooped out. Before Wilf went he kissed her again, longer this time, until she felt they were in danger of starting the honeymoon right there and then. Finally, he pulled away, breathing hard. 'I'll welcome the guests,' he said. 'Bar the door and give yourself an hour of peace.' He went out.

Ragna let out a long sigh. What a family, she thought: a man like a god, and relatives like a pack of yapping hounds. But she was marrying Wilf, not Wigelm or Dreng or Gytha or Milly.

She sat on a stool for Cat to do her hair. As the maid combed, teased and pinned, Ragna made herself calm. She knew how to behave at ceremonies: move slowly, smile at everyone, do what you're told and, if no one tells you what to do, stand still. Wilf had outlined the programme to her, and she had memorized every word. She might still make mistakes, not knowing anything about English rituals, but if she did, she would just smile and try again.

Cat finished the hairdo with a silk scarf the colour of autumn chestnuts. It covered Ragna's head and neck and was held in place by an embroidered headband. Now Ragna was ready for the dress.

She had bathed earlier and was already wearing the plain tan linen underdress, which would hardly be seen. Over it she donned a wool dress in a colour between green and blue that seemed to make her eyes brighter. It had flared sleeves, the cuffs of which were embroidered with a geometric pattern in gold thread. Cat put a silver cross on a silk band around Ragna's neck so that it hung outside the dress. Finally she put on a blue cloak with a gold-coloured lining.

When she was fully dressed, Cat stared at her and burst into tears.

'What's wrong?' Ragna said.

Cat shook her head. 'Nothing,' she sobbed. 'You're so beautiful.'

There was a knock at the door and a voice called: 'The ealdorman is ready.'

Bern said gruffly: 'That's a bit sooner than expected!'

'You know Wilf,' said Ragna. 'He's impatient.' She raised her voice to speak to the man outside. 'The bride is ready whenever Wilf cares to come and get her.'

'I'll tell him.'

A few minutes went by, then there was a banging at the door, and Wilf's voice said: 'The ealdorman comes for his bride!'

Bern picked up the chest containing the dowry. Cat opened the door. Wilf stood outside in a red cloak. Ragna held her head high and walked out.

Wilf took her arm and they walked slowly across the compound to the front of the great hall. A loud cheer went up from the waiting crowd. Despite the morning's showers, the townspeople had dressed up. None but the wealthiest could afford complete new outfits, but most had a new hat or kerchief, and the sea of brown and black was enlivened by celebratory flashes of yellow and red.

Ceremony was important. Ragna had learned from her father that gaining power was easier than keeping it. Conquest could be a matter merely of killing men and entering a stronghold, but holding on to power was never so simple – and appearances were crucial. People wanted their leader to be big and strong and handsome and rich, and his wife to be young and beautiful. Wilf knew this as well as Ragna did, and together they were giving his subjects what they wanted, and thereby consolidating his authority.

Wilf's family stood in front of the crowd in a semicircle. To one side Ithamar sat at a table with parchment, ink and pens. Although a wedding was not a religious sacrament, the details of property transfers had to be written down and witnessed, and the people who could write were mostly clergy.

Wilf and Ragna faced each other and held hands. When the cheering died down, Wilf said in a loud voice: 'I, Wilwulf, ealdorman of Shiring, take you, Ragna of Cherbourg, to be my wife, and I vow to love you and care for you and be true to you for the rest of my life.'

Ragna could not match the power of his voice, but she spoke clearly and confidently. 'I, Ragna, daughter of Count Hubert of Cherbourg, take you, Wilwulf of Shiring, to be my husband, and I vow to love you and care for you and be true to you for the rest of my life.'

They kissed, and the crowd cheered.

Bishop Wynstan blessed the marriage and said a prayer, then Wilf took from his belt a large ornamental key. 'I give you the key to my house, for it is now your house, to make a home for me by your side.'

Cat passed Ragna a new sword in a richly decorated sheath, and Ragna presented it to Wilf, saying: 'I give you this sword so that you can guard our house, and protect our sons and daughters.'

The symbolic gifts having been exchanged, they moved to the more important financial transactions.

Ragna said: 'As promised by my father to your brother, Bishop Wynstan, I give you twenty pounds of silver.'

Bern stepped forward and placed the chest at Wilwulf's feet.

Wynstan stepped out of the crowd to say: 'I witness that the chest contains the agreed amount.' He handed the key to Wilf.

Wilf said: 'Let the clerk record that I give you the Vale of Outhen, with its five villages and its quarry, and all the income therefrom, for you and your heirs to hold until the Day of Judgement.'

Ragna had not yet seen the Vale of Outhen. She had been told that it was a prosperous neighbourhood. She already owned the district of Saint-Martin in Normandy, and her income would be doubled by the addition of the Vale of Outhen. Whatever problems the future held for her, money was unlikely to be among them.

Grants of territory such as this were the everyday currency of politics in Normandy as well as England. The sovereign gave lands to the great noblemen, who in turned parcelled them out to lesser rulers – called thanes in England, knights in Normandy – thereby creating a web of people who were loyal because they had gained wealth and hoped for more. Every nobleman had to strike a careful balance between giving away enough to generate support and keeping enough to give him superiority.

Now, to everyone's surprise, Wigelm stepped out of the crowd and said: 'Wait.'

Wouldn't it be just like him, Ragna thought, to spoil my wedding somehow.

Wigelm said: 'The Vale of Outhen has been in our family for generations. I question whether my brother Wilf has the right to give it away.'

Bishop Wynstan said: 'It's in the marriage contract!'

'That doesn't make it right,' Wigelm said. 'It belongs in the family.'

'And it remains in the family,' said Wynstan. 'It now belongs to Wilf's wife.'

'And she will leave it to her children when she dies.'

'And they will be Wilf's children, and your nephews and nieces. Why do you raise this objection today? You've known the details of the contract for months.'

'I raise it in front of witnesses.'

Wilf intervened. 'Enough,' he said. 'Wigelm, you're not making any sense. Step back.'

'On the contrary—'

'Be quiet, or I shall become angry.'

Wigelm shut up.

The ceremony moved on, but Ragna was puzzled. Wigelm must have known that his protest would be spurned. Why had he chosen to court rejection at a very public moment? He could not possibly have expected Wilf to change his mind about Outhen. Why had he started a fight he was bound to lose? She shelved the mystery for later consideration.

Wilf said: 'As a pious gift, to mark my wedding, I give the village of Wigleigh to the Church, specifically to the minster at Dreng's Ferry, with the stipulation that the clergy there will pray for my soul, and the soul of my wife, and the souls of our children.'

This kind of gift was commonplace. When a man had achieved wealth and power, and was settling down with a wife to have children, his thoughts turned from earthly desires to heavenly blessings, and he did what he could to secure the comfort of his soul in the afterlife.

The formalities were coming to an end, and Ragna was happy that the ceremony had gone smoothly, except for Wigelm's strange intervention. Ithamar was now writing the names of the witnesses to the marriage, starting with Wilf himself, and followed by all the important people there: Wynstan, Osmund, Degbert and Sheriff Denewald. It was not a long list, and Ragna had expected other visiting clergy, perhaps the neighbouring bishops – Winchester, Sherborne and Northwood – and leading monks, such as the abbot of Glastonbury. But no doubt English customs were different.

She was sorry none of her family were present. But she had no relations in England, and the journey from Cherbourg could be long – it had taken her two weeks. It was never easy for a count to travel far from his domain, but she had hoped that her mother might make the effort, and perhaps bring her brother, Richard. However, Mother had been against this marriage, and perhaps she had been disinclined to give it her blessing.

She banished such thoughts.

Wilf raised his voice and said: 'And now, friends and neighbours, let us feast!' The crowd cheered, and the kitchen staff began to bring out great platters of meat, fish, vegetables and bread, plus jugs of ale for the common folk and mead for the special guests.

Ragna wanted nothing more than to get into bed with her husband, but she knew they had to join in the banquet. She would not eat much, but it was important for her to talk to as many people as possible. This was her chance to make a good impression on the townsfolk, and she seized it eagerly.

Aldred introduced her to Abbot Osmund, and she sat beside him for several minutes, asking questions about the monastery. She took the opportunity to praise Aldred, saying she shared his view that Shiring could become an international centre of scholarship – under Osmund's leadership, of course. Osmund was flattered.

She spoke to most of the leading townspeople: Elfwine, the master of the mint; the wealthy Widow Ymma, who traded in furs; the woman who owned the Abbey Alehouse, the most popular drinking place in town; the parchment maker; the jeweller; the dyer. They were pleased by her attention, for it marked them, in the eyes of their neighbours, as important people.

The task of chatting amiably to strangers became easier as the drink flowed. Ragna introduced herself to Sheriff Denewald, who was called Den, a tough-looking grey-haired man in his forties. He was at first wary of Ragna, and she guessed why: as a rival to Wilf he expected her to be hostile. But his wife was at his side and Ragna asked her about their children. She discovered that their first grandchild had just been born, a boy; whereupon the tough sheriff turned into a doting grandpa and became misty-eyed.

As Ragna moved away from Sheriff Den, Wynstan approached her and said in a challenging tone: 'What were you talking to him about?'

'I promised to tell him all your secrets,' she said; and she was rewarded by a momentary flash of anxiety in his eyes before he realized she was mocking him. She went on: 'In fact, I talked to Den about his new grandson. And now I have a question for you. Tell me about the Vale of Outhen, now that it's mine.'

'Oh, you don't need to worry about it,' said Wynstan. 'I've been collecting the rents for Wilf, and I'll continue to do the same for you. All you have to do is take the money when it comes in four times a year.'

She ignored that. 'There are five villages and a quarry, I believe.'

'Yes.' He offered no additional information.

'Any mills?' she tried.

'Well, there's a grindstone in each village.'

'No water mills?'

'Two, I think.'

She gave him a charming smile, as if he was being helpful. 'Any mining? Iron ore, silver?'

'Certainly no precious metals. There might be one or two groups of iron smelters working in the woods.'

'You're a bit vague,' she said mildly, holding her annoyance in check. 'If you don't know what's there, how can you be sure they're paying what they should?'

'I scare them,' he said in a matter-of-fact tone. 'They wouldn't dare cheat me.'

'I don't believe in scaring people.'

'That's all right,' said Wynstan. 'You can leave it to me.' He walked away.

This conversation is not finished, Ragna thought.

When the guests could eat no more, and the barrels were dry, people began to drift away. At last Ragna began to relax, and she sat down with a dish of roast pork and cabbage. While she was eating, Edgar the builder approached, greeted her politely, and bowed. 'I believe my work on your house is finished, my lady,' he said. 'With your permission, I will return to Dreng's Ferry with Dreng tomorrow.'

'Thank you for what you've done,' she said. 'It's made the place much more comfortable.'

'I'm honoured.'

She called Edgar's attention to Dunnere the carpenter, who had passed out with his head on a table. 'There's my problem,' she said.

'I'm sorry to see that.'

'Did you enjoy the ceremony today?'

He looked thoughtful, and said: 'No, not really.'

That surprised her. 'Why?'

'Because I'm envious.'

She raised her eyebrows. 'Of Wilf?'

'No –'

'Of me?'

He smiled. 'Much as I admire the ealdorman, I don't want to marry him. Aldred might.'

Ragna giggled.

Edgar became serious again. 'I'm envious of anyone who gets to marry the one they love. That chance was snatched away from me. Now weddings make me sad.'

Ragna was only a little surprised by his candour. Men often confided in her. She encouraged it: she was fascinated by other people's loves and hates. 'What was the name of the woman you loved?'

'Sungifu, called Sunni.'

'You remember her, and all the things you did together.'

'What hurts me most is the things we didn't do. We never cooked a meal together, washing vegetables, throwing herbs into the pot, putting bowls on our table. I never took her fishing in my boat – the boat I built was beautiful, that's why the Vikings stole it. We made love many times, but we never lay awake in each other's arms all night just talking.'

She studied his face, with its sparse beard and hazel eyes, and thought he was terribly young to have such grief. 'I think I understand,' she said.

'I remember my parents taking us to the river in spring to cut fresh rushes for the house, when we three boys were little. There must have been some romantic story about that riverside, with its rushes; perhaps my parents had made love there before they got married. I didn't think of that at the time – I was too young – but I knew they had a delicious secret that they loved to remember.' His smile was a sad smile. 'Things like that – you put them all together, and they make up a life.'

Ragna was surprised to find that she had tears in her eyes.

Edgar suddenly looked embarrassed. 'I don't know why I told you all that.'

'You'll find someone else to love.'

'I could, of course. But I don't want *someone else*. I want Sunni. And she's gone.'

'I'm so sorry.'

'It's unkind of me to tell sad stories on your wedding day. I don't know what got into me. I apologize.' He bowed, and walked away.

Ragna thought over what he had said. His loss made her feel very fortunate to have Wilf.

She drained her cup of ale, got up from the trestle table, and returned to her house. Suddenly she felt weary. She was not sure why: she had done nothing physically exhausting. Perhaps it was the strain of being on display to the world for hours on end.

She took off her cloak and her overdress and lay on her mattress. Cat barred the door so that people such as Dreng could not barge in. Ragna thought about the evening ahead. At some point she would be summoned to Wilf's house. To her surprise, she felt a bit nervous. That was silly. She had already had sexual intercourse with him: what was left to be nervous about?

She was also curious. When they had sneaked into the hay store at Cherbourg Castle at dusk, everything had been furtive and hurried and dimly lit. From now on they would make love at leisure. She wanted to spend time looking at his body, exploring it with her fingertips, studying and feeling the muscles and the hair and the skin and the bones of the man who was now her husband. Mine, she thought; all mine.

She must have dozed off, for the banging at the door woke her with a start.

She heard a muffled interchange, then Cat said: 'It's time.' Cat looked as excited as if it had been her own honeymoon night.

Ragna got up. Bern turned his back while she slipped out of her underdress and put on the new nightdress, dark ochre yellow, made especially for this occasion. She put on shoes, for she did not want to get into Wilf's bed with muddy feet. Finally she donned her cloak.

'You two stay here,' she said. 'I don't want any fuss.'

In that she was disappointed.

When she stepped outside she saw that Wigelm and the men-at-arms were lined up to cheer her along. Mostly drunk after the party, they blew whistles and banged cooking pots and pans. Wynstan's man Cnebba cavorted with a broomstick between his legs sticking up like a huge wooden penis, which made the men hoot with laughter.

Ragna was mortified, but tried not to show it: a protest by her would be seen as weakness. She walked slowly and with dignity between the two lines of mocking men. When they saw her hauteur they became more vulgar, but she knew she must not descend to their level.

At last she reached Wilf's door, opened it, then turned to the men. Their noise diminished as they wondered what she would do or say.

She gave them a grin, blew a kiss, then quickly stepped inside, closing the door behind her.

She heard them cheering, and knew she had done the right thing. Wilf stood beside his bed, waiting.

He too wore a new nightshirt. It was the blue of a starling's egg. She looked closely at his face and saw that he was remarkably sober for one who had appeared to be roistering all day. She guessed that he had been careful to limit his intake.

Impatiently, she dropped her cloak, kicked off her shoes, pulled the nightdress over her head and stood naked in front of him.

He stared at her hungrily. 'My immortal soul,' he said. 'You're even more beautiful than I remember.'

'You, now,' she said, indicating his nightshirt. 'I want to look at you.'

He pulled it off.

She saw again the scars on his arms, the fair hair on his belly, the long muscles of his thighs. Without shame she gazed at his cock, which was becoming larger by the second.

Then she had had enough of looking. 'Let's lie down,' she said.

She wanted no teasing, no stroking and whispering and kissing: she wanted him inside her, right away. He seemed to guess that, for instead of lying beside her he got on top immediately.

When he entered her, Ragna sighed deeply and said: 'At last.'

15

MOST OF RAGNA'S SERVANTS and men-at-arms were to return to Normandy. After the wedding she kept them with her as long as she reasonably could, but the time came when she had to relent, and they left on the last day of December.

A typical English drizzling rain fell on them as they carried their bags to the stables and loaded the packhorses. Only Cat and Bern were to stay: that had been the arrangement from the start.

Ragna could not help feeling sad and anxious. Although she was deliriously happy with Wilf, still she feared this moment. She was an Englishwoman now, surrounded by people she had met only a few weeks ago. As if she had lost a limb she missed the parents, the relations, the neighbours and the servants who had known her since before she could remember.

She told herself that thousands of noble brides must have felt the same. It was common for aristocratic girls to marry and move far from home. The wisest of them threw themselves into their new lives with energy and enthusiasm, and that was what Ragna was doing.

But that was small consolation today. She had known moments when the world seemed to be against her – and next time that happened, who would she turn to?

She would turn to Wilf, of course. He would be her friend and counsellor as well as her lover.

They made love in the evening and often again in the morning, and sometimes in the middle of the night too. After a week he had resumed his normal duties, riding out every day to visit some part of his domain. Fortunately there was no fighting: the Welsh raiders had gone home of their own accord, and Wilf said he would punish them in his own good time.

All the same, not every trip could be completed in a single day, so he began to spend some nights away. Ragna would have liked to go with him, but she was in charge of his home now, and she had not yet secured her grip on authority, so she stayed. The arrangement had an upside: he returned from such journeys hungrier than ever for her.

She was pleased when most of the residents of the compound came to say goodbye to the departing Normans. Although some of the English had at first been wary of the foreigners, that had quickly faded, and friendships had flourished.

As they were preparing to start the long journey home, the seamstress Agnes came to Ragna in tears. 'Madame, I am in love with the Englishman Offa,' she sobbed. 'I don't want to leave.'

Ragna was only surprised that it had taken Agnes this long to make up her mind. The signs of the romance had been obvious. She looked around and caught the eye of Offa. 'Come here,' she ordered him.

He stood in front of her. He would not have been Ragna's choice. He had the heavy look and flushed skin of someone who ate and drank a little too well. The broken nose was perhaps not his fault, but all the same Ragna felt he looked untrustworthy. However, he was Agnes's choice, not Ragna's.

Agnes was small and Offa was large, and as they stood side by side they looked faintly comical. Ragna had to smother a smile.

She said: 'Do you have something to say to me, Offa?'

'My lady, I beg permission to ask Agnes to be my wife.'

'You are the reeve of Mudeford.'

'But I have a house in Shiring. Agnes can still take care of your clothes.'

Agnes added hastily: 'If you so wish, my lady.'

'I do,' Ragna said. 'And I'm glad to give my consent to your marriage.'

They thanked her profusely. Sometimes, Ragna reflected, it was very easy to make people happy.

At last the group moved out. Ragna stood and waved them out of sight.

She would probably never see any of them again.

She did not allow herself to linger on her sense of loss. What did she need to do next? She decided to deal with Dunnere the carpenter. She was not going to put up with his slackness, even if he was Gytha's nephew.

She returned to her house and sent Bern to fetch Dunnere and his men. To receive them she sat on the kind of seat her father had used for formal occasions, a four-legged stool in the shape of a broad rectangle, with a cushion for comfort.

There were three carpenters: Dunnere, Edric and Edric's son Hunstan. She did not invite them to sit. 'From now on,' she said, 'you will go into the forest once a week to fell trees.'

'What for?' Dunnere said sullenly. 'We get wood when we need it.'

'You're going to have a stockpile, which will reduce delays.'

Dunnere looked mutinous, but Edric said: 'That's a good idea.'

Ragna marked him down as more conscientious than Dunnere.

She said: 'What's more, you're going to do it on the same day every week – Friday.'

'Why?' said Dunnere. 'One day's as good as another.'

'It's to help you remember.' In truth it was to help her keep tabs on them.

Dunnere was not ready to give in. 'Well, then, what if someone wants a repair done on a Friday? Milly, say, or Gytha?'

'You'll be gone from here so early that you won't know. You can take your breakfast with you. But if anyone asks you to do something different on a Friday – Milly or Gytha or anyone else – you just tell them to come and see me, because I'm in charge of you, and you're not allowed to change the schedule without my permission. Is that clear?'

Dunnere sulked, but Edric said: 'Very clear, mistress, thank you.'

'You may go now.'

They trooped out.

She knew this would cause trouble, but it was necessary. However, she would be wise to defend herself against a counter-attack. Gytha might go behind Ragna's back and complain to Wilf. Ragna needed to make sure of his response in that event.

She left the house, heading for Wilf's place. She passed the house her men-at-arms had lived in for the last twelve weeks, empty now; she would need to think about what should be done with it.

She was surprised to see a woman she did not recognize coming out of the place. She did not yet know everyone in Shiring, but this particular person was striking. In her thirties, she wore tight clothing and red shoes, and she had a lot of wild-looking hair that was not quite tamed under a large soft hat. Respectable women did not show much hair in public, and although a few stray locks might be overlooked, the woman in the red shoes was pushing the boundary of decorum. Yet she appeared unembarrassed, and walked with a confident stride. Ragna was curious to speak to her, but at that moment she caught sight of Wilf. She postponed speaking to the woman and followed him into his house.

As always, he kissed her enthusiastically. Then he said: 'I have to go to Wigleigh today. I need to make sure they've paid the correct rents to Dean Degbert.'

She said: 'I've told our carpenters to go into the forest and fell a tree every Friday. They need a stockpile, so that they can do repairs without delay.'

'Good thinking,' said Wilf with a touch of impatience. He did not like to be bothered with domestic issues.

Ragna said: 'I mention the carpenters to you only because Dunnere is a problem. He's lazy and he's a drunk.'

'You'd better come down hard on him.'

Despite Wilf's impatience, Ragna continued to nudge him towards saying what she wanted to hear. 'You don't think he deserves special indulgence because he's Gytha's nephew?'

'No! It doesn't matter who he is, he still owes me a good day's work.'

'I agree, and I'm glad to have your backing.' She kissed him with her mouth open, and he forgot his irritation and responded ardently. 'Now you must go,' she said.

They left the house together. The men-at-arms were assembling for the trip, and she watched Wilf join them, exchanging a joke or a few words with three or four. As they were about to leave, a young man of about sixteen years joined the group, and Ragna was surprised to see Wilf kiss him affectionately. Before she could ask who he was they mounted up and rode out.

As soon as Wilf had gone, Gytha approached Ragna. Here it comes, Ragna thought: she'll be angry about the carpenters. Dunnere must have wasted no time in complaining to his aunt.

But Gytha surprised her by talking about something else. 'The house that was occupied by your men-at-arms is empty now,' she said.

'Yes.'

'May I make a suggestion?'

Gytha was being carefully polite. That was a second surprise. Ragna responded: 'Of course.'

'Perhaps we could allow Wigelm and Milly to use it.'

Ragna nodded. 'Good idea – unless there's anyone else who might need it?'

'I don't think so.'

'I saw someone looking at it earlier – a woman in red shoes.'

'That's Milly's sister, Inge. She could look after the place while Wigelm and Milly are at Combe.'

'That sounds like a sensible arrangement.'

'Thank you,' said Gytha, but the note in her voice was not gratitude. It sounded to Ragna more like triumph.

Gytha went away. Ragna frowned as she returned to her own place. Why was she uneasy about the conversation? She suspected Gytha, feeling that her surface courtesy concealed an underlying hostility.

Ragna's intuition told her that something was wrong.

ÞÞÞ

RAGNA'S ANXIETY GREW through the day. Who was the boy her husband had kissed? He might be a close relative, a beloved nephew perhaps, but if so, why had he not been at the wedding? The kiss could not have been sexual: Ragna was as sure as a person could be that Wilf was not interested in sex with men. And what was Gytha up to, pretending to be so nice?

Ragna decided to question Wilf the minute he got home. But as the hours went by she wavered. She might need to be more cautious. Something was going on that she did not understand, and her ignorance put her at a disadvantage. Her father would never go to an important meeting until he was sure he knew everything that might be said there. Ragna was in a foreign country whose customs were still not entirely familiar. She had to tread carefully.

Wigleigh was not far, and Wilf returned mid-afternoon, but it was a short December day, and the light was already fading. A servant was lighting basket torches mounted on poles outside the main buildings. Ragna went with Wilf into his house and poured him a cup of ale.

He drank it in one draught then kissed her with the taste of ale on his tongue. He smelt of sweat and horse and leather. She was hungry for his love, perhaps because of the disquiet that had plagued her all day. She took his hand and pressed it between her thighs. He did not need much persuasion, and they made love right away.

Afterwards he fell into a light sleep, with his muscular arms outstretched and his long legs splayed, a strong man resting after an energetic day.

Ragna left him. She went to the kitchen and checked on the preparations for supper; she looked into the great hall to make sure it was ready for the evening meal; then she walked around the compound, observing who was working and who was lazing around, who was sober and who drunk, whose horse was fed and watered and whose had not even been unsaddled yet.

At the end of her peregrination she saw Wilf talking to the woman in the red shoes.

Something about them arrested her. She stopped and watched them from a distance. They were lit by the wavering light of the torch outside Wilf's door.

There was no reason why they should not talk: Inge was a kind of sister-in-law to Wilf, and they might be innocently fond of one another. All the same, Ragna was taken aback by the intimacy suggested by their bodies: they stood close, and she touched him several times, casually gripping his forearm to make a point, rapping his chest with the back of her hand in a dismissive gesture as if telling him not to be so foolish, and, once, putting the tip of her forefinger on his cheek affectionately.

Ragna could not move, could not tear her gaze away.

Then she saw the boy Wilf had kissed. He was young, with no beard, and though tall he gave the impression of being not quite full grown, as if the long limbs and wide shoulders had not yet knit together into a man's body. He joined Wilf and Inge, and the three talked for a minute with relaxed familiarity.

These people have clearly been part of my husband's life for many years, Ragna thought; how come I have no idea who they are?

Finally they split up, still without noticing her. Wilf headed for the stable, no doubt to make sure the grooms had taken care of his horse. Inge and the boy went into the house Ragna had agreed to allocate to Wigelm, Milly and Inge.

Ragna could not live in doubt and suspense any longer, but still she was unwilling to confront Wilf. So who could she talk to?

There was really only one possibility: Gytha.

She hated the thought. She would be revealing her ignorance, showing herself weak, and giving Gytha the position of the wise, knowing one – just when Gytha seemed to be accepting that she was no longer the ruler of Wilf's home.

But who else was there? Wynstan would be worse than Gytha. Aldred would be at prayers now. She did not know Sheriff Den well enough. She could not sink so low as to ask Gilda the kitchen maid.

She went to Gytha's house.

She was glad to find Gytha alone. Gytha offered her a cup of wine, and Ragna took it, needing courage. They sat on stools near the fire, facing one another. Gytha looked wary, but Ragna sensed something else: Gytha knew why Ragna had come, knew the questions she was going to ask, and had been waiting for this moment.

Ragna swallowed a mouthful of wine and tried to assume a casual tone of voice. 'I noticed a newcomer in the compound, an adolescent boy, about sixteen, tall.'

Gytha nodded. 'That would be Garulf.'

'Who is he, and what is he doing here?'

Gytha smiled, and Ragna saw with horror that the smile was loaded with malice. Gytha said: 'Garulf is Wilf's son.'

Ragna gasped. 'Son?' she said. 'Wilf has a son?'

'Yes.'

That explained the kiss, at least.

Gytha added: 'Wilf is forty years old. Did you think you married a virgin?'

'Of course not.' Ragna thought furiously. She knew that Wilf had been married before, but not that he had a child. 'Are there others?'

'Not that I know of.'

So, one son. It was a shock, but she could bear it. However, she had one more question. 'What connection does Garulf have with the woman in the red shoes?'

Gytha smiled broadly, and it was ominously clear that this was her great moment of triumph. 'Why,' she said, 'Inge is Wilf's first wife.'

Ragna was so shocked that she jumped to her feet and dropped her cup. She let it lie there. 'His first wife is dead!'

'Who told you that?'

'Wynstan.'

'Are you sure that's what he said?'

Ragna remembered clearly. 'He said: "Sadly, his wife is no longer with us." I'm sure of it.'

'I thought as much,' Gytha said. 'You see, *no longer with us* is not the same as *dead*, not at all.'

Ragna was incredulous. 'He deceived me, and my father and mother?'

'There was no deceit. After Wilf met you, Inge was set aside.'

'Set aside? What in heaven's name does that mean?'

'That she is no longer his wife.'

'So it's a divorce?'

'Of sorts.'

'Then why is she here?'

'Just because she's no longer his wife doesn't mean he can't see her. After all, they have a child together.'

Ragna was horrified. The man she had just married already had a family: a wife of many years, from whom he had had a divorce 'of sorts', and a son who was almost a man. And he was clearly fond of them both. And they had now moved into the compound.

She felt as if the world had shifted under her feet, and she struggled to keep her equilibrium. She kept thinking that surely this could not be true. It could not be that everything she had believed about Wilf was wrong.

Surely he could not have deceived her so badly.

She now felt she had to get away from Gytha's exultant gaze. She could not bear that woman's knowing eyes on her. She went to the door, then turned back. An even worse thought had struck her.

She said: 'But Wilf cannot continue to have marital relations with Inge.'

'Can't he?' Gytha shrugged. 'My dear, you must ask him about that.'

PART TWO
THE TRIAL
998 CE

16

IT WAS LONG PAST midnight when Ragna at last managed to stop crying.

She spent the night at her own house. She felt unable even to speak to Wilf. She ordered Cat to tell him that Ragna could not sleep with him because the woman's monthly curse was upon her. That bought her time.

Her servants watched her fearfully by the firelight, but she could not bring herself to explain her anguish. 'Tomorrow,' she kept saying. 'I'll tell you tomorrow.'

She thought she would never sleep again, but when her tears dried up, like an overused well, she did fall into a fitful doze. However, in her dreams she remembered the tragedy that had ruined her life, and she came wide awake with sudden horror, and wept again.

At this time of year the compound began to stir well before the late-arriving dawn. Morning sounds brought Ragna to full alertness: men shouting to one another, dogs barking, birdsong, and the clang and clatter of a big kitchen gearing up to feed a hundred people.

It's a new day, Ragna thought, and I don't know what to do. I'm lost.

If only she had learned the truth a day earlier, she might have gone home to Cherbourg with her men-at-arms, she thought; but immediately she realized that was not true. Wilf would have sent an army after her, and she would have been captured and brought back to Shiring. No nobleman would permit his wife to leave him. It would be too humiliating.

Could she sneak away unnoticed and get a few days' start? It was impossible, she saw. She was the ealdorman's wife: her absence would be remarked on within hours if not minutes. And she did not know the country well enough to evade pursuit.

What was more, to her dismay she found she did not really want to leave. She loved Wilf and desired him. He had deceived her and betrayed her but still she could not bear the thought of living without him. She cursed her weakness.

She needed someone to talk to.

She sat up and threw off her blanket. Cat, Agnes and Bern were staring at her, waiting apprehensively to see what she would do or say.

'Bishop Wynstan deceived us all,' she said. 'Wilf's first wife is not dead. Her name is Inge, and she has been "set aside", which seems to be a strange kind of divorce, for she has moved into the house that our men-at-arms vacated yesterday.'

Bern said: 'Nobody told us!'

'People probably assumed we knew. These English don't seem very shocked when a man has more than one wife. Remember Dreng the ferryman.'

Cat was looking thoughtful. She said: 'Edgar told me, more or less.'

'Did he?'

'The first time we met him, when he took us across the river, I said my lady was going to marry the ealdorman, and he said: "I thought he was already married." And I said: "He was, but his wife died." And Edgar said he had not realized that.'

Ragna said: 'The other thing they didn't tell us was that Inge has a son by Wilf, a young man called Garulf, who has moved in with his mother.'

Bern said: 'I still think it's strange that no one else mentioned the first wife to us.'

'It's more than strange,' said Ragna. 'They went farther than just staying quiet. They kept Inge and Garulf out of sight until after the wedding and after most of my people had gone home. That's not accidental. Wynstan organized it.' She was silent for a moment, then she voiced the most horrible thought: 'And Wilf must have been in on the plot.'

The others said nothing, and Ragna knew that meant they agreed.

Ragna felt an urge to talk to someone who was not her servant. She wanted a more detached point of view to help her get the calamity into some kind of perspective. She thought of Aldred. He had said: 'Let me know if there's anything I can do for you. Come to the abbey.'

'I'm going to talk to Brother Aldred,' she announced.

Then she recalled that Aldred had had second thoughts and added: 'Or just send a message.'

'Bern, go to the abbey,' she said. 'Wait. Let me think.' She did not want Aldred to come to the compound. Something held her back from that. Questioning the reason for her instinct, she decided that she did not want people such as Gytha and Inge to know who her allies might be.

So where could she meet Aldred?

The cathedral.

'Ask Aldred to come to the cathedral,' she said. 'Tell him I'll be waiting.' The doors of the big church were rarely locked. 'Wait. You can walk there with me.'

She dried her eyes and put a little oil on her face. Agnes fetched her cloak. Ragna put it on and pulled the hood over her head.

She and Bern went out of the compound and down the hill. On the way she kept her head bent and did not speak to anyone: she could not cope with normal conversation. When they reached the square, Bern went to the monastery and Ragna entered the cathedral.

She had been here several times before for services. It was the biggest church she had seen so far in England, with a nave twenty

307

or thirty yards long and about eight yards wide, and everyone in town crammed into it on special days such as Christmas. It was always cold. The stone walls were thick, and she guessed the place was chilly even in summer. Today it was icy. She stood by a carved stone baptismal font and looked around. The small windows dimly lit a colourful interior: red-and-black-patterned floor tiles, wall tapestries of biblical scenes, and a large painted wooden sculpture of the Holy Family. Peering through the arch into the chancel, she saw a stone altar covered with a white linen cloth. Behind the altar was a wall painting of the crucifixion in garish blue and yellow.

The storm in her heart eased a little. The gloom and the chill within the massive stone walls gave her a sense of eternity. Earthly troubles were temporary, even the worst of them, the church seemed to say. Her heart beat normally again. She found she could breathe without gasping. She knew her face was still red, despite the oil, but her eyes were dry, and no new tears came.

She heard the door open and close, and a moment later Aldred stood next to her. 'You've been crying,' he said.

'All night.'

'What on earth has happened?'

'My husband has another wife.'

Aldred gasped. 'You didn't know about Inge?'

'No.'

'And I never mentioned it. I thought you'd prefer not to talk about her.' Aldred was struck by a thought. '"He wants a son".'

'What?'

'You said that to me about Wilf. "He wants a son". I knew there was something odd in that conversation, but I couldn't figure out what. Now I know. Wilf already had a son – but you didn't know. What a fool I am.'

'I didn't come here to put the blame on you.' On the north wall was a built-in stone bench; at the Christmas service, when the whole town had crowded in here, older citizens who were unable to stand for a whole hour had sat tight-packed on that cold, narrow shelf. Now Ragna nodded towards it and said: 'Let's sit down.'

When they were settled, Aldred said: 'Inge was the reason King Ethelred gave for refusing to acknowledge your marriage.'

That shocked her. 'But Wynstan had royal approval in advance – he told us!' she said indignantly.

'Either Wynstan lied, or Ethelred changed his mind. But I think Inge is just a pretext. Ethelred was angry with Wilf for not paying the fine.'

'This is why the bishops didn't come to my wedding – because the king disapproved of the marriage.'

'I'm afraid so. Then Ethelred fined Wilf sixty pounds for marrying you. But Wilf hasn't paid the fine. Now he's even more out of favour.'

Ragna was dismayed. 'Can't Ethelred do anything?'

'He could ravage Shiring. That's what he did to Rochester about fifteen years ago, in a quarrel with Bishop Elfstan, but it was a bit extreme, and Ethelred later regretted it.'

'So a nobleman can just defy the king and get away with it?'

'Not indefinitely,' said Aldred. 'It reminds me of the famous case of Thane Wulfbald. He repeatedly ignored the rulings of the royal court and refused to pay fines, and got away with it. Eventually his lands passed into the possession of the king, but not until Wulfbald was dead.'

'I had no idea my husband was so badly at odds with his king – no one told me!'

'I assumed you knew, but did not want to talk about it. Wynstan would have told Wilf's family not to say anything to you. The servants probably don't even know about it, although they seem to find these things out eventually.'

'Am I even married to Wilf?'

'Yes, you are. Inge was set aside, and Wilf married you. The Church disapproves of the setting aside and of the marriage, but English law does not forbid either.'

'What am I to do?'

'Fight back.'

'It's not just Inge, it's Wynstan and Gytha and Wigelm and Milly and even Garulf.'

'I know. They form a powerful faction. But you have a magic weapon that will overcome them all.'

She wondered if he was going to turn pious on her. 'Do you mean God?'

'No, though it's always wise to ask for his help.'

'So what is my special weapon?'

'Wilf's love.'

Ragna gave him a sceptical look. What did he know about love?

Aldred read her mind. 'Oh, I realize everyone thinks monks are ignorant of love and marriage, but it's not quite true. Besides, anyone with eyes can see how much Wilf loves you. It's frankly embarrassing. He stares at you all the time. His hands are itching to touch you.'

Ragna nodded. After they were married she had somehow stopped feeling embarrassed by this.

'He adores you, he worships you,' Aldred went on. 'That makes you stronger than all the others put together.'

'I don't see what good it does me. Wilf has still brought his first wife to live next door to me.'

'That's not the end, it's the beginning.'

'I just don't understand what you want me to do.'

'First, don't lose his love. I can't tell you how to keep it, but I'm sure you know.'

I do, Ragna thought.

'Impose your will,' Aldred went on. 'Pick small fights with Gytha and Wynstan and Inge, and win small victories, then larger. Let everyone know that in a conflict Wilf's first instinct will always be to support you.'

Like the argument about Wigelm's house, she thought, or the one about Dunnere the carpenter.

'And build up your strength. Develop allies. You've got me, but you need more – all you can get. Men of power.'

'Such as Sheriff Den.'

'Very good. And Bishop Elfheah of Winchester: he hates Wynstan, so make Elfheah your friend.'

'You sound as if you're talking about war, not marriage.'

Aldred shrugged. 'I've spent twenty years living with monks. A monastery is awfully like a big, powerful family: rivalry, jealousy, squabbling, hierarchy – and love. And it's hard to escape from it. I'm glad when I see trouble coming, because I can deal with it. The real danger comes from surprises.'

They sat in silence for a minute, then Ragna said: 'You're a good friend.'

'I hope so.'

'Thank you.' She stood up, and Aldred did the same.

He said: 'Have you spoken to Wilf yet about Inge?'

'No. I'm still not sure what to say.'

'Whatever you do, don't leave him feeling guilty.'

Ragna felt herself flush with indignation. 'Why on earth not? He deserves to feel guilty.'

'You don't want to become the person who makes him unhappy.'

'But that's outrageous. He *should* be unhappy about what he has done to me.'

'Of course he should. But pointing it out won't help you.'

'I'm not sure about that.'

They left the cathedral and turned in opposite directions. Ragna was thoughtful as she walked up the hill to the compound. She began to see sense in Aldred's last remarks. She should not be a sad, defeated person this morning. She was Wilf's choice, his bride, the woman he loved. She had to walk and talk like a winner.

She returned to her house. It would soon be time for the midday meal. She got Cat to comb and arrange her hair, then she selected her favourite dress, made of a silk the rich colour of autumn leaves. She put on a necklace of amber beads. Then she went to the great hall and took her place on Wilf's right hand.

Throughout the meal she talked in her usual way, asking the people around her what they had done that morning, joking with the men and gossiping with the women. She caught several looking at her in surprise: they would be the ones who knew what a shock she had suffered yesterday. They expected her to be grief-stricken. She *was* grief-stricken, but she was hiding it.

Afterwards she left with Wilf and walked by his side to his house. As usual, he needed little encouragement to make love to her. She began by pretending her usual enthusiasm, but soon found pretence unnecessary, and in the end was almost as satisfied as normal.

All the same, she had forgotten nothing.

When he rolled off her, she did not let him fall into his habitual doze. 'I didn't know you had a son,' she said in a matter-of-fact voice.

She felt his body tense beside her, but he made his voice casual. 'Yes,' he said. 'Garulf.'

'And I didn't know that Inge was still alive.'

'I never said she was dead,' he shot back. It sounded like a rehearsed answer he had been holding in readiness.

Ragna ignored it. She did not want to get into a pointless argument about whether she had been lied to or merely told less than the whole truth. She said: 'I want to know all about you.'

He was watching her warily. Clearly he was not sure what she was up to. He was asking himself whether to prepare himself to be berated or get ready to make excuses.

Let him wonder, she thought. She was not going to accuse him, but she did not mind if his conscience made him uncomfortable. 'Your ways aren't the same as those of the Normans,' she said. 'I should ask you more questions.'

He could not object to that. 'All right.' He seemed relieved, as if he had feared worse.

'I do not want to be surprised again,' she said, and she heard the hardness in her own voice.

He was clearly not sure how to take this. She guessed that he was expecting rage, or tears, but this was different, and he had no response ready. He looked bewildered and said simply: 'I see.'

In the last few hours her anxieties had resolved into two burning questions, and she decided to ask them now. She felt he would be eager to give her what she wanted.

Ragna clasped her hands together to stop them shaking. 'I have a couple of things to ask you right now.'

'Go ahead.'

'Where is Inge from? What's her background?'

'Her father was a priest. In fact, he was secretary to my father.'

Ragna could easily imagine the scenario: the children of two men who worked closely together, the son of one and the daughter of the other, spending much time in each other's company, an adolescent romance, perhaps an unintended pregnancy, finally an early marriage. 'So Inge does not have noble blood.'

'No.'

'When my father agreed to my marriage with you, he certainly foresaw that my children would be your heirs.'

He did not hesitate. 'They will be.'

That was important. It meant she was the ealdorman's official wife, not just one of a number of women of unclear status. She was not going to be made number two.

Needing to be sure, she pressed him. 'Not Garulf.'

'No!' he said, annoyed to be asked twice.

'Thank you. I'm glad to have your solemn word on that.'

She was pleased to have extracted from him such an important promise. Perhaps he had never intended anything different, but the days were over when she took such things for granted.

He was mildly irritated at having been pushed up against the wall by her. In a voice that suggested his patience was running out he said: 'Anything else?'

'Yes, one more question. Do you intend to fuck Inge?'

He chuckled. 'If I have any energy left.'

'It's not a joke.'

His face hardened. 'Something you need to be in no doubt about,' he said. 'You will never tell me who I may or may not bring to my bed.'

Ragna felt as if she had been slapped.

Wilf said: 'I'm a man, an Englishman, and the ealdorman of Shiring, and I do not take orders from any woman.'

Ragna looked away to hide her sadness. 'I see,' she said.

He took her chin in his hand and turned her head back so that she was forced to look at him. 'I will fuck anyone I like. Is that clear?'

'Very clear,' said Ragna.

ÞÞÞ

THE DAMAGE TO Ragna's pride was painful but she could live with it. The wound to her heart was worse.

She mended her pride by holding her head high and concealing her sorrow. She also remembered Aldred's advice, and looked for an early opportunity to assert her authority. But nothing eased the hurt in her heart. She just nursed it, and hoped it would fade in time.

Garulf had received a gift of a ball, a piece of leather sewn with strong twine and stuffed with rags, and in January the adolescent boys of the compound began to play a rough game in which two teams competed, each trying to carry the ball into the opponents' 'castle', a square marked on the ground. Garulf was captain of one team, of course, and the other was led by his friend Stigand, called Stiggy. They played between the stable and the pond, irksomely near the main gate.

The rowdiness was a nuisance to the adults, but Garulf was the ealdorman's son, so a degree of tolerance was expected. However, as the days went by Ragna noticed the game becoming violent, while at the same time the boys were more careless of inconvenience to passers-by. It was worse when Wilf was away, and Ragna began to see it as a challenge to her authority.

Then one day when Wilf was away the ball struck the kitchen maid Gilda on the head, knocking her down.

Ragna happened to see it. She snatched up the ball, to stop the game, then knelt beside Gilda.

Gilda's eyes were open and after a moment she sat up, holding her head. 'That hurt,' she said.

The boys were standing around, panting with effort. Garulf did not express regret about the accident or concern for Gilda, Ragna noticed. He just seemed irritated that his fun had been disrupted. That annoyed her.

'Sit still for a minute,' Ragna said to Gilda. 'Catch your breath.'

But Gilda was impatient. 'I feel foolish sitting here in the mud,' she said. She struggled to her knees.

Ragna helped her stand. 'Come to my house,' she said. 'I'll give you a sip of wine to strengthen you.'

They walked to Ragna's door.

Garulf followed them and said: 'I want my ball.'

Ragna realized she was still holding it.

She ushered Gilda inside then, holding the door, turned to Garulf and said: 'What you want is a thrashing.' She went in and slammed the door.

She threw the ball into a corner.

She persuaded Gilda to lie on her bed, and Cat brought a little wine in a cup. Gilda soon felt better. Ragna established that she did not feel dizzy, and could walk without assistance, then let her return to the kitchen.

A minute later Gytha came in looking haughty. 'I gave my grandson a ball as a gift,' she said.

Garulf was Gytha's step-grandson, but Ragna did not quibble. 'So it came from you,' she said.

'He says you've taken it from him.'

'I have.'

Gytha looked around, spotted the ball in the corner, and quickly picked it up, then looked triumphant.

Ragna said: 'Did he tell you why I took it?'

'Something about a minor accident.'

'A kitchen maid was knocked off her feet. The game has become dangerous.'

'Boys will be boys.'

'Then they must be boys outside the compound. I won't allow the game to continue inside.'

'I will be responsible for my grandson's behaviour,' said Gytha, and she walked out, still holding the ball.

Not long afterwards the game began again.

Ragna summoned Bern, and the two of them stood outside watching. The boys saw them and tried to steer clear, but they could not keep the action within limits – that was the whole problem – and before long the ball came Ragna's way again.

She picked it up.

Both Garulf and Stiggy approached her. Stiggy was a strong boy who threw his weight around to compensate for his stupidity.

Garulf said: 'That's my ball.'

Ragna said: 'You can't play ball inside the compound.'

Stiggy made a sudden move. He stepped forward and struck

Ragna's arm with his fist to make her let go of the ball. The blow hurt, and she lost her grip, but she caught the ball with her other hand and stepped back out of Stiggy's reach.

Bern hit Stiggy a mighty punch on the side of his head, and Stiggy fell to the ground.

Bern looked hard at Garulf and said: 'Will anyone else try to lay hands on the ealdorman's wife?'

Garulf thought about it. His gaze went from the heavy body of Bern to the precious body of the ealdorman's wife and back. Then he stepped away.

Ragna said to Bern: 'Give me your knife.'

Bern's belt knife was a large dagger with a sharp blade. Ragna put the ball on the ground, inserted the point of the knife under the stitching of the ball, and cut the thread.

Garulf gave a cry of protest and stepped forward.

Ragna pointed the knife at him.

Bern took a step towards Garulf.

Ragna continued to cut the threads until she had opened the ball sufficiently to let out all the stuffing.

Finally she stood up and threw the mangled leather into the middle of the pond.

She handed the knife back to Bern, handle first, and said: 'Thank you.'

With Bern at her side she returned to her house. Her left arm hurt where Stiggy had punched her, but her heart sang with victory.

Wilf returned that afternoon, and not much later Ragna was summoned to his house. She was not surprised to find Gytha there.

Wilf looked bad-tempered. 'What's all this about a ball?' he said.

Ragna smiled. 'My beloved husband, you should not trouble yourself about foolish squabbles.'

'My stepmother has complained that you stole a gift she had given to my son.'

Ragna was pleased, but concealed it. Gytha had allowed indignation to impair her judgement. She was on to a loser. She could not win this argument.

Ragna spoke in a light tone appropriate for something trivial. 'The ball game has become too violent. One of your servants was injured by the ball today.'

Gytha snorted with derision. 'She slipped in the mud.'

'She was hit on the head. Worse injuries would have followed. I told them to play outside the compound, but they disobeyed me, so I stopped the game and destroyed the ball. Really, Wilf, I'm sorry you've been pestered with this.'

He looked sceptical. 'Is that really all that happened?'

'Well, no.' Ragna pulled up her left sleeve, showing a fresh bruise. 'The boy Stiggy punched me,' she said. 'So Bern knocked him down.'

Wilf looked darkly at Gytha. 'A boy laid hands on the ealdorman's wife? You didn't tell me that part, Mother.'

Gytha said: 'He just tried to grab the ball back!' But the bruise told its own story, and Gytha was on the defensive.

Wilf said: 'And what did Garulf do?'

'He looked on,' said Ragna.

'And did not defend his father's wife?'

'I'm afraid not.'

Wilf was furious, as Ragna had foreseen. 'Stiggy shall be flogged,' he said. 'A childish punishment for a childish man. Twelve strokes of the lash. But I don't know what to do with Garulf. My son should know what's right and wrong.'

Ragna said: 'May I suggest something?'

'Please.'

'Make Garulf do the flogging.'

Wilf nodded. 'Perfect,' he said.

ÞÞÞ

STIGGY WAS STRIPPED naked and tied facing a pole. The humiliation was part of the punishment.

Garulf stood behind him holding a leather whip, its end divided into three strips, each strip embedded with sharp stones. He looked resentful and unhappy.

Every resident of the compound was watching: men, women and children. The penalty was intended to educate everyone, not just the offender.

Wilf, standing by, said: 'Stiggy laid hands on my wife. This is his penalty.'

The crowd was silent. The only sound was the evening psalm of the birds.

Wilf said: 'Begin. One.'

Garulf raised the whip and struck Stiggy's naked back. The blow made a sharp snapping noise, and Stiggy flinched.

Ragna shuddered and wished she did not have to watch. But for her to leave now would appear weak.

Wilf shook his head. 'Not hard enough,' he said. 'Begin again. One.'

Garulf hit Stiggy harder. This time Stiggy gave a muted cry of pain. The whip left red marks on his white skin.

A woman in the crowd wept softly, and Ragna recognized Stiggy's mother.

Wilf was unmoved. 'Still too soft. Begin again. One.'

Garulf raised the whip high and struck with all his might. Stiggy screamed in pain, and drops of blood appeared where the stones had broken his skin.

The scream silenced the birds.

'Two,' said Wilf.

17

EDGAR WAS ANGERED BY the idea of people stealing from Ragna.

He had not cared so much about Gab the quarryman cheating Ealdorman Wilwulf. Wilf had plenty of money, and anyway it was none of Edgar's business. But he felt differently when Ragna was the victim, perhaps because she was a foreigner and therefore vulnerable – or perhaps, he thought wryly, because she was beautiful.

He had almost told her after the wedding, but he had hesitated. He wanted to be absolutely sure. He did not want to give her a false alert.

Anyway, he had to go to Outhenham again. The walls of the brewhouse were finished and the timber rafters were in place, but he wanted to complete the roof with thin stone tiles that would not burn. He told Dreng he could get the material for half the price if he transported it himself, which was true, and Dreng agreed, always keen to keep money rather than spend it.

Edgar built a simple raft of logs, long and broad. Last time he went to Outhenham he had followed the river upstream, so now he knew there were no major obstacles to overcome, just two places where the water became shallow and the raft might have to be pulled along with ropes for a few yards.

However, poling the raft upstream would be hard work, and roping it over the shallows even harder, so he persuaded Dreng to pay Erman and Eadbald a penny each to leave the farm for two days and help him.

Dreng handed Edgar a small leather purse, saying: 'There's twelve pennies in there. That should be plenty.' Ethel gave them bread and ham for the journey, and Leaf added a flagon of ale to quench their thirst.

They set off early. Brindle leaped onto the raft as they boarded. In dog philosophy it was always better to go somewhere than to be left behind. Edgar asked himself whether that was his philosophy too, and was not sure of the answer.

Erman and Eadbald were thin, and Edgar supposed he was too. A year ago, when they had been living at Combe, no one would have called them even a little fat, but all the same they had shed weight over the winter. They were still strong, but lean, their cheeks concave, their muscles ropy, their waists narrow.

It was a cold February morning but they perspired as they deployed the poles and pushed the raft upstream. One person could propel the vessel but it was easier with two, one on each side, the third man resting. They did not normally talk much, but there was nothing else to do on the journey, and Edgar asked: 'How are you getting on with Cwenburg?'

Eadbald answered: 'Erman lies with her on Monday, Wednesday and Friday, and me on Tuesday, Thursday and Saturday.' He grinned. 'Sunday is her day of rest.'

They were both good-humoured about it, and Edgar concluded that the unorthodox marriage was working surprisingly well.

Erman said: 'It's lying and nothing more, now – she's too pregnant for fucking.'

Edgar calculated when the baby was due. They had arrived in Dreng's Ferry three days before Midsummer, and Cwenburg had conceived more or less immediately. 'The baby is due three days before Lady Day,' he said. Erman gave him a sour look. Edgar's ability with numbers seemed almost miraculous to other people, and his brothers resented it.

321

Erman said: 'Anyway, Cwen can't help with the spring ploughing. Ma will have to guide the ploughshare while we pull.'

The soil at Dreng's Ferry was light and loamy, but their mother was no longer young. Edgar said: 'How is Ma with that?'

'She finds field work hard.'

Edgar saw his mother about once a week, but his brothers were with her every day. 'Does she sleep well?' he asked. 'Does she have a good appetite?'

They were not very observant. Eadbald shrugged, and Erman said snappishly: 'Look, Edgar, she's old, and one day she will die, and only God knows when that will be.'

After that they stopped talking.

Looking ahead, Edgar reflected that it might not be easy to establish Gab's cheating for certain. He needed to do it without arousing hostility. If he appeared too obviously inquisitive, Gab would become wary. And if he revealed his suspicions, Gab would be angry. It was curious, but a wrongdoer found out could often be morally indignant, as if the discovery was the offence, rather than the original transgression. More importantly, if Gab knew he was mistrusted, he would have a chance to cover up.

The raft moved faster than Edgar had when walking on the bank, and they reached the large village of Outhenham at midday. The soil here was clay, and an eight-ox team was pulling a heavy plough in the nearest field, the great clods of earth rising and falling like waves of mud breaking on a beach. In the distance men were sowing, trudging the furrows and throwing the seed, while small children followed, scaring off the birds with shrill cries.

They pulled the raft up onto a beach, and to be doubly safe Edgar tied it to a tree. Then they walked into the village.

Seric was again in his orchard, pruning the trees this time. Edgar stopped to talk to him. 'Am I going to have trouble with Dudda again?' he asked.

Seric glanced at the sky to check the time of day. 'Not this early,' he said. 'Dudda hasn't had his dinner yet.'

'Good.'

'Mind you, he's no sweetheart even when sober.'

'I can imagine.'

They walked on, and came across Dudda a minute later, outside the alehouse. 'Good day to you, lads,' he said. 'What's your business here?' His aggression was no doubt tempered by the sight of three strong young men. All the same Brindle growled, sensing underlying hostility.

Edgar said to his brothers: 'This is Dudda, headman of Outhenham.' To Dudda he said: 'I'm here to buy stone at the quarry, same as last time.'

Dudda looked blank. Clearly he had no memory of Edgar's previous visit. He said: 'Go to the east of the village and follow the track north.'

Edgar knew the way, but he just said: 'Thank you,' and walked on.

Gab and his family were working in the quarry as before. There was a large stack of cut stones in the middle of the clearing, suggesting that business was slow, which was probably a good thing for Edgar, the buyer. A handcart stood beside the stack.

All I have to do, Edgar thought, is watch how Gab marks the tally stick after I buy the stones I need. If he cuts the correct number of notches, my suspicions are groundless. If not, I've proved him guilty.

The slab that Gab was working on fell to the ground with a crash and a cloud of dust, and Gab coughed, put down his tools, and came to speak to the three brothers. He recognized Edgar and said: 'Dreng's Ferry, wasn't it?'

'I'm Edgar, and these are my brothers, Erman and Eadbald.'

Gab adopted a facetious tone. 'Did you bring them to protect you from Dudda?' Obviously he had heard about Edgar's altercation with the headman on the last visit.

Edgar did not find the joke funny. 'I don't need protection from a fat old drunk,' he said crisply. 'I'm here to buy stones, and I'm going to transport them myself this time, so my brothers are here to help me. This way we'll save a penny on every stone.'

'Oh, you will, will you?' Gab said archly. He did not like Edgar knowing his prices in advance. 'Who told you that?'

Cuthbert had, but Edgar decided to ignore the question. 'I need ten stones,' he said. He opened the purse Dreng had given him. To his surprise it contained more than the twelve pennies Dreng had said – in fact, he saw at a glance, twenty-four. Erman and Eadbald saw him hesitate and frown, and both could see the coins, but Edgar did not give them a chance to comment: he did not want to look indecisive in front of Gab. He postponed consideration of the mystery, and briskly counted out ten pennies.

Gab counted them again and pocketed them but, to Edgar's disappointment, he did not notch a stick. He just pointed at the stack of stones. 'Help yourselves,' he said.

Edgar did not have a plan for this contingency. He decided to move the stones while thinking about it. 'We have to take them to the river,' he said to Gab. 'Can we use your cart?'

'No,' said Gab with a sly little smile. 'You've decided to save money. You can carry the stones.' He walked away.

Edgar shrugged. He unslung his axe and handed it to Erman. 'You two go into the wood and cut two stout poles for carrying,' he said. 'I'll take a look at the stones.'

While his brothers were away he studied the pile. He had already tried cutting a stone into slim tiles, and had discovered that it was a delicate task. The thickness had to be just right: thin tiles sometimes fractured, thick ones would be too heavy for the rafters to bear. But he was confident his skill would improve.

When his brothers came back he trimmed the poles they brought then laid them parallel on the ground. He and Erman picked up a stone and placed it across the poles. Then they knelt on the ground, one in front of the stone and one behind, grasped the poles, and stood up, lifting the whole ensemble to hip height.

They set off down the track to the river. Edgar called back to Eadbald: 'Come with us – we'll need to set a guard on the raft.'

They took turns carrying, with the resting brother remaining at the riverside just in case some enterprising traveller should decide to make off with a stone or two. By the time the daylight began to fade they had sore shoulders and aching legs, and there was one more stone to move.

But Edgar had not achieved his other purpose. He had failed to confirm Gab's dishonesty.

The quarry was deserted. Gab and his sons had disappeared, presumably into their house. Edgar tapped on the door and went in. The family were eating their evening meal. Gab looked up with an annoyed expression.

Edgar said: 'Can we spend the night here? You were good enough to give me a place to sleep last time.'

'No,' said Gab. 'You're too many. And besides, there are more pennies in that purse of yours – you can afford to stay at the alehouse.'

Edgar was not surprised: the request was hardly reasonable. His question had been no more than a pretext for entering the house.

Gab's wife, Bee, said: 'The alehouse can be rowdy, but the food is all right.'

'Thank you.' Edgar turned around slowly, giving himself time to look carefully at the sticks hanging on the wall. There was a fresh-cut one, he observed, pale and new.

He saw immediately that it had five notches.

That proved it.

He masked his satisfaction, trying to look disappointed and mildly resentful at being refused accommodation. 'Goodbye, then,' he said, and walked out.

He felt jubilant as he and Eadbald carried the last stone to the river. He was not sure why, but he was pleased to be able to do Ragna a good turn. He looked forward eagerly to telling her all about it.

When the last stone had been added to the stack, Edgar said: 'I think the stones will be safe for an hour, if I leave Brindle here, especially now that it's getting dark. We can get our supper at the alehouse. You two can sleep there, but I'll spend the night on the raft. The weather's not too cold.'

He tied up Brindle on a long string, then the three brothers walked to the alehouse. They got bowls of mutton stew and plenty of rye bread, and a pot of ale each. Edgar noticed Gab in a corner with Dudda, deep in conversation.

Eadbald said: 'I saw that there was too much money in that purse.'

Edgar had been wondering when this would come up. He said nothing.

Erman said: 'What are we going to do with the extra?'

Edgar noticed the use of 'we' but did not comment on it. He said: 'Well, I think we're entitled to pay for our supper and beds for the night, but the rest goes back to Dreng, obviously.'

'Why?' said Erman.

Edgar disliked the question. 'Because it's his money!'

'He said he was giving you twelve pennies. How many were there?'

'Twenty-four.'

'How many extra is that?' Erman was not good with numbers.

'Twelve.'

'He made a mistake. So we can keep the extra twelve. We each get . . . a lot.'

Eadbald, who was smarter than Erman, said: 'Four each.'

Edgar said: 'So you're asking me to steal twelve pennies and give eight away!'

'We're all in this together,' said Erman.

'What if Dreng realizes his mistake?'

'We'll swear there were only twelve pennies in the purse.'

Eadbald said: 'Erman's right. This is a chance.'

Edgar shook his head firmly. 'I'm giving the extra back.'

Erman adopted a jeering tone. 'You'll get no thanks from Dreng.'

'I never get any thanks from Dreng.'

Eadbald said: 'He'd steal from you if he could.'

'He would, but I'm not like him – thank heaven.'

They gave up.

Edgar was not a thief, but Gab was. There had been only five notches on his stick, whereas Edgar had bought ten stones. If Gab recorded only half of what he sold, he would pay Ragna only half of what was due. But for that he would need the cooperation of the village headman, who was responsible for making sure the villagers paid the right dues. Dudda would betray Gab's scam – unless he were paid to keep quiet. And right now in front of Edgar's eyes Gab and Dudda were drinking together and talking seriously, as if they were discussing some important common interest.

Edgar decided to speak to Seric about it. Seric was in the alehouse, talking to a shaven-headed man in a black robe who must be the village priest. Edgar waited until he left, then followed him, saying to his brothers: 'I'll see you at dawn.'

He followed Seric to a house next to the orchard. Seric turned at the door and said: 'Where are you off to?'

'I'm going to spend the night on the river bank. I want to guard my stone.'

Seric shrugged. 'Probably unnecessary, but I won't discourage you. And it's a mild night.'

'May I ask you something in confidence?'

'Come inside.'

A grey-haired woman sat by the fire feeding a small child with a spoon. Edgar raised his eyebrows: Seric and his wife seemed too old to be the parents. Seric said: 'My wife, Eadgyth, and our grandson,

Ealdwine. Our daughter died in childbirth, and her husband went to Shiring to be a man-at-arms for the ealdorman.'

That explained the household.

'I wanted to ask you . . .' Edgar glanced at Eadgyth.

Seric said: 'You can speak freely.'

'Is Gab honest?'

Seric was not surprised by the question. 'I can't say. Has he tried to cheat you?'

'Not me, no. But I bought ten stones, and I noticed a new stick with only five notches.'

Seric said: 'Let me put it this way: if I were asked to swear to Gab's honesty, I would refuse.'

Edgar nodded. That was enough. Seric could prove nothing, but he had little doubt. 'Thank you,' said Edgar, and he took his leave.

The raft was pulled up on the beach. The brothers had not loaded it: that would have made theft of the stones too easy. Edgar lay down on the raft and pulled his cloak around him. He might not sleep, but perhaps that was no bad thing when he was guarding something valuable.

Brindle whimpered, and Edgar drew the dog under his cloak. Brindle would keep him warm, and warn him if anyone approached.

Edgar now had to tell Ragna that she was being defrauded by Gab and Dudda. He could go to Shiring tomorrow, he figured. Erman and Eadbald could manage the raft on the downstream trip, and he could go home by road, via the town. He needed lime for the mortar, and he could buy it in Shiring and carry it home on his shoulder.

Edgar slept fitfully and woke at first light. Soon afterwards Erman and Eadbald appeared, bringing Leaf's flagon topped up with Outhenham ale and a big loaf of rye bread to eat on the way. Edgar told them he was going to Shiring to buy lime.

'So we'll have to pole the raft back without your help!' Erman said indignantly.

'It won't cost you much effort,' Edgar said patiently. 'It's downstream. All you'll have to do is keep the raft away from the banks.'

The three of them pushed the raft into the water, still tied up, then loaded it with the stones. Edgar insisted on an interlocking pile, so that the cargo would not shift in transit, but in fact the river was so calm that it was not really necessary.

'You'd better unload before you drag the raft across the shallows,' Edgar said. 'Otherwise you might get stuck.'

'Then reload again – that's a lot of work,' Erman grumbled.

Eadbald said: 'And we'll have to unload the stones again at the other end!'

'You'd damn well better – you're being paid to.'

'All right, all right.'

Edgar untied the raft and the three boarded. 'Pole across and drop me on the opposite bank,' Edgar said.

They crossed the river. Edgar got off in the shallows. His brothers returned the vessel to midstream, and slowly the current caught it and took it away.

Edgar watched it out of sight, then set off on the road to Shiring.

ᚦᚦᚦ

THE TOWN WAS busy. The farriers were shoeing horses; the saddlers were sold out of tack; two men with rotating grindstones were sharpening every blade; and the fletchers were selling arrows as fast as they could make them. Edgar soon discovered the reason: Ealdorman Wilwulf was about to harry the Welsh.

The wild men of the west had raided into Wilf's territory in the autumn, but he had been busy with his wedding and had not retaliated. However, he had not forgotten, and now he was mustering a small army to punish them.

An English attack would be devastating to the Welsh. It would disrupt the agricultural cycle. Men and women would be killed, so there would be fewer to plough and sow. Adolescent boys and girls would be captured and sold as slaves, making money for the ealdorman and his men-at-arms, and leaving fewer fecund couples, and therefore, in the long term, fewer Welsh raiders, theoretically.

Harrying was meant to discourage raids, but since the Welsh generally raided only when they were starving, the punishment was a feeble deterrent, in Edgar's opinion. Revenge was the real motive, he thought.

He made his way to the abbey, where he planned to spend the night. It was a pale stone monument of peace in the middle of a town preparing for war. Aldred seemed pleased to see Edgar. The monks were about to go in procession to the church for the mid-afternoon services of Nones, but Aldred was allowed to skip it.

Edgar had had a long walk in the February cold, and Aldred said: 'You need to warm up. There's a fire in Osmund's room – let's sit there.' Edgar accepted gratefully.

All the other monks had left, and the monastery was silent. Edgar felt a moment of unease: Aldred's affection for him was a little too intense. He hoped this was not going to be the scene of an embarrassing interaction. He did not want to offend Aldred, but nor did he want to be embraced by him.

He need not have worried. Aldred had other things on his mind. 'It turns out that Ragna did not know about Wilf's first wife, Inge,' he said.

Edgar remembered a conversation with Agnes the seamstress. 'They thought she was dead,' he recalled.

'Until after they were married, and most of Ragna's servants had gone back to Cherbourg; then Wilf moved Inge back into the compound, along with their son, Garulf.'

Dread settled like a weight in the pit of Edgar's stomach. 'How is she?'

'Distraught.'

He felt desperately sorry for her, a stranger far from home and family, cruelly tricked by the English. 'Poor girl,' he said, but the phrase felt inadequate.

Aldred said: 'But that's not why I'm so keen to talk to you. It's about Dreng's Ferry.'

Edgar wrenched his thoughts away from Ragna.

Aldred went on: 'After I saw the state of the minster I proposed that it should be taken over by monks, and the archbishop agreed. But Wynstan kicked up a huge fuss, and Abbot Osmund backed down.'

Edgar frowned. 'Why did Wynstan care so much?'

'That's the question. It's not a rich church, and Degbert is no more than a distant relation to him.'

'Why would Wynstan quarrel with his archbishop over something so minor?'

'That's what I was going to ask you. You live at the alehouse, you operate the ferry, you see everyone who comes and goes. You must know most of what happens there.'

Edgar wanted to help Aldred, but did not know the answers to his questions. He shook his head. 'I can't imagine what's in Wynstan's mind.' Then a thought occurred to him. 'He does visit, though.'

'Really?' said Aldred, intrigued. 'How often?'

'Twice since I've been there. The first was a week after Michaelmas, the second just about six weeks ago.'

'You're good with dates. So both visits came soon after the quarter day. For what purpose?'

'Nothing apparent to me.'

'Well, what does he do there?'

'At Christmas he gave every house a piglet.'

'Strange. He's not normally open-handed. Rather the opposite.'

'And then he and Degbert went to Combe. Both times.'

Aldred scratched his shaved scalp. 'Something is going on, and I can't figure out what.'

Edgar had a notion, but he felt awkward about voicing it. 'Wynstan and Degbert could be . . . I mean, they could be having some kind of –'

'Love affair? Possibly, but I don't think so. I know a bit about that sort of thing, and neither man strikes me as the type.'

Edgar had to agree.

Aldred added: 'They might hold orgies with slave girls at the minster, that would be more credible.'

It was Edgar's turn to look dubious. 'I don't see how they could keep such a thing secret. Where would they hide the slaves?'

'You're right. They might hold pagan rites, though: they wouldn't necessarily need slaves for that.'

'Pagan rites? What's in that for Wynstan?'

'What's in it for anyone? But still there are pagans.'

Edgar was not convinced. 'In England?'

'Perhaps not.'

Edgar was struck by a thought. 'I vaguely remember Wynstan visiting Combe when we lived there. Young men aren't very interested in the clergy, and I never took much notice, but he used to stay at the house of his brother, Wigelm – I remember my mother commenting that you'd expect a bishop to stay at the monastery.'

'And why would he go to Combe?'

'It's a good place to indulge your lusts. At least, it was before the Vikings burned it, and it probably recovered quickly. There's a woman called Mags who keeps a bawdy house, several houses where men gamble for high stakes, and more alehouses than churches.'

'The fleshpots of Babylon.'

Edgar smiled. 'Also a lot of ordinary people like me just pursuing a trade. But, yes, the town gets a lot of visitors, mostly sailors, and that gives it a certain character.'

There was a moment of quiet, and they both heard a soft sound from outside the room. Aldred jumped to his feet and threw the door wide.

Edgar saw the figure of a monk moving away.

'Hildred!' said Aldred. 'I thought you were at Nones. Were you eavesdropping?'

'I had to come back for something.'

'What?'

Hildred hesitated.

'Never mind,' said Aldred, and he slammed the door.

ÞÞÞ

THE EALDORMAN'S COMPOUND was even busier than the town. The army was to leave at dawn, and all the men were getting ready, sharpening arrows and polishing helmets and loading saddlebags with smoked fish and hard cheese.

Edgar noticed that some of the women seemed dressed up, and he wondered why; then it occurred to him that they feared this night might be their last with their husbands, and they wanted to make it a memorable one.

Ragna looked different. The last time Edgar had seen her had been at her wedding, when she had shone with gladness and hope. She was still beautiful, but in a different way. Now the light she radiated was more like that of a full moon, bright but cold. She was as poised and composed as ever, and beautifully dressed in the rich brown colour that suited her so well; but a certain girlish enthusiasm had gone, to be replaced by an air of angry determination.

He looked carefully at her figure – never a burdensome task – and decided that she was not yet pregnant. She had been married only for a little more than three months, so it was early days yet.

She welcomed him into her house and gave him bread with soft cheese and a cup of ale. He wanted to know about Wilf and Inge, but he did not dare to ask her such personal questions. Instead he said: 'I've just been to Outhenham.'

'What were you doing there?'

'Buying stone for the new brewhouse I'm building at Dreng's Ferry.'

'I'm the new lord of the Vale of Outhen.'

'I know. That's why I wanted to see you. I think you're being cheated.'

'Go on, please.'

He told her the story of Gab and his sticks. 'I can't prove that you're being robbed, but I'm sure of it,' he said. 'You may want to check.'

'I certainly do. If Dudda the headman is defrauding me that way, he's probably doing it in a dozen other ways too.'

Edgar had not thought of that. Ragna had an instinct for government, he realized, just as he had an instinct for the construction of shapes in wood and stone. His respect for her rose higher.

She said thoughtfully: 'What are the other villagers like? I've never been there.'

'There's an elder called Seric who seems more sensible than most.'

'That's useful to know. Thank you. And how are you?' Her tone became bright and somewhat brittle. 'You're old enough to be married. Is there a girl in your life?'

Edgar was taken aback. After their conversation at her wedding, when he had told her about Sungifu, how could she ask him a light-hearted question about romance? 'I'm not planning to marry,' he said shortly.

She sensed his reaction, and said: 'I'm sorry. I forgot, for a moment, just how very serious you are, for someone your age.'

'I think we have that in common.'

She thought about that. He feared he had been impudent, but all she said was: 'Yes.'

It was an intimate moment, and he was emboldened to say: 'Aldred told me about Inge.'

A wounded look came over her lovely face. 'It was a shock to me,' she said.

Edgar guessed she was not that frank with everyone, and he felt privileged. 'I'm so sorry,' he said. 'I feel mortified that you've been so misled by the English.' In the back of his mind he was thinking that he was not as sad as he should have been. Somehow the idea that Wilf had turned out to be an unsatisfactory husband did not displease him as much as it ought to have. He put the ungenerous thought out of his mind and said: 'That's why I'm so cross about Gab the quarry master. You know that we English are not all the same, though, don't you?'

'Of course. But I only married one.'

Edgar risked a bold question. 'Do you still love him?'

She answered without hesitation. 'Yes.'

He was surprised.

He must have shown it for she said: 'I know. He's deceived me, and he's unfaithful, but I love him.'

'I see,' he said, though he did not.

'You shouldn't be shocked,' she said. 'You love a dead woman.'

That was harsh, but they were having a frank conversation. 'I suppose you're right,' he said.

Suddenly she seemed to feel they had gone far enough. She stood up and said: 'I have a lot to do.'

'I'm glad to have seen you. Thank you for the cheese.' He turned to go.

She stopped him with a hand on his arm. 'Thank you for telling me about the quarry master at Outhenham. I appreciate it.'

He felt a glow of satisfaction.

To his surprise she kissed his cheek. 'Goodbye,' she said. 'I hope I see you again soon.'

ÞÞÞ

IN THE MORNING Aldred and Edgar went out to see the army ride off.

Aldred was still chewing over the mystery of Dreng's Ferry. The place had something to hide. He had wondered why the ordinary villagers there were hostile to strangers. It was because they were guarding a secret – all except Edgar and his family, who were not in on it.

Aldred was determined to get to the bottom of it.

Edgar had with him the sack of lime he was going to carry for the next two days. 'It's a good thing you're strong,' Aldred said. 'I'm not sure I could carry it for two hours.'

'I'll manage,' said Edgar. 'It was worth it for the chance to talk to Ragna.'

'You're fond of her.'

Edgar's hazel eyes twinkled in a way that made Aldred's heart beat faster. 'Not in the way you seem to imply,' Edgar said. 'Which is just as well, since the daughters of counts never marry the sons of boatbuilders.'

Aldred was familiar with impossible love. He almost said so, but bit his tongue. He did not want his tendresse for Edgar to become embarrassing to them both. That might end their friendship, and friendship was all he had.

He glanced at Edgar and saw, with relief, that his expression was untroubled.

There was a noise from up the hill, hoof beats and cheering. The sound got louder, then the army appeared. At its head was a big iron-grey stallion with a mad look in its eye. Its rider, in a red cloak, was surely Wilf, but his identity was hidden by a gleaming full-face helmet with a plume. Looking more closely, Aldred saw that the helmet was made of more than one metal, and was engraved with complex designs that could not be made out at a distance. It was decorative, Aldred guessed, intended to impress: Wilf would probably wear a less valuable one into battle.

Wilf's brother Wigelm and son Garulf came next, riding side by side; then the men-at-arms, dressed less finely but still showing some bright colours. After them came a crowd of young men on foot, peasant boys and poor town lads, dressed in the usual worn brown tunics, most armed with home-made wooden spears, others having nothing more than a kitchen knife or a hand axe, all hoping to change their fortunes in battle and come home with a bag of looted jewellery or a valuable pair of teenage captives to sell as slaves.

They all crossed the square, waving at the townspeople, who clapped and cheered as they went by; then they disappeared to the north.

Edgar was going east. He shouldered his sack and took his leave.

Aldred returned to the abbey. It was almost time for the service of Terce, but he was summoned to Abbot Osmund.

As usual, Hildred was with the abbot.

Aldred thought: What now?

Osmund said: 'I'll get right to the point, Brother Aldred. I don't want you to make an enemy of Bishop Wynstan.'

Aldred understood immediately, but pretended not to. 'The bishop is our brother in Christ, of course.'

Osmund was too smart to be diverted by this sort of platitude. 'You were overheard talking to that lad from Dreng's Ferry.'

'Yes. I caught Brother Hildred eavesdropping.'

Hildred said: 'And a good thing too! You were plotting against your abbot!'

'I was asking questions.'

Osmund said: 'Listen to me. We had a difference of opinion with Wynstan about Dreng's Ferry, but the matter has been resolved, and is now closed.'

'Not really. The minster is still an abomination in the sight of the Lord.'

'That's as may be, but I have decided not to quarrel with the bishop. I don't accuse you of plotting against me, despite Hildred's hot words, but really, Aldred, you must not undermine me.'

Aldred felt shame mixed with indignation. He had no wish to offend his kindly but lazy superior. On the other hand, it was wrong for a man of God to overlook wickedness. Osmund would do anything for a quiet life, but a monk was obliged to do more than seek a quiet life.

However, this was not the time to make a stand. 'I'm sorry, my lord abbot,' he said. 'I will try harder to remember my vow of obedience.'

'I knew you'd see sense,' said Osmund.

Hildred looked sceptical. He did not believe that Aldred was sincere.

And he was right.

ÞÞÞ

EDGAR ARRIVED BACK in Dreng's Ferry on the afternoon of the following day. He was dead beat. It had been a mistake to carry a sack of lime that distance. He was strong, but not superhuman. He had a crippling backache.

The first thing he saw was a pile of stones on the bank of the river. His brothers had unloaded the raft but had not carried the stones to the site of the brewhouse. At that moment he felt he could have murdered them both.

He was too tired even to walk into the tavern. He dumped his sack by the stones and lay on the ground right there.

Dreng came out and saw him. 'So you're back,' he said superfluously.

'Here I am.'

'The stones have arrived.'

'So I see.'

'What have you brought?'

'A sack of lime. I saved you the cost of horse transport, but I'll never do it again.'

'Anything else?'

'No.'

Dreng smiled with an odd look of malicious satisfaction.

Edgar said: 'Except for one thing.' He took out the purse. 'You gave me too much money.'

Dreng looked startled.

Edgar said: 'The stones were a penny each. We paid a penny at the alehouse in Outhenham for supper and beds. The lime was four pence. There are nine pennies left.'

Dreng took the purse and counted the coins. 'So there are,' he said. 'Well, well.'

Edgar was puzzled. A man as mean as Dreng should have been horrified to learn that he had handed over more money than necessary. But he was just mildly surprised.

'Well, well,' Dreng said again, and he went back into the alehouse.

Lying supine, waiting for his back to stop hurting, Edgar mused. It was almost as if Dreng knew he had given too much and was surprised to get some back.

Of course, Edgar thought; that was it.

He had been given a test. Dreng had deliberately put temptation in his way, to see what he would do.

His brothers would have swallowed the bait. They would have stolen the money and been found out. But Edgar had simply given it back.

All the same, Erman and Eadbald had been right about one thing. They had said that Edgar would get no thanks from Dreng. And no thanks was just what he had got.

18

IT SHOULD HAVE BEEN a simple matter for Ragna to go to the Vale of Outhen.

She had mentioned it to Wilf the day before he left for Wales, and he had nodded agreement without hesitation. But after the army had left, Wynstan had come to her house. 'This is not a good moment for you to visit Outhen,' he said, using the soft voice and insincere smile he deployed when pretending to be reasonable. 'It's the time of spring ploughing. We don't want to distract the peasants.'

Ragna was wary. Wynstan had never before shown an interest in agricultural matters. 'Naturally, I don't want to do anything that would interfere with their work,' she said, temporizing.

'Good. Postpone your visit. Meanwhile, I'll collect your rents and hand the proceeds over to you, as I did at Christmas.'

It was true that Wynstan had given her a large sum of money a few days after Christmas, but he had offered no accounting, so she had no way of knowing whether she had received what was due to her. At the time she had been too distraught about Inge to care, but she did not intend to let this laxness continue. As he turned to leave, she put a hand on his arm. 'When would you suggest?'

'Let me think about that.'

Ragna suspected she knew more about the farming cycle than he did. 'You see, there's always something urgent to be done in the fields.'

'Yes, but—'

'After the ploughing comes the sowing.'

'Yes—'

'Then the weeding, then the reaping, then the threshing, then the grinding.'

'I know.'

'And then it's time for winter ploughing.'

He looked irritated. 'I'll let you know when the time is right.'

Ragna shook her head firmly. 'I have a better idea. I'll visit Outhen on Lady Day. It's a holiday, so they won't be working anyway.'

He hesitated, but apparently could not think of a rejoinder. 'Very well,' he said tersely and, as he walked away, Ragna knew she had not heard the last of this.

But she was not intimidated. On Lady Day she would receive her rents in Outhenham. And there she would ambush Gab the quarryman.

She wanted to take Edgar with her for the confrontation. She sent a messenger to summon him from Dreng's Ferry, pretending she needed him to do more carpentry.

An extra reason for her wanting to go away was that there was a tiresome atmosphere in the compound with the husbands away. The only males left were either too young to fight or too old. Ragna found that the women behaved badly when their men could not see them. They squabbled, shrieked, and ran each other down in ways that their husbands would have derided. No doubt men, too, misbehaved when the opposite sex was not there to be disdainful. She would have to ask Wilf about that.

She decided she would stay in the Vale of Outhen for a week or so after Lady Day. She was determined to make a personal tour of her property and find out in detail what she owned. She would show herself to her tenants and her subjects, getting to know them. She would hold court in each village and begin to establish a reputation as a fair judge.

When she spoke to the head groom, Wignoth, he shook his head and sucked in the air between his brown teeth. 'We haven't got enough horses,' he pointed out. 'Every spare mount has been commandeered for the harrying of the Welsh.'

Ragna could not possibly arrive on foot. People judged by appearances, and a noble who did not have a horse would be seen as lacking authority. 'But Astrid is still here,' she said. She had brought her favourite horse from Cherbourg.

'You'll have several people with you on your visit, of course,' said Wignoth.

'Yes.'

'Apart from Astrid, all we have is an elderly mare, a pony with one eye, and a packhorse that's never been ridden.'

There were other horses in the town: both the bishop and the abbot had several mounts, and the sheriff had a large stable. But they needed them for their own purposes. 'What we have here must suffice,' Ragna said firmly. 'It's not ideal, but I'll manage.'

As she walked away from the stable she saw two young townsmen lounging near the kitchen, talking to Gilda and the other kitchen maids. Ragna stopped and frowned. She had no moral objection to flirting – in fact, she was good at it herself when it suited her purpose. But with husbands away fighting, dalliances could be dangerous. Illicit affairs did not usually remain secret for long, and soldiers returning from battle could be quick to resort to violence.

Ragna changed direction and approached the two men.

A cook called Eadhild was skinning fish with a sharp knife and bloody hands. None of the maids noticed Ragna's approach. Eadhild was telling the men to go away, but in a playful tone that clearly showed she did not mean it. 'We don't want your sort here,' she said, but then she giggled.

Ragna noticed that Gilda looked disapproving.

342

One of the men said: 'Women never want our sort – until they do!'

'Oh, go on with you,' said Eadhild.

Ragna said abruptly: 'Who are you men?'

They looked startled and said nothing for a moment.

Ragna said: 'Give me your names or I'll have you both thrashed.'

Gilda pointed with a skewer. 'He's Wiga and the other one is Tata. They work at the Abbey Alehouse.'

Ragna said: 'And what do you think will happen, Wiga and Tata, when these women's husbands come home, with their swords as bloody as that fish knife of Eadhild's, and find out what you've been saying to their wives?'

Wiga and Tata looked shamefaced and made no answer.

'Murder,' Ragna said. 'That's what will happen. Now go back to your alehouse, and don't let me see you inside this compound until Ealdorman Wilf comes home.'

They scurried off.

Gilda said: 'Thank you, my lady. I'm glad to see the backs of those two.'

Ragna went to her house and turned her mind back to the Vale of Outhen. She decided to ride there on the eve of Lady Day. It was a morning's journey. She would spend the afternoon talking to villagers, then hold court the following morning.

One day before she was due to leave, Wignoth came to her, bringing the smell of the stables into her house. He looked insincerely mournful and said: 'The road to Outhenham has been washed out by a flood.'

She stared hard at him. He was a big man, but awkward. She said: 'Is it completely impassable?'

'Yes, completely,' he said. He was not a good liar, and he looked shifty.

'Who told you that?'

343

'Um, the Lady Gytha.'

Ragna was not surprised. 'I shall go to Outhenham,' she said. 'If there's a flood, I'll find a way around it.'

Wynstan seemed determined to prevent her visit, she reflected. He had recruited both Gytha and Wignoth to dissuade her. That made her all the more determined to go.

She was expecting Edgar from Dreng's Ferry that day, but he did not arrive. She was disappointed: she felt she needed him to give credence to her accusation. Could she charge Gab without Edgar's testimony? She was not sure.

Next day she got up early.

She dressed in rich fabrics of sombre colours, dark brown and deep black, to emphasize her seriousness. She felt tense. She told herself she was simply going to meet her people, something she had done dozens of times before – but never in England. Nothing would be quite as she expected; things never were here, she knew from experience. And it was so important to make a good first impression. Peasants had infuriatingly long memories. It could take years to recover from a false start.

She was pleased when Edgar showed up. He apologized for not appearing the day before, but said he had arrived late and gone straight to the abbey for the night. Ragna was relieved that she did not have to confront Gab alone.

They went to the stable. Bern and Cat were loading the packhorse and saddling the old mare and the one-eyed pony. Ragna took Astrid from her stall – and saw immediately that something was wrong.

As the horse walked she was bobbing her head in an unusual way. A moment's observation revealed that she lifted her head and neck as her left foreleg touched the ground. Ragna knew that this was a horse's way of reducing the weight bearing on an injury.

She knelt beside Astrid and touched the lower half of the leg with both hands. She palpitated gently at first and then with increasing

344

pressure. When she pressed hard, Astrid twitched and tried to free her leg from Ragna's grasp.

In this condition the horse could not carry her.

Ragna was furious. She stood up and looked hard at Wignoth. Controlling her anger with an effort, she said: 'My horse has been injured.'

Wignoth looked scared. 'One of the other beasts must have kicked her.'

Ragna looked at the other horses. They were a sorry lot. 'Which of these feisty creatures do you suspect?' she said sarcastically.

His voice took on a pleading tone. 'All horses kick sometimes.'

Ragna looked around. Her eye fell on a box of tools. Horses' hooves were protected by iron shoes nailed to their feet. One of the tools was a short, heavy wooden mallet. Her instinct told her that Wignoth had hit Astrid's foreleg with the mallet. But she could not prove it.

'Poor horse,' she said quietly to Astrid. Then she turned to Wignoth. 'If you can't keep the horses safe, you can't be in charge of the stable,' she said to him coldly.

He looked mulishly obstinate, as if he felt he was unjustly treated.

Ragna needed time to think. She said to Bern and Cat: 'Stay here. Don't unload the horses.' She left the stable and headed for her own house.

Edgar followed her.

As they passed the pond she said to him: 'That pig Wignoth deliberately lamed my horse. He must have hit her with his shoeing mallet. The bone isn't broken, but she's badly bruised.'

'Why would Wignoth do that?'

'He's a coward. Someone told him to do it, and he didn't have the guts to refuse.'

'Who would have given him that order?'

'Wynstan doesn't want me to go to Outhen. He's been putting

obstacles in my way. He has always collected the rents for Wilf, and he wants to continue to do so for me.'

'And skim off the cream for himself, I suppose.'

'Yes. I suspect he's already on his way there.'

They went into her house, but she did not sit down. 'I don't know what to do,' she said. 'I hate to give up.'

'Who might help you?'

Ragna recalled her conversation with Aldred about allies. She had some. 'Aldred would help me, if he could,' she said. 'So would Sheriff Den.'

'The abbey has horses, and so does Den.'

Ragna was thoughtful. 'If I go to Outhen now, there will be a confrontation. Wynstan is very determined; I fear he will refuse to let me receive my own rents, and I will have to find a way to enforce the law.'

'In that case you would have to appeal to the shire court.'

She shook her head. Ties of blood could matter more than the letter of the law in Normandy, and she had seen no sign that the legal system in England was any better. 'The shire court is presided over by Wilf.'

'Your husband.'

Ragna thought of Inge, and shrugged. Would Wilf side with his wife or his brother? She was not sure. The thought made her sad for a moment, but she shook off the feeling and said something different. 'I hate to play the role of moaner.'

Edgar said logically: 'Then you must make sure you receive the rents, not Wynstan, and let him be the complainer.'

That was a counsel of perfection. 'I'd need to be backed up by force.'

'Aldred might go with us. A monk has moral authority.'

'I'm not sure the abbot would let him. Osmund is timid. He doesn't want a quarrel.'

'Let me talk to Aldred. He likes me.'

'It's worth a try. But moral authority may not be enough. I need men-at-arms. All I've got is Bern.'

'What about Sheriff Den? He has men. If he backed you, he would be doing no more than enforcing the king's laws – which is his duty.'

This was a possibility, Ragna thought. As she had belatedly discovered, Wilf and Wynstan had defied the king over the Cherbourg treaty and her marriage. The sheriff might well be smarting from that. 'Den would probably relish an opportunity to restrain Bishop Wynstan.'

'I'm sure of it.'

Ragna felt she was beginning to see a way forward. 'You talk to Aldred. I'll go and see Den.'

'We should leave separately, so that it doesn't look like a conspiracy.'

'Good point. I'll go first.'

Ragna strode out of the house and across the compound. She spoke to no one: let them guess, fearfully, what her rage might bring about.

She went down the hill and turned towards the edge of town where Den lived.

She was deeply disappointed that Wynstan had been able to turn Wignoth against her. She had worked hard to win the loyalty of the servants in the compound, and she had imagined that she had succeeded. Gilda had been the first to adhere to Ragna, and the kitchen maids had followed her lead. The men-at-arms liked Garulf – they grinned and said he was a hell of a boy – and there was nothing she could do about that. But she had gone out of her way to befriend the stable hands, and now it seemed she had failed. People liked her better than Wynstan, she reflected, but they feared him more.

Now she needed all the support she could get. Would Den come to her aid? She thought there was a chance. He had no reason to fear Wynstan. And Aldred? He would help if he could. But if they failed her, she would be alone.

The sheriff's domestic establishment looked as formidable as the ealdorman's, an impression that was surely intentional. He had a stockaded compound with barracks, stables, a great hall and several smaller buildings.

Den had refused to join Wilf's army, saying that his responsibility was to maintain the king's peace within the district of Shiring, and he was needed all the more while the ealdorman was away – a view that was proved right by Wynstan's behaviour.

Ragna found Den in the great hall. He was pleased to see her, as men generally were. His wife and daughter were with him, and so was the grandson of whom he was so proud. Ragna spent a few minutes cooing over the baby, who smiled and babbled back at her. Then she got down to business.

'Wynstan is trying to rob me of my rents from the Vale of Outhen,' she said.

Den's answer made her exultant.

'Is he, now?' Den said with a pleased smile. 'Then we must do something about that.'

ÞÞÞ

RAGNA AND HER allies were careful not to speak about their plans beforehand, so their departure at dawn was unexpected, and no one had the chance to ride ahead and warn Wynstan. He was in for a shock.

Lady Day was the twenty-fifth day of March, the anniversary of the archangel Gabriel telling Mary that she was going to conceive a child miraculously. The air was cold but the sun was shining. This was the perfect moment, Ragna felt, to announce to the people of the valley that she was their new lord.

She left Shiring on a grey mare belonging to Den. The sheriff rode with her, and brought along a dozen men-at-arms led by their captain, Wigbert. She was thrilled by Sheriff Den's support. It proved to her that she was not a weakling, totally in the power of her husband's family. The conflict was not over yet, but she had already proved she was no pushover.

Bern, Cat and Edgar walked alongside the horses. Outside the town they met up with Aldred, who had sneaked away from the abbey without telling Osmund.

Ragna felt triumphant. She had overcome every problem, negotiated every impediment put in her way. She had refused to give in to discouragement.

She recalled Wigelm's rude intervention at her wedding. He had objected to her being given the Vale of Outhen, and had been quickly slapped down by Wilf. Ragna had wondered why Wigelm had troubled to make such an unwarranted protest, but now she thought she understood. He had been putting down a marker. He and Wynstan had a long-term plan to take Outhen from her, and they wanted to be able to say they had never accepted the legitimacy of the gift.

This had to be Wynstan's plan. Wigelm was not smart enough. She felt a surge of loathing for the bishop. He abused his priestly robes by using his position to gratify his greed. The thought made her momentarily nauseated.

She had defeated them so far, but she told herself not to celebrate yet. She had frustrated Wynstan's efforts to keep her at home, but that was only the start.

She turned her mind to what she needed to achieve with this visit. Endearing herself to the people was no longer the main objective. She first needed to make sure they understood that she was their lord, not Wynstan. She might not get another chance this good. The sheriff was not going to accompany her on every visit.

She questioned Edgar about the people of Outhenham, and memorized the names of the principal characters. Then she told him to walk at the back of the group entering the village, and remain inconspicuous until she called him forward.

As they arrived Ragna noted with pleasure that the place was affluent. Most houses had a pigsty, a henhouse or a cowshed, and some had all three. Where there was prosperity there was always trade, she knew, and she guessed that Outhenham's position at the mouth of the valley made it the natural marketplace for the district.

It would be her responsibility to maintain and increase that prosperity, for her own benefit as well as that of the people. Her father always said that nobles had duties as well as privileges.

The outskirts of the village had been almost deserted, and a minute later Ragna saw that most of the inhabitants had gathered on the green in the centre, between the church and the alehouse.

In the middle of the space, Wynstan sat on a broad four-legged stool with a cushion, the type of seat used on formal occasions. Two men stood either side of him. The one with the shaved head would be the village priest, whose name – Ragna now recalled from her conversation with Edgar – was Draca. The other, a heavy red-faced person, would be Dudda, the headman.

They were surrounded by goods. Some coins circulated in the countryside, but many peasants paid their rents in kind. Two large carts were being loaded with barrels and sacks, chickens in cages, and smoked and salted fish and meat. Piglets and young sheep were confined in temporary pens up against the wall of the church.

On a trestle table were numerous notched sticks and several piles of silver pennies. Wynstan's assistant Ithamar sat at the table, holding in his hand a long sheet of parchment, old and stained and worn at the edges, covered with close-packed writing in neat lines, possibly in Latin. That would be a list of payments due from each man. Ragna resolved to seize that parchment.

This was a familiar sight, no different in Normandy, and she took it all in at a glance, then focused on Wynstan.

He stood up from his seat and stared, open-mouthed, as he grasped the size and authority of the arriving contingent. His expression showed shock and dismay. No doubt he had thought that by causing Astrid to be lamed he had made sure Ragna could not leave Shiring. He was now beginning to realize how badly he had underestimated her. He said: 'How did you—?' But he changed his mind and did not finish the question.

She continued to walk her horse towards him, and the crowd parted for her. She held the reins in her left hand and a riding crop in her right.

Wynstan, always a quick thinker, changed his tune. 'Lady Ragna, welcome to the Vale of Outhen,' he said. 'We're surprised, but honoured, to see you here.' He seemed about to grasp the bridle of her horse, but Ragna was not having that: she raised her riding-crop, just a little, as if to strike his hand away; he saw her determination and aborted his move.

She rode past him.

She had often spoken to large groups in the open air, and she knew how to make her voice carry. 'People of the Vale of Outhen,' she said. 'I am the Lady Ragna, and I am your lord.'

There was a moment of silence. Ragna waited. A man in the crowd went down on one knee. Others followed suit, and soon everyone was kneeling.

She turned to her group. 'Take possession of those carts,' she ordered.

The sheriff nodded to his men-at-arms.

Their captain, Wigbert, was a small, wiry, mean-looking man with a temper as taut as a bowstring. His lieutenant was Godwine, tall and heavy. People were intimidated by Godwine's size, but he was the friendlier of the two. Wigbert was the man to be scared of.

Wynstan said: 'Those are my carts.'

Ragna said: 'And you shall have them back – but not today.'

Wynstan's companions were mostly servants, not men-at-arms,

and they backed away from the carts as soon as Wigbert and Godwine approached them.

The villagers were still on their knees.

Wynstan said: 'Wait! Are you going to be ruled by a mere woman?'

There was no response from the villagers. They were still on their knees, but kneeling was free. The real issue was not who they bowed to but who they paid rent to.

Ragna had an answer ready for Wynstan. 'Don't you know about the great princess Ethelfled, the daughter of King Alfred and lord of all Mercia?' she said. Aldred had told her that most people would have heard of this remarkable woman who had died only eighty years ago. 'She was one of the greatest rulers England ever saw!'

Wynstan said: 'She was English. You're not.'

'But Bishop Wynstan, you negotiated my marriage contract. You arranged for me to be given the Vale of Outhen. When you were in Cherbourg, making arrangements with Count Hubert, did you not notice that you were in Normandy, dealing with a Norman nobleman for the hand of his Norman daughter?'

The crowd laughed, and Wynstan flushed with anger. 'The people are used to paying their dues to me,' he said. 'Father Draca will confirm that.' He looked hard at the village priest.

The man looked terrified. He managed to say: 'What the bishop says is true.'

Ragna said: 'Father Draca, who is the lord of the Vale of Outhenham?'

'My lady, I'm just a poor village priest—'

'But you know who is the lord of your village.'

'Yes, my lady.'

'Then answer the question.'

'My lady, we have been informed that you are now lord of Outhen.'

'And so the people owe their rents to whom?'

Draca mumbled: 'You.'

'Louder, please, so that the villagers can hear you.'

Draca saw that he had no alternative. 'They owe their rents to you, my lady.'

'Thank you.' She looked over the crowd, paused a moment, then said: 'All stand.'

They got to their feet.

Ragna was satisfied. She had taken control. But it was not over yet.

She dismounted and went to the table. Everyone watched her silently, wondering what she would do next. 'You're Ithamar, aren't you?' she said to Wynstan's assistant. He stared at her anxiously. She snatched the parchment from his hand. Taken by surprise, he offered no resistance. The document specified, in Latin, what dues were payable by each man in the village, with many scribbled changes. It was old, and today's tenants would be the sons and grandsons of those originally listed.

She decided to impress the villagers with her education. 'How far have you got this morning?' she asked Ithamar.

'To Wilmund the baker.'

She ran a finger down the list. 'Wilmundus Pistor,' she read aloud. 'It says here that he owes thirty-six pence per quarter.' There was a murmur of surprise from the crowd: not only could she read, but she could translate Latin. 'Step forward, Wilmund.'

The baker was a plump young man with floury streaks of white in his dark beard. He stepped forward with his wife and a teenage son, each of them holding a small purse. Wilmund slowly counted out twenty pence in whole coins, then his wife counted another ten in halves.

Ragna said: 'What's your name, baker's wife?'

'Regenhild, my lady,' she said nervously.

'And is this your son?'

'Yes, my lady, he's Penda.'

'He's a fine lad.'

Regenhild relaxed a little. 'Thank you, my lady.'

'How old are you, Penda?'

'Fifteen, my lady.'

'You're tall, for fifteen.'

Penda blushed. 'Yes.'

He counted out six pence in quarters, and the family's rent was paid. They returned to the crowd, smiling at the attention they had received from a noblewoman. All she had done was to show interest in them as people, not just tenants, but they would remember it for years.

Ragna turned to Dudda, the headman. Feigning ignorance she said: 'Tell me about these notched sticks.'

'They are from Gab the quarry master,' Dudda replied. 'He keeps a different stick for each man who buys stone. One stone in five belongs to the lord.'

'Which is me.'

Dudda said sulkily: 'So we are told.'

'Which of you is Gab?'

A thin man with scarred hands stepped forward and coughed.

There were seven sticks, and only one of them bore five notches. She picked it up as if at random. 'So, Gab, to which buyer does this stick refer?'

'That would be Dreng the ferryman.' Gab's voice was hoarse, no doubt from breathing stone dust.

As if seeking to understand the system Ragna said: 'So Dreng bought five stones from you.'

'Yes, my lady.' Gab looked uneasy, as if wondering where this was leading. He added: 'And I owe you the price of one of them.'

She turned to Dudda. 'Is that right?'

He looked anxious, as if fearing a surprise but unable to figure out what it might be. 'Yes, my lady.'

'Dreng's builder is here with me today,' Ragna said.

She heard two or three startled exclamations, quickly supressed, and she guessed that some villagers must have known about Gab's fraud. Gab himself suddenly looked sick, and Dudda's red face paled.

Ragna said: 'Come forward, Edgar.'

Edgar emerged from the middle of the group of men-at-arms and servants, and came to stand beside Ragna. Dudda directed a look of hatred at him.

Ragna said: 'How many stones did you buy from my quarry, Edgar?'

Gab said quickly: 'It was five, wasn't it, young man?'

Edgar said: 'No. Five stones isn't enough to tile the roof of a brewhouse. I bought ten.'

Gab was panicking now. 'An innocent mistake, then, my lady, I swear it.'

Ragna made her voice cold. 'There are no innocent mistakes.'

'But my lady—'

'Be silent.' Ragna would have liked to get rid of Gab, but she needed a quarryman and did not have a replacement ready. She decided to make a virtue of necessity. 'I'm not going to punish you,' she said. 'I'm going to say to you what our Lord said to the adulteress: Go thy way, and sin no more.'

The crowd were surprised at that, but they seemed to approve. Ragna hoped she had shown herself to be a ruler who could not be fooled but might be merciful.

She turned to Dudda. 'However, I don't forgive you. Your duty was to make sure your lord was not cheated, and you failed. You are no longer headman.'

Once again she listened to the crowd. They sounded shocked, but she heard no note of protest, and she concluded that they did not much regret the dismissal of Dudda.

'Let Seric step forward.'

A man of about fifty with an alert look came out of the crowd and bowed to her.

She looked at the villagers and said: 'I'm told that Seric is an honest man.'

She had not asked them a question – that might have given the impression that the choice was theirs. But she paid attention to their reactions. Several people made approving noises, and others nodded assent. Edgar's instinct about Seric had been right, it seemed.

'Seric, you are now headman.'

'Thank you, my lady,' said Seric. 'I will be honest and true.'

'Good.' She looked at Wynstan's assistant. 'Ithamar, you are no longer required. Father Draca, you can take his place.'

Draca looked nervous, but he sat at the table, and Seric stood beside him.

Wynstan stalked off, and his men began to hurry after him.

Ragna looked around. The villagers were quiet, watching her, waiting to see what she would do next. She had their rapt attention, and they were ready to do her bidding. She had taken leadership. She was satisfied.

'Very well,' she said. 'Let us continue.'

19

ALDRED LEFT SHIRING ON the pony Dismas, heading for Combe. There was safety in numbers, and he travelled with Offa the reeve, who was going to Mudeford. Aldred was carrying a letter from Abbot Osmund to Prior Ulfric. The letter was about a routine matter of business having to do with some land that, awkwardly, was jointly owned by the two monasteries. In Aldred's saddlebag, carefully wrapped in linen, was a precious volume of the *Dialogues* of Pope Gregory the Great, copied and illuminated in Aldred's scriptorium, a gift to Combe Priory. Aldred was hoping to receive a reciprocal present, another book that would enlarge the library at Shiring. Books were sometimes bought and sold, though exchange of gifts was more usual. But Aldred's real reason for going to Combe was neither the letter nor the book. He was investigating Bishop Wynstan.

He wanted to be in Combe immediately after Midsummer Day, at the time when Wynstan and Degbert would visit, if they followed their usual routine. He was determined to find out what the corrupt cousins did there and whether it had any connection with the mystery of Dreng's Ferry. He had been firmly ordered to drop the whole thing, but he was determined to disobey.

The minster at Dreng's Ferry affected him profoundly. It made him feel stained. It was hard to take pride in being a man of God when others who wore the robes behaved like libertines. Degbert and his crew seemed to cast a shadow over everything Aldred did.

Aldred was willing to break his vow of obedience if he could put an end to the minster.

Now that he was on his way, he had misgivings. Just how was he going to find out what Wynstan and Degbert were up to? He could follow them around, but they might notice. Worse, there were houses in Combe that a man of God should not enter. Wynstan and Degbert might go to such places discreetly, or perhaps not care if they were seen, but Aldred would find it impossible to act the part of an habitué, and he would surely be spotted. And then he would be in all kinds of trouble.

His route lay via Dreng's Ferry, and he decided to ask Edgar's help.

On arriving at the hamlet he went first to the minster. He walked in with his head high. He had been unwelcome there before, but now he was hated. It was not surprising. He had tried to have the priests ejected and deprived of their life of comfort and idleness, and they would never forget it. Forgiveness and mercy were among the many Christian virtues they lacked. All the same Aldred insisted that they offer him the hospitality they owed to all clergy. He was not prepared to skulk in the alehouse. He was not the one who should feel ashamed. Degbert and his priests had given such offence by their behaviour that the archbishop had agreed to expel them: they should feel unable to hold up their heads. They were still here only because they had some clandestine usefulness to Bishop Wynstan – and that was the secret Aldred was determined to uncover.

He did not want to reveal that he was on his way to Combe, and would be there at the same time as Wynstan and Degbert, so he told a white lie, and said he was going to Sherborne, which was several days' journey from Combe.

After a begrudged evening meal and a perfunctory service of Collatio, Aldred went in search of Edgar. He found him outside the alehouse, dandling a baby on his knee in the warm evening air. They had not met since their triumph at Outhenham, and Edgar seemed pleased to see Aldred.

But Aldred was startled by the baby. 'Yours?' he said.

Edgar smiled and shook his head. 'My brother's. Her name is Wynswith. We call her Winnie. She's almost three months old. Isn't she beautiful?'

To Aldred she looked like every other baby: round-faced, bald as a priest, dribbling, charmless. 'Yes, she's beautiful,' he said. That was his second white lie today. He would have to pray for clemency.

'What brings you here?' said Edgar. 'It can't be the pleasure of visiting Degbert.'

'Is there somewhere we can talk without fear of being overheard?'

'I'll show you my brewhouse,' Edgar said eagerly. 'Just a minute.' He stepped inside the alehouse and came out again without the baby.

The brewhouse was close to the river, so that water did not have to be carried too far, and it was on the upstream side. As in all riverside settlements, the villagers dipped their buckets upstream and disposed of waste downstream.

The new building had a roof of oak tiles. 'I thought you planned a stone roof,' Aldred said.

'I made a mistake,' Edgar said. 'I found I couldn't cut stone into tiles. They were either too fat or too thin. I had to change my design.' He looked a bit abashed. 'In future I need to remember that not every bright idea I get is practicable.'

Inside, a strong, spicy odour of fermentation came from a big bronze cauldron suspended over a square stone-walled hearth. Barrels and sacks were stacked in a separate room. The stone floor was clean. 'It's a little palace!' said Aldred.

Edgar smiled. 'It's designed to be fireproof. Why did you want to talk privately? I'm eager to know.'

'I'm on my way to Combe.'

Edgar understood immediately. 'Wynstan and Degbert will be there in a few days.'

'And I want to see what they get up to. But I have a problem. I can't follow them around without being noticed, especially if they go into houses of ill fame.'

'What's the answer?'

'I want you to help me keep an eye on them. You're less likely to attract attention.'

Edgar grinned. 'Is it really a monk who is asking me to visit Mags's house?'

Aldred grimaced with distaste. 'I can hardly believe it myself.'

Edgar turned serious again. 'I can go to Combe to buy supplies. Dreng trusts me.'

Aldred was surprised. 'Does he?'

'He set a trap for me, gave me too much money for stones, expecting me to steal the surplus, and was shocked when I gave it back to him. Now he's glad to have me do the work, and take the strain off his famous bad back.'

'Do you need anything from Combe?'

'We're going to have to buy new ropes soon, and they're cheaper in Combe. I could probably leave tomorrow.'

'We shouldn't travel together. I don't want people to realize we're collaborating.'

'Then I'll leave the day after Midsummer, and take the raft.'

'Perfect,' Aldred said gratefully.

They stepped out of the brewhouse. The sun was going down. Aldred said: 'When you get there, you'll find me at the priory.'

'Travel safely,' said Edgar.

ÞÞÞ

FIVE DAYS AFTER Midsummer, Edgar was eating cheese in an alehouse known as the Sailors when he heard that Wynstan and

Degbert had arrived in Combe that morning and were staying with Wigelm.

Wigelm had rebuilt the compound that had been destroyed by the Vikings a year ago. It was easy for Edgar to keep an eye on the single entrance, especially as there was an alehouse a stone's throw away.

It was boring work, and he passed the time by speculating about Wynstan's secret. He could think of all kinds of nefarious activities that the bishop might indulge in, but he could not imagine how Dreng's Ferry fitted in, and his guesswork got him nowhere.

That first evening Wynstan and his brother and cousin caroused at home. Edgar watched the gate until the lights began to go out in the compound, then he returned to the abbey for the night, and told Aldred he had nothing to report.

He was worried about being noticed. Most people in Combe knew him, and it would not take them long to start wondering what he was up to. He had bought rope and a few other supplies; he had drunk ale with a handful of old friends; he had taken a good look around the rebuilt town; and now he needed a pretext to linger.

It was June, and he remembered a place in the woods where wild strawberries grew. They were a special treat at this time of year, hard to find but mouth-wateringly delicious. He left the town when the monks rose for their dawn service and walked a mile into the forest. He was lucky: the strawberries were just ripe. He picked a sackful, returned to the town, and began to sell them at Wigelm's gate. There was a good deal of traffic into and out of the compound so it was a logical place for a vendor to stand. He charged a farthing for two dozen.

By afternoon he had sold them all and had a pocket full of change. He returned to his seat outside the alehouse and ordered a cup of ale.

Brindle's behaviour at Combe was peculiar. The dog seemed

bewildered to be in the place she knew so well and find it different. She ran around the streets, renewing acquaintance with the town dogs, sniffing in a baffled way at rebuilt houses. She had yelped delightedly at coming across the stone-built dairy, which had survived the fire; then she had spent half a day sitting outside the place as if waiting for Sungifu to come.

'I know how you feel,' Edgar said to the dog.

Early that evening Wynstan, Wigelm and Degbert emerged from Wigelm's compound. Edgar was careful not to meet Wynstan's eye: the bishop might well recognize him.

But Wynstan had his mind on pleasure tonight. His brothers were brightly dressed, and the bishop himself had changed his long black priestly robes for a short tunic under a light cloak secured with a gold pin. His tonsured head was covered with a jaunty cap. The three men zig-zagged through the dusty streets in the evening light.

They went to the Sailors, the town's largest and best-furnished alehouse. The place was always busy, and Edgar felt able to go inside and order a cup of ale while Wynstan called for a jug of the strong fermented-honey liquor called mead, and paid with pennies from a bulging leather purse.

Edgar drank his ale slowly. Wynstan did nothing remarkable. He drank and laughed, ordered a plate of shrimps, and put his hand up the skirt of a serving wench. He was making no serious attempt to keep his revelry secret, though he was taking care not to be ostentatious.

The daylight was fading, and no doubt Wynstan was getting drunker. When the three left the alehouse Edgar followed them out, feeling that the chances of his being noticed were diminishing. Nevertheless, he maintained a discreet distance as he tailed them.

It occurred to him that if they spotted him they might pretend not to have, then ambush him. If that happened, they would beat him half to death. He would not be able to defend himself against three of them. He tried not to feel scared.

They went to Mags's house, and Edgar followed them in.

Mags had rebuilt the place and furnished it in a style as luxurious as that of any palace. There were tapestries on the walls, mattresses on the floor, and cushions on the seats. Two couples were shagging under blankets, and there were screens to hide those whose sexual practices were too embarrassing or too wicked to be seen. There seemed to be eight or ten girls and a couple of boys, some speaking with foreign accents, and Edgar guessed that most of them were slaves, bought by Mags at the market in Bristol.

Wynstan immediately became the centre of attention, as the highest-ranking customer in the place. Mags herself brought him a cup of wine, kissed him on the lips, then stood beside him, pointing out the attractions of different girls: this one had big breasts, that one was expert at sucking-off, and another had shaved all her body hair.

For a few minutes no one took any notice of Edgar, but eventually a pretty Irish girl showed him her pink breasts and asked him what would be his pleasure, and he muttered that he had come into the wrong house, and left quickly.

Wynstan was doing things a bishop ought not to do, and making only perfunctory attempts to be discreet, but again Edgar could not figure out what the great mystery might be.

It was full dark by the time the three merrymakers staggered out of Mags's house, but their evening was not over yet. Edgar followed them with little fear now of being spotted. They went to a house near the beach that Edgar recognized as belonging to the wool trader Cynred, probably the richest man in Combe after Wigelm. The door was open to the evening air, and they went inside.

Edgar could not follow them into a private house. Looking through the open door he saw them settle around a table, chatting in a relaxed and amiable manner. Wynstan took out his purse.

Edgar concealed himself in a dark alley opposite.

Soon a well-dressed middle-aged man he did not recognize approached the house. Apparently not sure he was in the right place, the man put his head round the door. In the light from inside, Edgar saw that his clothes looked costly and possibly foreign. He asked a question Edgar did not hear. 'Come in, come in!' someone shouted, and the man went in.

Then the door was closed.

However, Edgar could still hear something of what was going on inside, and soon the volume of conversation increased. He picked up the unmistakable rattle of dice in a cup. He heard shouted words:

'Ten pence!'

'Double six!'

'I win, I win!'

'The devil's in those dice!'

Clearly Wynstan had had enough of drinking and whoring and had turned at last to gambling.

After a long wait in the alley, Edgar heard the monastery bell strike for the midnight service of Nocturns, the first office of the new day. Soon afterwards the game seemed to come to an end. The players came out into the street, carrying branches from the fire to light their way. Edgar shrank back into his alley, but distinctly heard Wynstan say: 'Luck was with you tonight, Monsieur Robert!'

'You take your losses in good spirit,' said a voice with an accent, and Edgar deduced that the foreign-looking stranger was a French or Norman trader.

'You must give me a chance to win it all back some time!'

'With pleasure.'

Edgar reflected ruefully that he had followed Wynstan all evening only to learn that the bishop was a good sport.

Wynstan, Wigelm and Degbert turned towards Wigelm's place, and Robert went in the opposite direction. On impulse, Edgar followed Robert.

The foreigner went to the beach. There he hitched up the skirts of his tunic and waded out into the water. Edgar watched him, following the flame, until he boarded a ship. By the light of the torch Edgar could see that it was a broad-beamed, deep-hulled vessel, almost certainly a Norman cargo ship.

Then the light was doused, and Edgar lost sight of the man.

ÞÞÞ

EARLY NEXT MORNING Edgar met with Aldred and confessed himself at a loss. 'Wynstan spends the Church's money on wine, women and dice, but there's no mystery about that,' Edgar said.

But Aldred was intrigued by a detail Edgar had thought trivial. 'Wynstan didn't seem to mind having lost money, you say?'

Edgar shrugged. 'If he did mind, he concealed it well.'

Aldred shook his head sceptically. 'Gamblers always mind losing,' he said. 'There would be no thrill otherwise.'

'He just shook the man's hand and said he looked forward to a chance to win it back.'

'Something is wrong here.'

'I can't think what it might be.'

'And afterwards Monsieur Robert boarded a ship, presumably his own.' Aldred drummed his fingers on the table. 'I must talk to him.'

'I'll take you.'

'Good. Tell me, is there a money-changer in Combe? There must be, it's a port.'

'Wyn, the jeweller, buys foreign money and melts it down.'

'Jeweller? He must have a balance and accurate weights for small amounts of precious metals.'

'I'm sure.'

'We may need him later.'

Edgar was intrigued. He did not follow Aldred's thinking. He asked: 'But why?'

'Be patient. It's not clear in my own mind yet. Let's go and talk to Robert.'

They left the monastery. Until now they had not been seen together in Combe, but Aldred seemed too excited to worry about that this morning. Edgar led the way to the beach.

Edgar was excited too. Although he was baffled, he guessed they were nearer to solving the mystery.

The Norman cargo vessel was being loaded. On the beach was a small hill of iron ore. Men were shovelling the ore into barrels, carrying the barrels out to the ship, and emptying them into the hold. Monsieur Robert was on the beach, supervising. Edgar noticed that a leather purse bulging with coins was securely attached to his belt. 'That's him,' Edgar said.

Aldred approached the man and introduced himself, then said: 'I have something important and private to tell you, Monsieur Robert. I think you were cheated last night.'

'Cheated?' said Robert. 'But I won.'

Edgar shared Robert's mystification. How could he have been cheated when he came away with a purse full of cash?

Aldred said: 'If you will come with me to the jeweller's house, I will explain. I promise you won't feel it a wasted journey.'

Robert looked hard at Aldred for a long moment, then appeared to decide to trust him. 'Very well.'

Edgar led them to the home of Wyn, a stone house that had survived the Viking fire. They found the jeweller at breakfast with his family. Wyn was a small man of about fifty with receding hair. He had a young wife – his second, Edgar recalled – and two little children.

Edgar said: 'Good morning, sir. I hope I find you well.'

Wyn was amiable. 'Hello, Edgar. How is your mother?'

'Feeling her age, to tell the truth.'

'Aren't we all? Have you come back to Combe?'

'Just a visit. This is Brother Aldred, the armarius of Shiring Abbey, who's staying at Combe Priory for a few days.'

Wyn said politely: 'I'm glad to meet you, Brother Aldred.' He was puzzled but patient, waiting to find out what was going on.

'And this is Monsieur Robert, the owner of a ship in the harbour.'

'Happy to meet you, monsieur.'

Aldred then took over. 'Wyn, would you be so kind as to weigh some English pennies that Monsieur Robert has acquired?'

Edgar began to see where Aldred was heading, and he became riveted.

Wyn hesitated only for a moment. To do a good turn for an important monk was an investment that would be repaid one day. 'Of course,' he said. 'Come into my workshop.'

He led the way and the others followed, Robert looking mystified but not unwilling.

Wyn's workshop was similar to that of Cuthbert at the minster, Edgar saw, with a hearth, an anvil, an array of small tools, and a stout ironbound chest that probably contained precious metals. On the workbench was a delicate-looking balance, a T shape with trays dangling from each end of the crossbar.

Aldred said: 'Monsieur Robert, may we weigh the pennies you won at Cynred's house last night?'

Edgar said: 'Ah.' He was beginning to see how Robert might have been cheated.

Robert took the purse from his belt and opened it. It held a mixture of English and foreign currency. The others waited patiently while he picked out the English coins, all with a cross on one side and the head of King Ethelred on the other. He closed the purse carefully and reattached it to his belt, then counted out the pennies. There were sixty-three.

Aldred said: 'Did you win all these coins last night?'

'Most of them,' said Robert.

Wyn said: 'Please put sixty pennies in a tray – it doesn't matter which one.' As Robert did so, Wyn selected some small weights from a box. They were disc-shaped and looked, to Edgar, as if they were made of lead. 'Sixty pence should weight exactly three ounces,' Wyn said. He placed three weights in the opposite tray. The tray immediately sank to the bench. Edgar gasped, shocked. Wyn said to Robert: 'Your pennies are light.'

'What does that mean?' said Robert.

Edgar knew the answer, but he remained silent while Wyn explained.

'Most silver coins contain some copper to make the disc more hard-wearing,' Wyn said. 'English pennies have nineteen parts of silver to one part of copper. Just a moment.' He removed an ounce weight from the tray and began to replace it with smaller ones. 'Copper is lighter than silver.' When the two sides balanced he said: 'Your pennies contain about ten parts of copper to ten of silver. The difference is so small as to be imperceptible in normal use. But these are forgeries.'

Edgar nodded. That was the solution to the mystery: Wynstan was a forger. And furthermore, Edgar now realized, gambling was a way of changing bad coins for good. If Wynstan won at dice, he gained genuine silver pennies, but if he lost, he only sacrificed forgeries. Over the long run he was sure to come out ahead.

Robert's face was flushed with anger. 'I don't believe you,' he said.

'I'll prove it. Does anyone have a good penny?'

Edgar had Dreng's money. He gave Robert a penny. Robert drew his belt knife and scratched the coin on the side with the head of Ethelred. The scratch was hardly visible.

Wyn said: 'That coin is the same all the way through. No matter how deep you go, the colour showing will be silver. Now scratch one of your own.'

Robert gave Edgar his penny back, took a coin of his own from the tray, and repeated the exercise. This time the scratch mark was brown.

Wyn explained: 'The mixture of half silver, half copper is brown in colour. Forgers make their coins look silver by washing them in vitriol, which removes the copper from the surface; but underneath the metal is still brown.'

Robert said furiously: 'Those damned Englishmen were gambling with counterfeit money!'

Aldred said: 'Well, one of them was.'

'I shall go and accuse Cynred now!'

'Cynred may not be the guilty one. How many were around the table?'

'Five.'

'Who will you accuse?'

Robert saw the problem. 'So the cheat is going to get away with it?'

'Not if I can help it,' Aldred said resolutely. 'But if you make a wild accusation now, they will all deny it. Worse, the villain will be forewarned and it will become difficult to bring him to justice.'

'What am I to do with all this false money?'

Aldred was unsympathetic. 'You got it gambling, Robert. Have the forgeries melted down and made into a ring to wear to remind you not to gamble. Remember that the Roman soldiers at the Cross threw dice for our Lord's clothes.'

'I'll think about that,' Robert said sulkily.

Edgar doubted that Robert would melt down the counterfeit coins. More likely he would spend them in ones and twos so that their weight would not be noticed. But in fact that would suit Aldred's purpose, Edgar saw. Robert would not tell anyone about the false money if he planned to spend it. So Wynstan would not know that his secret had been revealed.

Aldred turned to Wyn. 'May I ask you to keep this to yourself, for the same reason?' he said.

'Very well.'

'I can assure you that I'm determined to bring the culprit to justice.'

'I'm glad to hear it,' said Wyn. 'Good luck.'

Robert said: 'Amen.'

ÞÞÞ

ALDRED WAS TRIUMPHANT, but he soon realized the battle was not yet won. 'All the clergy at the minster obviously know about this already,' he said thoughtfully as Edgar poled the raft upriver. 'It could hardly be hidden from them. But they keep quiet, and they're rewarded for their silence with a life of idleness and luxury.'

Edgar nodded. 'The villagers, too. They probably guess that something underhand goes on there, but they're bribed by the gifts Wynstan brings four times a year.'

'And this explains why he was so furious about my proposal to transform his corrupt minster into a God-fearing monastery. He would have to recreate the set-up in some other remote village – not an easy thing to do from scratch.'

'Cuthbert must be the forger. He's the only person with the skill to engrave the dies to make the coins.' Edgar looked uncomfortable. 'He's not such a bad man, just weak. He could never stand up to a bully like Wynstan. I almost feel sorry for him.'

They parted company at Mudeford Crossing, still keen to avoid calling attention to their association. Edgar continued upstream and Aldred rode Dismas towards Shiring by an indirect route. He was fortunate to join up with two miners driving a cartload of something that looked like coal but was in fact cassiterite, the mineral from which valuable tin was extracted. If the outlaw Ironface happened to be nearby, Aldred felt sure he would be deterred by the sight of the powerfully built miners with their iron-headed hammers.

Travellers loved to talk, but the miners did not have much to say, and Aldred was able to think at length about how he might bring Wynstan before a court and see him convicted of his crime and punished. Even with what Aldred now knew it would not be easy. The bishop would have no end of oath-helpers to swear he was an honest man who told the truth.

When witnesses disagreed there was a procedure for settling the matter: one of them had to undergo an ordeal, either pick up a red-hot iron bar and carry it ten paces, or plunge his hands into boiling water and pull out a stone. In theory, God would protect a man who was telling the truth. In practice, Aldred had never known anyone to volunteer for the ordeal.

Often it was clear which side was telling the truth, and the court would believe the more credible witness. But Wynstan's case would have to be heard in the shire court, which would be presided over by his brother. Ealdorman Wilwulf would be shamelessly biased in Wynstan's favour. Aldred's only chance would be to produce evidence so overwhelmingly clear, backed up by oaths from men of such high status, that even Wynstan's brother could not pretend to believe in his innocence.

He wondered what drove a man like Wynstan to become a forger. The bishop had a life of ease and pleasure: what more did he need? Why risk losing everything? Aldred supposed that Wynstan's greed was insatiable. No matter how much money and power he had, he would always crave more. Sin was like that.

He arrived at Shiring Abbey late in the evening on the next day. The monastery was quiet and he could hear, from the church, the psalm-singing of Compline, the service that signalled the end of the day. He stabled his horse and went straight to the dormitory.

In his saddlebag he had a gift from Combe Priory, a copy of St John's Gospel, with its profound opening words: *In principio erat Verbum, et Verbum erat apud Deum, et Deus erat Verbum.* In the beginning was the word, and the word was with God, and the word was God. Aldred felt he could spend his life trying to comprehend that mystery.

He would present the new book to Abbot Osmund at the first opportunity, he decided. He was unpacking his bag when Brother Godleof came out of Osmund's room, which was at the end of the dorm.

Godleof was Aldred's age, with dark skin and a wiry frame. His mother had been a milkmaid who was ravished by a passing nobleman. Godleof did not know the man's name and hinted that his mother had never known it either. Like most of the younger monks, Godleof shared Aldred's views and got impatient with the caution and parsimony of Osmund and Hildred.

Aldred was struck by Godleof's worried look. 'What's happened?' he said. He realized that Godleof had something on his mind that he was reluctant to say. 'Out with it.'

'I've been looking after Osmund.' Godleof had been a cowherd before he came to the monastery, and he used few words.

'Why?'

'He's taken to his bed.'

Aldred said: 'I'm sorry to hear that, but it's not really a shock. He's been ill for a while, and lately he's had trouble walking down the stairs, never mind up.' He paused, studying Godleof. 'There's something else, isn't there?'

'You'd better ask Osmund.'

'All right, I will.' Aldred picked up the book he had brought from Combe and went to Osmund's room.

He found the abbot sitting up in bed with a pile of cushions behind him. He was not well but he looked comfortable, and Aldred guessed he would be content to stay in bed for the rest of his life, however long or short it might be. 'I'm sorry to see you indisposed, my lord abbot,' said Aldred.

Osmund sighed. 'God in his wisdom has not granted me the strength to carry on.'

Aldred was not sure it had been entirely God's decision, but all he said was: 'The Lord is all wise.'

'I must rely on younger men,' Osmund said.

Osmund looked faintly embarrassed. Like Godleof, he seemed to be burdened with something he might have preferred not to say. Aldred had a premonition of bad news. He said: 'Are you perhaps thinking of appointing an acting abbot to manage the monastery during your illness?' It was an important point. The monk who was made acting abbot now had the best chance of becoming abbot when Osmund died.

Osmund did not answer the question, which was ominous. 'The problem with young men is that they make trouble,' he said. This was obviously a dig at Aldred. 'They are idealistic,' he went on. 'They offend people.'

It was time to stop tiptoeing around. Aldred said bluntly: 'Have you already appointed someone?'

'Hildred,' said Osmund, and he looked away.

'Thank you, my lord abbot,' said Aldred. He threw the book onto Osmund's bed and left the room.

20

WILF WAS AWAY THREE months longer than anyone expected, which was one third of the time Ragna had been married to him. There had been one message, six weeks ago, simply saying that he was penetrating deeper into Wales than he had originally planned, and that he was in good health.

Ragna missed him. She had grown to like having a man to talk to and discuss problems with and lie down beside at night. The shock of Inge had cast a shadow over that pleasure, but all the same she longed to have Wilf back.

Ragna saw Inge around the compound almost every day. Ragna was the official wife, and she held her head high and avoided speaking to her rival; but she still felt the humiliation constantly.

She wondered nervously how Wilf would feel about her when he returned. He would probably have lain with other women during his trip. He had made it brutally clear to her – not before the wedding, but after – that his love for her did not exclude sex with others. Had he met younger, more beautiful girls in Wales? Or would he return hungry for Ragna's body? Or both?

She got one day's notice of his return. He sent a messenger ahead on a fast horse to say he would be home tomorrow. Ragna threw the compound into action. The kitchen prepared a feast, slaughtering a young ox, building a fire for spit-roasting, tapping barrels of ale, baking bread. Those not needed in the kitchen were deployed

374

mucking out the stables, putting new rushes and straw on the floors, beating mattresses and airing blankets.

Ragna went into Wilf's house, where she burned rye to expel insects, took down shutters to let in fresh air, and made the bed inviting with lavender and rose petals. She set out fruit in a basket, a flagon of wine and a small barrel of ale, bread and cheese and smoked fish.

All this activity took her mind off her anxiety.

The next morning she got Cat to heat a cauldron of water and washed herself all over, paying special attention to the hairy parts. Then she rubbed perfumed oil into the skin of her neck, breasts, thighs and feet. She put on a freshly laundered dress and new silk shoes, and secured her headscarf with a gold-embroidered band.

He arrived at midday. She was forewarned by the sound of cheering from the town as he rode through at the head of the army, and she hurried to take a commanding position in front of the great hall.

He came through the gate at a canter, his red cloak flying, his lieutenants close behind. He saw her immediately and came at her dangerously fast, and she struggled against a reflex to leap out of the way; but she knew she had to show him – and the crowd – that she had complete faith in his horsemanship. In that last moment she saw that his hair and moustache were untrimmed, his normally clean-shaven chin now had a wild beard, and there was a new scar across his forehead. Then he reined in spectacularly late, causing his horse to rear a few inches away from her, while her heart beat like a hammer and she kept the welcoming smile undimmed on her face.

He leaped off his horse and took her in his arms, exactly as she had hoped he would. The people in the compound cheered and laughed: they loved to see his passion for her. She knew that he was showing off to his followers, and she accepted that as part of his role as leader. But there was no doubt about the sincerity of his embrace.

He kissed her lasciviously, his tongue in her mouth, and she eagerly responded in the same way.

After a minute he broke the clinch, bent down, and picked her up, with one arm under her shoulders and the other supporting her thighs. She laughed with joy. He carried her past the great hall to his own dwelling, as the crowd roared their approval. She was doubly glad that she had made his home clean and welcoming.

He fumbled for the latch and threw the door open, then he carried her inside. He put her down and slammed the door.

She took off her headdress and let her hair fall freely, then pulled her dress off with one swift move and lay down naked on his bed.

He stared at her body with delight and desire. He looked like a thirsty man about to drink from a mountain stream. He fell on her, still wearing his leather jerkin and cloth leggings.

She wrapped her arms and legs around him and drew him deep inside her.

It was over quickly. He rolled off her and was asleep in seconds.

She lay watching him for a while. She liked the beard, but she knew he would shave it tomorrow, for English noblemen did not wear beards. She touched the new scar on his brow. It started at his right temple, at the hair line, and followed a jagged course to his left eyebrow. She ran her fingertip along it, and he stirred in his sleep. Another half inch . . . Some brave Welshman had done that, she guessed. He had probably died for it.

She poured a cup of wine and ate a morsel of cheese. She was content just to look at him and feel glad that he had come back to her alive. The Welsh were not very formidable fighters, but they were by no means helpless, and she was sure that some wives in the compound were now weeping at the news that their husbands were never coming home.

As soon as he woke up they made love again. This time it was slower. He took off his clothes. She had time to relish every sensation, to rub her hands over his shoulders and his chest, to thrust her fingers into his hair and bite his lips.

When it was over he said: 'By the gods, I could eat an ox.'

'And I've roasted one for your dinner. But let me get you something for now.' She brought him wine and new bread and smoked eel, and he ate with relish.

Then he said: 'I met Wynstan on the road.'

'Ah,' she said.

'He told me what happened at Outhenham.'

Ragna tensed. She had been expecting this. Wynstan was never going to take his defeat lying down. He would try to get revenge by causing trouble between her and Wilf. But she had not anticipated that Wynstan would be so quick off the mark. As soon as the messenger had arrived yesterday, Wynstan must have set out to meet Wilf, keen to get his side of the story in first, hoping to put Ragna on the defensive.

But she had her strategy ready. The whole thing had been Wynstan's fault, not hers, and she was not going to make excuses for herself. She moved immediately to shift the ground of the discussion. 'Don't be angry with Wynstan,' she said. 'There should be no rift between brothers.'

Wilf was not expecting that. 'But Wynstan is angry with you,' he said.

'Of course. He tried to rob me while you were away, thinking to take advantage of me in your absence. But don't worry, I prevented him.'

'Is that how it was?' Clearly Wilf had not previously looked at the incident as an attack by a powerful man on an undefended woman.

'He failed, and that made him cross. But I can deal with Wynstan, and I don't want you to feel concerned about me. Don't reprove him, please.'

Wilf was still adjusting his picture of the incident. 'But Wynstan says you humiliated him in front of others.'

'A thief who is caught red-handed will naturally feel humiliated.'

'I suppose so.'

'His remedy is to stop stealing, isn't it?'

'It is.' Wilf smiled, and Ragna saw that she had successfully negotiated a difficult conversation. He added: 'Wynstan may have met his match at last.'

'Oh, I'm not his rival,' she said, knowing it was the opposite of the truth. But the conversation had gone far enough and ended well, so she changed the subject. 'Tell me about your adventures. Did you teach the Welsh a hard lesson?'

'I did, and I brought back a hundred captives to sell as slaves. We'll make a small fortune.'

'Well done,' said Ragna, but she did not mean it. Slavery was an aspect of English life that she found difficult. It had just about died out in Normandy, but here it was normal. There were a hundred or more slaves in Shiring, and several of them lived and worked in the compound. Many did dirty jobs, removing dunghills and cleaning stables, or heavy labouring such as digging ditches and carrying timber. No doubt the younger ones served in the town's brothels, although Ragna did not know from personal experience because she had never been inside one of those houses. Slaves were not generally kept in chains. They could run away, and some did, but they were easily identifiable, dressed as they were in rags, without shoes, and speaking in strange accents. Most runaways were caught and brought back, and a reward was paid by the owner.

Wilf said: 'You don't seem as pleased as you might.'

Ragna had no intention of having a discussion with him about slavery now. 'I'm thrilled with your triumph,' she said. 'And I'm wondering if you're man enough to fuck me three times in one afternoon.'

'Man enough?' he said in mock indignation. 'Get down on your hands and knees, and I'll show you.'

ÞÞÞ

THE CAPTIVES WERE put on display next day in the town square, standing in lines on the dusty ground between the cathedral and the abbey, and Ragna went out, accompanied by Cat, to look at them.

They were dirty and exhausted from their journey, and some had minor injuries, presumably having put up a struggle. Ragna imagined that any who had major injuries would have been left behind to die. In the square were men and women, boys and girls, roughly between eleven and thirty years of age. It was summer, and the sun was hot, but they had no shade. They were tied up in different ways: many had their feet hobbled so that they could not run; some were chained to one another; others were bound to their captors, who stood by them, waiting to haggle over a price. The regular soldiers had one or two to sell, but Wigelm and Garulf and the other captains all had several.

Ragna walked along the lines, finding the sight dispiriting. People said that slaves had done something to deserve their fate, and perhaps it was true sometimes, but not always. What crime could adolescent boys and girls have committed to deserve to be turned into prostitutes?

Slaves did whatever they were told, but they generally performed their tasks as badly as they could get away with; and since they had to be fed and housed and given minimal clothing they were in the end not much cheaper than the lowest-paid labourers. However, the financial aspect did not trouble Ragna as much as the spiritual. Owning a person had to be bad for the soul. Cruelty was normal: there were laws about ill-treatment of slaves, but they were feebly enforced and the punishments were mild. To be able to beat or rape or even murder someone brought out the very worst in human nature.

379

As she scanned the faces in the square she recognized Garulf's friend Stigand, with whom she had clashed over the ball game. He made a bow, too exaggerated to be sincere but not rude enough to merit a protest. She ignored him and looked at his three captives.

She was startled to realize that she knew one of them.

The girl was about fifteen. She had the black hair and blue eyes typical of Welsh people; the Bretons on the other side of the Channel were similar. She might have been pretty with the dirt washed off her face. She stared back, and her look of vulnerability imperfectly masked by defiance jogged Ragna's memory. 'You're the girl from Dreng's Ferry.'

The captive said nothing.

Ragna remembered her name. 'Blod.'

She remained silent, but her expression softened.

Ragna lowered her voice so that Stiggy could not hear. 'They said you had escaped. You must have been captured a second time.' That was remarkably bad luck, she thought, and she felt a warm surge of compassion for someone who had suffered that fate twice.

She remembered more. 'I heard that Dreng—' She realized what she was about to say and stopped, her hand flying to her mouth.

Blod knew what Ragna had hesitated to say. 'Dreng killed my baby.'

'I'm so sorry. Did no one help you?'

'Edgar jumped in the river to rescue the baby, but couldn't find him in the dark.'

'I know Edgar. He's a good man.'

'The only decent Englishman I ever met,' said Blod bitterly.

Ragna saw a certain look in her eye. 'Did you fall in love with him?'

'He loves someone else.'

'Sungifu.'

Blod gave Ragna an enigmatic look but said nothing.

Ragna said: 'The one the Vikings killed.'

'Yes, her.' Blod looked anxiously around the square.

'I suppose you're worried about who might buy you this time.'

'I'm frightened of Dreng.'

'I'm pretty sure he's not in town. He would have come to see me. He likes to pretend we're family.' Across the square, Ragna noticed Bishop Wynstan with his bodyguard, Cnebba. 'But there are other cruel men.'

'I know.'

'Maybe I should buy you.'

Blod's face lit up with hope. 'Would you?'

Ragna spoke to Stiggy. 'How much are you hoping to get for this slave?'

'One pound. She's fifteen, that's young.'

'It's too much. I'll give you half, though.'

'No, she's worth more than that.'

'Split the difference?'

Stiggy frowned. 'How much would that be?' He knew the phrase *split the difference* but he could not do the arithmetic.

'One hundred and eighty pence.'

Suddenly Wynstan was there. 'Buying a slave, my lady Ragna?' he said. 'I thought you high-minded Normans disapproved.'

'Like a high-minded bishop who disapproves of fornication, I find myself doing it anyway.'

'Always the smart answer.' He had been looking with curiosity at Blod, and now he said: 'I know you, don't I?'

Blod said loudly: 'You fucked me, if that's what you mean.'

Wynstan looked embarrassed, which was unusual. 'Don't be ridiculous.'

'You did it twice. That was before I was pregnant, so you paid Dreng three pence for each go.'

Wynstan made only a nominal pretence of priestly virtue, but all the same he was discomfited by this noisily public accusation of unchastity. 'Rubbish. You're making it up. You ran away from Dreng, I remember.'

'He murdered my baby boy.'

'Well, who cares? The child of a slave . . .'

'Perhaps he was your son.'

Wynstan went pale. Clearly he had not thought of that. He struggled to recover his dignity. 'You should be flogged for running away.'

Ragna interrupted. 'I was in the process of bargaining for this slave, my lord bishop, if you will excuse me from further conversation.'

Wynstan smiled maliciously. 'You can't buy her.'

'I beg your pardon?'

'She can't be sold.'

Stiggy said: 'Yes, she can!'

'No, she can't. She's a runaway. She must be returned to her legitimate owner.'

Blod whispered: 'No, please.'

'It's not my decision,' Wynstan said cheerfully. 'Even if the slave had not spoken disrespectfully to me, the outcome would be the same.'

Ragna wanted to argue, but she knew Wynstan was right. She had not thought of it, but a runaway still legally belonged to the original owner, even after months of freedom.

Wynstan said to Stiggy: 'You must take this girl back to Dreng's Ferry.'

Blod began to cry.

Stiggy had not understood. 'But she's my captive.'

'Dreng will give you the usual reward for returning a runaway, so you won't be out of pocket.'

Stiggy still looked puzzled.

Ragna believed in obeying the law. It could be cruel, but it was always better than lawlessness. However, on this occasion she would have defied it if she could. It was a harsh irony that the man now upholding the law was Wynstan.

Ragna said desperately: 'I will take charge of the girl, and recompense Dreng.'

'No, no,' said Wynstan. 'You can't do that, not to my cousin. If Dreng wants to sell the slave to you, he may, but she must be returned to him first.'

'I shall take her home, and send a message to Dreng.'

Wynstan said to Cnebba: 'Take that captive and lock her in the crypt of the cathedral.' He turned to Stiggy. 'She'll be released to you whenever you're ready to take her to Dreng's Ferry.' Finally he looked at Ragna. 'If you don't like it, complain to your husband.'

Cnebba began to untie Blod.

Ragna realized it had been a mistake to come out without Bern. If he had been present to provide a counterweight to Cnebba, she could at least have postponed any final decision on Blod's fate. But even that was impossible.

Cnebba took Blod firmly by the arm and walked her away.

Wynstan said: 'She's in for a serious flogging, I should think, when Dreng gets his hands on her.' He smiled, bowed, and walked after Cnebba.

Ragna could have screamed with frustration and rage. She bottled up her feelings and, with her head held high, walked away from the square and up the hill to the compound.

ÞÞÞ

JULY WAS THE hungry month, Edgar reflected as he looked over his brothers' farm. Most of the winter food was gone, and everyone was waiting for the grain harvest in August and September. At this season the cows were giving milk and the hens were laying, so people who had cows or hens did not starve. Others ate the early fruits and vegetables of the forest, leaves and berries and onions, a thin diet. People with large farms could afford to plant a few beans in spring to harvest in June and July, but not many peasants had land to spare.

Edgar's brothers were hungry, but not for much longer. For the second year running they had a good crop of hay on the low-lying land near the river. The three weeks before Midsummer had been wet, and the river was high now as a result, but the weather had cleared miraculously, and they had reaped the long blades of grass. Today Edgar had walked fifty yards downriver, to scrub out a cooking pot well away from the place where he drew clean water, and from there he could see several acres of cut grass drying and turning yellow in the strong sunshine. Soon the brothers would sell the hay and have money for food.

In the distance he saw a horse coming down the hill to the hamlet, and he wondered if it might be Aldred on Dismas. Shortly before they parted at Mudeford Crossing, Edgar had asked Aldred what he was going to do about Wynstan's forgery, and Aldred had said he was still thinking about it. Now Edgar wondered if he had come up with a plan.

But the rider was not Aldred. As the horse came nearer he saw that there was one person riding and another walking behind. He headed back to the tavern in case he was needed to operate the ferry. Moments later he was able to see that the walker was tied to the saddle. It was a woman, barefoot and ragged. Finally he realized, with a gasp of consternation, that it was Blod.

He had been sure she had escaped. How could she have been recaptured after this length of time? He recalled that Ealdorman Wilwulf had been harrying the Welsh: he must have brought her back among his captives. What tragic misfortune, to get free and then be enslaved a second time!

She raised her face and saw him but did not seem to have the strength to acknowledge him. Her shoulders were slumped and her shoeless feet were bleeding.

The man on the horse was about Edgar's age but bigger, and he wore a sword. When he saw Edgar he said: 'Are you the ferryman?'

Edgar got the impression the man was not very bright. 'I work for Dreng the ferryman.'

'I've brought his slave back.'

'So I see.'

Dreng came out of the tavern. He recognized the rider. 'Hello, Stiggy, what do you want? By the gods, is that little slut Blod?'

Stiggy said: 'If I'd known she was yours, I would have left her in Wales and captured another girl.'

'She is mine, though.'

'You have to pay me for bringing her back.'

Dreng did not like that idea. 'Do I, now?'

'Bishop Wynstan said.'

'Oh. And did he say how much?'

'Half what she's worth.'

'She's not worth much, the miserable whore.'

'I was asking a pound and the Lady Ragna offered half.'

'So you say I owe you half of half a pound, which is sixty pence.'

'Ragna might have paid a hundred and eighty.'

'She didn't, though. Go on, untie the bitch and come inside.'

'I'll have the money, first.'

Dreng softened his voice, pretending to be friendly. 'Don't you want a bowl of stew and a tankard of ale?'

'No. It's only midday. I'm going to head back right away.' Stiggy was not completely stupid, and he probably knew the ways of alehouse keepers. If he got drunk here and stayed the night, there was no telling how much would be deducted from his sixty pence in the morning.

'Very well,' said Dreng. He went inside. Stiggy got off his horse and untied Blod. She sat on the ground, waiting.

After a long pause Dreng came out with money wrapped in a rag and handed it to Stiggy, who put it into his belt pouch.

Dreng said: 'Aren't you going to count it?'

'I trust you.'

Edgar smothered a laugh. It took a fool to trust Dreng. But Stiggy probably could not count up to sixty.

Stiggy mounted his horse.

Dreng said: 'Sure we can't tempt you to some of my wife's famous ale?' He was still hoping to get some of those pennies back.

'No.' Stiggy turned the horse around and headed back the way he had come.

Dreng said to Blod: 'Get inside.'

As she passed him he kicked her backside. She let out a cry of pain, stumbled, and regained her balance. 'That's just the beginning,' he said.

Edgar followed them, but Dreng turned at the door and said: 'You stay outside.' He went in and shut the door.

Edgar turned and looked across the river. Moments later he heard Blod cry out in pain. It was inevitable, he told himself: a slave was bound to be chastised for running off. A slave owned little or nothing, so could not pay a fine, which meant that the only possible punishment was a beating. It was common practice and it was legal.

Blod cried out again and began to sob. Edgar heard Dreng grunting with the effort of his blows and cursing his victim at the same time.

Dreng was within his rights, Edgar told himself. And he was Edgar's master, too. Edgar had no right to intervene.

Blod began to beg for mercy. Edgar also heard the voices of Leaf and Ethel raised in protest, to no avail.

Then Blod screamed.

Edgar opened the door and burst in. Blod was on the floor, writhing in pain, her face covered with blood. Dreng was kicking her. When she protected her head he kicked her stomach, and when she protected her body he kicked her head. Leaf and Ethel were grabbing his arms and pulling him, trying to stop him, but he was too strong for them.

If this went on, Blod would die.

Edgar grabbed Dreng from behind and pulled him away.

Dreng wriggled out of Edgar's grasp, turned quickly, and punched Edgar's face. He was a strong man and the blow hurt. Edgar reacted reflexively. He punched Dreng on the point of the chin. Dreng's head flipped back like the lid of a chest, and he fell to the floor.

From the floor he pointed at Edgar. 'Get out of this house,' he yelled. 'And never come back!'

But Edgar had not finished. He dropped down with his knees on Dreng's chest, then put both hands to his throat and squeezed. Dreng's breath was cut off. He flailed at Edgar's arms uselessly.

Leaf screamed.

Edgar bent down until his face was inches from Dreng's. 'If you ever strike her again, I will come back,' he said. 'And I swear to God I will kill you.'

He released his grip. Dreng gasped and breathed hoarsely. Edgar looked at Dreng's two wives, who were standing back, looking scared. 'I mean it,' he said.

Then he got up and went out.

He walked along the river bank heading for the farmhouse. He rubbed his left cheekbone: he was going to have a black eye. He wondered whether he had done any good. Dreng might beat Blod again as soon as he caught his breath. Edgar could only hope that his threat would give the man pause.

Edgar had lost his job. Dreng would probably get Blod to pole the ferry now. She would be able to do it when she recovered from the beating. Perhaps that would discourage Dreng from crippling her. It was something to hope for.

Erman and Eadbald were not visible in the fields, and as it was midday Edgar guessed they would be having dinner at the farmhouse. He saw them as he approached the place. They were sitting outside in the sun, at a trestle table Edgar had made, evidently having just finished the meal. Ma was holding baby Winnie, now four months, singing her a little song that seemed familiar, and Edgar wondered whether he was remembering it from his own childhood. Ma had rolled up the sleeves of her dress, and Edgar was shocked to see how thin her arms were. She never complained, but she was obviously ill.

Eadbald looked at him and said: 'What happened to your face?'

'I had an argument with Dreng.'

'What about?'

'Blod the slave has been recaptured. He was killing her, but I stopped him.'

'What for? He owns her, he can kill her if he likes.'

This was almost true. Someone who killed a slave without justification might have to repent and do penance in the form of fasting, but justification was easy to invent and fasting was not much of a punishment.

But Edgar had a different objection. 'I won't let him kill her in front of me.'

The brothers had raised their voices, disturbing Winnie, who began to grizzle.

Erman said: 'Then you're a damn fool. If you're not careful, Dreng will dismiss you.'

'He already did.' Edgar sat at the table. The stew pot was empty, but there was a barley loaf, and he tore off a hunk. 'I'm not going back to the alehouse.' He began to eat.

Erman said: 'I hope you don't think we're going to feed you. If you were stupid enough to lose your position, that's your lookout.'

Cwenburg took the baby from Ma, saying: 'I've hardly got enough milk for Winnie as it is.' She uncovered her breast and put the baby to her nipple, giving Edgar a sultry glance from under her eyelids as she did so.

Edgar stood up. 'If I'm not welcome here, I'll leave.'

Ma said: 'Don't be foolish. Sit down.' She looked at the others. 'We're a family. Any child of mine – or grandchild – will be fed at my table as long as there's a crust in the house, and don't any of you ever forget it.'

þþþ

THAT NIGHT THERE was a storm. The wind shook the timbers of the house and waves of rain crashed on the thatch of the roof. They all woke up, including baby Winnie, who cried and was fed.

Edgar opened the door a crack and peeped out, but the night was black. He could see nothing but a sheet of rain like a crazed mirror reflecting the red glow of the fire behind him. He closed the door firmly.

Winnie went back to sleep, and the others seemed to doze, but Edgar remained wide awake. He was worried about the hay. If it remained wet for any length of time, it would rot. Was there a chance they might dry it, if the weather changed again and the sun shone in the morning? He was not enough of a farmer to know.

At first light the wind dropped and the rain eased, though it did not stop. Edgar opened the door again. 'I'm going to check on the hay,' he said, putting on his cloak.

His brothers and Ma came too, leaving Cwenburg behind with the baby.

As soon as they reached the low-lying land beside the river they saw that disaster had struck. The field was under water. The hay was not just wet, it was floating.

They all stared at it in the dawn light, horrified and afraid.

Ma said: 'It's ruined. Nothing can be done.' She turned away and walked back towards the house.

Eadbald said: 'If Ma says there's no hope, there's no hope.'

Edgar said: 'I'm trying to figure out how this happened.'

Erman said: 'What good will that do?'

'The rain was too much for the ground to soak up, I assume, so the water ran down the hill then pooled on the low ground.'

'My brother, the genius.'

Edgar ignored that. 'If the water could have drained away, the hay might have been saved.'

'So what? It didn't drain away.'

'I'm wondering how long it would take to dig a ditch from the top of the slope across the field to the bank to take the run-off and pour it into the river.'

'Too late for that now!'

The field was long and narrow, and Edgar guessed its width at about two hundred yards. A strong man could do it in a week or so, perhaps two if the digging proved difficult. 'There's a slight dip around the middle of the field,' he said, squinting through the rain. 'The best place for the ditch would be just there.'

Erman said: 'We can't start digging ditches now. We have to weed the oats then reap them. And Ma does no work these days.'

'I'll dig the ditch.'

'And what will we eat meanwhile – now there are six of us?'

'I don't know,' said Edgar.

They all trudged through the rain back to the house. Edgar saw that Ma was not there. He said to Cwenburg: 'Where did Ma go?'

Cwenburg shrugged. 'I thought she was with you.'

'She left us. I thought she came back here.'

'Well, she didn't.'

'Where else would she go, in this weather?'

'How should I know? She's your mother.'

'I'll look in the barn.'

Edgar went back out into the rain. Ma was not in the barn. He had a bad feeling.

He looked over the field. In this weather he could not see as far as the hamlet – but she had not gone in that direction, and if she had changed her mind she would have had to pass her three sons.

So where had she gone?

Edgar fought down a feeling of panic. He went to the edge of the forest. Why would she go into the wood in this weather? He walked downhill to the river. She could not have crossed over: she could not swim. He scanned the near bank.

He thought he saw something a few hundred yards downstream, and his heart faltered. It looked like a wet bundle of rags, but when he peered more closely he saw, protruding from the bundle, something that seemed horribly like a hand.

He hurried along the bank, impatiently shoving aside bushes and low branches. As he got closer his heart filled with dread. The bundle was human. It was half in the water. The worn brown clothes were female. The face was down, but the shape of the body was frighteningly familiar.

It did not move.

He knelt beside it. Gently, he turned the head. As he feared, the face was Ma's.

She was not breathing. He felt her chest. There was no heartbeat.

Edgar bowed his head in the rain, with his hand on the still body, and wept.

After a while he began to think. She had drowned – but why? She had no reason to go to the river. Unless . . .

Unless her death had been intentional. Had she killed herself so that her sons would have enough to eat? Edgar felt sick.

There was a weight inside him like a cold lump of lead in his heart. Ma was gone. He could imagine her reasoning: she was ill, she could no longer work, she had little time left on this earth, and all she was doing was eating food her family needed. She had sacrificed herself for their sakes, perhaps especially for the grandchild. If she had said all that to Edgar, he would have argued fiercely; but she had only thought it, and then taken the terrible, logical step.

He made up his mind that he would lie about this. If suicide was suspected, she might be denied a Christian burial. To avoid that, Edgar would say he had found her in the forest. Her wet clothes would be explained by the rain. She had been ill, perhaps she was losing her mind, she had wandered off, and the rain had acted on her already weakened body with fatal effect. He would even tell his brothers that story. Then she could lie in the graveyard alongside the church.

Water came from her mouth when he picked her up. She was light: she had got thinner during their time at Dreng's Ferry. Her body was still warm to the touch.

He kissed her forehead.

Then he carried her home.

ÞÞÞ

THE THREE BROTHERS dug the grave in the wet churchyard and they buried Ma the next day. Everyone in the hamlet came except Dreng. Ma's wisdom and determination had won people's respect.

The brothers had lost father and mother in just over a year. Erman said: 'As the eldest son, I'm head of the family now.' No one believed that. Edgar was the smart one, the resourceful one, the brother who came up with solutions to problems. He might never say so, but he was in practice head of the family. And that included the tiresome Cwenburg and her baby.

The rain stopped the day after the funeral, and Edgar started on the ditch. He did not know whether his plan would work. Was it an idea that would fail in practice, like the stone tiles for the roof of the brewhouse? He could only try it and see.

He used a wooden spade with a rusty iron tip. He did not want the ditch to have high banks – that would have defeated the purpose – so he had to carry the soil down to the river. He used it to raise the river bank.

Life at the farmhouse was barely tolerable without Ma. Erman watched Edgar eat, following every morsel from the bowl to Edgar's mouth. Cwenburg continued her campaign to make Edgar regret that he had not married her. Eadbald complained of backache from weeding. Only little Winnie was pleasant.

The ditch took two weeks. There was water in it from the start, a streamlet running slowly downhill; a hopeful sign, Edgar thought. He opened a gap in the river bank to let the water out. A pond formed behind the bank, its surface at the same height as that of the river, and Edgar realized there was a law of nature that made all water seek the same level.

He was barefoot in the pond, reinforcing the bank with stones, when he felt something move under his toes. There were fish in this pond, he realized. He was treading on eels. How had that happened?

He looked at what he had created, imagining the life of underwater creatures. They seemed to swim more or less randomly, and clearly some would pass from the river to the pond through the gap he had made in the bank. But how would they find their way out again? They would be ensnared, at least for a while.

He began to glimpse a solution to the food problem.

Fishing with a hook and line was a slow and unreliable way to get food. The fishermen of Combe made large nets and sailed in big ships to locations where fish swam in schools of a thousand or more. But there was another way.

Edgar had seen basketwork fish traps and he thought he could make one. He went into the forest and collected long, pliable green twigs from bushes and saplings. Then he sat on the ground outside the farmhouse and began to twist the twigs into the shape he remembered.

Erman saw him and said: 'When you've finished playing, you could help us in the fields.'

Edgar made a large basket with a narrow neck. It would catch fish the same way the pond did, by being easy to enter and difficult to leave – if it worked.

He finished it that evening.

In the morning he went to the tavern dunghill, looking for something he could use as bait. He found the head of a chicken and two decomposing rabbit feet. He put them in the bottom of the basket.

He added a stone, for stability, then sank the trap in the pond he had created.

He forced himself to leave it where it was, without checking it, for twenty-four hours.

Next morning, as he was leaving the farmhouse, Eadbald said: 'Where are you going?'

'To look at my fish trap.'

'Is that what you were making?'

'I don't know if it will work.'

'I'm coming to see.'

They all followed him, Eadbald and Erman and Cwenburg with the baby.

Edgar waded into the pond, which was thigh high. He was not sure exactly where he had sunk the trap. He had to bend down and feel around in the mud. It might even have moved in the night.

'You've lost it!' Erman jeered.

He could not have lost it; the pond was not big enough. But another time he would mark its location with some kind of buoy, probably a piece of wood tied to the basket by a string long enough to allow the wood to float on the surface.

If there was another time.

At last his hands came in contact with the basketwork.

He sent up a silent prayer.

He found the neck of the trap and upended it so that the entrance was at the top, then he lifted.

It seemed heavy, and he worried that it might somehow have got stuck.

With a heave he pulled it above the surface, water pouring away through the small holes between the woven twigs.

When the water was gone he could see clearly into the trap. It was full of eels.

Eadbald said delightedly: 'Would you look at that?'

Cwenburg clapped her hands. 'We're rich!'

'It worked,' Edgar said with profound satisfaction. This haul would allow them to eat well for a week or more.

Eadbald said: 'I see a couple of river trout in there, and some smaller fish I can't identify.'

'The tiddlers will serve as bait next time,' said Edgar.

'Next time? You think you can do this every week?'

Edgar shrugged. 'I'm not certain, but I don't see why not. Every day, even. There are millions of fish in the river.'

'We'll have more fish than we can eat!'

'Then we'll sell some and buy meat.'

They headed back to the house, Edgar carrying the basket on his shoulder. Eadbald said: 'I wonder why no one did this before.'

'I suppose the previous owner of the farm didn't think of it,' said Edgar. He thought some more and added: 'And no one else in this place is hungry enough to try new ideas.'

They put the fish into a large bowl of water. Cwenburg cleaned and skinned a big one, then roasted it over the fire for breakfast. Brindle ate the skin.

They decided they would have the trout for dinner and prepare the rest for smoking. The eels would hang from the rafters and be preserved for the winter.

Edgar put the small fish back in the basket as bait and returned the trap to the pond. He wondered how much he would haul up the second time. If it was even half as much as today's catch, he would have some to sell.

He sat looking at the ditch, the river bank and the pond. He had solved the flooding problem and might even have ensured that the family had enough to eat for the foreseeable future. So he wondered why he was not happy.

It did not take him long to figure out the answer.

He did not want to be a fisherman. Nor a farmer. When he had dreamed about the life ahead of him, he had never envisaged that his great achievement would be a fish trap. He felt like one of the eels, swimming round and round in the basket and always missing the narrow way out.

He knew he had a gift. Some men could fight, and some could recite a poem that went on for hours, and some could steer a ship by the stars. Edgar's gift had to do with shapes, and something about numbers; and somewhere in there was an intuitive grasp of weights and stress, pressure and tension, and the twisting strain for which there was no word.

There had been a time when he had not realized he was exceptional in this way, and he had caused offence sometimes, especially with older men, by saying things such as: 'Isn't that obvious?'

He just saw certain things. He had imagined the excess rain running off the field into his ditch, and down the ditch into the river; and his vision had come true.

And he could do more. He had built a Viking boat and a stone brewhouse and a drainage ditch, but that was only the start. His gift had to be used for greater things. He knew that, the way he had known that the fish would get caught in the trap.

It was his destiny.

21

ALDRED WAS PLAYING A dangerous game: trying to bring down a bishop. All bishops were powerful, but Wynstan was also ruthless and brutal. Abbot Osmund was right to be scared of him. To offend him was to put your head into the mouth of a lion.

But Christians had to do that sort of thing.

The more Aldred thought about it, the more sure he was that the man to prosecute Wynstan was Sheriff Den. First, the sheriff was the king's representative, and forgery was an offence against the king, whose duty it was to keep the currency sound. Second, the sheriff and his men formed a power group that rivalled Wilwulf and his brothers; each restrained the other, which caused animosity on both sides. Aldred was sure Den hated Wilf. Third, the successful prosecution of a high-ranking forger would be a personal triumph for the sheriff. It would please the king, who would surely reward Den handsomely.

Aldred spoke to Den after Mass on Sunday. He made it look casual, just two of the important men of the town exchanging courtesies: he was keen to avoid the appearance of conspiracy. Smiling amiably, he said quietly: 'I need to speak to you privately. May I call at your compound tomorrow?'

Den's eyes widened in surprise. He had an alert intelligence, and no doubt he could guess that this was no mere social request. 'Of course,' he replied, in the same tone of polite small talk. 'A pleasure.'

'In the afternoon, if that suits you.' That was the time when the monks' religious duties were light.

397

'Certainly.'

'And the fewer people who know, the better.'

'I understand.'

Next day Aldred slipped out of the abbey after the midday meal, when the townspeople were sleepily digesting their mutton and ale, and few people were on the streets to notice him. Now that he was about to tell the sheriff everything, he began to worry about what reaction he would get. Would Den have the nerve to go up against the mighty Wynstan?

He found Den alone in his great hall, using a hand-held whetstone to sharpen a favourite sword. Aldred began his story with his first visit to Dreng's Ferry: the unfriendliness of the inhabitants, the decadent atmosphere at the minster, and his instinct that there was a guilty secret there. Den looked intrigued by Wynstan's quarterly visits, and the gifts he brought; then he was amused at the idea of Aldred sending someone to follow Wynstan around the pleasure houses of Combe. But when Aldred began on the weighing of coins Den put down his sword and the stone, listening avidly.

'Clearly Wynstan and Degbert go to Combe to spend some of their forgeries and change others for genuine money in a large town where there is lots of commerce and the counterfeits are unlikely to be noticed.'

Den nodded. 'That makes sense. Pennies move from one person to another quickly in a town.'

'But the coins must be produced in Dreng's Ferry. To make perfect copies of the dies used in the royal mints requires the skill of a jeweller – and there is a jeweller in the minster at Dreng's Ferry. His name is Cuthbert.'

Den was both appalled and eager. He seemed genuinely shocked by the enormity of the crime. 'A bishop!' he said in an excited whisper. 'Counterfeiting the king's currency!' But he was also thrilled. 'If I expose this crime, King Ethelred will never forget my name!'

When he had calmed down Aldred got him to focus on just how they would pounce.

'We need to catch them at it,' Den said. 'I need to see the materials, the tools, the process. I need to see the false money being manufactured.'

'I think that can be arranged,' said Aldred, sounding more confident than he felt. 'They do it at regular times, always a few days after the quarter day. Wynstan collects his rents, takes genuine money to Dreng's Ferry, and there turns it into twice as many counterfeit coins.'

'It's diabolical. But for us to catch them, they mustn't be forewarned.' Den became thoughtful. 'I would have to leave Shiring before Wynstan, so that he wouldn't get the idea he was being followed. I'd need a pretext: I could pretend we're going to search for Ironface in, say, the woods around Bathford.'

'Good idea – I heard a report of goats being stolen there a few weeks ago.'

'Then we would have to hide out in the forest near Dreng's Ferry, well away from the road. However, we would need someone to tell us when Wynstan arrives at the minster.'

'I can arrange that. I have an ally in the village.'

'Trustworthy?'

'He already knows everything. It's Edgar the builder.'

'Good choice. He helped the Lady Ragna in Outhenham. Young, but smart. He would have to alert us as soon as they begin making the coins. Do you think he would do that?'

'Yes.'

'I believe we have the beginnings of a plan. But I need to think this over carefully. We'll talk more later.'

'Whenever you like, sheriff.'

ÞÞÞ

On Michaelmas, the twenty-ninth day of September, Bishop Wynstan sat in his residence at Shiring, receiving his rents.

Wealth poured into his treasury all day long, giving him a pleasure that was every bit as good as sex. The headmen of nearby villages appeared in the morning, driving livestock, steering loaded carts, and carrying bags and chests of silver pennies. Tribute from more distant places within Shiring arrived in the afternoon. Wynstan, as bishop, was also lord of villages in other shires, and their payments would arrive over the next day or two. He tallied it all as carefully as a hungry peasant counted the baby chicks in the henhouse. He liked the silver pennies best of all, for he could take them to Dreng's Ferry where they would miraculously be doubled.

The headman of Meddock was twelve pence short. The defaulter was Godric, the son of the priest, who had come to explain. 'My lord bishop, I beg your gracious mercy,' said Godric.

'Never mind that, where's my money?' said Wynstan.

'The rain has been terrible, before and after Midsummer. I have a wife and two children, and I don't know how I'm going to feed them this winter.'

This was not like last year's calamity at Combe, where everyone in town had been impoverished. Wynstan said: 'Everyone else in Meddock has paid their dues.'

'My land is on a west-facing slope, and my crops were washed out. I will pay you double next year.'

'No, you won't, you'll tell me another story.'

'I swear it.'

'If I accepted oaths instead of rents, I'd be poor and you'd be rich.'

'Then what am I to do?'

'Borrow.'

'I asked my father, the priest, but he doesn't have the money.'

'If your own father has refused you, why should I help you?'

'Then what can I do?'

'Get the money somehow. If you can't borrow it, sell yourself and your family into slavery.'

'Would you take us as slaves, my lord?'

'Is your family here?'

Godric pointed. A woman and two children were waiting anxiously in the background.

Wynstan said: 'Your wife is too old to be worth much, and your children are too small. I won't take any of you. Try someone else. Widow Ymma, the furrier, is rich.'

'My lord—'

'Get out of my sight. Headman, if Godric hasn't paid by the end of today, find another peasant for the west-sloping land. And make sure the new man understands the need for drainage furrows. This is the west of England, for heaven's sake – it rains here.'

There were several like Godric during the day, and Wynstan gave each the same treatment. If peasants were allowed to skip payments, they would all show up on quarter days with empty hands and sad stories.

Wynstan was also collecting rents for Wilwulf, and beside him Ithamar was carefully keeping the two sets of accounts separate. Wynstan took a modest rake-off from Wilf's money. The bishop was keenly aware that his wealth and power were magnified by his relationship to the ealdorman, and he was not going to endanger that relationship.

At the end of the afternoon Wynstan summoned servants to transport Wilf's rents-in-kind to the compound, but Wynstan carried the silver himself, liking to deliver it personally, so that it looked like a gift from him. He found Wilf in the great hall. 'There's not as much in the chest as there used to be, before you gave the Vale of Outhen to the Lady Ragna,' he said.

'She's there now,' Wilf said.

Wynstan nodded. This was the third quarter day on which Ragna had collected her rents personally. After her showdown with him on Lady Day she clearly was in no hurry to delegate to an underling. 'She's remarkable,' he said, speaking as if he liked her. 'So beautiful, and so smart. I understand why you seek her advice so often – even though she's a woman.'

The compliment was barbed. A man who was dominated by his wife was subject to many jibes, most of them obscene. Wilf did not miss the nuance. He said: 'I seek your advice, and you're a mere priest.'

'True.' Wynstan smiled, acknowledging the riposte. He sat down, and a servant poured him a glass of wine. 'She made a fool of your son over that ball game.'

Wilf made a sour face. 'Garulf is a fool, I'm sorry to say. He showed that in Wales. He's no coward – he'll fight against any odds. But he's no general, either. His notion of strategy is to charge into battle yelling at the top of his voice. However, the men follow him.'

They moved on to talk about the Vikings. This year the raids had been farther east, in Hampshire and Sussex, and Shiring had largely escaped, by contrast with the previous year, when Combe and other places in Wilf's domain had been ravaged. However, Shiring had suffered from this year's unseasonal rain. 'Perhaps God is displeased with the people of Shiring,' Wilf said.

'For not giving enough of their money to the Church, probably,' said Wynstan; and Wilf laughed.

Before returning to his residence, Wynstan went to see his mother, Gytha. He kissed her and sat by her fire. She said: 'Brother Aldred went to see Sheriff Den.'

Wynstan was intrigued. 'Did he, now?'

'He went alone, and was quite discreet. He probably thinks no one noticed. But I heard about it.'

'He's a sly dog. He went behind my back to the archbishop of Canterbury, and tried to take over my minster at Dreng's Ferry.'

'Does he have a weakness?'

'There was an incident in his youth, an affair with another young monk.'

'Anything since?'

'No.'

'Useful ammunition, perhaps, but if the behaviour hasn't been repeated then it's not enough to bring him down. Living without women, I should think half those monks are diddling one another in the dorm.'

'I'm not worried about Aldred. I squashed him once, I can do it again.'

Gytha was not reassured. 'I don't understand it,' she fretted. 'What would a monk want with the sheriff?'

'I'm more worried about the Norman bitch.'

Gytha nodded agreement. 'Ragna is smart and she's bold.'

'She outmanoeuvred me at Outhenham. Not many people can do that.'

'And she got Wilf to sack the head groom, Wignoth, who lamed her horse for me.'

Wynstan sighed. 'It was such a mistake for us to let Wilf marry her.'

'When you negotiated that, you were hoping to reinforce the treaty with Count Hubert.'

'It was more because Wilf wanted her so badly.'

'You could have prevented the marriage.'

'I know,' Wynstan said ruefully. 'I could have come home from Cherbourg saying we were too late, she was already engaged to marry Guillaume of Reims.' Wynstan considered his explanation. He could usually tell his mother the truth: she was on his side regardless. 'Wilf had only just got me appointed bishop, and the sad fact is that I didn't have the nerve. I was afraid he might guess what I'd done. I thought his wrath would be terrible. In fact, I could almost certainly have got away with it. But I didn't know that then.'

'Don't worry about Ragna,' said Gytha. 'We can handle her. She has no idea of the forces she's up against.'

'I'm not so sure.'

'In any case, we'd be foolish to move against her now. She holds his heart in her hand.' Gytha smiled with a twisted mouth. 'But a man's love is temporary. Give Wilf time to tire of her.'

'How long will that take?'

'I don't know. Be patient. The time will come.'

'I love you, Mother.'

'I love you too, my son.'

ÞÞÞ

SOME MORNINGS, THE fish trap was full, sometimes half full, occasionally empty but for a few tiddlers, but in any week there was more than the family could eat. They hung fish from the rafters to smoke until it seemed to be raining eels. One Friday when the trap came up full Edgar decided to sell some.

He found a stick a yard long and attached twelve fat eels to it, using green twigs as cords, then went to the alehouse. He found Ethel, Dreng's younger wife, sitting outside in the late summer sun, plucking doves for the pot, her bony hands red and greasy from the work. 'Do you want some eels?' he said. 'A farthing for two.'

'Where did you get them?'

'From our flooded hayfield.'

'Well done. They're nice and plump. Yes, I'll have two.'

She went inside to ask Dreng for the money, and he came out with her. 'Where did you get them?' he asked Edgar.

'I found an eel's nest in a tree,' Edgar said.

'Impertinent as always,' Dreng said, but he gave Edgar a quarter of a silver penny, and Edgar walked on.

He sold two to the laundress, Ebba, and four to fat Bebbe. Elfburg, who did the cleaning at the minster, said she did not have any money, but her husband, Hadwine, had gone into the forest for the day to collect nuts, and she knew another way to pay Edgar. He declined the offer.

With four farthings in his belt pouch, Edgar took the remaining fish to the priests.

Degbert's wife, Edith, was breast-feeding a baby outside the house. 'They look nice,' she said.

'You can have all four for half a penny,' he said.

'You'd better ask him,' Edith said, with a jerk of her head towards the open door.

Degbert heard the voices and came out. 'Where did you get those?' he said to Edgar.

Edgar suppressed a sarcastic answer. 'The flooding has made a fish pond in our hay field.'

'And who said you could take eels from it?'

'The fish didn't ask permission to swim to our farm.'

Degbert looked at Edgar's stick. 'You seem to have sold some already.'

Reluctantly, Edgar said: 'I've sold eight.'

'You forget that I'm the landlord here. You rent the farm, not the river. If you want to make a fish pond, you need my agreement.'

'Do I? I thought you were lord of the land, not lord of the river.'

'You're an uneducated peasant who doesn't know anything. The minster has a charter that gives me fishing rights.'

'In the time I've been here you've never caught a single fish.'

'Makes no difference. What's written is written.'

'Where is this charter?'

Degbert smiled. 'Wait there.' He went inside and returned holding a folded sheet of parchment. 'Here it is,' he said, pointing at a paragraph. 'If any man take fish from the river, he shall owe the dean one fish in three.' He grinned.

Edgar did not look at the parchment. He could not read, and

Degbert knew it. The charter might say anything. He felt humiliated. It was true, he was an ignorant peasant.

Degbert said triumphantly: 'You took twelve eels, so you owe me four.'

Edgar handed over his stick of eels.

Then he heard hoof beats.

He looked up the hill, and Degbert and Edith did the same. Half a dozen horsemen thundered down to the minster and reined in. Edgar recognized their leader as Bishop Wynstan.

While Degbert was welcoming his distinguished cousin, Edgar walked briskly away. He passed the tavern and crossed the field. His brothers were tying reaped stalks of oats into sheaves, but he did not speak to them. He bypassed the farmhouse and quietly slipped into the forest.

He knew his way. He followed a barely visible deer track through stands of oak and hornbeam for a mile and came to a clearing. Sheriff Den was there with Brother Aldred and twenty men and horses. They made a formidable group, the men heavily armed with swords, shields and helmets, the horses powerfully muscled. Two men drew weapons as Edgar appeared, and he recognized them: the short, nasty-looking one was Wigbert, the big man Godwine. Edgar raised his hands to show that he was unarmed.

Aldred said: 'It's all right, he's our spy in the hamlet,' and the men sheathed their blades.

Edgar winced. He did not like to think of himself as a spy.

He had agonized over this. The forgers were going to be found out, and their punishment would be cruel. Degbert deserved everything he would get, but what about Cuthbert? He was a weak man who did what he was told. He had been bullied into committing a crime.

However, Edgar had a horror of lawlessness. Ma would always argue with those in authority but never cheat them. Lawlessness was represented by the Vikings who had killed Sunni, and by Ironface the outlaw, and by people such as Wynstan and Degbert, who robbed the poor while pretending to care for their souls. The best people were rule keepers, clergymen such as Aldred and nobles such as Ragna.

Edgar sighed. 'Yes, I'm the spy,' he said. 'And Bishop Wynstan has just arrived.'

Den said: 'Good.' He glanced up. Little sky was visible between the leaves, but the strong light of noon had softened to a late afternoon radiance.

Edgar answered Den's unspoken question. 'They won't get much done in the forge today. It will take time to heat the fire and melt down the pennies.'

'So they'll start tomorrow.'

'I'd guess they'll be in full swing by mid-morning.'

Den looked uneasy. 'We can't take any chances. Can you check on their progress and let us know when it's a good time for us to raid?'

'Yes.'

'Will they let you into the workshop?'

'No, but that's how I'll know. I sometimes talk to the jeweller while he's working. We discuss tools and metals and—'

'How will you know?' Den interrupted impatiently.

'The only time Cuthbert closes his door is when Wynstan is there. So I'll knock and ask for Cuthbert. If I'm turned away, that will mean they're doing it.'

Den nodded his greying head. 'Good enough,' he said. 'Come and let me know. We'll be ready.'

ÞÞÞ

THAT EVENING WYNSTAN went around the hamlet and gave every household a side of bacon.

Before breakfast next morning, Cuthbert went into his workshop and started a fire, using charcoal, which burned hotter than wood or coal.

Wynstan made sure the outer door of the workshop was closed and barred, then stationed Cnebba outside to stand guard. Finally he handed Cuthbert an ironbound chest full of silver pennies.

Cuthbert took a large clay crucible and buried it in the charcoal up to the rim. As it heated, it gradually turned the red colour of the sun at daybreak.

He combined five pounds of copper, in thin slices cut off a cylindrical ingot, with the same weight of silver pennies, mixing them thoroughly, then poured the metal into the crucible. He boosted the flames with a pair of bellows, then as the mixture melted he stirred it with a puddling stick. The wood scorched in the hot metal, but that did no harm. The clay crucible continued to change colour, becoming the bright yellow of the sun at noon. The molten metal was a darker shade of yellow.

On his workbench he arranged ten clay moulds in a row. Each when full to the brim would hold a pound of the molten mixture: Wynstan and Cuthbert had established this, some time ago, by trial and error.

Finally Cuthbert took the crucible out of the fire, using two pairs of long-handled tongs, and poured the mixture into the clay moulds.

The first time Wynstan had witnessed this process he had been scared. Forgery was a very serious crime. Any act that subverted the coinage was treason against the king. The punishment was amputation of a hand, theoretically; but a worse sentence might be imposed.

On that first occasion, when Wynstan was only an archdeacon, he had paced around the minster, going in and out of the forge, ceaselessly looking to see whether anyone was coming. He had behaved, he now realized, like the picture of a guilty man. But no one had dared question him.

He had quickly realized that most people preferred not to know about the crimes of their superiors, for such knowledge could get them into trouble; and he had reinforced this feeling with gifts. Even now he doubted whether the residents of the hamlet guessed what happened four times a year in Cuthbert's forge.

Wynstan hoped he had not become careless; just more confident.

When the metal had cooled and hardened, Cuthbert turned the moulds upside-down and ejected fat discs of the copper-silver alloy. Next he hammered each disc, making them thinner and broader, until each one filled a large circle precisely scratched on the bench with dividers. One disc, Wynstan knew, would now provide two hundred and forty blank coins.

Cuthbert had made a punch of exactly the diameter of a penny, and now he used it to cut out blanks from the sheet of alloy. He carefully swept up the leftover fragments to be melted again.

On his bench he had three heavy iron objects of cylindrical shape. Two were dies, painstakingly engraved by Cuthbert with moulds for the two sides of a King Ethelred penny. The lower die, called the pile, showed the king's head, seen in profile, with the title 'King of the English' in Latin. Cuthbert set this piece firmly into its slot in the anvil. The upper die, called the trussel, had a cross, plus, deceitfully, the attribution 'Made by Elfwine in Shiring', also in Latin. Last year the design had been modified, making the arms of the cross longer; a change that made life difficult for forgers – which was why the king did it. At its other end the trussel was mushroom-shaped from much hammering. The third object was a collar that held the upper and lower dies perfectly aligned.

Cuthbert placed a blank on the pile, slipped the collar on, and inserted the trussel into the collar, letting it down until it rested on the blank. Then he gave the trussel a sharp tap with his iron-headed hammer.

He lifted the trussel and removed the collar. The top of the metal blank was now impressed with the cross. Cuthbert used a blunt knife to prise the coin off the pile, then turned it over to reveal the king's head on the other side.

It was the wrong colour, because the alloy was brown rather than silver. But there was a simple solution to that problem. Using his tongs, Cuthbert heated the coin in the fire then dipped it in a bowl containing dilute vitriol. As Wynstan watched, the acid took the copper away from the surface of the coin, leaving a sort of skin of pure silver.

Wynstan smiled. Money for nothing, he thought. Few sights pleased him more.

Two things gave him joy: money and power. And they were the same, really. He loved to have power over people, and money gave him that. He could not imagine ever having more power and money than he wanted. He was a bishop, but he wanted to be archbishop, and when he achieved that he would strive to become the king's chancellor, perhaps to be king; and even then he would want more power and money. But life was like that, he thought; you could eat your fill in the evening and still be hungry come breakfast time.

Cuthbert replaced the clay crucible in the fire and refilled it with another measure of mixed real coins and copper pieces.

While it was melting he hammered the trussel again and popped out another penny.

'Fresh as a virgin's tit,' Wynstan said appreciatively.

Cuthbert dropped the penny in the vitriol.

There was a sound from outside.

Cuthbert and Wynstan froze and listened in silence.

They heard the voice of Cnebba saying: 'Go away.'

A young man's voice said: 'I've come to see Cuthbert.'

Cuthbert whispered: 'That's Edgar the builder.'

Wynstan relaxed.

Outside, Cnebba said: 'Why do you want Cuthbert?'

'To give him an eel.'

'You can give it to me.'

'I can give it to the devil, but it's for Cuthbert.'

'Cuthbert is busy. Now piss off.'

'And a very good day to you, too, kind sir.'

'Insolent dog.'

They waited in silence, but there was no more conversation, and after a minute Cuthbert resumed his work. He speeded up, inserting the blanks and banging the trussel and popping the pennies out almost like a kitchen maid podding peas. The real moneyer, Elfwine of Shiring, working in a team of three, could produce something like seven hundred coins per hour. Cuthbert dropped the brown pennies in the acid and stopped his work every few minutes to retrieve the newly silvered coins.

Wynstan looked on, fascinated, hardly noticing the passage of time. The hard part, he reflected wryly, was spending the cash. Because copper was not as heavy as silver, the forged coins could not be used for any transaction large enough to require the money to be weighed. But Wynstan used Cuthbert's pennies in alehouses and whorehouses and gambling dens, where he enjoyed spending freely.

He was watching Cuthbert lift the crucible of molten metal out of the charcoal a second time when his reverie was disturbed by another noise outside. 'What now?' he murmured irritably.

This time Cnebba's tone was different. Speaking to Edgar, he had sounded scornful; now he seemed startled and intimidated, causing Wynstan to frown uneasily. Cnebba said: 'Who are you?' in a voice that was loud but anxious. 'Where did you all come from? What do you mean by sneaking up on a man like that?'

Cuthbert set the crucible down on the workbench and said: 'Oh, Jesus save me. Who is it?'

Someone rattled the door, but it was firmly barred.

Wynstan heard a voice he thought he knew. 'There's another entrance,' it said. 'Through the main house.'

Who was that? The name came to him in a moment: Brother Aldred from Shiring Abbey.

Wynstan remembered telling his mother that Aldred was no threat.

'I will have him crucified,' Wynstan muttered.

Cuthbert was standing stock still, paralysed by fright.

Wynstan looked around quickly. There was incriminating evidence everywhere: adulterated metal, illicit dies and forged coins. It would be impossible to hide everything: molten metal in a red-hot crucible could not be tucked away into a chest. His only hope was to keep the visitors out of the workshop.

He stepped through the interior door that led into the minster. The clergy and their families were around the room, the men talking, the women preparing vegetables, the children playing. They all looked up suddenly when Wynstan slammed the door.

A moment later, Sheriff Den came in through the main entrance.

He and Wynstan stared at one another for a moment. Wynstan was shocked and dismayed. Aldred had clearly brought Den here, and there could only be one reason for that.

My mother warned me, Wynstan thought, and I didn't listen.

He recovered his composure with an effort. 'Sheriff Den!' he said. 'This is a surprise visit. Come in, sit down, have a cup of ale.'

Aldred entered behind Den and pointed to the door behind Wynstan. 'The workshop is through there,' he said.

They were followed in by two armed men Wynstan knew as Wigbert and Godwine.

Wynstan had four men-at-arms. Cnebba was guarding the outer door of the workshop. The other three had spent the night in the stables. Where were they now?

More of the sheriff's men entered the minster, and Wynstan realized that it hardly mattered where his men were: they were hopelessly outnumbered. The wretched cowards had probably lain down their arms already.

Aldred strode across the room, but Wynstan stood squarely in front of the workshop door, blocking his way. Aldred looked at him but spoke to Den. 'It's in there.'

Den said: 'Stand aside, my lord bishop.'

Wynstan knew he had no defence now but his rank. 'Get out of this place,' he said. 'It's a priests' house.'

Den looked around at the priests and their families, all staring silently at the confrontation. 'It doesn't look like a priests' house,' said Den.

'You'll answer for this in the shire court,' Wynstan said.

'Oh, don't worry, we're going to the shire court, all right,' said Den. 'Now stand aside.'

Aldred pushed past Wynstan and put his hand on the door. Wynstan, furious, punched Aldred's face as hard as he could. Aldred fell back. Wynstan's knuckles hurt: he was not accustomed to fisticuffs. He rubbed his right hand with his left.

Den made a gesture to the men-at-arms.

Wigbert approached Wynstan. The bishop was bigger, but Wigbert seemed more dangerous.

'Don't you dare touch a bishop!' Wynstan said furiously. 'You'll bring God's curse down upon yourselves.'

The men hesitated.

Den said: 'A man as wicked as Wynstan can't bring down God's curse, even if he is a bishop.'

His scornful tone maddened Wynstan.

'Seize him,' said Den.

Wynstan moved, but Wigbert was faster. Before Wynstan could dodge, Wigbert grabbed him, lifted him off his feet, and moved him away from the door. Wynstan struggled in vain: Wigbert's muscles were like ships' ropes.

Wynstan's rage became as incandescent as the metal in Cuthbert's crucible.

Aldred darted into the workshop, with Den and Godwine right behind him.

Wynstan was still being held by Wigbert. For a moment he had no inclination to move. The experience of being manhandled by a sheriff's officer had shocked him. Wigbert slightly relaxed his grip.

Wynstan heard Aldred say: 'Look at this: copper to adulterate the silver, dies to counterfeit the king's currency, and brand new coins all over the bench. Cuthbert, my friend, what got into you?'

'They forced me,' said Cuthbert. 'I only wanted to make ornaments for the church.'

Lying dog, Wynstan thought; you were eager for this work, and you got fat on the profits.

He heard Den say: 'How long has that evil bishop had you debasing the king's coinage?'

'Five years.'

'Well, it's over now.'

Wynstan saw a river of silver coins change course and begin to flow away from him, and his fury boiled over. He pulled away from Wigbert with a sudden jerk.

þþþ

ALDRED WAS STARING in astonishment at the sophisticated counterfeit factory that was Cuthbert's workbench: the hammer and shears, the crucible in the fire, the dies and moulds, and the pile of shiny fake pennies; and at the same time he was rubbing his face where Wynstan had hit him, high on the left cheekbone; when he heard a roar of rage from Wynstan, followed by a surprised curse from Wigbert, and Wynstan charged into the workshop.

He was red in the face and there was spittle on his lips like the foam on the mouth of a sick horse. He was screaming obscenities like a lunatic.

Aldred had seen him angry but never like this: he appeared to have lost all control. Roaring with incoherent hatred, he hurled himself at Sheriff Den, who fell back against the wall, taken by surprise. But Den, who Aldred guessed must be experienced at this sort of thing, lifted one leg and kicked Wynstan hard in the chest, sending him lurching away.

Wynstan turned on Cuthbert, who cowered away. Then Wynstan grabbed the anvil and tipped it over, spilling tools and forged pennies.

Wynstan grabbed the iron-headed hammer and raised it high. There was murder in his eyes, Aldred saw, and for the first time in his life he felt he was in the presence of the devil.

Godwine bravely came at him. Wynstan changed his stance, drew back his arm, and swung the hammer at the crucible of molten metal standing on the workbench. The clay shattered and the metal sprayed.

Aldred saw a hot splash land full on Godwine's face. The big man's scream of terror and agony was cut off almost as soon as it began. Then something struck Aldred's leg below the knee. He felt a pain worse than anything he had known in his whole life, and he passed out.

ÞÞÞ

ALDRED SCREAMED WHEN he came round, and continued to scream for several minutes. Eventually his cries became groans. Someone made him drink strong wine, but that only made him feel confused as well as terrified.

When at last the panic subsided and he was able to focus, he looked at his leg. There was a hole in his calf the size of a robin's egg and the flesh was charred black. It hurt like hell. The metal that had done the damage had cooled and fallen to the floor, he guessed.

One of the priests' women brought ointment for his wound but he refused it: there was no telling what pagan magic ingredients had gone into it, bats' brains or crushed mistletoe or blackbird droppings. Spotting the trustworthy Edgar, he asked him to warm some wine and pour it into the hole to cleanse it, then find a clean rag.

Just before passing out, Aldred had seen a large splash of molten metal land on Godwine's face. Sheriff Den now told him that Godwine had died, and Aldred could understand how. A small drop of the molten metal had instantly made a hole in Aldred's leg, so the quantity that had hit Godwine's face must have burned all the way through to his brain in no time.

'I've arrested Degbert and Cuthbert,' Den said. 'I'll keep them prisoners until the trial.'

'What about Wynstan?'

'I hesitate to arrest a bishop. I don't want to turn the entire Church establishment against me. But it's not really necessary: Wynstan isn't likely to run away, and if he does I'll catch him.'

'I hope you're right. I've known him for years and I have never seen such a fit seize him. He's gone beyond ordinary wickedness. He seems possessed.'

'I think you're right,' said Den. 'This is a new level of evil. But don't worry. We've caught him just in time.'

22

THERE WOULD BE REPERCUSSIONS, Edgar knew. Wynstan would not accept what had happened. He would fight back, and he would be merciless with those involved in the exposure of his crime. Edgar felt fear like a small hard growth in his belly. Just how much danger was he in?

He had played an important role, but always clandestinely. During the raid he had been out of sight, and only when the excitement was over had he appeared at the minster with a group of curious villagers. He would not have been noticed by Wynstan, he felt sure.

He was wrong.

Wynstan's clerk Ithamar, with the round face and white-blond hair, came to Dreng's Ferry a week after the raid. After Mass he made an administrative announcement: in Degbert's absence the eldest of the priests remaining at the minster, Father Derwin, had been appointed acting dean. It hardly seemed worth the trip from Shiring when a letter would have done just as well.

As the congregation was leaving the little church, Ithamar approached Edgar, who was with his family: Erman, Eadbald, Cwenburg and six-month-old baby Winnie. Ithamar did not bother with polite small talk. He said bluntly to Edgar: 'You're a friend of Brother Aldred from Shiring Abbey.'

Was this the real reason for Ithamar's trip? Edgar felt a shiver of fear. He said: 'I don't know why you would say that.'

Erman put in stupidly: 'Because you are, idiot.'

Edgar wanted to punch him in the face. He said: 'No one's speaking to you, Erman, so keep your fool mouth shut.' He turned back to the clerk. 'I know the monk, certainly.'

'You bathed his wound after he was burned.'

'As anyone would. Why do you ask?'

'You've been seen with Aldred here in Dreng's Ferry, at Shiring, and at Combe; and I myself saw you with him at Outhenham.'

Ithamar was saying that Edgar knew Aldred, that was all. Ithamar did not seem to know that he had actually been Aldred's spy. So what was this about? He decided to ask outright. 'What point are you making, Ithamar?'

'Are you going to be one of Aldred's oath-helpers?'

So that was it. Ithamar's mission was to find out who Aldred's oath-helpers were going to be. Edgar felt relieved. It could have been a lot worse.

He said: 'I haven't been asked to be an oath-helper.'

This was true, but not completely honest. Edgar fully expected to be asked. When an oath-helper had personal knowledge of the facts in the case, it added weight to his vow. And Edgar had been in the workshop and seen the metals, the dies and the freshly minted coins, so his oath would be helpful to Aldred – and damaging to Wynstan.

Ithamar knew this. 'You will be asked, almost certainly,' he said. His rather childish face twisted with malice. 'And when that happens, I recommend you refuse.'

Erman spoke again. 'He's right, Edgar,' he said. 'People like us should stay out of priests' quarrels.'

'Your brother is wise,' said Ithamar.

Edgar said: 'Thank you both for your advice, but the fact remains that I haven't been summoned to appear at the trial of Bishop Wynstan.'

Ithamar was not satisfied. 'Remember,' he said, wagging a finger, 'that Dean Degbert is your landlord.'

Edgar was taken aback. He had not been expecting threats. 'What do you mean by that?' He moved closer to Ithamar. 'Exactly?'

Ithamar looked intimidated and took a step back, but he put on a belligerent face and said defiantly: 'We need our tenants to support the Church, not undermine it.'

'I would never undermine the Church. For example, I would not forge counterfeit coins in a minster.'

'Don't get clever with me. I'm telling you that if you offend your landlord he will evict you from your farm.'

Erman said: 'Jesus save us. We can't lose the farm. We're only just getting straight. Edgar, listen to the man. Don't be a fool.'

Edgar stared at Ithamar with incredulity. 'We're in a church, and you've just attended Mass,' he said. 'Angels and saints surround us, invisible but real. They all know what you're doing. You're trying to prevent the truth being told, and you're protecting a wicked man from the consequences of his crimes. What do you imagine the angels are whispering to one another now, as they watch you committing these sins, with the wine of the sacrament still on your lips?'

Eadbald protested: 'Edgar, he's the priest, not you!'

Ithamar paled, and took a moment to think how to reply. 'I'm protecting the Church, and the angels know it,' he said, though he looked as if he hardly believed that himself. 'And you should do the same. Otherwise you'll feel the wrath of God's priesthood.'

Erman spoke with a note of desperation. 'You have to do as he says, Edgar, or we'll be back where we were fifteen months ago, homeless and destitute.'

'I got that message,' Edgar said shortly. He was feeling bewildered and uncertain and he did not want to show it.

Eadbald put in: 'Tell us you won't testify, Edgar, please.'

Cwenburg said: 'Think of my baby.'

Ithamar said: 'Listen to your family, Edgar.' Then he turned away with the air of one who feels he has done all he can.

Edgar wondered what Ma would say. He needed her wisdom now. The others were no help. He said: 'Why don't you all go back to the farmhouse? I'll catch you up.'

Erman said suspiciously: 'What are you going to do?'

'I'm going to talk to Ma,' said Edgar, and he walked away.

He stepped outside the church and crossed the graveyard to Ma's resting place. The grass over it was young and bright green. Edgar stood at the foot of the plot and folded his hands in the attitude of prayer. 'I don't know what to do, Ma,' he said.

He closed his eyes and imagined she was alive, standing next to him, listening thoughtfully.

'If I swear the oath, I'll get us all evicted from the farm.'

He knew his mother could not answer him. However, she was in his memory, and her spirit was surely nearby, so she could speak to him in his imagination, if he just opened his mind.

'Just when we're starting to have a little to spare,' he said. 'Money for blankets and shoes and beef. Erman and Eadbald have worked hard – they deserve some reward.'

He knew she agreed with that.

'But if I give in to Ithamar, I'll be helping a wicked bishop escape justice. Wynstan will be able to carry on as he always has. I know you wouldn't want me to do that.'

He had laid it out plainly, he thought.

In his mind, she answered clearly. 'Family comes first,' she said. 'Take care of your brothers.'

'So I'll refuse to help Aldred.'

'Yes.'

Edgar opened his eyes. 'I knew you'd say that.'

He turned to leave, but as he did so she spoke again.

'Or you could do something clever,' she said.

'What?'

There was no reply.

'What clever thing could I do?' he said.

But she did not answer him.

ᚦᚦᚦ

EALDORMAN WILWULF PAID a call on Shiring Abbey.

Aldred was summoned from the scriptorium by a breathless novice. 'The ealdorman is here!' he said.

Aldred suffered a moment of fear.

'And he's asking for Abbot Osmund and you!' the novice added.

Aldred had been at the abbey since Wilwulf's father was ealdorman, and he could not remember either man ever entering the monastery. This was serious. He took a moment to calm his breathing and let his heartbeat return to normal.

He could guess what had brought about this unprecedented visit. The sheriff's raid on the minster at Dreng's Ferry was all anyone was talking about throughout the shire, and perhaps all over the west of England. And an attack on Wynstan was a personal affront to Wilwulf, his brother.

In Wilwulf's eyes, Aldred was probably the one who had caused the trouble.

Like all powerful men, Wilwulf would go to great lengths to keep his power. But would he go so far as to threaten a monk?

An ealdorman needed to be seen as a fair judge. Otherwise he lost moral authority. Then he might have trouble enforcing his decisions. Enforcement could be difficult for an ealdorman. He could use his small personal bodyguard of men-at-arms to punish occasional minor disobedience, and he could raise an army – albeit with considerable trouble and expense – to fight the Vikings or harry the Welsh, but it was hard for him to deal with a persistent undercurrent of disobedience among people who had lost faith in their overlords. He needed to be looked up to. Was Wilwulf now prepared to attack Aldred regardless?

Aldred felt a bit nauseated, and swallowed hard. He had known, when he began to investigate Wynstan, that he was going up against ruthless people, and he had told himself it was his duty. But it was easy to take risks in a theoretical way. Now the reality was on him.

He limped up the stairs. His leg still hurt, especially when he walked. Molten metal was worse than a knife in the flesh.

Wilwulf was not a man to be kept waiting outside the door, and he had already gone into Osmund's room. In his yellow cloak he was a garish worldly presence in the grey-and-white monastery. He stood at the end of the bed with his legs apart and his hands on his hips in a classic stance of aggression.

The abbot was still bedridden. He was sitting up, wearing a nightcap, looking scared.

Aldred acted more confident than he felt. 'Good day to you, ealdorman,' he said briskly.

'Come in, monk,' said Wilwulf, as if he were at home and they were the visitors. With a note of complacency he added: 'I believe my brother gave you that black eye.'

'Don't worry,' Aldred said with a deliberate note of condescension. 'If Bishop Wynstan confesses and begs forgiveness, God will have mercy on him for his unpriestly violence.'

'He was provoked!'

'God doesn't accept that excuse, ealdorman. Jesus told us to turn the other cheek.'

Wilwulf grunted with exasperation and shifted his ground. 'I'm highly displeased by what happened at Dreng's Ferry.'

'So am I,' said Aldred, going on the offensive. 'Such a wicked crime against the king! Not to mention the murder of the sheriff's man, Godwine.'

Osmund said timorously: 'Be quiet, Aldred, let the ealdorman speak.'

The door opened and Hildred came in.

Wilwulf was irritated by both interruptions. 'I didn't summon you,' he said to Hildred. 'Who are you?'

Osmund answered the question. 'This is Treasurer Hildred, whom I have made acting abbot during my illness. He should hear whatever you have to say.'

'All right.' Wilwulf picked up the conversation where it had been left off. 'A crime has been committed, and that is shameful,' he conceded. 'But now the question is what should be done.'

'Justice,' said Aldred. 'Obviously.'

'Shut up,' said Wilwulf.

Osmund spoke in a pleading tone. 'Aldred, you're only making things worse for yourself.'

'Making what worse?' Aldred said indignantly. 'I'm not in trouble. I didn't forge the king's currency. That was Wilwulf's brother.'

Wilwulf was on weak ground. 'I'm not here to discuss the past,' he said evasively. 'The question, as I said a moment ago, is what is to be done now.' He turned to Aldred. 'And don't say "justice" again or I'll knock your bald head off your skinny neck.'

Aldred said nothing. It hardly needed pointing out that for a nobleman to threaten a monk with personal violence was undignified, to say the least.

Wilwulf seemed to realize he had lowered himself, and he changed his tone. 'Our duty, Abbot Osmund,' he said, flattering the abbot by putting the two of them on the same level, 'is to make sure this incident doesn't damage the authority of the nobility or the Church.'

'Quite so,' said Osmund.

Aldred found this ominous. Wilwulf bullying was normal; Wilwulf sounding conciliatory was sinister.

Wilwulf said: 'The forgery has ended. The dies have been confiscated by the sheriff. What is the point of a trial?'

Aldred almost gasped. The effrontery was astonishing. Not have a trial? It was outrageous.

Wilwulf went on: 'The trial will achieve nothing except to bring disgrace to a bishop who is also my half-brother. Think how much better it would be if no more were heard of this incident.'

Better for your evil brother, Aldred thought.

Osmund prevaricated. 'I see your point, ealdorman.'

Aldred said: 'You're wasting your breath here, Wilwulf. Whatever we might say, the sheriff will never agree to your proposal.'

'Perhaps,' said Wilwulf. 'But he might become discouraged if you were to withdraw your support.'

'What do you mean, exactly?'

'I presume he will want you to be one of his oath-helpers. I'm asking you to refuse – for the sake of the Church and the nobility.'

'I must tell the truth.'

'There are times when the truth is best unsaid. Even monks must know that.'

Osmund spoke pleadingly. 'Aldred, there's a lot in what the ealdorman says.'

Aldred took a deep breath. 'Imagine that Wynstan and Degbert were dedicated, self-sacrificing priests giving their lives to the service of God, and abstaining from the lusts of the flesh; but they had made one foolish mistake that threatened to end their careers. Then, yes, we would need to discuss whether the punishment would do more harm than good. But they aren't priests of that kind, are they?' Aldred paused, as if waiting for Wilwulf to answer the question, but the ealdorman wisely said nothing. Aldred went on: 'Wynstan and Degbert spend the Church's money in alehouses and gambling dens and whorehouses, and an awful lot of people know it. If they were both unfrocked tomorrow, it would do nothing but good for the authority of nobility and the Church.'

Wilwulf looked angry. 'You don't want to make an enemy of me, Brother Aldred.'

'I certainly don't,' Aldred replied, with more sincerity than might have been apparent.

'Then do as I say, and withdraw your support.'

'No.'

Osmund said: 'Take time to think about it, Aldred.'

'No.'

Hildred spoke for the first time. 'Won't you submit to authority, as a monk should, and show obedience to your abbot?'

'No,' said Aldred.

ÞÞÞ

RAGNA WAS PREGNANT.

She had not told anyone yet, but she was sure. Cat probably guessed, but no one else knew. Ragna hugged the secret to herself, a new body growing inside her. She thought about it as she walked around, ordering people to clear, tidy and repair, keeping the place running, making sure there was nothing to bother Wilf.

It was bad luck to tell people too early, she knew. Many pregnancies ended in spontaneous abortion. In the six years between Ragna's birth and her brother's, their mother had suffered several miscarriages. Ragna would not make the announcement until the bulge became too large to be hidden by the drape of her dress.

She was thrilled. She had never daydreamed of having a baby, as many girls did, but now that it was happening she found she longed to hold and love a tiny scrap of life.

She was also pleased to be fulfilling her role in English society. She was a noblewoman married to a nobleman, and it was her job to give birth to heirs. This would dismay her enemies and strengthen her bond with Wilf.

She was scared, too. Childbirth was dangerous and painful, everyone knew that. When a woman died young it was usually because of a difficult delivery. Ragna would have Cat at her side, but

Cat had never given birth. Ragna wished her mother were here. However, there was a good midwife in Shiring: Ragna had met her, a calm, competent grey-haired woman called Hildithryth, known as Hildi.

Meanwhile, she was pleased that Wynstan's sins were at last catching up with him. Forgery was undoubtedly only one of his crimes, but it was the one that had been exposed, and she hoped for a severe punishment. Perhaps the experience would puncture the bishop's arrogance. Good for Aldred, she thought, for finding him out.

This would be the first major trial she had attended in England, and she was eager to learn more about the country's legal system. She knew it would be different from Normandy's. The biblical principle of an eye for an eye and a tooth for a tooth did not apply here. The punishment for murder was normally a fine paid to the family of the victim. The murder price was called *wergild*, and it varied according to the wealth and status of the dead man: a thane was worth sixty pounds of silver; an ordinary peasant ten pounds.

She learned more when Edgar came to see her. She was sorting apples on a table, picking out the bruised ones that would not last the winter, so that she could teach Gilda the kitchen maid the best way to make cider; and she saw Edgar coming through the main gate and across the compound, a sturdy figure with a confident stride.

'You've changed,' he said with a smile as soon as he saw her. 'What happened?'

He was perceptive, of course, especially of shapes. 'I've been eating too much English honey,' she said. It was true: she was always hungry.

'You look well on it.' Remembering his manners he added: 'If I may be permitted to say so, my lady.'

He stood on the other side of the table and helped her sort the apples, handling the good ones gently, throwing the bad into a barrel. She sensed that he was worried about something. She said: 'Has Dreng sent you here to buy supplies?'

'I am no longer Dreng's servant. I was dismissed.'

Perhaps he wanted to work for her. She quite liked the idea. 'Why were you dismissed?'

'When Blod was returned to him, he beat her so badly I thought he would kill her, so I intervened.'

Edgar always tried to do the right thing, she reflected. But how much trouble was he in? 'Can you go back to the farm?' Perhaps this was what was on his mind. 'As I recall, it isn't very productive.'

'It's not, but I made a fish pond, and now we have enough to eat and some left over to sell.'

'And is Blod all right?'

'I don't know. I told Dreng I would kill him if he hurt her again, and perhaps that has made him think twice about beating her.'

'You know I tried to buy her, to save her from him? But Wynstan overruled me.'

He nodded. 'Speaking of Wynstan . . .'

He had tensed up, Ragna saw, and she guessed that what he was about to say was the real reason for his visit. 'Yes?'

'He sent Ithamar to threaten me.'

'What's the threat?'

'If I testify at the trial, my family will be evicted from the farm.'

'On what grounds?'

'The Church needs tenants who support the clergy.'

'That's outrageous. What will you do?'

'I want to defy Wynstan, and testify for Aldred. But my family needs a farm. I've got a sister-in-law and a baby niece now, as well as my brothers.'

Ragna could see that he was torn, and she felt sympathy for him. 'I understand.'

'That's why I've come to you. In the whole of the Vale of Outhen it must happen that a farm becomes vacant quite often.'

'Several times a year. Usually there's a son or a son-in-law to take it over, but not always.'

'If I knew I could rely on you to give my family a farm, I would be one of Aldred's oath-helpers, and defy Wynstan.'

'I'll give you a farm, if you're evicted,' she said without hesitation. 'Of course I will.'

She saw his shoulders slump with relief. 'Thank you,' he said. 'You've no idea how much . . .' To her surprise, his hazel eyes filled with tears.

She reached across the table and took his hand. 'You can rely on me,' she said. She held his hand a moment longer, then let it go.

ÞÞÞ

HILDRED AMBUSHED ALDRED in the chapter meeting.

Chapter was the hour of the day in which the monks remembered their democratic origins. They were all brothers, alike in the eyes of God and equals in the running of the abbey. This conflicted directly with their vow of obedience, so neither principle was obeyed fully. Day to day, the monks did what the abbot told them to do; but at the chapter meeting they sat in a circle and decided major issues of principle as equals – including the election of a new abbot when the old one died. If no consensus emerged, they would hold a vote.

Hildred began by saying that he had to bring before the monks an issue that grieved both him and poor Abbot Osmund upstairs on his sick bed. He then reported Wilwulf's visit. As he told the story, Aldred looked around at the faces of the monks. None of the older ones looked surprised, and Aldred realized that Hildred had secured their support in advance. The younger ones looked surprised and shocked. They had not been forewarned for fear that they would give Aldred a chance to prepare his defence.

Hildred finished by saying that he had raised this in chapter because Aldred's role in the investigation of Wynstan and the upcoming trial was an issue of principle. 'Why is the abbey here?' he said. 'What is our role? Are we here to play a part in power struggles among the nobility and the higher priesthood? Or is it our duty to withdraw from the world, and worship God in tranquillity, ignoring the storms of earthly life that rage around us? The abbot has asked Aldred to take no part in the trial, and Aldred has refused. I believe the brothers here assembled have the right to consider what the will of God is for our monastery.'

Aldred saw that there was a measure of general agreement. Even those who had not been previously buttonholed by Hildred thought that monks ought not to get involved in politics. Most monks liked Aldred better than Hildred, but they also liked a quiet life.

They were waiting for him to speak. It was like a gladiatorial contest, he thought. He and Hildred were the two leading monks under the abbot. One of them would take Osmund's place sooner or later. This tussle could make a difference to the final battle.

He would give his point of view, but he feared too many of the monks had already made up their minds. Rationality might not be enough.

He decided to raise the stakes.

'I agree with much of what Brother Hildred says,' he began. In an argument it was always wise to show respect for your opponent: people disliked antipathy. 'This is indeed an issue of principle, a question of the role of monks in the world. And I know Hildred is sincere in his concern for our abbey.' This was going to the far edge of generosity, and Aldred decided it was enough. 'However, let me put a slightly different point of view.'

The room was quiet now, and they were all agog.

'Monks must be concerned with this world as well as the next. We're told to store up treasure in heaven, but we do so by good works here on earth. We live in a world of cruelty and ignorance and pain, but we make it better. When evil is done in front of our eyes we cannot remain silent. At least . . . I cannot.' He paused for effect.

'I have been asked to withdraw from the trial. I refuse. It is not God's will for me. I ask you, my brothers, to respect my decision. But if you decide to expel me from this abbey, then of course I will have to leave.' He looked around the room. 'For me that would be a sad day.'

They were shocked. They had not expected him to make this a resigning issue. No one wanted it to go that far – except Hildred, perhaps.

There was a long silence. What Aldred needed was for one of his friends to suggest a compromise. But he had had no chance to prearrange this, so he had to hope that one of them would work something out on his own.

In the end it was Brother Godleof, the taciturn ex-cowherd, who figured it out. 'No need for expulsion,' he said with characteristic brevity. 'Man shouldn't be forced to do what he thinks wrong.'

Hildred said indignantly: 'But what about your vow of obedience?'

Godleof was economical with words but he did not lack intelligence, and he could match Hildred in an argument. 'There are limits,' he said simply.

Aldred saw that many of the monks agreed with this. Their obedience was not absolute. He sensed the mood moving to his side.

To Aldred's surprise his colleague in the scriptorium, the old scribe Tatwine, raised his hand. Aldred could not remember him speaking in chapter before. 'I haven't been outside the precincts of this abbey for twenty-three years,' Tatwine said. 'But Aldred went to Jumièges. That isn't even in England! And he brought back marvellous volumes, books we'd never seen before. Marvellous. There are more ways than one to be a monk, you see.' He smiled and nodded, as if agreeing with himself. 'More ways than one.'

The older monks were moved by this intervention, the more so because it was so rare. And Tatwine worked with Aldred daily: that made his opinion more weighty.

Hildred knew that he was beaten, and he did not push the matter to a vote. 'If the chapter is minded to pardon Aldred's disobedience,' he said, trying to hide his annoyance under a mask of tolerance, 'then I feel sure Abbot Osmund would not want to insist otherwise.'

Most of the monks nodded assent.

'Then let us move on,' Hildred said. 'I understand there has been a complaint about mouldy bread . . .'

ÞÞÞ

THE DAY BEFORE the trial, Aldred and Den shared a cup of ale and reviewed their prospects. Den said: 'Wynstan has done his best to undermine our oath-helpers, but I don't think he's succeeded.'

Aldred nodded. 'He sent Ithamar to threaten Edgar with eviction, but Edgar persuaded Ragna to promise him a farm if necessary, so he's solid now.'

'And I gather you prevailed in chapter.'

'Wilwulf tried to bully Abbot Osmund, but in the end the chapter backed me, just.'

'Wynstan isn't liked in the religious community – he brings them all into disrepute.'

'There's a lot of interest in this case, not just in Shiring. There will be several bishops and abbots present, and I would expect them to support us.'

Den offered Aldred more ale. Aldred declined, but Den took another cupful.

Aldred said: 'How will Wynstan be punished?'

'One law says that a forger's hand should be cut off and nailed over the door to the mint. But another prescribes the death penalty for forgers who work in the woods, which might include Dreng's

Ferry. And anyway judges don't always read the books of law. Often they do as they please, especially men such as Wilwulf. But we have to get Wynstan convicted first.'

Aldred frowned. 'I don't see how the court can fail to convict. Last year King Ethelred made every ealdorman swear an oath with his twelve leading magnates. They had to vow not to conceal any guilty person.'

Den shrugged. 'Wilwulf will break that oath. So will Wigelm.'

'The bishops and abbots will keep theirs.'

'And there's no reason why other thanes, unrelated to Wilwulf, should imperil their immortal souls to save Wynstan.'

'God's will be done,' said Aldred.

23

DURING THE PRE-DAWN SERVICE of Matins, Aldred's mind wandered. He tried to concentrate on the prayers and their meaning, but all he could think about was Wynstan. Aldred had caught a lion by the tail, and if he did not kill the beast then it would kill him. Failure in court today would be a catastrophe. Wynstan's revenge would be brutal.

The monks returned to bed after Matins, but got up again soon afterwards for Lauds. They crossed the courtyard in the cold November air and entered the church shivering.

Aldred found that every hymn, psalm and reading had something in it that reminded him of the trial. One of today's psalms was number seven, and Aldred chanted the words with feeling: 'Save me from them that persecute me, and deliver me, lest he tear my soul like a lion.'

He ate little at breakfast but drained his cup of ale and wished for more. Before the service of Terce, which was about the crucifixion, Sheriff Den knocked at the abbey door, and Aldred put on his cloak and went out.

Den was accompanied by a servant carrying a basket. 'It's all in there,' he said. 'The dies, the adulterated metal, the false coins.'

'Good.' Physical evidence could be important, especially if someone was prepared to swear to its authenticity.

They headed for the ealdorman's compound, where Wilwulf normally held court in front of the great hall; but as they passed the cathedral they were stopped by Ithamar. 'The trial will be held here,' he said smugly. 'At the west door of the church.'

Den said indignantly: 'Who decided that?'

'Ealdorman Wilwulf, of course.'

Den turned to Aldred. 'This is Wynstan's doing.'

Aldred nodded. 'It will remind everyone of Wynstan's high status as a bishop. They will be reluctant to convict him in front of the cathedral.'

Den looked at Ithamar. 'He's still guilty, and we can prove it.'

'He is God's representative on earth,' said Ithamar, and he walked away.

Aldred said: 'This may not be entirely a bad thing. Probably more townspeople will come to listen to the proceedings – and they'll be against Wynstan: anyone who messes with the currency is unpopular, because it's the town tradesmen who end up with dud coins in their purses.'

Den looked dubious. 'I don't suppose the feelings of the crowd will make much difference.'

Aldred was afraid he was right.

The townspeople began to gather, early arrivers securing places with a good view. People were curious about the contents of Den's basket. Aldred told him to let them look. 'Wynstan may try to prevent your showing the evidence during the proceedings,' he said. 'Better if everyone sees it beforehand.'

A group gathered around them, and Den answered their questions. Everyone had already heard about the forgery, but seeing the precision dies, the perfect imitation coins and the big cold lump of brown alloy made the whole thing real to them, and they were shocked all over again.

Wigbert, the captain of the sheriff's men, brought the two prisoners, Cuthbert and Degbert, their hands tied and their ankles roped together so that they could not make a sudden dash for freedom.

A servant arrived carrying the ealdorman's seat and its red plush cushion. He placed it just in front of the great oak door. Next, a priest set a small table beside the seat and placed on it a reliquary – an engraved silver container for the relics of a saint – on which people could swear.

The crowd thickened, and the air became heavy with the dunghill smell of unwashed people. Soon the bell tolled in the tower, announcing the court, and the magnates of the region – the thanes and senior clergy – arrived and stood around the ealdorman's still-empty seat, pushing the ordinary townspeople back. Aldred bowed to Ragna as she appeared, and nodded to Edgar, who was beside her.

When the booming notes died away, a choir inside the church began a hymn. Den was furious. 'This is a court, not a service!' he said. 'What does Wynstan think he's doing?'

Aldred knew exactly what Wynstan was doing. In the next moment the bishop came out through the great west door. He wore a white ecclesiastical robe embroidered with biblical scenes and a tall conical hat with fur trim. He was doing all he could to make it difficult for people to regard him as a criminal.

Wynstan walked to the ealdorman's seat and stood beside it, eyes closed, hands folded in prayer.

'This is outrageous,' Den fumed.

'It won't work,' Aldred said. 'People know him too well.'

Finally Wilwulf arrived with a large escort of men-at-arms. Aldred wondered briefly why he had such a large bodyguard. The crowd fell quiet. Somewhere a hammer rang on iron as a busy blacksmith worked on despite the attraction of a big trial. Wilwulf strode through the crowd, nodding to the assembled magnates, and made himself comfortable on the cushion. He was the only person sitting.

The proceedings opened with the swearing of oaths. Everyone who was to be accused, accuser or oath-helper had to put his hand on the silver box and promise God that he would tell the truth, convict the guilty and free the innocent. Wilwulf looked bored, but Wynstan watched carefully, as if he thought he might catch someone making an imperfect vow. He was normally careless of ritual details, Aldred knew, but today he was pretending to be meticulous.

When it was done, Aldred felt Sheriff Den tense up, ready to begin his prosecution speech. But Wilwulf turned to Wynstan and nodded, and to Aldred's astonishment Wynstan addressed the court. 'A dreadful crime has been committed,' he said, his voice booming out in tones of deep sorrow. 'A crime, and a terrible sin.'

Den stepped forward. 'Wait!' he shouted. 'This is wrong!'

Wilwulf said: 'Nothing is wrong, Den.'

'I am the sheriff and I am here to prosecute this case. Forgery is a crime against the king.'

'You'll have your chance to speak.'

Aldred frowned worriedly. He could not quite figure out what the two brothers were up to, but he was sure it was not good.

Den said: 'I insist! I speak for the king, and the king must be heard!'

'I, too, speak for the king, who appointed me ealdorman,' said Wilwulf. 'And now you will shut your mouth, Den, or I will shut it for you.'

Den put his hand on the hilt of his sword.

Wilwulf's men-at-arms tensed.

Aldred looked around swiftly and counted twelve men-at-arms with Wilwulf. Now he understood why there were so many. Den, who had not foreseen violence, had only Wigbert.

Den made the same calculation and took his hand off his sword.

Wilwulf said: 'Carry on, Bishop Wynstan.'

This was why King Ethelred wanted courts to follow procedures, Aldred reflected; so that noblemen could not make arbitrary decisions as Wilwulf had just done. Opponents of Ethelred's reform argued that rules made no difference, and justice was guaranteed only by having a wise nobleman use his judgement. The people who said that were usually noblemen.

Wynstan pointed at Degbert and Cuthbert. 'Untie those priests,' he said.

Den protested: 'They are my prisoners!'

Wilwulf said: 'They are the court's prisoners. Untie them.'

Den had to give in. He nodded to Wigbert, who undid the ropes. The two priests looked less guilty now.

Wynstan raised his voice again so that all could hear. 'The crime, and the sin, is forgery of the king's currency.' He pointed straight at Wigbert, who looked startled. 'Come forward,' Wynstan said. 'Show the court what is in the basket.'

Wigbert looked at Den, who shrugged.

Aldred was mystified. He had expected Wynstan to try to conceal the physical evidence, yet here he was demanding that it be shown. What was he up to? He had made an elaborate pretence of innocence – but now he seemed to be prosecuting himself.

He took the objects out of the basket one by one. 'The adulterated metal!' he said dramatically. 'The pile. The trussel. The collar. And finally, the coins, half silver, half copper.'

The assembled magnates looked as puzzled as Aldred felt. Why was Wynstan underlining his own wickedness?

'And worst of all,' Wynstan cried, 'these belonged to a priest!'

Yes, Aldred thought; they belonged to you.

Then Wynstan pointed dramatically and said: 'Cuthbert!'

Everyone looked at Cuthbert.

Wynstan said: 'Imagine my surprise – imagine my horror – when I learned that this foul crime was being committed under my very nose!'

Aldred's mouth dropped open in shock.

There was a stunned silence in the crowd: everyone was astonished. They had all thought Wynstan was the culprit.

Wynstan said: 'I should have known. I accuse myself of negligence. A bishop must be vigilant, and I failed.'

Aldred found his voice. He shouted at Wynstan: 'But you were the instigator!'

Wynstan said sorrowfully: 'Ah – I knew wicked men would try to implicate me. It's my own fault. I gave them the opening.'

Cuthbert said: 'You told me to forge money. I just wanted to make ornaments for the church. You made me do it!' He was crying.

Wynstan maintained his regretful expression. 'My son, you think you will make your crime seem less if you pretend you were talked into it by your superiors—'

'I was!'

Wynstan shook his head sadly. 'It won't work. You did what you did. So don't add perjury to your list of crimes.'

Cuthbert turned to Wilwulf. 'I confess,' he said miserably. 'I forged pennies. I know I will be punished. But the bishop dreamed up the whole scheme. Don't let him escape blame.'

Wilwulf said: 'Remember that false accusation is a serious matter, Cuthbert.' He turned to Wynstan. 'Carry on, bishop.'

Wynstan turned his attention to the assembled magnates, all of whom were watching raptly. 'The crime was well hidden,' he said. 'Dean Degbert himself did not know what Cuthbert was up to in his little workshop attached to the minster.'

Cuthbert said piteously: 'Degbert knew everything!'

Wynstan said: 'Step forward, Degbert.'

Degbert did as he was told, and Aldred noted that he was now standing among the magnates, as if one of them, rather than a criminal they had to judge.

Wynstan said: 'The dean admits his fault. Like me, he was negligent – but in his case the fault was worse, because he was at the minster every day, whereas I was only an occasional visitor.'

Aldred said: 'Degbert helped you spend the money!'

Wynstan ignored that. 'I have taken it upon myself, as bishop, to punish Degbert. He has been expelled from the minster and stripped of his title of dean. Today he is a simple, humble priest, and I have brought him under my personal supervision.'

Aldred thought: So he moves from the minster to the cathedral – no great hardship.

Could this possibly be happening?

Den shouted out: 'That's no punishment for a forger!'

'I agree,' said Wynstan. 'And Degbert is no forger.' He looked around. 'Nobody here denies that it was Cuthbert who made the coins.'

That was the truth, Aldred thought ruefully. It was not the whole truth, not by a long way, but it was not actually a lie.

And he could see that the magnates were beginning to come round to Wynstan's version of events. They might not believe him – they knew what he was like, after all – but his guilt could not be proved. And he was a bishop.

Wynstan's masterstroke had been to prosecute the case himself, thereby robbing the sheriff of the chance to tell the whole convincing story: Wynstan's visits to Dreng's Ferry after each quarter day, his gifts to the residents, his trips to Combe with Degbert, and their free-spending evenings in the town's alehouses and brothels. None of that had come out, and if raised now it would seem feeble and circumstantial.

Wynstan had gambled with forged money, but no one could prove that. His victim, Monsieur Robert, was the skipper of an oceangoing ship and might now be at any port in Europe.

The only hole in Wynstan's story was that he had not 'discovered' Cuthbert's crime until the minster was raided by the sheriff. That was surely too much of a coincidence for the magnates to swallow.

Aldred was about to point this out when Wynstan forestalled him. 'I see the hand of God in this,' said the bishop, his voice increasingly sonorous, like a church bell. 'It must have been divinely ordained that, at the very hour I discovered Cuthbert's crime, Sheriff Den came to Dreng's Ferry – just in time to arrest the wicked priest! Heaven be praised.'

Aldred was amazed by Wynstan's sheer nerve. The hand of God! Did the man have no concern for how he might explain himself on the Day of Judgement? Wynstan was constantly changing. At Combe he had seemed no worse than a slave to pleasure, a clergyman who had lost his self-discipline; then when he had been found out at Dreng's Ferry he had become possessed, screaming and foaming at the mouth; but now he was sane again, and more wily than ever, yet plunging more deeply into wickedness. This must be how the devil made a man his own, Aldred thought; by stages, one sin leading to a worse.

Wynstan's logic, and the confidence with which he told his deceitful story, were so overwhelming that Aldred almost found himself wondering if it could be true; and he could see by the faces of the magnates that they were going to go along with it, even if they might have private reservations.

Wilwulf sensed the mood and moved to take advantage of it. 'Degbert having been dealt with already, we need only sentence Cuthbert.'

'Wrong!' shouted Sheriff Den. 'You have to deal with the accusation against Wynstan.'

'No one has accused Wynstan.'

'Cuthbert did.'

Wilwulf mimed astonishment. 'Are you suggesting that the oath of a lowly priest is worth more than that of a bishop?'

'Then I accuse Wynstan myself. When I entered the minster I found Wynstan in the workshop with Cuthbert while the forgery was going on!'

'Bishop Wynstan has explained that he had at that very moment discovered the crime – by divine providence, no doubt.'

Den looked around, meeting the eyes of the magnates. 'Do any of you really believe that?' he said. 'Wynstan was in the workshop, standing by Cuthbert as he made false coins out of base metal, but he had only just discovered it was going on?' He swivelled to Wynstan. 'And don't tell us that was the hand of God. This is something much more earthly, a plain old-fashioned lie.'

Wilwulf said to the magnates: 'I think we may agree that the charge against Bishop Wynstan is malicious and false.'

Aldred gave it one last try. 'The king will hear of this, naturally. Do you really think he will believe Wynstan's story? And how will he feel about the magnates who have exonerated Wynstan and Degbert and punished no one but a lowly priest?'

They looked uneasy, but no one spoke up in support of Aldred, and Wilwulf said: 'Then the court is agreed that Cuthbert is guilty. Because of his wicked attempt to put the blame on two senior clergymen, his punishment will be more severe than is usual. I sentence Cuthbert to be blinded and castrated.'

Aldred said: 'No!' But it was hopeless to protest further.

Cuthbert's legs gave way under him and he fell to the ground.

Wilwulf said: 'See to it, sheriff.'

Den hesitated, then reluctantly nodded to Wigbert, who picked up Cuthbert and carried him away.

Wynstan spoke again. Aldred thought the bishop had already won everything he wanted, but there was more drama to come. 'I accuse myself!' Wynstan said.

Wilwulf showed no surprise, and Aldred deduced that this, like everything that had happened so far, had been planned in advance.

Wynstan said: 'When I discovered the crime, I was so enraged that I destroyed much of the forger's equipment. With his hammer I smashed a red-hot crucible, and molten metal flew through the air and killed an innocent man called Godwine. It was an accident, but I accept the blame.'

Once again, Aldred saw, Wynstan gained an advantage by prosecuting himself. He could put the murder in its best light.

Wilwulf said gravely: 'What you did was still a crime. You are guilty of unlawful killing.'

Wynstan bowed his head in a gesture of humility. Aldred wondered how many people were fooled.

Wilwulf went on: 'You must pay the murder price to the victim's widow.'

An attractive young woman with a baby in her arms emerged from the crowd, looking intimidated.

Wilwulf said: 'The murder price of a man-at-arms is five pounds of silver.'

Ithamar stepped forward and handed a small wooden chest to Wynstan.

Wynstan bowed to the widow, handed her the chest, and said: 'I pray constantly that God and you will forgive me for what I have done.'

Around him, many of the magnates were nodding approval. It made Aldred want to scream. They all knew Wynstan! How could they believe he was humbly repentant? But his display of Christian remorse had made them forget his true nature. And the large fine was a severe punishment – which also diverted attention from the way he had wriggled out of a more serious charge.

The widow took the box and left without speaking.

And so, Aldred thought, great ones sin with impunity while lesser men are brutally chastised. What could God's purpose be in this travesty of justice? But perhaps there was some small advantage to be gained. It occurred to Aldred that he should act now, while Wynstan was still pretending to be virtuous. Almost without thinking he said: 'Ealdorman Wilwulf, after what we've heard today it's clear that the minster at Dreng's Ferry should be closed.' This was the time to clean out the rat's nest, he thought, but he did not need to say it: the implication was obvious.

He saw a flash of rage cross Wynstan's face, but it vanished quickly and the look of pious meekness returned.

Aldred went on: 'The archbishop has already given his approval to a plan to turn the minster into a branch of Shiring Abbey and staff it with monks. When first broached the plan was shelved, but this seems a good moment to reconsider it.'

Wilwulf looked at Wynstan for guidance.

Aldred could guess what Wynstan was thinking. The minster had never been rich, and it was of little benefit to him now that the forgery racket had been stopped. It had been a useful sinecure for his cousin Degbert, but now Degbert had had to be moved. Its loss cost him next to nothing.

No doubt, Aldred thought, Wynstan was unhappy letting Aldred have even such a small victory, but he needed also to think about the impression he would make if he now tried to protect the minster. He had pretended to be shocked and appalled by the forgery, and people would expect him to be glad to turn his back on the place where it had happened. If he renewed his opposition to Aldred's plan, sceptical people might even suspect that Wynstan wanted to revive the counterfeit workshop.

'I agree with Brother Aldred,' said Wynstan. 'Let all the priests be reassigned to other duties, and let the minster become a monastery.'

Aldred thanked God for one piece of good news.

Wilwulf turned to Treasurer Hildred. 'Brother Hildred, is this still the wish of Abbot Osmund?'

Aldred was not sure what Hildred would say. The treasurer generally opposed anything Aldred wanted. But this time he concurred. 'Yes, ealdorman,' he said. 'The abbot is keen to see this plan implemented.'

'Then be it so,' said Wilwulf.

But Hildred was not finished. 'And furthermore . . .'

'Yes, Brother Hildred?'

'It was Aldred's notion to turn the minster into a monastery, and he has now revived the idea. All along, Abbot Osmund thought the best choice for prior of the new institution would be . . . Brother Aldred himself.'

Aldred was taken by surprise. He had not anticipated this. And he did not want it. He had no wish to run a tiny monastery in the middle of nowhere. He wanted to become abbot of Shiring and create a world-class centre of learning and scholarship.

This was Hildred's way of getting rid of him. With Aldred gone, Hildred would surely succeed Osmund as abbot.

He said: 'No, thank you, Treasurer Hildred, I am not worthy of such a post.'

Wynstan joined in with barely concealed glee. 'Of course you are worthy, Aldred,' he said.

You, too, want me out of the way, Aldred thought.

Wynstan went on: 'And as bishop I'm happy to give my immediate approval to your promotion.'

'It's hardly a promotion – I'm already armarius of the abbey.'

'Oh, don't be churlish,' said Wilwulf with a smile. 'This will give free rein to your leadership qualities.'

'It is for Abbot Osmund to appoint the prior. Is this court trying to usurp his prerogative?'

'Of course not,' said Wynstan oilily. 'But we can approve Treasurer Hildred's proposal.'

Aldred saw that he had been outmanoeuvred. Now that the appointment had been endorsed by all the most powerful people in Shiring, Osmund would not have the guts to reverse their decision. He was trapped. He thought: Why did I ever imagine that I was clever?

Wynstan said: 'One thing I should point out now – if I may, brother Wilf?'

Aldred thought: What now?

'Go ahead,' said Wilwulf.

'Over the years pious men have donated lands for the upkeep of the minster at Dreng's Ferry.'

Aldred had a bad feeling.

Wynstan went on: 'Those lands were given to the diocese of Shiring, and they remain the property of the cathedral.'

Aldred was outraged. When Wynstan said 'the diocese' and 'the cathedral' he meant himself. 'This is nonsense!' Aldred protested.

Wynstan said condescendingly: 'The village of Dreng's Ferry I grant to the new monastery, as a sign of my goodwill; but the village of Wigleigh, donated by you, brother, at your wedding, and the other lands that have supported the minster remain the property of the diocese.'

'This is wrong,' Aldred said. 'When Archbishop Elfric turned Canterbury into a monastery, the departing priests did not take all the assets of Canterbury Cathedral with them!'

'Different circumstances completely,' said Wynstan.

'I disagree.'

'Then the ealdorman will have to decide.'

'No, he won't,' said Aldred. 'This is a matter for the archbishop.'

Wilwulf said: 'I intended my wedding gift to benefit the minster, not a monastery, and I believe the other donors felt the same way.'

'You have no idea what the other donors felt.'

Wilwulf looked angry. 'I rule in favour of Bishop Wynstan.'

Aldred persisted: 'The archbishop will rule, not you.'

Wilwulf was offended to be told he had no jurisdiction. 'We shall see,' he said angrily.

Aldred knew how it would be. The archbishop would command Wynstan to return the lands to the new monastery, but Wynstan would ignore him. Wilwulf had already defied the king twice, first over the treaty with Count Hubert and then over the marriage to Ragna, and now Wynstan would treat the ruling of the archbishop with the same kind of scorn. And there was little a king or an archbishop could do about a magnate who simply refused to obey orders.

He noticed Wigbert speaking to Den quietly. Wilwulf saw the interaction and said: 'Is everything ready for the punishment?'

Den said reluctantly: 'Yes, ealdorman.'

Wilwulf stood up. Surrounded by his men-at-arms he walked through the crowd to the centre of the square. The magnates followed him.

A tall stake stood in the middle of the square for occasions such as this. While everyone had been looking at Wilwulf on his seat and listening to the arguments, poor Cuthbert had been stripped naked and roped to the stake so tightly that he could not move any part of his body, not even his head. Everyone gathered around him to watch. The townspeople jostled to see better.

Wigbert produced a large pair of shears, blades gleaming from recent sharpening. A murmur rose up from the crowd. Looking at the faces of his neighbours, Aldred saw with disgust that many of them were avid for blood.

Sheriff Den said: 'Go ahead and carry out the ealdorman's sentence.'

The purpose of this punishment was not to kill the wrongdoer, but to doom him to life as merely half a man. Wigbert manipulated the shears so that the twin blades could close on Cuthbert's testicular sack without removing his penis.

Cuthbert was moaning, praying and weeping all at the same time. Aldred felt ill.

Wigbert cut off Cuthbert's testicles with one decisive motion. Cuthbert screamed, and blood ran down his legs.

A dog appeared from nowhere, snatched up the testicles in his jaws, and fled; and the crowd roared with laughter.

Wigbert put down the bloodstained shears. Standing in front of Cuthbert he put his hands on the priest's temples, touched the eyelids with his thumbs, and then, with another practised motion, thrust his thumbs deep into the eyes. Cuthbert screamed again, and the fluid from his burst eyeballs dribbled down his cheeks.

Wigbert undid the ropes binding Cuthbert to the stake, and Cuthbert fell to the ground.

Aldred caught sight of Wynstan's face. The bishop was standing next to Wilwulf, and both were staring at the bleeding man on the ground.

Wynstan was smiling.

24

ONLY ONCE BEFORE IN Aldred's life had he felt utterly defeated, humiliated and despondent about the future. That had been when he was a novice at Glastonbury and had been caught kissing Leofric in the herb garden. Until then he had been the star among the youngsters: best at reading, writing, singing, and memorizing the Bible. Suddenly his weakness became the subject of every conversation, discussed even in chapter. Instead of talking in admiring tones of his bright future, people asked one another what was to be done with a boy so depraved. He had felt like a horse that could not be ridden or a dog that bit its master. He had wanted only to crawl into a hole and sleep for a hundred years.

And now that feeling was back. All the promise he had shown as armarius of Shiring, all the talk of his becoming abbot one day, had come to nothing. His ambitions – the school, the library, the world-class scriptorium – were now mere daydreams. He had been exiled to the remote hamlet of Dreng's Ferry and put in charge of a penniless priory, and this would be the end of the story of his life.

Abbot Osmund had told him he was too passionate. 'A monk should develop an accepting disposition,' he had said when saying goodbye to Aldred. 'We can't correct all the evil in the world.' Aldred had lain awake night after night chewing over that judgement in bitterness and anger. Two passions had undone him: first his love for Leofric, then his rage at Wynstan. But in his heart he still could not agree with Osmund. Monks ought never to accept evil. They had to fight against it.

He was weighed down with despair, but not crippled by it. He had said that the old minster was a disgrace, so now he could throw his energy into making the new priory a shining example of what men of God ought to do. The little church already looked different: the floor had been swept and the walls whitewashed. The old scribe Tatwine, one of the monks who had chosen to migrate to Dreng's Ferry with Aldred, had begun a wall painting, a picture of the Nativity, a birth scene for the reborn church.

Edgar had repaired the entrance. He had taken out the stones of the arch one by one, trimmed them to shape, and re-set them so that they sat precisely on the spokes of an imaginary wheel. That was all that was needed, he said, to make it stronger. Aldred's sole consolation in Dreng's Ferry was that he saw more of the clever, charming young man who had captured his heart.

The house looked different too. When Degbert and his crew left they had naturally taken with them all their luxuries, the wall hangings and the ornaments and the blankets. The place was now bare and utilitarian, as monks' accommodation ought to be. But Edgar had welcomed Aldred with a gift of a lectern he had made of oak, so that while the monks were eating they could listen to one of their number reading from the Rule of St Benedict or the life of a saint. It had been made with love, and although this was not the kind of love Aldred sometimes dreamed of, not a love of kisses and caresses and embraces in the night, nevertheless the gift brought tears to his eyes.

Aldred knew that work was the best solace. He told the brothers that the history of a monastery normally began with the monks rolling up their sleeves and clearing ground, and here in Dreng's Ferry they had already started to fell trees on the wooded hillside above the church. A monastery needed land for a vegetable garden, an orchard, a duck pond, and grazing for a few goats and a cow or two. Edgar had made axes, hammering out the blades on the anvil in Cuthbert's old workshop, and had taught Aldred and the other monks how to chop down trees efficiently and safely.

The rents Aldred got as landlord of the hamlet were not sufficient to feed even the monks, and Abbot Osmund had agreed to pay the priory a monthly subsidy. Hildred had, of course, argued for an amount that was hopelessly inadequate. 'If it's not enough, you can come back and discuss it,' Hildred had said, but Aldred had known that once the subvention was fixed the treasurer would never agree to an increase. The upshot had been an allowance that would keep the monks alive and the church functional but no more. If Aldred wanted to buy books, plant an orchard and build a cowshed, he would have to find the funds himself.

When the monks had arrived here and looked around, the old scribe Tatwine had said to Aldred, not unkindly: 'Perhaps God wants to teach you the virtue of humility.' Aldred thought Tatwine might be right. Humility had never been one of his strengths.

On Sunday Aldred celebrated Mass in the little church. He stood at the altar in the tiny chancel while the six monks who had come here with him – all volunteers – stood in two neat rows on the ground floor of the tower, which served as the nave. The villagers gathered behind the monks, quieter than usual and awed by the unfamiliar sense of discipline and reverence.

During the service a horse was heard outside, and Aldred's old friend Wigferth of Canterbury came into the church. Wigferth visited the west of England frequently, to collect rents. His mistress in Trench had recently given birth, according to monastic gossip. Wigferth was a good monk in other respects, and Aldred remained friendly to him, restricting himself to the occasional disapproving frown if Wigferth was so tactless as to mention his illicit family.

As soon as the service was over Aldred spoke to him. 'It's good to see you. I hope you have time to stay for dinner.'

'Certainly.'

'We're not rich, so our food will save you from the sin of gluttony.'

Wigferth smiled and patted his belly. 'I stand in need of such salvation.'

'What news from Canterbury?'

'Two things. Archbishop Elfric has ordered Wynstan to return the village of Wigleigh to the ownership of the church at Dreng's Ferry, which means you.'

'Good!'

'Wait, don't celebrate. I have already taken that message to Wynstan, who said the matter was outside the archbishop's jurisdiction.'

'In other words he will ignore the ruling.'

'That one, and another. Wynstan has made Degbert an archdeacon at Shiring Cathedral.'

'In effect, deputy to Wynstan, and his likely successor.'

'Exactly.'

'Some punishment.' The promotion, coming so swiftly after the trial and Degbert's demotion, told everyone that Wynstan's people would always do well, and those who opposed him – such as Aldred – would suffer.

'The archbishop refused to ratify the appointment – and Wynstan ignored him.'

Aldred scratched his shaved head. 'Wynstan defies the archbishop and Wilwulf defies the king. How long can this go on?'

'I don't know. Maybe until the Day of Judgement.'

Aldred looked around. Two of the congregation were watching him expectantly. 'We'll talk more at dinner,' he said to Wigferth. 'I must speak to the villagers. They're a discontented lot.'

Wigferth left, and Aldred turned to the waiting couple. A woman called Ebba, with chapped hands, said: 'The priests used to pay me to do their laundry. Why don't you?'

'Laundry?' said Aldred. 'We do our own.' There was not much.

Monks usually washed their robes twice a year. Other people might have loincloths, strips of material wound around the waist and between the legs and tied in front. Women used them during the monthly flux, and washed them afterwards; men wore them for riding, and probably never washed them at all. Babies were sometimes wrapped in something similar. Monks had no use for such things.

The woman's husband, Cerdic, said: 'I used to gather firewood for the priests, and rushes for their floor, and bring them fresh water from the river every day.'

'I have no money to pay you,' Aldred said. 'Bishop Wynstan has stolen all the wealth of this church.'

'The bishop was a very generous man,' said Cerdic.

With the proceeds of forgery, Aldred thought; but there was no point in making such accusations to the villagers. Either they believed Wynstan's story of innocence or they would pretend to believe it: anything else would make them complicit. He had lost that argument in court and he was not going to rerun it for the rest of his life. So he said: 'One day the monastery will be prosperous and bring employment and trade to Dreng's Ferry, but that will require time and patience and hard work, for I have nothing else to offer.'

He left the disgruntled couple and moved on. What he had said to them depressed him. This was not the life he had dreamed of: struggling to make a new monastery viable. He wanted books and pens and ink, not a vegetable garden and a duck pond.

He approached Edgar, who still had the power to brighten his day. Edgar had created a weekly fish market in the hamlet. There were no large villages near Dreng's Ferry, but there were many small settlements and lonely farms such as Theodberht Clubfoot's sheepfold. Every Friday a handful of people, mostly women, showed up to buy Edgar's fish. But Degbert had claimed he was entitled to one fish in three of Edgar's catch. 'You asked me about Degbert's charter,' Aldred said. 'It's attached to that of the new monastery, since some of the rights are the same.'

'And did Degbert tell the truth about it?' Edgar asked.

Aldred shook his head. 'There's no mention of fish in the charter. He had no right to tax you.'

'I thought as much,' said Edgar. 'The lying thief.'

'I'm afraid he is.'

'Everyone wants something for nothing,' Edgar complained. 'My brother Erman said I should share the money with him. I made the pond, I make the traps, I empty the traps every morning, and I give my family all the fish they can eat. But they want money too.'

'Men are greedy.'

'Women too. My sister-in-law Cwenburg probably told Erman what to say. Never mind. Can I show you something?'

'Of course.'

'Come with me to the graveyard.'

They left the building and walked around to the north side. Edgar said conversationally: 'My father taught me that in a well-made boat the joints should never be too tight. A small amount of movement between the timbers absorbs some of the shock of the endless buffeting of wind and waves. But there's no looseness in a stone building.' Near the place where the little chancel extension joined the tower he pointed up. 'See that crack?'

Aldred certainly did see it. Where the tower met the chancel was a gap he could have put his thumb into. 'Good Lord,' he said.

'Buildings move, but there's no looseness between mortared stones, so cracks appear. In some ways they're useful, because they tell us what's happening in the structure and forewarn us of problems.'

'Can you fill the crack with mortar?'

'Of course, but that's not enough. The problem is that the tower is slowly tilting downhill, and leaving the chancel behind. I can fill the gap, but the tower will continue to move, and then the crack will reappear. But that's the least of your problems.'

'What is the greatest of my problems?'

'The tower will fall down.'

'How soon?'

'I can't tell.'

Aldred wanted to weep. As if his tribulations were not already as much as a man could bear, now his church was falling down.

Edgar saw the expression on his face, touched his arm lightly, and said: 'Don't despair.'

The touch heartened Aldred. 'Christians never despair.'

'Good, because I can stop the tower falling down.'

'How?'

'By building buttresses to support it on the downhill side.'

Aldred shook his head. 'I have no money for stone.'

'Well, perhaps I could get some free.'

Aldred brightened. 'Could you, really?'

'I don't know,' said Edgar. 'I can try.'

ÞÞÞ

EDGAR WENT TO ask Ragna for help. She had always been kind to him. Other people spoke of her as formidable, something of a dragon, a woman who knew exactly what she wanted and was determined to get it. But she seemed to have a soft spot for Edgar. However, that did not mean she would give him anything he asked for.

He felt eager to see her, and he asked himself why. Of course he wanted to help Aldred out of the morass of gloom. But Edgar suspected himself of a desire he despised in others, the wish to be friends with aristocrats. He thought of the way Dreng acted around them, fawning on Wilwulf and Wynstan and constantly mentioning that he was related to them. He hoped his keenness to talk to Ragna was not part of a similar, shameful aspiration.

He went by river to Outhenham and spent a night at the home of Seric, the new headman, and his wife and grandchild. Perhaps it was Edgar's imagination, but the village seemed a calmer, happier place with Seric in charge.

In the morning he left his raft in Seric's care and walked on to Shiring. If his plan worked, he would be able to return to Dreng's Ferry with a load of stone on the raft.

It was a cold journey. Icy rain turned to sleet. Edgar's leather shoes became sodden and his feet hurt. If ever I have money, he thought, I'm going to buy a pony.

His thoughts turned to Aldred. He felt sorry for the monk, a man who wanted only to do good. Aldred had been brave, to go up against a bishop. Too brave, perhaps: justice might be something to hope for in the next world, not this one.

The streets of Shiring were almost deserted: in this weather most people stayed indoors, huddled around their fires. But there was a small crowd outside Elfwine's stone house, where silver pennies were made under the king's licence. Elfwine, the moneyer, stood outside, and his wife was beside him, weeping. Sheriff Den was there with his men, and Edgar saw that they were bringing Elfwine's equipment out onto the street and smashing it up.

Edgar spoke to Den. 'What's going on?'

'King Ethelred ordered me to close the mint,' said Den. 'He's displeased about the forgery at Dreng's Ferry, and believes the trial was a sham; and this is his way of showing it.'

Edgar had not foreseen this, and clearly Wilwulf and Wynstan had not either. All the most important towns in England had a mint. The closure would be a blow to Wilwulf. It was a loss of prestige but, worse, the mint drew business to the town, business that would now go elsewhere. A king did not have many ways of enforcing his will, but coinage was under his control, and closing the mint was a punishment he could inflict. However, Edgar guessed this would not be enough to change Wilwulf's behaviour.

Edgar found Ragna in a pasture next to the ealdorman's compound.

She had decided the weather was too bad for the horses to be out-of-doors, and was supervising the stable hands as they rounded up the beasts to bring them inside. She wore a coat of fox furs, red-gold like her hair, and she looked like a wild woman of the forest, beautiful but dangerous. Edgar found himself wondering whether her body hair was the same colour. He quickly pushed the thought away: it was foolish for a working man to think such thoughts about a noblewoman.

She smiled at him and said: 'Have you walked here in this weather? Your nose looks as if it could drop off at any moment! Come with me and have some hot ale.'

They entered the compound. Here, too, most people were staying indoors, though a handful of busy folk scurried from one building to another with their cloaks over their heads. Ragna led Edgar into her house. When she took her coat off he thought she had gained some weight.

They sat close to the fire. Her maid Cat heated a fire iron then plunged it into a tankard of ale. She offered it to Ragna, who said: 'Give it to Edgar – he's colder than me.'

Cat handed the cup to Edgar with a pleasant smile. Perhaps I should marry a girl like her, he thought. I could feed a wife, now that we have the fish pond, and it would be nice to have someone to sleep with. But as soon as he formed the idea he knew it was wrong. Cat was a perfectly nice woman, but he did not feel about her the way he had felt about Sungifu. He was momentarily embarrassed, and hid his face by drinking from the cup. The ale warmed his belly.

Ragna said: 'I had a nice little farm picked out for you in the Vale of Outhen, but in the end you didn't need it. Aldred is your landlord now, so you should be safe.'

She seemed a little distracted, and Edgar wondered if she had something on her mind. 'I'm grateful to you all the same,' he said. 'You gave me the courage to be one of Aldred's oath-helpers.'

She nodded acknowledgement, but clearly was not interested in going back over the events of the trial. Edgar decided to get right to the point: he did not want to make her impatient. 'I'm here to ask another favour,' he said.

'Go ahead.'

'The church at Dreng's Ferry is falling down, but Aldred can't afford to repair it.'

'How could I help with that?'

'You could let us have the stone free of charge. I could quarry it myself, so it would cost you nothing. And it would be a pious gift.'

'So it would.'

'Will you do it?'

She looked into his eyes with an expression of amusement and something else he could not read. 'Of course I will,' she said.

Her ready assent threatened to bring tears to his eyes, and he felt a surge of gratitude that was almost like love. Why were there not more people like this in the world? 'Thank you,' he said.

She sat back, breaking the spell, and said briskly: 'How much stone will you need?'

He suppressed his emotions and became practical. 'About five raft-loads of stones and rubble, I think. I'm going to have to build buttresses with deep foundations.'

'I'll give you a letter to Seric saying you can take as much as you like.'

'You're so kind.'

She shrugged. 'Not really. There's enough stone in Outhenham to last a hundred years.'

'Well, I'm very thankful.'

'There's something you could do for me.'

'Name it.' There was nothing he would like better than to perform some service for her.

'I still have Gab as quarry master.'

457

'Why do you keep someone who stole from you?'

'Because I can't find anyone else. But perhaps you could take over as quarry master, and supervise him.'

The idea of working for Ragna thrilled Edgar. But how was it to be managed? He said: 'And repair the church at the same time?'

'I'm thinking you could spend half your time at Outhenham and half at Dreng's Ferry.'

He nodded slowly. That might work. 'I'm going to be travelling often to Outhenham for stone.' But he would have to hand over the fish pond to his brothers, so he would lose the income from the fish market.

Ragna solved that problem with her next sentence. 'I'll pay you sixpence a week, plus a farthing per stone sold.'

This would amount to a lot more than the fish brought in. 'You're generous.'

'I want you to make sure Gab doesn't get up to his old tricks again.'

'That's easy enough. I can tell how much stone he's removed just by looking at the quarry.'

'And he's lazy. Outhenham could produce more stone if someone was willing to make the effort to sell it.'

'And that someone is me?'

'You can do anything – that's the kind of person you are.'

He was surprised. Even if it was not true, he was pleased that she thought it.

She said: 'Don't blush!'

He laughed. 'Thank you for having faith in me. I hope I can justify it.'

'Now, I have some news,' she said.

Ah, he thought; this will be the reason why she seemed distracted earlier.

She said: 'I'm going to have a baby.'

'Oh!' The announcement took his breath away – which was

strange, for it was hardly surprising that a healthy young bride should get pregnant. And he had even noticed that she had put on weight. 'Baby,' he said stupidly. 'My goodness.'

'It's due in May.'

He did not know what to say. What question did people ask a pregnant woman? 'Are you hoping for a boy or a girl?'

'A boy, to please Wilf. He wants an heir.'

'Of course.' A nobleman always wanted heirs.

She smiled. 'Are you happy for me?'

'I am,' Edgar said. 'Very happy.'

He wondered why that felt like a lie.

ÞÞÞ

CHRISTMAS EVE WAS a Saturday this year. Early that morning Aldred got a message from Mother Agatha asking him to go and see her. He put on a cloak and walked down to the ferry.

Edgar was there, unloading stones from his raft. 'Ragna agreed to give us the stone free,' he said, smiling at his triumph.

'Great news! Well done.'

'I can't start building yet – the mortar might freeze overnight instead of setting. But I can get everything ready.'

'But I still can't pay you.'

'I won't starve.'

'Is there something I can do for you by way of reward, something that doesn't require money?'

Edgar shrugged. 'If I think of something, I'll ask.'

'Good enough.' Aldred looked towards the alehouse. 'I need to cross to the nunnery. Is Blod around?'

'I'll take you.' Edgar untied the ferry as Aldred boarded, then picked up a pole and pushed the boat across the narrow channel to the island.

Edgar waited at the waterside while Aldred knocked at the door of the convent and Agatha came out in a cloak. She would not let men into the nunnery, but because of the cold she took Aldred into the church, which was empty.

At the east end, near the altar, was a chair carved from a block of stone, with a rounded back and a flat seat. 'A sanctuary stool,' he commented. By tradition, anyone sitting on such a chair in a church was immune from prosecution, regardless of his or her crimes, and those who flouted that rule, and captured or killed someone who had taken refuge there, were themselves subject to the death penalty.

Agatha nodded. 'It's not easily accessible, of course, here on this island. But a fugitive who is innocent will show determination.'

'Has it often been used?'

'Three times in twenty years, each time by a woman who had decided to be a nun against the wishes of her family.'

They sat on a cold stone bench on the north wall, and Agatha said: 'I admire you. It takes guts to stand up to a man such as Wynstan.'

'It takes more than guts to defeat him, though,' said Aldred ruefully.

'We have to try. It's our mission.'

'I agree.'

Her tone became practical. 'I have a suggestion to make,' she said. 'A way of lifting our spirits in midwinter.'

'What do you have in mind?'

'I'd like to bring the nuns to the church tomorrow for the Christmas service.'

Aldred was intrigued. 'What gave you that idea?'

Agatha smiled. 'The fact that it was a woman who brought our Lord into the world.'

'That's true. So we should have female voices joining in with our Christmas hymns.'

'That's what I thought.'

'In addition, the women might improve the singing.'

'They might,' said Agatha, 'especially if I leave Sister Frith behind.'

Aldred laughed, but said: 'Don't do that. Bring everyone.'

'I'm so glad you like the idea.'

'I love it.'

Agatha stood up, and Aldred did the same. It had been a short conversation, but she was not one for idle chatter. They walked out of the church.

Aldred saw that Edgar was talking to a man dressed in a filthy robe. He was barefoot despite the cold. He had to be one of the wretches the nuns fed.

Agatha said: 'Oh, dear, poor Cuthbert has got lost again.'

Aldred was shocked. Coming closer, he saw the dirty rag that bandaged the man's eyes like a blindfold. Cuthbert must have been brought here from Shiring, by some kind soul, to join the community of lepers and other helpless people who depended on the nuns, Aldred thought; and then he felt guilty that he had not been that kind soul. He had been too occupied with his own troubles to think in a Christ-like way about helping others.

Cuthbert was speaking to Edgar in low, harsh tones. 'It's your fault I'm like this,' he said. 'Your fault!'

'I know,' said Edgar.

Agatha raised her voice. 'Cuthbert, you've wandered into the nuns' zone again. Let me lead you back.'

Edgar said: 'Wait.'

Agatha said: 'What is it?'

Edgar said: 'Aldred, a few minutes ago you asked if there was something you could do for me by way of reward for buttressing the church.'

'I did.'

'I've thought of something. I want you to take Cuthbert into the priory.'

Cuthbert gasped with shock.

Aldred was moved. For a few moments he could not speak. After a few moments he said in a choked voice: 'Would you like to become a monk, Cuthbert?'

Cuthbert said: 'Yes, please, Brother Aldred. I've always been a man of God – it's the only life I know.'

'You'd have to learn our ways. A monastery is not like a minster, not really.'

'Would God want someone like me?'

'He cares especially for people like you.'

'But I'm a criminal.'

'Jesus said: "I come not to call the righteous, but sinners, to repentance".'

'This isn't a joke, is it? A trick, to torture me? Some people are very cruel to the blind.'

'No trick, my friend. Come with me now, on the ferry.'

'Right away?'

'Right away.'

Cuthbert shook with sobs. Aldred put one arm around him, ignoring the dreadful smell. 'Come,' he said. 'Let's get on board the boat.'

'Thank you, Aldred, thank you.'

'Thank Edgar. I'm ashamed I didn't think of it myself.'

They waved to Agatha, who said: 'God bless you.'

As they crossed the water Aldred reflected that even if he could not achieve his grand ambitions in this out-of-the-way priory, he might still do some good.

They disembarked and Edgar tied up the ferry. Aldred said: 'This doesn't count, Edgar. I still owe you a reward.'

Edgar said: 'Well, there is something else I want.' He looked embarrassed.

'Out with it,' said Aldred.

'You used to talk about starting a school.'

'It's my dream.'

Edgar hesitated again, then blurted it out. 'Would you teach me to read?'

PART THREE
THE MURDER
1001–1003 CE

25

RAGNA WAS GIVING BIRTH to her second child, and it was going badly. Bishop Wynstan could hear her screams from where he sat in the home of his mother, Gytha. A steady rain outside did little to muffle the noise. Ragna's cries gave Wynstan hope. 'If mother and child die, all our problems are over,' he said.

Gytha picked up a jug. 'I was like that with you,' she said. 'It took a day and a night to get you out. No one thought either of us would survive.'

It sounded to him like an accusation. 'Not my fault,' he said.

She poured more wine into his cup. 'And then you were born howling and waving your fists.'

Wynstan did not feel comfortable in his mother's house. She always had sweet wine and strong ale, bowls of plums and pears in season, ham and cheese on a platter, and thick blankets for cold nights, but for all that he was never at ease. 'I was a good child,' he protested. 'A scholar.'

'Yes, when forced. But if I took my eye off you, you would sneak away from your lessons to play.'

A childhood memory struck Wynstan. 'You wouldn't let me see the bear.'

'What bear?'

'Someone brought a bear on a chain. Everyone went to look at it. But Father Aculf wanted me to finish copying the Ten Commandments first, and you backed him.' Wynstan had sat with a slate and a nail, hearing the others boys laughing and yelling outside. 'I kept making mistakes in the Latin, and by the time I got it right the bear had gone.'

She shook her head. 'I don't remember that.'

Wynstan remembered it vividly. 'I hated you for it.'

'And yet I did it out of love.'

'Yes,' he said. 'I suppose you did.'

She picked up his doubt. 'You had to become a priest. Let peasant brats play.'

'Why were you so sure I should be a priest?'

'Because you're a second son, and I'm a second wife. Wilwulf was going to inherit your father's wealth, and probably become ealdorman, and you might have been an unimportant person, only wanted just in case Wilf should die. I was determined not to let that happen to us. The Church was your route to power and wealth and high status.'

'And yours.'

'I'm nothing,' she said.

Her modesty was utterly insincere and he ignored it. 'After me, you had no offspring for five years. Was that deliberate? Because of my difficult birth?'

'No,' she said indignantly. 'A noblewoman does not shirk childbirth.'

'Of course.'

'But I had two miscarriages between you and Wigelm, not to mention a stillbirth later.'

'I remember the arrival of Wigelm,' Wynstan mused. 'When I was five years old I wanted to murder him.'

'An older child often has such feelings. It's a sign of spirit. He rarely does anything about it, but I kept you away from Wigelm's cradle just the same.'

'What was his delivery like?'

'Not so bad, though childbirth is rarely easy. The second child is normally less agonizing than the first.' She glanced in the direction of the noise. 'Though clearly that's not so for Ragna. Something may be going wrong.'

'Death in childbirth is a common occurrence,' Wynstan said cheerfully; then he caught a black look from Gytha and realized he had gone too far. She was on his side, whatever he did, but she was still a woman. 'Who is attending Ragna?' he asked.

'A Shiring midwife called Hildi.'

'Local woman with heathen remedies, I suppose.'

'Yes. But if Ragna and the newborn were to die, that would still leave Osbert.'

Ragna's first child was coming up to two years old, a ginger-haired baby Norman, named Osbert after Wilwulf's father. Osbert was Wilf's legitimate heir, and would be even if Ragna's newborn died today. But Wynstan waved a hand dismissively. 'A child without a mother is little threat,' he said. A two-year-old was not difficult to get rid of, he was thinking; but he did not say so, remembering Gytha's black look.

She just nodded.

He studied her face. Thirty years ago that face had terrified him. She was in her middle fifties now, and her hair had been grey for years; but lately her dark eyebrows had grown silver strands, there were new little vertical lines above her upper lip, and her figure was not so much voluptuous as lumpy. But she still had the power to strike fear into his heart.

She was patient and still. Women could do that. Wynstan could not: he tapped his foot, shifted in his seat, and said: 'Dear God, how much longer?'

'If the baby gets stuck, both mother and child usually die.'

'Pray for that. We need Garulf to inherit from Wilf. It's the only way to hold on to everything we've won.'

'You're right, of course.' Gytha made a sour face. 'Although Garulf is not the wisest of men. Fortunately we can control him.'

467

'He's popular. The men-at-arms like him.'

'I'm not sure why.'

'He's always willing to buy a barrel of ale and let them take turns raping a prisoner.'

His mother gave him that look again. But her scruples were disposable. In the end she would do what was necessary for the family.

The screaming stopped. Wynstan and Gytha fell silent and waited, tense. Wynstan began to think his wish had come true.

Then they heard the unmistakable wail of a newborn. 'It's alive,' Wynstan said. 'Hell.'

A minute later the door opened and a fifteen-year-old maid called Winthryth, daughter of Gilda, poked her head in, her hair wet with rain. 'It's a boy,' she said, grinning happily. 'Strong as a bull calf and a big chin like his father's.' She disappeared.

Wynstan muttered: 'To hell with his damn chin.'

'So, the dice did not roll our way.'

'This changes everything.'

'Yes.' Gytha looked thoughtful. 'This calls for a completely new approach.'

Wynstan was taken aback. 'Does it?'

'We've been looking at this situation the wrong way.'

Wynstan did not see that, but his mother was usually right. 'Go on,' he said.

'Our real problem is not Ragna.'

Wynstan raised his eyebrows. 'Isn't it?'

'Wilf is our problem.'

Wynstan shook his head. He did not see what she was getting at. But she was no fool, and he waited patiently to learn what she was thinking.

After a moment she said: 'Wilf is so taken with her. He's never before fallen so hard for a woman. He likes her, he loves her, and she seems to know how to please him in and out of bed.'

'That doesn't stop him fucking Inge once in a while.'

Gytha shrugged. 'A man's love is never really exclusive. But Inge's no great threat to Ragna. If Wilf had to choose between the two, he'd pick Ragna in a heartbeat.'

'I don't suppose there's any chance Ragna could be seduced into betraying him?'

Gytha shook her head. 'She's fond of that clever boy from Dreng's Ferry, but nothing will ever come of it. He's far beneath her.'

Wynstan remembered the boatbuilder from Combe who had moved to the farm at Dreng's Ferry. He was a person of no importance. 'No,' he said dismissively. 'If she falls, it will be for some good-looking town boy who charms his way up her skirt while Wilf is away fighting Vikings.'

'I doubt it. She's too smart to jeopardize her position for a dalliance.'

'I agree, unfortunately.'

Winthryth surprised them by reappearing in the doorway, wetter than before but beaming even more. 'And another boy!' she said.

Gytha said: 'Twins!'

'This one is smaller and dark-haired, but healthy.' Winthryth left.

'God damn them both,' said Wynstan.

Gytha said: 'Now three males stand in Garulf's way, instead of one.'

They were silent for a while. This was a major shift in the power politics of the ealdormanry. Wynstan mulled over the consequences, and he was sure his mother was doing the same.

Eventually he said frustratedly: 'There must be something we can do to drive Wilf and Ragna apart. She's not the only sexy woman in the world.'

'Perhaps another girl will come along and fascinate him. She'd be younger than Ragna, of course, and probably even more of a spitfire.'

'Can we make it happen?'

'Maybe.'

'Do you think it would work?'

'It might. And I can't think of a better plan.'

'Where would we find such a woman?'

'I don't know,' said Gytha. 'Perhaps we could buy one.'

ÞÞÞ

AFTER A PEACEFUL Christmas, Ironface struck again in January.

Edgar was unloading stone from his raft at the waterside near the farmhouse on a cold, bright morning. He was preparing to build a smokehouse on his family's farm. They often had more fish than they could sell, and their ceiling had started to look like an upside-down forest in winter, the eels like bare saplings growing down from the thatch. A stone-built smokehouse would have plenty of room and also be less likely to catch on fire.

He was more and more confident as a stonemason. He had long ago finished buttressing the church, which was now stable. For two years he had been managing Ragna's quarry at Outhenham, selling more stone than ever, making money for her and for himself. But demand was slack in winter and he had taken the opportunity to stockpile stones for his personal project.

His brother Eadbald appeared, rolling an empty barrel along the rough path on the bank of the river. 'We need more ale,' he said. They could afford it now, thanks to the fish pond.

'I'll give you a hand,' said Edgar. One man could manage an empty barrel but it took two to move a full one over uneven ground.

The two brothers took the empty to the alehouse, with Brindle trotting behind. While they were paying Leaf, two passengers arrived for the ferry. Edgar recognized them as Odo and Adelaide, a husband-and-wife courier team from Cherbourg. They had passed through Dreng's Ferry two weeks earlier on their way to Shiring, accompanied by two men-at-arms, carrying letters and money to Ragna.

Edgar greeted them and said: 'On your way home?'

Odo spoke with a French accent. 'Yes, we hope to find a ship at

470

Combe.' He was a big man of about thirty with fair hair cut in the Norman style, shaved to the scalp at the back. He wore a sturdy-looking sword.

They had no bodyguards, but this time they were not carrying a large sum of money.

Adelaide said excitedly: 'We're in a hurry, because we have good news to take home. The Lady Ragna has given birth – to twin boys!' A small blonde, she was wearing a pendant of silver wire with an amber bead; it would suit Ragna, Edgar thought.

He was pleased about the twins. Wilwulf's heir would probably be one of Ragna's offspring now, rather than Inge's son, Garulf, who was both stupid and brutal. 'Good for Ragna,' he said.

Dreng, who had heard the announcement, said: 'I'm sure everyone would like to drink a toast to the new young princelings!' He made it sound as if the ale would be on the house, but Edgar knew that was one of his tricks.

The Normans did not fall for it. 'We want to get to Mudeford Crossing before nightfall,' Odo said, and they took their leave.

Edgar and Eadbald rolled their new, full barrel to the farmhouse, then Edgar resumed unloading his raft, roping the stones and dragging them from the waterside up the slope to the site of the smokehouse.

The winter sun was high and he was about to unload the last stone when he heard a shout from the other side of the river: 'Help me, please!'

He looked across the water and saw a man with a woman in his arms. Both were naked and the woman appeared to be unconscious. Shading his eyes, he saw that they were Odo and Adelaide.

He jumped onto the raft and poled across the river. They had been robbed of everything, including their clothes, he guessed.

He reached the far bank and Odo stepped onto the raft, still cradling Adelaide, and sat down heavily on the one remaining rough-hewn quarry stone. He had blood on his face and one eye half closed, and some kind of injury to one leg. Adelaide's eyes were shut and blood was congealing in her fair hair, but she was breathing.

Edgar felt a surge of compassion for the slight young figure, and a spasm of hatred for the men who had done this to her. He said: 'There's a nunnery on the island. Mother Agatha has some skill with injuries. Shall I take you straight there?'

'Yes, please, quickly.'

Edgar poled vigorously upstream. 'What happened?' he said.

'It was a man in a helmet.'

'Ironface,' Edgar said, and he muttered ferociously: 'The spawn of Satan.'

'And he had at least one companion. I was knocked unconscious. I suppose they left us for dead. When I came round we were naked.'

'They need weapons. It might have been your sword that attracted them. And Adelaide's pendant.'

'If you know these men are in the forest, why don't you capture them?' Odo's tone was challenging, almost as if he thought Edgar condoned the thieves.

Edgar pretended not to notice the veiled accusation. 'We've tried, believe me. We've searched every yard of the south bank. But they disappear into the undergrowth like weasels.'

'They had a boat. I saw it just before they attacked us.'

Edgar was startled. 'What kind?'

'Just a small rowboat.'

'I didn't know that.' Everyone had always assumed that Ironface hid out on the south bank, as he always robbed there; but if he had a boat then his hidey-hole could just as easily be on the north bank.

'Have you ever seen him?' Odo asked.

'I put an axe into his arm one night when he tried to steal our pig, but he got away. Here we are.' Edgar beached the raft on Leper

Island and stood holding the rope while Odo stepped off, still holding Adelaide.

He carried her to the nunnery door, and Mother Agatha opened it. She ignored his nakedness and looked at the wounded woman.

Odo said: 'My wife . . .'

'Poor woman,' said Agatha. 'I will try to help her.' She reached for the unconscious form.

'I'll bring her in.'

Agatha just shook her head silently.

Odo let her lift Adelaide from his arms. Agatha took the weight effortlessly and went back inside. An invisible hand closed the door.

Odo stood staring at the door for several moments, then turned away.

They boarded the raft. 'I'd better go to the alehouse,' Odo said.

'You won't be welcome there, with no money,' Edgar said. 'But the monastery will take you in. Prior Aldred will give you a monk's robe and some shoes, and clean your wounds, and feed you for as long as you need it.'

'Thank God for monks.'

Edgar poled across to the bank and tied up. 'Come with me,' he said.

Odo stumbled as he disembarked, and went down on his knees. 'Sorry,' he said. 'My legs feel weak. I carried her a long way.'

Edgar hauled him up. 'Just a bit farther.' He walked Odo to the building that had been the priests' house and was now the monastery. He lifted the latch and half carried Odo inside. The monks were at dinner around the table, all but Aldred, who stood at the lectern Edgar had made, reading aloud.

He stopped when Edgar and Odo came in. 'What happened?' he said.

'On his way home to Cherbourg, Odo and his wife were beaten, robbed, stripped and left for dead,' Edgar said.

Aldred closed the book and took Odo's arm gently. 'Come over

473

here and lie down near the fire,' he said. 'Brother Godleof, bring me some wine to clean his wounds.' He helped Odo lie down.

Godleof brought a bowl of wine and a clean rag, and Aldred began to wash the injured man's bloody face.

Edgar said to Odo: 'I'll leave you. You're in good hands.'

Odo said: 'Thank you, neighbour.'

Edgar smiled.

ÞÞÞ

RAGNA NAMED THE elder twin Hubert, after her father, and called the younger Colinan. They were not identical, and it was easy to tell which was which because one was big and fair and the other small and dark. Ragna had enough milk to feed them both: her breasts felt swollen and heavy.

She had no shortage of help looking after them. Cat had been present at the birth and doted on them from the start. Cat had married Bern the Giant, and had a baby of her own the same age as Ragna's Osbert. She seemed happy with Bern, although she had told the other women that his belly was so big that she always had to get on top. They had all giggled, and Ragna had wondered how men would feel if they knew the way woman talked about them.

The seamstress Agnes was equally fond of the twins. She had married an Englishman, Offa, the reeve of Mudeford, but they had no children, and all her frustrated maternal feelings were focused on Ragna's babies.

Ragna left the twins for the first time when she heard what had happened to Odo and Adelaide.

She was terribly worried. The couriers had come to England on a mission for Ragna's benefit, and she felt responsible. The fact that they were Normans, as she was, made her sympathy sharper. She had to see them, and find out how badly they were hurt and whether she could do anything for them.

474

She put Cat in charge of the children, with two wet nurses to make sure they did not go hungry. She took Agnes as her maid and Bern as her bodyguard. She packed clothes for Odo and Adelaide, having been told that they had been left naked. She rode out of the compound with a heavy heart: how could she leave her little ones behind? But she had her duty.

She missed them every minute of the two-day journey to Dreng's Ferry.

She arrived late in the afternoon and immediately took the ferry to Leper Island, leaving Bern at the alehouse. Mother Agatha welcomed her with a kiss and a bony hug.

Without preamble Ragna said: 'How is Adelaide?'

'Recovering fast,' Agatha said. 'She's going to be fine.'

Ragna slumped with relief. 'Thank God.'

'Amen.'

'What injuries does she have?'

'She suffered a nasty blow to the head, but she's young and strong, and it seems there are no long-term effects.'

'I'd like to speak to her.'

'Of course.'

Adelaide was in the dormitory. She had a clean rag tied over her blonde head, and she was dressed in a drab nun's shift, but she was sitting upright in bed, and she smiled happily when she saw Ragna. 'My lady! You shouldn't have troubled to come all this way.'

'I had to be sure you were recovering.'

'But your babies!'

'I'll hurry back to them now that I've seen you're all right. But who else would have brought you fresh clothes?'

'You're so kind.'

'Nonsense. How is Odo? They told me he wasn't hurt as badly as you.'

'Apparently he's fine, but I haven't seen him – men aren't allowed here.'

'I'm going to have Bern the Giant escort you to Combe, whenever you both feel well enough to go.'

'I can go tomorrow. I don't even feel ill.'

'All the same I'm going to lend you a horse.'

'Thank you.'

'You can ride Bern's mount, and he can ride it back to Shiring after he's seen you off on a ship to Cherbourg.'

Ragna gave Adelaide money and a few feminine necessities: a comb, a small jar of oil for cleaning her hands, and a linen loincloth. Then she took her leave – with another kiss from Agatha – and returned to the mainland.

Odo was at the priory with Aldred. His face was bruised, and he favoured his left leg when he stood up and bowed to her, but he looked cheerful. She handed him the men's clothes she had brought from Shiring. 'Adelaide wants to leave tomorrow,' Ragna told him. 'How do you feel?'

'I think I'm fully recovered.'

'Be guided by Mother Agatha. She has taken care of many sick people.'

'Yes, my lady.'

Ragna left the monastery and returned to the waterfront. She would take the ferry back to the island and spend the night in the nunnery.

Edgar was outside the alehouse. 'I'm very sorry that this has happened to your couriers,' he said, although it obviously was not his fault.

Ragna said: 'Do you think they were attacked by the same thieves who stole the wedding present I had for Wilf three years ago?'

'I'm sure of it. Odo described a man in an iron helmet.'

'And I gather that all efforts to catch him have failed.' Ragna frowned. 'When he steals livestock he and his gang just eat it; and they keep weapons and money; but they must turn clothes and jewellery into cash. I wonder how they manage that?'

Edgar said thoughtfully: 'Perhaps Ironface takes the stuff to Combe. There are several dealers in second-hand clothes there, and two or three jewellers. The jewellery can be melted down, or at least altered so that it's not easily recognizable, and any distinctive clothes can be remade.'

'But outlaws look disreputable.'

'There must be people willing to buy things without asking too many questions.'

Ragna frowned. 'I just think outlaws would be noticed. On the few occasions when I've seen such men they looked ragged and unhealthy and dirty. You lived in Combe. Do you recall men who looked as if they lived rough in the forest coming into town to sell things?'

'No. And I don't remember people talking about such visitors, either. Do you think Ironface might use a go-between?'

'Yes. Someone respectable who has a reason for visiting Combe.'

'But that includes hundreds of people. It's a big town. They go there to buy and sell.'

'Anyone you'd suspect, Edgar?'

'Dreng, the tavern-keeper here, is evil enough, but he doesn't like to travel.'

Ragna nodded. 'This wants thinking about,' she said. 'I'd like to put a stop to this lawlessness, and Sheriff Den feels the same way.'

'Don't we all,' said Edgar.

Þ Þ Þ

RAGNA AND CAT were putting the twins down in their cots for an afternoon sleep when they heard a commotion outside. A girl howled in fury, several women began to shout, and then a lot of men started laughing and jeering. The twins closed their eyes, oblivious, and went to sleep in seconds, then Ragna stepped outside to see what the fuss was about.

It was cold. A north wind with ice in its blast scoured the compound. A crowd had gathered around a barrel of water. As Ragna got closer she saw that at the centre of the group was a naked girl in a rage. Gytha and two or three other women were trying to wash her, using brushes and rags and oil and water, while others struggled to hold her still. As they poured cold water over her she shivered uncontrollably while at the same time yelling a stream of what sounded to Ragna like swear words in Welsh.

Ragna said: 'Who is she?'

The new head groom, Wuffa, standing in front of Ragna, replied without turning his head. 'It's Gytha's new slave,' he said, then he shouted: 'Scrub her tits!' and the men around him chortled.

Ragna could have stopped the mistreatment of an ordinary young woman, but not a slave. People were entitled to be cruel to slaves. There were some feeble laws against killing a slave for no good reason, but even they were difficult to enforce, and the punishments were mild.

The girl was about thirteen, Ragna saw. Her skin, when the dirt came off, was pale. The hair on her head and between her legs was dark, almost black. She had slender arms and legs and perfect small breasts. Even though her face was twisted with fury, she was pretty.

Ragna said: 'Why would Gytha want a slave girl?'

Wuffa turned to reply, grinning, but he realized who he was talking to and changed his mind. The grin vanished and he muttered: 'I don't know.'

Clearly he did know, but was embarrassed to say.

Wilf appeared out of the great hall and approached the crowd, evidently curious as Ragna had been. She watched him, wondering how he would react to this. Gytha quickly ordered her companions to stop washing the girl and hold her still for Wilf to look at.

The crowd parted respectfully for the ealdorman to pass. The girl was more or less clean now. Her black hair hung wetly either side of her face, and her skin glowed with the scrubbing it had suffered. Her scowl seemed only to make her more alluring. Wilf grinned broadly. 'Who is this?' he said.

Gytha answered. 'Her name is Carwen,' she said. 'She's a gift from me to you, to thank you for being the best stepson a mother could ask for.'

Ragna stifled a cry of protest. This was not fair! She had done everything to please Wilf and keep him loyal, and in the three years they had been married he had been a good deal more faithful than most English noblemen. He slept with Inge now and again, as if for old times' sake, and he probably lay with peasant girls when he went away, but while he was here he hardly looked at other women. And now all her work was going to be undone by a slave girl – given to him by Gytha! Ragna knew right away that Gytha's plan was to drive a wedge between her and Wilf.

Wilf stepped forward with his arms outstretched, as if to embrace Carwen.

She spat in his face.

Wilf stopped in his tracks, and the crowd went silent.

A slave could be executed for that. Wilf might well draw his knife and cut her throat on the spot.

He wiped his face with his sleeve, then put his hand on the hilt of the dagger in his belt. He stared at Carwen for a long moment. Ragna could not tell what he would do.

Then he took his hand off his knife.

He could still simply reject Carwen. Who wanted a gift that spat in your face? Ragna thought this might be her salvation.

Then Wilf relaxed. He grinned and looked around. The crowd tittered uneasily. Then Wilf began to laugh.

The crowd laughed with him, and Ragna knew that she was lost.

Wilf's expression became serious again, and the crowd quietened.

He slapped the slave's face once, hard. He had big, strong hands.

Carwen cried out and began to weep. Her cheek turned bright red and a trickle of blood ran from her lips down her chin.

Wilf turned to Gytha. 'Tie her up and put her in my house,' he said. 'On the floor.'

He watched as the women tied the slave's hands behind her back, with some difficulty as she struggled to resist. Once that was done they tied her ankles.

The men in the crowd were looking at the naked girl but the women were surreptitiously watching Ragna. She realized they were curious to see how she would react. She did her best to keep her face a dignified blank.

Gytha's women lifted the trussed Carwen and carried her to Wilf's house.

Ragna turned and walked slowly away, feeling distraught. The father of her three sons was going to spend tonight with a slave girl. What was she to do?

She would not allow this to ruin her marriage, she resolved. Gytha could hurt her but not destroy her. She would keep her hold on Wilf, somehow.

She entered her own house. Her servants did not speak to her. They had found out what was happening, and they could see the expression on her face.

She sat down, thinking. It would be a mistake to try to stop Wilf sleeping with Carwen, she saw right away. He would not heed her wishes – a man such as he did not take orders from a woman, even one he loved – and the demand would only sour his feelings. Should she pretend not to care? No, that would be going too far. The right note to strike might be rueful acceptance of a man's desires. She could fake that, if she had to.

It was approaching suppertime. At all costs she must not appear defeated and sad. She had to look so gorgeous that he might even suffer a pang of regret at spending the night with another woman.

She picked a dark-yellow dress that she knew he liked. It was a bit tight across the bust, but that was good. She got Cat to tie up her hair in a kerchief of chestnut silk. She put on a cloak of dark red wool, to protect her back from the cold draughts that pierced the timber walls of the great hall. She finished the outfit with a brooch of gold-coloured enamel inlay.

At supper she sat on Wilf's right, as usual. He was in convivial mood, bantering with the men, but every now and again she caught him looking at her with something in his eyes that intrigued her. It was not quite fear, but it was stronger than mere anxiety, and she realized that he was actually nervous.

How should she respond? If she showed her pain, he would feel manipulated and become angry, and then he would want to teach her a lesson, probably by paying all the more attention to Carwen. No, there had to be a more subtle way.

All through the meal Ragna made sure she was more alluring than ever, though she felt miserable. She laughed at Wilf's jokes and, whenever he made some allusion to love or sex, she looked at him from under her eyelids in a way that always made him feel amorous.

When the food was finished and the men were getting drunk she left the table, along with most of the women. She returned to her own house, carrying a rush lamp to light her way. She did not take off her cloak, but stood in the doorway looking out, watching the movements dimly visible around the compound, thinking, trying out speeches in her mind.

Cat said: 'What are you doing?'

'Waiting for a quiet moment.'

'Why?'

'I don't want Gytha to see me going to Wilf's house.'

Cat sounded fearful. 'That's where the slave is. What are you going to do to her?'

'I'm not sure. I'm thinking about it.'

'Don't make Wilf angry with you.'

'We'll see.'

A few minutes later Ragna saw a silhouette move from Gytha's house to Wilf's, carrying a candle. She guessed Gytha was checking on her gift, making sure Carwen was still presentable.

Ragna waited patiently. Soon Gytha left Wilf's house and returned to her own. Ragna gave her a minute to settle. A woman and her drunk husband came out of the great hall and staggered across the compound. At last the coast was clear, and Ragna quickly crossed the short distance and went into Wilf's house.

Carwen was still bound, but able to sit upright. Being naked, she was cold, and she had squirmed closer to the fire. The left side of her face bore a huge purple bruise where Wilf had slapped her.

Ragna sat on a stool and wondered whether the slave spoke English. She said: 'I'm sorry this has happened to you.'

Carwen showed no response.

'I'm his wife,' Ragna said.

Carwen said: 'Ha!'

So she understood.

'He's not a cruel man,' Ragna went on. 'At least, no more cruel than men generally are.'

Carwen's face relaxed a fraction, perhaps with relief.

'He's never hit me the way he hit you today,' Ragna said. 'Mind you, I've been careful not to displease him.' She held up a hand as if to forestall argument. 'I'm not judging you, just telling you how it is.'

Carwen nodded.

That was progress.

Ragna took a blanket from Wilf's bed and put it around Carwen's thin white shoulders. 'Would you like some wine?'

'Yes.'

Ragna went to the table and poured wine from a jug into a wooden cup. She knelt beside Carwen and held the cup to her lips. Carwen drank. Ragna half expected her to spit the wine at her, but she swallowed it gratefully.

Then Wilf came in.

'What the devil are you doing here?' he said immediately.

Ragna stood up. 'I want to talk to you about this slave.'

Wilf folded his arms.

Ragna said: 'Would you like a cup of wine?' Without waiting for an answer she poured for two, handed him one, and sat down.

He sipped the wine and sat opposite her. His expression said that if she wanted a fight he would give her a damn good one.

A half-formed thought took more definite shape in Ragna's mind and she said: 'I don't think Carwen should live in the slave house.'

Wilf looked surprised and did not know how to respond. This was the last thing he had been expecting. 'Why?' he said. 'Because the slave house is so filthy?'

Ragna shrugged. 'It's dirty because we lock them in at night and they can't go outside to piss. But that's not what bothers me.'

'What, then?'

'If she spends nights there, she'll be fucked by one or more of the men, who probably have disgusting infections that she will pass to you.'

'I never thought of that. Where should she live?'

'We don't have a spare house in the compound at the moment, and anyway a slave can't have her own place. Gytha bought her, so perhaps Carwen should live with Gytha ... when she's not with you.'

'Good idea,' he said. He was visibly relieved. He had been expecting trouble, but all he got was a practical problem with a ready solution.

Gytha would be furious, but Wilf would not change his mind once he had given his agreement. For Ragna this was a small but satisfying act of revenge.

She stood up. 'Enjoy yourself,' she said, though in truth she was hoping he would not.

'Thank you.'

She went to the door. 'And when you tire of the girl, and you want a woman again, you can come back to me.' She opened the door. 'Goodnight,' she said, and she went out.

26

THINGS DID NOT WORK out the way Ragna expected. Wilf slept with Carwen every night for eight weeks, then he went to Exeter.

At first Ragna was baffled. How could he bear to spend that much time with a thirteen-year-old girl? What did he and Carwen talk about? What could an adolescent girl have to say that could possibly interest a man of Wilf's age and experience? In bed with Ragna, in the mornings, he had chatted about the problems of governing the ealdormanry: collecting taxes, catching criminals, and most of all defending the region from Viking attacks. He certainly did not discuss those issues with Carwen.

He still chatted to Ragna, just not in bed.

Gytha was delighted with the change and made the most of it, never missing an opportunity to refer to Carwen in Ragna's presence. Ragna was humiliated, but hid her feelings behind a smile.

Inge, who hated Ragna for taking Wilf from her, was delighted to see Ragna supplanted and, like Gytha, tried to rub it in. But she did not have Gytha's nerve. She said: 'Well, Ragna, you haven't spent a night with Wilf for weeks!'

'Nor have you,' Ragna replied, and that shut her up.

Ragna made the best of her new life, but with bitterness in her heart. She invited poets and musicians to Shiring. She doubled the size of her home, making it a second great hall, to accommodate her visitors – all with Wilf's permission, which he gave readily, so eager was he to placate her while he fucked his slave girl.

She worried that as Wilf's passion for her faded so her political position might weaken, therefore to compensate she strengthened her relationships with other powerful men: the bishop of Norwood, the abbot of Glastonbury, Sheriff Den, and others. Abbot Osmund of Shiring was still alive but bedridden, so she befriended Treasurer Hildred. She invited them to her house to listen to music and hear poems declaimed. Wilf liked the idea that his compound was becoming a cultural centre: it enhanced his prestige. Nevertheless, his great hall continued to feature jesters and acrobats, and the discussion after dinner was of swords and horses and battleships.

Then the Vikings came.

They had spent the previous summer peacefully in Normandy. No one in England knew why, but all were grateful, and King Ethelred had felt confident enough to go north and harry the Strathclyde Britons. But this spring the Vikings came back with a vengeance, a hundred ships with prows like curved swords sailing fast up the river Exe. They found the city of Exeter strongly defended, but mercilessly ravaged the countryside around about.

All this Shiring learned from messengers who came to seek help. Wilf did not hesitate. If the Vikings took control of the area around Exeter, they would have a base easily accessible from the sea, and from there they could attack anywhere in the West Country at will. They would be only a step from conquering the region and taking over Wilf's ealdormanry – something they had already achieved in much of the north-east of England. That outcome could not be contemplated, and Wilf assembled an army.

He discussed strategy with Ragna. She said he should not simply dash there with a small Shiring force and attack the Vikings as soon as he could find them. Speed and surprise were always good, but with an enemy force this large there was a risk of early defeat and humiliation. Wilf agreed, and said he would first make a tour of the West Country, recruiting men and swelling his ranks, in the hope of having an overwhelming army by the time he met the Vikings.

Ragna knew this would be a dangerous time for her. Before Wilf left she needed to establish publicly that she was his deputy. Once he was gone, her rivals would try to do her down while he was not there to protect her. Wynstan would not go with Wilf to fight the Vikings, for as a man of God he was forbidden to shed blood, and he generally kept that rule, while breaking many others. He would remain in Shiring, and would certainly attempt to take charge of the ealdormanry with Gytha's backing. Ragna would need to be on her guard every day.

She prayed that Wilf would spend one night with her before leaving, but it did not happen, and her bitterness deepened.

On the day he was to depart Ragna stood with him at the door of the great hall while Wuffa brought his favourite horse, Cloud, an iron-grey stallion. Carwen was nowhere to be seen: no doubt Wilf had said goodbye to her privately, which was considerate of him.

In front of everyone, Wilf kissed Ragna on the lips – for the first time in two months.

She spoke loudly so that all could hear. 'I promise you, my husband, that I will rule your ealdormanry well in your absence,' she said, with emphasis on the word *rule*. 'I will dispense justice as you would, and safeguard your people and your wealth, and I will allow no one to prevent me from doing my duty.'

It was an obvious challenge to Wynstan, and Wilf understood that. His guilt was still causing him to give Ragna anything she asked for. 'Thank you, my wife,' he said, equally loudly. 'I know you will rule as I would if I were here.' He, too, emphasized *rule*. 'Who defies the Lady Ragna, defies me,' he said.

Ragna lowered her voice. 'Thank you,' she said. 'And come back safe to me.'

ᚦᚦᚦ

RAGNA BECAME QUIET, deep in thought, hardly talking to the people around her. Gradually she realized she had to face up to a hard fact: Wilf would never love her the way she wanted to be loved.

He was fond of her, he respected her, and sooner or later he would probably begin to spend some nights with her again. But she would always be just one of the mares in his stable. This was not the life she had dreamed of when she fell in love with him. Could she get used to it?

The question made her want to cry. She held her feelings in during the day, when she was with others, but at night she wept, heard only by the intimates who shared her house. It was like a bereavement, she thought; she had lost her husband, not to death but to another woman.

She decided to make her usual Lady Day visit to Outhenham, in the hope that it would give her something to think about other than the shipwreck of her life. She left the children with Cat, and took Agnes with her as her personal maid.

She entered Outhenham with a smile on her face and a stone in her heart. However, the village raised her spirits. It had prospered in the three years of her rule. They called her Ragna the Just. No one had done well when everyone was cheating and stealing. Now, with Seric in charge, people were more willing to pay their dues, knowing they were not being robbed, and they worked harder when they felt confident they would reap the rewards.

She slept at Seric's house and held court in the morning. She ate a light midday meal, for there would be a feast later. She had arranged to visit the quarry in the afternoon, and when she was ready she found Edgar waiting for her, wearing a blue cloak. He had his own horse now, a sturdy black mare called Buttress. 'May I show you something on the way?' he asked as she got on her own mount.

'Of course.'

She thought he seemed uncharacteristically nervous. Whatever he had to say to her must be important to him, she guessed. Everyone had important things to say to the ealdorman's wife, but Edgar was special, and Ragna was intrigued.

They rode to the riverside, then followed the cart track that led to the quarry. On one side were the backs of village houses, each with its small plot of land containing a vegetable garden, some fruit trees, one or two animal shelters, and a dunghill. On the other side was the East Field, partly ploughed, the damp clay furrows gleaming, though no work was being done as it was a holiday.

Edgar said: 'Notice that the gap between the East Field and the village gardens is wide.'

'Much wider than necessary, enough for two roads.'

'Exactly. Now, it takes most of a day for two men to bring a boatload of stone from the quarry along this track to the river. That makes our stone more expensive. If they use a cart, it's easier, but it takes about the same length of time.'

She guessed he was making an important point, but she did not yet see it. 'Is this what you want to show me?'

'When I tried to sell stone to the monastery at Combe, they told me they have started to buy it from Caen, in Normandy, because that's cheaper.'

She was interested. 'How can that be?'

'It travels all the way on one ship, down the Orne river to the sea and across the Channel to Combe harbour.'

'And our problem is that our quarry isn't on a river.'

'Not quite.'

'What does that mean?'

'The river is only half a mile away.'

'But we can't make that half-mile disappear.'

'I think we can.'

She smiled. She could see that he was enjoying this gradual revelation. 'How?'

'Dig our own channel.'

That surprised her. 'What?'

'They've done it at Glastonbury,' he said with the air of one who produces a winning card. 'Aldred told me.'

'Dig our own river?'

'I've worked it out. Ten men with picks and shovels would take about twenty days to dig a channel, three feet deep and a bit wider than my raft, from the river to the quarry.'

'Is that all?'

'The digging is the easy part. We might need to reinforce the banks, depending on the consistency of the soil as we dig down, but I can do that myself. More difficult is getting the depth right. Obviously it has to go down far enough to make sure water flows in from the river. But I think I can work that out.'

He was smarter than Wilf and perhaps even than Aldred, she thought, but all she said was: 'What would it cost?'

'Assuming we don't use slaves—'

'I'd rather not.'

'Then a halfpenny a day for each man plus a penny a day for a ganger, so one hundred and twenty pennies, which is half a pound of silver; and we'd have to feed them, as most of them would be away from home.'

'And it would save money in the long term.'

'A lot of money.'

Ragna felt bucked by Edgar and his project. It would be a great new thing. It was costly, but she could afford it.

They arrived at the quarry. There were two houses now. Edgar had built a place for himself so that he did not have to share with Gab and his family. It was a fine house, with walls of vertical planks linked by tongue-and-groove joints. It had two shuttered windows, and the door was made of a single piece of oak. The door had a lock, and Edgar inserted a key and turned it to open the door.

Inside, it was a masculine domain, with pride of place given to tools, coils of rope and balls of cord, and harness. There was a barrel of ale but no wine, a truckle of hard cheese but no fruit, no flowers.

On the wall Ragna noticed a sheet of parchment hanging from a nail. Looking more closely she saw a list of customers, with details of the stones they had received and the money they had paid. Most craftsmen kept track of such things with notches on sticks. 'You can write?' she said to Edgar.

He looked proud. 'Aldred taught me.'

He had kept that quiet. 'And obviously you can read.'

'I could if I had a book.'

Ragna resolved to give him a present of a book when his canal was finished.

She sat on the bench and he drew a cup of ale from the barrel for her. 'I'm glad you don't want to use slave labour,' he said.

'What makes you say that?'

'There's something about having slaves that brings out the worst in people. Slave owners become savage. They beat and kill and rape as if it was all right.'

Ragna sighed. 'I wish all men were like you.'

He laughed.

She said: 'What?'

'I remember having exactly the same thought about you. I asked you to find me a farm, and you just said yes, without hesitation, and I said to myself: Why aren't they all like her?'

Ragna smiled. 'You've cheered me up,' she said. 'Thank you.' Impulsively she sprang to her feet and kissed him.

She meant to kiss his cheek but somehow she kissed his mouth. Her lips were on his for only a moment, and she would have thought nothing of it, but he was startled. He jumped back, away from her, and his face turned deep red.

She realized right away that she had made a mistake. 'I'm sorry,' she said. 'I shouldn't have done that. I was just grateful to you for making me feel better.'

'I didn't know you were feeling bad,' he said. He was beginning to recover his composure, but she noticed that he touched his mouth with his fingertips.

She was not going to explain to him about Carwen. 'I'm missing my husband,' she said. 'He's raising an army to fight the Vikings. They've sailed up the river Exe. Wilf is very worried.' She saw a shadow cross his face at the mention of Vikings, and she remembered that they had killed his lover. 'I'm sorry,' she said again.

He shook his head. 'It's all right. But there's something else I need to mention to you.'

Ragna was grateful for the change of subject. 'Go on.'

'Your maid Agnes is wearing a new ring.'

'Yes. Her husband gave it to her.'

'It's made of silver wires twisted together, and has an amber stone.'

'It's rather pretty.'

'It put me in mind of the pendant that was stolen from your courier Adelaide. It was made of silver wires with an amber stone.'

Ragna was startled. 'I never noticed that!'

'I remember thinking that the amber would have suited you.'

'But how could Agnes have a ring made of Adelaide's pendant?'

'The pendant was stolen and refashioned to disguise it. The question is how her husband got it.'

'She's married to Offa, the thane of Mudeford.' Ragna began to see the connections. 'He probably bought it from a jeweller in Combe. That jeweller knows the go-between, and the go-between knows where Ironface is to be found.'

'Yes,' said Edgar.

'The sheriff needs to question Offa.'

'Yes,' said Edgar.

'Offa may have bought the ring innocently.'

'Yes,' said Edgar.

'I don't want to risk getting Agnes's husband in trouble.'

'You have to,' said Edgar.

ꝧꝧꝧ

EDGAR ESCORTED RAGNA back to the centre of the village and left her surrounded by a crowd. He slipped away and returned to the quarry. He set Buttress to graze at the edge of the wood. Then, at last, he lay down in his house and thought about that kiss.

He had been surprised and discomfited. He knew he must have blushed. He had jumped away. She had seen all of that, and had apologized for embarrassing him. But what she saw was only the surface. Something else happened, deep down, and he had managed to keep it hidden. When Ragna's lips touched his, he had found himself instantly and totally overwhelmed by love for her.

A clap of thunder, a bolt of lightning, a man stricken in a second –

No, it had only seemed that way. Lying in the rushes by his fireplace, alone, eyes closed, he examined his soul and saw that he had fallen in love with her long ago. For years he had told himself that he had lost his heart to Sungifu, and no one could take her place. But at some point – he could not tell when – he had begun to love Ragna. He had not known it at the time, but it seemed obvious now.

In his memory he relived the last four years and realized that Ragna had become the most important person in his life. They helped each other. He liked nothing better than talking to her – how long had that been his favourite occupation? He admired her brains and her determination and, especially, the way she combined unchallengeable authority with a common touch that made people love her.

He liked her, he admired her, and she was beautiful. That was not the same as the fire of passion, but it was like a pile of summer-dry

493

wood that would burst into flames with a single spark, and today's kiss had been the spark. He wanted to kiss her again, kiss her all day, all night –

Which would never happen. She was the daughter of a count: even if she had been single she would never marry a mere builder. And she was not single. She was married to a man who must never, ever find out about that kiss, for if he did he would have Edgar killed in a heartbeat. Worse, she showed every sign of loving her husband. And if that were not enough, she had three sons with him.

Is there something wrong with me? Edgar asked himself. I used to love a dead girl, now I love a woman who might as well be dead for all the chance I have of being with her.

He thought of his brothers, happily sharing a wife who was coarse and self-centred and not very intelligent. Why can't I be like them, and take whatever woman comes my way? How could I be so foolish as to fall for a married noblewoman? I'm supposed to be the clever one.

He opened his eyes. There would be a feast in the village tonight. He could be near Ragna all evening. And tomorrow he would start work on the canal. That would give him plenty of reasons to talk to her over the next few weeks. She would never kiss him again, but she would be part of his life.

That would have to be enough.

ÞÞÞ

RAGNA SPOKE TO Sheriff Den as soon as she got back to Shiring. She was eager to catch Ironface, who was a blight on the entire district. And Wilf would be very pleased to come home and find she had solved that problem – the kind of thing Carwen could never achieve.

The sheriff was equally keen, and agreed with her that Offa might provide clues to the whereabouts of the outlaw. They decided to question Offa the following morning.

Ragna just hoped she was not going to learn that Agnes and Offa were guilty of something, perhaps receiving stolen property.

At dawn the next day Ragna met Den outside the home of Offa and Agnes. It had been raining all night and the ground was sodden. Den was accompanied by Captain Wigbert, two other men-at-arms, and two servants with shovels. Ragna wondered what the shovels were for.

Agnes opened the door. When she saw the sheriff and his men she looked frightened.

Ragna said: 'Is Offa here?'

'What on earth do you want Offa for, my lady?'

Ragna felt sorry for her, but had to be stern. Ragna was the ruler of the ealdormanry, and she could not show indulgence during a criminal inquiry. She said: 'Be quiet, Agnes, and speak when you're spoken to. You'll find out everything soon enough. Now let us in.'

Wigbert told the two men-at-arms to stay outside but beckoned the servants to follow him.

Ragna saw that the house was comfortably furnished, with wall hangings to keep out the draughts, a bed with a mattress, and a row of metal-rimmed cups and bowls on a table.

Offa sat up in bed, threw off a thick wool blanket, and stood up. 'What's the matter?'

Ragna said: 'Agnes, show the sheriff the ring you were wearing in Outhenham.'

'I still have it on.' She held out her left hand to Den.

Ragna said: 'Offa, where did you get this?'

He thought for a moment, scratching his twisted nose, as if he was trying to remember – or thinking of a plausible story. 'I bought it in Combe.'

'Who sold it to you?' She was hoping to be given the name of a jeweller, but she was disappointed.

'A French sailor,' said Offa.

If this was a lie, it was a clever one, Ragna thought. A particular Combe jeweller could have been questioned, but a foreign sailor could not be found.

She said: 'His name?'

'Richard of Paris.'

It was a name you might make up on the spur of the moment. There were probably hundreds of men called Richard of Paris. She began to feel suspicious of Offa, but she hoped for Agnes's sake that her suspicions were unfounded. She said: 'Why was a French sailor selling women's jewellery?'

'Well, he told me he had bought it for his wife, then regretted the purchase when he lost all his money at dice.'

Ragna could usually tell when people were lying, but she could not read Offa. She said: 'Where had Richard of Paris bought the ring?'

'I assumed he got it from a Combe jeweller, but he didn't say. What is this about? Why are you questioning me? I paid sixty pennies for that ring. Is there something wrong?'

Ragna guessed that Offa must have known or at least suspected that the ring was stolen property, but wanted to protect whoever had sold it to him. She was not sure what to ask next. After a pause, Den took over. Turning to the two servants he said brusquely: 'Search the house.'

Ragna was not sure how that would help. They needed to loosen Offa's tongue, not search his home.

There were two locked chests and several boxes storing food. Ragna watched patiently while the servants went through everything thoroughly. They patted down the clothing hanging from pegs, dipped into a barrel of ale all the way to the bottom, and overturned all the rushes on the floor. Ragna was not sure what they were looking for, but in any event they found nothing of interest.

Ragna was relieved. She wanted Offa to be innocent, for Agnes's sake.

Then Den said: 'The fireplace.'

Now Ragna saw what the shovels were for. The servants used them to scoop up the embers in the fire and throw them through the door. The hot logs hissed as they hit the wet ground outside.

Soon the earth below the fireplace was revealed, then the servants began to dig.

A few inches down their shovels hit wood.

Offa ran out of the door. It happened so fast that no one in the house could stop him. But there were two men-at-arms outside. Ragna heard a roar of frustration and the sound of a heavy body hitting the mud. A minute later the men-at-arms brought Offa back, each man holding one of his arms very firmly.

Agnes began to sob.

'Keep digging,' Den told the servants.

A few minutes later they pulled a wooden chest a foot long out of the hole. Ragna could see by the way they handled it that it was heavy.

It was not locked. Den lifted the lid. Inside were thousands of silver pennies, together with a few items of jewellery.

Den said: 'The proceeds of many years of thievery – plus a few souvenirs.'

On top of it all was a belt of soft leather with a silver buckle and strap end. Ragna gasped.

Den said: 'Do you recognize something?'

'The belt. It was to be my present to Wilf – until it was stolen by Ironface.'

Den turned to Offa. 'What is Ironface's real name, and where does he hide out?'

'I don't know,' said Offa. 'I bought that belt. I know I shouldn't have. I'm sorry.'

Den nodded to Wigbert, who stood in front of Offa. The two men-at-arms gripped Offa tighter.

Wigbert took from his belt a heavy club made of polished oak. With a swift movement he smashed the club into Offa's face. Ragna cried out, but Wigbert ignored her. With a rapid series of well-aimed blows he hit Offa's head, shoulders and knees. The crack of the hard wood hitting bones sickened Ragna.

When he paused, Offa's face was covered in blood. He was unable to stand but the men-at-arms held him upright. Agnes moaned as if in pain herself.

Den repeated: 'What is Ironface's real name, and where does he hide out?'

Through smashed teeth and bloody lips Offa said: 'I swear I don't know.'

Wigbert raised the club again.

Agnes shrieked: 'No, please, don't! Ironface is Ulf! Don't hit Offa again, please!'

Den turned to Agnes. 'The horse-catcher?' he said.

'Yes, I swear it.'

'You'd better be telling me the truth,' said Den.

Þ Þ Þ

EDGAR DID NOT believe that Ulf the horse-catcher was Ironface. He had met Ulf a few times and recalled him as a small man, though energetic and strong, as he would need to be to tame wild forest ponies. Edgar had vivid memories of the two occasions on which he had seen Ironface, and felt sure the man was of medium height and build. 'Agnes might be mistaken,' he said to Den, when the sheriff came to Dreng's Ferry on his way to arrest Ulf.

'You might be mistaken,' said Den.

Edgar shrugged. Agnes could have been lying, too. Or she might have shouted out a name at random, just to stop the torture, having in fact no idea whose head was inside the rusty iron helmet.

Edgar and the other men of the village joined Den and his group.

Den had no need of reinforcements, but the villagers did not want to miss the excitement, and they had the excuse that they were responsible for upholding the law in their hundred.

On the way they picked up Edgar's brothers, Erman and Eadbald.

A dog barked as they approached Theodberht Clubfoot's sheepfold. Theodberht and his wife asked what they were doing, and Den said: 'We're looking for Ulf the horse-catcher.'

'You'll find him at home this time of year,' said Theodberht. 'The wild horses are hungry. He puts out hay and they come to him.'

'Thanks.'

A mile or so farther on they came to Ulf's fenced corral. The mastiff tied up by the gate did not bark, but the horses neighed, and soon Ulf and his wife, Gwen, came out of the house. As Edgar had remembered, Ulf was a slight man with muscles like ropes, somewhat shorter than his wife. Both had dirty faces and hands. Edgar remembered that Gwen had had a brother, called Begstan, who had died around the time Edgar and family moved to Dreng's Ferry. Dreng had been suspicious about the death, because the body had not been buried at the minster.

The sheriff's men surrounded them, and Den said to Ulf: 'I've been told that you're Ironface.'

'You been told wrong,' said Ulf. Edgar sensed that he was telling the truth about that but hiding some other knowledge.

Den told the men to search the place.

Wigbert said to Ulf: 'You'd better tie that mastiff up close to the fence, because if he goes for one of my people, I'll put my spear through his chest faster than you can blink.'

Ulf shortened the rope so that the mastiff could not move more than a few inches.

They searched the ramshackle house. Wigbert came out with a chest and said: 'He's got more money than you'd think – there's four or five pounds of silver in here, I'd say.'

Ulf said: 'My life savings. That's twenty years of hard work, that is.'

It might be true, Edgar thought. In any event the sum of money was not really enough to prove criminality.

Two men with shovels walked around the outside of the corral, scanning the ground for signs of a place where Ulf might have buried something. They jumped the fence and did the same inside the corral, making the wild horses retreat nervously. They found nothing.

Den began to look frustrated. Speaking quietly to Wigbert and Edgar, he said: 'I don't believe Ulf is innocent.'

'Not innocent, no,' said Edgar. 'But he's not Ironface. Seeing him again makes me sure.'

'So why do you say he's not innocent?'

'Just a hunch. Perhaps he knows who Ironface is.'

'I'm going to arrest him anyway. But I wish we'd found something incriminating.'

Edgar looked around. Their house was ramshackle, with a sagging roof and holes in the wattle-and-daub walls; but Gwen looked well-fed and her coat was fur-lined. The pair were not poor, just slovenly.

Edgar looked at the mastiff's shelter. 'Ulf is kind to his dog,' he said. Not many people bothered to keep the rain off a guard dog. Frowning, he went closer. The mastiff growled a threat, but he was securely tied. Edgar took his Viking axe from his belt.

Ulf said: 'What are you doing?'

Edgar did not reply. With a few blows of the axe he demolished the dog's shelter. Then he used the blade to excavate the ground beneath. After a few minutes his axe rang on something metal.

He knelt by the hole he had dug and began to scoop out the mud with his hands. Slowly the round outline of a rusty iron object began to emerge. 'Ah,' he said as he recognized the shape.

Den said: 'What is it?'

Edgar pulled the object out of the hole and held it up triumphantly. 'Ironface's helmet,' he announced.

'That settles it,' said Den. 'Ulf is Ironface.'

Ulf said: 'I'm not, I swear!'

Edgar said: 'It's true. He's not.'

'Then who does the helmet belong to?' said Den.

Ulf hesitated.

'If you won't say, it's you.'

Ulf pointed at his wife. 'It's hers! I swear it! Gwen is Ironface!'

Den said: 'A woman?'

Gwen suddenly dashed away, dodging the sheriff's men near her. They turned to give chase and crashed into one another. Others followed, a few crucial seconds too late; and it looked as if she might get away.

Then Wigbert threw his spear. It struck Gwen's hip and she fell to the ground.

She lay face down, moaning in pain. Wigbert went to her and pulled his spear out of her body.

In the fall her left sleeve had been pushed up her arm. On the soft, pale skin at the back of her upper arm was a scar.

Edgar remembered a moonlit night at the farmhouse, only a few days after he and his family had arrived at Dreng's Ferry. The farm had been silent until Brindle barked. Edgar had seen someone in an iron helmet running away with the piglet under his arm, and had brought the thief down with his Viking axe.

And Ma had cut the throat of one of the other two thieves. That must have been Begstan, the brother of Gwen.

Edgar knelt beside Gwen and measured her scar against the blade of his axe. They were exactly the same length.

'That settles it,' he said to Den. 'I gave her that scar. She's Ironface.'

ÞÞÞ

RAGNA FELT TERRIBLE. She had brought Agnes here from Cherbourg, and had happily consented to her marriage to Offa. Now Ragna had to preside over a trial that could end in a death sentence for Offa. She was desperate to pardon Offa, but she had to uphold the law.

The shire court was a small affair this time. Most of the thanes and other notables who normally attended were away with Wilwulf, fighting the Vikings. Ragna sat under a makeshift canopy. The world seemed to be waiting for spring: it was a cold day, overcast and intermittently wet, with no hint in it of warm sunshine to come.

The big event was the trial of Gwen, now known to be Ironface. Offa was accused with her, along with Ulf, both clearly Gwen's collaborators. They all faced the death penalty.

Ragna was not sure how much Agnes had understood of her husband's crimes. In a moment of desperation she had shouted that Ulf was Ironface, so she must have suspected something; but she had named the wrong person, which suggested she had not actually known the truth. There was a generally agreed legal principle that a wife was not guilty of her husband's crimes unless she collaborated and, on balance, Ragna and Sheriff Den had decided not to prosecute Agnes.

All the same Ragna felt torn. Could she now condemn Offa to death, and leave Agnes a widow?

She knew she should. She had always argued for the rule of law. She had a reputation for scrupulous fairness. In Normandy they had called her Deborah, after the biblical judge, and in Outhenham she was Ragna the Just. She believed that justice ought to be objective, and it was not acceptable that powerful men should influence a court to rule in favour of their kin; and she had argued the point fiercely. She had been disgusted when Wilwulf condemned Cuthbert for forgery and let Wynstan get away with it. She could not now do a similar thing herself.

The three accused stood in a line, bound hand and foot to discourage escape attempts. Ulf and Gwen were dirty and ragged, Offa was upright and well-dressed. Gwen's rusty iron helmet stood on a low table in front of Ragna's seat, next to the holy relics on which witnesses had to swear.

Sheriff Den was the accuser, and his oath-helpers included Captain Wigbert, Edgar the builder, and Dreng the ferryman.

Both Gwen and Ulf admitted their guilt and said that Offa had bought some of the loot from them and had sold it in Combe.

Offa denied everything, but his only oath-helper was Agnes. Nevertheless a small part of Ragna's mind hoped he would come up with a defence that would permit her to find him innocent, or at least give him a reduced sentence.

Sheriff Den told the story of the arrest, then recited the list of people who had been robbed – and in a few cases killed – by the person who had worn the helmet. The notables attending the court, mostly senior clergy and those thanes who were too old or infirm to fight, muttered their anger at the people who had terrorized the road to Combe, used by most of them.

Offa defended himself spiritedly. He said that Gwen and Ulf were lying. He swore that the stolen goods found in his house had been bought in good faith at jewellery shops. When he had tried to run away from Sheriff Den he had simply been in a panic, he claimed. He said that when his wife had named Ulf she was just picking someone at random.

No one believed a word of it.

Ragna said the consensus was that all three accused were guilty, and there was no disagreement.

At that moment, Agnes threw herself on the wet ground in front of Ragna, sobbing, and said: 'Oh, but my lady, he's a good man, and I love him!'

Ragna felt as if there was a knife in her heart, but she kept her voice level. 'Every man who ever robbed or raped or murdered had a mother, and many had wives who loved them and children who needed them. But they killed other women's husbands, and sold other men's children into slavery, and took other people's life savings to spend in alehouses and brothels. They must be punished.'

'But I've been your maid for ten years! You have to help me! You have to pardon Offa, or he will be hanged!'

'I serve justice,' Ragna said. 'Think of all the people who have been wounded and robbed by Ironface! How would they feel if I set him free because he's married to my seamstress?'

Agnes screeched: 'But you're my friend!'

Ragna longed to say *Oh, very well, perhaps Offa meant no harm, I will not condemn him to death.* But she could not. 'I'm your mistress, and I'm the ealdorman's wife. I will not twist justice for you.'

'Please, madam, I beg you!'

'The answer is no, Agnes, and that is the end of the matter. Someone take her away.'

'How could you do this to me?' As the sheriff's men took hold of Agnes her face twisted in hatred. 'You're killing my husband, you murderer!' Drool came from her mouth. 'You witch, you devil!' She spat, and the saliva landed on the skirt of Ragna's green dress. 'I hope your husband dies too!' she screamed, and then they dragged her away.

ÞÞÞ

WYNSTAN WATCHED THE altercation between Ragna and Agnes with great interest. Agnes was in a poisonous rage, and Ragna felt guilty. Wynstan could use that, although he did not immediately see how.

The guilty were hanged at dawn the next day. Later Wynstan gave a modest banquet for the notables who had attended the court. March was not a good month for a feast, because the year's lambs and calves had not yet been born; so the table in the bishop's residence was laid with smoked fish and salt meat, plus several dishes of beans flavoured with nuts and dried fruit. Wynstan made up for the poor food by serving plenty of wine.

He listened more than he talked during the meal. He liked to know who was prospering or running out of money, which noblemen bore grudges against others, and what the ugly rumours were, whether true or false. He was also mulling over the Agnes question. He made only one significant contribution to the conversation, and that had to do with Prior Aldred.

The frail Thane Cenbryht of Trench, too old for battle, mentioned that Aldred had visited him and asked for a donation to the priory at Dreng's Ferry, either money or – preferably – a grant of land.

Wynstan knew about Prior Aldred's fund-raising. Unfortunately he had enjoyed some successes, albeit small: the priory was now landlord of five hamlets in addition to Dreng's Ferry. However, Wynstan was doing all he could to discourage donors. 'I hope you weren't over-generous,' he said.

'I'm too poor to be generous,' said the thane. 'But what makes you say that?'

'Well . . .' Wynstan never missed an opportunity to belittle Aldred. 'I hear unpleasant stories,' he said, feigning reluctance. 'Perhaps I shouldn't say too much, as it may be no more than gossip, but there's talk of orgies with slaves.' This was not even gossip: Wynstan was making it up.

'Oh, dear,' said the thane. 'I only gave him a horse, but now I wish I hadn't.'

Wynstan pretended to backtrack. 'Well, the reports may not be true – although Aldred has misbehaved before, when he was a novice at Glastonbury. Right or wrong, I would have clamped down right away, if only to dispel rumours, but I'm no longer in authority at Dreng's Ferry.'

Archdeacon Degbert, at the other end of the table, said: 'More's the pity.'

Thane Deglaf of Wigleigh started talking about the news from Exeter, and no more was said about Aldred; but Wynstan was satisfied. He had planted a doubt, not for the first time. Aldred's ability to raise funds was severely limited by the perpetual undercurrent of nasty tales. The monastery at Dreng's Ferry must always be a backwater, with Aldred doomed to spend the rest of his life there.

When the guests left, Wynstan retired to his private room with Degbert and they discussed how the court had gone. Ragna had dispensed justice rapidly and fairly, it could not be denied. She had a good instinct for guilt and innocence. She had shown much mercy to the unfortunate and none to the wicked. Naively, she made no attempt to use the law to further her own interests by winning friends and punishing enemies.

In fact, she had made an enemy of Agnes – a foolish mistake, in Wynstan's view, but one that he might be able to exploit.

'Where do you think Agnes could be found at this hour?' he asked Degbert.

Degbert rubbed his bald pate with the palm of his hand. 'She's in mourning, and will not leave her house without a pressing reason.'

'I might pay her a visit.' Wynstan stood up.

'Shall I come with you?'

'I don't think so. This will be an intimate little chat: just the grieving widow and her bishop, come to give her spiritual consolation.'

Degbert told Wynstan where Agnes lived, and Wynstan put on his cloak and went out.

He found Agnes at her table, sitting over a bowl of stew that appeared to have gone cold without being touched. She was startled to see him and jumped to her feet. 'My lord bishop!'

'Sit down, sit down, Agnes,' Wynstan said in a low, quiet voice. He studied her with interest, never having taken much notice of her before. She had bright blue eyes and a sharp nose. Her face had a shrewd look that Wynstan found attractive. He said: 'I come to offer you God's solace in your time of grief.'

'Solace?' she said. 'I don't want solace – I want my husband.'

She was angry, and Wynstan began to see how he could make use of that. 'I can't bring back your Offa, but I might be able to give you something else,' he said.

'What?'

'Revenge.'

'God offers me that?' she said sceptically. She was quick-witted, he realized. That made her all the more useful.

'God's ways are mysterious.' Wynstan sat down and patted the bench beside him.

Agnes sat. 'Revenge on the sheriff, who prosecuted Offa? Or Ragna, who condemned him to death? Or Wigbert, who hanged him?'

'Whom do you hate most?'

'Ragna. I'd like to claw her eyes out.'

'Try to stay calm.'

'I'm going to kill her.'

'No, you're not.' A plan had been forming gradually in Wynstan's mind, and now he saw it entire. But would it work? He said: 'You're going to do something much smarter,' he said. 'You're going to take revenge on her in ways that she will never know about.'

'Tell me, tell me,' said Agnes breathlessly. 'If it hurts her, I'll do it.'

'You're going to go back to her house and return to your old position of seamstress there.'

'No!' Agnes protested. 'Never!'

'Oh, yes. You're going to be my spy in Ragna's house. You'll tell me everything that goes on there, including those things that are meant to be kept secret – especially those things.'

'She'll never take me back. She'll suspect my motives.'

That was what Wynstan feared. Ragna was no fool. But her

instinct was to look for the best in people, not the worst. Besides, she was terribly sorry about what had happened to Agnes – he had seen that at the trial. 'I think Ragna feels horribly guilty about sentencing your husband to death. She's desperate to make up for that somehow.'

'Is she?'

'She may hesitate, but she'll do it.' Even as he said it he wondered if it was true. 'And then you will betray her, just as she betrayed you. You will ruin her life. And she will never know.'

Agnes's face shone. She looked like a woman in the ecstasy of sexual intercourse. 'Yes!' she said. 'Yes, I'll do it!'

'Good girl,' said Wynstan.

ÞÞÞ

RAGNA LOOKED AT Agnes, feeling an agony of conscience and regret.

Yet it was Agnes who apologized. 'I have done you a terrible wrong, my lady,' she said.

Ragna was sitting on a four-legged stool by the fire. She felt that it was she who had done Agnes a wrong. She had killed the woman's husband. It had been the right decision, but it felt dreadfully cruel.

She hesitated to show her feelings. She let Agnes remain standing. She thought: What should I do?

Agnes said: 'You might have had me flogged for the things I said to you, but you did nothing, which was more kindness than I deserved.'

Ragna waved a dismissive hand. Insults uttered in anger were the least of her concerns.

Cat, who was listening, took a different view. She said severely: 'It was a lot more kindness than you deserved, Agnes.'

Ragna said: 'That's enough, Cat. I can speak for myself.'

'I beg your pardon, my lady.'

Agnes said: 'I have come to ask your forgiveness, my lady, even though I know I don't merit it.'

Ragna felt that they both needed forgiveness.

Agnes said: 'I have lain awake nights thinking and I can see, now, that you did the right thing, the only thing you could. I'm so sorry.'

Ragna did not like apologies. When there was a rift between people it could not be mended by the utterance of a form of words. But she wanted to heal this rift.

Agnes went on: 'I couldn't think straight at the time, I was too distraught.'

Ragna thought: I, too, might curse someone who let my husband be executed, even if he deserved his punishment.

Ragna wondered what to say. Could she reconcile with Agnes? Wilf would have scoffed at the idea, but he was a man.

From a practical point of view she would like to have Agnes back. It was difficult for Cat to manage Ragna's three sons plus her own two daughters, all under the age of two. Since Agnes had left Ragna had been looking for a replacement, but she had not found the right sort of woman. If Agnes were to come back, that problem would be solved. And the children liked her.

Could she trust Agnes, after what had happened?

'You don't know what it's like, my lady, to find that you have chosen the wrong husband.'

Ah, but I do, Ragna thought; then she realized this was the first time she had admitted that to herself.

She felt a surge of compassion. Whatever sins Agnes had committed had been done under the strong influence of Offa. She had married a dishonest man, but that did not make her a dishonest woman.

'It would mean so much to me if you would just say a kind word before I go,' Agnes said, and she did seem pathetic. 'Just say, "God bless you", please, my lady.'

Ragna could not refuse her. 'God bless you, Agnes.'

'May I just kiss the twins? I do miss them so.'

She did not have children of her own, Ragna reflected. 'All right.'

Agnes expertly picked up both babies at the same time, holding one in each arm. 'I do love you both,' she said.

Colinan, the younger twin by a few minutes, was the more advanced. He met Agnes's eye, gurgled, and smiled.

Ragna sighed and said: 'Agnes, do you want to come back?'

27

Prior Aldred had high hopes of Thane Deorman of Norwood. Deorman was rich. Norwood was a market town, and a market was always a big earner. And Deorman's wife of many years had died a month ago. That would have put the thane in mind of the afterlife. The death of someone close often prompted a nobleman to make a pious donation.

Aldred needed donations. The priory was not as poor as it had been three years ago – it had three horses, a flock of sheep and a small herd of milk cows – but Aldred had ambitions. He accepted that he would never take charge of Shiring Abbey, but he now believed he might turn the priory into a centre of learning. For that he needed more than a few hamlets. He had to win something big, a prosperous village or a small town, or some moneymaking enterprise such as a port or the fishing rights to a river.

Thane Deorman's great hall was richly furnished with wall hangings and blankets and cushions. His servants were preparing the table for a lavish midday meal, and there was a powerful aroma of roasting meat. Deorman was a middle-aged man with failing eyesight, unable to join Wilwulf in fighting the Vikings. Nevertheless, with him he had two women in brightly coloured dresses who seemed too fond of him to be merely servants, and Aldred wondered disapprovingly what their exact status was. At least six small children ran in and out of the house, playing some game that involved much high-pitched squealing.

Deorman ignored the children and did not respond to the women's touches and smiles, but gave his affection to a large black dog that sat beside him.

Aldred got right to the point. 'I was sorry to hear of the death of your dear wife, Godgifu. May her soul rest in peace.'

'Thank you,' said Deorman. 'I have two other women, but Godgifu was with me for thirty years, and I miss her.'

Aldred did not comment on Deorman's polygamy. That might be a discussion for another time. Today he had to focus on his target. He spoke in a deeper, more emotional tone. 'The monks of Dreng's Ferry would be glad to give solemn daily prayers for the dear lady's immortal soul, if you should wish to commission us.'

'I have a cathedral full of priests praying for her right here in Norwood.'

'Then you are truly blessed, or rather she is. But I'm sure you know that the prayers of celibate monks carry more weight, in that other world that awaits us all, than those of married priests.'

'So people say,' Deorman conceded.

Aldred changed his tone and became more brisk. 'As well as Norwood, you're lord of the little hamlet of Southwood, which has an iron mine.' He paused. It was time to make his request specific. With a quick silent prayer of hope he said: 'Would you consider making a pious gift of Southwood and its mine to the priory, in memory of Lady Godgifu?'

He held his breath. Would Deorman pour scorn on such a demand? Would he burst out laughing at Aldred's effrontery? Would he be offended?

Deorman's response was mild. He looked startled, but also amused. 'That's a bold request,' he said non-committally.

'*Ask, and it shall be given you,* Jesus told us; *seek, and ye shall find; knock, and it shall be opened unto you.*' Aldred often remembered this verse from Matthew's gospel when he was soliciting gifts.

'You certainly don't get much in this world if you don't ask,' Deorman said. 'But that mine makes me a lot of money.'

'It would transform the fortunes of the priory.'

'I don't doubt it.'

Deorman had not said no, but there was a negative undertone, and Aldred waited to find out what the problem was.

'How many monks are there at your priory?' Deorman asked after a moment.

He was playing for time, Aldred thought. 'Eight, including me.'

'And are they all good men?'

'Most certainly.'

'Because, you see, there are rumours.'

Here it comes, Aldred thought. He felt a bubble of anger in his guts, and told himself to stay calm. 'Rumours,' he repeated.

'To be frank, I've heard that your monks hold orgies with slaves.'

'And I know who you heard it from,' said Aldred. He could not completely hide his rage, but he managed to speak quietly. 'Some years ago I had the misfortune to discover a powerful man committing a terrible crime, and I'm still being punished for doing so.'

'*You're* being punished?'

'Yes, by this kind of slander.'

'You're telling me the orgy story is a deliberate lie?'

'I'm telling you that the monks of Dreng's Ferry follow the Rule of St Benedict strictly. We have no slaves, no concubines, no catamites. We are celibate.'

'Hmm.'

'But please don't take my word for it. Pay us a visit – preferably with no forewarning. Surprise us, and you will see us as we are every day. We work, we pray, and we sleep. We will invite you to share our dinner of fish and vegetables. You will see that we have no servants, no pets, no luxuries of any kind. Our prayers could not be more pure.'

'Well, we'll see.' Deorman was backing down, but was he convinced? 'Meanwhile, let's eat.'

Aldred sat at the table with Deorman's family and senior servants. A pretty young woman sat next to him and engaged him in a teasing conversation. Aldred was polite, but flintily unresponsive to her flirting. He guessed he was being tested. It was the wrong test: he might have revealed a weakness if confronted with an alluring young man.

The food was good, suckling pig with spring cabbage, and the wine was strong. Aldred ate sparingly and drank one sip, as always.

At the end of the meal, as the bowls and platters were being cleared away, Deorman announced his decision. 'I'm not going to give you Southwood,' he said. 'But I'll give you two pounds in silver to pray for the soul of Godgifu.'

Aldred knew he should not show his disappointment. 'Your kindness is much appreciated, and you can be sure that God will hear our prayers,' he said. 'But could you not make it five pounds?'

Deorman laughed. 'I'll make it three, to reward your persistence, on condition you ask for no more.'

'I'm most grateful,' Aldred said, but in his heart he was angry and resentful. He should have got much more, but Wynstan's slanders had sabotaged him. Even if Deorman did not really believe the lies, they gave him an excuse to be less generous.

Deorman's treasurer got the money from a chest and Aldred stashed it in his saddlebag. 'I won't travel alone with this money,' he said. 'I'll go to the Oak alehouse and find companions for tomorrow's journey.'

He took his leave. The town centre was only a few steps from Deorman's compound, so Aldred did not mount Dismas, but walked him to the stable of the tavern, brooding over his failure. He had hoped that Wynstan's malign influence would not reach this far, for Norwood had its own cathedral and bishop, but he had been disappointed.

When he reached the Oak he walked past the alehouse, from which came the sound of a boisterous group enjoying the drink, and went straight to the stable. As he arrived he was surprised to see the familiar lean frame of Brother Godleof unsaddling a piebald. He looked anxious, and seemed to have hurried here. 'What is it?' Aldred said.

'I thought you'd want to hear the news as soon as possible.'

'What news?'

'Abbot Osmund is dead.'

Aldred crossed himself and said: 'May his soul rest in peace.'

'Hildred has been made abbot.'

'That was quick.'

'Bishop Wynstan insisted on an immediate election, which he oversaw.'

Wynstan had made sure that his preferred candidate won, and had then ratified the monks' decision. In theory, both the archbishop and the king had a say in the appointment, but it would be difficult now for them to overturn Wynstan's fait accompli.

Aldred said: 'How do you know all this?'

'Archdeacon Degbert brought the news to the priory. I think he was hoping to tell you himself. Especially the part about the money.'

Aldred had a bad feeling. 'Go on.'

'Hildred has cancelled the abbey's subsidy to our priory. From now on we must manage on whatever sums we can raise for ourselves – or close down.'

That was a blow. Aldred was suddenly grateful for Deorman's three pounds. It meant the priory was not in danger of immediate closure.

He said to Godleof: 'Get yourself something to eat. We should leave as soon as possible.'

They sat on the ground beside the oak tree that gave the house its name. While Godleof ate bread and cheese and drank a pot of ale, Aldred brooded. There were advantages to the new arrangement, he told himself. The priory would now be independent, in practice: the abbot could no longer control it by threatening to cut off funds – that was an arrow that could be shot only once. Aldred would now ask the archbishop of Canterbury for a charter that would make the priory's independence official.

However, Deorman's gift would not last for ever, and Aldred's search for some means of financial security was now urgent. What could he do?

Most monasteries depended on the accumulation of wealth from numerous donations. Some had large flocks of sheep, some drew rents from villages and towns, some owned fisheries and quarries. For three years Aldred had worked tirelessly to attract such gifts, and his success had been no more than modest.

His mind strayed to Winchester and St Swithun, who had been bishop there in the ninth century. Swithun had worked a miracle on the bridge over the Itchen river. Taking pity on a poor woman who had dropped her basket of eggs, he had made the smashed eggs whole again. His tomb in the cathedral was a popular destination for pilgrims. Sick people experienced miraculous cures there. The pilgrims donated money to the cathedral. They also bought souvenirs, lodged in alehouses owned by the monks, and generally brought prosperity to the town. The monks spent the profits enlarging the church so that it could accommodate more pilgrims, who brought more money.

Many churches possessed holy relics: the whited bones of a saint, a splintered piece of the True Cross, a worn square of ancient cloth miraculously imprinted with the face of Christ. Provided the monks managed their affairs shrewdly – making sure pilgrims were welcomed, placing the sacred objects in an impressive shrine, publicizing miracles – the relics would attract pilgrims who would bring prosperity to the town and to the monastery.

Unfortunately, Dreng's Ferry had no relics.

Such things could be bought, but Aldred did not have enough money. Would anyone give him something so valuable? He thought of Glastonbury Abbey.

He had been a novice at Glastonbury, and knew that the abbey had such a large collection of relics that the sacrist, Brother Theodric, did not know what to do with them all.

He began to feel excited.

The abbey had the grave of St Patrick, patron saint of Ireland, and twenty-two complete skeletons of other saints. The abbot would not give Aldred a priceless complete skeleton, but the abbey also owned numerous odd bones and scraps of clothing, one of the bloodstained arrows that had killed St Sebastian, and a sealed jug of wine from the wedding at Cana. Would Aldred's old friends take pity on him? He had left Glastonbury in disgrace, of course, but that had been a long time ago. Monks generally sided with monks against bishops, and no one liked Wynstan: there was a chance, Aldred decided with mounting optimism.

Anyway, he had no better ideas.

Godleof finished his meal and took his wooden tankard back into the alehouse. Coming out, he said: 'So, are we heading back to Dreng's Ferry?'

'Change of plan,' said Aldred. 'I'll accompany you part of the way – then I'm going to Glastonbury.'

Þ Þ Þ

HE WAS NOT prepared for the intense wave of nostalgia that overwhelmed him when he came in sight of the place where he had spent his adolescence.

He crested a low hill and looked down on a flat, swampy plain, green with spring foliage interlaced with pools and runnels that glinted in the sun. To the north a canal five yards wide came arrow-straight along the gently sloping hillside and ended in a wharf at a marketplace bright with bales of red cloth and truckles of yellow cheese and stacks of green cabbages.

Edgar had questioned Aldred closely about this canal, severely taxing Aldred's memory, before beginning construction of the canal at Outhenham.

Beyond the village stood two buildings of pale grey stone, a church and a monastery. A dozen or more timber structures were clustered around: animal shelters, storehouses, kitchens and servants' quarters. Aldred could even see the herb garden where he had been caught kissing Leofric, bringing down on himself a cloud of shame that had never lifted.

As he rode closer he remembered Leofric, whom he had not seen for twenty years. He pictured a boy, tall and skinny, pink-faced with a few blond hairs on his upper lip, full of adolescent energy. But Leo must have changed. Aldred himself was different: slower and more dignified in his movements, solemn in his demeanour, with the dark shadow of a beard even when he had just shaved.

Sadness possessed him. He mourned the passing of the tireless lad he had once been, reading and learning and absorbing knowledge as the parchment soaked up the ink, and then, when lessons were over, deploying just as much energy in breaking all the rules. Coming to Glastonbury was like visiting the grave of his youth.

He tried to shake off the feeling as he rode through the village, which was noisy with buying and selling, carpentry and ironwork, men shouting and women laughing. He made his way to the monastery stable, which smelled of clean straw and brushed horses. He unsaddled Dismas and let the tired beast drink its fill from the horse trough.

Would his history here help or hinder his mission? Would people remember him with affection, and do their best to help him, or would they treat him as a renegade who had been expelled for bad behaviour and whose return was unwelcome?

He knew none of the stable hands, who were not monks but

employees, but he asked one of the older men if Elfweard was still abbot. 'Yes, and in good health, praise God,' said the groom.

'And is Theodric the sacrist?'

'Yes, though getting older, now.'

Pretending to ask casually, Aldred added: 'And Brother Leofric?'

'The kitchener? Yes, he's well.'

The kitchener was an important monastery officer, responsible for purchasing all supplies.

One of the lads said: 'Well fed, anyhow,' and the others laughed.

From that Aldred deduced that Leo had put on weight.

The older groom, clearly curious, said: 'May I direct you to a part of the abbey, or any particular one of the monks?'

'I should pay my respects to Abbot Elfweard first. I assume I'll find him at his own house?'

'More than likely. The monks' midday dinner is over, and it'll be another hour or two before they ring the Nones bell.' Nones was the mid-afternoon service.

'Thank you.' Aldred left without satisfying the groom's curiosity.

He headed not for the abbot's house but for the cookhouse.

In a monastery this big, the kitchener did not carry sacks of flour and sides of beef to the cooking fires, but held a pen and sat at a table. All the same a wise kitchener would work near the cooks, to keep an eye on what came in and went out, and make it difficult for anyone to steal.

From the kitchen came the sound of clashing pots as the monastery servants scrubbed the utensils.

Aldred recalled that in his day the kitchener had worked in a lean-to shed attached to the cookhouse but now, he saw, there was a more substantial building in the same place, with a stone-built extension that was undoubtedly a safe room for storage.

He approached apprehensively, full of trepidation about how Leo would receive him.

He stood in the doorway. Leo sat on a bench at a table, side-on to the entrance so that the light could fall on his work. He had a stylus in his hand and was making notes on a wax tablet in front of him. He did not look up, and Aldred had a few moments to study him. He was not really fat, though he certainly was not the bony boy Aldred remembered. The circle of hair around his tonsure was still fair, and his face was, if anything, pinker. Aldred's heart missed a beat as he remembered how passionately he had loved this man. And now, twenty years later?

Before Aldred could examine his heart, Leo looked up.

At first he did not recognize Aldred. A busy man dealing courteously with an unwelcome interruption, he gave a perfunctory smile and said: 'How can I help you?'

'By remembering me, you idiot,' Aldred said, and he stepped inside.

Leo stood up, mouth open in surprise, doubt creasing his forehead. 'Are you Aldred?'

'The same,' Aldred said, walking towards him with open arms.

Leo raised his hands in a protective gesture, and Aldred understood at once that Leo did not want to be embraced. That was probably wise: people who knew their history might suspect that they were resuming their old relationship. Aldred stopped immediately and took a step back, but he continued to smile, and said: 'It's so good to see you.'

Leo relaxed a little. 'You, too,' he said.

'We could shake hands.'

'Yes, we could.'

They shook across the table. Aldred held Leo's hand in both of his, just for a moment, then let go. He had great affection for Leo but, he now realized, he had lost all desire for physical intimacy with him. He experienced the same surge of fondness that he sometimes felt for old Tatwine the scribe, or poor blind Cuthbert, or Mother Agatha, but none of that formerly irresistible yearning to touch body to body, skin to skin.

'Draw up a stool,' said Leo. 'Can I give you a cup of wine?'

'I'd prefer a tankard of ale,' said Aldred. 'The weaker, the better.'

Leo went into his storeroom and returned with a large wooden mug of a dark brew.

Aldred drank thirstily. 'It's been a long and dusty road.'

'And dangerous, if you encounter the Vikings.'

'I took a northerly route. The fighting is in the south, I believe.'

'What brings you here after all these years?'

Aldred told him the story. Leo already knew about the forgery – everybody knew about it – but he was not fully aware of Wynstan's campaign of revenge against Aldred. As Aldred talked, Leo relaxed, no doubt feeling reassured that Aldred had no wish to resume their affair.

'We certainly have more old bones than we need,' Leo said when Aldred finished. 'Whether Theodric will be willing to part with any of them is another question.'

Leo was now almost completely amiable – but not quite. He was holding something back, perhaps guarding a secret. So be it, thought Aldred; I don't need to know everything about his life now, as long as he's on my side.

Aldred said: 'Theodric was a grumpy old stick-in-the-mud while I was here. He seemed to resent young people particularly.'

'And he's got worse. But let's go and see him now, before Nones. He'll be in a relatively good mood after his dinner.'

Aldred was pleased: Leo had become an ally.

Leo stood up but, as he did so, another monk appeared, entering and speaking at the same time. He was about ten years younger than Aldred and Leo, and handsome, with dark eyebrows and full lips. 'They're charging us for four wheels of cheese, but they've only sent three,' said the newcomer, then he saw Aldred. 'Oh!' he said, and his eyebrows went up. 'Who's this?' He walked around the table and stood beside Leo.

Leo said: 'This is my assistant, Pendred.'

Aldred said: 'I'm Aldred, prior of Dreng's Ferry.'

Leo explained: 'Aldred and I were novices together here.'

Aldred knew immediately, just by the way Pendred stood close to Leo, and by the hint of nervousness in Leo's voice, that they were intimate friends – how intimate, he could not tell and did not want to know.

No doubt this was the secret Leo had been hoping to hide.

Aldred felt that Pendred might be dangerous. He could become jealous and try to discourage Leo from helping. Aldred needed urgently to show that he was no threat. He gave a frank look and said: 'I'm glad to meet you, Pendred.' He spoke in a serious voice so that Pendred would know this was not mere courtesy.

Leo said: 'Aldred and I used to be great friends.'

Aldred immediately said: 'But that was a long time ago.'

Pendred nodded slowly, three times, then said: 'I'm pleased to meet you, Brother Aldred.'

He had got the message, and Aldred felt relieved.

Leo said: 'I'm going to take Aldred to see Theodric. Give the dairy the price of three cheeses and say we'll pay for the fourth when we get it.' He led Aldred out.

One ally confirmed, Aldred thought, and a potential opponent neutralized: so far, so good.

As they crossed the grounds Aldred caught sight of the canal and said: 'Does the channel run through clay all the way?'

'Almost,' said Leo. 'Just at this end the ground is a bit sandy. It has to be lined with puddled clay, and the banks are braced – the technical term is "revetted" – with planks. I know that because I ordered the timber last time it was renewed. Why do you ask?'

'A builder called Edgar has been interrogating me about the Glastonbury canal, because he's digging one at Outhenham. He's a brilliant young man, but he's never attempted a canal.'

They went into the abbey church. Some younger monks were singing, perhaps learning a new hymn or practising an old one. Leo led the way to the east side of the south transept, where a heavy ironbound door with two locks stood open. This was the treasury, Aldred remembered. They stepped into a windowless room, dark and cold and smelling of dust and age. As Aldred's eyes adapted to the dim illumination of a rush light, he saw that the walls were lined with shelves bearing a variety of gold, silver and wooden containers.

At the back of the room – the east end, therefore the most holy zone – a monk knelt before a small, simple altar. On the altar stood an elaborate box of silver and carved ivory, undoubtedly a reliquary, a container for relics.

In a low voice, Leo explained: 'The feast day of St Savann is next week. The bones will be carried into the church in procession for the celebration. I expect Theodric is asking the saint's pardon for disturbing him.'

Aldred nodded. Saints did in some sense live on in their remains, and were very present in whatever holy institution guarded their bones. They were pleased to be remembered and venerated, but they had to be treated with great respect and caution. Elaborate ritual surrounded any movement to which they were subjected. 'You don't want to displease him,' Aldred murmured.

Despite their whispers, Theodric heard them. He stood up with some difficulty, turned around, peered at them, then approached on unsteady legs. He was about seventy years old, Aldred reckoned, and the skin of his face was loose and wrinkled. He was naturally bald, and would not need to shave his tonsure.

Leo said: 'We're sorry to disturb your prayers, Brother Theodric.'

'Don't worry about me, just hope you haven't upset the saint,' Theodric said sharply. 'Now come outside before you say any more.'

Aldred stayed where he was and pointed to a small chest made of yellowish-red yew wood, normally used for longbows. He thought he had seen it before. 'What's in there?'

'Some bones of St Adolphus of Winchester. Just the skull, an arm and a hand.'

'I think I remember. Was he killed by a Saxon king?'

'For possessing a Christian book, yes. Now, please, outside.'

They stepped into the transept, and Theodric closed the door behind them.

Leo said: 'Brother Theodric, I don't know if you remember Brother Aldred.'

'I never forget anything.'

Aldred pretended to believe him. 'I'm glad to see you again,' he said.

'Oh, it's you!' said Theodric, recognizing the voice. 'Aldred, yes. You were a troublemaker.'

'And now I'm prior of Dreng's Ferry – where I deal severely with troublemakers.'

'So why aren't you there now?'

Aldred smiled. Leo was right, age had not blunted Theodric's edge. 'I need your help,' Aldred said.

'What do you want?'

Aldred again told the story of Wynstan and Dreng's Ferry, and explained his need for some means of attracting pilgrims.

Theodric pretended to be indignant. 'You want me to give you precious relics?'

'My priory has no saint to watch over it. Glastonbury has more than twenty. I ask you to take pity on your poorer brethren.'

'I've been to Dreng's Ferry,' Theodric said. 'That church was falling down five years ago.'

'I've had the west end buttressed. It's stable now.'

'How could you afford that? You said you were penniless.' Theodric looked triumphant, thinking he had caught Aldred in a lie.

'The Lady Ragna gave me the stone free, and a young builder called Edgar did the work in exchange for being taught to read and write. So I got the work done for no money.'

Theodric changed tack. 'That church is a poor showcase for a saint's remains.'

It was true. Aldred improvised. 'If you give me what I want, Brother Theodric, I will build an extension to the church, with the help once again of Ragna and Edgar.'

'Makes no difference,' Theodric said firmly. 'The abbot would never allow me to give away relics even if I wanted to.'

Leo said: 'Perhaps you're right, Theodric – but let's ask the abbot himself, shall we?'

Theodric shrugged. 'If you insist.'

They left the church and headed for the abbot's house. One ally and one enemy, Aldred thought. Now it's up to Abbot Elfweard.

As they walked, Leo said: 'What's Edgar like, Aldred?'

'A wonderful friend to the priory. Why do you ask?'

'You've mentioned his name three times.'

Aldred gave Leo a sharp look. 'I'm fond of him, as you've cleverly guessed. He in turn is devoted to the Lady Ragna.' Aldred was telling Leo, without saying it explicitly, that Edgar was not his lover.

Leo got the message. 'All right, I understand.'

Abbot Elfweard lived in a great hall. It had two doors in its side, suggesting two separate rooms, and Aldred guessed the abbot slept in one and held meetings in the other. It was a luxury to sleep alone, but the abbot of Glastonbury was a great magnate.

Leo led them into what was clearly the meeting room. Because there was no fire here, the air was pleasantly fresh. On one wall hung a large tapestry of the Annunciation, with the Virgin Mary in a blue dress edged with costly gold thread. A young man who was apparently the abbot's assistant said: 'I'll tell him you're here.' A minute later Elfweard entered the room.

He had been abbot for a quarter of a century, and he was now an old man, walking with a cane held in a shaky hand. His expression was stern, but his eyes were bright with intelligence.

Leo introduced Aldred. 'I remember you,' said Elfweard severely. 'You were guilty of the sin of Sodom. I had to send you away, to separate you from your partner in iniquity.'

That was a bad start. Aldred said: 'You told me that life is hard, and being a good monk makes it harder.'

'I'm glad you remember.'

'I've spent twenty years remembering, my lord abbot.'

'You've done well since you left us,' Elfweard said, softening. 'I'll give you credit for that.'

'Thank you.'

'Not that you've kept out of trouble.'

'But it was good trouble.'

'Perhaps.' Elfweard did not smile. 'What brings you here today?'

Aldred told his story for the third time.

When he had finished, Elfweard turned to Theodric. 'What does our sacrist say?'

Theodric said: 'I can't imagine that a saint would thank us for sending his remains to a tiny priory in the back of beyond.'

Leofric weighed in on Aldred's side. 'On the other hand, a saint who receives little attention here might be glad to work miracles somewhere else.'

Aldred watched Elfweard, but the abbot's face was unreadable.

Aldred said: 'I recollect, from my time here, that many treasures were never brought into the main body of the church, never shown to the monks, let alone the congregation.'

Theodric said disparagingly: 'A few bones, some bloodstained clothing, a lock of hair. Precious, yes, but unimpressive when compared to a complete skeleton.'

Theodric's scornful tone was a mistake. 'Exactly!' said Aldred, seizing the advantage. 'Unimpressive here at Glastonbury, as Brother Theodric says – but at Dreng's Ferry such things would work miracles!'

Elfweard looked inquiringly at Theodric.

Theodric said: 'I didn't say "unimpressive", I feel sure.'

'Yes, you did,' said the abbot.

Theodric began to look defeated. He backtracked. 'Then I should not have said that, and I withdraw it.'

Aldred sensed that he was close to success, and he pushed his advantage, at the risk of appearing grasping. 'The abbey has a few bones of St Adolphus – the skull and an arm.'

'Adolphus?' said Elfweard. 'Martyred for possessing the gospel of St Matthew, if I remember rightly.'

'Yes,' said Aldred, delighted. 'He was killed over a book. That's why I remembered him.'

'He should be the patron saint of librarians.'

Aldred felt he was an inch away from triumph. He said: 'It's my dearest wish to create a great library at Dreng's Ferry.'

'A creditworthy ambition,' Elfweard said. 'Well, Theodric, the remains of St Adolphus certainly do not constitute the greatest treasure of Glastonbury.'

Aldred remained silent, afraid of breaking the spell.

Theodric said sulkily: 'I don't suppose anyone will even notice their absence.'

Aldred fought to conceal his glee.

Elfweard's assistant reappeared carrying a cope, a wide-shouldered liturgical cloak made of white wool embroidered with biblical scenes in red. 'It's time for Nones,' he said.

Elfweard stood up and the assistant placed the cope over his shoulders and fastened it at the front. Dressed for the service, Elfweard turned to Aldred. 'You realize, I'm sure, that the nature of the relic doesn't matter as much as the use you make of it. You must create the circumstances in which miracles are likely.'

'I promise you, I will make the most of the bones of St Adolphus.'

'And you'll have to transport them to Dreng's Ferry with all due ceremony. You don't want the saint to take against you from the start.'

'Never fear,' said Aldred. 'I have great things planned.'

ÞÞÞ

Bishop Wynstan stood at an upstairs window in his palace at Shiring, looking across the busy market square to the silent monastery on the opposite side. There was no glass in the window – glass was a luxury for kings – and the shutter had been thrown open to let in a fresh spring breeze.

A four-wheeled cart pulled by an ox was approaching along the Dreng's Ferry road. It was escorted by a small group of monks led by Prior Aldred.

It was astounding that the penniless prior of a remote monastery could be so irritating. The man just did not know when he was defeated. Wynstan turned to Archdeacon Degbert, who was there with his wife, Edith. Between them, Degbert and Edith picked up most of the town gossip. 'What the devil is that damned monk up to now?' he said.

Edith said: 'I'm going out to look.' She left the room.

'I can guess,' said Degbert. 'Two weeks ago he was at Glastonbury. The abbot gave him a partial skeleton of St Adolphus.'

'Adolphus?'

'He was martyred by a Saxon king.'

'Yes, I remember now.'

'Aldred is on his way to Glastonbury again, this time to perform the necessary rites for removal of the relics. But that's only a box of bones. I don't know why he needs a cart.'

Wynstan watched the cart pull up at the entrance to Shiring Abbey. A small crowd gathered, curious. He saw Edith join them. He said: 'How could Aldred even pay for a four-wheel cart and an ox?'

528

Degbert knew the answer to that. 'Thane Deorman of Norwood gave him three pounds.'

'More fool Deorman.'

The people crowded closely around. Aldred pulled away a covering of some kind, but Wynstan could not see what was on the cart. Then the covering was replaced, the cart entered the abbey, and the crowd dispersed.

Edith returned a minute later. 'It's a life-sized effigy of St Adolphus!' she said excitedly. 'He has a lovely face, holy and sad at the same time.'

Wynstan said contemptuously: 'An idol for the ignorant to worship. I suppose it's painted, too?'

'The face is white, and the hands and feet. The robe is grey. But the eyes are so blue you'd think they were looking at you!'

Blue was the most costly paint, being made with crushed gems of lapis lazuli. Wynstan said slowly: 'I know what that sly devil is up to.'

Degbert said: 'I wish you'd tell me.'

'He's going to take the relics on a tour. He'll stop at every church between Glastonbury and Dreng's Ferry. He needs money, now that Hildred has stopped his subsidy, and he wants to use the saint to raise funds.'

'It will probably work,' said Degbert.

'Not if I have anything to do with it,' said Wynstan.

28

ON THE OUTSKIRTS OF the village of Trench, the monks began to sing.

All eight from the Dreng's Ferry priory were present, including blind Cuthbert, plus Edgar to work the mechanism. They walked in solemn procession each side of the cart, with Godleof leading the ox by the ring in its nose.

The effigy of the saint and the yew chest containing the bones were on the cart, but covered by cloths that also prevented their shifting.

The villagers were working in the fields. They were busy, but it was the time for weeding, and that task was easy to abandon. As they heard the singing they unbent from the green shoots of barley and rye, stood upright rubbing their backs, saw the procession, and came across the fields to the road to find out what was going on.

Aldred had ordered the monks not to speak to anyone until afterwards. They continued to sing, solemn-faced, looking straight ahead. The villagers joined the procession, following the cart, talking amongst themselves in excited whispers.

Aldred had planned everything carefully, but this was the first time he had tried it out. He prayed for success.

The cart passed between houses, drawing out all those who were not working in the fields: old men and women, children too young to tell the difference between crops and weeds, a shepherd with a sickly lamb in his arms, a carpenter with a hammer and chisel, a

530

milkmaid carrying a butter churn that she continued to agitate as she fell in behind the cart. The dogs came too, excitedly sniffing the robes of the strangers.

They all arrived at the centre of the village. There was a pond, an unfenced communal pasture where a few goats grazed, an alehouse, and a small wooden church. A large house presumably belonged to old Thane Cenbryht, but he did not appear, and Aldred presumed he was away from home.

Godleof brought the cart around so that its rear end was in line with the church door, then released the ox and put it to graze in the pasture.

The relics and the effigy could now be smoothly lifted and carried into the church by the monks: they had practised this manoeuvre to be confident of doing it in a dignified manner.

That was Aldred's plan. But now he saw the village priest standing in front of the church door with his arms folded. He was young, and he looked scared but determined.

That was strange.

'Keep singing,' Aldred murmured to the others, then he approached the priest. 'Good day, Father.'

'Good day to you.'

'I'm Prior Aldred of Dreng's Ferry, and I bring the holy relics of St Adolphus.'

'I know,' said the priest.

Aldred frowned. How did he know? Aldred had told no one his plans. But he decided not to get into that discussion. 'The saint wishes to spend tonight in the church.'

The man looked troubled, but he said: 'Well, he can't.'

Aldred stared at him, astonished. 'You're willing to provoke the anger of the saint, with his sacred bones there in front of you?'

The priest swallowed hard. 'I have my orders.'

'You do God's will, of course.'

'God's will, as explained to me by my superiors.'

'Which superior told you to deny St Adolphus a temporary resting place in your church?'

'My bishop.'

'Wynstan.'

'Yes.'

Wynstan had ordered the priest to do this – and, worse, he had probably sent the same message to every church between Glastonbury and Dreng's Ferry. He must have moved quickly, to get word out so fast. And for what purpose? Merely to make it difficult for Aldred to raise money? Was there no limit to the bishop's malice?

Aldred turned his back on the priest. The poor man was more terrified of Wynstan than he was of St Adolphus, and Aldred did not blame him. But Aldred was not ready to give up. The villagers were waiting for a spectacle, and Aldred was going to give them one. If it could not be in the church, it would just have to be outside.

He spoke quietly to Edgar. 'The mechanism will work with the effigy on the cart, won't it?'

'Yes,' said Edgar. 'It will work anywhere.'

'Then get ready.'

Aldred moved in front of the cart, faced the villagers, looked around as they fell silent, and started to pray. He began in Latin. They did not understand the words but they were used to that; in fact, the Latin would convince doubters, if there were any, that this was a genuine church service.

Then he switched to English. 'O most omnipotent and eternal God, who reveals to us through the merits of St Adolphus your mercy and compassion, may your saint intercede for us.'

He said the Lord's Prayer, and the villagers joined in.

After the prayers, Aldred told the story of the saint's life and death. Only the bare facts were known, but Aldred embroidered freely. He portrayed the Saxon king as a raging egomaniac and Adolphus as amazingly sweet-tempered and pure-hearted, which could not have been far from the truth, he felt sure. He credited Adolphus with numerous invented miracles, believing that the saint must have performed them or similar wonders. The crowd was rapt.

Finally he addressed the saint personally, reminding people that Adolphus was actually present here in Trench village, moving among them, watching and listening. 'O holy Adolphus, if there is anyone here, in the Christian village of Trench, who is feeling grief today, we beg you to bring consolation.'

This was Edgar's cue. Aldred wanted to look back, but resisted the temptation, trusting Edgar to do what had been arranged.

Aldred made his voice boom out over the crowd. 'If there is anyone here who has lost something precious, we beg you, O holy saint, to restore it.'

Behind him he heard faint creaking which told him that Edgar, behind the cart, was pulling smoothly on a stout cord.

'If there is anyone here who has been robbed or cheated, bring justice.'

Suddenly there was a reaction. In the crowd, people began to point at the cart. Others stepped back, murmuring in surprise. Aldred knew why: the effigy, which had been lying on its back on the cart's flatbed, was beginning to rise up, emerging from its wraps.

'If anyone here is sick, bring healing.'

Everyone in front of Aldred was staring past him in shock. He knew what they were looking at. He had rehearsed this many times with Edgar. The feet of the effigy remained on the cart but the body tilted upwards. Edgar could be seen pulling on a cord, but the mechanism he was operating was not visible. To peasants who had never seen pulleys and levers, the statue seemed to be rising up of its own volition.

There was a collective gasp, and Aldred guessed the face had appeared.

'If anyone is tormented by demons, cast them out!'

Aldred had agreed with Edgar that the effigy's rise would begin slowly then speed up; and now, as it stood upright with a jerk, the eyes came into clear view. A woman screamed and two children ran away. Several dogs barked in fear. Half the people crossed themselves.

'If there is anyone here who has committed a sin, turn your gaze upon him, O holy saint, and give him the courage to confess!'

A young woman near the front fell to her knees and moaned, staring up at the blue-eyed statue. 'It was I who stole it,' she said. Tears streamed down her face. 'I stole Abbe's knife. I'm sorry, forgive me, I'm sorry.'

From the back of the crowd came the indignant voice of another woman. 'Frigyth! You!'

Aldred had not been expecting this. He had hoped for a miraculous cure. However, St Adolphus had given him something different, so he would improvise. 'The saint has touched your heart, sister,' he announced. 'Where is the stolen knife?'

'In my house.'

'Fetch it now, and bring it to me.'

Frigyth got to her feet.

'Quickly, run!'

She ran through the crowd and entered a nearby house.

Abbe said: 'I thought I'd lost it.'

Aldred prayed again. 'O holy saint, we thank you for touching the sinner's heart and making her confess!'

Frigyth reappeared with a shiny knife having an elaborately carved bone handle. She passed it to Aldred. He called Abbe, and she stepped forward. She wore a faintly sceptical look; she was older than Frigyth, and perhaps not so ready to believe in miracles.

Aldred said: 'Do you forgive your neighbour?'

'Yes,' said Abbe without enthusiasm.

'Then give her the kiss of mercy.'

Abbe kissed Frigyth's cheek.

Aldred handed Abbe the knife then said: 'All kneel!'

He began a prayer in Latin. This was the cue for the monks to go round with begging bowls. 'A gift for the saint, please,' they said quietly to the villagers, who could not easily move away because they were on their knees. A few shook their heads and said: 'No money, sorry.' Most fished in their belt purses and came up with farthings and halfpennies. Two men went to their houses and returned with silver. The alehouse keeper gave a penny.

The monks thanked each donor, saying: 'St Adolphus gives you his blessing.'

Aldred's spirits were high. The villagers had been awestruck. A woman had confessed a theft. Most people had given money. The event had achieved what he wanted, despite Wynstan's attempt to undermine it. And if it worked in Trench, it would work elsewhere. Perhaps the priory would survive after all.

Aldred's plan had been that the monks would spend the night in the church, guarding the relics, but that had to be abandoned now. He made a quick decision. 'We'll leave the village in procession and find somewhere else to spend the night,' he said to Godleof.

Aldred had one more message for the villagers. 'You may see the saint again,' he said. 'Come to the church at Dreng's Ferry on Whit Sunday, the feast of Pentecost. Bring the sick and the troubled and the bereaved.' He thought of telling them to spread the word then realized that was unnecessary: everyone would be telling the story of today for months to come. 'I look forward to welcoming you all.'

The monks returned with their bowls. Edgar lowered the effigy slowly, then covered it with cloths. Godleof returned the ox to the shafts.

The beast lumbered into action. The monks began to sing, and slowly they left the village.

ÞÞÞ

ON WHIT SUNDAY Aldred led the monks to the church for the pre-dawn service of Matins, as always. It was a cloudless May morning in the season of hope, when the world was full of promising green shoots, plump piglets, young deer and fast-growing calves. Aldred's hope was that the tour he had made with St Adolphus would achieve its object of attracting pilgrims to Dreng's Ferry.

Aldred planned a stone extension to the church, but there had not been enough time to build it, so Edgar had put up a temporary version in wood. A wide round arch opened from the nave into a side chapel where the effigy of Adolphus lay on a plinth. The congregation in the nave would observe the service taking place in the chancel and then turn, at the climax of the rite, to see the saint rise up miraculously and stare at them with his blue eyes.

And then, Aldred hoped, they would make donations.

The monks had trudged from village to village with the cart and the effigy, Aldred had repeated his rousing sermon every day for two weeks, and the saint had struck awe into the hearts of the people. There had even been a miracle, albeit a small one: an adolescent girl suffering from severe stomach pain had suddenly recovered when she saw the saint rise up.

The people had given money, mostly in halfpennies and farthings, but it had added up, and Aldred had arrived home with almost a pound of silver. That was very helpful, but the monks could not spend their lives on tour. They needed the people to come to them.

Aldred had urged everyone to visit on Whit Sunday. It was in God's hands now. There was only so much a mere human could do.

After Matins, Aldred paused outside the church to survey the hamlet in the early light. It had grown a little since he moved here. The first newcomer had been Bucca Fish, the third son of a Combe fishmonger and an old pal of Edgar's. Edgar had persuaded Bucca to set up a stall selling fresh and smoked fish. Aldred had encouraged the project, hoping that a reliable supply of fish would help people in the area to observe more strictly the Church's rules on fasting: they should eat no meat on Fridays, nor on the twelve festivals of the apostles or certain other special days. Demand was strong, and Bucca sold everything caught in Edgar's traps.

Aldred and Edgar had discussed where Bucca should build a house for himself, and the question had prompted them to draw a village plan. Aldred had suggested a grid of squares for household groups, the way it was usually done, but Edgar had proposed something new, a main street going up the hill and a high street at right angles along the ridge. To the east of the main street they zoned a site for a new, larger church and monastery. It was probably a daydream, Aldred thought, albeit a pleasant one.

All the same, Edgar had spent a day marking the sites of houses in the main street, and Aldred had decreed that anyone willing to build on one of the sites could take timber from the woods and have a year rent-free. Edgar himself was building a house: although he spent a lot of time at Outhenham, nevertheless on the days he was at Dreng's Ferry he preferred not to sleep at his brothers' house, where he often had to listen to Cwenburg have sex with one or other of them, noisily.

Following Bucca's lead three more strangers had settled in Dreng's Ferry: a rope maker, who used the entire length of his back yard for plaiting his cords; a weaver, who built a long house and put his loom at one end and his wife and children at the other; and a shoemaker, who built a house next to Bucca's.

Aldred had built a one-room schoolhouse. At first his only pupil had been Edgar. But now three small boys, the sons of prosperous men in the surrounding countryside, came to the priory every Saturday, each clutching half a silver penny in a grubby hand, to learn letters and numbers.

All this was good but not good enough. At this rate Dreng's Ferry might become a great monastery in a hundred years. All the same,

Aldred had forged on as best he could – until Osmund died and Wynstan cut off the money.

He looked across the river and was heartened to see a small group of pilgrims on the far side, sitting on the ground near the water's edge, waiting for the ferry. That was a good sign so early in the morning. But it looked as if Dreng was still asleep and no one was operating the boat. Aldred went down the hill to wake him.

The alehouse door was closed and the windows shuttered. Aldred banged on the door but got no reply. However, there was no lock, so Aldred lifted the latch and went in.

The house was empty.

Aldred stood in the doorway, looking around, baffled. Blankets were piled neatly, and the straw on the floor was raked. The barrels and jars of ale had been put away, probably in the brewhouse, which had a lock. There was a smell of cold ashes: the fire was out.

The inhabitants had gone.

There was no one to operate the ferry. That was a blow.

Well, Aldred thought, we'll operate it ourselves. We have to get those pilgrims across. The monks can take turns. We can do it.

Puzzled but determined, he went back outside. That was when he noticed that the ferry was not at its mooring. He looked up and down the bank, then scanned the opposite side with a sinking heart. The boat was nowhere to be seen.

He reasoned logically. Dreng had gone, with his two wives and his slave girl, and they had taken the boat.

Where had he gone? Dreng did not like to travel. He left the hamlet about once a year. His rare trips were usually to Shiring, and you could not get there by river.

Upstream, to Bathford and Outhenham? Or downstream, to Mudeford and Combe? Neither made much sense, especially as he had taken his family.

Aldred might have been able to guess *where* if he had known *why*. What reason could Dreng possibly have for going away?

He realized grimly that this was not a coincidence. Dreng knew all about St Adolphus and the Whitsun invitation. The malicious ferry owner had left on the very day when Aldred was hoping that hundreds of people would come to his church. Dreng had known that the absence of the ferry would ruin Aldred's plan.

It must have been deliberate.

And once Aldred had figured that out, the next logical deduction was inevitable.

Dreng had been put up to this by Wynstan.

Aldred wanted to strangle them both with his bare hands.

He suppressed such irreligious passions. Rage was pointless. What could he do?

The answer came immediately. The boat was gone, but Edgar had a raft. It was not moored here by the tavern, but that was not unusual: Edgar sometimes tied it up near the farmhouse.

Aldred's spirits lifted. He turned from the river and set off up the hill at a fast walk.

Edgar had decided to build his new house opposite the site of the new church, even though there was no church there yet and might never be. The walls of the house were up but the roof was not yet thatched. Edgar sat on a bale of straw, writing with a stone on a large piece of slate that he had fixed into a wooden frame. He was making a calculation, frowning with his tongue between his teeth, perhaps adding up the materials he would need to rebuild the saint's chapel in stone.

Aldred said: 'Where's your raft?'

'On the river bank by the tavern. Has something happened?'

'The raft is not there now.'

'Damn.' Edgar stepped outside to see, and Aldred followed. They both looked down the hill to the riverside. There were no vessels of any kind in sight. 'That's odd,' said Edgar. 'They can't both have come untied accidentally.'

'No. We're not talking about an accident here.'

'Who . . . ?'

'Dreng has vanished. The tavern is empty.'

'He must have taken the ferry . . . and taken my raft, too, to prevent us using it.'

'Exactly. He will have set it adrift several miles away. He'll claim he has no idea what happened to it.' Aldred felt defeated. 'With no ferry and no raft, we can't bring the visitors across the river.'

Edgar snapped his fingers. 'Mother Agatha has a boat,' he said. 'It's very small – with one person rowing and two passengers it's crowded – but it floats.'

Aldred's hopes rose again. 'A little boat is better than nothing.'

'I'll swim across and beg a loan. Agatha will be happy to help, especially when she finds out what Dreng and Wynstan are trying to do.'

'If you'll start rowing the visitors over, I'll send a monk to relieve you after an hour.'

'They're also going to want to buy food and drink at the alehouse.'

'There's nothing there, but we can sell them everything in the priory stores. We've got ale and bread and fish. We'll manage.'

Edgar ran down the hill to the riverside and Aldred hurried to the monks' house. It was still early: there was time to get passengers across the river and turn the monastery into a tavern.

Fortunately, it was a fine day. Aldred told the monks to set up trestle tables outside and round up all the cups and bowls in the hamlet. He mustered barrels of ale from the stores and loaves of bread both fresh and stale. He sent Godleof to buy all the stock Bucca Fish had in his store. He built a fire, spitted some of the fresh fishes, and started cooking them. He was run off his feet, but he was happy.

Soon the pilgrims began to come up the hill from the river. More arrived from the opposite direction. The monks started selling. There were rumbles of discontent from people who had been looking forward to meat and strong ale, but most of them cheerfully entered into the spirit of emergency arrangements.

When Edgar was relieved he reported that the queue for the boat was getting longer, and some people were turning around and going home rather than waiting. Aldred's fury with Dreng surged up again, but he forced himself to be calm. 'Nothing we can do about that,' he said, pouring ale into wooden cups.

An hour before midday the monks herded the pilgrims into the church. Aldred had hoped the nave would be packed shoulder-to-shoulder, and was prepared to repeat the service for a second congregation, but that was not necessary.

With an effort he turned his mind from managing an improvised alehouse to conducting Mass. The familiar Latin phrases soon calmed his soul. They had the same effect on the congregation, who were remarkably quiet.

At the end, Aldred told the now-familiar story of the life of St Adolphus, and the congregation watched the effigy rise. By now most people knew what to expect, and few were actually terrified, but it was still an impressive and marvellous sight.

Afterwards they all wanted dinner.

Several people asked about staying the night. Aldred told them they could sleep in the monks' house. Alternatively they could take shelter in the alehouse, even though the owner was away and there would be no food or drink.

They did not like either option. A pilgrimage was a holiday, and they looked forward to convivial evenings with other pilgrims, drinking and singing and, sometimes, falling in love.

In the end, most of them set out for home.

At the end of the day Aldred sat on the ground between the church and the monks' house, looking downstream, watching a red sun sink to meet its reflection in the water. After a few minutes Edgar joined him. They sat in silence for a while, then Edgar said: 'It didn't work, did it?'

'It worked, but not well enough. The idea is sound, but it was undermined.'

'Will you try again?'

'I don't know. Dreng operates the ferry, and that makes it difficult. What do you think?'

'I have an idea.'

Aldred smiled. Edgar always had ideas, and they were usually good. 'Tell me.'

'We wouldn't need the ferry if we had a bridge.'

Aldred stared at him. 'I never thought of that.'

'You want your church to become a pilgrim destination. The river is a major obstacle, especially with Dreng in charge of the ferry. A bridge would make this place easy to reach.'

It had been a day of emotional ups and downs, but now Aldred's mood went from deeply pessimistic to wildly hopeful in the biggest switch yet. 'Can it be done?' he said eagerly.

Edgar shrugged. 'We have plenty of timber.'

'More than we know what to do with. But do you know how to build a bridge?'

'I've been thinking about it. The hard part will be making the pillars secure in the river bed.'

'It must be possible, because bridges exist!'

'Yes. You have to fix the foot of the pillar into a large box of stones on the river bed. The box has to have sharp corners pointing upstream and downstream, and be firmly fixed on the river bed, so that the current can't dislodge it.'

'How do you know such things?'

'By looking at existing structures.'

'But you've already thought about this.'

'I have time to think. There's no wife to talk to me.'

'We must do this!' Aldred said excitedly. Then he thought of a snag. 'But I can't pay you.'

'You've never paid me for anything. But I'm still taking lessons.'

'How long would the bridge take?'

'Give me a couple of strong young monks as labourers and I think I can probably do it in six months to a year.'

'Before next Whit Sunday?'

'Yes,' said Edgar.

ÞÞÞ

THE HUNDRED COURT took place on the following Saturday. It almost turned into a riot.

The pilgrims were not the only people who had been inconvenienced by Dreng's disappearance. Sam the shepherd had attempted to cross the river with hoggets, year-old sheep, to sell at Shiring; but he had been obliged to turn around and drive the flock home. Several more inhabitants on the far side of the river had been unable to take their produce to market. Others who liked to come to Dreng's Ferry just on special holy days had returned home dissatisfied. Everyone felt they had been let down by someone they were entitled to rely upon. The headmen of the villages berated Dreng.

'Am I a prisoner here?' Dreng protested. 'Am I forbidden to leave?'

Aldred was sitting outside the church on the big wooden stool, presiding over the court. He said to Dreng: 'Where did you go, anyway?'

'What business is that of yours?' Dreng said. There were shouts of protest, and he backed down. 'All right, all right, I went to Mudeford Crossing with three barrels of ale to sell.'

'On the very day when you knew there would be hundreds of ferry passengers?'

'No one told me.'

Several people shouted: 'Liar!'

They were right: it was impossible that the alehouse keeper should be ignorant of the special Whit Sunday service.

Aldred said: 'When you go to Shiring you normally leave your family in charge of the ferry and tavern.'

'I needed the boat to transport the ale, and I needed the women to help me manhandle the barrels. I've got a bad back.'

Several people groaned mockingly: they had all heard about Dreng's bad back.

Edgar said: 'You've got a daughter and two strong sons-in-law. They could have opened the alehouse.'

'There's no point in opening the alehouse if there's no ferry.'

'They could have borrowed my raft. Except that the raft disappeared at the same time as you did. Wasn't that strange?'

'I don't know anything about that.'

'Was my raft tied up alongside the ferry when you left?'

Dreng looked hunted. He could not figure out whether to say yes or no. 'I don't remember.'

'Did you pass the raft on your way downstream?'

'I might have.'

'Did you untie my raft and set it adrift?'

'No.'

Once again there were shouts of: 'Liar!'

Dreng said: 'Look! There's nothing that says I have to operate the ferry every day. I was given this job by Dean Degbert. He was lord of this place and he never said anything about a seven-day-a-week service.'

Aldred said: 'Now I'm lord, and I say it is essential that people are able to cross the river every day. There's a church here and a fish shop, and it's on the road between Shiring and Combe. Your unreliable service is not acceptable.'

'So are you saying you'll give the service to someone else?'

Several people shouted: 'Yes!'

Dreng said: 'We'll see what my powerful relatives in Shiring have to say about that.'

Aldred said: 'No, I'm not going to give the ferry to someone else.'

There were groans, and someone said: 'Why not?'

'Because I have a better idea.' Aldred paused. 'I'm going to build a bridge.'

The crowd went quiet as people took that in.

Dreng was the first to react. 'You can't do that,' he said. 'You'll ruin my business.'

'You don't deserve your business,' Aldred said. 'But, as it happens, you'll be better off. The bridge will bring more people to the village and more customers to your alehouse. You'll probably get rich.'

'I don't want a bridge,' he said stubbornly. 'I'm a ferryman.'

Aldred looked at the crowd. 'How does everyone else feel? Do you want a bridge?'

There was a chorus of cheers. Of course they wanted a bridge. It would save them time. And no one liked Dreng.

Aldred looked at Dreng. 'Everyone else wants a bridge. I'm going to build one.'

Dreng turned and stamped away.

29

RAGNA WAS LOOKING AT her three sons when she heard the noise.

The twins were asleep side by side in a wooden cradle, seven months old, Hubert plump and contented, Colinan small and agile. Osbert, two years old and toddling, was sitting on the ground, stirring a wooden spoon around an empty bowl in imitation of Cat making porridge.

The sound from outside caused Ragna to glance through the open door. It was the afternoon of a summer day: the cooks were sweating in the kitchen, the dogs were sleeping in the shade, and the children were splashing at the edges of the duck pond. Just visible in the distance, beyond the outskirts of the town, fields of yellow wheat ripened in the sun.

It looked peaceful, but there was a rising hullabaloo from the town, shouts and cries and neighing, and she knew immediately that the army was home. Her heart beat faster.

She was wearing a teal-blue gown of lightweight summer cloth: she always dressed carefully, a habit for which she was now grateful, for there was no time to change. She stepped outside and stood in front of the great hall to welcome her husband. Others quickly joined her.

The return of the army was a moment of agonizing tension for the women. They longed to see their men, but they knew that not all the combatants would return from the battlefield. They looked at one another, wondering which of them would soon be weeping tears of grief.

Ragna's own feelings were even more mixed. In the five months that he had been away, her feelings for Wilf had hardened from disappointment and sadness to anger and disgust. She had tried not to hate him, tried to remember how much they had loved each other once; then something had happened that tipped the balance. During his absence Wilf sent her no message, but a wounded soldier had returned to Shiring with a looted Viking bangle as a gift from Wilf to his slave girl, Carwen. Ragna had wept, she had stormed and raged, and finally she had just felt numb.

Yet she feared his death. He was the father of her three sons, and they needed him.

Wilf's stepmother, Gytha, well dressed in her habitual red, came and stood a yard away from Ragna. Inge, his first wife, and Carwen, his slave girl, followed close behind. Inge had made the mistake of dressing down while the men were away, and now she looked shabby. Young Carwen, who felt constrained in the floor-length dresses of English women, wore a colourless shift as short as a man's tunic, and her bare feet were dirty: the poor girl looked as if she would be more at home with the children playing in the pond.

If Wilf was alive, Ragna felt sure he would greet her first: anything else would be a gross insult to his official wife. But who would he spend tonight with? No doubt they were all wondering that. The thought further soured Ragna's mood.

The noise from the town had at first sounded like a celebration, male roars of welcome and female squeals of delight, but now Ragna realized that there was no triumphant braying of horns or thudding of vainglorious drums, and there was a discouraged feel to the hoof beats. The exultant greetings turned into exclamations of dismay.

She frowned, concerned. Something had gone wrong.

The army appeared at the entrance to the compound. Ragna saw a cart drawn by an ox, with two men riding each side. A driver sat at the front of the vehicle. Behind him on the flatbed of the cart was a supine form. It was a man, Ragna saw, and she recognized the fair hair and beard of Wilf. She let out a short scream: was he dead?

The entourage was moving slowly, and Ragna could not wait. She ran across the compound, and heard the other women behind her. All her resentment of Wilf for his infidelity faded into the background, and she felt nothing but excruciating worry.

She reached the cart and the procession stopped. She stared at Wilf: his eyes were closed.

She hitched up her skirts and leaped onto the cart. Kneeling beside Wilf she leaned over him, touched his face, and looked at his closed eyes. His face was deathly pale. She could not tell whether he was breathing. 'Wilf,' she said. 'Wilf.'

There was no response.

He was lying on a stretcher placed on top of a pile of blankets and cushions. Ragna scanned his body. The shoulders of his tunic were dark with old blood. She looked more closely at his head and saw that it seemed misshapen. He had a swelling, or perhaps more than one, on his skull. He had suffered a head injury. That was ominous.

She looked at the outriders but they said nothing and she could not read their expressions. Perhaps they did not know whether he was alive or dead.

'Wilf,' she said. 'It's me, Ragna.'

The corners of his mouth were touched by the ghost of a smile. His lips opened and he murmured: 'Ragna.'

'Yes,' she said. 'It's me. You're alive, thank God!'

He opened his mouth to speak again. She leaned closer to hear. He said: 'Am I home?'

'Yes,' she said, weeping. 'You're home.'

'Good.'

She looked up. Everyone seemed to be waiting. She realized she was the one who must decide what should be done next.

In the next instant she realized something more: while Wilwulf was incapacitated, *whoever had his body also had his power.*

'Drive the cart to my house,' she said.

The carter cracked his whip and the ox lumbered forward. The cart was drawn across the compound to Ragna's house. Cat, Agnes and Bern stood at the door, and Osbert was half hiding in Cat's skirts. The escort dismounted, and the four men gently picked up the stretcher and Wilf.

'Stop!' said Gytha.

The four men stood still and looked at her.

She said: 'He must go to my house. I will take care of him.'

She had come to the same realization as Ragna, but not so quickly.

Gytha gave Ragna an insincere smile and said: 'You have so much else to do.'

Ragna said: 'Don't be ridiculous.' She could hear the venom in her own voice. 'I am his *wife.*' She turned to the four men. 'Take him inside.'

They obeyed Ragna. Gytha said no more.

Ragna followed them in. They put the stretcher down in the rushes on the floor. Ragna knelt beside him and touched his forehead: he was too warm. 'Give me a bowl of water and a clean rag,' she said without looking up.

She heard little Osbert say: 'Who's that man?'

'This is your father,' she said. Wilf had been away for almost half a year and Osbert had forgotten him. 'He would kiss you, but he's hurt.'

Cat put a bowl on the floor beside Wilf and handed Ragna a cloth. Ragna dipped the cloth in the water and dampened Wilf's face. After a minute she thought he looked relieved, though that might have been her imagination.

Ragna said: 'Agnes, go into town and fetch Hildi, the midwife who attended me when I gave birth to the twins.' Hildi was the most sensible medical practitioner in Shiring.

Agnes hurried away.

'Bern, talk to the soldiers and find someone who knows what happened to the ealdorman.'

'Right away, my lady.'

Wynstan came in. He said nothing but stood staring at the supine form of Wilf.

Ragna concentrated on her husband. 'Wilf, can you understand me?'

He opened his eyes and took a long moment to fix his gaze on her, but then she could tell that he knew her. 'Yes,' he said.

'How were you wounded?'

He frowned. 'Can't remember.'

'Are you in pain?'

'Headache.' The words came slowly but they were clear.

'How bad?'

'Not bad.'

'Anything else?'

He sighed. 'Very tired.'

Wynstan said: 'It's serious.' Then he left.

Bern returned with a soldier called Bada. 'It wasn't even a battle, more of a skirmish,' Bada said in a tone of apology, as if his commander should not have been hurt in something as inglorious as a minor brawl.

Ragna said: 'Just tell me how it happened.'

'Ealdorman Wilwulf was riding Cloud, as usual, and I was right behind him.' He spoke succinctly, a soldier reporting to a superior, and Ragna was grateful for his clarity. 'We came upon a group of Vikings all of a sudden, on the bank of the river Exe a few miles upstream of Exeter. They had just raided a village and were loading the loot onto their ship – chickens, ale, money, a calf – before returning to their camp. Wilf jumped off his horse and stuck his sword into one of the Vikings, killing him; but he slipped on the riverside mud, and fell. Cloud stamped on Wilf's head, and Wilf lay like one dead. I couldn't check right then – I was under attack myself. But we killed most of the Vikings and the rest escaped in their ship. Then I went back to Wilf. He was breathing, and eventually he came round.'

'Thank you, Bada.'

Ragna saw Hildi in the background, listening, and beckoned her forward.

A woman of about fifty, she was small in stature and grey-haired. She knelt beside Wilf and studied him, taking her time. She touched the lump on his head with gentle fingertips. When she pressed, Wilf winced without opening his eyes, and she said: 'Sorry.' She peered closely at the wound, parting his hair to see the skin. 'Look,' she said to Ragna.

Ragna saw that Hildi had lifted a patch of loose skin to show a crack in the skull beneath. It looked as if a sliver of bone had come away.

'This explains all the blood on his clothes,' Hildi said. 'But the bleeding stopped long ago.'

Wilf opened his eyes.

Hildi said: 'Do you know how you were hurt?'

'No.'

She held up her right hand with three fingers sticking up. 'How many fingers?'

'Three.'

She lifted her left hand with four fingers showing. 'How many altogether?'

'Six.'

Ragna was dismayed. 'Wilf, can you not see clearly?'

He made no reply.

Hildi said: 'His eyesight is fine, but I'm not sure about his mind.'

'God save him.'

Hildi said: 'Wilwulf, what is your wife's name?'

'Ragna.' He smiled.

That was a relief.

'What's the king's name?'

There was a long pause, then he said: 'King.'

'And his wife?'

'I forget.'

'Can you name one of Jesus's brothers?'

'St Peter . . .'

Everyone knew that Jesus's brothers were James, Joseph, Jude and Simeon.

'What number comes after nineteen?'

'Don't know.'

'Rest now, Ealdorman Wilwulf.'

Wilf closed his eyes.

Ragna said: 'Will the wound heal?'

'The skin will grow back and cover the hole, but I don't know whether the bone will regrow. He needs to keep as still as possible for several weeks.'

'I'll make sure of that.'

'It will help to tie a bandage around his head, to reduce movement. Give him watered wine or weak ale to drink, and feed him soup.'

'I will.'

'The most worrying sign is the loss of much of his memory, and it's hard to say how serious that is. He remembers your name, but not the king's. He can count up to three but not to seven, and certainly not to twenty. There's nothing you can do about that but pray. After a head wound, sometimes people recover all their mental abilities, and sometimes they don't. I know no more than that.' She looked up, noticing someone else entering, and she added: 'And nor does anyone else.'

Ragna followed her glance. Gytha had come in with Father Godmaer, a priest at the cathedral who had studied medicine. He was a big, heavy man with a shaved head. A younger priest followed him in. 'What is that midwife doing here?' said Godmaer. 'Stand aside, woman. Let me look at the patient.'

Ragna considered telling him to leave. She had more faith in Hildi. But a second opinion could do no harm. She stepped back, and others followed suit, allowing Godmaer to kneel beside Wilf.

He was not as gentle as Hildi, and when he touched the swelling Wilf groaned in pain. It was too late for Ragna to protest.

Wilf opened his eyes and said: 'Who are you?'

'You know me,' Godmaer said. 'Have you forgotten?'

Wilf closed his eyes.

Godmaer turned Wilf's head to one side, looked into his ear, then turned it again to look into the other ear. Hildi frowned anxiously and Ragna said: 'Gently, please, Father.'

'I know what I'm doing,' Godmaer said haughtily, but he became a little less rough. He opened Wilf's mouth and peered in, then pushed up his eyelids, and finally sniffed his breath.

He stood up. 'The problem is an excess of black bile, especially in the head,' he announced. 'This is causing fatigue, dullness and memory loss. The treatment will be trepanning, to let the bile out. Pass me the bow drill.'

His young companion handed him the tool, which was used by carpenters to drill small holes. The sharpened iron bit was twisted into the string of the bow so that, when the bit was held firmly against a plank and the shaft of the bow moved to and fro, the point spun fast and pierced the wood.

Godmaer said: 'I will now drill a hole in the patient's skull to allow the accumulated choler to escape.'

Hildi made an exasperated sound.

Ragna said: 'Just a minute. There is already a hole in his skull. If there was an excess of any fluid, it would surely have come out by now.'

Godmaer looked taken aback, and Ragna realized that he had not lifted the loose skin and therefore did not know about the crack in the skull. But he recovered quickly, squared his shoulders, and looked indignant. 'I trust you're not questioning the judgements of a medically trained man.'

Ragna could play that game. 'As the wife of the ealdorman I question the judgement of everyone except my husband. I thank you for your attendance, Father, even though I did not invite you, and I will bear your advice in mind.'

Gytha said: 'I invited him because he is the leading medical practitioner in Shiring. You have no right to deny the ealdorman the recommended treatment.'

'I'll tell you something, stepmother-in-law,' said Ragna angrily. 'I'll make a hole in the throat of anyone who tries to make another hole in my husband's head. Now take your pet priest out of my house.'

Godmaer gasped. Ragna realized she had gone too far – referring to Godmaer as 'your pet priest' was close to sacrilege – but she hardly cared. Godmaer was arrogant, which made him dangerous. Medically trained priests rarely cured anyone, in her experience, but they often made sick people worse.

Gytha murmured something to Godmaer, who nodded, lifted his head and stalked out, still carrying the bow drill. His assistant followed.

There were still too many people standing around uselessly. 'Everyone except my servants please leave now,' Ragna said. 'The ealdorman needs peace and quiet to get well.'

They all went out.

Ragna bent over Wilf again. 'I will take care of you,' she said. 'I will do as I have for the last half a year, and govern your territory as you would govern it.'

There was no response.

She said: 'Do you think you can answer one more question?'

He opened his eyes, and his lips twitched in the ghost of a smile.

'What is the most important thing you need me to do now, as your deputy?'

She thought she saw a look of intelligence come over his face. He said: 'Appoint a new commander for the army.' Then he closed his eyes.

Ragna sat on a cushioned stool and looked thoughtfully at him. He had given her a clear instruction in a moment of lucidity. From it she deduced that the army's work was not yet done, and the Vikings had not been driven off. The men of Shiring needed to regroup and attack again. And for that they needed a new leader.

Wynstan would want his brother Wigelm to be in charge. Ragna dreaded that: the more power Wigelm acquired, the more likely he was to challenge her authority. Her choice would be Sheriff Den, an experienced leader and fighter.

In the shire court, where most decisions were reached by consensus, she could often get her way by force of personality, but with this decision she foresaw a problem. The men would have strong views and they would be quick to dismiss the opinion of a woman, who could not know much about warfare. She would have to be sly.

It was evening. The hours had gone by quickly. Ragna said to Agnes: 'Go to Sheriff Den and ask him to come to me now. Don't walk with him – I don't want people to know I summoned him. It must look as if he heard the news and came to see the ealdorman, like everyone else.'

'Very well,' said Agnes, and she left.

Ragna said to Cat: 'Let's see if Wilf will drink some soup. Warm, not hot.'

There was a pot of mutton bones simmering over the fire. Cat ladled some of the juice into a wooden bowl, and Ragna inhaled the fragrance of rosemary. She broke a few morsels of bread from the inside of a loaf and dropped them in the soup, then knelt beside Wilf with a spoon. She took a piece of soaked bread, blew on it to cool it, and put it to his lips. He swallowed it with some sign of relish and opened his mouth for another.

By the time Ragna had finished feeding him, Agnes was back, and Den followed a few minutes later. He looked at Wilf and shook his head pessimistically. Ragna reported what Hildi had said. Then she told him of Wilf's instruction to appoint a new army commander. 'It's you or Wigelm, and I want you,' she finished.

'I'd be better than Wigelm,' he said. 'And he can't do it anyway.'

Ragna was surprised. 'Why not?'

'He's indisposed. He hasn't taken part in any action for two weeks. That's why he's not here – he stayed down near Exeter.'

'What's the problem?'

'Piles – anal haemorrhoids – exacerbated by months of campaigning. They hurt so much that he can't sit on a horse.'

'How do you know?'

'I've been talking to the thanes.'

'Well, that makes it easy,' said Ragna. 'I'll pretend to favour Wigelm, then, when his debility is revealed, you will reluctantly agree to step into the gap.'

Den nodded. 'Wynstan and his friends will oppose me, but most of the thanes will support me. I'm not their favourite person, of course, because I make them pay their taxes, but they know I'm competent.'

Ragna said: 'I will hold court tomorrow morning after breakfast. I want to make it clear from the start that I'm still in charge.'

'Good,' said Den.

ÞÞÞ

THE NEXT DAY was warm, even first thing in the morning, but the cathedral was as cool as ever when Wynstan celebrated early Mass. He went through the ceremony with maximum solemnity. He liked to do what was expected of a bishop: it was important to maintain appearances. Today he prayed for the souls of the men who had died fighting the Vikings, and he begged for healing of those wounded, especially Ealdorman Wilwulf.

All the same his mind was not on the liturgy. Wilwulf's incapacity had upset the balance of power in Shiring, and Wynstan was desperate to learn Ragna's intentions. This could be a chance to weaken her position or even get rid of her altogether. He had to be alert to all possibilities, and he needed to find out what she was up to.

The congregation was larger than usual for a weekday, swollen by the bereaved families of the men who had not returned from the fighting. Looking into the nave, Wynstan noticed Agnes among them, a small, thin woman in the drab clothes of a housemaid. She looked unremarkable, but her eyes met Wynstan's with a clear message: she was here to see him. His hopes rose.

It was half a year since Ragna had condemned Agnes's husband to death, half a year since Agnes had agreed to be Wynstan's spy in Ragna's house. In that time she had brought him no useful information. Nevertheless, he had continued to speak to her at least once a month, feeling sure that one day she would justify his efforts. Fearing that her desire for revenge might fade, he had engaged Agnes emotionally, treating her as an intimate rather than a servant, speaking to her in conspiratorial tones, thanking her for her loyalty. He was subtly taking the place of her late husband, being affectionate but dominant, expecting to be obeyed without question. His instinct told him this was the way to control her.

Today he might be rewarded for his patience.

When the service was over Agnes lingered and, as soon as the other worshippers had gone, Wynstan beckoned her into the chancel, put his arm around her bony shoulders, and drew her into a corner. 'Thank you for coming to see me, my dear,' he said, making his voice quiet but intense. 'I was hoping you would.'

'I thought you'd like to know what she's planning.'

'I would, I would.' Wynstan tried to sound keen but not needy. 'You are my pet mouse, creeping on silent feet into my room at night, lying on my pillow, and whispering secrets into my ear.'

She flushed with pleasure. He found himself wondering what she would do if he put his hand up her skirt right there in the church. He would do no such thing, of course: she was driven by desire for what she could not have, the strongest of all human motives.

She stared at him for a long moment, and he felt the need to break the spell. 'Tell me,' he said.

She collected herself. 'Ragna will hold court today, after breakfast.'

'Moving fast,' Wynstan said. 'Characteristic. But what's her agenda?'

'She will appoint a new commander for the army.'

'Ah.' He had not thought of that.

'She will say she wants Wigelm.'

'He can't ride at the moment. That's why he's not here.'

'She knows that, but she will pretend to be surprised.'

'Crafty.'

'Then someone will say that the only alternative is Sheriff Den.'

'Her strongest ally. Dear God, with her running the court and Den commanding the army, Wilf's family would be practically impotent.'

'That's what I thought.'

'But now I'm forewarned.'

'What will you do?'

'I don't know, yet.' He would not have confided in her in any case. 'But I'll think of something, thanks to you.'

'I'm glad.'

'This is a dangerous time. You must tell me everything she does from now on. It's really important.'

'You can count on me.'

'Go back to the compound and keep listening.'

'I will.'

'Thank you, my little mouse.' He kissed her lips then ushered her out.

ᚦᚦᚦ

THE COURT FORMED a small group. This was not one of the regular meetings, and there had been no more than an hour's notice. But the most important thanes had arrived with the army. Ragna held court in front of the great hall, sitting on the cushioned stool usually occupied by Wilwulf. Her choice of seat was deliberate.

However, she stood up to speak. Her height was an advantage. Leaders needed to be smart, not tall, she believed; but she had noticed that men were readier to defer to a tall person; and as a woman she used any weapon that came to hand.

She was wearing a brown-black dress, dark for authority, a bit loose so that her figure was not accentuated. All her jewellery today was chunky: pendant, bangles, brooch, rings. She had on nothing feminine, nothing dainty. She was dressed to rule.

The morning was her preferred time for meetings. The men were more sensible, less boisterous, having drunk only a cup of weak ale with their breakfast. They could be much more difficult after the midday meal.

'The ealdorman is seriously wounded, but we have every hope that he will recover,' she said. 'He was fighting a Viking when he slipped in the riverside mud, and his horse kicked him in the head.' Most of them would know that already, but she said it to show them that she was not ignorant of the haphazard nature of battle. 'You all know how easily something like that can happen.' She was gratified to see nods of approval. 'The Viking died,' she added. 'His soul is now suffering the agonies of hell.' Once again she saw that they approved of her words.

'In order to recover, Wilf needs peace and quiet and, most importantly, he must lie still so that his skull can mend. That is why my door is barred from the inside. When he wants to see someone he will tell me, and I will summon the person. No one will be admitted unless invited.'

She knew that this news would be unwelcome, and she was expecting some opposition.

Sure enough, Wynstan pushed back. 'You can't keep the ealdorman's brothers away.'

'I can't keep anyone away. All I can do is follow Wilf's orders. He will see whomever he wants, of course.'

Garulf, Wilf's twenty-year-old son by Inge, said: 'That's not right. You could tell us to do anything, and pretend the orders came from him.'

That was exactly what Ragna intended.

She had expected someone to make this point, and she was glad it came from a lad rather than a respected older man: this made it easier to dismiss.

Garulf went on: 'He might be dead. How would we know?'

'By the smell,' Ragna said crisply. 'Don't talk nonsense.'

Gytha spoke up. 'Why did you refuse to let Father Godmaer perform the trepanning operation?'

'Because Wilf's skull already has a hole. You don't need two holes in your arse and Wilf doesn't need two in his head.'

The men laughed, and Gytha shut up.

Ragna said: 'Wilf has briefed me on the military situation.' It had been Bada, but this sounded better. 'The fighting has been inconclusive so far. Wilwulf wants the army to regroup, rearm, go back and finish the job – but he can't lead you. So the main task of the court this morning is to appoint a new commander. Wilf did not express a wish, but I assume his brother Wigelm must be the preferred candidate.'

Bada spoke up. 'He can't do it – he can't ride.'

Ragna pretended ignorance. 'Why not?'

Garulf said: 'He's got a sore arsehole.'

The men chuckled.

Bada said: 'He has piles – very badly.'

'So he really can't get on a horse?'

'No.'

'Well,' Ragna said, as if thinking on her feet, 'the next choice would have to be Sheriff Den.'

As agreed, Den pretended reluctance. 'Perhaps a nobleman would be better, my lady.'

'If the thanes can agree on one of their number . . .' Ragna said dubiously.

Wynstan stood up from the bench where he had been sitting and stepped forward, making himself the centre of attention. 'It's obvious, isn't it?' he said, spreading his arms in a gesture of appeal and looking around the group.

Ragna's heart sank. He's got a plan, she thought, and I didn't foresee it.

Wynstan said: 'The commander should be Wilf's son.'

Ragna said: 'Osbert is two years old!'

'I mean his eldest son, of course.' Wynstan paused, smiling. 'Garulf.'

'But Garulf is only—' Ragna stopped, realizing that although she thought of Garulf as a lad he was in fact twenty, with a man's muscular body and a full beard. He was old enough to lead an army.

Whether he was wise enough was another question.

Wynstan said: 'Everyone here knows Garulf to be a brave man!'

There was general agreement. Garulf had always been popular with the men-at-arms. But did they really want him to decide strategy?

Ragna said: 'And do we feel that Garulf has the brains to lead the army?'

She probably should not have said it. The question would have come better from one of the thanes, a fighting man. They were predisposed to scorn anything a woman might say on such a subject. Her intervention shored up support for Garulf.

Bada said: 'Garulf is young, but he has the aggressive spirit.'

Ragna saw the men nodding. She tried one more time. 'The sheriff is more experienced.'

Wynstan said: 'At collecting taxes!'

They all laughed, and Ragna knew she had lost.

ÞÞÞ

EDGAR WAS NOT used to failure. When it came, it bowled him over.

He had tried to build a bridge across the river at Dreng's Ferry, but it had proved impossible.

He sat with Aldred on the bench outside the alehouse, listening to the sound of the river and staring at the ruins of his plan. He had succeeded, with great difficulty, in building a foundation on the river bed for one of the pillars of the bridge, a simple box filled with stones to hold the base of the column firmly in place. He had fashioned a mighty beam of heart of oak, stout enough to bear the weight of people and carts as they crossed. But he could not insert the pillar into its socket.

It was evening, and he had been trying in the hot sun all day. At the end almost everyone in the village had been helping. The pillar had been held in place by long ropes, made at high cost by the newcomer Regenbald Roper. People on both banks had hauled on the ropes to keep the timber stable. Edgar and several others had stood on his raft in midstream trying to manoeuvre the enormous beam.

But everything moved: the water, the raft, the ropes, and the pillar. The timber itself insisted on rising to the surface.

At first it had been like a game, and there was laughter and banter as they all struggled. Several people had fallen into the water, to general hilarity.

To keep the pillar under water and at the same time position it in its socket should have been possible, but they had not done it. They had all become frustrated and bad-tempered. In the end Edgar had given up.

Now the sun was sinking, the monks had returned to the monastery, the villagers had returned to their homes, and Edgar was defeated.

Aldred was not yet willing to abandon the project. 'It can be done,' he said. 'We need more men, more ropes, more boats.'

Edgar did not think that would work. He said nothing.

Aldred said: 'The problem was that your raft kept shifting. Whenever you pushed the pillar into the water, the raft would move away from the foundation.'

'I know.'

'What we really need is a whole row of boats, stretching out from the bank, tied together so that they can't move so much.'

'I don't know where we'd get that many boats,' Edgar said gloomily; but he could picture what Aldred was suggesting. The boats could be roped or even nailed together. The whole row would still move, but more slowly, more predictably, less capriciously.

Aldred was still fantasizing. 'Maybe two rows, one each side of the river.'

Edgar was so weary and downhearted that he was reluctant to entertain new ideas, but despite his mood he was intrigued by Aldred's notion. It would provide a much more stable set-up for the awkward task. All the same it might not be enough. However, something else was nagging at him as he pictured the two rows of boats growing out of the banks and reaching out into midstream. They would be steady, they would provide a sturdy platform on which to stand . . .

He said suddenly: 'Perhaps we could build the bridge on the boats.'

Aldred frowned. 'How?'

'The roadbed of the bridge could rest on boats, instead of on the river bed.' He shrugged. 'Theoretically.'

Aldred snapped his fingers. 'I've seen that!' he said. 'When I was travelling in the Low Countries. A bridge built on a row of boats. They called it a pontoon bridge.'

Edgar felt bemused. 'So it can be done!'

'Yes.'

'I've never seen such a thing.' But Edgar was already designing it in his head. 'They would have to be firmly braced at the shore line.'

Aldred thought of a snag. 'We can't block the river. There's not much traffic, but there is some. The ealdorman would object, and so would the king.'

'There can be a gap in the line of boats, spanned by the roadbed but wide enough for any normal riverboat to pass through.'

'Do you think you could build that?'

Edgar hesitated. Today's experience had undermined his confidence. All the same, he thought a pontoon bridge was a possibility. 'I don't know,' he said with new-found caution. 'But I think so.'

þþþ

THE SUMMER WAS over, the harvest had been gathered in, and the nip of autumn was in the breeze when Wynstan rode with Garulf to join forces with the men of Devon.

Priests were not supposed to shed blood. This rule was often broken, but Wynstan normally found it a convenient excuse to avoid the discomfort and danger of war.

However, he was no coward. He was bigger and stronger than most men, and he was well armed. As well as the spear carried by everyone he had a sword with a steel blade, a helmet, and a sort of sleeveless shirt of mail.

He was riding with the army, breaking his usual habit, in order to stay close to Garulf. He had connived to have Garulf made commander-in-chief because it was the only way to keep control of the army in the family's hands. But it would be a disaster if Garulf were to die in battle. With Wilf so ill, Garulf had become important. While Ragna's children were small, Garulf had a chance of inheriting Wilf's fortune and his title. He could be the means by which the family kept its hold, not just on the army, but on Shiring.

The road was a track through forested hills. One day before they were due at their rendezvous, they emerged from a wood and looked up a long valley. At the far, narrower end the river was a fast stream hurrying towards them. Then it widened and ran shallow over rocky falls, and finally consolidated into a deeper, slower waterway.

Six Viking ships were moored just below the falls, tied to the near bank, making a neat line. They were about two miles upstream from where Wynstan and the Shiring army stood staring out from among the trees.

This was the army's first encounter with the enemy since Garulf became leader. Wynstan felt his stomach clench in anticipation. A man who did not suffer a spasm of fear before a battle was a fool.

The Vikings had made a small encampment on the mud beach, with a scatter of makeshift tents and numerous cooking fires giving up wisps of smoke. About a hundred men were visible.

Garulf's army was three hundred strong, fifty mounted noblemen and two hundred and fifty foot soldiers.

'We outnumber them!' Garulf said excitedly, seeing an easy victory.

He might have been right, but Wynstan was not so sure. 'We outnumber the ones we can see,' he said cautiously.

'Who else do we need to worry about?'

'Each of those ships could carry fifty men, more if crowded. At least three hundred came to England in them. Where are the rest?'

'What does it matter? If they're not here, they can't fight!'

'We might do better to wait until we've met up with the men of Devon – we'd be much stronger. And they're only a day away, if that.'

'What?' said Garulf scornfully. 'We outnumber the Vikings three to one, yet you want to wait until it's six to one?'

The men laughed.

Encouraged, Garulf went on: 'That seems timid. We must seize our opportunity.'

Perhaps he's right, Wynstan thought. Anyway, the men were eager for action. The enemy seemed weak and they smelled blood. Cool-headed logic did not impress them. And perhaps logic did not win battles.

Nevertheless, Wynstan said warily: 'Well, then, let's take a closer look before we make a final decision.'

'Agreed.' Garulf looked around. 'We'll go back into the woods and tie up the horses. Then we'll get behind that ridge and stay out of sight while we approach nearer.' He pointed into the distance. 'When we reach that bluff we'll spy out the enemy from close up.'

All that sounded right, Wynstan thought as he tied his horse to a tree. Garulf understood tactics. So far, so good.

The army moved through the woods and crossed the gentle crown of the ridge, hidden by trees. On the far side they turned, moving parallel with the valley in an upstream direction. The men bantered, making jokes about bravery and cowardice, keeping their courage up. One said it was a shame there would be no one to rape after the battle; another said they could rape the Viking men; a third said that was a matter of personal taste, and everyone guffawed. Did they know from experience that they were too far away from the Vikings to be heard, Wynstan wondered – or were they just careless?

Wynstan soon lost track of how much ground they had covered, but Garulf showed no such uncertainty. 'This is far enough,' he said eventually, his voice quieter now. He turned uphill, walked a few yards, then dropped to a crawl to approach the summit of the ridge.

Wynstan saw that they were indeed close to the bluff Garulf had indicated earlier. The thanes wriggled on their bellies to the vantage point, keeping their heads low to avoid being spotted by the enemy below. The Vikings were going about their casual business, stoking fires and fetching water from the river, unaware that they were being watched.

Wynstan felt queasy. He could see their faces and hear their desultory talk. He could even make out a few words: their language was similar to English. He was nauseated by the thought that he was here to cut these men with his sharp blade, to shed their blood and chop off their limbs and pierce their living, beating hearts, to make them fall helpless to the earth screaming in agony. People saw him as a cruel man – which he was – but what was about to happen was a different kind of brutality.

He looked up and down the river. On the far bank the ground rose to a low hill. If there were more Vikings in the area, they were probably farther upstream, having passed the falls on foot and gone on in search of a village or a monastery to raid.

Garulf wriggled backwards on his belly, and the others followed suit. When they were well behind the ridge they stood up. Without speaking, Garulf beckoned them to follow him. They all remained silent.

Wynstan expected that they would withdraw for a further discussion, but that did not happen. Garulf moved a few yards farther, remaining behind the ridge, then turned down a ravine that led to the beach. The thanes followed, with the rest of the men close behind.

They were now in full view of the Vikings. It had happened with a suddenness that took Wynstan by surprise. As the men of Shiring moved downhill over the scrubby ground they remained quiet, gaining a few extra seconds of surprise. But soon one of the Vikings happened to glance up, saw them, and let out a cry of warning. With that the army broke its silence. Whooping and yelling, they ran pell-mell down the ravine, brandishing their weapons.

Wynstan took his sword in one hand and his spear in the other and joined the pack.

The Vikings realized immediately that they could not win. They abandoned their fires and their tents and dashed to the boats. They splashed through the shallows, severed the ropes with knives, and began to scramble aboard; but as they did so the English reached the beach, raced across it in a few moments, and caught up.

The two sides met at the edge of the river. A tidal wave of bloodlust swamped all lesser emotions, and Wynstan waded into the water, possessed by nothing but the overwhelming hunger for slaughter. He plunged his spear into the chest of a man who turned to face him, then swiped with his sword, left-handed, at the neck of another who tried to flee. Both men fell into the water. Wynstan did not wait to see whether they were dead.

The English had the advantage of always being in slightly shallower water, therefore freer to move. The thanes in the lead thrust with spears and swords and quickly killed dozens of Vikings. Wynstan saw that the enemy were mostly older men and poorly armed – some appeared to have no weapons, perhaps having left them on the beach when fleeing. He guessed that the best fighters in this group had been chosen for the raiding party.

After the initial explosion of hatred he managed to regain enough self-possession to stay close to Garulf.

Some of the Vikings made it to the ships, but then they were not able to go anywhere. To move six ships off their moorings and into midstream was a complex manoeuvre even when the ships each had a full complement of oarsmen. With just a few men aboard each, and too much panic for co-ordination, the vessels merely drifted and collided. The men standing up in the ships were also easy targets for a handful of English archers, who were standing back from the fray and shooting over the heads of their comrades.

The battle began to turn into a massacre. With all the Shiring men engaged there were three English to kill each Viking. The river became dark with blood and swollen with dead and dying men. Wynstan stood back, breathing hard, holding his bloodstained weapons. Garulf had been right to seize this chance, he thought.

Then he looked across the river, and cold dread seized him.

Hundreds of Vikings were coming. The raiding party must have been just out of sight over that hill. They were running down to the river and crossing the falls, jumping from stone to stone and splashing through shallow water. In a few moments they were on the beach, weapons held high, eager for battle. The dismayed English turned to meet them.

With a stab of pure fear Wynstan saw that it was now the English who were outnumbered. Worse, the Viking newcomers were well armed with long spears and axes, and they seemed younger and stronger than the men they had left behind to guard their encampment. They dashed along the bank and fanned out across the beach, and Wynstan guessed they hoped to surround the English and drive them into the water.

Wynstan looked at Garulf and saw a bewildered look on his face. 'Tell the men to fall back!' Wynstan yelled. 'Along the bank, downstream – otherwise we'll get trapped!'

But Garulf seemed unable to think and fight at the same time.

I was so wrong, Wynstan thought in a whirlwind of desperation and fear. Garulf can't command, he just hasn't got the intelligence. That mistake could cost me my life today.

Garulf was defending himself vigorously against a big red-bearded Viking. As Wynstan looked, Garulf took a glancing blow to his right

569

arm, dropped his sword, fell to one knee, and was hit on the head by a hammer wildly swung by a berserk Englishman, who then smashed it into the red beard.

Wynstan put his regrets aside, fought down panic, and thought fast. The battle was lost. Garulf was in danger of being killed or taken prisoner and enslaved. Retreat was the only hope. And those who retreated first were most likely to survive.

The red-bearded Viking was occupied with the berserk Englishman. Wynstan had a few seconds of respite. He sheathed his sword and stuck his spear into the mud. Then he bent down, picked up the unconscious Garulf, and slung the limp body over his left shoulder. He grabbed his spear in his right hand, turned, and moved away from the battle.

Garulf was a big lad, densely muscled, but Wynstan was strong, and not yet forty years old. He carried Garulf without undue effort, but he could not move fast with such a weight, and he broke into a stumble that was half walking, half running. He headed up the ravine.

He glanced back and saw one of the newly arrived Vikings break away from the battle on the beach and run after him.

He found the strength to move faster, and began to breathe hard as the upward slope became steeper. He could hear the pounding footsteps of his pursuer. He kept glancing back, and the man was closer every time.

At the last possible moment he turned, went down on one knee, slid Garulf off his shoulder onto the ground, and sprang forward with his spear uptilted. The Viking raised his axe over his head for the fatal blow, but Wynstan got under his guard. He thrust the sharpened iron point of his spear into the Viking's throat and pushed with all his might. The blade penetrated the soft flesh, sliced through muscles and tendons, passed through the brain, and came out at the back of the head. The man died without a sound.

Wynstan picked Garulf up and went on up the ravine. At the top he turned and looked back. Now the English were surrounded, and the beach was carpeted with their dead. A few had broken away and fled along the bank in the downstream direction. They might be the only other survivors.

No one was looking at Wynstan.

He crossed the ridge, went downhill until he felt sure he was out of sight, then turned and trudged along the hillside towards the woods where the horses waited.

ÞÞÞ

DURING ONE OF Wilf's lucid moments, Ragna told him about the battle. 'Wynstan brought Garulf home, without serious injuries,' she said in conclusion. 'But almost the entire army of Shiring was wiped out.'

Wilf said: 'Garulf is a brave lad, but he's no leader. He should never have been put in command.'

'It was Wynstan's idea. He's virtually admitted he was wrong.'

'You should have stopped it.'

'I tried, but the men wanted Garulf.'

'They like him.'

This was just like old times, Ragna thought; Wilf and her talking as equals, each interested in the other's opinion. They were together more than they had ever been. She was with him day and night, taking care of every need, and she ruled the ealdormanry in his place. He seemed grateful for everything. His injury had made them close again.

This had happened against her deepest wishes. No matter what happened, she would never feel about him as she once had. But suppose he wanted to resume their former passionate relationship? How would she react?

She did not have to decide just yet. They could not have sex now – Hildi had stressed that any sudden movement could be harmful

– but when he was recovered he might want to go back to the passionate lovemaking of their early years. His brush with death might have brought him to his senses. Perhaps he would forget Carwen and Inge and cling to the woman who had nursed him back to health.

She would have to go along with whatever he wished for, she knew. She was his wife, she had no choice. But it was not what she wanted.

She took up the conversation again. 'And now the Vikings have left as suddenly as they came. I suppose they got bored.'

'It's their way: sudden attack, random raiding, instant success or failure, then home.'

'In fact, they seem to have gone to the Isle of Wight. Apparently they show every sign of spending the winter there.'

'Again? It's becoming a permanent base.'

'But I'm afraid they may come back.'

'Oh, yes,' said Wilf. 'That's one thing you can be sure of with the Vikings. They will be back.'

30

'YOUR BRIDGE IS A marvel,' said Aldred.

Edgar smiled. He was extremely pleased, especially after his initial failure. 'It was your idea,' he said modestly.

'And you made it happen.'

They were standing outside the church, looking down the slope to the river. Both wore heavy cloaks against the winter cold. Edgar had a fur hat, but Aldred made do with his monkish hood.

Edgar studied the bridge with pride. As Aldred had envisaged, on each side of the river was a row of boats sticking out into the water like twin peninsulas. Each row was linked to a stout riverside mooring by ropes that allowed the bridge a small degree of movement. Edgar had built flat-bottomed boats, low-sided near the banks and rising in height towards the centre. They were linked by oak beams bearing a framework that supported the timber roadbed above. There was a gap in the middle, where the span was highest, to allow river traffic to pass.

He wanted Ragna to see it. It was her admiration he craved. He imagined her looking at him with those sea-green eyes and saying *How marvellous, you're so clever to know how to do that, it looks perfect*, and a sensation of warmth spread though his body, as if he had drunk a cup of mead.

Looking over Dreng's Ferry, he recalled the rainy day when she had arrived here with all the grace of a dove curving down to a branch. Had he fallen in love with her right away? Perhaps just a little bit, even then.

He wondered when Ragna would come here again.

Aldred said: 'Who are you thinking about?'

Edgar was startled by Aldred's perception. He did not know what to say.

'Someone you love, obviously,' Aldred said. 'It shows on your face.'

Edgar was embarrassed. 'The bridge will need maintenance,' he said. 'But if it's looked after, it will last a hundred years.'

Ragna might never return to Dreng's Ferry, of course. It was not an important place.

'Look at the people crossing,' said Aldred. 'It's a triumph.'

The bridge was already much used. People came to buy fish and to attend services. More than a hundred had crowded into the church at Christmas, and had witnessed the elevation of St Adolphus.

Everyone who crossed paid a farthing, and another farthing to go back. The monks had an income, and it was growing. 'You did this,' Aldred said to Edgar. 'Thank you.'

Edgar shook his head. 'It's your persistence. You've been through one setback after another, mostly due to the malice of evil men, and yet you never give up. Every time you're knocked to the ground you just get up and start again. You amaze me.'

'My goodness,' said Aldred, looking inordinately pleased. 'High praise.'

Aldred was in love with Edgar, and Edgar knew it. Aldred's love was hopeless, for Edgar would never reciprocate. He would never fall in love with Aldred.

Edgar felt the same way about Ragna. He was in love with her, and it would never come to anything. She would never fall in love with him. There was no hope.

There was a difference, though. Aldred seemed reconciled with the way things were right now. He could feel sure he would never sin with Edgar, because Edgar would never want it.

By contrast, Edgar yearned with all his heart to consummate his love for Ragna. He wanted to make love to Ragna, he wanted to marry her, he wanted to wake up in the morning and see her head sharing his pillow. He wanted the impossible.

There was nothing to be gained by brooding on it. He said conversationally: 'The tavern is busy.'

Aldred nodded. 'That's because Dreng isn't there to be rude to everyone. The place always gets more customers when he's away from home.'

'Where did he go?'

'Shiring. I don't know why, some nefarious purpose, I expect.'

'He's probably protesting about the bridge.'

'Protesting? To whom?'

'Good point,' said Edgar. 'Wilwulf is still ill, apparently, and Dreng won't get much sympathy from Ragna.'

Edgar was glad the village was busy. He shared Aldred's affection for the place. They both wanted it to prosper. It had been a dump just a few years ago, a scatter of poor houses supporting two lazy and venal brothers, Degbert and Dreng. Now it had a priory, a fish shop, a saint and a bridge.

That led Edgar's thoughts to another topic. He said: 'Sooner or later we're going to need to build a wall.'

Aldred looked dubious. 'I've never felt in danger here.'

'Every year the Vikings raid deeper into the west of England. And if our village continues to prosper, before long we'll be worth raiding.'

'They always attack up rivers – but there's an obstacle at Mudeford, that shallow stretch.'

Edgar remembered the wrecked Viking vessel on the beach at Combe. 'Their ships are light. They can be dragged over the shallows.'

'If that happened, they would attack us from the river, not from land.'

'So first we would need to fortify the river bank all the way around the bend.' Edgar pointed upstream, to where the river turned a right angle. 'I'm talking about an earth rampart, possibly revetted with timber or stone in places.'

'Where would you put the rest of the wall?'

'It should start at the waterfront just beyond Leaf's brewhouse.'

'Then your brothers' farm would be outside.'

Edgar cared about his brothers more than they cared about him, but they were not in serious danger. 'The Vikings don't raid isolated farms – there's not enough to steal.'

'True.'

'The wall would run uphill at the back of the houses: Bebbe's place, then Cerdic and Ebba, then Hadwine and Elfburg, then Regenbald Roper, Bucca Fish, and me. Past my place it would turn right and go all the way to the river, to enclose the site of the new church, just in case we ever get to build it.'

'Oh, we'll build it,' said Aldred.

'I hope so.'

'Have faith,' said Aldred.

ÞÞÞ

RAGNA WATCHED AS Hildi the midwife examined Wilf carefully. She made him sit upright on a stool, then brought a candle close to look at his head wound.

'Take that away,' he said. 'It hurts my eyes.'

She moved it behind him so that it did not shine in his face. She touched the wound with her fingertips and nodded with satisfaction. 'Are you eating well?' she said. 'What did you have for breakfast?'

'Porridge with salt,' he replied glumly. 'And a flagon of weak ale. A poor meal for a nobleman.'

Hildi met Ragna's eye. 'He had smoked ham and wine,' said Ragna quietly.

'Don't contradict me,' Wilf said irritably. 'I know what I had for breakfast.'

576

Hildi said: 'How are you feeling?'

'I get headaches,' he replied. 'Otherwise I'm fine – never better.'

'Good,' she said. 'I think you're ready to resume normal life. Well done.' She stood up. 'Step outside with me for a moment, Ragna,' she said.

The bell was ringing for the midday meal as Ragna followed her out. 'He has recovered physically,' Hildi said. 'The wound has healed and he no longer needs to stay in bed. Let him have dinner in the great hall today. He can ride again as soon as he wants to.'

Ragna nodded.

'Sex, too,' Hildi said.

Ragna said nothing. She had lost all desire for sex with Wilf, but if he wanted it she would of course permit it. She had had a lot of time to think about it, and she was reconciled to a future of intimacy with a man she no longer loved.

Hildi went on: 'But you must have noticed that his mind is not what it was.'

Ragna nodded. Of course she had.

'He can't bear bright light, he's bad-tempered and down-hearted, and his memory is poor. I have seen several men with head injuries since the renewal of Viking raids, and his condition is typical.'

Ragna knew all that.

Hildi looked apologetic, as if she might be to blame for what she was reporting. 'It's been five months, and there are no signs of improvement.'

Ragna sighed. 'Will there ever be?'

'No one can tell. It's in God's hands.'

Ragna took that as a no. She gave Hildi two silver pennies. 'Thank you for being gentle with him.'

'I'm at your service, my lady.'

Ragna left Hildi and went back inside the house. 'She says you

577

can have your dinner in the great hall,' Ragna said to Wilf. 'Would you like to?'

'Of course!' he said. 'Where else would I have it?'

He had not dined in the great hall for almost a year, but Ragna did not correct him. She helped him get dressed then took his arm and walked him the short distance across the compound.

The midday meal was already under way. Ragna noticed that both Bishop Wynstan and Dreng were at the table. As Wilf and Ragna entered, the sound of talk and laughter quietened and then stopped as people stared in surprise: no one had been forewarned of Wilf's reappearance. Then there was applause and cheering. Wynstan stood up, clapping, and finally everyone stood.

Wilf smiled happily.

Ragna took him to his usual chair, then sat beside him. Someone poured him a cup of wine. He drank it down and asked for more.

He ate heartily and guffawed at all the usual jokes the men made, seeming like his old self. Ragna knew this was an illusion that would not survive any attempt at serious conversation, and she found herself trying to protect him. When he said something foolish she laughed, as if he were just being amusing; and if it was extremely foolish, she hinted that he was drinking too much. It was amazing how much idiocy could be passed off as men's drunken humour.

Towards the end of the meal he became amorous. He put his hand under the table and stroked her thigh through the wool of her dress, moving slowly higher.

Here it comes, she thought.

Even though she had not held a man in her arms for almost a year, she was dismayed by the prospect. But she would do it. This was her life, now, and she had to get used to it.

Then Carwen came in.

She must have slipped away from the dinner table and gone to change her clothes, Ragna thought, for now she was wearing a black dress that made her look older and red shoes that would have suited a whore. She had washed her face, too, and now she glowed with youthful health and vigour.

She caught Wilf's eye immediately.

He smiled broadly, and then looked puzzled, as if trying to remember who she was.

Standing in the doorway she smiled back, then turned to leave, and with a slight motion of her head invited him to follow.

Wilf looked unsure. So he should, Ragna thought. He is sitting next to the wife who has cared for him constantly for the last five months – he can hardly walk away from her to chase a slave girl.

Wilf stood up.

Ragna stared at him with her mouth open, horrified. She could not conceal her distress: this was too much. I can't bear it, she thought.

'Sit down, for God's sake,' she hissed. 'Don't be a fool.'

He looked at her, and seemed surprised; then he looked away and addressed the assembled diners. 'Unexpectedly,' he began; and they all started to laugh. 'Unexpectedly, I find I am called away.'

No, Ragna thought; this can't be happening.

But it was. She struggled to hold back tears.

'I shall return later,' Wilf said, walking to the exit.

At the door he paused and turned back, with the instinctive feeling for dramatic timing that he had always had.

He said: 'Much later.'

The men roared with laughter, and he went out.

ÞÞÞ

WYNSTAN, DEGBERT AND Dreng left Shiring quietly, in the dark, leading their horses until they were outside the town. Only a few trusted servants knew they were leaving, and Wynstan was determined that no one else should find out. They had a packhorse loaded with a small barrel and a sack as well as food and drink, but they took no men-at-arms with them. Their mission was a dangerous secret.

They were careful not to be recognized on the road. Even with no entourage, anonymity was not easy. Degbert's bald head was conspicuous, Dreng had a distinctive reedy voice, and Wynstan was one of the best-known men in the region. So they wrapped up in heavy cloaks, buried their chins in the folds, and shrouded their faces by pulling forward their hoods – none of which was unusual in the cold, wet February weather. They hurried past other travellers, spurning the usual exchanges of information. Rather than seek hospitality at an alehouse or monastery where they would have had to reveal their faces, they spent the first night at the home of a family of charcoal burners in the forest, surly unsociable people who paid Wynstan a fee for the licence to follow their occupation.

The nearer they got to Dreng's Ferry, the greater the danger that they would be recognized. They had a mile or two to go on the second day when they suffered a tense moment. They met a group coming in the opposite direction: a family on foot, the women holding a baby, the man with a bucket of eels that he must have bought from Bucca Fish, and two more children trailing behind. Dreng murmured: 'I know that family.'

'So do I,' said Degbert.

Wynstan kicked his horse into a trot, and his companions did likewise. The family scattered to the sides of the road. Wynstan and the others rode past without speaking. The family were too busy getting out of the way of the flying hooves to take a good look at the riders. Wynstan thought they had got away with it.

Soon afterwards they turned off the road onto a near-invisible track through the trees.

Now Degbert took the lead. The woods thickened, and they had to dismount and walk the horses. Degbert found his way to an old ruined house, probably once the home of a forester, long abandoned.

Its broken walls and half-collapsed roof would provide some shelter for their second night.

Dreng gathered an armful of deadfalls and lit a fire with a spark from a flint. Degbert unloaded the packhorse. The three men made themselves as comfortable as they could as night fell.

Wynstan took a long pull from a flask and passed it around. Then he gave instructions. 'You'll have to carry the barrel of tar with you to the village,' he said. 'You can't take the horse – it might make a noise.'

Dreng said: 'I can't carry a barrel. I've got a bad back. A Viking—'

'I know. Degbert can take it. You'll carry the sack of rags.'

'That looks heavy enough.'

Wynstan ignored his grumbling. 'What you have to do is simple. You dip the rags in the tar, then tie them to the bridge, ideally to the ropes and the smaller wooden components. Take your time, tie them tight, don't rush the job. When they're all attached, light a good dry stick, then use that to ignite all the rags, one by one.'

'This is the part that worries me,' said Degbert.

'It will be the middle of the night. A few burning rags won't wake anyone. You'll have all the time in the world. When the rags are alight, walk quietly back up the hill. Don't make a noise, don't run until you're out of earshot. I'll be waiting for you here with the horses.'

'They'll know it was me,' said Dreng.

'They'll suspect you, perhaps. You were foolish enough to oppose the building of the bridge, a protest that was doomed to be ignored, as you should have known.' Wynstan was often infuriated by the stupidity of men such as Dreng. 'But then they'll recall that you were in Shiring when the bridge was set on fire. You were seen in the great hall two days ago, and you'll be seen there again the day after tomorrow. If anyone is smart enough to realize that you were out of sight during a period long enough to get to Dreng's Ferry and back, I will swear that the three of us were at my residence the whole time.'

Degbert said: 'They'll blame outlaws.'

Wynstan nodded. 'Outlaws are useful scapegoats.'

Dreng said: 'I could hang for this.'

'So could I!' said Degbert. 'Stop whining – we're doing it for you!'

'No, you're not. You're doing it because you hate Aldred, both of you.'

It was true.

Degbert detested Aldred for getting him kicked out of his comfortable minster. Wynstan's hatred was more complex. Aldred had challenged him again and again. Each time, Wynstan had punished him; but Aldred never learned his lesson. This maddened Wynstan. People were supposed to be afraid of him. Someone who had defied him should never be seen to prosper. Wynstan's curse had to be fatal. If Aldred could oppose him, others might get the same idea. Aldred was a crack in the wall that might one day bring down the whole building.

Wynstan made himself calm. 'Who cares why we're doing it?' he said, and his fury sounded in his voice despite his effort at self-control, so that the other two looked scared. 'None of us is going to hang,' he said in a more emollient tone. 'If necessary, I shall swear that we're innocent, and the oath of a bishop is too powerful.' He passed the wineskin around again.

After a while he put more wood on the fire and told the others to settle down to rest. 'I'll stay awake,' he said.

They lay down, wrapped in their cloaks, but Wynstan remained sitting upright. He would have to guess when it was the middle of the night. Perhaps the exact hour did not matter, but he needed to feel sure the villagers were in the deepest trough of slumber, and the monks were a few hours away from their pre-dawn service of Matins.

He was uncomfortable, feeling the aches and pains of a body almost forty years old, and he asked himself whether it had really been necessary for him to sleep rough in the forest with Degbert and Dreng; but he knew the answer. He had to make sure they did the job thoroughly and at the same time discreetly. As with all the most important tasks, his hands-on supervision was the only guarantee of success.

He was glad he had gone into battle with Garulf. If he had not been there, the boy would surely have been killed. These were things a bishop should not have to do. But Wynstan was no ordinary bishop.

While he waited for the hours to pass he brooded over the illness of his half-brother Wilf and its consequences for Shiring. It was plain to Wynstan, though not to everyone, that Wilf's recovery was partial. Ragna was still the main conduit for his instructions: she decided what was to be done and then pretended that her decisions were his wishes. Bern the Giant was still in charge of Wilf's personal bodyguard and Sheriff Den was in command of the Shiring army, what was left of it. Wilf's recovery served mainly to allow him to confirm her authority.

Wynstan and Wigelm had been cleverly sidelined. They retained authority in their respective spheres, Wynstan in the diocese and Wigelm at Combe, but they had little general power. Garulf had recovered from his injuries, but the disastrous battle with the Vikings had destroyed his reputation and he had no credibility. Gytha had long been stripped of influence in the compound. Ragna still reigned supreme.

And there was nothing Wynstan could do about it.

He had no trouble staying alert as the night wore on. A maddeningly intractable problem would always keep him awake. He took a few sips of wine now and again, never very much. He threw wood on the fire, just enough to keep it going.

When he judged it was past midnight, he woke Degbert and Dreng.

ÞÞÞ

BRINDLE GROWLED IN the night. The sound did not quite wake Edgar. He was vaguely aware and recognized it as the muted warning the dog gave when he heard someone pass the house at night but recognized the step of a person he knew. Edgar understood that he did not need to respond, and went back to sleep.

Some time later, the dog barked. That was different. It was an urgent, frightened bark that said: *Wake up quickly, now, I'm really scared.*

Edgar smelled burning.

The air was always smokey in his house, as it was in every house in England, but this was a different aroma, sharper and slightly ripe, pungent. In the first moment of wakefulness he thought of tar. In the second moment he realized this was some kind of emergency, and he leaped to his feet, full of fear.

He threw open the door and stepped out. He saw with horror where the smell came from: the bridge was alight. Flames flickered maliciously in a dozen different places, and on the surface of the water their reflections danced with insane glee.

Edgar's masterpiece was burning.

He ran down the hill in his bare feet, hardly noticing the cold. The fire blazed higher in the few seconds it took him to reach the waterside, but the bridge could still be saved, he thought, if enough water could be thrown on it. He stepped into the river, cupped his hands in the water, and splashed a burning timber.

He realized immediately that this was hopelessly inadequate. He had allowed panic to direct him for a few moments. He stopped, breathed, and looked around. Every house was daubed with orange-red reflections. No one else was awake. 'Help!' he yelled desperately. 'Everybody, come quickly! Fire! Fire!'

He ran to the alehouse and banged on the door, shouting. It was opened a moment later by Blod, big-eyed and scared, her dark hair tangled. 'Bring buckets and pots!' Edgar yelled. 'Quickly!' Blod, showing impressive presence of mind, immediately reached behind the door and handed him a wooden bucket.

Edgar dashed into the river and began throwing bucketfuls of water over the flames. Seconds later he was joined by Blod with Ethel, who carried a big clay jar, and Leaf, staggering with an iron cookpot.

It was not enough. The flames were spreading faster than the people could put them out.

Other villagers appeared: Bebbe, Bucca Fish, Cerdic and Ebba, Hadwine and Elfburg, Regenbald Roper. As they ran to the river, Edgar saw that they were all empty-handed. Maddened with frustration, he yelled: 'Bring pots! You idiots, bring pots!' They realized they could do little without water containers, and turned back to their houses to find what was needed.

Meanwhile, the fire grew quickly. The smell of tar was diminishing, but the flat-bottomed boats were burning strongly and even the oak timbers were now catching alight.

Then Aldred came out of the monastery followed by the rest of the monks, all carrying pots, jars and small barrels. 'Go to the downstream side!' Edgar shouted, accompanying his words with an arm gesture. Aldred led the monks into the river on the other side of the bridge and they all began throwing water on the flames.

Soon the whole village had joined in. Some who could swim crossed the cold river and attacked the blaze at the far end of the bridge. But even at the near end, Edgar saw with despair, they were losing the battle.

Mother Agatha arrived with two other nuns in their tiny boat.

Leaf, Dreng's elder wife, who was probably drunk as well as sleepy, stumbled out of the river, exhausted. Edgar noticed her and feared she was in danger of reeling into the flames. She dropped to her knees in the riverside mud and swayed sideways. She managed to right herself, but not before her hair caught fire.

She screamed in pain, came upright, and ran, blindly heading away from the water that could save her. Ethel went after her, but Edgar was quicker. He threw down his bucket and ran. He caught Leaf easily, but saw that she was already badly burned, the skin of her face blackened and cracking. He threw her to the ground. There was no time to carry her back to the river: she would be dead before they got there. He pulled his tunic off and wrapped it around her head, smothering the flames instantly.

Mother Agatha appeared beside him. She bent over and gently removed Edgar's garment from around Leaf's head. It came away scorched, with some of Leaf's hair and face attached to the woollen fibres. She touched Leaf's chest, feeling for a heartbeat, then shook her head sadly.

Ethel burst into tears.

Edgar heard a great creak, like the groan of a giant, then a mammoth splash. He turned to see that the far end of the bridge had crashed into the river.

He glimpsed something on the bank just downstream of the ruined bridge. It piqued his curiosity. Not caring that he was stark naked, he stepped to the bank and picked it up. It was a half-burned rag. He sniffed it. As he had suspected, it had been soaked in tar.

In the light of the dying flames he saw his brothers, Erman and Eadbald, hurrying along the bank from the farmhouse. Cwenburg was close behind them, carrying eighteen-month-old Beorn and holding the hand of Winnie, aged four. Now the whole village was here.

He showed the rag to Aldred. 'Look at this.'

At first Aldred did not understand. 'What is it?'

'A rag soaked in tar and set alight. It obviously fell in the water, which put out the flames.'

'You mean it was originally tied to the bridge?'

'How do you think the bridge caught fire?' The other villagers began to gather around Edgar, listening. 'There's been no storm, no lightning. A house might burn, because a house has a fire in the middle of it, but what could set light to a bridge in the middle of winter?'

The cold got to his naked body at last, and he began to shiver.

Aldred said: 'Someone did this.'

'When I discovered the fire, the bridge was burning in a dozen separate places. An accidental fire starts in one place. This was arson.'

'But who did it?'

Bucca Fish was listening. 'It must have been Dreng,' he said. 'He hates the bridge.' Bucca, by contrast, loved it: his business had multiplied.

Fat Bebbe overheard. 'If it was Dreng, he's killed his own wife,' she said.

The monks crossed themselves, and old Tatwine said: 'God bless her soul.'

Aldred said: 'Dreng is in Shiring. He can't have started the fire.'

Edgar said: 'Who else?'

No one answered the question.

Edgar studied the dying flames, assessing the damage. The far end of the bridge was gone. At the near end, the embers still glowed, and the entire structure was leaning downstream precipitously.

It was utterly beyond repair.

Blod came to him holding a cloak. After a moment he realized it was his own. She must have gone to his house and fetched it. She also had his shoes.

He put the cloak on. He was shivering too much to manage the shoes, so Blod knelt in front of him and put them on his feet.

'Thank you,' said Edgar.

Then he began to cry.

31

JUNE 1002

RAGNA SAT ASTRIDE HER horse and looked down the slope at the village of Dreng's Ferry. The ruined bridge stood out like a gallows in a marketplace. The blackened timbers were twisted and broken. At the far end nothing was left but the deeply embedded abutment: the boats and the superstructure had become detached, and scorched beams littered the downstream banks. At the near side the flat-bottomed boats were still in place, but the framework and the roadbed had collapsed into them, forming a tragic heap of destroyed carpentry.

She felt for Edgar. He had talked passionately about this bridge, whenever they met in Outhenham and Shiring: the challenge of building in the river, the need for strength enough to bear the weight of loaded carts, the beauty of well-fitting oak joinery. He had put his soul into that bridge, and now he must be heartbroken.

No one knew who had set the fire, but Ragna had no doubt about who was behind it. Only Bishop Wynstan was malicious enough to do such a thing and clever enough to get away with it.

She hoped to see Edgar today, to talk about the quarry, but she was not sure whether he was here or at Outhenham. She would be disappointed if she had missed him. However, that was not her main purpose here.

She touched Astrid's flanks with her heels and moved slowly down the hill, followed by her entourage. Wilwulf was with her, and she had brought Agnes as her maid – Cat was back at the compound taking care of the children. Ragna was guarded by Bern and six men-at-arms.

Wilf now spent his days being cared for by Ragna and his nights with Carwen. He pleased himself, as he always had; in that respect he had not changed. He saw Ragna as a banquet table from which he could select what he wanted, leaving the rest. He had loved her body until he was distracted by another one; he relied more than ever on her intelligence to help him govern; and he acted as if she had no more soul than his favourite horse.

In the days since his physical recovery she had developed a sense that he was in danger, an intuition that was getting stronger. She had come to Dreng's Ferry to do something about it. She had a plan, and she was here to win support for it.

Dreng's Ferry smelled of brewing ale, as it often did. She rode past a house with a display of silvery fish on a stone slab outside the door: the village had acquired its first shop. There was a new extension on the north side of the little church.

By the time she and Wilf reached the monastery, Aldred and the monks were lined up outside to greet them. Wilf and the men would sleep here tonight; Ragna and Agnes would cross to Leper Island and spend the night at the nunnery, where Ragna would be welcomed only too warmly by Mother Agatha.

For some reason she was reminded of her first meeting with Aldred, back in Cherbourg. He was still handsome, but his face now had worry lines that had not been there five years ago. He was not yet forty, she calculated, but he looked older.

She greeted him and said: 'Are the others here?'

'Waiting in the church, in accordance with your instructions,' he replied.

She turned to Wilf. 'Why don't you go to the stable with the men and make sure the horses are looked after?'

'Good idea,' said Wilf.

Ragna went with Aldred to the church. 'I see you've built an extension,' she said as they approached the entrance.

'Thanks to free stone from you, and a builder who takes reading lessons instead of pay.'

'Edgar.'

'Of course. The new transept is a side chapel for the relics of St Adolphus.'

They went in. A trestle table had been set up in the nave with parchment, a bottle of ink, several quills, and a pen knife with which to sharpen the points of the quills. Sitting on benches at the table were Bishop Modulf of Norwood and Sheriff Den.

Ragna felt confident of the support of Aldred for her scheme. The hard-faced Sheriff Den had consented in advance. She was not so sure of Modulf, a thin man with a sharp mind. He would help her if her plan made sense to him, but not otherwise.

She sat down with them. 'Thank you, bishop, and you, sheriff, for agreeing to meet me here.'

Den said: 'Always a pleasure, my lady.'

Modulf said warily: 'I'm eager to hear the reason for this mysterious invitation.'

Ragna got straight down to business. 'Ealdorman Wilwulf is now physically well, but as you eat supper with him this evening you'll wonder about his mind. I can tell you now that he is not the man he used to be, mentally, and all the signs are that he will never return to normal.'

Den nodded. 'I had wondered . . .'

Modulf said: 'And what, exactly, do you mean when you say "mentally"?'

'His memory is erratic and he has difficulty with numbers. This leads him to make embarrassing mistakes. He addressed Thane Deorman of Norwood as "Emma" and offered him a thousand pounds for his horse. If I'm present, which is nearly always, I laugh and try to brush it off.'

Modulf said: 'This is bad news.'

'I'm sure Wilf is now incapable of leading an army against the Vikings.'

Aldred said: 'I noticed, a few minutes ago, that you told him to go to the stable with the men, and he just obeyed you like a child.'

Ragna nodded. 'The old Wilf would have bristled at orders from his wife. But he's lost his aggression.'

Den said: 'That makes it serious.'

Ragna went on: 'For the most part people accept my explanations, but that can't last. The shrewder men are already noticing a change, as Aldred and Den have, and before long people will talk of it openly.'

Den said: 'A weak ealdorman offers an opportunity to an ambitious and unscrupulous thane.'

Aldred said: 'What do you think might happen, sheriff?'

Den did not answer immediately.

Ragna said: 'I think someone will kill him.'

Den gave the briefest of nods: it was what he had thought but hesitated to say.

There was a long silence.

Finally Modulf said: 'But what can Aldred, Den and I do about it?'

Ragna suppressed a sigh of satisfaction. She had won her point; she had convinced the bishop that there was a problem. Now she had to sell him her solution.

'I think there is one way to protect him,' she said. 'He's going to make a will. It will be in English, so that Wilf can read it.'

'And me,' said Den. Noblemen and royal officials could often read English but not Latin.

Modulf said: 'And what will the deed say?'

'He will make our son Osbert heir to his fortune and the ealdormanry, with me to manage everything on Osbert's behalf until he comes of age. Wilf will agree to it today, here in the church, and

I'm asking you three dignitaries to witness his agreement and put your names to the document.'

Modulf said: 'I'm not a worldly man. I'm afraid I don't see how this protects Wilwulf from assassination.'

'The only motive for anyone to murder Wilf would be the hope of succeeding him as ealdorman. The will pre-empts that by making Osbert the successor.'

Den, who was the king's man in Shiring, said: 'Such a will would have no validity unless endorsed by the king.'

'Indeed,' said Ragna. 'And when I have your names on the parchment I will take it to King Ethelred and beg his consent.'

'Will the king agree?' said Modulf.

Den said: 'Inheritance is by no means automatic. It is the king's prerogative to choose the ealdorman.'

'I don't know what the king will say,' Ragna said. 'I only know I have to ask.'

Aldred said: 'Where is the king now – does anybody know?'

Den knew. 'As it happens, he's on his way south,' he said. 'He'll be at Sherborne in three weeks' time.'

'I will see him there,' said Ragna.

þþþ

EDGAR KNEW THAT Ragna had arrived in Dreng's Ferry, but he was not sure he would see her. She was with Wilwulf, and they had come for a meeting at the monastery that involved two other nobles whose identities were being kept secret. So he was surprised and overjoyed when she walked into his house.

It was like the sun coming from behind a cloud. He felt short of breath, as if he had been running uphill. She smiled, and he was the happiest man on earth.

She looked around his house, and suddenly he saw it through her eyes: the neat rack of tools on the wall, the small wine barrel and cheese safe, the cooking pot over the fire giving off a pleasant herby odour, Brindle wagging a greeting.

She pointed to the box on the table. 'That's beautiful,' she said. Edgar had made it, and carved a design of interlocking serpents to symbolize wisdom. 'What do you keep in such a lovely container?' she asked.

'Something precious. A gift from you.' He lifted the lid.

Inside was a small book called *Enigmata*, a collection of riddles in poem form, a favourite of Ragna's. She had given it to him when he learned to read. 'I didn't know you'd made a special box for it,' she said. 'How nice.'

'I must be the only builder in England who owns a book.'

She gave him that smile again and said: 'God didn't make two like you, Edgar.'

He felt warm all over.

She said: 'I'm so sorry about the burning of the bridge! I'm sure Wynstan had something to do with it.'

'I agree.'

'Can you rebuild it?'

'Yes, but what's the point? It could be burned down again. He got away with it once, he may do so again.'

'I suppose so.'

Edgar was sick of talking about the bridge. To change the subject he asked her: 'How are you?'

She seemed about to make a conventional reply, then appeared to change her mind. 'To tell you the truth, I'm utterly miserable.'

Edgar was taken aback. It was an intimate confession. He said: 'I'm so sorry. What's happened?'

'Wilwulf doesn't love me, and I'm not sure he ever did, not as I understand love.'

'But . . . you seemed so fond of each other.'

'Oh, he couldn't get enough of me for a while, but that wore off.

He treats me like one of his men friends now. He hasn't come to my bed for a year.'

Edgar could not help feeling glad about that. It was an unworthy thought, and he hoped it did not show on his face.

Ragna appeared not to notice. 'He prefers his slave girl at night,' she said with contempt in her voice. 'She's fourteen years old.'

Edgar wanted to express the sympathy he was feeling, but it was difficult to find words. 'That's shameful,' he said.

She let her anger show. 'And it's not what we promised when we made our vows! I never agreed to this kind of marriage.'

He wanted to keep her talking because he yearned to know more. 'How do you feel about Wilf now?'

'For a long time I tried to go on loving him, hoped to win him back, dreamed that he would tire of others. But now something else has happened. The head injury he suffered last year has damaged his mind. The man I married is gone. Half the time I'm not sure he even remembers that he's married to me. He treats me more like a mother.' Her eyes filled with tears.

Tentatively, Edgar reached for her. She did not move away. He took both her hands in his, and was thrilled when he felt her answering grasp. He looked at her face and felt closer to contentment than he had ever been. He watched the tears overflow her eyes and run down her face, raindrops on rose petals. Her expression was a grimace of pain, but to him she had never been more beautiful. They stood still for a long time.

At last she said: 'I'm still married, though.' And she withdrew her hands.

He said nothing.

She wiped her face with her sleeve. 'May I have a sip of wine?'

'Anything.' He drew wine from the barrel into a wooden cup.

She drank it and handed back the cup. 'Thank you.' She began to look more normal. 'I have to cross the river to the nunnery.'

Edgar smiled. 'Don't let Mother Agatha kiss you too much.'
Everyone liked Agatha, but she did have a weakness.

Ragna said: 'Sometimes it's a comfort to be loved.' She gave him
a direct look, and he understood that she was talking about him as
well as Agatha. He felt bewildered. He needed time to think about
that.

After a moment she said: 'How do I look? Will they know what
we've been doing?'

And what have we been doing? Edgar wondered. 'You look fine,'
he said. What a stupid thing to say, he thought. 'You look like a sad
angel.'

'I wish I had the powers of an angel,' she said. 'Think what I could
do.'

'What would you do first?'

She smiled, shook her head, turned around, and left.

ÞÞÞ

ONCE AGAIN WYNSTAN spoke to Agnes in a corner of the chancel,
near the altar but out of sight of the nave. There was a Bible on the
altar and, near his feet, a chest containing holy water and the
sacramental bread. Wynstan had no qualms about conducting
business in the holiest part of the church. He worshipped Jehovah,
the Old Testament God who had ordered the genocide of the
Canaanites. What needs to be done must be done, and God had no
use for the squeamish, he believed.

Agnes was excited but nervous. 'I don't know the whole story, but
I have to tell you anyway,' she said.

'You're a wise woman,' he said. She was not, but he needed her to
calm down. 'Just tell me what happened, and leave me to figure out
its significance.'

'Ragna went to Dreng's Ferry.'

Wynstan had heard as much, but he did not know what to make

of it. There was nothing for Ragna in that little hamlet. She had a soft spot for the young builder, but Wynstan felt sure she was not fucking him. 'What did she do there?'

'She and Wilf met with Aldred and two other men. The identities of the others were supposed to be secret, but it's a small place, and I saw them. They were Bishop Modulf of Norwood and Sheriff Den.'

Wynstan frowned. That was interesting, but it raised more questions than it answered. 'Did you get any hint of the purpose of the meeting?'

'No, but I think they all witnessed a parchment.'

'A written agreement,' Wynstan mused. 'I don't suppose you caught a glimpse of it.'

She smiled. 'What would such a thing mean to me?' She could not read, of course.

'I wonder what that French bitch is up to,' Wynstan said, mainly to himself. Most documents were about land being sold, leased or gifted. Had Ragna persuaded Wilf to transfer land to Prior Aldred or Bishop Modulf, a pious gift? But that would not have needed a secret meeting. Marriage contracts might be written, if property was to change hands, but it seemed no marriage had taken place at Dreng's Ferry. Births were not recorded, even royal births, but deaths were – and wills were written. Had someone made a will? Ragna might have persuaded Wilf to do so. Wilf had not recovered fully from his head wound, and might yet die of it.

The more Wynstan thought about it, the more sure he felt that the purpose of Ragna's clandestine meeting was to get the ealdorman's will secretly written and witnessed.

The problem with that was that a nobleman's will meant little. The king had control of every dead nobleman's property, including that of widows. No will had any force unless it was ratified in advance by the king.

Wynstan asked Agnes: 'Was anything said about going to see King Ethelred?'

'How did you know that?' she said. 'You're so clever! Yes, I heard Bishop Modulf say he would see Ragna at Sherborne when the king is there.'

'That's it,' said Wynstan decisively. 'She's written Wilf's will, it's been witnessed by a bishop, a sheriff and a prior, and now she's going to ask for royal approval.'

'Why would she do that?'

'She thinks Wilf is going to die, and she wants her son to inherit.' Wynstan thought further. 'She will have got Wilf to designate her to rule as regent for Osbert until he comes of age, I'm sure.'

'But Garulf is also Wilf's son, and he's twenty. Surely the king would prefer him to a child.'

'Unfortunately Garulf's a fool, and the king knows it. Last year Garulf lost most of the Shiring army in one injudicious battle, and Ethelred was furious about the waste of all those fighting men. Ragna is a woman, but she's as clever as a cat, and the king would probably rather have her in charge of Shiring than Garulf.'

'You understand everything,' Agnes said admiringly.

She was gazing at him in adoration, and he wondered whether he should gratify her evident desire, but he decided it was better to keep her hoping. He touched her cheek, as if he were about to whisper an endearment, but what he said was: 'Where would Ragna keep such a document?'

'At the house, in the locked chest with her money,' Agnes said in an ardent whisper.

He kissed her lips. 'Thank you,' he said. 'You'd better go.'

He watched her walk away. She had a nice trim figure. Maybe one day he would give her what her heart desired.

But the news she had brought him was no light matter. It could mean the final demise of his powerful family. He had to talk to his younger brother about it. Wigelm happened to be in Shiring, and staying at the bishop's residence, but Wynstan wanted to have a plan of action worked out before he opened the conversation. He remained in the cathedral, alone, glad of the chance to think without interruption.

As he brooded, it became clear to him that his troubles would never be over until he had destroyed Ragna. The problem was not just the will. As the wife of a disabled ealdorman Ragna had power, and she was sufficiently intelligent and determined to make the most of it.

Whatever Wynstan decided, he had to act quickly. If Ethelred endorsed the will, its provisions would be set in stone: nothing Wynstan could do thereafter would change anything. Ragna must not be allowed even to show it to the king.

Ethelred was due in Sherborne in eighteen days' time.

Wynstan left the cathedral and crossed the market square to his residence. He found Wigelm on the upstairs floor, sitting on a bench, sharpening a dagger on a stone. He looked up and said: 'What's made you glum?'

Wynstan shooed a couple of servants out and closed the door. 'In a minute you're going to be glum too,' he said, and he told Wigelm what Agnes had reported.

'King Ethelred must never see that will!' said Wigelm.

'Obviously,' said Wynstan. 'It's a knife at my throat, and yours.'

Wigelm thought for a minute, then said: 'We have to steal the will and destroy it.'

Wynstan sighed. Sometimes it seemed he was the only person who understood anything. 'People make copies of documents to guard against that sort of thing. I imagine that all three witnesses took away duplicates from the meeting at Dreng's Ferry. In the unlikely event that there are no copies, Ragna could just write another will and get it witnessed again.'

Wigelm's face took on a familiar petulant look. 'Well, what can we do, then?'

'We can't let the situation continue.'

'I agree.'

'We have to destroy Ragna's power.'

'I'm in favour of that.'

Wynstan led Wigelm step by step. 'Her power depends on Wilf.'

'And we don't want to take that away from him.'

'No.' Wynstan sighed. 'I hate to say it, but all our problems will be solved if Wilf dies soon.'

Wigelm shrugged. 'That's in God's hands, as you priests like to say.'

'Perhaps.'

'What?'

'His demise could be hastened.'

Wigelm was baffled. 'What are you talking about?'

'There's only one answer.'

'Well, come on, spit it out, Wynstan.'

'We have to kill Wilf.'

'Ha, ha!'

'I mean it.'

Wigelm was shocked. 'He's our brother!'

'Half-brother. And he's losing his mind. He's more or less under control of the Norman cow, something that would shame him if he wasn't too demented to know that it's happening. It will be a kindness to end his life.'

'Still . . .' Wigelm lowered his voice, even though the room was empty but for the two of them. 'To kill a brother!'

'What needs to be done must be done.'

'We can't,' said Wigelm. 'It's out of the question. Think of something else. You're the great thinker.'

'And I think you'll hate it when you're replaced, as reeve of Combe, by someone who hands over taxes to the ealdorman without skimming a fifth off the top.'

'Would Ragna replace me?'

'In a heartbeat. She'd have done it already, except that no one would believe Wilf had agreed to it. Once he's gone . . .'

Wigelm looked thoughtful again. 'King Ethelred wouldn't stand for it.'

'Why not?' said Wynstan. 'He did the same thing himself.'

'I've heard some such story.'

'Twenty-four years ago, Ethelred's older half-brother Edward was king. Ethelred was living with his mother, Elfryth, who was stepmother to the king. Edward went to visit them and was murdered by their men-at-arms. Ethelred was crowned the following year.'

'Ethelred must have been about twelve years old.'

Wynstan shrugged. 'Young? Yes. Innocent? God knows.'

Wigelm made a sceptical face. 'We can't kill Wilf. He has a squad of bodyguards, commanded by Bern the Giant, who is a Norman and a long-time servant of Ragna's.'

One day, Wynstan thought, I won't be here to do all the thinking for my family. I wonder if then they will just stand still and do nothing, like an ox team when the ploughman walks away.

He said: 'The killing itself is easy. It's the management of the aftermath we have to worry about. We'll need to move into action the minute he's dead, while Ragna is still stunned with shock. We don't want to eliminate Wilf only to find that she takes charge anyway. We have to become masters of Shiring before she recovers her composure.'

'How do we do that?'

'We need a plan.'

ÞÞÞ

RAGNA WAS NOT sure about the feast.

Gytha had come to her with a reasonable request. 'We should

celebrate Wilf's recovery,' she said. 'Let everyone know that he's fit and well again.'

He was not, of course, but the pretence was important. However, Ragna did not like him to drink to excess: he became even more fuddled than a normal drunk. 'What kind of celebration?' she said, prevaricating.

'A feast,' said Gytha. 'The way *he* likes,' she added pointedly. 'With dancing girls, not poets.'

He was entitled to some fun, Ragna thought guiltily. 'And a juggler,' she said. 'And a jester, perhaps?'

'I knew you'd agree,' Gytha said quickly, nailing it down.

'I have to leave for Sherborne on the first day of July,' Ragna said. 'Let's do it on the night before.'

That morning she made her plans and packed her bags. She was ready to depart next day, but first she had to sit through tonight's feast.

Gytha donated a barrel of mead to the festivities. Made from fermented honey, mead was both sweet and strong, and men could get drunk on it quickly. Ragna would have forbidden it if she had been asked, but now she did not want to seem a killjoy, so she made no objection. She could do no more than hope that Wilf would not drink too much. She spoke to Bern and ordered him to remain sober, so that he could look after Wilf if necessary.

Wilf and his brothers were in convivial mood, but to her relief they seemed to be drinking moderately. Some of the men-at-arms were not so judicious, perhaps because for them mead was a rare treat, and the evening became raucous.

The jester was very funny, and came dangerously close to lampooning Wynstan, pretending to be a priest and blessing a dancing girl then grabbing her breasts. Happily, Wynstan was not in a mood to take offence, and he laughed as heartily as anyone.

Darkness fell, the lamps were lit, the table was cleared of dirty bowls, and the drinking continued. Some people became sleepy or amorous, or both. Adolescents flirted, and married women giggled when their friends' husbands took minor liberties. If major liberties were taken, it happened outside, in the dark.

Wilf began to look tired. Ragna was about to suggest that Bern help him to bed, but his brothers took charge: Wynstan and Wigelm held an arm each and escorted him out.

Carwen followed close behind.

Ragna summoned Bern. 'The bodyguards are all more or less drunk,' she said. 'I want you to stand guard with them all night.'

'Yes, my lady,' said Bern.

'You can sleep tomorrow morning.'

'Thank you.'

'Goodnight, Bern.'

'Goodnight, my lady.'

ÞÞÞ

Wynstan and Wigelm went to Gytha's house and sat up into the small hours, talking in desultory fashion, making sure they did not fall asleep.

Wynstan had explained the plan to Gytha, and she had been shocked and horrified at the idea that her sons wanted to murder her stepson. She had challenged Wynstan's deduction about the document written at Dreng's Ferry: could he be sure it was Wilf's last will and testament? As it happened, Wynstan was able to reassure her, for he had received confirmation of his speculation. Bishop Modulf had indiscreetly confided in his neighbour Thane Deorman of Norwood, and Deorman had told Wynstan.

Gytha had agreed to Wynstan's plan, as he had known she would in the end. 'What needs to be done must be done,' she had said. All the same she looked troubled.

Wynstan was tense. If this went seriously wrong, and the plot was revealed, both he and Wigelm would be executed for treason.

He had tried to envisage every possible obstacle in his way, and plan how to overcome each one, but there were always unexpected snags, and that thought kept him stressed.

When he judged the time was right he stood up. He picked up a lamp, a leather strap, and a small cloth bag, all of which he had got ready earlier.

Wigelm got to his feet and nervously touched the long-bladed dagger in its sheath at his belt.

Gytha said: 'Don't make Wilf suffer, will you?'

Wigelm replied: 'I'll do my best.'

'He's not my son, but I loved his father. Remember that.'

Wynstan said: 'We'll remember it, Mother.'

The two brothers left the house.

Here we go, Wynstan thought.

There were always three bodyguards outside Wilf's house: one at the door and one at each of the two front corners of the building. Wigelm had spent two nights observing them, partly through cracks in Gytha's walls and partly by going outside to piss frequently. He had found that all three bodyguards spent most of the night sitting on the ground with their backs to the walls of the house, and they often dozed off. Tonight they were probably in a drunken stupor and would not even know that two murderers were entering the house they were guarding. However, Wynstan had a story ready in case they were wide awake.

They were not, but he was taken aback to find Bern standing in front of Wilf's door.

'God be with you, my lord bishop, and you, Thane Wigelm,' said Bern in his French accent.

'And with you.' Wynstan recovered quickly from the shock and implemented the fall-back plan he had devised in case the bodyguards were not asleep. 'We have to wake Wilf,' he said, speaking low but clearly. 'It's an emergency.' He glanced at the other two guards, who slept on. Improvising, he said to Bern: 'Come inside with us – you need to hear this.'

'Yes, my lord.' Bern looked puzzled, as well he might – how would the brothers have learned of this emergency, in the middle of the night, when no one appeared to have entered the compound to bring news? But though he frowned, he opened the door. His task was to protect Wilf, but it would not occur to him that the ealdorman was in danger from his own brothers.

Wynstan knew exactly what had to happen now to counteract the surprise interference of Bern – it was obvious to him – but would Wigelm figure it out? Wynstan could only hope.

Wynstan went in, walking quietly on the straw. Wilf and Carwen were asleep on the bed, wrapped in blankets. Wynstan put the lamp and the cloth bag on the table but kept hold of the strap. Then he turned to look back.

Bern was closing the door behind him. Wigelm reached for his dagger. Wynstan heard a noise from the bed.

He looked at the two in bed and saw that Carwen was opening her eyes.

He grasped the ends of the strap and stretched a length of about a foot between his two hands. At the same time he went down on one knee beside the slave girl. She came awake quickly, sat up, looked terrified, and opened her mouth to shout. Wynstan dropped the belt over her head, drew it into her open mouth like a horse's bit, and pulled it tight. Thus gagged, she could make only desperate gargling sounds. He twisted the belt tighter, then looked behind him.

He saw Wigelm cut Bern's throat with a powerful slash of his long dagger. Well done, Wynstan thought. Blood spurted and Wigelm jumped out of the way. Bern fell. The only noise was the thud his body made as it hit the ground.

That's it, Wynstan thought; now there's no turning back.

He turned to see Wilf waking up. Carwen's grunting took on fresh urgency. Wilf's eyes opened wide. Even with his reduced mental capacity he could grasp what was happening in front of him. He sat bolt upright and reached for the knife beside his bed.

But Wigelm was quicker. He reached the bed in two strides and fell on Wilf just as Wilf grasped his weapon. Wigelm brought his knife hand down in a long overhand swing, but Wilf raised his left arm and knocked aside Wigelm's blow. Then Wilf thrust at Wigelm, but Wigelm dodged.

Wigelm lifted his arm for another slash, but suddenly Carwen moved, surprising Wynstan, who did not have her restrained as tightly as he had thought. Still gagged, she jumped on Wigelm, pummelling him and trying to scratch his face, and it took Wynstan a moment to tug on the belt and jerk her back. He jumped on her, landing with both knees. Keeping hold of the belt with his right hand, he drew his own dagger with his left.

Wilf and Wigelm were still grappling and it seemed neither had struck a telling blow. Wynstan saw Wilf open his mouth to yell for help. That would have been disastrous: the plan required a silent murder. Wynstan leaned over as a roar began in Wilf's throat. Using all the force he could muster in his left arm, he plunged the dagger into Wilf's mouth and thrust it as hard as he could down Wilf's throat.

The roar was cut off almost before it began.

Wynstan suffered a moment of paralysed horror. He saw the panic of extreme pain in Wilf's eyes. He jerked the knife out, as if that would somehow mitigate the atrocity.

Wilf gave a strangled grunt of agony and blood poured out of his mouth. He writhed in pain, but he did not die. Wynstan had been in battle, and he knew that men with fatal wounds might suffer a long time before they died. He needed to put Wilf out of his misery but he could not bring himself to do it.

Then Wigelm administered the coup de grâce, plunging his knife into the left side of Wilf's chest, aiming accurately for the heart. The blade sunk in deep and stilled Wilf in an instant.

Wigelm said: 'May God forgive us both.'

Carwen began to cry.

Wynstan listened hard. He could hear nothing from outside the house. The killing had been done quietly and the guards had not been disturbed from their drunken slumbers.

He took a deep breath and pulled himself together. 'That's only the beginning,' he said.

He climbed off Carwen, still holding the gag tightly, and pulled her to her feet. 'Now you listen to me carefully,' he said.

She stared at him with terrified eyes. She had seen two men stabbed to death and she thought she might be next.

'Nod if you understand me,' Wynstan said.

She nodded with frantic energy.

'Wigelm and I are going to swear that you murdered Wilf.'

She shook her head from side to side vigorously.

'You could deny it. You could tell everyone the truth about what happened here tonight. You could accuse me and Wigelm of cold-blooded murder.'

He could tell by her expression that she was bewildered.

He said: 'But who will believe you? The oath of a slave is worthless – doubly so against that of a bishop.'

He saw understanding dawn in her eyes, followed by despair.

'You see the position you're in,' he said with satisfaction. 'But I'm going to offer you a chance. I'm going to let you escape.'

She stared at him incredulously.

'In two minutes' time you're going to leave the compound and walk out of Shiring by the Glastonbury road. Travel by night and hide in the woods by day.'

She looked at the door, as if making sure that it was there.

Wynstan did not want her to be recaptured, so he had prepared some things that would help her. 'Take that bag on the table beside the lamp,' he said. 'It contains bread and ham, so that you won't need to find food for a couple of days. It also contains twelve silver pennies, but don't spend them until you're a long way away.'

He could see from her eyes that she understood.

'Tell anyone you meet that you're going to Bristol to find your husband, who is a sailor. In Bristol you can get a boat across the estuary to Wales, and then you'll be safe.'

She nodded again, slowly this time, taking in his meaning and thinking about it.

He held his knife to her throat. 'Now I'm going to take this gag out of your mouth, and if you scream, it will be the last sound you ever make.'

She nodded again.

He released the strap.

She swallowed and rubbed her cheeks where the leather had left red marks.

Wynstan noticed that Wigelm had splashes of blood on his hands and face. He assumed that his own body showed similar tell-tale signs. There was a bowl of water on a table and he washed himself quickly and gestured to Wigelm to do the same. They probably had blood on their clothes, too, but Wigelm was wearing brown and Wynstan was in black so it showed only as unidentifiable stains that told no particular story.

The water in the bowl was now pink so Wynstan emptied it onto the floor.

Then he said to Carwen: 'Put on your shoes and cloak.'

She did as she was told.

He handed her the bag.

'We're going to open the door. If the remaining two guards are awake, Wigelm and I will kill them. If they're asleep, we will tiptoe past them. Then you will walk, briskly but quietly, to the gate of the compound and silently let yourself out.'

She nodded.

'Let's go.'

Wynstan opened the door softly and peeped out.

Both bodyguards were slumped against the wall. One was snoring.

Wynstan stepped out, waited for Carwen and Wigelm, then closed the door.

He gestured to Carwen and she walked away, quickly and silently.

He allowed himself a moment of satisfaction. Her flight would be seen by everyone as proof of guilt.

Wynstan and Wigelm walked to Gytha's house. At her door, Wynstan looked back. The guards had not moved.

He and Wigelm went into their mother's house and shut the door.

ÞÞÞ

RAGNA HAD BEEN sleeping badly for months. She had too many worries: Wilf, Wynstan, Carwen, Osbert and the twins. When at last she fell asleep she often had bad dreams. Tonight she dreamed that Edgar had murdered Wilf, and she was trying to protect the builder from justice, but every time she said something her voice was drowned out by shouting from outside. Then she realized that she was dreaming but the shouting was real, and she woke quickly and sat upright, her heart pounding.

The cries were urgent. Two or three men were calling out, and a woman was speaking in a high-pitched scream. Ragna jumped up and looked for Bern, who normally slept just inside her door; then she remembered that she had assigned him to guard Wilf.

She heard Agnes say: 'What's that?' in a frightened voice.

Then Cat said: 'Something's happened.'

Their fearful voices woke the children, and the twins began to cry.

Ragna pulled on her shoes, snatched up her cloak, and went out.

It was still dark, and she saw immediately that there were lights in Wilf's house, and his door was wide open. Her breath caught in her throat. Had something happened to him?

She ran across the short distance to his door and stepped inside.

At first she could not make sense of the scene in front of her. Men and women were milling around, all speaking at the tops of their voices. There was a metallic smell in the air, and she saw blood on the floor and on the bed, lots of blood. Then she made out Bern, lying in a congealed puddle, his throat horribly slashed, and she gasped with horror and dismay. At last her gaze went to the bed. In among the red-stained blankets was her husband.

She let out a scream, and cut it short with a fist in her mouth. He was horribly wounded, his mouth full of dried black blood. His eyes were open and staring at the ceiling. A knife lay on the bed beside his open fist: he had tried to defend himself.

There was no sign of Carwen.

Staring at the ruin of Wilf she remembered the tall, fair-haired man in a blue cloak who had walked off a ship in Cherbourg harbour and said in bad French: 'I have come to speak with Count Hubert.' She began to cry but, even while she wept, she had to ask a question, and she forced the words out: 'How did this happen?'

She was answered by Wuffa, the head groom. 'The bodyguards were asleep,' he said. 'They must die for their negligence.'

'They will,' Ragna said, dashing the tears from her eyes with her fingers. 'But what do they say happened?'

'They woke up and noticed that Bern was gone. They searched for him, eventually looked inside the house, and saw' – he spread his arms – 'this.'

Ragna swallowed and made her voice calmer. 'No one else here?'

'No. Obviously the slave did it and fled.'

Ragna frowned. Carwen would have to be stronger than she looked to kill two such big men with a knife, she thought, but she set the suspicion aside for the moment. 'Fetch the sheriff,' she told Wuffa. 'He must start the hue and cry as soon as dawn breaks.' Whether Carwen was the killer or not, she must be recaptured, for her testimony would be crucial.

'Yes, my lady.' Wuffa hurried away.

As he went out, Agnes came in carrying the twins. Just over a year old, the children did not understand what they were looking at, but Agnes screamed and they began to bawl.

Cat entered holding three-year-old Osbert by the hand. She stared at the corpse of Bern, her husband, in horrified disbelief. 'No, no, no,' she said, and she let go of Osbert's hand and knelt beside the body, shaking her head, sobbing.

Ragna struggled to think straight. What did she need to do next? Although she had thought about Wilf's death, and feared that he might be murdered, the actual event had rocked her so hard that she could hardly digest what had happened. She knew she should react quickly and decisively but she was too shocked and bewildered.

She listened to her sons crying and realized they should not be here. She was about to tell Agnes to take them away when she was distracted by the sight of Wigelm moving towards the door with a heavy oak chest in his arms. She recognized it as Wilf's treasury, the box in which he kept his money.

She stood in front of Wigelm and said: 'Stop!'

Wigelm said: 'Get out of my way or I'll knock you down.'

The room went quiet.

Ragna said: 'That's the treasury of the ealdormanry.'

'It *was*.'

Ragna let her voice express the contempt and loathing she felt. 'Wilf's blood isn't dry yet, and you're already stealing his money.'

'I'm taking charge of it, as his brother.'

Ragna realized that Garulf and Stiggy had moved to stand either side of her, trapping her. She spoke defiantly. 'I will decide who takes charge of the treasury.'

'No, you won't.'

'I am the ealdorman's wife.'

'No, you're not. You're his widow.'

'Put the box down.'

'Get out of the way.'

Ragna slapped Wigelm's face hard.

She expected him to drop the box, but he restrained himself and nodded to Garulf.

The two young men seized Ragna, taking one arm each. She knew she could not escape from their grasp, so she maintained her dignity and did not struggle. She looked at Wigelm with narrowed eyes. 'You're not quick-thinking,' she said. 'Therefore you must have planned this. It's a coup. Did you murder Wilf so that you could take over?'

'Don't be disgusting.'

She looked at the men and women around her. They were watching the scene avidly. They knew this was about who was going to rule them after Wilf. She had planted in their minds the suspicion that Wigelm had killed Wilf. For now she could do no more.

Wigelm said: 'The slave killed Wilf.' He walked around Ragna and out through the door.

Garulf and Stiggy released Ragna.

She looked again at Agnes and Cat and the children, and realized there was no one left in her home. Her treasury, containing Wilf's will, was unguarded. She hurried out, leaving Cat and Agnes to follow her.

She crossed the compound quickly and entered her house. She went to the corner where the treasury was kept. The blanket that normally covered it had been cast aside, and the chest had gone.

She had lost everything.

32

RAGNA ARRIVED AT SHERIFF Den's compound an hour before dawn. The men, and a few women, were already gathering for the hue and cry, milling around in the dark, talking excitedly. The horses sensed the mood and stamped and snorted impatiently. Den finished saddling his black stallion then invited Ragna into his house so that they could talk in private.

Ragna's panic was over and she had postponed her grief. She now knew what she had to do. She realized she was under attack by utterly ruthless people, but she was not defeated, and she was going to fight back.

And Den would be her principal ally – if she handled him right.

She said to him: 'The slave Carwen knows exactly what happened in Wilf's house tonight.'

'You don't think it's obvious,' he commented without surprise.

Good, she thought; he hasn't prejudged the matter. 'On the contrary, I think the obvious explanation is the wrong explanation.'

'Tell me why.'

'Firstly, Carwen did not seem to be unhappy. She was well fed, no one beat her, and she was sleeping with the most attractive man in town. What could she have been running from?'

'She may simply have been homesick.'

'True, though she showed no sign of it. But, secondly, if she wanted to escape, she could have gone at any time – she was never closely guarded. She could have left without killing Wilf or anyone else.

Wilf slept heavily, especially after drink. She could have slipped away.'

'And if the guards happened to be awake?'

'She would just have said she was going to Gytha's house, which is where she slept when Wilf didn't want her. And then her absence might not have been noticed for a day or more.'

'All right.'

'But thirdly, and most importantly, I don't believe that little girl could have killed either Wilf or Bern, let alone both. You saw the wounds. They were done with a strong arm by someone who had the confidence and the power to overcome two big men, both of whom were accustomed to violence. Carwen is fourteen.'

'It would be surprising, I agree. But if not her, who?'

Ragna had a strong suspicion, but she did not state it right away. 'It must have been someone Bern knew.'

'How can you be sure of that?'

'Because Bern let the murderer enter the house. If it had been a stranger, Bern would have been on his guard. He would have stopped the visitor, questioned him, refused him entry, and fought with him – all outside the house, where the noise would have awakened the guards. And Bern's body would have been found outside the house.'

'The killer could have dragged it inside.'

'The sound of the fight would have awakened Wilf, who would have got out of bed and attacked the intruder. Clearly that didn't happen, for Wilf died in his bed.'

'So someone known to Bern appeared and was ushered into the house. As soon as they were inside, the unsuspecting Bern was surprised and killed quickly and silently. Then the visitor killed Wilf, and persuaded the slave to run away so that she would be blamed.'

'That's what I think happened.'

'And the reason for the murder?'

'The key to that lies in two things that happened in the confusion immediately after the bodies were discovered. When everyone else was shocked and bewildered, Wigelm calmly made off with Wilf's treasury.'

'Really?'

'And then someone stole mine.'

'This changes everything.'

'It means Wigelm is making a bid for power.'

'Yes – but that doesn't prove he was the murderer. His power grab might be opportunistic. He could be taking advantage of something he didn't instigate.'

'Possibly, but I doubt it. Wigelm is not sufficiently quick-thinking. This whole thing seems to me to have been carefully planned.'

'You may be right. It smells of Wynstan.'

'Exactly.' Ragna was pleased and relieved. Den had questioned her closely but had ended up coming round to her point of view. She moved on quickly. 'If I am to defeat this coup, I need Carwen to tell her story at the shire court.'

'She may not be believed. The word of a slave . . .'

'Some people will believe her, especially when I explain what drove Wynstan to do this.'

Den did not comment on that. He said: 'Meanwhile, you're penniless. Your treasury has been stolen. You can't win a power battle without money.'

'I can get more. Edgar will have money for me from the sale of stone at my quarry. And in a few weeks I'll have my rents from Saint-Martin.'

'Presumably Wilf's will was in the same chest?'

'Yes – but you have a copy.'

'However, the will has no force without the king's approval.'

'All the same I'll read it out in court. Wilf's intentions prove Wynstan's motive. The thanes will be influenced by that: they all want their dying wishes to be respected.'

'True.'

Ragna returned her attention to the day's challenges. 'None of this will matter unless you can catch Carwen.'

'I'll do my best.'

'But don't lead the hue and cry yourself. Send Wigbert.'

Den was surprised. 'He's reliable . . .'

'And as mean as a starving cat. But I need you here. They'll do a lot of things, but they won't actually murder me if you're in town. They know you'd go after them, and you're the king's man.'

'Perhaps you're right. Wigbert is more than capable of leading a hue and cry. He's done it many times.'

'Where might Carwen have gone?'

'West, presumably. I imagine she wants to go home to Wales. Assuming she left here around midnight, she will have walked at least ten miles along the Glastonbury road by now.'

'She might take shelter somewhere near Trench, perhaps?'

'Exactly.' He glanced through the open door. 'First light. Time for them to get started.'

'I hope they find her.'

ÞÞÞ

WYNSTAN WAS SATISFIED with progress. His plan had gone not perfectly but well enough. It had been a nasty shock to find Bern outside Wilf's door, alert and sober; but Wynstan had reacted quickly and Wigelm had known what to do; and after that everything had happened as intended.

The story that Carwen had killed both Bern and Wilf was a good deal less plausible than Wynstan's original, which was that she had cut Wilf's throat while he slept; but people were fools and they seemed to believe it. They were all frightened of their slaves, Wynstan thought: the slaves had every reason to hate their owners and, if they had the chance, why would they not kill the people who had stolen their lives? A slave owner never slept easy. And all that stored-up fear burst like a boil when a slave was accused of murdering a nobleman.

Wynstan was hoping that the hue and cry would fail to find Carwen. He did not want her to tell her story in court. He would deny everything she said, and swear an oath, but a few might believe her rather than him. Much better if she vanished. Runaway slaves were usually caught, betrayed by their ragged clothes and their foreign accents and their pennilessness. However, Carwen had good clothes and some money, so she had a better-than-average chance.

Failing that, he had a contingency plan.

He was at the house of his mother, Gytha, with his brother Wigelm and their nephew Garulf, late in the afternoon, waiting for the search party to return, when Sheriff Den appeared. With mock courtesy Wynstan said: 'It's an honour to receive a visit from you, sheriff, and all the more prized for its rarity.'

Den was impatient with facetious banter. A grey-haired man of about fifty, he had probably seen too much violence to be baited by mere jeering. He said: 'You understand, don't you, that not everyone is fooled?'

'I have no idea what you can be talking about,' said Wynstan with a smile.

'You think you're clever, and you are, but there's a limit to what you can get away with. And I'm here to tell you that you're now perilously close to that limit.'

'It's kind of you.' Wynstan continued to make fun of Den, but in fact he was paying close attention. This kind of threat from a sheriff to a bishop was unusual. Den was serious and he was not without power. He had authority, he had men-at-arms, and he had the ear of the king. Wynstan was only pretending not to care.

But what had prompted this display of menace? Not just the murder of Wilf, Wynstan thought.

In the next second he found out.

Den said: 'Keep your hands off the Lady Ragna.'

So that was it.

Den went on: 'I want you to understand that if she should die, I will come after you, Bishop Wynstan.'

'How dreadful.'

'Not your brother or your nephew or any of your men – you. And I will never give up. I will bring you all the way down. You will live as a leper and die, as lepers do, in misery and filth.'

Despite himself Wynstan was chilled. He was thinking up a sarcastic riposte when Den simply turned around and left the house.

Wigelm said: 'I should have ripped his guts open, the arrogant fool.'

Wynstan said: 'He's not a fool, unfortunately. If he was, we could ignore him.'

Gytha commented: 'The foreign cat has got her claws into him.'

It was partly that, Wynstan had no doubt – Ragna had the ability to enchant most men – but there was something else. Den had long wanted to restrain the power of Wynstan's family, and the murder of Ragna might provide him with a strong enough pretext, especially if it followed quickly after a power grab by Wynstan.

His ruminations were interrupted by Garulf's bone-headed friend Stiggy, who burst in, breathing hard, excited. He had gone with the hue and cry, under instructions from Wynstan, who had told him to race home ahead of the group if Carwen should be recaptured, a task so simple that even Stiggy could hardly fail to understand it.

'They got her,' he said now.

'Alive?'

'Yes.'

'Shame.' It was time for the contingency plan. Wynstan got to his feet, and Wigelm and Garulf did the same. 'Where was she?'

'In the woods this side of Trench. The dogs sniffed her out.'

'Did she say anything?'

'A lot of Welsh cursing.'

'How far behind you are they now?'

'At least an hour.'

'We'll meet them on the road.' Wynstan looked at Garulf. 'You know the plan.'

'I do.'

They went to the stables and saddled four horses, one each for Wynstan, Wigelm and Garulf, plus a fresh mount for Stiggy; then they set out.

Half an hour later they came upon the hue and cry, now relaxed and triumphant. Wigbert, the sheriff's quick-tempered captain, led the group, with Carwen stumbling along behind his horse, roped to his saddle, hands tied behind her back.

Wynstan said quietly: 'All right, men, you know what you have to do.'

The four horsemen spread across the road in a line and reined in, forcing the hue and cry to halt. 'Congratulations, everyone,' Wynstan said heartily. 'Well done, Wigbert.'

'What do you want?' Wigbert said suspiciously, then added as an afterthought: 'My lord bishop.'

'I will take charge of the prisoner now.'

There was a mutter of resentment from the group. They had captured the miscreant and they were looking forward to returning to the city in triumph. They would receive the congratulations of the citizenry, and free drinks all evening in the alehouses.

Wigbert said: 'My orders are to hand the prisoner over to Sheriff Den.'

'Your orders have been changed.'

'You must speak to the sheriff about that.'

Wynstan knew he was going to lose this argument, but he continued anyway, because it was merely a distraction. 'I have already spoken to Den. His instructions are that you must hand over the prisoner to the victim's brothers.'

'I can't accept that from you, my lord bishop.' This time there was a distinct irony in the way he said *my lord bishop*.

Suddenly Garulf seemed to lose it. He yelled: 'She killed my father!' then drew his sword and spurred his horse forward.

Those on foot scattered out of his way. Wigbert snarled a curse and drew his sword, but too late: Garulf was already past him. Carwen gave a cry of terror and cowered back, but she was roped to Wigbert's saddle and unable to get away. Garulf was on her in a flash. Her hands were tied and she was defenceless. Garulf's sword gleamed in the sunlight as he stabbed her in the chest. The momentum of man and horse drove the blade deep into her and she screamed. For a moment Wynstan thought Garulf would lift the girl and carry her away spitted on his weapon, but as his horse passed her she fell on her back and he was able to pull the sword out of her slender body. Blood spurted from the wound in her chest.

Amid howls of protest from the hue and cry, Garulf turned his horse, came back to where Wynstan was, and reined in, facing the crowd with his bloodstained sword held upright as if ready for more carnage.

Wynstan spoke loudly and insincerely. 'You fool, you should not have killed her!'

'She stabbed my father in the heart!' Garulf shouted hysterically. Wynstan had instructed him to say these words, but his grief-stricken rage seemed genuine – which was strange, for Wynstan had told him who had really killed Wilf.

'Go!' said Wynstan. In a low voice he added: 'Not too slow, not too fast.'

Garulf turned his horse then looked back. 'Justice has been done!' he cried. He left at a trot, heading back towards Shiring.

Wynstan adopted a calming tone. 'This should not have happened,' he said, although, in fact, all had gone exactly as he intended.

Wigbert was furious, but all he could do was protest. 'He has murdered the slave!'

'Then he will be prosecuted in the shire court, and will pay the appropriate fine to the slave's owner.'

Everyone looked at the girl bleeding to death on the ground.

Wigbert said angrily: 'She knew what happened last night in Wilwulf's house.'

'So she did,' said Wynstan.

ÞÞÞ

EDGAR'S CANAL WAS a success. It ran dead straight from the Outhenham quarry to the river, and was three feet deep for its entire length. Its clay sides were firm and slightly sloped.

He was working in the quarry today, using a hammer that had a short handle for accuracy and a heavy iron head for impact. He placed an oak wedge into a crack in the stone then hammered it with quick, powerful strokes, forcing the wedge deeper, widening the crack until a slab of stone fell away. It was a warm summer day, and he had taken off his tunic and wrapped it around his waist to be cooler.

Gab and his sons were working nearby.

Edgar was still mulling over Ragna's visit to Dreng's Ferry. 'Sometimes it's a comfort to be loved,' she had said, and he was sure she was speaking of his love for her. She had let him hold her hands. And afterwards she had said: 'Will they know what we've been doing?' and he had asked himself what, exactly, they had been doing.

So she knew that he loved her, and she was glad that he loved her, and she felt that in holding hands they had done something that she would not like others to know about.

What did all this add up to? Could it possibly be that she returned his love? It was unlikely, almost impossible, but what else could it mean? He was not sure, but just thinking about it gave him a warm glow.

Edgar had won a large order for stone from Combe Priory, where the monks had royal permission to defend the town with an earth rampart and a stone barbican. Instead of carrying each stone half a mile to the river, Edgar had to transport it only a few yards to the head of the canal.

The raft was now almost completely loaded. Edgar had laid the heavy stones one deep on the deck, in order to spread the load and keep the vessel stable. He had to be careful not to overload the raft otherwise it would sink below the surface.

He added one last stone and was getting ready to leave when he heard the distant drumbeat of fast horses. He looked to the north of the village. The roads were dry and he could see a cloud of dust approaching.

His mood changed. The arrival of a large number of men on horseback was rarely good news. Thoughtfully, he hooked his iron hammer into his belt, then locked the door of his house. He left the quarry and walked briskly to the village. Gab and his family followed.

Many others had the same idea. Men and women left the weeding of their fields and returned to the village. Others emerged from their houses. Edgar shared their curiosity but was more cautious. As he approached the centre he ducked between two houses and took cover, creeping between the henhouses and the apple trees and the dunghills, progressing from one back yard to the next, listening.

The sound of the hooves diminished to a rumble then stopped, and he heard men's voices, loud and commanding. He looked about for a vantage point. He could watch from a roof, but he would be noticed. At the back of the alehouse was a mature oak tree in full leaf. He scrambled up the trunk to a low bough and pulled himself into the foliage. Careful not to reveal himself, he climbed higher until he could see over the alehouse roof.

The horsemen had reined in on the green between the tavern and the church. They wore no armour, evidently feeling they had little to fear from peasants, but they carried spears and daggers, clearly ready to inflict violence. Most dismounted, but one remained on horseback, and Edgar recognized Wilwulf's son Garulf. His companions were herding the villagers together, an exercise in control that was superfluous since they were all pressing into the centre anyway, anxious to find out what was going on. Edgar could see the grey hair of the village headman, Seric, speaking first to Garulf then to Garulf's men, getting no responses. The shaven-headed village priest, Draca, was moving through the crowd looking fearful.

Garulf stood up in his stirrups. A man standing beside him shouted: 'Silence!' and Edgar recognized Garulf's friend Stiggy.

A few villagers who carried on talking were tapped on the head with clubs, and the crowd went quiet.

Garulf said: 'My father, Ealdorman Wilwulf, is dead.'

There was a murmur of shock from the villagers.

Edgar whispered to himself: 'Dead! How did that happen?'

Garulf said: 'He died the night before last.'

Edgar realized that Ragna was now a widow. He felt hot, then cold. He became conscious of his heartbeat.

It makes no difference, he told himself; I must not get excited. She is still a noblewoman and I'm still a builder. Noble widows marry noble widowers. They never marry craftsmen, no matter how good.

All the same he *did* feel excited.

Seric voiced the question that had occurred to Edgar. 'How did the ealdorman die?'

Garulf ignored Seric and said: 'Our new ealdorman is Wilf's brother Wigelm.'

Seric shouted: 'That's not possible. He cannot have been appointed by the king so soon.'

Garulf said: 'Wigelm has made me lord of the Vale of Outhen.'

He was continuing to ignore the headman, who spoke for the villagers; and they began to mutter discontentedly.

'Wigelm can't do that,' said Seric. 'The Vale of Outhen belongs to the Lady Ragna.'

Garulf said: 'You also have a new village headman. It is Dudda.'

Dudda was a thief and a cheat, and everyone knew it. There were sounds of indignation from the crowd.

This was a coup, Edgar realized. What should he do?

Seric turned his back on Garulf and Stiggy, a deliberate act that repudiated their authority, and addressed the villagers. 'Wigelm is not ealdorman, because he has not been appointed by the king,' he said. 'Garulf is not lord of Outhen, because the valley belongs to Ragna. And Dudda is not headman, because I am.'

Edgar saw Stiggy draw his sword. 'Look out!' he yelled, but at that moment Stiggy ran his sword into Seric's back until it stuck out of the front of his belly. Seric cried out like a wounded animal and collapsed. Edgar found himself breathing hard, as if he had run a mile. It was the shock of such a cold-blooded murder.

Stiggy calmly drew his sword out of Seric's guts.

Garulf said: 'Seric is not your headman now.'

The men-at-arms laughed.

Edgar had seen enough. He was horrified and frightened. His first instinct was to tell Ragna what he had seen. He climbed rapidly down from the tree. But when he reached the ground he hesitated.

He was close to the river and could swim across and get on the Shiring road in a couple of minutes. That way he would have a good chance of getting away without being seen by any of Garulf's men. He could leave his raft and his load of stone at the quarry: Combe Priory would have to wait.

But his horse, Buttress, was at the quarry, and so was Ragna's money. Edgar had almost a pound of silver for her in his chest, the proceeds of sales of stone, and she might need that money.

He made a snap decision. He had to risk his life by staying in Outhenham a few minutes longer. Instead of heading for the river he ran in the opposite direction, towards the quarry.

It took him only a few minutes to get there. He unlocked his house and retrieved his money chest from its hiding place. He tipped Ragna's money into a leather purse that he attached to his belt then locked up his house again.

Buttress stepped onto the raft willingly, being used to sailing. Brindle jumped on too, eager as ever despite her age. Then Edgar untied the raft and pushed off.

He had never before noticed how slowly the raft travelled along the canal. There was no stream to drive it, so the only impetus came from the pole he wielded. He pushed with all his might, but his speed barely increased.

As he passed along the ends of the back yards, the noise from the village green increased in volume – and, he thought, anger. Despite the murder of Seric, the villagers were courageously protesting against Garulf's announcements. There was going to be more violence, he had no doubt. Could he bypass it?

He drew level with the oak that had concealed him, and began to hope that he would get away without being noticed. A moment later that hope was dashed. He saw two men and a woman running from the alehouse towards the river. By their dress he knew they were villagers. A man-at-arms came after them, sword in hand, and Edgar recognized Bada. Fighting had broken out.

Edgar cursed. He could not pass them: they were faster than the raft. This was dangerous. If he was captured, Garulf would not let him leave Outhenham. He was known to be an associate of Ragna, and in the middle of a coup that might be enough reason for Garulf to kill him.

One of the peasant men stumbled and fell. Edgar saw that he had floury white streaks in his dark beard: he was Wilmund, the baker, and the two with him were his wife, Regenhild, and their son, Penda, now nineteen and taller than ever.

Regenhild stopped and turned to help Wilmund. As Bada raised his sword she flew at him, weaponless, her hands extended to scratch his face. He swung his sword through the air uselessly and pushed her away with his left hand, raising his right to strike at Wilmund again.

Then Penda intervened. He picked up a rock the size of a fist and hurled it. It hit Bada in the chest, hard enough to throw him off balance so that his second sword stroke also went wild.

The raft drew level with the fighters.

Edgar was full of fear, and desperate to get away, but he could not watch and do nothing while people he knew were murdered. He dropped his pole, leaped from the raft to the bank of the canal, and drew his iron-headed hammer from his belt.

Wilmund got to his knees. Bada thrust with his sword and this time hit his target, though obliquely. His point entered the soft part of Wilmund's thigh, next to the hip, and went in deep. Regenhild screamed and knelt beside her husband. Bada lifted his weapon to dispatch her.

Edgar ran at him, hammer raised high, and hit him with all his might.

At the last moment Bada moved to the left, and Edgar's hammer landed on his shoulder. There was an audible snap as a bone broke. Bada roared with pain. His right arm went limp and his sword fell from his hand. He dropped to the ground, groaning.

But Bada was not alone. Pounding steps from the village alerted Edgar. He looked back to see another man-at-arms approaching. It was Stiggy.

Regenhild and Penda got Wilmund to his feet. He was crying out in agony but he managed to put one foot in front of the other and the three of them staggered away. Stiggy ignored the helpless peasants and headed for Edgar, who with his hammer in his hand was evidently the one who had wounded Stiggy's comrade, Bada. Edgar knew he was only moments away from death.

He turned and dashed towards the canal. The raft had drifted several yards. He heard running steps behind him. Reaching the edge he leaped through the air and landed on the stones.

Turning back, he saw the baker's family disappear into the houses. They were safe, at least for now.

He saw Stiggy picking up rocks from the ground.

Fighting down panic he lay flat, sticking his hammer into his belt, and rolled into the water on the far side of the raft just as a large rock flew over his head. Brindle jumped into the water alongside him.

He grabbed the side of the raft with one hand and ducked his head. He heard a series of thuds and guessed that Stiggy's rocks were hitting the quarry stones. He heard Buttress's hooves stamp, and hoped his pony would not be hurt.

His feet touched the far bank of the canal. He turned in the water and pushed the raft in the direction of the river as hard as he could. He put his face above the surface just long enough to fill his lungs, then submerged again.

He noticed a slight change in the water temperature and guessed he was at the end of the canal and feeling the colder river water.

The raft emerged from the mouth of the canal and he felt the current. He put his head up – and saw Stiggy leap from the bank towards the raft.

The distance looked too great, and he allowed himself to hope that Stiggy would land in the water or, even better, miss by an inch and injure himself on the timbers. But Stiggy just made it. For a moment he stood precariously on the edge of the raft, windmilling his arms, and Edgar prayed he would fall backwards into the river; but he regained his balance and crouched with both hands flat on the cargo of quarry stones.

Then he stood up and drew his sword.

Edgar knew he was in danger, more danger than he had faced since he confronted a Viking in Sunni's dairy at Combe. Stiggy was standing on the deck with a sword in his hand and Edgar was in the water with a hammer in his belt.

Perhaps, he thought hopefully, Stiggy would jump into the river to grapple, thereby losing the advantage of a solid footing. In the water, the short-handled hammer would be easier to deploy than the long sword.

Unfortunately, there was a limit to Stiggy's stupidity. He remained on the raft and thrust at Edgar. Edgar dodged the sword and ducked under the raft.

Here Stiggy could not hurt him, but on the other hand Edgar could not breathe. He was a strong swimmer and could hold his breath for a long time, but eventually he would have to put his head up above the surface again.

He might have to abandon the raft. He still had Ragna's money and the hammer. He swam as deep as he could go, hoping to get beyond the length of Stiggy's sword, then turned away from the raft and moved towards the far bank, fearing that at any second he would feel the point of the sword in his back. The water became shallower and he knew he was at the river's edge. He rolled over and surfaced, gasping.

He was several yards from the raft. Stiggy stood on the deck, sword in hand, looking around desperately, not seeing Edgar lying in the shallows.

If Edgar could crawl a few yards and vanish into the woods before Stiggy spotted him, he could get away. Stiggy would not know where he had gone. Edgar would be sorry to lose Buttress but his life was more precious. Alive, he could build another raft and buy another pony.

Then Brindle came out of the water, shook himself dry, and barked at Stiggy, who looked at the dog then spotted Edgar. Too late, Edgar thought, and got to his feet.

Stiggy sheathed his sword, picked up the pole and pushed the raft towards the bank.

Edgar was no match for Stiggy, who was taller and heavier and well practised in violence. He realized his only chance would be to attack Stiggy as soon as he jumped, before he had the chance to steady himself on land and draw his sword.

Edgar drew the hammer from his belt and ran along the bank after the raft, which was slowly drifting downstream. Stiggy poled towards the water's edge. They were on a collision course.

Stiggy drew his sword and jumped, and Edgar saw his chance.

The man-at-arms landed in the shallows and Edgar lashed out with his hammer; but Stiggy stumbled and Edgar missed, landing only a glancing blow on Stiggy's left arm.

Stiggy stepped onto the riverside mud and reached for his sword.

Edgar was quick. He kicked Stiggy, striking his knee. It was not a severe blow but it sufficed to keep Stiggy off balance. Drawing his sword, Stiggy swung wildly, missing Edgar, then slipped on the mud and fell.

Edgar jumped onto Stiggy's chest, landing with his knees, feeling ribs break, getting too close for Stiggy to use his long sword.

Edgar knew he probably had the chance to strike one blow, no more. The first might be the last, so it had to be fatal.

He swung the short hammer as he did when forcing an oak wedge into a crack in the limestone quarry, putting all the power of his right arm into the one blow that had to save his life. His arm was strong, the hammerhead was iron, and Stiggy's forehead was mere skin and bone. It was like breaking thick ice on a winter pond. Edgar felt the hammer smash the skull and saw it plunge into the soft brain beneath. Stiggy's body went limp.

Edgar remembered Seric, the wise headman, the caring grandfather, and he saw again the way Stiggy had plunged his sword into that good man's body; and as he looked at Stiggy's smashed head he thought: I just made the world a better place.

He looked across the river. No one had seen the fight. No one would know who had killed Stiggy. Garulf and his men did not know that Edgar was in the vicinity, and the villagers would not tell them.

Then he realized that the raft was a giveaway. If he left it here, it would be obvious that he had killed Stiggy and fled.

He waded to the raft, accompanied by Brindle, and climbed aboard. He gave the trembling Buttress a reassuring pat. He retrieved the pole, which Stiggy had dropped in the water.

Then he pushed off, heading downstream towards Dreng's Ferry.

þþþ

IT WAS A hot day in the compound. Ragna got a large, shallow bronze bowl from the kitchen and filled it with cool water from the well. She placed the bowl in front of her house and let her sons play with the water. The twins, eighteen months old, splashed with their hands and screamed with laughter. Osbert devised an elaborate game with several wooden cups, pouring one into another. Soon they were all soaking wet and happy.

Watching them, Ragna experienced a rare moment of contentment. These boys would grow up to be men like her father, she thought: strong but not cruel, wise but not sly. If they became rulers, they would enforce the laws, not their own whims. They would love women without using them. They would be respected, not feared.

Her mood was soon spoiled. Wigelm approached her and said: 'I must speak to you.'

Wigelm might have been mistaken for Wilf, though not for long. He had the same big nose, fair moustache and jutting chin, and he walked with the same swagger; but he had none of Wilf's easy charm, and always looked as though he were on the point of making a complaint.

Ragna was certain that Wigelm had been involved somehow in the murder of Wilf. She might never know the details, now that Carwen had been killed, but she had no doubt. She felt a loathing so intense that it nauseated her. 'I have no wish to talk to you,' she said. 'Go away.'

'You are the most beautiful woman I have ever seen,' he said.

She was mystified. 'What are you talking about?' she said. 'Don't be stupid.'

'You're an angel. There is no one like you.'

'This is a crude joke.' She looked around. 'Your dopey friends are at the side of the house, listening and sniggering, hoping you'll make a fool of me. Go away.'

He produced an arm ring from inside his tunic. 'I thought you might like to have this.' He offered it to her.

She took it. It was silver with an engraved pattern of intertwining serpents, beautifully done, and she recognized it instantly. It was the one she had bought from Cuthbert and given to Wilf on their wedding day.

Wigelm said: 'Aren't you going to thank me?'

'Why? You stole Wilf's treasury and found this in the chest. But I'm Wilf's heir, so the arm ring is already mine. I won't thank you until you give me back everything.'

'That might be possible.'

Here it comes, she thought. Now I'll find out what he really wants. She said: 'Possible? How?'

'Marry me.'

She let out a short, sharp laugh, shocked by the absurdity of the proposal. 'Ridiculous!' she said.

Wigelm flushed angrily, and she sensed that he wanted to hit her. He clenched his fists but restrained himself from raising them. 'Do not dare to call me ridiculous,' he said.

'But you're already married – to Milly, Inge's sister.'

'I have put her aside.'

'I'm afraid I don't like your English "putting aside".'

'You're not in Normandy now.'

'Doesn't the English Church forbid the marriage of a widow to a near kinsman? You're my brother-in-law.'

'Half-brother-in-law. That's separation enough, according to Bishop Wynstan.'

She realized she had taken the wrong tack. People like Wigelm could always find ways around the rules. Feeling exasperated, she said: 'You don't love me! You don't even like me.'

'But our marriage will solve a political problem.'

'How flattering for me.'

'I'm Wilf's half-brother and you're his widow. If we married, no one could challenge us for the ealdormanry.'

'Us? You're saying we would rule together? Do you imagine I'm stupid enough to believe you?'

Wigelm looked angry and frustrated. He was telling a completely dishonest story and he was not smart enough to make it even halfway believable. Realizing that Ragna was not so easily fooled, he did not know what to say next. He tried to look as confident and charming as Wilf. 'You will come to love me, once we're married,' he said.

'I will never love you.' How much clearer could she make it? 'You are all the bad things about Wilf and none of the good. I hate and loathe you, and that will never change.'

'Bitch,' he muttered, and walked away.

Ragna felt as if she had been in a fight. Wigelm's proposal had been shocking and his persistence had been brutal. She felt battered and exhausted. She leaned against the side of her house and closed her eyes.

Osbert started to cry. He had got mud in his eye. She picked him up and washed his face with her sleeve, and he was quickly pacified.

She no longer felt shaky. It was strange how the needs of children swamped everything else – for women, at least. No crude English thane was as tyrannical as a baby.

Her breathing returned to normal as she watched the children playing with the water. But once again she did not enjoy the peaceful moment for long. Bishop Wynstan appeared. 'My brother Wigelm is very upset,' he said.

'Oh, for goodness' sake,' Ragna said impatiently. 'Don't pretend he's lovelorn.'

'We both know that love has nothing to do with this.'

'I'm glad you're not as stupid as your brother.'

'Thank you.'

'It's not much of a compliment.'

'Take care,' he said with suppressed anger. 'You're not in a strong position to insult me and my family.'

'I'm the ealdorman's widow, and nothing you can do will change that. My position is strong enough.'

'But Wigelm is in control of Shiring.'

'I'm still lord of the Vale of Outhen.'

'Garulf went there yesterday.'

Ragna was startled. She had not heard about this.

Wynstan went on: 'He told the villagers that Wigelm has made him lord of Outhen.'

'They will never accept him. Seric, the headman—'

'Seric is dead. Garulf made Dudda headman.'

'Outhen is mine! It's in the marriage contract that *you* negotiated!'

'Wilf had no right to give it to you. It's been in our family for generations.'

'All the same he did give it to me.'

'He obviously intended a lifetime gift. Wilf's lifetime, not yours.'

'That's a lie.'

Wynstan shrugged. 'What are you going to do about it?'

'I don't have to do anything. King Ethelred will appoint the new ealdorman, not you.'

'I thought you might be labouring under that illusion,' Wynstan said, and the seriousness of his tone chilled Ragna. 'Let me explain to you what the king has on his mind today. The Viking fleet is still in English waters – they spent the winter at the Isle of Wight instead of returning home. Ethelred has now negotiated a truce with them – for which he must pay twenty-four thousand pounds of silver.'

Ragna was shocked. She had never heard of such a large sum of money.

'You may imagine,' Wynstan went on, 'that the king is preoccupied with raising money. On top of that he is planning his wedding.'

Ethelred had been married to Elfgifu of York, who had died giving birth to their eleventh child.

Wynstan went on: 'He is going to marry Emma of Normandy.'

Ragna was surprised again. She knew Emma, the daughter of Count Richard of Rouen. Emma had been a child of twelve when Ragna left Normandy five years ago. She would now be seventeen. It occurred to Ragna that a young Norman woman marrying the English king could become an ally.

Wynstan had a different agenda. 'With all that to worry about, how much time do you think the king is going to spend deciding who is to be the new ealdorman of Shiring?'

Ragna said nothing.

'Very little,' said Wynstan, answering his own question. 'He will look at who is in control of the region and simply ratify that person. The de facto ruler will become the de jure ealdorman.'

If that were true, Ragna thought, you would not be so keen for me to marry Wigelm. But she did not say it, because she had been struck by another thought. What would Wynstan do when she steadfastly refused Wigelm's proposal? He would cast about for an alternative solution. There might be several options open to him, but one stood out to Ragna.

He could kill her.

33

EDGAR HAD NOW KILLED two men. The first had been the Viking; the second Stiggy. It might be three, if Bada had died of his broken collarbone. Edgar asked himself whether he was a killer.

Men-at-arms never had to ask themselves that question: killing was their role in life. But Edgar was a builder. Combat did not come naturally to a craftsman. Yet Edgar had defeated men of violence. Perhaps he should have felt proud: Stiggy had been a cold-blooded murderer. All the same Edgar was troubled.

And the death of Stiggy had solved no problems. Garulf had taken control of Outhen, and undoubtedly was even now tightening his grip on the villagers.

When Edgar reached Shiring he went straight to the ealdorman's compound. He unsaddled Buttress, took her to the pond to drink, then turned her loose in the adjoining pasture with the other horses.

As he approached Ragna's house he wondered – foolishly, perhaps – whether she would look different now that she was a widow. He had known her for five years, and for all that time she had belonged to another man. Would there be a different look in her eye, a new smile on her face, an unaccustomed liberty to the way she walked? She was fond of him, he knew; but would she express that feeling more freely now?

He found her at home. Despite the sunshine she was indoors, sitting on a bench, staring at nothing, brooding. Her three sons and Cat's two daughters were taking their afternoon nap, supervised by

Cat and Agnes. Ragna brightened a little when she saw Edgar, which pleased him. He handed her the leather bag of silver. 'Your earnings from the quarry. I thought you might need money.'

'Thank you! Wigelm took my treasury – I was penniless, until now. They want to steal everything from me, including the Vale of Outhen. But the king is responsible for aristocratic widows, and sooner or later he'll have something to say about what Wigelm and Wynstan have done. And how are you?'

He sat down on the bench next to her and spoke in an undertone so that the servants could not hear. 'I was at Outhen. I saw Stiggy murder Seric.'

Her eyes widened. 'Stiggy died . . .'

Edgar nodded.

She mouthed a question soundlessly: 'You?'

He nodded again. 'But nobody knows,' he whispered.

She squeezed his wrist, as if to thank him silently, and he felt a tingle in the place where her skin touched his. Then she resumed a normal voice. 'Garulf is mad with rage.'

'Of course.' Edgar thought of the despondent expression he had seen on her face when he arrived, and he said: 'But what about you?'

'Wigelm wants to marry me.'

'God forbid!' Edgar was appalled. He did not want Ragna to marry anyone, but Wigelm was a particularly repellent choice.

'It's not going to happen,' she added.

'I'm glad to hear it.'

'But what will they do?' Ragna's face bore a look he had never seen before, of anxiety so desperate that Edgar wanted to take her in his arms and tell her that he would look after her. She went on: 'I'm a problem they need to solve, and they aren't going to leave it to King Ethelred – he doesn't like them and he may not do what they want.'

'But what can they do?'

'They could kill me.'

Edgar shook his head. 'Surely that would cause an international scandal—'

'They would say I fell ill and died suddenly.'

'Dear God.' It had not occurred to Edgar that they might go so far. They were ruthless enough to kill Ragna, but it could get them into major trouble. However, they were risk-takers. He was seriously alarmed. 'We have to protect you, somehow!' he said.

'I have no bodyguard now. Bern is dead and the men-at-arms switched their loyalty to Wigelm.'

The two women servants could hear their conversation now, for they were speaking at normal volume, and Cat reacted to Ragna's last remark. 'Filthy beasts,' she said in Norman French. Bern had been her husband.

Edgar said to Ragna: 'You probably have to leave this compound.'

'It would seem like giving up.'

'This would be temporary, until you can put your case to the king. Which you can't do if you're dead.'

'Where could I go?'

Edgar considered. 'What about Leper Island? There's a sanctuary stool in the nuns' church. Even Wigelm wouldn't dare to murder a noblewoman there. Every thane in England would consider it a duty to kill him in revenge.'

Her eyes sparkled. 'That's a clever idea.'

'We should leave immediately.'

'You would come with me?'

'Of course. When could you leave?'

She hesitated, then made up her mind. 'Tomorrow morning.'

Edgar felt it was sounding too easy, too good to be true. 'They may try to stop you.'

'You're right. We'll go before sunrise.'

'You'll have to be discreet until then.'

'Yes.' Ragna turned to Cat and Agnes, who were both listening, wide-eyed. 'You two, do nothing before supper – just carry on as normal. Then, when it's dark, pack what we need for the children.'

Agnes said: 'We should take food. Shall I get some from the kitchen?'

'No, that would give us away. Buy bread and ham in the town.' She gave Agnes three silver pennies from the purse Edgar had brought.

Edgar said: 'Don't use your own horses. Sheriff Den will lend you mounts.'

'Do I have to lose Astrid?'

'I'll come back for her later.' He stood up. 'I'll stay at Den's place tonight. I'll speak to him about borrowing horses. Will you let me know, later this evening, that everything is ready for the morning?'

'Of course.' She took both his hands in hers, reminding him of their piercingly intimate conversation at his house in Dreng's Ferry. Were there more intimate moments ahead? He hardly dared hope. 'And thank you, Edgar, for everything. I've lost track of all you've done for me.'

He wanted to tell her that it was done out of love, but not in front of Cat and Agnes, so he said: 'You deserve it. More.'

She smiled and released his hands, and he turned and left.

ÞÞÞ

'We could just kill Ragna,' said Wigelm. 'It would make everything simple.'

'I've thought about it, believe me,' said Wynstan. 'She stands in our way.'

They were in the bishop's residence, on the upper floor, drinking cider: it was thirsty weather.

Wynstan recalled Sheriff Den's threat to kill him if anything happened to Ragna. But he dismissed it. Many people would have liked to kill Wynstan. If he feared them, he would never step out of the door.

637

Wigelm said: 'Without Ragna, I would have no rival for the ealdormanry.'

'No very convincing one. Who is the king going to choose? Deorman of Norwood is half blind. Thurstan of Lordsborough is a ditherer who could hardly lead a sing-song, let alone an army. All the other thanes are little more than wealthy farmers. No one has your experience and connections.'

'So . . .'

Wynstan often felt exasperated that he had to explain things to Wigelm more than once, but on this occasion he was also getting the problem straight in his own mind. 'We just need to keep her under control,' he said.

'How is that better than killing her? We could set it up so that someone else gets the blame, as we did with Wilf.'

Wynstan shook his head. 'It's possible, but it would be pushing our luck. Yes, we got away with it once, just about, even though plenty of people still don't believe Carwen killed Wilf. However, a second convenient murder so soon after the first would be highly suspicious. Everyone would assume we were guilty.'

'King Ethelred might believe us.'

Wynstan laughed scornfully. 'He wouldn't even pretend to. We're usurping his prerogatives in two ways. First, we're forcing a choice of ealdorman on him. Second, we're interfering with the fate of a widow.'

'Surely he's more worried about raising his twenty-four thousand pounds?'

'For now, yes, but once he's got the money he'll do whatever he wants.'

'So we need to keep Ragna alive.'

'If at all possible, yes. Alive, but under control.' Wynstan looked up to see Agnes entering. 'And here is the little mouse that will help us do that.' He saw that she was carrying a basket. 'Have you been shopping, my mouse?'

'Supplies for a journey, my lord bishop.'

'Come here, sit on my lap.'

She looked surprised and embarrassed, but also thrilled. She put down her basket and sat on Wynstan's knee, perching with a straight back.

He said: 'Now, what journey is this?'

'Ragna wants to go to Dreng's Ferry. It takes two days.'

'I know how long it takes. But why does she want to go there?'

'She thinks you might kill her when you realize she will never marry Wigelm.'

Wynstan looked at Wigelm. This was the kind of thing he had feared. A good thing he had found out in advance. How clever he had been to place a spy in Ragna's house. 'What brought this on?' he said.

'I'm not sure, but Edgar showed up with some money for her, and it was his idea. She will live in the nunnery and she thinks she will be safe from you there.'

She was probably right, Wynstan thought. He did not want to make all England his enemy. 'When will she leave?'

'Tomorrow at sunrise.'

Wynstan ran his hand over Agnes's breasts, and she shuddered with desire. 'You've done well, my little mouse,' he said warmly. 'This is important information.'

In a shaky voice she said: 'I'm so glad to have pleased you.'

He winked at his brother then put his hand up her dress. 'So wet, already!' he said. 'I seem to have pleased you too.'

She whispered: 'Yes.'

Wigelm laughed.

Wynstan eased Agnes off his lap. 'Kneel down, my little mouse,' he said. He lifted his tunic. 'Do you know what to do with this?'

She bent her head over his lap.

'Ah, yes,' he sighed. 'I see that you do.'

ÞÞÞ

As DARKNESS WAS falling Ragna slipped out of the compound. She pulled her hood over her head and hurried across the town. She was happy to be on her way to see Edgar. It was a familiar feeling, she realized. She had always been happy to see him. And he had been an unfailingly good friend to her ever since she came to England.

She found Sheriff Den and his wife preparing to go to bed. Edgar was occupying an empty house in the compound, Den told her, and he took her there. The place was lit by a single rush light. Edgar stood by the fireplace, but there was no fire: the weather was warm.

Den said briskly: 'Your horses will be ready at first light.'

'Thank you,' Ragna said. Some of the English were decent folk and others were pigs, she reflected; perhaps it was the same everywhere. 'You've probably saved my life.'

'I'm doing what I believe the king would wish,' he said, then he added: 'And I'm glad to help you.' He looked at the two of them with a faint smile. 'I'll leave you to make final arrangements.' He went out.

Ragna's heart beat faster. She had seldom been alone with Edgar – so seldom, in fact, that she could clearly recall each occasion. The first had been five years ago at Dreng's Ferry when he had rowed her across to Leper Island. She remembered the darkness, the patter of the rain falling on the surface of the river, and the warmth of his strong arms as he carried her from the boat through the shallows to dry land. The second had been four years later, at Outhenham, in his house at the quarry, when she had kissed him, and he had almost died of embarrassment. And the third time had been at Dreng's Ferry, when he had showed her the box he had made for the book she had given him, and she had as good as admitted that his love comforted her.

This was the fourth time.

She said: 'Everything is ready.' She meant for the escape.

'Here, too.' He looked ill at ease.

'Relax,' she said. 'I'm not going to bite you.'

He gave a sheepish grin. 'Worse luck.'

Looking at him in the dim light, she wanted nothing more than to take him in her arms. It seemed the most natural thing in the world. She stepped closer. 'I've realized something,' she said.

'What?'

'We're not friends.'

He understood right away. 'Oh, no,' he said, shaking his head. 'We're something else entirely.'

She put her hands on his cheeks, feeling the soft hair of his beard. 'Such a good face,' she said. 'Strong, intelligent and kind.'

He dropped his eyes.

She said: 'Am I embarrassing you?'

'Yes, but don't stop.'

She thought of Wilwulf, and wondered how she could have loved a warrior. It had been a girlish love, she thought. What she was feeling now was grown-up desire. But she could not say any of that, so she kissed him instead.

It was a long, soft kiss, their lips exploring gently. She stroked his cheeks and his hair, and she felt his hands on her waist. After a long minute she broke the kiss, panting. 'Oh, my,' she said. 'Can I have some more of that?'

'As much as you like,' he said. 'I've been saving it up.'

She felt guilty. 'I'm sorry.'

'Why?'

'That you waited so long. Five years.'

'I'd have waited ten.'

Tears came to her eyes. 'I don't deserve such love.'

'Yes, you do.'

She longed to do something to please him. She said: 'Do you like my breasts?'

'Yes. That's why I've been staring at them all these years.'

'Would you like to touch them?'

'Yes,' he said hoarsely.

She bent and lifted the hem of her dress, pulling it over her head with a swift motion, and stood naked in front of him.

'Oh, my,' he said. He caressed her with both hands, squeezing lightly, touched her nipples with feathery fingertips. His breath was coming faster. She thought he looked like a thirsty man finding a stream. After a while he said: 'Can I kiss them?'

'Edgar,' she said, 'you can kiss anything you like.'

He bent his head and she stroked his hair, watching him in the flickering light as his lips moved over her skin.

His kisses became more urgent and she said: 'If you suck, you'll get milk.'

He laughed. 'Would I like it?'

She loved how he could be passionate and laugh all at the same time. She smiled. 'I don't know,' she said.

Then he turned serious again. 'Can we lie down?'

'Wait a minute.' She bent and lifted the skirt of his tunic. When it was up to his waist she kissed the tip of his cock. Then she pulled the garment over his head.

They lay side by side and she explored his body with her hands, feeling his chest, his waist, his thighs; and he did the same to her. She felt his hand between her legs, and his fingertip in the wet cleft. She shuddered with pleasure.

Suddenly she was impatient. She rolled on top of him and guided his cock inside her. She moved slowly at first, then faster. Looking down at his face, she thought: I didn't know how much I was longing for this. It was not just the sensation, the pleasure, the excitement; it was more, it was the intimacy, the openness with one another; it was the love.

He closed his eyes, but she did not want that, and she said: 'Look at me, look at me.' He opened his eyes. 'I love you,' she said. Then she was swamped by the sheer joy of doing this with him, and she cried out, and at the same time felt him convulse inside her. It went on for a long moment, then she collapsed on his chest, exhausted with emotion.

As she lay on him, the memories of the last five years came to her like a remembered poem. She recalled the terrifying storm when she had been aboard the *Angel*; the helmeted outlaw who had stolen her wedding gift for Wilf; the loathsome Wigelm groping her breasts the first time they met; the shock of learning that Wilf was already married with a son; the misery of his infidelity with Carwen; the horror of his murder; the malice of Wynstan. And through it all there had been Edgar, whose kindness had turned into affection and then passionate love. Thank God for Edgar, she thought. Thank God.

ÞÞÞ

AFTER SHE HAD gone, Edgar lay for a long time in a daze of happiness. He had thought that he was doomed to have two impossible loves, one for a dead woman and one for an unattainable one. And now Ragna had said that she loved him. Ragna of Cherbourg, the most beautiful woman in England, loved Edgar the builder.

He relived every minute: the kiss; her taking off her dress; her breasts; the way she had kissed his cock, lightly, affectionately, almost in passing; her telling him to open his eyes and look at her. Had two people ever enjoyed each other so intensely? Had two people ever loved each other so much?

Well, probably, he thought, but perhaps not very many.

With his head full of the most pleasant thoughts he drifted off to sleep.

The monastery bell woke him. His first thought was: Did I really make love to Ragna? His second: Am I late?

Yes, he had made love to her, and no, he was not late. The monks got up an hour before dawn. He had plenty of time.

He and Ragna had not thought beyond the next two days. They would get out of Shiring, they would travel to Dreng's Ferry, Ragna would take refuge in the nunnery, and then they would think about the future. But now he could not help speculating.

The social distance between them was not as great as it had been. Edgar was a prosperous craftsman, an important man in both Dreng's Ferry and Outhenham. Ragna was a noblewoman, but a widow, and her financial resources were under attack by Wynstan. The gap was smaller – but still too large. Edgar saw no way out of this, but he was not going to let that spoil his happiness today.

He found Sheriff Den in the kitchen, breakfasting off cold beef and ale. Edgar was too tense and excited to feel hungry, but he made himself eat something: he might need his strength.

Den looked through the door up at the sky and said: 'It's getting light.'

Edgar frowned. It was not like Ragna to be late for anything.

He went to the stable. The grooms were saddling three horses, for Ragna, Cat and Agnes, and loading a packhorse with panniers for the supplies. Edgar saddled Buttress.

Den appeared and said: 'Everything is ready – except for Ragna.'

'I'll go to her,' said Edgar.

He hurried through the town. Dawn was brightening and smoke rose from a bakery, but he did not see anyone on his way to the ealdorman's compound.

Sometimes the gate entrance was barred and guarded, but not now: this year there was a truce with the Vikings, and the Welsh were going through a dormant phase. He opened the gate quietly. The compound was silent.

He walked quickly towards Ragna's house. He knocked sharply on the door then tried the handle. It was not barred from the inside. He opened the door and stepped inside.

There was no one there.

He frowned, suddenly terribly fearful. What could have happened?

There were no lights. He peered into the gloom. A mouse scampered across the hearth: it must be cold. As his eyes grew accustomed to the faint light from the open doorway, he saw that most of Ragna's possessions were here – dresses hanging from pegs, cheese box and meat safe, cups and bowls – but the children's cots had gone.

She had gone. And the cold fireplace proved she had left hours ago, probably not long after saying goodnight to him at Sheriff Den's compound. By now she might be miles away in any direction.

She must have changed her plans. But why had she sent him no message? She could have been prevented from doing so. That strongly suggested she had been taken against her will and held incommunicado. Wynstan and Wigelm had to be responsible. She had been made prisoner, then.

Anger flamed inside him. How dare they? She was a free woman, the daughter of a count and the widow of an ealdorman – they had no right!

If they had found out that she was planning to flee, who had told them? One of the sheriff's servants, perhaps, or even Cat or Agnes.

Edgar had to find out where they had taken her.

Furious, he left the house. He was ready to confront either Wigelm or Wynstan, but Wigelm was probably nearer. When in Shiring he slept at the house of his mother, Gytha. Edgar strode across the grass to Gytha's house.

A man-at-arms was outside the door, sitting on the ground with his back to the wall, dozing. Edgar recognized Elfgar, big and strong but an amiable youngster. Ignoring him, Edgar banged on the door.

Elfgar jumped up, suddenly awakened and unsteady on his feet. He looked at the floor around his feet and belatedly picked up a club, a length of gnarled oak roughly carved. He looked as though he was not sure what to do with it.

The door was thrown open and another man-at-arms stood there. He must have been sleeping across the threshold. It was Fulcric, older and meaner than Elfgar.

Edgar said: 'Is Wigelm here?'

Fulcric said aggressively: 'Who the hell are you?'

Edgar raised his voice. 'I want to see Wigelm!'

'You'll get your head bashed in if you're not careful.'

A voice from within said: 'Don't worry, Elfgar, it's only the little builder from Dreng's Ferry.' Wigelm emerged from the gloom within. 'But he'd better have a damned good reason for banging on my door at this hour of the morning.'

'You know the reason, Wigelm. Where is she?'

'Don't presume to question me, or you'll be punished for insolence.'

'And you'll be punished for kidnapping a noble widow – a more serious offence in the eyes of the king.'

'No one has been kidnapped.'

'Then where is the Lady Ragna?'

Behind Wigelm, his wife Milly and his mother appeared, both of them tousled and sleepy-eyed.

Edgar went on: 'And where are her children? The king will want to know.'

'In a safe place.'

'Where?'

Wigelm sneered. 'Surely you didn't think you could have her?'

'You're the one who asked her to marry you.'

Milly said: 'What?' Clearly she had not been told about her husband's proposal to Ragna.

Edgar said recklessly: 'But Ragna rejected you, didn't she?' He knew it was foolish to provoke Wigelm, but he was too enraged to stop. 'That's why you kidnapped her.'

'That's enough.'

'Is that the only way you can get a woman, Wigelm? By kidnapping her?'

Elfgar sniggered.

Wigelm took a step forward and punched Edgar's face. Wigelm was a strong man whose only skill was fighting, and the blow hurt. Edgar felt as if the whole left side of his face was on fire.

While Edgar was dazed Fulcric swiftly stepped behind him and grabbed him in an expert hold, then Wigelm punched him in the stomach. Edgar had the panicky feeling that he could not breathe. Wigelm kicked him in the balls. Edgar caught his breath and roared in agony. Wigelm punched his face again.

Then he saw Wigelm take the club from Elfgar.

Terror possessed Edgar. He feared he would be beaten to death, and then there would be no one to protect Ragna. He saw the club come swinging towards his face. He turned his head and the heavy wood struck his temple, sending a lightning bolt of pain around his skull.

Next it smashed into his chest, and he felt as if his ribs had broken. He slumped, half unconscious, held up only by Fulcric's grip.

Through the ringing in his ears he heard the voice of Gytha say: 'That's enough. You don't want to kill him.'

Then Wigelm said: 'Throw him in the pond.'

He was picked up by his wrists and ankles and carried across the compound. A minute later he felt himself flying through the air. He hit the water and sank. He was tempted to lie there and drown, to end his pain.

He rolled over and put his hands and knees on the sludgy bottom of the pond, then managed to raise his head above the surface and breathe.

Slowly, in agony, he crawled like a baby until he reached the edge.

He heard a woman's voice say: 'You poor thing.'

It was Gilda, the kitchen maid, he realized.

He tried to get to his feet. Gilda gripped his arm and helped him up. Mumbling through smashed lips, Edgar said: 'Thank you.'

'God curse Wigelm,' she said. She got under his armpit and slung his arm across her shoulders. 'Where are you going?'

'Den's.'

'Come on, then,' said Gilda. 'I'll help you there.'

34

ALDRED WAS PLEASED WITH the way his library was growing. He favoured books in English rather than Latin, so that they could be used by all literate people, not just educated clergy. He had the Gospels, the Psalms, and some service books, all of which could be consulted by ordinary country priests who had few or no books of their own. His little scriptorium produced low-cost copies for sale. He also had some commentaries and secular poetry.

The priory was prospering, collecting more and more rents from the town and now, at last, getting gifts of land from noblemen. There were new novice monks in the monastery and resident pupils in the school. On a mild October afternoon the young students were chanting psalms in the churchyard.

All was well, except that Ragna had vanished, along with her children and servants. Edgar had spent two months going from town to town and village to village, but he had found no trace of her. He had even visited the new hunting lodge Wigelm was building near Outhenham. No one had seen Ragna pass by. Edgar was distraught but helpless, and Aldred pitied him.

Meanwhile, Wigelm was collecting all the rents from the Vale of Outhen.

Aldred had asked Sheriff Den how come the king did nothing about it. 'Look at it from King Ethelred's point of view,' Den had said. 'He sees Ragna's marriage as illegitimate. He declined to ratify it, but Wilwulf went ahead anyway. The royal court fined Wilf for

649

disobedience, and he refused to pay the fine. Ethelred's authority has been challenged and, what's worse, his pride has been hurt. He's not going to carry on as if this were a perfectly normal marriage.'

Aldred said indignantly: 'So he's punishing Ragna for Wilwulf's sins!'

'What else can he do?'

'He could harry Shiring!'

'That's an extreme measure: raising an army, burning the villages, killing the opposition, making off with the best horses and cattle and jewellery. It's a king's ultimate weapon, to be used only in extreme circumstances. Is he going to do that for a foreign widow whose marriage he never sanctioned in the first place?'

'Does her father know that she has disappeared?'

'Possibly. But a rescue operation from Normandy would be an invasion of England, and Count Hubert can't manage that – especially when his neighbour's daughter is about to marry the English king. Ethelred's wedding to Emma of Normandy is set for November.'

'The king has to rule, come what may; and one of his duties is to take care of noble widows.'

'You should put that point to him yourself.'

'All right, I will.'

Aldred had written a letter to King Ethelred.

In response, the king had ordered Wigelm to produce the person of his brother's widow.

Aldred thought Wigelm would simply ignore the order, as he had ignored royal decrees in the past, but this time it was different: Wigelm had announced that Ragna had gone home to Cherbourg.

If true, that would at least explain why no one had been able to find her in England. And she would naturally have taken her children and her Norman servants with her.

Edgar had made a second visit to Combe and had found no one who could confirm that Ragna had boarded a ship there – but she might have sailed from a different port.

While Aldred was worrying about Edgar, the man himself appeared. He had recovered from the beating he had suffered, except that his nose was slightly twisted now, and he was missing a front tooth. He approached the churchyard in the company of two others whom Aldred recognized. The man with the Norman-style haircut was Odo, and the small blonde woman was his wife, Adelaide. They were the couriers from Cherbourg who brought Ragna her rents from Saint-Martin every three months. Close behind were three men-at-arms, their escort. They needed fewer bodyguards since the execution of Ironface.

Aldred greeted them, then Edgar said: 'Odo has come to ask a favour, Prior Aldred.'

'I'll do my best,' said Aldred.

'I would like you to look after Ragna's money for her,' said Odo in his French accent.

'You can't find her, of course,' Aldred said.

Odo threw up his hands in a gesture of frustration. 'In Shiring they say she has gone to Outhenham, and at Outhenham they say she is in Combe, but we came via Combe and she was not there.'

Aldred nodded. 'No one can find her. Of course I will take care of her money, if that is your wish. But our latest information is that she has gone home to Cherbourg.'

Odo was astonished. 'But she is not there! If she were, we would not have come to England!'

'Of course not,' said Aldred.

Edgar said: 'Then where on earth is she?'

ÞÞÞ

RAGNA AND CAT and their children had been grabbed in their house and tied up and gagged by Wigelm and a group of men-at-arms. Under cover of darkness they had been carried out of the compound then bundled onto a four-wheeled cart and covered with blankets.

The children had been terrified, and the worst of it was that Ragna could not speak words of comfort to them.

The cart had jolted along dry-rutted dirt roads for hours. From what Ragna could hear, it had an escort of half a dozen men on horseback. However, they were quiet, speaking as little as possible and doing so in low voices.

The children had cried themselves to sleep.

When the cart stopped and the blankets were removed it was daylight. Ragna saw that they were in a clearing in the forest. Agnes was with the escort, and that was when Ragna realized that she was a traitor. Agnes must have betrayed Ragna by telling Wynstan of Ragna's plan to flee with Edgar. All this time the seamstress had been nursing a secret hatred of Ragna for the execution of her husband, Offa. Ragna cursed the merciful impulse that had led her to re-employ the woman.

She now saw that the children's cots were on the cart with the prisoners. But everything was covered up. What had this looked like, to villagers who saw the group pass by? Certainly not a kidnapping, for the women and children had not been visible. Ragna herself would have assumed, from the armed escort, that the blankets hid a large quantity of silver or other valuables that a wealthy nobleman or clergyman was transferring from one place to another.

Now, with no one around to see, Agnes untied the children and let them pee at the edge of the clearing. They would not run off, of course, for that would mean leaving their mothers behind. They were given bread soaked in milk, then tied up and gagged again. Then the mothers were released, one at a time, and watched carefully by the men as they relieved themselves then ate and drank a little. When all that was done, the prisoners were covered up again and the cart jolted on.

They stopped twice more at intervals of several hours.

That evening they arrived at Wilwulf's hunting lodge in the forest.

Ragna had been there before, in the happy early days of her marriage. She had always loved hunting, and it had reminded her of when she had hunted with Wilf in Normandy, and they had killed a boar together and then kissed passionately for the first time. But after the marriage started to go wrong she had lost her enthusiasm for the chase.

The lodge was remote and isolated, she recalled. There were stables, kennels, stores and a large house. A caretaker and his wife lived in one of the smaller buildings, but other than them no one had any reason to come here unless there was a hunting party.

Ragna and the others were carried into the big house and untied. The caretaker nailed boards over the two windows, making it impossible to open the shutters, and fixed a bar to the outside of the door. His wife brought a pot of porridge for their supper. Then they were left until morning.

That had been two months ago.

Agnes always brought them their food. They were allowed to exercise once a day, but Ragna was never let out at the same time as the children. There were always two of Wigelm's personal bodyguard outside, Fulcric and Elfgar. As far as Ragna could tell there were never visitors.

Wigelm and Wynstan could not have done this to an English noblewoman. She would have had a powerful family, parents and siblings and cousins with money and men-at-arms, who would have come looking for her, would have demanded that the king enforce her rights, and failing that would have come to Shiring with an army. Ragna was vulnerable because her family was too far away to intervene.

Agnes enjoyed bringing bad news with the food. 'Your boyfriend Edgar kicked up a fuss,' she had said early on.

'I knew he would,' Ragna had replied.

Cat had added: 'He is a *loyal* friend.'

Agnes ignored that jibe. 'He got beaten black and blue,' she said with malign satisfaction. 'Fulcric held him still while Wigelm beat him with a club.'

Ragna whispered: 'God save him.'

'I don't know about God, but Gilda took him to Sheriff Den's place. He couldn't stand upright for twenty-four hours.'

At least he was alive, Ragna thought. Wigelm had not killed him. Already in trouble with the king, Wigelm had perhaps not wanted to add to his list of offences.

Agnes was malign, but Ragna could beguile her into revealing information. 'They can't hide us here long,' she had said one day. 'People know Wilwulf had a hunting lodge here – soon someone will show up looking for us.'

'No, they won't,' Agnes had said with a triumphant look. 'Wigelm has told people that this place burned down. He has even built a new hunting lodge near Outhenham. He says the game is more abundant there.'

That had been Wynstan's idea, Ragna thought in despair; Wigelm was not clever enough to have thought of it.

All the same, there was a limit to how long their imprisonment could be kept secret. The forest was not empty of people: there were charcoal burners, horse-catchers, woodcutters, miners and outlaws. They might be frightened off by the men-at-arms, but it was impossible to stop them peeping from the bushes. Sooner or later someone would wonder whether prisoners were being kept at the hunting lodge.

Then rumours would start. People would say the house held a monster with two heads, or a coven of witches, or a corpse that came back to life at full moon and tried to break open its coffin. But someone would connect the prison with the missing noblewoman.

How long would that take? The forest folk's way of life meant they had little contact with ordinary peasants or townspeople. They did not speak to strangers for months on end. At some point they had to go to market with a string of newly broken horses or a cartload of iron ore, but that would most likely happen next spring.

As the weeks turned into months Ragna sank into depression. The children grizzled all the time, Cat was bad-tempered, and Ragna found she could not think of a reason to wash her face in the morning.

And then she found out that there was worse in store; much worse.

She was making scratch marks on the wall to count the days, and it was not long before Hallowe'en when Wigelm arrived.

It was dark outside, and the children were already asleep. Ragna and Cat were sitting on a bench by the fire. The room was lit by a single rush lamp – they were allowed only one at a time. Fulcric opened the door for Wigelm then closed it, remaining outside.

Ragna looked carefully and saw that Wigelm was not armed.

'What do you want?' she said, and she immediately felt ashamed of the note of fear she heard in her own voice.

With a gesture of his thumb Wigelm ordered Cat to get up, then he took her place. Ragna shifted along the bench to be as far from him as possible.

He said: 'You've had plenty of time to think about your position.'

With an effort, she summoned some of her old spirit. 'I've been illegally imprisoned. I worked that out in no time at all.'

'You're powerless and penniless.'

'I'm penniless because you stole my money. By the way, a widow is entitled to the return of her dowry. Mine was twenty pounds of silver. You stole Wilf's treasury, too, so you owe me twenty pounds from that. How soon can you let me have the money?'

Wigelm said: 'If you marry me, you can have it all.'

'And lose my soul. No, thank you, I'll just take my money.'

He shook his head as if saddened. 'Why do you have to be such a bitch? What's wrong with being nice to a man?'

'Wigelm, why have you come here?'

He sighed theatrically. 'I made you a good offer. I will marry you—'

'So condescending!'

'– and together we will ask the king to appoint us to rule Shiring. I was hoping that by now you might have seen the sense of accepting my proposal.'

'No, I haven't.'

'You won't get a better one.' He grasped her upper arm with a strong hand. 'Come, now, you can't pretend to find me unattractive.'

'Pretend? Let go of me.'

'I promise you, after one shag with me you'll be begging for more.'

She wrenched her arm from his grasp and stood up. 'Never!'

To Ragna's surprise he went to the door and tapped on it, then turned back to her. 'Never is a long time,' he said. The guard opened and Wigelm went out.

'Thank God,' said Ragna as the door closed.

'A lucky escape,' said Cat. She returned to the bench and sat beside Ragna.

Ragna said: 'He doesn't usually give up that easily.'

'You're still worried.'

'Actually, I think Wigelm is worried. Why do you think he's so keen to marry me?'

'Who wouldn't be?'

Ragna shook her head. 'He doesn't really want me for a wife. I'm too much trouble. He'd rather sleep with someone who will never stand up to him.'

'What, then?'

'They're worried about the king. They've got control of Shiring, and of me, for now, but they've done a lot to antagonize Ethelred in the process, and the time may come when he decides to teach them who rules England.'

'Or it may not,' said Cat. 'Kings like a quiet life.'

'True. But Wynstan and Wigelm can't predict which way Ethelred will jump. However, they'd have a better chance of getting the result they want if I married Wigelm. And that's why they keep trying.'

The door opened, and Wigelm came back in.

This time he was accompanied by four men-at-arms whom Ragna did not recognize. He must have brought them with him. They looked like ruffians.

Cat screamed.

Two men grabbed each woman, threw them to the floor, and held them down.

All the children cried.

Wigelm grasped the neckline of Ragna's dress and ripped it off, leaving her spreadeagled naked, held by her ankles and wrists.

One of the men said: 'Now, there's a pair of plump pigeons, by the gods!'

'They're not for you,' Wigelm said, lifting the skirt of his tunic. 'When I've finished you can fuck the maid, but not this one. She's going to be my wife.'

ÞÞÞ

THERE WAS A cold wind coming off the sea, and Wynstan walked gratefully into the warm, smoky atmosphere of Mags's house in Combe, with Wigelm behind him. Mags saw him at once and threw her arms around him. 'My favourite priest!' she exulted.

Wynstan kissed her. 'Mags, you sweet thing, how are you?'

She looked over his shoulder. 'And your equally handsome younger brother,' she said, and embraced Wigelm.

'Every rich man is handsome to you,' Wigelm said sourly.

She ignored that. 'Sit down, dear friends, and have a cup of mead. It's newly brewed. Selethryth!' She snapped her fingers, and a flagon and cups were brought by a middle-aged woman – undoubtedly a former prostitute now considered too old for the work, Wynstan thought.

657

They drank the ultra-sweet potion and Selethryth poured more.

Wynstan looked at the women sitting at the sides of the room on benches. Some were dressed, others draped in loose wraps, and one pale girl was stark naked. 'What a lovely sight,' he said with a sigh.

'I have a new girl I've been saving,' Mags said. 'But which of you will take her virginity?'

Wigelm said: 'How many men have taken it so far?'

Wynstan chuckled.

Mags protested. 'You know I'd never lie to you. I don't even allow her in here – she's locked up in the house next door.'

Wynstan said: 'Let Wigelm have the virgin. I'm in the mood for a more experienced woman.'

'How about Merry? She likes you.'

Wynstan smiled at a voluptuous dark-haired woman of about twenty. She waved to him. 'Yes,' he said. 'Merry would be lovely. Such a big arse.'

Merry came and sat beside him, and he kissed her.

Mags said: 'Selethryth, fetch the virgin from next door for Thane Wigelm.'

After a few minutes Wynstan said to Merry: 'Lie down in the straw, my dear, and let's get at it.'

Merry pulled her dress over her head and lay on her back. She was pink-skinned and plump: he was glad he had chosen her. He lifted the skirt of his tunic and knelt between her legs.

Merry screamed.

Wynstan flinched away, bewildered. 'What the devil is wrong with the woman?' he said.

Merry screeched: 'He's got a chancre!' She leaped to her feet and covered her vagina protectively.

'No, I haven't,' Wynstan said.

Mags spoke in a new tone of voice. Her former anything-you-like-darling attitude had been replaced by a brisk sense of authority. 'Let me see, bishop,' she said in a matter-of-fact way. 'Show me your prick.'

Wynstan turned.

'Oh, Jesus,' said Mags. 'It's a chancre.'

Wynstan looked down at his penis. Near the head was an oval ulcer an inch long with an angry red spot at its centre. 'That's nothing,' he said. 'It doesn't even hurt.'

Mags's jollity had all fallen away and her voice was cold. 'It's not nothing,' she said firmly. 'It's the Great Pox.'

'That's impossible,' said Wynstan. 'Great Pox leads to leprosy.'

Mags softened, but only slightly. 'Perhaps you're right,' she said, and Wynstan felt she was humouring him. 'But whatever it is I can't let you fuck my girls. If any kind of pox got around this house, half the clergy in England would be out of action before you could say "fornicate".'

'Well, that's a blow.' Wynstan felt cast down. An illness was a weakness, and he was supposed to be strong. Besides, he was aroused, and wanted a fuck. 'What am I going to do?' he said.

Mags's demeanour regained some of its usual coquetry. 'You're going to get the best hand-fuck you've ever had, and I'm going to give it to you myself, my sweet priest.'

'Well, if that's the best you can do . . .'

'The girls will put on a show for you at the same time. What would you like to watch?'

Wynstan considered. 'I'd like to see Merry's arse flogged with a strap.'

'Then you shall,' Mags said.

Merry said: 'Oh, no.'

'Don't complain,' Mags told her. 'You get extra pay for flagellation, you know that.'

Merry was contrite. 'I'm sorry, Mags. I didn't mean to complain.'

'That's better,' said Mags. 'Now, turn around and bend over.'

35

RAGNA AND CAT WERE teaching the children a counting song. Osbert, almost four, could more or less carry a tune. The twins were just two, and they could only drone, but they were able to learn the words. Cat's daughters, aged two and three, were somewhere in between. They all liked the singing and, as a bonus, they were learning their numbers.

Ragna's main occupation in prison was keeping the children busy with activities that taught them something. She remembered poems, made up stories, and described every place she had ever visited. She told them about the ship the *Angel* and the storm in the Channel, the thief Ironface who had stolen the wedding present, and even the fire in the stables at Cherbourg Castle. Cat was not as good at stories but had a bottomless fund of French songs and a pure voice.

Entertaining the children also kept the two women from sinking into a swamp of suicidal despair.

As the song was ending the door opened and a guard looked in. It was Elfgar, the youngster, not as hardened as Fulcric and inclined to be sympathetic. He often told Ragna the news. From him she had learned that the Vikings were attacking the West Country again, with the dreaded King Swein at their head. The truce that Ethelred had bought for twenty-four thousand pounds of silver had not lasted into a second year.

Ragna almost hoped that the Vikings might conquer the West Country. She could be captured and ransomed. At least she might get out of this prison.

Elfgar said: 'Exercise time.'

'Where's Agnes?' said Ragna.

'She's feeling ill.'

Ragna was not sorry. She hated seeing Agnes, the woman who had betrayed her, the one responsible for her imprisonment.

The open door let in cold air, so Ragna and Cat put the impatient children into their cloaks, then released them to run outside. Elfgar closed the door and barred it from the outside.

With the children gone, Ragna gave herself up to misery.

She had been here seven months, according to the almanac she had scratched on the wall. There were fleas in the rushes on the floor and nits in her hair, and she had a cough. The place stank: two adults and five children used a single pot for their toilet, for they were not allowed to go outside for that purpose.

A day spent here was a day stolen from her life, and she felt a resentment as sharp as an arrowhead every morning when she woke up to find herself still a prisoner.

And Wigelm had come again yesterday.

His visits were mercifully less frequent now. At first he had appeared once a week; now it was more like once a month. She had learned to close her eyes and think about the view from the ramparts of Cherbourg Castle, and the clean salty air blowing in her face, until she felt him withdraw like a slug leaving her body. She prayed he would soon lose interest altogether.

The children returned, red-faced from the cold, and it was the turn of the two women to put on cloaks and go out.

They walked up and down to keep warm, and Elfgar walked with them. Cat asked him: 'What's wrong with Agnes?'

'Some kind of pox,' he said.

'I hope she dies of it.'

There was a pause, then Elfgar said conversationally: 'I won't be here much longer, I shouldn't think.'

Ragna said: 'Why? We'd be sorry to lose you.'

'I shall have to go and fight the Vikings.' He was pretending to be pleased, but Ragna detected an undertone of fear beneath his bravado. 'The king is raising an army to come and defeat Swein Forkbeard.'

Ragna stopped walking. 'Are you sure?' she said. 'King Ethelred is coming to the West Country?'

'So they say.'

Ragna's heart leaped with hope. 'Then he must surely learn of our imprisonment,' she said.

Elfgar shrugged. 'Maybe.'

'Our friends will tell him: Prior Aldred, and Sheriff Den, and Bishop Modulf.'

'Yes!' said Cat. 'And then King Ethelred is bound to free us!'

Ragna was not sure.

'Isn't he, my lady?'

Ragna said nothing.

ÞÞÞ

'THIS IS OUR chance to find Ragna,' Prior Aldred said to Sheriff Den. 'We must not let the opportunity slip through our fingers.'

Aldred had come from Dreng's Ferry to Shiring specifically to talk to Den about this. Now he studied the sheriff for his reaction. Den was fifty-eight, exactly twenty years older than Aldred, but they had much in common. Both were rule keepers. Den's compound testified to his liking for order: his stockade was well built, the houses stood in lines, and the kitchen and dunghill were in opposite corners, as far from each other as possible. Dreng's Ferry had acquired a similar orderly look since Aldred had taken over. But there were differences, too: Den served the king; Aldred served God.

Aldred went on: 'We now know for sure that Ragna never went

to Cherbourg. Count Hubert has confirmed that to us and has sent a formal complaint to King Ethelred. Wynstan and Wigelm lied.'

Den's response was cautious. 'I'd like to see Ragna safe and well, and I believe King Ethelred would too,' he said. 'But a king has multiple needs, and the different pressures on him sometimes conflict with one another.'

Den's wife, Wilburgh, a middle-aged woman with grey hair under her cap, had a more trenchant opinion. 'The king should put that devil Wigelm in a prison.'

Aldred agreed with her, but took a more practical line. 'Will the king hold court in the West Country?'

'He must,' said Den. 'Everywhere he goes, his subjects come to him with demands, accusations, pleas, proposals. He cannot help but hear them, and then people want decisions.'

'In Shiring?'

'If he comes here, yes.'

'Here or elsewhere, he must do *something* about Ragna, surely!'

'Sooner or later. His authority has been defied, and he can't let that stand. But the timing is another matter.'

Every answer was maybe, Aldred thought with frustration, but perhaps that was normal with royalty. In a monastery, by contrast, a sin was a sin, and there was nothing to dither about. He said: 'Ethelred's new wife, Queen Emma, will surely be a strong ally to Ragna. They're both Norman aristocrats, they knew each other when younger, they both married powerful English noblemen. They must have experienced similar joys and sorrows in our country. Queen Emma will want Ethelred to rescue Ragna.'

'And Ethelred would do so, were it not for Swein Forkbeard. Ethelred is gathering armies to do battle, and as always he relies on the thanes to muster men from the towns and villages. It's a bad time for him to quarrel with powerful magnates such as Wigelm and Wynstan.'

Which boiled down to another maybe, Aldred thought. 'Is there anything that could sway the decision?'

Den thought for a moment, then said: 'Ragna herself.'

'What do you mean?'

'If Ethelred meets her, he will do anything she asks. She is beautiful and vulnerable, and a noble widow. He will not be able to find it in himself to refuse justice to an alluring woman who has been ill-treated.'

'But that's our problem. We can't bring her before him because we can't find her.'

'Exactly.'

'So anything could happen.'

'Yes.'

'By the way,' said Aldred, 'while I was on my way here, Wigelm passed me on the road, going in the opposite direction, with a small group of men-at-arms. You don't know where he was headed, do you?'

'Wherever he was going, his route must have led through Dreng's Ferry, for there's no other place of note on that stretch.'

'I hope he wasn't intending to make trouble for me.'

Aldred rode home with a worried mind, but when he arrived Brother Godleof told him that in fact Wigelm had not visited Dreng's Ferry. 'He must have changed his mind on the road and turned back, for some reason,' Godleof said.

Aldred frowned. 'I suppose so,' he said.

ÞÞÞ

ALDRED HEARD THE army when they were still a mile or more away from Dreng's Ferry. At first he did not know what he was listening to. It was a noise something like the sound of Shiring city centre on market day: the cumulative result of hundreds of people, perhaps thousands, talking and laughing, shouting orders, cursing, whistling and coughing, plus horses braying and whinnying, and carts creaking and bumping. He could also hear the destruction of foliage either side of the mud road, men and horses treading down plants, carts rolling over bushes and saplings. It could only be an army.

Everyone knew that King Ethelred was on his way, but his route had not been announced, and Aldred was surprised that he would choose to cross the river at Dreng's Ferry.

When Aldred heard the din he was at work in the monastery's new building, a stone edifice housing the school, the library and the scriptorium. Resting a sheet of parchment on a board on his knees, he was painstakingly copying St Matthew's gospel in the insular minuscule script used for literature in English. He worked prayerfully, for this was a holy task. Writing out a part of the Bible had a double purpose: it created a new book, of course, but it was also a perfect way to meditate on the deeper meaning of the holy scriptures.

He had a rule that worldly developments should never be allowed to interrupt spiritual work – but this was the king, and he stopped.

He closed St Matthew's book, put the stopper back into his ink horn, rinsed the nib of his quill in a bowl of clean water, blew on his parchment to dry the ink, then put everything back into the chest where such costly articles were kept. He did so methodically, but his heart was racing. The king! The king was the hope of justice. Shiring had become a tyranny, and only Ethelred could change that.

Aldred had never seen the king. He was called Ethelred the Misled, for people said that his fault was to follow bad advice. Aldred was not sure he believed that. Saying that the king was ill-advised was usually a way of attacking the monarch without seeming to.

Anyway, Aldred was not convinced that Ethelred's decisions were disastrous. He had become king when he was twelve years old and, despite that, he had reigned for twenty-five years so far – an achievement in itself. True, Ethelred had failed to inflict a decisive defeat on the marauding Vikings, but they had been raiding England for something like two hundred years, and no other king had done much better against them.

Aldred reminded himself that Ethelred might not be in company with the approaching troops today. He might have diverted on some errand, arranging to rejoin the army later. Kings were not the servants of their own plans.

By the time Aldred stepped outside, the first soldiers were visible on the far bank of the river. Most were boisterous young men carrying home-made weapons, mainly spears with a few hammers and axes and bows. There was a sprinkling of greybeards and a few women too.

Aldred walked down to the riverside. Dreng was there, looking bad-tempered.

Blod was already poling the ferry across. A few men swam the river immediately, impatient to get across, but most people could not swim; Aldred himself had never learned. One man led his horse into the water and clung to the saddle while the mount swam across, but most of the horses were heavily laden pack animals. Soon a waiting crowd gathered. Aldred wondered how many men there were in total, and how long it would take for them all to cross the river.

The time could have been halved if Edgar had been here with his raft, but he had gone to Combe, where he was helping the monks build town defences. These days Edgar seized on any excuse to travel, so that he could continue his search for Ragna. He never gave up.

Blod landed on the far side and announced the fare. The soldiers ignored her demand and crowded onto the boat, fifteen, twenty, twenty-five. They had little sense of how many the vessel could hold safely, and Aldred saw Blod argue fiercely with several before they reluctantly got off to wait for the next shuttle. When she had fifteen aboard she poled away.

As they reached the near bank Dreng shouted: 'Where's the money?'

'They say they haven't got any money,' Blod replied.

The soldiers disembarked, shoving Blod aside.

Dreng said: 'You shouldn't have let them board if they wouldn't pay.'

Blod looked at Dreng with contempt. 'You go across and see if you do any better.'

One of the soldiers was listening to the interchange. He was an older man armed with a good sword, so he was probably some kind of captain. He said to Dreng: 'The king doesn't pay tolls. You'd better ferry the men across. Otherwise we'll probably burn this entire village.'

Aldred said: 'There will be no need for violence. I'm Aldred, prior of the monastery.'

'I'm Cenric, one of the quartermasters.'

'How many men in your army, Cenric?'

'About two thousand.'

'This one slave girl will not be able to ferry them all across. It's going to take a day or two. Why don't you operate the boat yourselves?'

Dreng said: 'What business is this of yours, Aldred? It's not your boat!'

Aldred said: 'Be quiet, Dreng.'

'Who do you think you are?'

Cenric said to Dreng: 'Shut up, you stupid oaf, or I'll cut out your tongue and stuff it down your gullet.'

Dreng opened his mouth to reply, then seemed to realize that Cenric was not making an empty threat, but meant exactly what he said. Dreng changed his mind and quickly closed his mouth.

Cenric said: 'You're right, prior, it's the only way. We'll make a rule: last man aboard poles the boat back then across again. I'll stand here for an hour and make sure they do it.'

Dreng looked over his shoulder and saw some of the soldiers entering the tavern. In a frightened voice he said: 'Well, they'll have to pay for their ale.'

'Then you'd better go and serve them,' said Cenric. 'We'll try to make sure the men don't expect free drinks.' Sarcastically he added: 'As you've been so helpful about the ferry.'

Dreng hurried inside.

Cenric spoke to Blod. 'One more trip, slave girl, then the men will take over from you.'

Blod stepped into the boat and poled off.

Cenric said to Aldred: 'We'll want to buy any stores you monks have of food and drink.'

'I'll see what we can spare.'

Cenric shook his head. 'We're going to buy them whether you can spare them or not, Father Prior.' His tone was without malice but brooked no opposition. 'The army doesn't take no for an answer.'

And they would set the prices of everything they bought, Aldred thought, and no haggling.

He asked the question that had been on his mind all through the conversation. 'Is King Ethelred with you?'

'Oh, yes. He's near the front of the horde, with the senior noblemen. He'll be here shortly.'

'Then I'd better prepare a meal for him at the monastery.'

Aldred left the riverside and walked up the hill to the home of Bucca Fish, where he bought all the fresh fish on the slab, promising to pay later. Bucca was glad to sell, fearing that otherwise his stocks might be commandeered or stolen.

Aldred returned to the monastery and gave orders for dinner. He told the monks that any quartermasters who demanded stores should be told that everything was earmarked for the king. They began to lay the table, putting out wine and bread, nuts and dried fruit.

Aldred opened a locked box and took out a silver cross on a leather thong. He put it around his neck and re-locked the box. The cross would indicate to all the visitors that he was the senior monk.

What was he going to say to the king? After years of wishing that Ethelred would come and set matters right in the semi-lawless region of Shiring, suddenly Aldred found himself searching for the words he needed. The wrongs committed by Wilwulf, Wynstan and Wigelm made a long and complicated story, and many of their crimes could not easily be proved. He considered showing the king his copy of Wilwulf's will; but that told only part of the story, and anyway the king might be offended to be shown a will he had not authorized. Aldred really needed a week to write it all down – and then the king probably would not read it: many noblemen were literate but reading was not usually their favourite occupation.

He heard cheering. That must be for the king. He left the monastery and hurried down the hill.

The ferry was approaching. A soldier was poling it, and on board was only one man, standing at the forward end of the boat, and a horse. The man wore a patterned red tunic with gold-coloured embroidery and a blue cloak with silk edging. His cloth leggings were secured by narrow leather binding straps, and he had laced boots of soft leather. A long sword in a scabbard hung from a yellow silk sash. This was undoubtedly the king.

Ethelred was not looking towards the village. His head was turned to the left and he was staring at the scorched ruins of the bridge, the blackened beams still disfiguring the waterfront.

As Ethelred led his horse off the ferry onto dry land, Aldred saw that he was in a fury.

Ethelred addressed Aldred, knowing by the cross that he was in authority here. 'I expected to cross by a bridge!' he said accusingly.

That explains why he chose to come this way, Aldred thought.

'What the devil happened?' the king demanded.

'The bridge was burned down, my lord king,' said Aldred.

Ethelred narrowed his eyes shrewdly. 'You didn't say it *burned*, you said it *was* burned. By whom?'

'We don't know.'

'But you suspect.'

Aldred shrugged. 'It would be foolish to make accusations that cannot be substantiated – especially to a king.'

'I would suspect the ferryman. What's his name?'

'Dreng.'

'Of course.'

'But his cousin, Bishop Wynstan, swore that Dreng was at Shiring on the night the bridge burned.'

'I see.'

'Please come with me to our humble monastery and take some refreshment, my lord king.'

Ethelred left his horse for someone else to deal with and walked up the slope beside Aldred. 'How long is it going to take for my army to cross this cursed river?'

'Two days.'

'Hell.'

They went inside. Ethelred looked around in some surprise. 'Well, you said "humble", and you meant it,' he said.

Aldred poured him a cup of wine. There was no special chair, but the king sat on a bench without complaint. Aldred guessed that even a king could not be too fastidious when on the road with his army. Studying his face surreptitiously, Aldred realized that although Ethelred was not yet forty years old he looked nearer fifty.

Aldred still had not figured out how best to broach the large issue of tyranny in Shiring, but the conversation about the bridge had given him a new idea, and he said: 'I could build a new bridge, if I had the money.' This was disingenuous, for the old one had cost him nothing.

'I can't pay for it,' said Ethelred immediately.

Aldred said thoughtfully: 'But you could help me pay for it.'

Ethelred sighed, and Aldred realized that he probably heard similar words from half the people he met. 'What do you want?' said the king.

'If the monastery could collect tolls, and hold a weekly market and an annual fair, the monks would get their money back, and also be able to pay for the maintenance of the bridge in the long term.' Aldred was thinking on his feet, improvising. He had not anticipated this conversation but he knew he had an opportunity and he was determined to seize it. This might be the only time in his life that he talked to the king.

Ethelred said: 'What's stopping you?'

'You've seen what happened to our bridge. We're monks, we're vulnerable.'

'What do you need from me?'

'A royal charter. At present we're just a cell of Shiring Abbey, formed when the old minster was closed for corruption – they were forging coins here.'

Ethelred's face darkened. 'I remember. Bishop Wynstan denied all knowledge.'

Aldred did not want to get into that. 'We have no guaranteed rights, and that makes us weak. We need a charter that says the monastery is independent, and is entitled to build a bridge and charge a toll and hold markets and a fair. Then predatory noblemen would hesitate to attack us.'

'And if I give you this charter, you will build me a bridge?'

'I will,' said Aldred, silently hoping that Edgar would be as helpful as previously. 'And fast,' he added optimistically.

'Then consider it done,' said the king.

Aldred would not consider it done until it was done. 'I will have the charter drawn up immediately,' he said. 'It can be witnessed before you leave here tomorrow.'

'Good,' said the king. 'Now, what have you got for me to eat?'

ÞÞÞ

WIGELM SAID TO Wynstan: 'The king is on his way. We don't know exactly where he is, but he will be here in a matter of days.'

'Very likely,' said Wynstan anxiously.

'And then he will confirm me as ealdorman.'

They were in the ealdorman's compound. Wigelm was acting ealdorman, though he had never received the king's blessing. The two brothers were standing in front of the great hall, looking east, at the road that led into the town of Shiring, as if Ethelred's army might appear there at any moment.

So far there was no sign, though a single rider was approaching at a trot, his horse's breath steaming in the cold air.

Wynstan said: 'There's still a chance he might nominate little Osbert, with Ragna acting as the boy's regent.'

Wigelm said: 'I've mustered four hundred men already and more are coming in every day.'

'Good. If the king attacks us, the army can defend us, and if he doesn't, they can fight the Vikings.'

'Either way, I will have proved my ability to raise an army, and therefore to be ealdorman of Shiring.'

'I bet Ragna could muster armies equally well. But fortunately the king doesn't know what she's like. With luck, he'll think that if he wants his troops he has to have your help.'

Wynstan himself should have been the one to claim the title of ealdorman. But it was too late for that, too late by about thirty years. Wilwulf had been the elder brother, and their mother had set Wynstan firmly on the second-best route to power, the Church. But no one could see the future, and the unforeseen consequence of his mother's careful planning had been that the mulish youngest brother, Wigelm, was now playing the role of ealdorman.

'But we've got another problem,' Wynstan said. 'We can't stop Ethelred holding court, and we can't prevent him from talking about Ragna. He is going to order us to produce her, and then what can we do?'

Wigelm sighed. 'I wish we could just kill her.'

'We've been over that. We barely got away with killing Wilf. If we murder Ragna, the king will declare war on us.'

The rider Wynstan had seen on the road now trotted into the compound, and Wynstan recognized Dreng. He grunted with irritation. 'What does that fawning idiot want now?'

Dreng left his horse at the stable and came to the great hall. 'Good day to you, my cousins,' he said, smiling unctuously. 'I hope I see you well.'

Wynstan said: 'What brings you here, Dreng?'

'King Ethelred came to our village,' Dreng said. 'His army crossed on my ferry.'

'That must have taken a while. What did he do while he was waiting?'

'He gave the priory a charter. They have royal approval for a toll bridge, a weekly market and an annual fair.'

'Aldred building his power base,' Wynstan mused. 'These monks renounce the things of the world, but they know how to look after their own interests.'

Dreng seemed disappointed that Wynstan was not more shocked. 'Then the army left,' he said.

'When do you think they'll get here?'

'They're not coming here. They re-crossed the river.'

'What?' This was the real news, even though Dreng had not recognized it. 'They turned around and went back eastwards? Why?'

'A message came to say that Swein Forkbeard has attacked Wilton.'

Wigelm said: 'The Vikings must have sailed up the river from Christchurch.'

Wynstan did not care how King Swein had reached Wilton. 'Don't you see what this means? Ethelred has gone back!'

'So he's not coming to Shiring,' said Wigelm.

'Not now, anyway.' Wynstan was profoundly relieved. He added hopefully: 'And perhaps not any time soon.'

36

EDGAR WAS SHAPING A beam with an adze, a tool like an axe but with an arched blade, its edge at right angles to the handle, designed for scraping a length of timber to a smooth, even surface. In past times work such as this had been a delight to him. He had found profound satisfaction in the fresh smell of the scraped wood, the sharpness of the cutting edge, and, most of all, the clear, logical picture he had in his head of the structure he was creating. But now he worked joylessly, as mindless as a millwheel going round and round.

He paused, straightened his back, and took a long swallow of weak ale. Looking across the river he saw that the trees on the far side were now in full leaf, fresh green in the pale morning sun. That woodland had formerly been a dangerous place on account of Ironface, but now travellers ventured there with less trepidation.

On the near side, his family's farmland was just turning from green to yellow as the oats ripened, and he could see in the distance the stooped figures of Erman and Cwenburg as they weeded. Their children were with them: Winnie, now five, was old enough to help with the weeding, but Beorn, three, was sitting on the ground, playing with the earth. Nearer to Edgar, Eadbald was at the fish pond, up to his waist in the water, pulling up a fish trap and examining the contents.

Nearer still, there were new houses in the village, and many of the old buildings had been extended. The alehouse had a brewhouse, which was even now giving off the yeasty aroma of fermenting barley:

Blod had taken over the brewing after Leaf died, and she had turned out to have something of a flair for it. Right now Fat Bebbe was sitting on the bench in front of the alehouse drinking a flagon of Blod's ale.

The church had an extension, and the monastery had a stone building for the school, library and scriptorium. Halfway up the hill, opposite Edgar's house, a site was slowly being cleared for the new, larger church that would be built there one day, if Aldred's dreams came true.

Aldred's optimism and ambition were infectious, and most of the village now looked to the future with eager hope; but Edgar was an exception. Everything that he and Aldred had achieved in the last six years tasted sour in his mouth. He could think of nothing but Ragna, languishing in some place of captivity all this time while he was powerless to help her.

He was about to restart his work when Aldred came down from the monastery. Rebuilding the bridge was quicker than the original construction, but not much, and Aldred was desperately impatient. 'When will it be finished?' he asked Edgar.

Edgar surveyed the site. He had used his Viking axe to chop away the charred remains. He had let the useless ashes float downstream, and had stacked half-burned timbers by the riverside to be recycled as firewood. He had renewed the stout abutments on both banks, then had rapidly built a series of simple flat-bottomed boats to be fixed together and moored to the abutments to form the pontoons. He was now fashioning the framework that would rest on the boats and support the roadbed.

'How long?' said Aldred.

'I'm not dawdling,' Edgar said irritably.

'I didn't say you were dawdling, I asked you how long. The priory needs the money!'

Edgar hardly cared about the priory and he resented Aldred's tone.

Lately he had found that several of his friends were becoming uncongenial. Everyone seemed to want something from him, and he found their demands annoying. 'I'm on my own!' he said.

'I can give you more monks to use as labourers.'

'I don't need labourers. Most of the work is skilled.'

'Perhaps we can get other builders to help you.'

'I'm probably the only craftsman in England willing to work in exchange for reading lessons.'

Aldred sighed. 'I know we're lucky to have you, and I'm sorry to badger you, but we really are eager to get this finished.'

'I hope the bridge might be ready to use by the autumn.'

'Could you make it sooner, if I could find the money for another skilled man to work with you?'

'Good luck finding one. Too many builders around here have gone to Normandy for higher wages. Our neighbours across the Channel have long been ahead of us in building castles and now, apparently, the young Duke Richard is turning his attention to churches.'

'I know.'

Edgar was impatient about something else. 'I saw that a travelling monk spent last night at the monastery. Did he have news of King Ethelred?' After all his months of searching, Edgar now believed that the king represented the only hope of finding Ragna and freeing her.

'Yes,' said Aldred. 'We learned that Swein Forkbeard sacked Wilton and left. Ethelred got there too late. The Vikings, meanwhile, had sailed for Exeter, so our king and his army headed there.'

'They must have taken the coast road, as Ethelred didn't pass through Shiring this time.'

'Correct.'

'Has the king held court anywhere in the Shiring region?'

'Not as far as we know. He has neither confirmed Wigelm as ealdorman nor issued any new orders about Ragna.'

'Hell. She's been a prisoner for nearly ten months now.'

'I'm sorry, Edgar. Sorry for her and sorry for you.'

Edgar did not want anyone's pity. He glanced towards the tavern and saw Dreng outside. He was standing near Bebbe but looking at Edgar and Aldred. Edgar shouted: 'What are you staring at?'

'You two,' Dreng said. 'Wondering what you're plotting now.'

'We're building a bridge.'

'Aye,' said Dreng. 'Take care, though. It would be a shame if this one were to burn down too.' He laughed, then turned around and went inside.

Edgar said: 'I hope he goes to hell.'

'Oh, he will,' said Aldred. 'But while we wait for that I have another plan.'

ÞÞÞ

ALDRED WENT TO Shiring and returned a week later with Sheriff Den and six men-at-arms.

Edgar heard the horses and looked up from his work. Blod came out of the brewhouse to see. Within a couple of minutes most of the village had gathered at the riverside. Despite the season the weather was cool, with a chill breeze. The sky was grey and threatened rain.

The men-at-arms were grim-faced and silent. Two of them dug a narrow hole in the ground outside the alehouse and fixed a stake into it. The villagers asked questions but got no answers, which made them all the more curious.

However, they could guess that someone was about to be punished.

Edgar's brothers had got wind that something was happening, and showed up with Cwenburg and the children.

When the stake was firmly embedded, the men-at-arms seized Dreng.

'You let me go!' he shouted, struggling.

They pulled off his clothes, causing everyone to laugh.

'My cousin is the bishop of Shiring!' he yelled. 'You'll all pay a heavy price for this!'

Ethel, Dreng's surviving wife, rained feeble blows on the men-at-arms with her fist, saying: 'Leave him alone!'

They ignored her and roped her husband to the stake.

Blod looked on expressionlessly.

Prior Aldred spoke to the crowd. 'King Ethelred has ordered a bridge to be built here,' he said. 'Dreng threatened to burn it down.'

'I did not!' said Dreng.

Fat Bebbe was watching. 'You did, though,' she said. 'I was there, I heard you.'

Sheriff Den said: 'I represent the king. He is not to be defied.'

Everyone knew that.

'I want each person to go home, find a bucket or a pot, and bring it back here, quickly.'

The villagers and the monks obeyed with alacrity. They were keen to see what was going to happen. Among the few who declined to join in were Cwenburg, Dreng's daughter, and her two husbands, Erman and Eadbald.

When they had reassembled Den said: 'Dreng threatened a fire. We will now put out his flames. Everyone, fill your vessel from the river and pour the water over Dreng.'

Edgar guessed that Aldred had devised this punishment. It was more symbolic than painful. Few people would have dreamed up something so mild. On the other hand it was humiliating, especially for a man such as Dreng who boasted of his connections in high places.

And it was a warning. Dreng had got away with burning down the bridge before, because that bridge had belonged to Aldred, who was no more than the prior of a small monastery, whereas Dreng had the support of the bishop of Shiring. But the sheriff's action today announced that the new bridge would be different. This one belonged to the king, and even Wynstan would struggle to protect someone who set fire to it.

The villagers began to throw their containers of river water over Dreng. He was not much liked, and people clearly enjoyed what they were doing. Some took care to throw the water directly into his face, which made him curse. Others laughed and poured it over his head. Several people went back for another bucketful. Dreng began to shiver.

Edgar did not fill a bucket but stood watching, with his arms folded. Dreng will never forget this, he thought.

Eventually Aldred called: 'Enough!'

The villagers stopped.

Den said: 'He is to remain here until dawn tomorrow. Anyone who releases him before then will take his place.'

Dreng was going to spend a cold night, Edgar thought, but he would live.

Den led his men-at-arms to the monastery, where presumably they would stay the night. Edgar hoped they liked beans.

The villagers dispersed slowly, realizing there was no more fun to be had.

Edgar was about to restart his work when Dreng caught his eye.

'Go on, laugh,' said Dreng.

Edgar was not laughing.

Dreng said: 'I heard a rumour about your precious Norman lady, Ragna.'

Edgar froze. He wanted to walk away, but he could not.

'I hear she's pregnant,' Dreng said.

Edgar stared at him.

Dreng said: 'Now laugh at that.'

ÞÞÞ

EDGAR BROODED OVER Dreng's taunt. He might have been making it up, of course. Or the rumour might simply be untrue: many rumours were. But Ragna might really be pregnant.

And if she was pregnant, Edgar might be the father.

He had made love to her only once, but once could be enough. However, their night of passion had been in August, so the baby would have been born in May, and it was now June.

The baby might be late. Or perhaps it had already been born.

That evening he asked Den if he had heard the rumour. Den had.

'Do they say when the baby is due?' he asked.

'No.'

'Did you pick up any hint of where Ragna is?'

'No, and if I did, I would have gone there and rescued her.'

Edgar had had the conversation about Ragna's whereabouts a hundred times. The pregnancy rumour took him no nearer to an answer. It was just an additional torture.

Towards the end of June he realized he needed nails. He could make them in what had once been Cuthbert's forge, but he had to go to Shiring to buy the iron. Next morning he saddled Buttress and joined up with two trappers heading for the city to sell furs.

At mid-morning they stopped at a wayside alehouse known as Stumpy's on account of the proprietor's amputated leg. Edgar fed Buttress a handful of grain, then she drank from a pond and cropped the grass around it while Edgar ate bread and cheese, sitting on a bench in the sunshine with the trappers and some local men.

He was about to leave when a troop of men-at-arms rode by. Edgar was startled to see Bishop Wynstan at their head, but happily Wynstan did not notice him.

He was even more surprised to see, riding with them, a small grey-haired woman he recognized as Hildi, the midwife from Shiring.

He stared at the group as they receded in a cloud of dust, heading for Dreng's Ferry. Why would Wynstan be escorting a midwife?

Could it be a coincidence that Ragna was rumoured to be pregnant? Perhaps, but Edgar was going to assume the opposite.

If they were taking the midwife to attend on Ragna, they could lead Edgar to her.

He took his leave of the trappers, climbed onto Buttress, and trotted back the way he had come.

He did not want to catch up with Wynstan on the road: that could lead to trouble. But they had to be heading for Dreng's Ferry. They would either stay the night there or ride on, perhaps to Combe. Either way Edgar could continue to follow them, at a discreet distance, to their destination.

Since Ragna had vanished he had had many surges of exhilarating hope followed by heartbreaking disappointments. He told himself that this could be another such one. But the clues were promising, and he could not help feeling a thrill of optimism that banished, at least for now, his depression.

He saw no one else on the road before he arrived back in Dreng's Ferry at midday. He knew immediately that Wynstan and the group had not stopped here: it was a small place and he would have seen some of them outside the alehouse, men drinking and horses grazing.

He went into the monks' house and found Aldred, who said: 'Are you back already? Did you forget something?'

'Did you speak to the bishop?' Edgar asked without preamble.

Aldred looked puzzled. 'What bishop?'

'Didn't Wynstan come through here?'

'Not unless he walked on tiptoe.'

Edgar was bewildered. 'That's strange. He passed me on the road, with his entourage. They must have been on their way here – there's nowhere else.'

Aldred frowned. 'The same thing happened to me, back in February,' he said thoughtfully. 'I was returning from Shiring, and Wigelm passed me on the road, going in the opposite direction. I thought he must have been here, and I worried about what mischief he might have been making. But when I arrived Brother Godleof told me they had not seen any sign of him.'

'Their destination must be somewhere between here and Stumpy's.'

'But there's nothing between here and Stumpy's.'

Edgar snapped his fingers. 'Wilwulf had a hunting lodge deep in the forest on the south side of the Shiring road.'

'That burned down. Wigelm built a new lodge in the Vale of Outhen, where the hunting is better.'

'They said it had burned down,' said Edgar. 'That might not have been true.'

'It's what everyone believed.'

'I'm going to check.'

'I'll go with you,' said Aldred. 'But shouldn't we get Sheriff Den to come with us, and bring some men?'

'I'm not prepared to wait,' Edgar said firmly. 'It would take two days to get to Shiring then a day and a half to return to Stumpy's. I can't wait four days. Ragna might be moved in that time. If she's at the old hunting lodge, I'm going to see her today.'

'You're right,' said Aldred. 'I'll saddle a horse.'

He also put on a silver cross on a leather thong. Edgar approved: Wynstan's men might hesitate to attack a monk wearing a cross. On the other hand, they might not.

A few minutes later the two of them were on the road.

Neither had ever been to the hunting lodge. Fire or no fire, it had not been used for years. Wilwulf had gone away to war and come back severely wounded, and after his death Wigelm had hunted elsewhere.

But they knew roughly where it must be. Between Dreng's Ferry and Stumpy's there had to be a track leading away from the road into the forest to the south. All Edgar and Aldred had to do was find it. If the lodge truly had burned and was no longer in use, then the task would be difficult: the entrance to the side track would be overgrown and hard to see. But if the story of the fire was a lie intended to divert suspicion, and people were still using the track to get to the lodge, to bring supplies – and a midwife – then there would be a roadside gap visible where the undergrowth had been trodden down and saplings had been damaged or destroyed.

Edgar and Aldred made several fruitless excursions, along tracks leading to isolated cottages, homesteads, and one small village that neither man had ever heard of. They were almost at Stumpy's when Edgar noticed a place where several horses had passed today: there were freshly snapped twigs on the bushes and recent droppings on the path. His heart beat faster and he said: 'I think this could be it.'

They turned in. The path got narrower but the evidence of recent passage became stronger. Now Edgar began to feel fear as well as hope. He might find Ragna, but if he did, he would also come across Wynstan, and what would Wynstan do? Beside Edgar, Aldred looked unafraid, but he probably thought God would protect him.

The woods were full of lush new growth. Every minute or two Edgar glimpsed a deer moving silently through the dappled shadows, evidence that there had been no hunting here recently. Progress slowed. Where low branches overhung the path they had to dismount. They walked a mile, then another.

Then Edgar heard the voices of children.

They tied up their horses and walked forward slowly, trying to make no noise. They approached the edge of a clearing and stopped in the shadow of a massive oak.

Edgar recognized the children right away: the four-year-old boy was Osbert, the two-year-old twins were Hubert and Colinan, and the little girls were Cat's daughters, Mattie, who was four, and Edie, two. Although pale, they looked well enough otherwise, running around after a ball.

However, Cat's appearance shocked him. Her black hair was lank and lifeless and her skin was blemished. There was a boil on the side of her tip-tilted nose. Worst of all, the spark of mischief had gone from her eyes and her expression was lethargic. She stood with her shoulders slumped, watching the children without apparent interest.

Edgar looked past Cat to the timber house behind her. Its windows had been boarded over so that the shutters could not be opened. The door was secured from the outside by a heavy bar, and a guard sat nearby on a bench, looking the other way and picking his nose. Edgar recognized a Shiring boy called Elfgar. His right arm was covered with a dirty bandage.

There were several more buildings and a field where horses grazed, presumably the mounts of Wynstan and his men.

Aldred whispered: 'This is the secret prison. We should leave now, before we're seen. We can go to Shiring and fetch Den.'

Edgar knew Aldred was right, but now that he was this close he could not tear himself away. 'I have to see Ragna,' he said.

'You don't need to. She must be here. It's dangerous to linger.'

'You go and fetch Den. I don't care if they imprison me for a few days.'

'Don't be such a fool!'

Their murmured conversation was interrupted by a loud voice from behind: 'Who the hell are you?'

Both turned. The speaker was a man-at-arms called Fulcric. He had a spear in his hand and a long dagger in a wooden sheath hanging from his belt. Scars on his hands and face showed he had survived many fights. Edgar realized at once that physical resistance would be useless.

Aldred adopted an authoritative tone. 'I am Prior Aldred and I'm here to speak to the Lady Ragna,' he said.

'You'll speak to Bishop Wynstan before you see anyone else,' said Fulcric.

'Very well,' said Aldred, as if he had a choice.

'Over there.' Fulcric nodded towards a house on the far side of the clearing.

Edgar turned and stepped out of the trees. 'Hello, Cat,' he said quietly. 'How are you?'

Cat gave a little cry of shock. 'Edgar!' She looked around with a frightened expression. 'This is dangerous for you.'

'Never mind,' he said. 'Is Ragna here?'

'Yes.' Cat hesitated. 'She's pregnant.'

So it was true. 'I heard a rumour.'

He was about to ask when the baby was due when Elfgar awoke from his reverie, jumped to his feet, and said: 'Hey, you!'

Fulcric said: 'You're half asleep, boy. They were hiding in the trees.'

Edgar said: 'You know me, Elfgar. I mean no harm. What happened to your arm?'

'I was in the king's army and I got a spear wound from a Viking,' Elfgar said proudly. 'It's healing, but I can't fight until it's better, so they sent me home.'

Fulcric said: 'Keep moving, you two.'

They crossed the clearing but, before they came to the house, the door opened and Wynstan came out. When he saw Edgar and Aldred he registered surprise but – strangely – not dismay. 'So, you found the place!' he said cheerfully.

Aldred said: 'I am here to see the Lady Ragna.'

'I haven't seen her myself yet,' said Wynstan. 'I've been . . . busy.' He glanced back through the open door of the house he had left, and Edgar thought he saw Agnes there.

That confirmed another rumour.

Edgar said: 'You have kidnapped her and imprisoned her here against her will. That's a crime, and you shall be called to account.'

'On the contrary,' said Wynstan mildly. 'The Lady Ragna wished to retire from the public eye and mourn her late husband in solitude for a year. I offered her the use of this isolated lodge so that she could be undisturbed. She accepted my offer gratefully.'

Edgar looked at him through narrowed eyes. Widows did sometimes withdraw for a period of mourning, but they went to nunneries, not hunting lodges. Was there any chance at all that this fairy tale might be believed? Everyone present knew it was a blatant lie, but others might not. Wynstan had escaped the charge of forgery with a similarly devious ruse. Edgar said: 'I insist you free the Lady Ragna immediately.'

'There's no question of freeing her,' Wynstan said, still pretending to be all sweet reason. 'She has expressed a wish to return to Shiring, and I have come to escort her there.'

Edgar stared, incredulous. 'You're taking her back to the compound?'

'Yes. Quite naturally, she wants to see King Ethelred.'

'The king is coming to Shiring?'

'Yes, so we're told. We're not sure when.'

'And you're taking Ragna to meet him?'

'Naturally.'

Edgar was confounded. What was Wynstan up to now? His tone of goodwill was of course completely false, but what did he intend in reality?

Edgar said: 'Will she tell me the same?'

'Go and ask her,' said Wynstan. 'Elfgar, let him in.'

Elfgar unbarred the door, and Edgar went inside. The door closed behind him.

The room was dark: the shutters were closed over the windows. It smelled bad, like the slave quarters in the ealdorman's compound, where the people were not allowed out at night. Flies circled around a covered pot in a corner. The rushes on the floor should have been changed months ago. Mice rustled underfoot. It was hot and airless.

As his eyesight adjusted to the gloom Edgar saw two women

sitting facing each other on a bench, holding hands. Evidently he had interrupted an intimate conversation. One of the women was Hildi; she got up and left immediately. The other had to be Ragna, but she was almost unrecognizable. He hair was dirty brown rather than red-gold, and her complexion was spotty. Her dress might once have been blue, but now it was a mottled grey-brown. Her shoes were in tatters.

Edgar held out his arms to embrace her, but she did not come to him.

He had lived this moment many times in his imagination: the happy smiles, the non-stop kisses, her body pressed hard against his, the murmured words of love and joy. The reality was nothing like his dream.

He took a step towards her, but she stood up and moved back.

He had to make allowances, he realized. Her spirit had been crushed. She was not herself. He must help her to act normally.

He found his voice and said gently: 'May I kiss you?'

She lowered her eyes.

Still speaking in a low, loving tone, he said: 'Why not?'

'I'm hideous.'

'I've seen you better dressed.' He smiled. 'But that doesn't matter. You're you. We're together. That's all I care about.'

She shook her head.

Edgar said: 'Say something.'

'I'm pregnant.'

'I can see that.' He studied her figure. The bulge was clearly visible, but not enormous. 'When is the baby due?'

'August.'

He had suspected this, but confirmation came like a blow. 'So it's not mine.'

She shook her head.

'Who, then?'

'Wigelm.' She lifted her head at last. 'His men held me down.' Defiance showed in her face. 'Many times.'

Edgar felt as if he had been knocked over. He could hardly breathe. No wonder she was in the depths of despair. It was a miracle she had not gone mad.

When he recovered his voice he did not know what to say. Eventually he managed: 'I love you.'

His words made no impression.

She seemed numb, stunned, like one barely conscious, a sleepwalker. What could he do? He wanted to comfort her, but nothing he said seemed to register. He would have touched her but, when he lifted his hands, she backed away. He might have overcome her resistance and embraced her regardless, but he sensed that would just remind her of what Wigelm had done. He was helpless.

She said: 'I want you to go.'

'I'll do anything you ask.'

'Then go.'

'I love you.'

'Please go.'

'I'm going.' He went to the door. 'We'll be together one day. I know it.'

She said nothing. He thought he saw the glint of tears in her eyes, but the room was dark and it might have been wishful thinking.

'Say goodbye to me, at least,' he said.

'Goodbye.'

He knocked at the door and it was opened immediately.

'*Au revoir*,' he said. 'I'll see you again soon.'

She turned her back, and Edgar walked out.

ÞÞÞ

RAGNA LEFT THE hunting lodge the next day with Cat and the children. They rode on the same cart that had brought them. They

688

departed early and arrived as darkness was falling. The two women were tired and the children were cranky, and they all went to sleep as soon as they got into the house.

Next morning Cat borrowed a big iron pot from the kitchen and they heated water on the fire. They washed the children from head to toe, then themselves. After putting on clean clothes, Ragna began to feel less like penned livestock and more like a human being.

Gilda the kitchen maid appeared with a loaf of bread, fresh butter, eggs and salt, and they all fell on the food as if starving.

Ragna needed to rebuild her household, and she decided to start with Gilda. 'Would you like to come and work for me?' she said as Gilda was leaving. 'And your daughter, Winthryth, too, perhaps?'

Gilda smiled. 'Yes, please, my lady.'

'I haven't any money to pay you now, but I will soon.' Before too long a courier would arrive from Normandy.

'That's all right, my lady.'

'I'll speak to the kitchen master later. Don't say anything to anyone for the moment.'

All Ragna's possessions seemed to be here. Her robes were on pegs around the walls, and looked as if they had been aired. Most of the chests appeared to be here too, with her brushes and combs, scented oils, belts and shoes, and even her jewellery. Only her money was missing.

She was going to see the kitchen master, a mere servant, but she needed to assert her authority right from the start. She put on a silk dress in a rich dark brown colour and tied a gold-coloured sash around her middle. She chose a tall pointed hat. She picked out a jewelled headband to secure the hat, and added a pendant and an arm ring.

She walked across the compound with her head held high.

Everyone was interested to see her and curious about how she looked. She met the eyes of each person she passed, determined not to appear cowed by her ill-treatment. People were at first unsure how to react, then they decided to play safe and bow to her. She spoke to several and they responded warmly. She guessed they might look back nostalgically to the times when Wilwulf and Ragna ruled the compound: it was unlikely that Wigelm had been equally congenial.

The kitchen master was called Bassa. She walked up to him and said: 'Good morning to you, Bassa.'

He looked startled. 'Good morning,' he said, then, after a brief hesitation, he added: 'My lady.'

'Gilda and Winthryth are coming to work at my house,' she said in a tone that did not invite discussion.

Bassa was uncertain, but just said: 'Very good, my lady.' People never got in trouble for saying that.

'They can begin tomorrow morning,' Ragna said in a softer voice. 'That will give you time to make other arrangements.'

'Thank you, my lady.'

Ragna left the kitchen, feeling better. She was behaving like a powerful noblewoman, and people were treating her as such.

As she returned to her house, Sheriff Den appeared, followed by two of his men. 'You need bodyguards,' he said.

It was true. After the death of Bern had left her unprotected, it had been easy for Wigelm to kidnap her quietly in the middle of the night. She wanted never to be so vulnerable again.

Den said: 'I'm lending you Cadwal and Dudoc until you're able to hire your own.'

'Thank you.' Ragna was struck by a thought. 'Where will I find bodyguards for hire, I wonder?'

'This autumn there will be a lot of soldiers returning from the Viking war. Most will go back to their farms and workshops, but some will be looking for employment, and they will have had the kind of experience a bodyguard needs.'

'Good point.'

'You may need to equip them with decent weapons. And I'd recommend heavyweight leather jerkins. They will keep the men warm in winter and give some protection too.'

'As soon as I get some money.'

It was another week before money arrived. It came with Prior Aldred, who had been looking after the cash brought every three months by Odo and Adelaide.

He also brought a folded sheet of parchment. It was a copy, made in his scriptorium, of Wilwulf's will. 'This may help you when you see King Ethelred,' he said.

'Do I need help? I'm going to accuse Wigelm of kidnap and rape. Both crimes were witnessed by my maid Cat.' She put her hand on her belly. 'And if further proof were needed, there's this.'

'And that would be sufficient, if we lived in a world that was ruled by laws.' Aldred sat on a stool, leaned forward, and spoke quietly. 'But the man matters more than the law, as you know.'

'Surely King Ethelred must be mortally offended by what Wigelm has done.'

'True. And he could turn his army on Shiring and arrest Wigelm and Wynstan. Goodness knows, they've done enough to deserve that. But the king has his hands full battling the Vikings, and he may feel this is the wrong time to fight English noblemen who are his allies.'

'Are you telling me that Wigelm is going to get away with it?'

'I'm saying that Ethelred will see this as a political problem, rather than a simple matter of crime and punishment.'

'Hell. So how might he solve the problem?'

'He may think the simplest answer is for you to marry Wigelm.'

Ragna stood up, furious. 'Never!' she cried. 'Surely he wouldn't force me to marry the man who raped me?'

'I don't think he would force you, no. And even if he were inclined that way, I suspect his new Norman queen would take your side. But you don't want to clash with the king if you can help it. You need him to think of you as a friend.'

Ragna struggled to accept all this. She recalled that she had once been quite shrewd about politics. She felt passionately angry and indignant, but that was not helping her to develop her strategy. She was lucky that Aldred was here to open her eyes. She said: 'What do you think I should do?'

'Before Ethelred gets the chance to suggest the marriage, you should ask him to make no decision about your future before the baby is born.'

It was a sensible idea, Ragna thought. The whole picture would be changed if the baby died. Or the mother. And both happened frequently.

Aldred must have been thinking that, but he said something different. 'Ethelred will like the idea because it will offend nobody.'

More importantly, Ragna thought, it would give her time to renew her friendship with Queen Emma and win her as an ally. There was nothing so valuable as a friend at court.

Aldred stood up. 'I'll leave you to think about that.'

'Thank you for taking care of my money.'

'Edgar travelled here with me. Will you see him?'

Ragna hesitated. She thought with regret of their last encounter. She had been too paralysed with self-disgust to talk sensibly. He must have been terribly upset by her pregnancy, and her mood must have made that even worse. 'Of course I'll see him,' she said.

When he came in she noticed how well dressed he was, in a fine wool tunic and leather shoes. He wore no jewellery, but his belt had a decorated silver buckle and strap end. He was prospering.

And his face bore an expression of eager optimism that she knew well.

She stood up and said: 'I'm glad to see you.'

He opened his arms and she stepped into his embrace.

He was careful of her belly, but he hugged her shoulders hard. It almost hurt, but she did not care, she was so pleased to be touching him. They stayed like that for a long moment.

When they broke apart he was smiling like the boy who won the race. She smiled back. 'How are you?' she said.

'I'm all right, now that you're free.'

'Have you finished your bridge?'

'Not yet. What about you, what's your plan?'

'I have to stay here until the king comes.'

'Will you come to Dreng's Ferry afterwards? Our plan could still work. You could take refuge in the nunnery for as long as necessary. And we could talk at leisure about . . . our future.'

'I'd like that. But I can't make any plans until I see the king. He is in charge of noble widows. I don't know what he might do.'

Edgar nodded. 'I'll leave you for now. I have to buy iron. But will you invite me to dinner?'

'Of course.'

'I'm happy to sit around the table with the servants and children, you know that.'

'I know.'

'I have one more question.' He took her hands.

'Go ahead,' she said.

'Do you love me?'

'With all my heart.'

'Then I'm a happy man.'

He kissed her lips. She let her mouth linger on his for a long moment. Then he left.

37

KING ETHELRED HELD COURT in the marketplace outside
Shiring Cathedral. Every citizen was there, plus hundreds from the
surrounding villages, and most of the noblemen and senior clergy
in the region. Ragna's bodyguards made a path through the crowd
so that she could get to the front, where Wynstan and Wigelm and
all the other magnates stood, waiting for the king. She knew most
of the thanes and made a point of speaking to each. She wanted
everyone to know she was back.

In front of the crowd stood two cushioned four-legged stools
under a temporary canopy put up to shade the royals from the August
sun. To one side was a table with writing materials, and two priests
sitting ready to pen documents at the king's command. They also
had a stilyard balance to weigh large sums of money if the king
imposed fines.

The townspeople were excited. Kings travelled from town to town
all the time, but even so an ordinary English person seldom got to
see one in the flesh. Everyone was keen to see whether he seemed
in good health, and what his new queen was wearing.

A king was a remote personage. In theory he was all-powerful but,
in practice, edicts issued from a faraway royal court might not be
enforced. The decisions of local overlords often had more effect on
everyday life. But that changed when the king came to town. It was
hard for tyrants such as Wynstan and Wigelm to defy a royal edict
that had been pronounced in front of thousands of local people.

Victims of injustice hoped for restitution when the king came to visit.

At last Ethelred appeared with Queen Emma. The townspeople knelt and the noblemen bowed. Everyone made way for the royal couple to walk to their seats.

Emma at eighteen was young and pretty, much the same as when Ragna last saw her six years ago, except that now she was pregnant. Ragna smiled, and Emma recognized her immediately. To Ragna's delight the queen came straight to her and kissed her. Speaking Norman French, she said: 'How wonderful to see a familiar face!'

Ragna was thrilled to be acknowledged as the queen's friend in front of the men who had treated her so cruelly. She replied in the same language. 'Congratulations on your marriage. I'm so happy that you're England's queen.'

'We're going to be such friends.'

'I hope so – if they don't imprison me again.'

'They won't – not if I can help it.' Emma turned away and moved to her seat. She spoke a word of explanation to Ethelred, who nodded and smiled at Ragna.

That was a good start. Ragna was heartened by Emma's friendliness, but recalled with trepidation the words *not if I can help it*. Clearly Emma was not sure she could control events. And she was young, perhaps too young to have learned the tricks Ragna knew.

Ethelred spoke in a loud voice, though even so he probably could not be heard by those on the outskirts of the crowd. 'Our first and most important task is to choose a new ealdorman for Shiring.'

Aldred boldly interrupted. 'My lord king, Ealdorman Wilwulf made a will.'

Bishop Wynstan called out: 'Never ratified.'

Aldred said: 'Wilwulf intended to show his will to you, my lord king, and to ask you to approve it – but before he could do so he was murdered in his bed right here in Shiring.'

Wynstan said scornfully: 'Where is this will, then?'

'It was in the Lady Ragna's treasury, which was stolen minutes after Wilwulf died.'

'A non-existent will, it seems.'

The crowd enjoyed this, a ding-dong between two men of God, right at the start of the court. But then Ragna spoke up. 'On the contrary,' she said. 'Several copies were made. Here is one, my lord king.' She took the folded parchment from the bosom of her dress and handed it to Ethelred.

He took it, but did not unroll it.

Wynstan said: 'It doesn't matter if a hundred copies were made – the will is invalid.'

Ragna said: 'As you can see from the document, my lord king, it was my husband's wish that you should make our eldest son Osbert ealdorman—'

'A child four years of age!' Wynstan jeered.

'– with me to rule as his representative until he comes of age.'

Ethelred said: 'Enough!' He paused, and they all remained silent for a moment. Having asserted his power he went on: 'In times such as these, the ealdorman must have the ability to muster an army and lead men into battle.'

The assembled noblemen nodded and murmured their agreement. Ragna realized that, much as they liked her, they did not believe in her as a military leader. She was not really surprised.

Wynstan said: 'My brother Wigelm has recently proved his ability in this regard, by assembling an army to fight alongside you, my lord king, at Exeter.'

'He has,' said Ethelred.

The battle of Exeter had been lost, and the Vikings had looted the city and then gone home; but Ragna decided not to say that. She saw that she was going to lose this argument. Immediately after a Viking victory the king was not going to appoint a woman ealdorman to lead the men of Shiring. But that had always been a faint hope.

She had lost the first round. But she might yet gain from this decision, she told herself; perhaps Ethelred might now wish to balance the concession to Wigelm with one to her.

She had regained her ability to strategize, she realized. The torpor of prison was wearing off rapidly. She felt enlivened.

Aldred said: 'My lord king, Wigelm and Wynstan have imprisoned the Lady Ragna for almost a year, taken over her lands in the Vale of Outhen and stolen her income, and refused to return her dowry to which she is entitled. I now ask you to protect this noble widow from her predatory in-laws.'

Ragna realized that Aldred was coming as close as he could to accusing Ethelred of failing in his duty to care for widows.

Ethelred looked at Wigelm. There was an undertone of anger in his voice as he said: 'Is this true?'

But it was Wynstan who answered. 'The Lady Ragna sought solitude in which to mourn. We merely provided her with protection.'

'Nonsense!' said Ragna indignantly. 'My door was barred on the outside! I was a prisoner.'

Wynstan said smoothly: 'The door was barred so that the children could not wander out and get lost in the forest.'

It was a feeble excuse, but would Ethelred accept it?

The king did not hesitate. 'Locking a woman in is not protection.'

He was not so easily fooled, Ragna saw.

Ethelred went on: 'Before I confirm Wigelm as ealdorman, I will require both Wigelm and Wynstan to swear an oath not to imprison the Lady Ragna.'

Ragna allowed herself a moment of sheer relief. She was free – for now, at least: oaths could be broken, of course.

Ethelred went on: 'Now, what's this about Outhen? I thought she had received that land as part of her marriage contract.'

'True,' said Wynstan. 'But my brother Wilwulf had no right to give it to her.'

Ragna said indignantly: 'You negotiated the marriage contract with my father! How can you repudiate it now?'

Wynstan said smoothly: 'It has belonged to my family since time immemorial.'

'No, it hasn't,' said the king.

Everyone stared at him. This was a surprise intervention.

Ethelred went on: 'My father gave it to your grandfather.'

Wynstan said: 'There may be legends—'

'No legends,' said the king. 'It was the first deed I witnessed.'

That was an unexpected piece of luck for Ragna.

Ethelred went on: 'I was nine years old when I witnessed it. That's not time immemorial, I'm only thirty-six now.' The noblemen laughed.

Wynstan looked sick – clearly he had not known the history of the land.

Ethelred said firmly: 'The Lady Ragna is to have the Vale of Outhen and all the income from it.'

Ragna said gratefully: 'Thank you. And my dowry?'

Ethelred said: 'A widow is entitled to the return of her dowry. How much was it?'

'Twenty pounds of silver.'

'Wigelm shall pay Ragna twenty pounds.'

Wigelm looked furious and said nothing.

Ethelred said: 'Do it now, Wigelm. Go and fetch twenty pounds.'

Wigelm said: 'I don't think I have that much.'

'Then you're not a very good ealdorman. Perhaps I should reconsider.'

'I'll go and look.' Wigelm stormed off.

'Now,' Ethelred said to Ragna, 'what is to be done about you and the child you're carrying?'

'I have a request, my lord king. Please don't make that decision today.' This was the approach Aldred had counselled, and Ragna had decided it was wise. But she added a further demand. 'I would like to go to the convent on Leper Island, and give birth there, cared for by Mother Agatha and the nuns. I will leave tomorrow morning, if I gain your permission. Please, wait until the baby is born before you decide my future.' She held her breath.

Aldred spoke up again. 'If I may say so, my lord king, any plan you make today may be overtaken by the unpredictable events of childbirth. Heaven forbid, but the child may not live. If it lives, the picture will change depending on whether it is a boy or a girl. Worst of all, the mother may not survive the ordeal. All these things are in God's hands. Would it not make sense to wait and see?'

Ethelred did not need persuading. In fact, he looked relieved not to have to make a decision. 'So be it,' he said. 'Let us reconsider the matter of the widow Lady Ragna after her child is born. Sheriff Den is responsible for her safety as she travels to Dreng's Ferry.'

Ragna had got everything she had reasonably hoped for. She could leave Shiring in the morning with enough money to make her independent. She would find blessed sanctuary with the nuns. She would put things right with Edgar. They would make a plan.

It had not escaped her attention that the king had not responded to Aldred's accusation of kidnapping. And no one had mentioned rape. But she had expected that. Ethelred could not make Wigelm ealdorman and then convict him of rape. So the charge had been conveniently forgotten. However, the king's other decisions came as such a relief to her that she was willing to accept the whole package gratefully.

Wigelm came back, followed by Cnebba carrying a small chest. He set it in front of Ethelred.

'Open it,' said the king.

It contained several leather bags of coins.

Ethelred pointed to the scale on the side table. 'Weigh the coins.'

Ragna felt a sudden sharp jab in her abdomen. She froze. There was something familiar about the pain. She had felt it before, and she knew what it meant.

The baby was coming.

þþþ

RAGNA CALLED THE baby Alain. She wanted a French name, for an English name would have reminded her of the English father. And it was similar to the word for 'handsome' in the Celtic language of the Breton people.

Alain was handsome. Every baby was lovely to its mother, but this was Ragna's fourth child and she thought she was capable of being somewhat objective. Alain was a healthy pink colour, with a head of dark hair and large blue eyes that looked out with a baffled expression, as if puzzled that the world should be such a strange place.

He cried hard when hungry, drank his fill rapidly from Ragna's breasts, and fell asleep immediately afterwards, as if following a timetable that he considered perfectly sensible. Remembering how Osbert, her first, had seemed so unpredictable and incomprehensible, she wondered whether the children really were so dissimilar. Perhaps it was she who was different, more relaxed and confident now.

The birth had not been easy, but it had been a little less painful and exhausting than previously, for which she was grateful. Alain's only mistake so far had been to arrive early. Ragna had not had the chance to go to Dreng's Ferry for her confinement. However, she now planned to go there to recuperate, and Den had told her that King Ethelred had agreed to that.

Cat was as pleased as if she had given birth herself. The children stared at Alain, with curiosity and a touch of resentment, as if unsure whether there was space in the family for another one.

A less welcome admirer was Gytha, mother to Wynstan and

Wigelm. She came to Ragna's house and cooed over the baby, and Ragna did not feel she could forbid her to pick him up: she was his grandmother, and the fact that he was the result of a rape did not change that.

All the same Ragna was uncomfortable when she saw Alain in Gytha's arms. She felt uneasily that Gytha was assuming some kind of ownership. 'The newest member of our family,' Gytha said, 'and so handsome!'

'It's time for his feed,' Ragna said, and took him back. Ragna put the baby to her breast and he began to suck enthusiastically. She had thought Gytha might leave, but instead she sat down and watched, as if to make sure Ragna was doing it right. When he paused, he puked a little of the milk and – to Ragna's surprise – Gytha leaned over and wiped his chin with the sleeve of her costly wool gown. It was a gesture of genuine affection.

Ragna still did not trust Gytha, all the same.

A few minutes later one of Ragna's bodyguards put his head around the door and said: 'Will you see Ealdorman Wigelm?'

He was the last person on earth Ragna wanted to see. However, she thought she had better find out what he was up to. She said: 'He may come in, but alone – no sidekicks. And you stay with me while he's here.'

Gytha heard all this and her face hardened.

Wigelm entered looking offended. 'You see, Mother?' he said to Gytha. 'I have to be questioned by a guard before I can see my own son!' He stared at Ragna's uncovered breast.

She said: 'Consider how much of a fool I would have to be to trust you.' She took Alain off her nipple, but he had not had enough and he cried, so she had to put him back, and suffer Wigelm's gawking.

He said: 'I'm the ealdorman!'

'You're the rapist.'

Gytha made a disapproving noise, as if Ragna had said something discourteous. It wasn't half as discourteous as what your son did to me, Ragna thought. It was odd, she reflected, that someone who had failed to condemn the rape would disapprove audibly of the mention of it.

Wigelm seemed about to continue, then changed his mind and choked back his retort. He took a deep breath. 'I didn't come here for an argument.'

'So why did you come?'

He looked uneasy. He sat down, then stood up again. 'To talk about the future,' he said vaguely.

What was bugging him? Ragna guessed that he was simply unable to get to grips with politics at the royal level. He understood bullying and coercion, but the king's need to balance conflicting pressures was beyond Wigelm's intellect. It was best to speak simply to him. She said: 'My future has nothing to do with you.'

Wigelm scratched his head, loosened his belt then tightened it, rubbed his chin, and at last said: 'I want to marry you.'

Ragna felt cold dread in her heart. 'Never,' she said. 'Please don't even mention it.'

'But I love you.'

That was so obviously untrue that she almost laughed. 'You don't even know what that means.'

'Everything will be different, I swear.'

'So . . .' She looked at Gytha then back at Wigelm. 'So you won't have your men-at-arms hold me down while you fuck me?'

Gytha made the disapproving noise again.

'Of course I won't,' Wigelm said in a tone of indignation, as if he would never dream of such a thing.

'That's the kind of promise a woman longs to hear.'

Gytha said: 'Don't you want to be part of our family?'

Ragna stared at her in astonishment. 'No!'

'Why not?'

'How can you even ask me that question?'

Wigelm said: 'Why do you have to be so sarcastic?'

Ragna took a breath. 'Because I don't love you, you don't love me, and talk of us getting married is so ludicrous that I can't even pretend to take you seriously.'

Wigelm frowned, figuring out what she meant: he was not quick to grasp long sentences, she had noticed. Eventually he said: 'So that's your answer.'

'My answer is no.'

Gytha stood up. 'We tried,' she said.

Then she and Wigelm left.

Ragna frowned. That was an unexpected exit line.

Alain was asleep at Ragna's breast. She put him in his cradle and refastened the front of her dress. The material was milk-stained, but she did not worry: at this point it suited her not to be too alluring.

She puzzled over the words *We tried*. Why had Gytha said that? It sounded like a veiled threat, as if she was saying *Don't blame us for what will happen next*. But what could happen next?

She did not know, and it troubled her.

ÞÞÞ

WYNSTAN AND GYTHA went to see King Ethelred, who was living in the great hall. Wynstan did not feel his usual self-confidence. The king was not predictable. Wynstan could normally foresee his neighbours' responses to problems: it was not difficult to figure out what they were going to do in order to get what they wanted. But the king's challenges were much more complex.

He touched his pectoral cross in the hope of divine assistance.

When they entered the great hall, Ethelred was deep in conversation with one of his clerks. Queen Emma was not present. Ethelred held up a hand to tell Wynstan and Gytha to wait. They stood a few paces away while the king finished his conversation. Then the clerk left and Ethelred beckoned.

Wynstan began: 'The child of my brother Wigelm and the Lady Ragna is a healthy boy who seems likely to live, my lord king.'

'Good!' said Ethelred.

'It is indeed good news, though it threatens to destabilize the ealdormanry of Shiring.'

'How so?'

'First, you have given Ragna permission to go to the nunnery at Dreng's Ferry. There, of course, she will be away from the influence of the ealdorman. Second, she has the ealdorman's only child. Third, even if the baby should die, Ragna also has Wilwulf's three young sons.'

'I see what you're getting at,' said the king. 'You think she could easily become the figurehead of a rebellion against Wigelm. People might say that her children were the true heirs.'

Wynstan was pleased that the king saw the point so quickly. 'Yes, my lord king.'

'And do you propose a course of action?'

'There is only one. Ragna must marry Wigelm. Then Wigelm has no rivals.'

'Of course, that would resolve the issue,' said Ethelred. 'But I'm not going to do it.'

Wynstan burst out: 'Why on earth not?'

'First, because she has set her face against it. She might well refuse to take the vows.'

'You may leave it to me to deal with that,' Wynstan said. He knew how to make people do what they did not want to do.

Ethelred looked disapproving, but did not comment. Instead he said: 'Second, because I have promised my wife that I will not force the marriage.'

Wynstan gave a man-to-man chuckle. 'My lord king, a promise to a woman . . .'

'You don't know much about marriage, do you, bishop?'

Wynstan bowed his head. 'Of course not, my lord king.'

'I'm not willing to break my promise to my wife.'

'I understand.'

'Go away and think of a different solution.' Ethelred turned away dismissively.

Wynstan and Gytha bowed and left the house.

As soon as they were out of earshot Wynstan said: 'So one troublemaking Norman bitch supports the other!'

Gytha said nothing. Wynstan glanced at his mother. She was deep in thought.

They went to Gytha's house, and she poured a cup of wine for him.

He took a long draught and said. 'I don't know what to do now.'

'I have a suggestion,' said Gytha.

ÞÞÞ

WYNSTAN CAME TO Ragna's house and said: 'We need to have a serious talk.'

She looked at him with suspicion. He wanted something, of course. 'Don't ask me to marry your brother,' she said.

'I don't think you understand your situation.'

He was his usual arrogant self, except that he touched his pectoral cross. She thought that was a sign of a hidden lack of confidence, which was unusual in Wynstan. She said: 'Enlighten me.'

'You can leave here any time you like.'

'The king said so.'

'And you can take Wilwulf's children.'

It took a moment for her to see the implication, but when she did she was horrified. 'I will take *all* my children!' she said. 'Including Alain.'

'You're not being offered that option.' Wynstan touched the cross

705

again. 'You can leave Shiring, but you can't take the ealdorman's only son with you.'

'He's my baby!'

'He is, and naturally you want to raise him yourself. That's why you have to marry Wigelm.'

'Never.'

'Then you must leave your baby here. There is no third choice.'

A cold weight settled in the pit of Ragna's stomach. Involuntarily, she looked over at the cradle, as if to make sure Alain was still there. He was sleeping soundly.

Wynstan put on a treacly voice. 'He's a beautiful baby. Even I can see that.'

There was something so malign in the insincere compliment that Ragna felt nauseated.

'I have to raise him,' Ragna said. 'I'm his mother.'

'There's no shortage of mothers. Gytha, my own mother, is longing to take charge of her first grandchild.'

That infuriated Ragna. 'So that she can raise him the way she raised you and Wigelm?' she said. 'To be cruel and selfish and violent!'

To her surprise, Wynstan stood up. 'Take your time,' he said. 'Think about it. Let us know your decision in due course.' He went out.

Ragna knew she had to resist immediately and fiercely. 'Cat,' she said. 'Please go and ask if Queen Emma can see me as soon as possible.'

Cat left, and Ragna brooded. Had she been granted a false liberation? To be allowed to go only if she left her baby behind was no freedom at all. Surely Ethelred could not have meant that?

Ragna expected Cat to come back with a message saying when she could see Queen Emma, but when Cat returned she said breathlessly: 'My lady, the queen is here.'

Emma walked in.

Ragna stood up and bowed, then Emma kissed her.

'I've just seen Bishop Wynstan,' Ragna said. 'He says that if I don't marry Wigelm they will take my baby from me.'

'Yes,' said Emma. 'Gytha explained that to me.'

Ragna frowned. Gytha must have gone to see Emma at the same time as Wynstan spoke to Ragna. This was planned and co-ordinated. Ragna said: 'Does the king know?'

'Yes,' Emma said again.

Emma's face frightened Ragna. She looked worried, but not horrified or even shocked. What her face showed was pity. That was scary.

Ragna felt that she was losing control of her life again. 'But the king freed me. What does that mean?'

'It means that you cannot be imprisoned, and the king will not force you to marry a man you loathe; but also you cannot take away the ealdorman's son. His only son, I believe.'

'But then I'm not free after all!'

'You face a hard choice. I didn't foresee this.' The queen went to the door. 'I'm very sorry.' She left.

Ragna felt as if she was in a nightmare. For a moment she considered taking the first option, abandoning her child to be raised by Gytha. Anything to avoid marriage to the loathsome Wigelm. And after all Alain was the product of a rape. But as soon as she looked at him, lying in his cot sleeping peacefully, she knew she could not do it, not if they made her marry five Wigelms.

Edgar walked in. She recognized him through her tears. She stood up, and he enfolded her in his arms. 'Is it true?' he said to Ragna. 'Everyone says you have to marry Wigelm or give up Alain!'

'It's true,' Ragna said. Her tears soaked into the wool of his tunic.

'What are you going to do?' said Edgar.

Ragna did not answer.

'What are you going to do?' he repeated.

'I'm going to leave my baby,' she said.

ÞÞÞ

'NO, NO, THIS won't do!' Wynstan said angrily.

'It's happening,' said Wigelm. 'Edgar is helping her pack all her possessions. She's going to leave the baby behind.'

'She will still have Wilwulf's three young sons. People will say they are the genuine heirs. We're hardly better off.'

Wigelm said: 'We have to kill her. It's the only way to be rid of her.'

They were at their mother's house, and now she interrupted them. 'You can't kill Ragna,' Gytha said. 'Not right under the nose of the king. He couldn't let you get away with it.'

'We could put the blame on someone else.'

Gytha shook her head. 'Nobody really believed that last time. They won't even pretend to believe a second time.'

Wigelm said: 'We'll do it when the king's gone.'

Wynstan said: 'Idiot, Ragna will be safely ensconced in the nunnery on Leper Island by then.'

'Well, what are we going to do?'

Gytha said: 'We're all going to calm down.'

'What good is that?' said Wigelm.

'You'll see. Just wait.'

ÞÞÞ

THAT NIGHT EDGAR and Ragna slept together in her house. They lay on the rushes, in each other's arms, but they did not make love: they were much too distressed. Edgar took consolation from holding Ragna. She pressed her body to his in a way that seemed loving but also desperate.

She fed the baby twice in the night. Edgar dozed but he

suspected that Ragna did not sleep at all. They got up as soon as it was light.

Edgar went into the town centre and rented two carts for the journey. He had them brought into the compound and stationed outside Ragna's house. While the children were given breakfast, he loaded most of the baggage on one cart. He put all the cushions and blankets on the other, for the women and children to sit on. He saddled Buttress and put Astrid on a leading rein.

He was getting what he had longed for over many years, but he could not rejoice. He thought Ragna might eventually get over the loss of Alain, but he feared it could take a long time.

They all had their travelling clothes and shoes on. Gilda and Winthryth were coming with them, as well as Cat and the bodyguards. They all walked out of the house, Ragna carrying Alain.

Gytha was waiting to take him.

The servants and children climbed onto the cart.

Everyone looked at Ragna.

She walked up to Gytha, and Edgar walked by her side. Ragna hesitated. She looked at Edgar, then at Gytha, then at the baby in her arms. Tears were streaming down her face. She turned away from Gytha, then turned back. Gytha reached for Alain, but Ragna did not let her take him. She stood between the two of them for a long moment.

Then she said to Gytha: 'I can't do it.'

She turned to Edgar and said: 'I'm sorry.'

Then, holding Alain tightly to her chest, she walked back into her house.

ÞÞÞ

THE WEDDING WAS huge. People came from all over southern England. A major dynastic conflict had been settled, and everyone wanted to make friends with the winning side.

Wynstan looked around the great hall with a feeling of profound satisfaction. The trestle table was loaded with the products of a warm summer and a fine harvest: great joints of meat, loaves of new bread, pyramids of nuts and fruit, and jugs of ale and wine.

People were falling over one another to show deference to Ealdorman Wigelm and his family. Wigelm was seated next to Queen Emma, and looked smug. As a ruler he would be uninspired but brutally firm, and with Wynstan's guidance he would make the right decisions.

And now he was married to Ragna. Wigelm had never really liked her, Wynstan felt sure, but he desired her in the way a man sometimes craved a woman just because she rejected him. They were going to be miserable together.

Ragna, the only threat to Wynstan's dominance, had been crushed. She sat at the top table next to the king, with her baby in her arms, looking as if she would like to commit suicide.

The king seemed satisfied with his visit to Shiring. Looking at it from the royal point of view, Wynstan guessed that Ethelred was glad to have appointed the new ealdorman and disposed of the old one's widow, righted the wrong of Ragna's imprisonment but prevented her from running off with the ealdorman's baby, and all without bloodshed.

There was little sign of the Ragna faction. Sheriff Den was here, looking as if he had detected a bad smell, but Aldred had gone back to his little priory, and Edgar had vanished. He might have gone back to manage Ragna's quarry at Outhenham, but would he have wanted to, now that the love of his life had married someone else? Wynstan did not know and really did not care.

There was even a good piece of medical news. The sore on Wynstan's penis had gone. He had been frightened, especially when the whores said it could lead to leprosy, but that had evidently been a false alarm, and he was back to normal.

My brother is the ealdorman and I'm the bishop, Wynstan thought proudly. And neither of us is yet forty years old.

We've only just begun.

ÞÞÞ

EDGAR AND ALDRED stood at the waterside and looked back at the hamlet. The Michaelmas Fair was on. Hundreds of people were crossing the bridge, shopping at the market, and queueing to see the bones of the saint. They were talking and laughing, happy to spend what little money they had.

'The place is thriving,' Edgar said.

'I'm very pleased,' said Aldred, but there were tears on his face.

Edgar was both embarrassed and moved. He had known for years that Aldred was in love with him, though it had never been said.

Edgar looked the other way. His raft was tied up at the river bank downstream of the bridge. Buttress, his pony, stood on it. Also on the raft were his Viking axe, all his tools, and a chest containing a few precious possessions, including the book Ragna had given him. Missing was Brindle, his dog, who had died of old age.

That had been the last straw. He had been contemplating leaving Dreng's Ferry, and the death of Brindle had finally made up his mind.

Aldred wiped his eyes on his sleeve and said: 'Must you go?'

'Yes.'

'But Normandy is so far.'

Edgar planned to pole his raft downriver to Combe and there get a ship to Cherbourg. He would see Count Hubert and tell him the news of Ragna's marriage to Wigelm. In return he would ask the count to direct him to a large building site. He had heard that a good craftsman could easily get work in Normandy.

He said: 'I want to be as far away as possible from Wigelm and Wynstan and Shiring – and Ragna.'

Edgar had not seen Ragna since the wedding. He had tried, but

711

had been turned away by servants. In any case he did not know what he would have said to her. She had been given a hard choice and she had put her child first, something most women would have done. Edgar was heartbroken, but he could not blame her.

Aldred said: 'Ragna is not the only person who loves you.'

'I'm fond of you,' said Edgar. 'But, as you know, not that way.'

'Which is all that saves me from sin.'

'I know.'

Aldred took Edgar's hand and kissed it.

Edgar said: 'Dreng should sell the ferry boat. Ragna might buy it for Outhenham. They have no boat there.'

'I'll suggest that.'

Edgar had said his farewells to his family and the villagers. There was nothing more for him to do here.

He untied the raft, stepped aboard, and pushed away from the bank.

Gathering speed, he passed the family farm. At his suggestion, Erman and Eadbald were building a water mill, copying one they had seen farther downstream. They were good enough craftsmen; their father had taught them well. They were prosperous, important men in the town. They waved to him as he passed, and he noticed they were both becoming rather stout. Edgar waved back. He was going to miss Wynswith and Beorn, his niece and nephew.

The vessel gathered speed. Normandy would be warmer and drier than England, he guessed, as it was to the south. He thought of the few French words he had picked up from listening to Ragna talk to Cat. He knew some Latin, too, from his lessons with Aldred. He would get by.

It would be a new life.

He took one last glance back. His bridge dominated the view. It had changed the hamlet dramatically. Most people no longer referred to the place by its old name of Dreng's Ferry.

Nowadays they called it King's Bridge.

PART FOUR

THE CITY

1005–1007 CE

38

THE NAVE OF CANTERBURY Cathedral was cold and dark on a
November afternoon. Candles lit the scene fitfully, throwing shadows
like restless ghosts. In the chancel, the holiest part of the church,
Archbishop Elfric was slowly dying. His pale hands clasped a silver
cross, holding it over his heart. His eyes were open but they moved
very little. His breathing was regular though shallow. He seemed to
like the chanting of the monks who surrounded him, for whenever
it stopped he frowned.

Bishop Wynstan knelt in prayer at the archbishop's feet for a long
time. He felt ill himself. He had a headache. He was sleeping badly.
He ached with tiredness like an old man, though he was only forty-
three. And he had an unsightly reddish lump over his collarbone
that he hid by fastening his cloak high on his throat.

Feeling as he did, he had not wished to travel across the width of
England in winter weather, but he had a compelling motive. He
wanted to be the next archbishop of Canterbury. That would make
him the senior clergyman in southern England. And a power struggle
could not be fought at a distance: he had to be here.

He judged that he had prayed long enough to impress the monks
with his piety and respect. He got to his feet and suddenly felt dizzy.
He put his arm out and managed to lay his hand on a stone pillar
to steady himself. He felt angry: he hated to show weakness. All his
adult life he had been the strong man, the one others feared. And
the last thing he wanted was for the Canterbury monks to think he

was in poor health. They would not want a sick archbishop.

After a minute his head cleared and he was able to turn and walk away with reverent slowness.

Canterbury Cathedral was the largest building Wynstan had ever seen. Made of stone, it was cross-shaped, with a long nave, side transepts, and a short chancel. The tower over the crossing was topped by a golden angel.

Shiring Cathedral would have fitted inside it three times.

Wynstan met his cousin Degbert, archdeacon of Shiring, in Canterbury's north transept. Together they went out into the cloisters. A cold rain lashed the green of the quadrangle. A group of monks sheltering under the roof fell respectfully silent as they approached. Wynstan pretended first not to notice them then to be startled out of his meditations.

He spoke in the tones of one devastated by grief. 'The soul of my old friend seems reluctant to leave the church he loved.'

There was a moment of silence, then a lanky young monk said: 'Elfric is a friend of yours?'

'But of course,' said Wynstan. 'Forgive me, brother, what's your name?'

'I'm Eappa, my lord bishop.'

'Brother Eappa, I got to know our beloved archbishop when he was the bishop of Ramsbury, which is not far from my cathedral at Shiring. When I was a young man he took me under his wing, so to speak. I was infinitely grateful for his wisdom and guidance.'

None of this was true. Wynstan despised Elfric and the feeling was probably mutual. But the monks believed Wynstan. He was often amazed at how easy it was to fool people, especially if you had some kind of status. Men who were so gullible deserved everything that was coming to them.

Eappa said: 'What sort of thing did he say to you?'

Wynstan made something up on the spur of the moment. 'He said that I should listen more and speak less, because you learn while you're listening but not when you're speaking.' Enough of that, he thought. 'Tell me, who do you think will be the next archbishop?'

Another monk spoke up. 'Alphage of Winchester,' he said.

The man was familiar. Wynstan looked more closely. He had seen that round face and brown beard before. 'We know each other, don't we, brother?' he said warily.

Degbert interrupted. 'Brother Wigferth visits Shiring regularly. Canterbury owns property in the West Country, and he comes to collect rents.'

'Yes, of course, Brother Wigferth, it's good to see you again.' Wynstan remembered that Wigferth was a friend of Prior Aldred's, and resolved to be cautious. 'Why do people assume that Alphage will succeed to the archbishopric?'

'Elfric is a monk, and so is Alphage,' Wigferth replied. 'And Winchester is our senior cathedral after Canterbury and York.'

'Very logical,' said Wynstan, 'although perhaps not decisive.'

Wigferth persisted. 'And Alphage ordered the building of the famous church organ at Winchester. They say you can hear it a mile away!'

Wigferth was clearly an admirer of Alphage's, Wynstan thought – or perhaps he was simply against Wynstan, being a friend of Aldred's.

Wynstan said: 'According to the Rule of St Benedict, the monks have the right to elect their abbot, don't they?'

'Yes, but Canterbury doesn't have an abbot,' Wigferth said. 'We're led by the archbishop.'

'Or, to put it another way, the archbishop is the abbot.' Wynstan knew that the monks' privileges were not clear. The king claimed the right to appoint the archbishop, and so did the Pope. As always, the rules did not matter as much as the men. There would be a struggle, and the strongest and smartest would win.

Wynstan went on: 'In any case, it will take a great man to live up to the example set by Elfric. From all I hear, he has ruled wisely and fairly.' He left the hint of a question at the end of his sentence.

Eappa took the bait. 'Elfric has strict ideas about bedding,' he said, and the others laughed.

'How so?'

'He thinks a monk should be denied the luxury of a mattress.'

'Ah.' Monks often slept on boards, sometimes without any kind of cushion. The bony Eappa must have found that uncomfortable. 'I've always believed that monks need their sleep, so that they can be fully alert when they perform their devotions,' said Wynstan, and the monks nodded eagerly.

A monk called Forthred, who had medical knowledge, disagreed. 'Men can sleep perfectly well on boards,' he said. 'Self-denial is our watchword.'

Wynstan said: 'You're right, brother, though there is a balance to be struck, is there not? Monks should not eat meat every day, of course, but beef once a week helps to build up their strength. Monks should not indulge themselves by having pets, but sometimes a cat is needed to keep down the mice.'

The monks murmured their approval.

Wynstan had done enough for one day to establish himself as a lenient leader. Any more and they might begin to suspect that he was merely currying favour – which was the truth. He turned back into the church.

'We need to do something about Wigferth,' he murmured to Degbert as soon as they were out of earshot. 'He might become the leader of an anti-Wynstan faction.'

'He has a wife and three children in Trench,' Degbert said. 'The peasants there don't know he's a monk, they think he's a regular priest. If we revealed his secret here in Canterbury, that would undermine him.'

Wynstan reflected for a moment then shook his head. 'Ideally Wigferth should be absent from Canterbury when the monks make their decision. I'll have to think about that. Meanwhile, we should talk to the treasurer.'

Treasurer Sigefryth was the most senior monk under the archbishop, and Wynstan needed to get him on side.

'He has the timber house just outside the west end of the church,' Degbert said.

They walked down the nave and passed through the great west doorway. Wynstan pulled his hood over his head to keep the rain off. They hurried across the muddy ground to the nearest building.

The treasurer was a small man with a large bald head. He greeted Wynstan warily but without fear. Wynstan said: 'There's no change in the condition of our beloved archbishop.'

Sigefryth said: 'Perhaps we may be blessed with his presence a little longer.'

'Not much, sadly,' Wynstan said. 'I think the monks here are thankful to God that you are here, Sigefryth, to watch over the affairs of Canterbury.'

Sigefryth acknowledged the compliment with a nod.

Wynstan smiled and spoke in a light tone. 'I always think a treasurer has an impossible job.'

Sigefryth looked intrigued. 'How so?'

'He is supposed to make sure there is always enough money, but he has no control over the spending of it!'

Sigefryth at last permitted himself a smile. 'That is true.'

Wynstan went on: 'I think an abbot – or prior, or whoever fulfils the role – should consult the treasurer about expenditure, not just about income.'

'It would prevent a lot of problems,' Sigefryth said.

That was enough, Wynstan thought again. He needed to ingratiate himself, but in a way that was not too obvious. Now to deal with

Wigferth. 'This year of all years a treasurer has reason to look anxious.' There had been a poor harvest, and people had starved.

'Dead men pay no rent.'

An unsentimental man, Wynstan thought. I like that. He said: 'And the bad weather is continuing. There's flooding all over southern England. On my way here I kept having to make long diversions.' This was much exaggerated. There had been heavy rain, but it had not delayed him more than a few days.

Sigefryth tutted sympathetically.

'And it seems to be getting worse. I hope you're not planning a journey.'

'Not for a while. We'll have rents to collect at Christmas, from those of our tenants who are still alive. I'll be sending Brother Wigferth to your neighbourhood.'

'If you want Wigferth to get there by Christmas, send him soon,' said Wynstan. 'It's going to take him a long time.'

'I'll do that,' said Sigefryth. 'Thank you for the warning.'

So gullible, Wynstan thought with satisfaction.

Wigferth left the next day.

ÞÞÞ

RAGNA'S SONS WERE having a snowball fight. The twins, four years old, were ganging up on Osbert, who was six. Alain, two years old and toddling, was screaming with laughter.

Ragna's small household watched with her: Cat, Gilda, Winthryth and Grimweald, the bodyguard. Grimweald was no use: as one of Wigelm's men-at-arms, he probably would not protect Ragna from the person most likely to attack her.

However, this was a happy moment. All four boys were in good health. Osbert was already learning to read and write. This was not the life Ragna had wanted, and she yearned for Edgar still, but she had things to be thankful for.

When Wigelm became ealdorman he no longer wanted to be bothered with the detailed administration of Combe, so Ragna deputized, and in practice she was reeve of Combe and of Outhen, although Wigelm still visited and held court.

Wigelm appeared now, accompanied by a young concubine, Meganthryth. They stood beside Ragna, watching the boys play. Ragna did not speak to Wigelm or even look at him. Her loathing of him had only deepened in the two years they had been husband and wife. He was both cruel and stupid.

Fortunately, she did not have to be with him much. Most nights he got drunk and was carried to bed. When sober enough he spent the night with Meganthryth, who nevertheless had borne him no children. Occasionally, the old desire overcame him and he visited Ragna. She did not resist him, but closed her eyes and thought about something else until he had finished. Wigelm enjoyed sex against the woman's will, but he disliked indifference, and Ragna's apparent apathy helped to discourage him.

Osbert threw a large snowball wildly and it hit Alain full in the face. The little boy was shocked, and he burst into tears and ran to Ragna. She wiped his cheeks with her sleeve and comforted him.

Wigelm said: 'Don't be a crybaby, Alain. It's only snow, it doesn't hurt.'

His harsh tone made Alain sob harder.

Ragna muttered: 'He's only two.'

Wigelm did not like arguments: he was better at fights. 'Don't mollycoddle the boy,' he said. 'I don't want a namby-pamby son. He's going to be a warrior, like his father.'

Ragna prayed every day that Alain would grow up to be as different as possible from his father. But she said no more: discussion with Wigelm was profitless.

'Don't you start teaching him to read,' Wigelm added. Wigelm himself could not read. 'That's for priests and women.'

We'll see about that, Ragna thought, but she said nothing.

'You raise him right,' Wigelm said. 'Or else.' He walked away, and his concubine trailed after him.

Ragna felt chilled. What did he mean by *or else*?

She saw Hildi the midwife approaching across the snowy compound. Ragna was always pleased to speak to her. She was a wise old woman, and her medical skill extended much beyond childbirth.

Hildi said: 'I know you don't like Agnes.'

Ragna stiffened. 'I liked her well enough until she turned traitor.'

'She's dying, and she wants to beg your forgiveness.'

Ragna sighed. Such a request was hard to refuse, even when it came from the woman who had ruined Ragna's life.

She told Cat to watch the boys, and left with Hildi.

In the town the pure white of the snow had already been defiled by garbage and muddy footsteps. Cat led the way to a small house behind the bishop's palace. The place was dirty and smelled bad. Agnes lay in the straw on the floor, wrapped in a blanket. On her cheek, beside her nose, was a hideous red lump with a scabbed crater in its centre.

Her gaze roamed around the room as if she did not know where she was. Her eyes fell on Ragna and she said: 'I know you.'

It was an odd thing to say. Agnes had lived with Ragna for more than a decade, but she spoke as if they were distant acquaintances.

Hildi said: 'She gets confused. It's part of the illness.'

'I've got a terrible headache,' Agnes said.

Hildi addressed her. 'You asked me to bring the Lady Ragna to see you so that you could tell her how sorry you are.'

Agnes's face changed. Suddenly she appeared to have all her mental faculties. 'I did a wicked thing,' she said. 'My lady, can you ever forgive me for betraying you?'

The plea was irresistible. 'I forgive you, Agnes,' Ragna said sincerely.

Agnes said: 'God is punishing me for what I did. Hildi says I've got Whore's Leprosy.'

Ragna was shocked. She had heard of this disease. It was spread by sexual contact, hence the name. Starting with headaches and dizziness, it caused mental deterioration and eventually drove the sufferer mad. In a quiet tone she said to Hildi: 'Is it fatal?'

'In itself, no, but the sufferer is so weakened and accident-prone that death comes soon from other causes.'

Ragna raised her voice and spoke to Agnes. 'Did Offa have it?' she asked incredulously.

Hildi shook her head. 'Agnes didn't get it from her husband.'

'Who, then?'

Agnes said: 'I sinned with the bishop.'

'Wynstan?'

Hildi said: 'Wynstan has the disease. It's progressing more slowly with him than it did with Agnes, so he doesn't know it yet, but I've seen the signs. He's tired all the time and he gets dizzy spells. And he has a lump on his throat. He tries to hide it under his cloak, but I've seen it, and it's just like the one on Agnes's face.'

Ragna said: 'If he finds out, he'll keep it deadly secret.'

'Yes,' said Hildi. 'If people knew he was going mad, he might lose his power.'

'Exactly,' said Ragna.

'I will never tell anyone. I'm too frightened.'

'Me, too,' said Ragna.

ÞÞÞ

ALDRED FELT A little dazed as he looked at the stacks of silver pennies on the table.

Brother Godleof was the treasurer of King's Bridge Priory, and he had brought the money chest from the safe in Cuthbert's old workshop and placed it on the table. Together they had counted out the silver coins. They could have weighed them faster, but they did not have a scale.

Until now they had not needed one.

'I thought we would be short of money this year, after the famine,' Aldred said.

'The upside of that was it caused the Vikings to go home,' said Godleof. 'We earned less than usual, but still plenty. We have the tolls from the bridge, the rents from stallholders in the marketplace, and donations from pilgrims. And don't forget that we've received four grants of substantial lands in the past year, and we're now collecting rents from them.'

'Success breeds success. But we must have spent a lot, too.'

'We have fed starving people from miles around. But we've also built a schoolhouse, a scriptorium, a refectory and a dormitory for all the new monks who have joined us.'

It was true. Aldred was well on the way to achieving his dream of a centre of learning and scholarship.

Godleof went on: 'Most of them are timber buildings, so they didn't cost much.'

Aldred stared at the money. He had worked hard to strengthen the priory's finances, but now he found himself feeling uncomfortable about so much wealth. 'I took a vow of poverty,' he said, half to himself.

'It's not your money,' said Godleof. 'It belongs to the priory.'

'True. Still, we can't just sit and gloat over it. Jesus told us not to store up treasure on earth, but in heaven. This was given to us for a purpose.'

'What purpose?'

'Perhaps God wants us to build a bigger church. We certainly need it. We have to hold three separate Masses on Sundays now, and the church is packed for each one. Even on weekdays the pilgrims sometimes queue for hours to see the bones of the saint.'

'Whoa,' said Godleof. 'What you see in front of you is not enough to pay for a stone church.'

'But more money will continue to come in.'

'I certainly hope so, but we can't see the future.'

Aldred smiled. 'We must have faith.'

'Faith isn't money.'

'No, it's much better than money.' Aldred stood up. 'Let's lock all this away, then I'll show you something.'

They put the chest back in the safe, left the monastery, and walked up the hill. There were new houses on both sides of the street – all of which were paying rent to the monastery, Aldred recalled. They drew level with Edgar's house. Aldred should have rented it to a new tenant, but he had sentimentally kept it empty.

Opposite Edgar's house was the marketplace. Today was not a market day, but nevertheless, a handful of hopeful traders were there, despite the cold weather, offering fresh eggs, sweet cakes, woodland nuts and home-made ale. Aldred led Godleof across the square.

On the far side the forest began, but here much of it had been cut down for timber. 'This is where the new church will stand. Edgar and I made a town plan, years ago.'

Godleof stared at the jungle of bushes and tree stumps. 'All this will have to be properly cleared.'

'Of course.'

'Where would we get the stone?'

'Outhenham. The Lady Ragna will probably give it to us free, as a pious donation, but we'll have to employ a quarryman.'

'There's a lot to be done.'

'Indeed – so the sooner we begin, the better.'

'Who's going to design the church? It's not like building a house, is it?'

'I know.' Aldred's heart beat faster. 'We need to get Edgar back.'

'We don't even know where he is.'

'He can be found.'

'By whom?'

Aldred was tempted to lead the search himself. However, that was impossible. The priory was thriving, but he was the leader. If he absented himself for the weeks or months that a trip to Normandy would take, all kinds of things could go wrong. 'Brother William could go,' he said. 'He was born in Normandy and lived there until he was twelve or thirteen. And I'll send young Athulf with him, because Athulf is always restless.'

'Today is not the first time you've thought about this.'

'True.' Aldred did not want to admit how often he had daydreamed of bringing Edgar home. 'Let's go and talk to William and Athulf.'

As they walked downhill to the monastery, Aldred noticed a man in monk's robes riding across the bridge. The figure looked familiar, and as he came closer Aldred recognized Wigferth of Canterbury.

He welcomed Wigferth and took him to the kitchen for bread and hot ale. 'This is early for you to be collecting your Christmas rents,' he said.

'They sent me ahead of time to get rid of me,' Wigferth said sourly.

'Who wanted to get rid of you?'

'The bishop of Shiring.'

'Wynstan? What's he doing in Canterbury?'

'Trying to be made archbishop.'

Aldred was horrified. 'But it's supposed to be Alphage of Winchester!'

'I still hope it will be Alphage. But Wynstan has cleverly ingratiated himself with the monks, and in particular with Sigefryth, the treasurer. A lot of them are now opposed to Alphage. And a discontented body of monks can be a frightful nuisance. King Ethelred may appoint Wynstan just for the sake of a quiet life.'

'Heaven forbid!'

'Amen,' said Wigferth.

ÞÞÞ

A FRESH FALL of snow gave Ragna the chance to teach the children some letters. She gave each boy a stick and said: 'What letter starts Osbert's name?'

'I know, I know!' said Osbert.

'Can you draw it?'

'Easy.' Osbert drew a large, uneven circle in the snow.

'The rest of you, draw the letter that starts Osbert. See, it's round, like the shape of your lips when you say the beginning of his name.'

The twins managed rough circles. Alain had trouble, but he was only two, and Ragna's main purpose was to teach them that words were made of letters.

'What letter starts Hubert?' she said.

'I know, I know!' Osbert said again, and he drew a passable H in the snow. The twins copied it, more or less. Alain's effort looked like three random sticks, but she praised it anyway.

Out of the corner of her eye, Ragna saw Wigelm. She cursed under her breath.

'What's going on here?' Wigelm said.

Ragna invented something on the spur of the moment. Pointing at the circles she said: 'The English are here, on these hills. And all around them . . .' She indicated the other scrawls. 'The Vikings. What happens next, Wigelm?'

He looked at her with suspicion. 'The Vikings attack the English,' he said.

Ragna said: 'And who wins, boys?'

'The English!' they all shouted.

If only that were true, Ragna thought.

Then Alain gave the game away. Pointing at the rough circle Osbert

727

had drawn, he said: 'That's Osbert's name.' He smiled proudly, and looked to his father for praise.

It was not forthcoming. Wigelm gave Ragna a hard look. 'I've warned you.'

Ragna clapped her hands. 'Let's go inside and have breakfast,' she said.

The boys ran indoors and Wigelm stalked off.

Ragna followed the boys more slowly. How was she going to educate Alain? Living so close to Wigelm made it hard to deceive him. Twice now he had hinted that he would hand over the raising of Alain to someone else. Ragna could not bear that. But neither could she bring Alain up to be an ignoramus, especially when his brothers were learning.

As they were finishing breakfast Prior Aldred came in. He had probably arrived from King's Bridge yesterday and spent the night at Shiring Abbey. He accepted a cup of warm ale and sat on a bench. 'I'm going to build a new church,' he said. 'The old one is too small.'

'Congratulations! The priory must be prospering, for you to plan such a project.'

'I think we'll be able to afford it, God willing. But it would be a great help if you would continue to let us take stone from Outhenham free of charge.'

'I'll be glad to.'

'Thank you.'

'But who will be your master builder?'

Aldred lowered his voice so that the servants could not hear. 'I've sent messengers to Normandy to beg Edgar to come back.'

Ragna's heart leaped. 'I hope they can find him.'

'They'll sail to Cherbourg and start by speaking to your father. Edgar told me he would ask Count Hubert where he might find work.'

Hope filled Ragna's heart. Would Edgar really come home? He might not want to. She shook her head sadly. 'He left because I married Wigelm – and I'm still married to Wigelm.'

Aldred said brightly: 'I'm trusting that the prospect of designing and building his own church from scratch will be enough to tempt him.'

'It might be – he'd love that,' Ragna said with a smile. Then she thought of another possibility. 'He might have met a girl there.'

'Perhaps.'

'He might even be married by now,' she said dismally.

'We must wait and see.'

'I hope he comes,' Ragna whispered.

'So do I. I've kept his house empty for him.'

Aldred loved him too, Ragna knew – and with even less expectation than she had.

Aldred's tone became brisk, as if he had read her thoughts and wanted to change the subject. 'There's something else I need to ask you – another favour.'

'Go ahead.'

'The archbishop of Canterbury is dying, and Wynstan is making a bid to succeed him.'

Ragna shuddered. 'The idea of Wynstan as the moral leader of the entire south of England is just obscene.'

'Would you say that to Queen Emma? You know her, she likes you, she would listen to you more than to anyone.'

'You're right, she'd listen to me,' Ragna said. And there was something Aldred did not know. Ragna could tell the queen that Wynstan had a disease that would slowly drive him mad. That would certainly be enough to prevent his being made archbishop.

But Ragna would never do it. She could not pass her information to Emma or anyone else. Wynstan would easily find out what had blocked his appointment, and there would be reprisals. Wigelm would take Alain away from Ragna, knowing that was the most severe punishment he could inflict.

She looked at Aldred and felt sad. His face showed optimism and determination. He was a good man, but she could not give him what he needed. The evil men always seemed to get their way, she thought: Dreng, Degbert, Wigelm, Wynstan. Perhaps it would always be so, on this earth.

'No,' she said. 'I'm too scared of what Wynstan and Wigelm would do to me in revenge. I'm sorry, Aldred, I can't help you.'

39

THE CRAFTSMEN WORKING ON the new stone church stopped for a break at mid-morning. The master mason's daughter, Clothild, brought her father a pot of ale and some bread. Giorgio, a builder from Rome, soaked his bread in ale to soften it before eating.

Edgar was the master's deputy, and during the break he usually went to the lodge, a lean-to hut, to discuss what orders should be given for the rest of the day. After more than two years of speaking nothing but Norman French, Edgar was now fluent.

Clothild had got into the habit of bringing ale and bread for Edgar, too. Edgar gave some of the bread to his new dog, Coalie, who was black with a whiskered muzzle.

The church was being built on a site that sloped down from west to east, which presented a challenge in itself. In order to keep the floor level throughout, a deep crypt with massive squat pillars would provide a platform to hold up the east end.

Edgar was thrilled by Giorgio's design. The nave would have two parallel rows of huge semicircular arches supported by mighty pillars, so that people in the side aisles could see the entire width of the church, and a large congregation could watch the Mass. Edgar had never imagined such a bold design, and he was pretty sure no one else in England had either. The French workers were equally startled: this was something brand new.

Giorgio was a thin, grumpy man in his fifties, but he was the most skilled and imaginative builder Edgar had ever known. He sat

731

drawing in the dirt with a stick, explaining how the voussoirs, the stones in the arches, would be carved with moulding in such a way that, when they were set side by side, they would look like a series of concentric rings. 'Do you understand?' he said.

'Yes, of course,' Edgar said. 'It's extremely clever.'

'Don't say you understand unless it's true!' Giorgio said with irritation.

Giorgio often expected to spend a long time explaining things that Edgar grasped immediately. It reminded Edgar of conversations with his father. 'You describe things so clearly,' he said, smoothing Giorgio's feathers.

Clothild handed him a platter with bread and cheese, and he ate hungrily. She sat opposite him. As he continued to discuss the shape of voussoirs with Giorgio, she crossed and uncrossed her knees repeatedly, showing him her strong brown legs.

She was attractive, with an easygoing personality and a trim figure, and she had made it clear that she liked Edgar. She was twenty-one, just five years younger than he. She was lovely, except that she was not Ragna.

He had long ago realized that he did not love as most men did. He seemed to become almost blind to all women but one. He had remained faithful to Sungifu for years after her death. Now he was being true to a woman who had married another man – two other men, in fact. At times he wished he had been made differently. Why should he not marry this likeable girl? She would be kind and affectionate to him, as she was with her father. And Edgar would be able to lie between those strong brown legs every night.

Giorgio said: 'We draw a half-circle on the ground the same size as the arch, draw a radius from the centre to the circumference, then place a stone on the circumference so that it is square to the radius. But the sides of the stone, where it butts onto the neighbouring voussoirs, must be slightly angled.'

'Yes,' said Edgar. 'So we draw two more radii, one on each side, and they give us the correct slant for the edges of the stone.'

Giorgio stared at him. 'How did you know that?' he said tetchily.

Edgar needed to be careful not to offend Giorgio by knowing too much. Builders jealously guarded what they called the 'mysteries' of their craft. 'You told me, a while ago,' Edgar lied. 'I remember everything you tell me.'

Giorgio was mollified.

Edgar saw two monks walking across the site. They were looking around open-mouthed, probably never having seen a church as large as this one would be. Something about them made Edgar think they were English. But the older one spoke Norman French. 'Good day to you, master mason,' he said courteously.

'What do you want?' said Giorgio.

'We're looking for an English builder called Edgar.'

Messengers from home, Edgar thought, and he felt a mixture of excitement and fear. Would it be good news or bad?

He noticed that Clothild looked dismayed.

'I'm Edgar,' he said, speaking in the now-unfamiliar language of English.

The monk slumped with relief. 'It has taken us a long time to find you,' he said.

Edgar said: 'Who are you?'

'We're from King's Bridge Priory. I'm William and this is Athulf. May we have private words with you?'

'Of course.' Neither man had been at the monastery when Edgar left. The place must be expanding, he realized. He led them across the site to the timber stack, where there was less noise. They sat on the piles of planks. 'What's happened?' Edgar said. 'Did someone die?'

'Our news is different,' William said. 'Prior Aldred has decided to build a new stone church.'

'Halfway up the slope? Opposite my house?'

'Exactly where you planned it.'

'Has work begun?'

'When we left the monks were clearing tree stumps from the site, and we were starting to receive deliveries of stone from Outhenham quarry.'

'Who will design the church?'

William paused and said: 'You, we hope.'

So that was it.

'Aldred wants you to come home,' William went on, verifying Edgar's deduction. 'He has kept your house empty for you. You will be the master builder. He has ordered us to find out how much a master is paid here in Normandy, and to offer you the same wages. And anything else you care to demand.'

There was really only one thing Edgar wanted. He hesitated to bare his heart to these two strangers, but probably everyone in Shiring knew the story. After a moment he just blurted it out. 'Is the Lady Ragna still married to Ealdorman Wigelm?'

William looked as though he had expected this question. 'Yes.'

'She still lives with him at Shiring?'

'Yes.'

The flicker of hope in Edgar's heart died away. 'Let me think about this. Do you two have somewhere to lodge?'

'There is a monastery nearby.'

'I'll give you an answer tomorrow.'

'We will pray for your agreement.'

The monks moved away, and Edgar stayed where he was, thinking, staring at a muscular woman stirring a mountain of mortar with a wooden paddle, hardly seeing her. Did he want to go back to England? He had left because he could not bear to see Ragna married to Wigelm. If he returned, he would meet them often. It would be torture.

On the other hand, he was being offered the top job. He would be the master. Every detail of the new church would be for him to decide. He could create a magnificent building in the radical new style Giorgio had shown him. It might take ten years, perhaps twenty, possibly more. It would be his life.

He got up from his perch on the wood pile and went back to his work. Clothild had gone. Giorgio was working on a sample voussoir, and had drawn the circle and radii he had described earlier. Edgar was about to resume his current task, which was to make the wooden support, called formwork, that would hold the stones in place while the mortar hardened; but Giorgio detained him.

'They asked you to go home,' Giorgio said.

'How did you know?'

Giorgio shrugged. 'Why else would they come from England?'

'They want me to build a new church.'

'Will you go?'

'I don't know.'

To Edgar's surprise, Giorgio put down his tools. 'Let me tell you something,' he said. His tone changed, and suddenly he seemed vulnerable. Edgar had never seen him like this. 'I married late,' Giorgio said, as if reminiscing. 'I was thirty when I met Clothild's mother, rest her soul.' He paused, and for a moment Edgar thought he might weep; then Giorgio shook his head and carried on. 'Thirty-five when Clothild was born. Now I'm fifty-six. I'm an old man.'

Fifty-six was not ancient, but this was not a moment to quibble.

Giorgio said: 'I get pains in my stomach.'

That would account for the bad temper, Edgar thought.

'I can't keep food down,' Giorgio said. 'I live on sops.'

Edgar had thought Giorgio soaked his bread because he liked it that way.

'I probably won't die tomorrow,' Giorgio went on. 'But I may have only a year or so.'

I should have known, Edgar thought. All the clues were there. I could have guessed. Ragna would have figured it out long ago. 'I'm so sorry,' he said. 'I hope it doesn't come true.'

Giorgio dismissed that possibility with a wave of his hand. 'As I think about the life to come, I realize that two things on earth are precious to me,' he said. He looked around the site. 'One is this church.' His gaze came back to Edgar. 'The other is Clothild.'

Giorgio's face changed again, and Edgar saw naked emotion. The man was revealing his soul.

Giorgio said: 'I want someone to take care of them both when I'm gone.'

Edgar stared, thinking: He's offering me his job and his daughter.

'Don't go home,' Giorgio said. 'Please.'

It was a heartfelt appeal, and hard to resist, but Edgar managed to say: 'I have to think about this.'

Giorgio nodded. 'Of course.' The moment of intimacy was over. He turned away and resumed his work.

Edgar thought about it for the rest of the day and most of the night.

It never rains but it pours, he thought. To be a master builder was the summit of his ambition, and he had been offered two such posts in one day. He could be master mason here or at home. Both would give him profound satisfaction. But the other half of the choice was what kept him awake: Clothild or Ragna?

It was not a real choice. Ragna might be married to Wigelm for the next twenty years. Even if Wigelm died young, she might again be forced to remarry to a nobleman chosen by the king. As dawn approached Edgar realized that back in England he might well spend the rest of his life longing for someone he could never have.

He had spent too many years living like that, he thought. If he stayed in Normandy and married Clothild, he would not be happy, but he might be tranquil.

In the morning he told the monks he was staying.

ÞÞÞ

WIGELM CAME TO Ragna's bed on a warm spring night when the trees were in bud. The opening of the door awakened her and her servants. She heard the maids shift in the rushes on the floor, and Grimweald, her bodyguard, grunted, but the children remained asleep.

With no forewarning she did not have the chance to oil herself. Wigelm lay beside her and pushed her shift up around her waist. She hastily spat on her hand and moistened her vagina, then opened her legs obediently.

She was resigned to this. It happened only a few times a year. She just hoped she would not become pregnant again. She loved Alain, but she did not want another child by Wigelm.

But this time it was different. Wigelm shoved in and out but seemed unable to reach satisfaction. She did nothing to help him. She knew, from female conversations, that when there was no love other women often pretended to be aroused, just to get it over faster; but she could not bring herself to play that role.

Soon his erection softened. After a few more hopeless thrusts he withdrew. 'You're a cold bitch,' he said, and punched her face. She sobbed, expecting a beating, and knowing that her bodyguard would do nothing to protect her; but Wigelm stood up and went out.

In the morning the left side of her face was swollen and her upper lip felt huge. She told herself it could have been worse.

Wigelm came into the house when the children were having their breakfast. She noticed that his big nose was now marked with wine-coloured lines like a red spiderweb from drinking so much, an ugly feature she had not seen last night in the firelight.

He looked at her and said: 'I should have punched the other side to match.'

A sarcastic remark came to her mind but she suppressed it. She sensed that he was in a dangerous mood. She felt a cold dread: perhaps her punishment was not over. She spoke in a neutral tone through her damaged mouth. 'What do you want, Wigelm?'

'I don't like the way you're raising Alain.'

This was an old song, but she heard a new level of malice in his tone. She said: 'He's only two and a half years old – still a baby. There's plenty of time for him to learn to fight.'

Wigelm shook his head determinedly. 'You want to give him womanish ways – reading and writing and such.'

'King Ethelred can read.'

Wigelm refused to be drawn into an argument. 'I'm going to take charge of the boy's upbringing.'

What could that mean? Ragna said desperately: 'I'll get him a wooden sword.'

'I don't trust you.'

Much of what Wigelm said could normally be ignored. He uttered abuse and curses that meant little, and forgot what he had said within minutes. But now Ragna had a feeling that he was not just making empty threats. In a scared voice she said: 'What do you mean?'

'I'm taking Alain to live at my house.'

The idea was so ludicrous that at first Ragna hardly took it seriously. 'You can't!' she said. 'You can't look after a two-year-old.'

'He's my son. I shall do as I please.'

'Will you wipe his bum?'

'I'm not alone.'

Ragna said incredulously: 'Are you talking about Meganthryth? You're going to give him to Meganthryth to raise? She's sixteen!'

'Many girls of sixteen are mothers.'

'But she's not!'

'No, but she will do as I say, whereas you completely ignore my wishes. Alain hardly knows he's got a father. But I will have him raised according to my principles. He must become a man.'

'No!'

Wigelm moved towards Alain, who was sitting at the table, looking scared. Cat stepped between the two. Wigelm grabbed the front of her dress with both hands, lifted her off her feet, and threw her at the wall. She screamed, hit the timber planks, and crumpled to the floor.

All the children were crying.

Wigelm picked Alain up. The boy screamed in terror. Wigelm tucked him under his left arm. Ragna grabbed Wigelm's arm and tried to detach Alain. Wigelm punched the side of her head so hard that momentarily she blacked out.

She came to lying on the floor. She looked up to see Wigelm going out, with Alain kicking and screaming under his arm.

She struggled to her feet and staggered to the door. Wigelm was marching across the compound to his own house. Ragna was too dazed to run after him, and anyway she knew she would only be knocked down again.

She turned back inside. Cat was sitting on the floor rubbing her head through her mop of black hair. Ragna said: 'How badly are you injured?'

'I don't think anything's broken,' Cat said. 'What about you?'

'My head hurts.'

Grimweald spoke. 'What can I do to help?'

Ragna's answer was sarcastic. 'Just carry on protecting us, as usual,' she said.

The bodyguard stamped out.

The children were still wailing. The women began to comfort them. Cat said: 'I can't believe he's taken Alain.'

'He wants Meganthryth to raise the boy to be a stupid bully like his father.'

'You can't let him get away with this.'

Ragna nodded. She could not let things stand. 'I'm going to talk to him,' she said. 'Perhaps I can get him to see sense.' She was not optimistic, but she had to try.

She left the house and crossed to Wigelm's place. As she approached she could hear Alain crying. She went in without knocking.

Wigelm and Meganthryth stood talking, Meganthryth holding Alain and trying to quiet him. As soon as the child saw Ragna he screamed: 'Mudder!' That was what he had always called Ragna.

Instinctively, Ragna went towards him, but Wigelm stopped her. 'Leave him,' he said.

Ragna stared at Meganthryth. She was short and plump, and would have been pretty but for a twist about her mouth that suggested greed. Still, she was a woman: would she really refuse to let a child go to his mother?

Ragna stretched out her arms towards Alain.

Meganthryth turned her back.

Ragna was horrified that any woman could do such a thing, and her heart filled with loathing.

With an effort, she turned from Alain and spoke to Wigelm, doing her best to use a calm, reasonable voice. 'We need to discuss this,' she said.

'No. I don't discuss. I tell you what's going to happen.'

'Will you make a prisoner of Alain, and keep him locked in this house? That will turn him into a weakling, not a warrior.'

'Of course I won't.'

'Then he will play in the compound with his brothers, and he will go with them when they come home, and every day you will have to do what you've just done. And when you're not here, which is often, who is going to drag the little boy away from his family while he kicks and screams for his mother?'

Wigelm looked baffled. Clearly he had thought of none of this. Then his face cleared and he said: 'When I travel I'll take him with me.'

'And who will look after him on the road?'

'Meganthryth.'

Ragna glanced at her. She looked appalled. Clearly she had not been consulted. But she clamped her mouth shut.

Wigelm went on: 'I leave for Combe tomorrow. He can come with me. He'll get to know about the life of an ealdorman.'

'You're going to take a two-year-old on a four-day journey.'

'I don't see why not.'

'And when you come back?'

'We'll see. But he's not going to live with you, not ever again.'

Ragna could no longer control herself, and she began to cry. 'Please, Wigelm, I beg you, don't do this. Forget about me, but take pity on your son.'

'I pity him being raised by a gaggle of women and turned effeminate. If I allowed that to happen, he would grow up to curse his father. No, he stays here.'

'No, please—'

'I'm not listening to any more of this. Get out.'

'Just think, Wigelm—'

'Do I have to pick you up and throw you through the door?'

Ragna could not take any more beating. She hung her head. 'No,' she sobbed. Slowly she turned and walked to the door. She looked back at Alain, still screaming hysterically and holding his arms out to her. With a huge effort she turned away and walked out.

ÞÞÞ

THE LOSS OF her youngest child left a hole in Ragna's heart. She thought about him constantly. Did Meganthryth keep him clean and fed? Was he well, or suffering from a childish ailment? Did he wake at night and cry for her? She had to force herself to put him out of her mind for at least part of the day, otherwise she would go mad.

She had not given him up – she never would. So when the king and queen came to Winchester, Ragna went there to plead with them.

By this time Ragna had not seen Alain for a month. Wigelm's visit to Combe turned into a spring tour of his region, and he kept the child with him. Apparently he intended staying away from Shiring for an extended period.

Wynstan was still at Canterbury, for the tussle over who was to be the new archbishop was dragging out; so both brothers managed to miss the royal court, which encouraged Ragna.

However, she preferred not to plead her cause in open court. She was distraught, but she could still strategize. Open court was unpredictable. The noblemen of the region might side with Wigelm. Ragna preferred to talk quietly to individuals.

After the grand service in the cathedral on Easter Sunday, Bishop Alphage gave a dinner at his palace for the magnates gathered in Winchester. Ragna was invited, and saw her chance. Full of hope, she rehearsed again and again what she would say to the king.

Easter was the most important festival of the Church year, and this was a royal occasion too, so it was a great social event. People wore their finest clothes and most costly jewellery, and Ragna did the same.

The bishop's house was richly furnished with carved oak benches and colourful tapestries. Someone had put fragrant apple tree twigs on the fire to perfume the smoke. The table was set with silver-rimmed cups and bronze dishes.

Ragna was greeted warmly by the royal couple, which gave her encouragement. She immediately told them that Wigelm had taken Alain from her. Queen Emma was a mother – she had given birth to a son and a daughter in the first four years of her marriage to Ethelred – so she would undoubtedly sympathize.

But Ethelred interrupted Ragna before she had finished the first sentence of her prepared speech. 'I know about this,' he said. 'On our way here we happened to meet Wigelm and the child.'

That was news to Ragna – bad news.

Ethelred went on: 'I discussed this problem with him.'

Ragna despaired. She had been hoping her story would shock the king and queen and excite their compassion. But unfortunately Wigelm had got in first. Ethelred had already heard his version, which would have been distorted.

Ragna would just have to combat that. As an experienced ruler, Ethelred must know not to believe everything he heard.

She spoke emphatically. 'My lord king, it can't be right for a two-year-old to be torn from his mother.'

'I think it's very harsh, and I told Wigelm so.'

Queen Emma said: 'Quite right. The boy is the same age as our Edward, and if he were taken from me it would break my heart.'

'I don't disagree, my love,' said Ethelred. 'But it's not for me to tell my subjects how to order their families. The king's responsibilities are defence, justice and a sound currency. The raising of children is a private matter.'

Ragna opened her mouth to argue. The king was a moral leader, too, and he had the right to reprove misbehaving magnates. But then she saw Emma give a quick shake of her head. Ragna closed her mouth. A moment's reflection told her that Emma was right. When a ruler had spoken so decisively he would not be talked around. For her to persist would only alienate Ethelred. It was hard, but she controlled her disappointment and rage. She bowed her head and said: 'Yes, my lord king.'

How long would she be separated from Alain? Surely not for ever?

Someone else caught the attention of the royal couple, and Ragna turned aside. She tried not to cry. Her position seemed hopeless. If the king would not help her get her son back, who would?

Wigelm and Wynstan had all the power, that was the curse. They could get away with just about anything. Wynstan was clever, Wigelm was thuggish, and both of them were willing to defy the king and the law. If she could have done something to weaken them, she would have. But it seemed nothing could stop them.

Aldred approached her. She said: 'Are your messengers back from Normandy yet?'

'No,' he said.

'They've been away months.'

'They must be having trouble finding him. Builders often move around. They have to go where the work is.'

He looked worried and distracted, she now saw. She said: 'How are you?'

'I understand that kings avoid conflict whenever they can,' he said angrily. 'But sometimes a king should rule!'

Ragna had exactly the same complaint, but such things should be said privately. She looked around uneasily. However, no one seemed to have heard. 'What's brought that on?'

'Wynstan has stirred up everyone at Canterbury so that there's now an anti-Alphage faction, and Ethelred is hesitating because he doesn't want trouble with the monks.'

'You want the king to put his foot down, announce that Wynstan is unfit to be archbishop, and impose Alphage regardless of the monks' opinion.'

'It strikes me that a king should take a moral stand!'

'Those monks, living so far away from Shiring, simply don't know what we all know about Wynstan.'

'True.'

Ragna suddenly recalled something that could damage Wynstan. She had almost forgotten it in her anguish about Alain. 'What if . . .'

She hesitated. She had decided to keep this secret, for fear of reprisals. But Wigelm had already done his worst. He had carried out the threat he had hinted at for so long. He had taken away Ragna's child. And his cruelty had a consequence that undoubtedly he had not foreseen: he no longer had a hold over her.

As she drank in this realization she felt liberated. From now on, she would do anything in her power to undermine Wigelm and Wynstan. It would still be dangerous, but she was prepared for risk. It was worth it to undermine the brothers.

She said: 'What if you could prove to the monks that Wynstan is unfit?'

Aldred looked suddenly alert. 'What do you mean?'

Ragna hesitated again. She was eager to weaken Wynstan but at the same time afraid of him. She took her courage in both hands. 'Wynstan has Whore's Leprosy.'

Aldred's mouth fell open. 'God save us! Really?'

'Yes.'

'How do you know?'

'Hildi has seen a growth on his neck that is characteristic of the disease. And Agnes, his mistress, had the same kind of growth, and died.'

'But this changes everything!' Aldred said eagerly. 'Does the king know?'

'No one knows except Hildi and me – and now you.'

'Then you must tell him!'

Fear made Ragna pause. 'I'd rather Wynstan did not know that I had spread the news.'

'Then I'll tell the king, without mentioning your name.'

'Hold on . . .' Aldred was in a rush, but Ragna was figuring out the best approach. 'You have to be careful with a king. Ethelred knows you favour Alphage, and he might view your intervention as opposition to his will.'

Aldred looked frustrated. 'We have to use this information!'

'Of course,' Ragna said. 'But there might be a better way.'

ÞÞÞ

BISHOP WYNSTAN AND Archdeacon Degbert often attended meetings in the chapter house, where the monks discussed the daily business of the monastery and the cathedral. It was not usual for visitors to take part but Brother Eappa had suggested it, and Treasurer Sigefryth had become an ally of Wynstan's. They went along to the first meeting after Easter.

After the chapter had been read Sigefryth, who chaired the meetings, said: 'We have to decide what to do about the riverside pasture. Local people are using it for grazing, even though it belongs to us.'

Wynstan had no interest in such a topic, but he put on an earnest expression. He had to pretend that anything affecting the monks was of concern to him.

Brother Forthred, the medical monk, said: 'We don't use that field. You can't blame them.'

'True,' said Sigefryth, 'but if we allow it to be treated as communal property, we may have trouble in the future when we need it for ourselves.'

Brother Wigferth, who had just returned from Winchester, spoke up. 'My brethren, forgive me for interrupting, but there is something much more important that I believe we should talk about right away.'

Sigefryth could hardly refuse such a strong plea from Wigferth. 'Very well,' he said.

Wynstan perked up. He had agonized over whether to go to Winchester for Easter. He hated to miss a royal court so close to home. But in the end he had decided it was more important to keep his finger on the pulse here in Canterbury. Now he was eager to learn what had gone on.

'I attended the Easter court,' Wigferth said. 'Many people spoke to me about the question of who is to be the next archbishop of Canterbury.'

Sigefryth was offended. 'Why would they speak to you?' he said.

'Did you pretend to be our representative? You're just a rent collector!'

'Indeed I am,' said Wigferth. 'But if people speak to me, I'm obliged to listen. It's only good manners.'

Wynstan had a bad feeling. 'Never mind about that,' he said, impatient with this quarrel about mere etiquette. 'What were they saying, Brother . . . Brother . . . ?' He could not think of the name of the monk who had gone to Winchester.

'You know me well, bishop. My name is Wigferth.'

'Of course, of course, what did they say?'

Wigferth looked scared but determined. 'People are saying that Bishop Wynstan is unfit to be archbishop of Canterbury.'

Was that all? 'It's not up to *people*!' Wynstan said scornfully. 'It's the Pope who awards the podium.'

Wigferth said: 'You mean the pallium.'

Wynstan realized he had mis-spoken. The pallium was an embroidered sash given by the Pope to new archbishops as a symbol of his approval. Embarrassed, Wynstan denied his error. 'That's what I said, the pallium.'

Sigefryth said: 'Brother Wigferth, did they say why they object to Bishop Wynstan?'

'Yes.'

The room went quiet, and Wynstan's unease deepened. He did not know what was coming, and ignorance was dangerous.

Wigferth seemed glad to have been asked that question. He looked around the chapter house and raised his voice to make sure everyone heard. 'Bishop Wynstan has a disease called Whore's Leprosy.'

Pandemonium broke out. Everybody spoke at once. Wynstan jumped to his feet yelling: 'It's a lie! It's a lie!'

Sigefryth stood in the middle of the room saying: 'Quiet, please, everyone, quiet, please,' until the others got tired of shouting. Then he said: 'Bishop Wynstan, what do you say to this?'

Wynstan knew he should stay calm but he was unnerved. 'I say that Brother Wigferth has a wife and child in the west of England village of Trench, and that as a fornicating monk he has no credibility.'

Wigferth said coolly: 'Even if the accusation were true, it would have no bearing on the question of the bishop's health.'

Wynstan realized immediately that he had taken the wrong tack. What he had said sounded like a tit-for-tat accusation, something he might have made up on the spot. He seemed to be losing his touch. He thought: What's the matter with me?

He sat down, to look less bothered, and said: 'How would those *people* know anything about my health?'

As soon as the words were out of his mouth he realized he had made another mistake. In an argument it was never good to ask a question: that simply gave the opponent an opening.

Wigferth seized his chance. 'Bishop Wynstan, your mistress, Agnes of Shiring, died of Whore's Leprosy.'

Wynstan was silenced. Agnes had never been his mistress, just an occasional indulgence. He knew she was dead – the news had reached him in a letter from Deacon Ithamar. But the deacon had not specified what had killed her – and Wynstan had not been interested enough to ask.

Wigferth went on: 'One of the symptoms is mental confusion: forgetting people's names, and mixing up words. Saying *podium* for *pallium*, for example. The sufferer's mental state gets worse and eventually he goes mad.'

Wynstan found his voice. 'Am I to be condemned for nothing more than a sip of the tongue?'

The monks burst out laughing, and Wynstan realized he had made another mistake: he had intended to say *a slip of the tongue*. He was humiliated and enraged. 'I'm not going mad!' he roared.

Wigferth had not finished. 'The infallible sign of the disease is a large red lump on the face or neck.'

Wynstan's hand flew to his throat, covering the carbuncle; and a second later he realized he had given himself away.

Wigferth said: 'Don't try to hide it, bishop.'

'It's just a boil,' Wynstan said. Reluctantly, he moved his hand away.

Forthred said: 'Let me see.' He approached Wynstan. Wynstan was obliged to let him: anything else would have been an admission. He sat still while Forthred examined the lump.

Finally Forthred straightened up. 'I have seen sores like this before,' he said. 'On the faces of some of the most wretched and unfortunate sinners in this city. I'm sorry, my lord bishop, but what Wigferth says is true. You have Whore's Leprosy.'

Wynstan stood up. 'I'm going to find out who started this filthy lie!' he yelled, and he had the small consolation of seeing fear on the faces of the monks. He walked to the door. 'And when I find him – I will kill him! I will kill him!'

þþþ

WYNSTAN FUMED THROUGHOUT the long journey back to Shiring. He abused Degbert, yelled at tavern keepers, slapped maids, and whipped his horse mercilessly. The fact that he kept forgetting the simplest things made him even more angry.

When he got home he grabbed Ithamar by the front of his tunic, slammed him up against the wall, and yelled: 'Someone has been going around saying I've got Whore's Leprosy – who is it?'

Ithamar's childish face was white with terror. He managed to stutter: 'No one, I swear it.'

'Someone told Wigferth of Canterbury.'

'He probably made it up.'

'What did that woman die of? The reeve's wife – what was her name?'

'Agnes? The palsy.'

'What kind of palsy, fool?'

'I don't know! She fell ill, then she got a huge pustule on her face, then she went mad and died! How should I know what kind?'

'Who attended her?'

'Hildi.'

'Who's she?'

'The midwife.'

Wynstan let go of Ithamar. 'Bring the midwife to me, now.'

Ithamar hurried off, and Wynstan took off his travelling clothes and washed his hands and face. This was the greatest crisis of his life. If everyone came to believe that he had a debilitating disease, then power and wealth would slip away from him. He had to kill the rumours, and the first step was to punish whoever had started them.

Ithamar returned in a few minutes with a small grey-haired woman. Wynstan could not figure out who she was or why Ithamar had brought her.

Ithamar said: 'Hildi, the midwife who attended Agnes when she was dying.'

'Of course, of course,' Wynstan said. 'I know who she is.' Now he recalled that he had got to know her when he took her to the hunting lodge to check on Ragna's pregnancy. She was prim but she possessed a calm confidence. She looked nervous, but not as frightened as most people were on being summoned by Wynstan. Bluster and bullying would not work with this woman, he guessed.

He put on a sad face and said: 'I am in mourning for beloved Agnes.'

'Nothing could be done to save her,' said Hildi. 'We prayed for her, but our prayers were not answered.'

'Tell me how she died,' he said lugubriously. 'The truth, please, I don't want comfortable illusions.'

'Very well, my lord bishop. At first she was tired and suffered headaches. Then she became confused. She developed a large lump on her face. Finally she lost her mind. At the end she caught a fever and died.'

The list was horrifying. Most of the same symptoms had been mentioned by Wigferth.

Wynstan suppressed the fear that threatened to overwhelm him. 'Did anyone visit Agnes during her illness?'

'No, my lord bishop. They were frightened of catching the disease.'

'Who did you talk to about her symptoms?'

'No one, my lord bishop.'

'Are you sure?'

'Quite sure.'

Wynstan suspected that she was lying. He decided to spring a surprise. 'Did she have Whore's Leprosy?' He saw just a flicker of fear in Hildi's expression.

'There is no such disease, my lord bishop, to the best of my knowledge.'

She had recovered quickly, but he had seen the reaction, and now he was sure she was lying. But he decided not to say so. 'Thank you for consoling me in my grief,' he said. 'You may go now.'

Hildi seemed very self-possessed, he thought as she went out. 'She doesn't seem the type of woman to spread scandalous gossip,' he said to Ithamar.

'No.'

'But she told someone.'

'She's friendly with the Lady Ragna.'

Wynstan shook his head doubtfully. 'Ragna and Agnes hated one another. Ragna sentenced Agnes's husband to death, then Agnes took revenge by warning me of Ragna's attempt to escape.'

'Could there have been a deathbed reconciliation?'

Wynstan considered this. 'It's possible,' he said. 'Who would know?'

'Her French maid, Cat.'

'Is Ragna here in Shiring right now?'

751

'No, she went to Outhenham.'

'Then I shall go and see Cat.'

'She won't tell you anything.'

Wynstan smiled. 'Don't you be so sure.'

He left his residence and walked up the hill to the ealdorman's compound. He felt energized. For the moment his mind was clear of the confusion that sometimes afflicted him nowadays. The more he thought about it, the more likely it seemed that there was a link from Agnes through Hildi and Ragna to Wigferth of Canterbury.

Wigelm was still away from home, and the compound was quiet. Wynstan went straight to Ragna's house and found the three maids taking care of the children.

'Good day to you,' he said. The prettiest of the three was the important one, he knew, but he could not remember her name.

She looked at him with fear. 'What do you want?' she said.

Her French accent reminded him who she was. 'You're Cat,' he said.

'The Lady Ragna isn't here.'

'That's a shame, because I came to thank her.'

Cat looked slightly less fearful. 'Thank her?' she said sceptically. 'What did she do for you?'

'She visited my dear Agnes on her deathbed.'

Wynstan waited for Cat's reaction. She might say, *but my lady never visited her,* in which case Wynstan would have to wonder whether she was telling the truth or not. But Cat said nothing.

Wynstan said: 'It was kind of her.'

Another silence followed, then Cat said: 'More kind than Agnes deserved.'

There it was. Wynstan worked hard not to smile. His guess had been accurate. Ragna had gone to see Agnes. She must have observed the symptoms, which would then have been explained to her by Hildi. It was the French bitch who was behind the rumours.

But he continued the pretence. 'I am most grateful to her, especially as I myself was far away and unable to give dear Agnes comfort. Will you please tell your mistress what I said?'

'I certainly will,' said Cat in a bemused tone.

'Thank you,' said Wynstan. Nothing wrong with me, he thought; I'm as sharp as ever.

Then he left.

Þ Þ Þ

WIGELM RETURNED A week later and Wynstan went to see him the following morning.

In the compound he saw Alain running around with Ragna's other three sons, all of them clearly overjoyed to be together again. A moment later, Meganthryth came out of Wigelm's house and called Alain to come for his dinner. The boy said: 'I don't want to.'

She repeated the summons, and he ran away.

She was obliged to run after him. He was not yet three, and could not outrun a healthy adult, so she soon caught him and picked him up. He threw a tantrum, yelling and wriggling and trying to hit her with his little fists. 'I want Mudder!' he screamed. Embarrassed and annoyed, Meganthryth carried him into Wigelm's house.

Wynstan followed.

Wigelm was sharpening a long-bladed dagger on a whetstone. He looked up with irritation at the screaming child. 'What is the matter with that boy?' he said angrily.

Meganthryth replied with equally ill temper: 'I don't know, he's not my son.'

'This is Ragna's fault. By God, I wish I'd never married her. Hello, Wynstan. You priests are wise to remain single.'

Wynstan sat down. 'I've been thinking that it may be time to get rid of Ragna,' he said.

Wigelm looked eager. 'Can we?'

'Three years ago we needed her to join our family. It was a way of neutralizing any opposition to your becoming ealdorman. But you're established now. Everyone has accepted you, even the king.'

'And Ethelred still needs me,' Wigelm said. 'The Vikings are back in force, raiding all along the south coast of England. There will be more battles this summer.'

Meganthryth sat Alain at the table and put buttered bread in front of him, and he quietened down and started to eat.

'So we no longer need Ragna,' said Wynstan. 'In addition, she has become a nuisance. Alain won't forget her while she's still living in this compound. And she is a spy in our camp. I believe she's the one spreading rumours that I've got Whore's Leprosy.'

Wigelm lowered his voice. 'Can we kill her?'

He had never learned subtlety.

'It would cause trouble,' Wynstan said. 'Why don't you just set her aside?'

'Divorce?'

'Yes. It's easily done.'

'King Ethelred won't like it.'

Wynstan shrugged. 'What can he do? We've been defying him for years. All he does is impose fines which we don't pay.'

'I'd be glad to see the back of her.'

'Then do it. And order her to leave Shiring.'

'I could marry again.'

'Not yet. Give the king time to get used to the divorce.'

Meganthryth overheard this and said to Wigelm: 'Will we be able to get married?'

'We'll see,' Wigelm prevaricated.

Wynstan said to her: 'Wigelm needs more sons, and you seem to be barren.'

It was a cruel remark, and tears came to her eyes. 'I might not be.

And if I become the ealdorman's wife, you'll have to treat me with respect.'

'All right,' said Wynstan. 'As soon as cows lay eggs.'

ÞÞÞ

RAGNA WAS FREE at last.

She was sad, too. She would not have Alain, and she would not have Edgar. But she would not have Wigelm or Wynstan either.

Under their domination for almost nine years, she now realized how repressed she had felt for almost all that time. In theory English women had more rights than Norman women – control over their own property being the major one – but in practice it had proved difficult to enforce the law.

She had told Wigelm that she would continue to rule the Vale of Outhen. She planned to stay in England at least until Aldred's messengers returned from Normandy. When she knew what Edgar's plans were she could make her own.

She would write to her father, telling him what had happened, and entrust the letter to the couriers who brought her money four times a year. Count Hubert was going to be angry, she felt sure, though she did not know what he would do about it.

Her maids packed. Cat, Gilda and Winnie all wanted to go with Ragna.

She asked Den to lend her a couple of bodyguards for the journey. As soon as she was settled she would hire her own.

She was not allowed to say goodbye to Alain.

They loaded the horses and left early in the morning, with little fuss. Many of the women in the compound came out of their houses to say quiet goodbyes. Everyone felt that Wigelm's behaviour had been shameful.

They rode out of the compound and took the road to King's Bridge.

40

RAGNA MOVED INTO EDGAR's house.

It was Aldred's idea. She asked him, as landlord, where she might set up home in King's Bridge, and he told her he had been keeping the house empty in the hope that Edgar would return. Neither of them doubted that Edgar would want to live with Ragna – if he came home.

The place was the same size and shape as most houses, just better built. The edge-to-edge upright planks were sealed with wool soaked in tar, as in the hull of a ship, so that rain could not enter even in the stormiest weather. There was a second door, at one end of the building, leading out into an animal pen. There were smoke holes in the gable ends that made the air in the room more pleasant.

Edgar's spirit was here, Ragna felt, in the combination of meticulousness and invention with which the house had been built.

She had been here once before. That was the occasion on which he showed her the box he had made for the book she had given him. She remembered the neat rack of tools, the wine barrel and the cheese safe, and Brindle wagging her tail – all gone now. She also remembered how he had held her hands while she wept.

She wondered where he was living now.

As she settled in, she hoped every morning that this would be the day the messengers returned with news of him, but no word came. Normandy was a big region, and Edgar might not even be there: he could have moved on to Paris or even Rome. The messengers might well have got lost. They could have been robbed and murdered. They might even have liked France better than England and decided not to come home.

Even if they found Edgar, he might not want to return. He could be married. By now he could have a child learning to talk in Norman French. She knew she should not get her hopes up.

However, she was not going to live like a poor rejected woman. She was wealthy and powerful and she would show it. She hired a dressmaker, a cook and three bodyguards. She bought three horses and employed a groom. She began to build stables and storehouses and a second house on the neighbouring plot for all her extra servants. She made a trip to Combe and bought tableware, cooking equipment and wall hangings. While there she commissioned a boatbuilder to make her a barge to take her from King's Bridge to Outhenham. She also ordered a great hall to be built for herself at Outhenham.

She would visit Outhenham soon, to make sure Wigelm did not try to usurp her authority there; but for now she concentrated on her new life at King's Bridge. In Edgar's absence the main attraction of the place was Aldred's school. Osbert was seven and the twins five, and all three had morning lessons six days a week, along with three novice monks and a handful of boys from the neighbourhood. Cat did not want her daughters educated – she feared it would give them ideas above their station – but when the boys came home they shared what they had learned.

Ragna would never get used to being without Alain. She worried about him all the time: when she woke up she wondered if he was hungry, in the afternoon she hoped he was not tired, in the evening she knew he should soon be put to bed. Such hopeless thoughts gradually came to occupy her less, but her grief was always in the back of her mind. She refused to accept that her separation from her child was permanent. Something would happen. Ethelred might change his mind and order Wigelm to give the child back. Wigelm might die. Every night she thought about such happy possibilities, and every night she cried herself to sleep.

She renewed her acquaintance with Blod, Dreng's slave. The two got on well, which was surprising: they were so far apart socially that they might have lived in different worlds. But Ragna enjoyed Blod's no-nonsense attitude to life. And they shared a fondness for Edgar. At the alehouse Blod now brewed the beer, did the cooking, and took care of Dreng's wife Ethel. Happily, Blod was seldom prostituted these days, she told Ragna. 'Dreng says I'm too old,' she said wryly, one day when Ragna went to the tavern to buy a barrel of ale.

'How old are you?' Ragna asked.

'Twenty-two, I think. But anyway I was always too sulky to please the men. So he's bought a new girl, now that he's making so much money on market days.' They were standing outside the brewhouse, and Blod pointed to a girl in a short dress who was dipping a bucket in the river. Her lack of any kind of hat or headdress marked her as a slave and a prostitute, but also revealed a head of thick dark-red hair falling in waves to her shoulders. 'That's Mairead. She's Irish.'

'She looks terribly young.'

'She's about twelve – the age I was when I came here.'

'Poor girl.'

Blod was brutally practical. 'If men are going to pay for sex, they want something they can't get at home.'

Ragna studied the girl more carefully. There was a roundness to her that did not come from eating well. 'Is she pregnant?'

'Yes, and she's farther gone than she looks, but Dreng hasn't realized yet. He's ignorant about such things. However, he's going to be furious. Men won't pay as much for a pregnant woman.'

Despite Blod's tough practicality, Ragna detected in her tone a fondness for Mairead, and she felt glad that the slave girl had someone to look out for her.

She paid Blod for the ale, and Blod rolled a barrel out of the brewhouse.

Dreng himself emerged from the henhouse with a few eggs in a basket. He was getting fat, and limping more than ever. He gave Ragna a cursory nod – he no longer troubled to toady to her, now that she had fallen from favour – and walked past. He was breathing hard even though he was hardly exerting himself.

Ethel came to the door of the alehouse. She, too, looked ill. She was in her late twenties, Ragna knew, but she appeared older. The cause was not just a decade of marriage to Dreng. According to Mother Agatha, Ethel had an internal ailment requiring that she rest.

Blod looked worried and said: 'Do you need something, Ethel?' Ethel shook her head and took the eggs from Dreng, then disappeared back inside. 'I have to look after her,' Blod said. 'No one else will.'

'What about Edgar's sister-in-law?'

'Cwenburg? You won't see her taking care of her stepmother.' Blod began to push the barrel up the hill. 'I'll bring this to your house.' She leaned into her work. She was a strong woman, Ragna saw.

Across from Ragna's house, Aldred was supervising a mixed group of monks and labourers who were pulling up tree stumps and clearing bushes on the site of the proposed new church. He saw Ragna and Blod, and came over. 'You'll have a rival soon,' he said to Blod. 'I'm planning to build an alehouse here in the marketplace and lease it to a man from Mudeford.'

Blod said: 'Dreng will be outraged.'

'He's always outraged about something,' Aldred replied. 'The town is big enough now for two alehouses. On market days we could do with four.'

Ragna said: 'Is an alehouse an appropriate thing for a monastery to own?'

'This one will have no prostitutes,' Aldred said with a severe look.

Blod said: 'Good for you.'

Ragna looked towards the river and saw two monks crossing the bridge on horseback. The King's Bridge monks travelled a lot, now that the monastery owned property all over the south of England, but something about these two made her heart beat faster. Their clothes were grubby, the leather of their baggage looked battered, and their horses were tired. They had come a long way.

Aldred followed Ragna's gaze, and spoke with a frisson of excitement. 'Could those two be William and Athulf, back from Normandy at last?'

If so, Edgar was not with them. Ragna felt the pain of disappointment so severely that she winced as if she had been lashed.

Aldred hurried down the hill to meet them, and Ragna and Blod followed.

The monks dismounted and Aldred embraced them both. 'You've come safely home,' he said. 'Praise God.'

'Amen,' said William.

'Did you find Edgar?'

'Yes, though it took a long time.'

Ragna hardly dared to hope.

Aldred said: 'And what did he say to our proposal?'

'He declined the invitation,' William said.

Ragna put her hands over her mouth to stop herself moaning in despair.

Aldred said: 'Did he give a reason?'

'No.'

Ragna found her voice. 'Is he married?'

'No . . .'

She heard the hesitation. 'What, then?'

'People in the town where he's living say he will marry the daughter of the master mason and eventually become master himself.'

Ragna began to cry. They were all looking at her now, but she cared nothing for her dignity. 'He's made a new life for himself there, then?'

'Yes, my lady.'

'And he doesn't want to leave it.'

'So it seems. I'm sorry.'

Ragna could not contain herself. She burst into sobs. She turned away and hurried up the slope, finding her way through a blur of tears to her house. Inside, she threw herself down in the straw and cried her heart out.

ÞÞÞ

'I'LL GO BACK to Cherbourg,' Ragna said firmly to Blod a week later.

It was a warm day, and the children were splashing in the shallows at the edge of the river. Ragna was sitting on the bench outside the alehouse, watching them and thirstily drinking a cup of Blod's ale. On the pasture alongside the alehouse, a well-trained dog was watching over a small flock of sheep. The shepherd, Theodberht Clubfoot, was inside.

Blod was standing beside Ragna, having served her the drink then stayed to chat. 'That's a shame, my lady,' Blod said.

'Not necessarily.' Ragna was determined not to feel defeated. True, nothing had gone the way she planned, but she was going to make the best of things. She still had most of her life ahead of her, and she was going to live it to the full.

Blod said: 'When would you go?'

'Not yet. I need to spend time at Outhenham before I leave. Long term, my idea is to have two good houses, one here and one at Outhenham, and return to England every year or two to keep an eye on my property.'

'Why? You might get someone else to do the work so that you can just sit back and count the money.'

'I couldn't do that. I always thought it was my destiny to be a ruler, dispensing justice, helping to make a place more prosperous.'

'It's usually men who rule.'

'Usually, but not always. And I've never enjoyed idleness.'

'I've never tried it.'

Ragna smiled. 'I feel sure you wouldn't like it.'

Cwenburg, the wife of Erman and Eadbald, walked by with a basket of silvery fish fresh from the pond, some of them still flipping their tails. Ragna guessed she was heading for the house of Bucca Fish. Cwenburg had always been plump, Ragna recalled, but now she was quite fat. In her twenties she had lost the vigorous freshness of youth, and was no longer even mildly attractive. However, Edgar's brothers seemed content with her. It was an unusual arrangement but it had worked for nine years now.

Cwenburg stopped to speak to Dreng, her father, who was just coming out of a storehouse with a wooden shovel in his hand. It was always a little surprising to see unkind, unpleasant people showing affection, Ragna mused. Then her thoughts were interrupted by an angry shout from inside the alehouse.

A moment later Theodberht hobbled out, fastening his belt. 'She's pregnant!' he said angrily. 'I'm not paying a penny for a pregnant whore!'

Dreng came hurrying up, still holding the shovel. 'What's this?' he said. 'What's the matter?'

Theodberht repeated his complaint at the top of his voice.

'I didn't know that!' said Dreng. 'I paid a pound for her at Bristol market and that was not even a year ago.'

'Give me back that penny!' said Theodberht.

'Cursed girl, I'll teach her a lesson.'

Ragna said: 'It's your fault she's pregnant, Dreng – don't you understand that?'

Dreng replied to Ragna with surly formality. 'My lady, they only get pregnant if they enjoy the shagging, everyone knows that.' He fumbled in his belt purse and gave Theodberht a silver penny. 'Have another cup of ale, my friend, forget about the whore.'

Theodberht took the money with ill grace and walked towards the pasture, whistling to his dog.

'He would have drunk a gallon of ale and stayed the night,' Dreng said sourly. 'Might even have paid for another tumble in the morning. Now I've lost that money.' He limped inside.

Ragna said to Blod: 'What a fool. If he prostitutes the poor girl, she's almost certain to get pregnant sooner or later – doesn't he know that?'

'Who told you Dreng was a rational man?'

'I hope he isn't going to punish her?'

Blod shrugged.

Ragna said: 'The law is that a man can't kill or beat a slave unreasonably.'

'But who says what is unreasonable?'

'I do, usually.'

They heard a cry of pain from inside, then a grunt of rage, then sobbing. Both women got to their feet, then hesitated. There was a silence for several seconds. Blod said: 'If that's all . . .'

Then they heard Mairead scream.

They rushed inside.

She was on the floor, covering her belly with her arms. She had a head wound, and bright red blood was soaking into her dark-red hair. Dreng stood over her, the shovel held in both hands and raised above his head. He was yelling incoherently. His wife, Ethel, was crouching in a corner, watching with a terrified face.

Ragna shouted: 'Stop that at once!'

Dreng brought the shovel down hard on Mairead's body.

Ragna repeated: 'Stop that!'

From the corner of her eye she saw Blod grab the oak bucket that was kept on a peg behind the door. As Dreng raised the shovel to hit Mairead again, Blod lifted the heavy bucket to strike him. Then Dreng staggered.

He dropped the shovel, and one hand went to his chest.

Blod lowered the bucket.

Dreng groaned and fell to his knees, saying: 'Jesus, it hurts!'

Ragna froze, staring at him. Why was he in pain? He had been giving a beating, not suffering one. Was this an act of a vengeful God?

Dreng toppled forwards and fell with his face on the stone surround of the hearth. Ragna leaped to him, grabbed his ankles, and pulled him away from the flames. His body was limp. She rolled him over. His long nose had been smashed in the fall and there was blood all over his mouth and chin.

He was not moving.

She put her hand on his chest. He seemed not to be breathing. She could not feel a heartbeat.

She turned to Mairead. 'How badly are you hurt?' she said.

'My head is agony,' she answered. She rolled over and sat upright with one hand on her belly. 'But I don't think he injured the baby.'

Ragna heard Cwenburg's voice from the doorway. 'Father! Father!'

Cwenburg ran in, dropped her basket of fish and fell to her knees beside Dreng. 'Speak to me, Father!'

Dreng did not move.

Cwenburg looked over her shoulder at Blod. 'You've killed him!' She leaped to her feet. 'You murdering slave, I'm going to kill you!'

She flew at Blod, but Ragna intervened. She grabbed Cwenburg from behind, grasping both her arms, restraining her. 'Stand still!' she commanded.

Cwenburg ceased to struggle but yelled: 'She killed him! She hit him with that bucket!'

Blod still had the oak bucket in her hand. 'I didn't hit anyone,' she said. She put the bucket back on its peg. 'Your father was the only person doing that.'

'Liar!'

'He used that shovel on Mairead.'

Ragna said: 'She's telling the truth, Cwenburg. Your father was beating Mairead and he suffered some kind of seizure. He fell face-down onto the hearth, and I pulled him out of the fire. But he was already dead.'

Cwenburg went limp. Ragna released her and she sat down abruptly on the floor, weeping. She was probably the only person who would weep for Dreng, Ragna thought.

Several villagers crowded into the house, staring at the corpse in the centre of the room. Then Aldred came in. Seeing the body on the floor he crossed himself and murmured a short prayer.

Ragna was the most high-ranking person there, but Aldred was the landlord, and normally took responsibility for justice. However, he had no interest in squabbles over precedence, and he came straight to Ragna and said: 'What happened?'

She told him.

Ethel stood up and spoke for the first time. 'What am I going to do?' she said.

Aldred said: 'Well, you own the alehouse, now.'

Ragna had not thought of that.

Cwenburg made a sudden recovery. 'No she doesn't.' She got to her feet. 'My father wanted me to inherit the alehouse.'

Aldred frowned. 'Did he make a will?'

'No, but he told me.'

'That doesn't count. The widow inherits.'

'She can't run an alehouse!' Cwenburg said scornfully. 'She's always sick. I can, especially with Erman and Eadbald to help me.'

Ragna was sure Edgar would disapprove of this. She said: 'Cwenburg, you and Erman and Eadbald are already rich, with your fish pond and your water mill, and paid labourers who do all the work on your farm. Do you really want to rob a widow of her livelihood?'

Cwenburg was abashed.

Ethel said: 'But I'm not very strong. I don't think I can manage it.'

Blod said: 'I'll help you.'

Ethel came over to her. 'Will you, really?'

'I'll have to. You own me, now, as well as the house.'

Mairead stood the other side of Ethel. 'You own me, too.'

'I'll free you in my will, I promise. Both of you.'

There was a murmur of approval from the watching villagers: freeing slaves was considered an act of piety.

Aldred said: 'A lot of witnesses have heard your generous promise, Ethel. If you want to change your mind, you should probably do it now.'

'I will never change my mind.'

Blod put her arm around Ethel, and Mairead did the same from the other side. Blod said: 'We three women can manage the alehouse and look after Mairead's baby – and make more money than Dreng ever did.'

'Yes,' said Ethel. 'Perhaps we can.'

ÞÞÞ

WYNSTAN FOUND HIMSELF in a strange place. Puzzled, he looked around. It was an unfamiliar market square on a summer day, with people buying and selling eggs and cheese and hats and shoes all around him. He could see a church, large enough to be a cathedral. Alongside it was a fine house. Opposite was what looked like a monastery. On a hill beyond the square was a fenced compound that suggested the residence of a wealthy thane, perhaps an alderman. He felt scared. How had he got so lost? He could not even remember how he had come here. He felt himself shaking with terror.

A stranger bowed to him and said: 'Good morning, bishop.'

He thought: Am I a bishop?

The stranger looked more closely at him and said: 'Are you all right, your reverence?'

Suddenly everything fell into place. He was the bishop of Shiring, the church was his cathedral, and the house next to it was his residence. 'Of course I'm all right,' he snapped.

The stranger, whom Wynstan now recognized as a butcher he had known for twenty years, walked rapidly away.

Feeling bewildered and frightened, Wynstan hurried to his house.

Inside was his cousin, Archdeacon Degbert, and Ithamar, a deacon of the cathedral. Ithamar's wife, Eangyth, was pouring a cup of wine.

Degbert said: 'Ithamar has some news.'

Ithamar looked scared. He said nothing while the maid set the wine on the table in front of him.

Wynstan was angry about his episode of forgetfulness, and he said impatiently: 'Well, come on, spit it out.'

Ithamar said: 'Alphage has been made archbishop of Canterbury.'

Wynstan was expecting this. Nevertheless, he felt a mad rage rise within him. Unable to control himself, he picked up a cup from the table and dashed the contents in Ithamar's face. Not satisfied with that, he overturned the table. Eangyth screamed, so he clenched his fist and hit her across the head as hard as he could. She lay still, and he thought he had killed her; then she stirred, got up, and ran out of the room. Ithamar followed her, wiping his eyes with the sleeve of his robe.

Degbert said nervously: 'Calm yourself, cousin. Sit down. Have a cup of wine. Are you hungry? Shall I get you something to eat?'

'Oh, shut up,' Wynstan said, but he sat down and drank the wine that Degbert gave him.

When he had calmed down Degbert said accusingly: 'You promised to make me bishop of Shiring.'

'I can't now, can I?' Wynstan said. 'There's no vacancy, you fool.'

Degbert looked as if that was a poor excuse.

'It's Ragna's fault,' Wynstan said. 'She started the stupid rumour that I had leprosy.' His rage began to return, and he seethed. 'Her punishment was much too light. All we did was take away one of her children. She has three left to console her. I should have thought of something worse. I should have put her to work in Mags's house until some filthy sailor gave *her* Whore's Leprosy.'

'You know she was in the room when my brother Dreng died? I suspect she killed him. They put it about that he had some kind of seizure while beating his slave girl, but I'm sure Ragna had something to do with it.'

'I don't care who killed Dreng,' Wynstan said. 'He may have been my cousin but he was a fool, and so are you. Get out.'

Degbert left, and Wynstan was alone.

Something was wrong with him. He had flown into a berserk rage on being given news that merely confirmed his expectations. He had nearly murdered a priest's wife. Worse, a few minutes earlier he had forgotten not only where he was but who he was.

I'm going mad, he said to himself, and the thought filled him with terror. He could not be mad. He was clever, he was ruthless, he always got his way. His allies were rewarded and his enemies were destroyed. The prospect of insanity was so horrifying as to be unbearable. He closed his eyes tight and banged both fists on the table in front of him, saying: 'No, no, no!' He had a sensation of falling, as if he had jumped off the roof of the cathedral. He was going to hit the ground any second, and he would be smashed up and then he would die. He struggled to restrain himself from screaming.

As the terror eased, he thought more about jumping off the roof. He would hit the ground, then suffer a moment of unbearable agony, then die. But how badly would he be punished for the sin of suicide?

He was a holy priest, he could expect forgiveness. But for suicide?

He could confess his sins, say Mass, and die in a state of grace, could he not?

He could not. He would die condemned.

Degbert came back carrying the embroidered cope that Wynstan wore for services. 'You're due in the cathedral,' he said. 'Unless you would prefer me to say Mass?'

'No, I'll do it,' said Wynstan, and he stood up.

Ithamar draped the vestment over Wynstan's shoulders.

Wynstan frowned. 'I was worrying about something a moment ago,' he said. 'I can't think what it was.'

Ithamar said nothing.

'Never mind,' said Wynstan. 'It can't have been important.'

ÞÞÞ

ETHEL WAS DYING.

Ragna sat in the alehouse late at night, with Blod and Mairead and Mairead's new baby, Brigid, long after the last customers had staggered out of the door. The room was lit by a smoky rush light. Ethel lay still with her eyes closed. Her breathing was shallow and her face was grey. Sister Agatha had said that the angels were calling her, and she was getting ready to go.

Blod and Mairead were planning to raise the baby together. 'We don't want men and we don't need them,' Blod said to Ragna. Ragna was not surprised by their feelings, after the lives they had been forced to lead; but there was something else. Ragna had a feeling that Blod's passion for Edgar might have been transferred to Mairead. It was only a feeling, and she was not sure and certainly would not ask.

Not long after dawn Ethel passed gently away. There was no crisis: she simply stopped breathing.

Blod and Mairead undressed her and washed the body. Ragna

asked the two slaves what they planned to do now. Ethel had said she would free them, and Aldred had assured them that she had made a will. They could return to their homes, if they wished; but it seemed they were planning to stay together.

'I can't travel to Ireland with a baby in my arms and no money,' Mairead said. 'Not that I would know where in Ireland my home is. It's a hamlet on the coast, but that's all I could tell you. If the place had a name, I never heard it. I'm not even sure how many days I was on the Viking ship before we got to Bristol.'

Ragna would help her with a little money, of course, but money would not solve the problem. She said: 'What about you, Blod?'

Blod looked thoughtful. 'It's ten years since I saw my home in Wales. All my young friends must now be married with children. I don't know whether my parents are alive or dead. I'm not sure how much I can remember of the Welsh language. I never imagined I would ever say this, but I almost feel as if this place is home.'

Ragna was not convinced. Was there something else at work here? Had Blod and Mairead become so attached to one another that they did not want to part?

The news of Ethel's death soon got around, and shortly after dawn Cwenburg showed up with her two husbands. The men looked sheepish but Cwenburg was aggressive. 'How dare you wash the body?' she said. 'That was my job – I'm her stepdaughter!'

Ragna said: 'They were only being helpful, Cwenburg.'

'I don't care. This alehouse is mine, now, and I want those slaves out of here.'

'They're no longer slaves,' Ragna said.

'If Ethel kept her promise.'

'Anyway, you can't throw them out of their home at a minute's notice.'

'Who says?'

'I do,' said Ragna.

Cwenburg said: 'Erman, go and fetch the prior.'

Erman left.

Cwenburg said: 'The slaves should wait outside.'

Ragna said: 'Perhaps you should wait outside, until Aldred confirms that the alehouse is now yours.'

Cwenburg looked sullen.

'Go on,' said Ragna. 'Out you go. Otherwise it will be the worse for you.'

Reluctantly, Cwenburg left, and Eadbald followed her out.

Ragna knelt beside the body, and Blod and Mairead did the same.

Aldred appeared a few minutes later, wearing a silver cross on a leather thong. Cwenburg and her husbands came in behind him. He made the sign of the cross and said a prayer over the corpse. Then he took a small sheet of parchment from the pouch at his belt.

'This is Ethel's last will and testament,' he said. 'Written by me at her dictation, and witnessed by two monks.'

Of the others present only Ragna could read, so they had to rely on Aldred to tell them what Ethel had done.

'As she promised, she frees both Blod and Mairead,' he said.

The two slaves embraced and kissed each other, smiling. Their celebration was muted by the presence of the corpse, but they were happy.

'There is only one other bequest,' Aldred said. 'She leaves all her worldly possessions, including the alehouse, to Blod.'

Blod's mouth fell open. 'It's mine?' she said incredulously.

'Yes.'

Cwenburg screamed: 'She can't do that! My stepmother can't steal my father's alehouse and then give it to a Welsh whore slave!'

'She can,' said Aldred.

Ragna said: 'And she just did.'

'It's unnatural!'

771

'No, it's not,' Ragna said. 'When Ethel was dying, it was Blod who cared for her, not you.'

'No, no!' Cwenburg stormed out, still screaming protests, and Erman and Eadbald followed her, looking embarrassed.

The noise died down as Cwenburg walked away.

Blod looked at Mairead. 'You'll stay and help me, won't you?'

'Of course.'

'I'll teach you to cook. But no more whoring.'

'And you can help me with the baby.'

'Of course.'

Tears came to Mairead's eyes, and she nodded wordlessly.

'It will be fine,' said Blod. She reached out and took Mairead's hand. 'We'll be happy.'

Ragna was glad for them, and something else.

After a few moments she figured out what it was.

She was envious.

ÞÞÞ

EVERY FEW MONTHS Giorgio, the master mason, sent Edgar to Cherbourg to buy supplies. It was a two-day journey, but there was nowhere nearer where they could get iron for making tools, lead for windows, and lime for mortar.

When he left this time, Clothild kissed him and told him to hurry back. He still had not proposed marriage to her, but everyone treated him as if he were already a member of Giorgio's family. He was not really comfortable with the way he had slipped, by imperceptible steps, into the role of Clothild's fiancé without a formal decision: it seemed weak. But he was not sufficiently unhappy about it to break away.

A few hours after he arrived in Cherbourg, a messenger found him and ordered him to go and see Count Hubert.

Edgar had met Hubert only once before, on his arrival in

772

Normandy almost three years ago. Hubert had been kind to him then. Glad to hear news of his beloved daughter, he had talked at length to Edgar about life in England, and had advised him of building sites where he might find employment.

Now Edgar again climbed the hill to the castle, and marvelled anew at its size. It was bigger than Shiring Cathedral, which had previously been the largest building he had ever seen. A servant showed him to a large room on the upstairs floor.

Hubert, now in his fifties, was at the far end of the room talking to Countess Genevieve and their handsome son, Richard, who looked about twenty.

Hubert was a small man with quick movements: Ragna's very different build, tall and statuesque, came from her mother. But Hubert had the red-gold hair and sea-green eyes, somewhat wasted on a man – in Edgar's view – but so overpoweringly alluring in Ragna.

The servant motioned Edgar to wait by the door, but Hubert caught his eye and beckoned.

Edgar expected Hubert to regard him benignly, as he had before, but now, approaching the count, Edgar saw that he looked angry and hostile. He wondered what he could possibly have done to infuriate Ragna's father.

Hubert said loudly: 'Tell me, Edgar, do Englishmen believe in Christian marriage, or not?'

Edgar had no idea what this was about, and all he could do was answer to the best of his ability. 'My lord, they are Christians, though they don't always obey the teachings of the priests.' He was about to add *just like Normans* but he stopped himself. He was no longer an adolescent and he had learned not to make clever ripostes.

Genevieve said: 'They are barbarians! Savages!'

Edgar assumed this must somehow be about their daughter. He said anxiously: 'Has something happened to the Lady Ragna?'

Hubert said: 'She has been set aside!'

'I didn't know that.'

'What the devil does it mean?'

'It means divorce,' Edgar said.

'For no reason?'

'Yes.' Edgar needed to be sure he had understood correctly. 'So Wigelm has set Ragna aside?'

'Yes! And you tell me this is legal in England!'

'Yes.' But Edgar was thunderstruck. Ragna was single!

Hubert said: 'I've written to King Ethelred demanding that he make recompense. How can he allow his noblemen to behave like farmyard animals?'

'I don't know, my lord,' said Edgar. 'A king can give orders, but enforcing them is another matter.'

Hubert snorted, as if he considered that a feeble excuse.

Edgar said: 'I'm terribly sorry this has been done to her by my countrymen.'

But he was lying.

41

RAGNA REBUILT HER LIFE, making her days busy so that she would not brood over the loss of both Edgar and Alain. At Michaelmas she went to Outhenham in her new barge to collect her rents.

The barge needed two strong oarsmen. Ragna took her horse, Astrid, with her so that she could ride all the way along the Vale of Outhen. She also took a new maid, Osgyth, and a young man-at-arms, a black-haired boy called Ceolwulf, both of them from King's Bridge. They fell for each other on the journey, teasing and giggling on the barge when they thought Ragna was not looking; so both were somewhat distracted from their duties. Ragna was inclined to be indulgent: she knew what it was to be in love. She hoped that Osgyth and Ceolwulf never learned what she knew about the misery that love could bring.

Her new great hall at Outhenham was not yet finished, but Edgar's old house in the quarry was empty, so she lodged there with Osgyth and Ceolwulf. She liked it for sentimental reasons. The only other house in the quarry belonged to Gab.

The oarsmen stayed at the alehouse.

She held court, but there was not much justice needed. This was a happy time of year, with the harvest in the barns, bellies full of bread, and red-cheeked apples lying on the ground to be picked up; and this year the Vikings had not come this far west to spoil everything. When people were happy they were slow to quarrel and committed fewer crimes. It was in the miserable depths of winter that men strangled their wives and knifed their rivals, and it was in the hungry spring that women stole from their neighbours to feed their children.

She was pleased to see that Edgar's canal was still in good condition, its edges straight and its banks sturdy. However, she was annoyed that the villagers had got into the lazy habit of throwing rubbish into the water. There was no through flow, so the canal did not clean itself the way a river did, and in places it smelled like a privy. She instituted a strict rule.

To enforce this and any other edicts she dismissed Dudda and appointed a new headman, one of the elders of the village, the roly-poly alehouse keeper Eanfrid. A taverner was usually a good choice for headman: his house was already the centre of village life and he himself was often a figure of unofficial authority. Eanfrid was also good-humoured and well liked.

Sitting outside the alehouse with a cup of cider she talked to Eanfrid about her income from the quarry, which had fallen since Edgar left. 'Edgar is just one of those people who does everything well,' said Eanfrid. 'Find us another one like him and we'll sell more stone.'

'There isn't another one like Edgar,' said Ragna with a sad smile.

They went on to discuss a murrain that had killed a number of sheep, and which Ragna thought was caused by grazing them on wet clay soil; but their conversation was interrupted. Eanfrid cocked his head, and a moment later Ragna heard what had caught his attention: the sound of thirty or more horses approaching, not cantering or even trotting but walking with weary steps. It was the noise made by a wealthy nobleman and his entourage on a long journey.

The autumn sun was red in the west: the visitors would undoubtedly decide to stay the night at Outhenham. The village would welcome them with mixed feelings. Travellers brought silver: they would buy food and drink, and pay for accommodation. But they might also get drunk and pester girls and start fights.

Ragna and Eanfrid stood up. A minute later the horsemen appeared, winding through the houses to the centre of the village.

At their head was Wigelm.

Ragna was possessed by fear. This was the man who had imprisoned her, raped her, and stolen her child. What new torture had he devised for her? She controlled her trembling. She had always stood up to him. She would do so again.

Riding beside Wigelm was his nephew Garulf, the son of Wilwulf and Inge. He was twenty-five now, but Ragna knew that he was no wiser than he had been as an adolescent. He looked like Wilf, with the fair beard and broad-shouldered swagger of the family men. She winced to think she had married two of them.

Eanfrid murmured: 'What does Wigelm want here?'

'Only God knows,' Ragna replied in a shaky voice, then she added: 'And maybe Satan.'

Wigelm reined in his dusty horse. 'I didn't expect to see you here, Ragna,' he said.

She was somewhat relieved. His remark indicated that he had not planned this meeting. Any evil he tried to do her would be improvised. 'I don't know why you'd be surprised,' she said. 'I'm lord of the Vale of Outhen. What do you want here?'

'I'm ealdorman of Shiring, I'm travelling in my territory, and I intend to spend the night here.'

'Outhenham welcomes you, Ealdorman Wigelm,' Ragna said with cold formality. 'Please enter the alehouse and take refreshment.'

He remained on his horse. 'Your father complained to King Ethelred,' he said.

'Of course he did.' She got some of her nerve back. 'Your behaviour has been disgraceful.'

'Ethelred fined me one hundred pounds of silver for setting you aside without his permission.'

'Good.'

'I didn't pay the fine, though,' said Wigelm; and he laughed heartily, then dismounted.

His men followed suit. The younger ones set about unsaddling the horses while the seniors settled in the alehouse and called for drink. Ragna would have liked to retire, but she felt she could not leave Eanfrid alone to cope with this visitation – he might struggle to keep order, and her authority would help.

She moved around the village, doing her best to stay out of Wigelm's sight. She told the young men to put the horses to graze in a neighbouring pasture. Then she picked out the houses where Wigelm and his entourage might spend the night, choosing the homes of older couples or young marrieds with small babies, avoiding those where there were adolescent girls. It was usual to pay the householder a penny for accommodating four men, and the family were expected to share their breakfast with the guests.

The village priest, Draca, who raised beef cattle, butchered a young steer and sold it to Eanfrid, who built a fire behind the tavern and roasted the joints on a spit. While the men were waiting for the meat they drank ale, and Eanfrid emptied two barrels and opened a third.

They spent an hour singing raucous anthems of violence and sex, then became argumentative. Just when Ragna feared a fight was imminent, Eanfrid served the beef, with bread and onions, which shut them up. After eating they began to drift off to their lodgings, and Ragna judged she could safely go to bed.

She returned to the house in the quarry with Osgyth and Ceolwulf. They barred the door firmly. They had brought blankets with them, but it was not yet winter-cold, and they lay down in the straw wrapped only in their cloaks. Ceolwulf lay across the door, the approved position for a bodyguard, but Ragna caught a look between the two young people and guessed they planned to move closer together later.

Ragna lay awake for an hour or more, unnerved by the surprise appearance of her enemy Wigelm; but finally she drifted into a perturbed sleep.

She awoke with the sense that she had not been asleep long. She sat up and looked around, frowning, wondering uneasily what had disturbed her. In the firelight she saw that Osgyth and Ceolwulf had gone. She guessed they wanted to be alone, and had slipped away into the woods, where they were now probably under a bush, discovering sex in the moonlight.

She was less inclined to be indulgent now. They were supposed to care for her and protect her, not sneak off and leave her alone in the middle of the night. They would both be sacked when they got back to King's Bridge.

She heard a drunk man talking loudly and incoherently, and guessed it was Gab. The voice must be what had awakened her. However, she was safe behind a barred door, she thought; then she realized that Osgyth and Ceolwulf must have unbarred the door to get out.

The drunk came closer, and she recognized the voice. It was not Gab, but Wigelm, she realized with a fearful chill.

He had found her house easily, despite his state, she guessed in a dreadful flash – he had simply followed the canal – but it was a tragic miracle that he had not fallen in the water and drowned.

She leaped to secure the door, but she was a moment too late. As she put her hands on the heavy timber bar, the door opened and Wigelm stepped in. She sprang back with a cry of fear.

Wigelm was barefoot and without a cloak, despite the chill of the autumn night. He was not wearing a belt or carrying a sword or knife, which gave some relief to Ragna. He looked as if he had got up from his bed and had not troubled to get properly dressed.

There was a strong, sour smell of ale.

He peered at her in the firelight as if unsure who she was. He was swaying, and she realized that he was very drunk. For a moment she optimistically hoped he might pass out right there and then, but his puzzled expression cleared and he said in a slurred voice: 'Ragna. Yes. I was looking for you.'

I can't take this, Ragna thought. I can't suffer any more by this man. I want to die.

She tried to hide her despair. 'Please go away.'

'Lie down.'

'I'll scream. Gab and his wife will hear me.' She was not sure that was true: the two houses were widely separated.

Her threat was ineffective for a different reason. 'What will they do?' he said scornfully. 'I'm their ealdorman.'

'Get out of my house.'

He shoved her hard. Caught off balance, and surprised by how strong he was despite being drunk, she fell on her back. The impact knocked the wind out of her.

He said: 'Shut your mouth and open your legs.'

She caught her breath. 'You can't do this, I'm no longer your wife.'

He toppled forward. Clearly he intended to land on her, but at the last moment she rolled sideways, and he fell on his face. She got up on her hands and knees, but at the same time he turned on his back and grabbed her arm, pulling her towards him.

Trying to keep her balance, she moved her leg and, without intending it, planted her knee squarely in his belly. He said: 'Oof!' and gasped.

Ragna moved the other leg so that both knees were in his belly, then she grabbed his arms and pressed them to the ground. In normal circumstances he could have thrown her off easily, but now he was unable to shake her.

It was an ironic reversal. For the first time ever, she had him at her mercy.

But what was she going to do?

His head moved from side to side, his eyes closed, and he gasped: 'Can't breathe.'

She realized that her knees were constricting his lungs, but she did not move to ease him, because she was terrified that he might regain his strength.

He seemed to convulse, and there was a smell of vomit. Liquid trickled from the corners of his mouth. His arms and legs went limp.

Ragna had heard of drunk men passing out and choking to death on their own puke. She realized, in a moment, that if Wigelm were to die now she would get Alain back: no one would say he should be raised by Meganthryth. A momentary wave of hope passed over her. She would have prayed for Wigelm to die, except that such a prayer seemed blasphemous.

Wigelm was not dying. His nose was full of liquid vomit but air was bubbling through it.

Could she kill him?

It would be a sin, and it would be dangerous. She would be a murderess and, although there was no one here to see what she was doing, she might nevertheless be found out somehow.

But she wanted him dead.

She thought of the year in prison, and the repeated rape, and the theft of her child. By forcing his way into her house tonight he had shown that his torture of her would never end, not while he lived. She had taken all she could stand; it had to end here and now.

God forgive me, she thought.

Tentatively, she took her hands away from his arms. He did not move.

She closed his mouth, then placed her left hand over his lips and pressed firmly.

He could still breathe through his nose, just.

She put her right forefinger and thumb either side of his nose and squeezed his nostrils.

Now he could not breathe.

She had not killed him, not yet; there was still time to change her mind, to release her grip. She could roll him over and clear the fluid from his mouth and enable him to breathe. He would probably survive.

Survive to attack her again.

She maintained her hold on his mouth and nose. She waited, watching his face. How long did a man live without air? She had no idea.

He twitched, but he seemed barely conscious, and could not struggle. Ragna remained with her knees in his belly, closing his mouth with one hand and his nose with the other. All his motion ceased.

Was he dead now?

The house was silent. The embers in the fire made no sound, and there was no rustle of small creatures in the rushes on the floor. She listened for footsteps outside but heard none.

Suddenly Wigelm opened his eyes. The shock made her shriek with fear.

He looked with terror at Ragna. He tried to shake his head but she leaned forward, pressing down harder with her two hands, holding him still.

He stared into her eyes, in a half-conscious panic, for a long moment of high tension. He was in fear of his life but he could not move, like a man in a nightmare. 'This is how it feels, Wigelm,' she said, her voice taut with loathing. 'This is what it's like to be helpless at the mercy of a killer.'

Suddenly his feeble efforts ceased and his eyes rolled up into his head.

Still Ragna held her grip. Was he really dead? She could hardly believe that the man who had tormented her for so long might have left this world for good.

At last she summoned the courage to release her pressure on his nose and mouth. His face showed no change. She put her hand on his chest and felt no heartbeat.

She had killed him.

'God forgive me,' she prayed.

She found herself shaking uncontrollably. Her hands trembled, her shoulders shuddered, and her thighs felt so weak she wanted to lie down.

She struggled to control her body. What she needed to worry about right now was how men would react. No one would believe her innocent. The ealdorman, her great enemy, had died in the middle of the night with no one present but her. The evidence was incriminating.

She was a murderess.

At last she became steady and stood up.

It was not over yet. What would tell against her most was that the body was here with her. She had to move it. But where could she put it? The answer was obvious.

In the canal.

Wigelm's drunken companions would have assumed he had gone to take a piss. In his state he could easily have passed out, fallen in the canal, and drowned before he could come round. That was exactly the kind of thing drunken fools did.

But no one must see her disposing of the body. She needed to move quickly, before Osgyth and Ceolwulf tired of canoodling and came back, before one of Wigelm's half-conscious men began to wonder what was taking him so long and decided to go in search.

She grabbed one leg and heaved. It took more effort than she had expected. She moved him a yard then stopped. It was too much. He was a heavy man and, literally, a dead weight.

She could not be defeated by such a simple problem. Her horse, Astrid, was in a nearby pasture. If necessary, Ragna would fetch the horse to drag the body – though that would take time and increase the risk of discovery. It would be quicker if she could put Wigelm on something, like a board. She remembered the blankets.

She took one and spread it on the floor next to Wigelm. With considerable effort she rolled him onto the blanket. Then she seized the head end and pulled. It was not easy, but it was possible, and she dragged him across the floor and out through the door.

She looked around in the moonlight and saw no one. Gab's house was dark and quiet. Osgyth and Ceolwulf must still be in the woods, and there was no sign of a search party looking for Wigelm. Only the inhabitants of the night surrounded her: an owl hooting in the trees, a small rodent scurrying past so quickly that she saw it only out of the corner of her eye, the distinct swooping movement of a silent bat.

She decided she could manage without Astrid, just about. She hauled Wigelm slowly across the quarry floor. The body made a scraping noise as it moved, but not loud enough to be heard in Gab's house.

From the quarry the ground sloped up gently, and her work became harder. She was already panting from the effort. She rested for a minute, then forced herself to resume the task. It was not much farther.

At last she reached the canal. She lugged him to the edge and rolled him in. There was a splash that sounded loud to her, and a smell of waste and rot from the disturbed water. Then the surface calmed, and Wigelm steadied, face down. She saw a dead squirrel floating next to his face.

She rested, breathing hard, exhausted, but after a minute she realized this was not good enough. The corpse was still close enough to the house to arouse suspicion. She had to move it farther away.

If she had had a rope, she could have tied it to him then walked along the bank, pulling Wigelm through the water. But she did not have a rope.

She thought of riding equipment. Astrid was in a field but her saddle and other tack were in the house. She returned there. She folded the blanket and put it at the bottom of the pile, hoping its dirty state would not be noticed for many days. Then she detached the reins from the bridle.

She returned to the canal. Still there was no one in sight. She reached across the water and grabbed the corpse by the hair. She pulled it to her, then fastened the strap around the neck. She stood up, tugged on the strap, and walked along the canal bank towards the village.

A part of her exulted to think that Wigelm was now so powerless that she could lead him along like a dumb animal.

She scanned all around her, peering into the shadows under the trees, scared that at any second she might run into some night-time wanderer. In the moonlight she saw a pair of yellow eyes, which gave her a momentary fright, until she realized she was looking at a cat.

As she neared the village she heard raised voices. She cursed. It sounded as though Wigelm's absence had been noticed.

She was not yet far enough from the quarry to divert suspicion. To rest her arm she changed hands and walked backwards, but she could not see where she was going and, after stumbling twice, she put the tired arm back to work again. Her legs began to ache too.

She saw lights moving among the houses. Wigelm's men were looking for him, almost certainly. They were too drunk to search systematically, and their calls to one another were incoherent. But all the same one of them might spot her by chance. And if she were caught dragging Wigelm's corpse along the canal, there would be no doubt about her guilt.

She kept moving. One of the searchers came towards the canal with a lamp. Ragna stopped, got down on the ground, and lay still, watching the jerky movement of the light. What would she do if it came nearer? What story could she possibly tell to explain Wigelm's corpse and her strap?

But the light seemed to go in the opposite direction and fade. When it disappeared she got to her feet and carried on.

She passed the back of one village house, then another, and decided that was far enough. Wigelm had been incapable of walking in a straight line so it would be assumed he had not taken the most direct route to the canal, but had staggered around at random on his way.

She knelt down, put her hands in the water, and unfastened the strap from Wigelm's neck. Then she pushed his body out into the middle of the canal. 'That way to hell,' she murmured.

She turned and hurried back to the quarry.

There was no movement around Gab's house or Edgar's. She hoped the lovebirds had not returned in her absence: she was not sure how she would explain what she had been doing.

She crossed the quarry with quiet steps and entered the house. No one was there.

She took her place in the straw and closed her eyes.

I believe I got away with it, she thought.

She knew she should have been full of guilt, but all she could do was rejoice.

She did not sleep. She relived the night in her head, from the moment she had heard Wigelm's slurred voice to her final rush back along the bank of the canal. She asked herself whether she had done enough to make the death look like a drunken accident. Was there anything about the corpse that might cause suspicion? Had she perhaps been seen by someone who did not reveal himself? Had her absence from the house somehow been noticed?

She heard the door creak and guessed that Osgyth and Ceolwulf had returned. She pretended to be fast asleep. There was a soft thud as the bar was replaced – too late, she thought resentfully. She heard their tiptoed footsteps, a smothered giggle, and soft rustling as they lay down. She guessed that Ceolwulf had resumed his guard position, lying across the doorway, so that no one could get in without waking him.

Both young people were soon breathing rhythmically.

Clearly they had no idea of the night's drama. And now Ragna saw that their negligence would work in her favour. If asked, they would swear that they had been in the house all night, guarding their mistress as was their duty. Their dishonesty would give her an alibi.

Soon it would be a new day, a happy day, her first in a world without Wigelm.

She hardly dared to think about Alain. With Wigelm dead, surely she would get her child back? No one would want Meganthryth to raise him, now that Wigelm was no longer around to bully them – would they? It would make no sense, but it might be done out of spite. Wigelm was gone, but his evil brother, Wynstan, was still alive. People said Wynstan was going mad, but that only made him even more dangerous.

She fell into a fretful doze and was awakened by a knock at the door, three sharp taps, polite but urgent. A voice said: 'My lady! Eanfrid here.'

Now for the aftermath, she thought.

She stood up, brushed off her dress, and smoothed her hair, then said: 'Let him in, Ceolwulf.'

Dawn was breaking, she saw when the door was opened. Eanfrid entered, red-faced and panting from the effort of carrying his considerable bulk at a fast walk. Without preamble he said: 'Wigelm is missing.'

Ragna adopted a tone of brisk efficiency. 'Where was he when you last saw him?'

'He was in my alehouse, still drinking with Garulf and others, when I fell asleep.'

'Has anyone looked for him?'

'His men have been wandering around calling his name half the night.'

'I didn't hear anything.' Ragna turned to her servants. 'Did you?'

Osgyth said quickly: 'Nothing, my lady. It was quiet here the whole night through.'

Ragna was keen to get them both to commit to lying. She said: 'Did either of you go outside at all in the night, even just to piss or anything?'

Osgyth shook her head, and Ceolwulf said firmly: 'I didn't move from my place by the door.'

'Right.' She was satisfied. It would now be difficult for them to change their story. 'It's daylight, so we must organize a systematic search.'

They walked to the village. Passing the canal brought grim thoughts but Ragna pushed them to the back of her mind. She went to the priest's house and banged on the door. The church did not have a bell tower, but Draca had a handbell. The shaven-headed priest appeared and Ragna said briskly: 'Lend me your bell, please.' He produced it and she rang vigorously.

People who were already up and about came immediately to the green between the church and the alehouse. Others followed, buckling their belts and rubbing their eyes. Most of Wigelm's party looked much the worse for their revels.

The sun was rising by the time everyone had assembled. Ragna spoke so that all could hear. 'We'll form three search parties,' she said in a tone that did not invite discussion. She pointed at the priest. 'Draca, take three villagers and search the west pasture. Go around the edges and all the way to the river bank.' Next she chose the baker, a solidly reliable man. 'Wilmund, you take three men-at-arms and search the east ploughland. Again, make sure you're thorough and go all the way to the canal.' Wilmund would find the corpse if he was meticulous. Finally she turned to Garulf, whom she wanted out of the way. 'Garulf, take everyone else to the north wood. That's where your uncle is most likely to be. My guess is he lost his way in a drunken stupor. You'll probably find him asleep under a bush.' The men laughed. 'All right, move out!'

The three search parties left.

Ragna knew she had to act normally. 'I could do with some breakfast,' she said to Eanfrid, though in truth she was still too wound up to be hungry. 'Get me some ale and bread and an egg.' She led the way into the tavern.

Eanfrid's wife brought her a jug and a loaf and quickly cooked an egg. Ragna drank the ale and forced herself to eat, and she felt better despite her lack of sleep.

What would the men-at-arms say when the body was found? In the night Ragna had assumed that they would jump to the obvious conclusion; that Wigelm had died in a drunken accident. But now she saw that there were other possibilities. Would they suspect foul play? And if they did, what could they do about it? Fortunately, there was no one here who ranked high enough to challenge Ragna's authority.

As she had intended, Wilmund's group found the body.

What she had not expected was the shock she felt when she looked at the corpse of the man she had killed.

Wigelm was carried into the village by Wilmund and one of Wigelm's entourage, Bada. As soon as Ragna saw his body she began to feel the horror of what she had done.

Last night she had been full of fear until Wigelm died, and then suffused with relief that he was gone. Now she remembered that she had suffocated Wigelm, and had watched his face while, moment by moment, the life left his body. At the time she had felt nothing but terror but now, when she remembered the scene, she was sick with guilt.

She had seen dead people plenty of times, but this was different. She felt she was going to faint, or cry, or scream.

She struggled to remain calm. She had to conduct an inquest, and she needed to manage it carefully. She must not seem too eager to reach the obvious verdict. And she must show no fear.

She ordered the men to lay the corpse on a trestle table in the church, and she sent messengers to recall the other two search parties.

Everyone crowded into the little church, whispering out of respect, staring at the dead white face of Wigelm, and watching his clothes drip canal water onto the floor.

Ragna began by speaking to Garulf, the highest-ranking man among Wigelm's entourage. 'Last night,' she said to him, 'you were among the last drinkers in the alehouse.' Her voice seemed to her to sound unnaturally calm, but no one noticed. 'Did you see Wigelm fall asleep?'

Garulf looked shocked and scared, and had trouble answering the simple question. 'Um, I don't know, wait, no, I think I closed my eyes before he did.'

Ragna led him along. 'Did you see him again after that?'

He scratched his stubbled chin. 'After I fell asleep? No, I was asleep. But hold on. Yes. He must have got up, because he stumbled over me and that woke me.'

'You saw his face.'

'In the firelight, yes, and heard his voice.'

'What did he say?'

'He said: "I'm going to piss in Edgar's canal".'

Some of the men laughed, then stopped abruptly when they realized it was inappropriate.

'And then he went out?'

'Yes.'

'What happened next?'

Garulf was regaining his composure, and making more sense. 'Some time later, someone woke me by saying: "Wigelm seems to be having a very long piss".'

'What did you do?'

'I went back to sleep.'

'Did you see him again?'

'Not alive, no.'

'What do you think happened?'

'I think he fell into the canal and drowned.'

There was a murmur of agreement from the crowd. Ragna was pleased. She had led them to the result she wanted while letting them think it had been their own decision.

She looked around the church. 'Did anyone see Wigelm after he left the tavern in the middle of the night?'

No one answered.

'To the best of our knowledge, then, the cause of death was accidental drowning.'

To her surprise Bada, the man-at-arms who had helped carry Wigelm from the canal to the church, spoke up in dissent. 'I don't think he drowned,' he said.

Ragna had been afraid of something like this. She hid her anxiety and put on an expression of interest. 'What makes you say that, Bada?'

'I've taken a drowned man out of the water before. When you lift him, a lot of fluid comes out of his mouth. It's the water he breathed in, the water that killed him. But when we lifted Wigelm, nothing came out.'

'Now that's curious, but I'm not sure it gets us anywhere.' Ragna turned to the baker. 'Did you see that, Wilmund?'

'I didn't notice it,' the baker said.

Bada said insistently: 'I did, though.'

'What do you think it signifies, Bada?'

'It shows that he was dead before he went in the water.'

Ragna remembered holding Wigelm's mouth and nose so that he could not breathe. The picture kept returning to her mind no matter how hard she tried. With an effort she thought of the next question. 'So how did he die?'

'Maybe someone killed him, then threw the body in the water.' Bada looked defiantly around the church. 'Someone who hated him, perhaps. Someone who felt wronged by him.'

Ragna was being accused by implication. Everyone knew she had hated Wigelm. If the charge were made openly, she was confident that the villagers would loyally take her side; but she did not want things to go that far.

She walked slowly and deliberately around the body. With difficulty, she made her voice calm and confident. 'Come closer, Bada,' she said. 'Look carefully.'

The room went quiet.

Bada did as she said.

'If he didn't drown, how was he killed?'

Bada said nothing.

'Do you see a wound? Any blood? A bruise, even? Because I don't.'

She was suddenly scared by a new thought. The strap she had used to pull the corpse along the canal might have left a red mark. Discreetly, she looked hard at the skin of his throat, but to her relief nothing was visible.

'Well, Bada?'

Bada just looked sulky.

'Anybody,' Ragna said to the crowd. 'Come as near as you like. Inspect the body. Look for signs of violence.'

Several people stepped forward and peered closely at Wigelm. One by one they shook their heads and stepped back.

Ragna said: 'Sometimes a man just drops dead, especially one who has been getting drunk every evening for years. It's possible Wigelm suffered some kind of seizure while pissing in the canal. Perhaps he died and then fell into the water. We may never know. But there's no sign that it was anything but an accident, is there?'

Once again the crowd murmured assent.

Bada looked mulish. 'I've heard tell,' he said, 'that if a murderer touches the corpse of his victim, the dead man will bleed afresh.'

A chill went through Ragna. She had heard that, too, though she had never seen it happen and did not really believe it. But she was going to have to test the truth of the superstition now.

She said to Bada: 'Who would you like to see touch the body?'

'You,' said Bada.

Ragna struggled to hide her fear. Pretending supreme confidence, she said: 'Watch, everyone.' Unfortunately she could not quite stop the tremor in her voice. She lifted her right arm high, then brought it down slowly.

In the version she had heard, when she touched Wigelm blood would pour from his nose, mouth and ears.

At last she laid a hand on Wigelm's heart.

She kept it there for a long moment. The church was silent. The body was horribly cold. She felt faint.

Nothing happened.

The corpse did not move. No blood appeared. Nothing.

Feeling as if her life had been saved, she lifted her hand, and the crowd gave a collective sigh of relief.

Ragna said: 'Anyone else you suspect, Bada?'

Bada shook his head.

Ragna said: 'Wigelm died in the canal when drunk. That is the verdict, and this inquest is over.'

The people began to leave the church, talking among themselves. Ragna listened to the tone of the collective murmur and heard satisfied conviction.

But they were not the only people she needed to convince. The city of Shiring was much more important. She needed to make sure her version of events, as backed up by the Outhenham verdict, was the one repeated in the alehouses and brothels tomorrow.

And for that she had to get there first.

The men most likely to make trouble for her were Garulf and Bada. She thought of a way to make sure they were detained here in Outhenham.

She summoned them. 'You two are responsible for the ealdorman's body,' she said. 'Go now to Edmund the carpenter and tell him I command him to make a coffin for Wigelm. He should be able to finish it by this evening or tomorrow morning. Then you are to escort the body to Shiring for burial in the cathedral graveyard. Is that clear?'

Bada looked at Garulf.

'Yes,' Garulf said. He seemed glad to have someone tell him what to do.

Bada was not so compliant.

Ragna said: 'Bada, is that clear?'

He was forced to back down. 'Yes, my lady.'

Ragna would leave immediately, but without warning. Quietly, she said: 'Ceolwulf, find the oarsmen and bring them to the quarry.'

Ceolwulf was young enough to be cheeky. He said: 'What for?'

She made her voice coldly severe. 'Don't you dare question me. Just do as you're told.'

'Yes, my lady.'

'Osgyth, come with me.'

Back at the house she told Osgyth to pack. When Ceolwulf arrived she ordered him to saddle Astrid.

One of the oarsmen said: 'Are we going back to King's Bridge?'

Ragna did not want to give anyone a chance to betray her plans. 'Yes,' she said. It was half true.

When they were ready she rode along the side of the canal with her servants accompanying her on foot. At the riverside they boarded the barge.

Then she told the oarsmen to row her to the opposite bank. Having heard Ceolwulf snapped at for insolence, they did not question her.

They tied up and she walked Astrid off the barge.

'Ceolwulf and Osgyth, come with me,' she said. 'You two, row the barge back to King's Bridge and wait for me there.'

Then she turned her horse in the direction of Shiring.

ÞÞÞ

RAGNA WAS NERVOUS about being reunited with her child.

She had not seen Alain for six months, which was a long time in the life of a toddler. He was now three years old. Did he now think Meganthryth was his mother? Would he even remember Ragna? When she took him away, would he cry for Meganthryth? Should Ragna tell him that his father was dead?

She did not have to confront these questions immediately upon arrival. It was dark. The search and the inquest at Outhenham had taken up most of the morning, so she arrived in Shiring in the evening, when little children were asleep and the grown-ups were preparing supper. She would not wake Alain. When she was married to Wigelm he had sometimes taken it into his head to visit his son late in the evening, and always insisted on waking the child. Alain would grizzle sleepily until he was put down again, and then Wigelm would accuse Ragna of turning his son against him. But the fault was his own. Ragna would not make the same mistake. She would not go to the ealdorman's compound until the morning. 'We'll stay with Sheriff Den tonight,' she said to her servants.

She found Den sitting with his wife, Wilburgh, while supper was prepared in his great hall. 'I've just come from Outhenham,' Ragna said. 'Wigelm died there last night.'

Wilburgh said: 'Heaven be praised.'

Den asked the key question. 'How did he die?' he said calmly.

'He got drunk and fell in the canal and drowned.'

'No surprise.' Den nodded. 'It's a pity you were there, though. People will suspect you.'

'I know. But there were no signs of violence on the body, and the villagers are satisfied that it was an accident.'

'Good.'

'I need to spend the night here in your compound.'

'Of course. Let's get you settled in, then you and I must talk about what happens next.'

Den assigned her an empty house. It might have been the one in which she had lain with Edgar, for the first and only time, four years ago. She remembered every detail of their lovemaking, but she was not sure which house they had had. She wished she could make love to him again.

She left Osgyth and Ceolwulf to light the fire and make the place comfortable, and she returned to Den's house. 'I'm going to take my son Alain back tomorrow morning,' she said. 'There's no reason for him to stay with Wigelm's concubine.'

Wilburgh said: 'I should think so too.'

'I agree,' said Den.

'Sit down, my lady, please,' said Wilburgh. She brought a jug of wine and three cups.

Ragna said: 'I hope King Ethelred will support me.'

'I believe he will,' said Den. 'In any case, it will be the least of his concerns.'

Ragna had not thought about the king's other concerns. 'What do you mean?'

'The main question is who will become ealdorman now.'

Ragna had had too much else to worry about: the body, the inquest, getting to Shiring first, and most of all Alain. But now that Den had raised the subject she saw that it was a matter of pressing urgency. It would affect her future profoundly. She wished she had given it more thought.

Den said: 'I'm going to tell the king that there's only one practical answer.'

Ragna could not guess what he meant. 'Tell me.'

'You and I have to rule Shiring together.'

Ragna was thunderstruck. She said nothing for a long moment. Finally she managed: 'Why?'

'Think about it,' Den said. 'Wigelm's heir is Alain. Your son inherits the town of Combe. And the king ruled that Wigelm was Wilwulf's heir, so all of Wilwulf's lands also now come to Alain.' He paused, to let that sink in, then he said: 'Your little boy is now one of the richest men in England.'

'Of course he is.' Ragna felt stupid. 'I just hadn't thought it through.'

'He's two years old, isn't he?'

Wilburgh said: 'More like three, now.'

'Yes,' said Ragna. 'He's three.'

'So you will be lord of all his lands for the next decade at least. In addition to the Vale of Outhen.'

'This depends on the king's approval.'

'True, but I can't imagine him doing anything else. Every nobleman in England will be watching to see how Ethelred handles this. They like to see wealth passed from father to son, because they want their own sons to inherit.'

Ragna sipped wine thoughtfully. 'The king doesn't have to do everything the nobles want, of course, but if he doesn't, they can make trouble.'

'Exactly.'

'But who will be named as the new ealdorman?'

'If it could be a woman, Ethelred would choose you. You have the wealth and status, and you're known to be a fair judge. They call you Ragna the Just.'

'But a woman can't be ealdorman.'

'No. Nor raise armies and lead them into battle against the Vikings.'

'So you will do that.'

'I'm going to propose to the king that he make me regent until Alain is old enough to rule as ealdorman. I will manage the defence of Shiring against Viking raids, and continue to collect taxes for the king. You will hold court, on behalf of Alain, in Shiring and Combe as well as Outhenham, and administer all the smaller courts. That way the king and the nobles get what they want.'

Ragna felt excited. She had no greed for wealth, perhaps because she had never lacked for money, but she was eager to gain the power to do good. She had long felt it was her destiny. And now she seemed on the brink of becoming the ruler of Shiring.

She found that she badly wanted the future that Den painted for her. She began to think about how to make sure of it.

'We should do more,' said Ragna. Her strategic brain was back on track. 'Remember what Wynstan and Wigelm did after they killed Wilwulf? They took charge the very next day. No one had time to figure out how to stop them.'

Den looked thoughtful. 'You're right. They still needed royal approval, of course – but once they were in place it was difficult for Ethelred to dislodge them.'

'We should hold court tomorrow morning – in the ealdorman's compound, in front of the great hall. Announce to the townspeople that you and I are taking charge – no, that we already *have* taken charge – pending the king's decision.' She thought for a minute. 'The only opposition will come from Bishop Wynstan.'

'He's ill, and losing his mind; and people know that,' Den said. 'He's not the power he once was.'

'Let's make sure of that,' Ragna insisted. 'When we go to the compound, you should take all your men with you, fully armed, a show of strength. Wynstan has no men-at-arms: he never needed them because his brothers had plenty. Now he has no brothers and no men. He may protest at our announcement, but there will be nothing he can do about it.'

'You're right,' said Den. He looked at Ragna with an odd little smile.

She said: 'What?'

He said: 'You've just proved it. I made the right choice.'

Þ Þ Þ

IN THE MORNING Ragna could hardly wait to see Alain.

She forced herself not to hurry. This was a hugely important public event, and she had long ago learned the importance of giving the right impression. She washed thoroughly, to smell like a noblewoman. She let Osgyth do her hair in an elaborate style with a high hat, to make her even taller. She dressed carefully, in the richest clothes she had with her, to look as authoritative as possible.

But then she could not discipline herself any longer, and she went ahead of Sheriff Den.

The townspeople were already climbing the hill to the ealdorman's compound. The news had evidently got around town already. No doubt Osgyth and Ceolwulf had talked last night of the events in Outhenham, and half the townspeople had heard the story – Ragna's version – by morning. They were avid to learn more.

Den had written to the king last night, before going to bed, and his messenger had left already. It would be some time before a reply came: Den was not sure where the king was, and it could take the messenger weeks to find him.

Ragna went straight to Meganthryth's house.

She saw Alain immediately. He was sitting at the table eating porridge with a spoon, watched by his grandmother, Gytha, and Meganthryth, plus two maids. Ragna realized with a shock that he was no longer a baby. He was taller, his dark hair was getting long, and his face had lost its podgy roundness. He had the beginnings of the nose and chin that characterized the men of Wigelm's family.

She cried: 'Oh, Alain, you've changed!' and she burst into tears.

Gytha and Meganthryth both turned around, startled.

Ragna went to the table and sat by her son. He stared at her thoughtfully with his large blue eyes. She could not tell whether he knew her or not.

Gytha and Meganthryth looked on without speaking.

Ragna said: 'Do you remember me, Alain?'

'Mudder,' he said, in a matter-of-fact tone, as if he had been searching for the right word and was satisfied to have found it; then he put another spoonful of porridge into his mouth.

Ragna felt a wave of relief overwhelm her.

She wiped the tears from her eyes and looked at the other women. Meganthryth's eyes were red and sore. Gytha was dry-eyed, but her face was white and drawn. They had heard the news, evidently, and both were possessed by grief. Wigelm had been evil, but he had been Gytha's son and Meganthryth's lover, and they mourned him. But Ragna felt little compassion. They had connived in the monumental cruelty of taking Alain away from Ragna. They deserved no sympathy.

Ragna said firmly: 'I have come to take back my child.'

Neither woman protested.

Alain put down his spoon and turned his bowl to show that it was empty. 'All gone,' he said. He placed the bowl back on the table.

Gytha looked defeated. All her deviousness had come to nothing in the end. She seemed much changed. 'We were cruel to you, Ragna,' she said. 'It was wicked of us to take your child.'

It was a shocking turnaround, and Ragna was not ready to take it at face value. 'Now you admit it,' she said. 'When you've lost the power to keep him.'

Gytha persisted. 'You won't be as wicked as us, will you? Please don't cut me off from my only grandchild.'

Ragna made no reply. She turned her attention back to Alain. He was watching her carefully.

She reached for him and he held out his arms to be picked up. She lifted him onto her lap. He was heavier than she remembered: she would no longer be able to carry him around half the day. He leaned into her, resting his head on her chest, and she felt the heat of his little body through the wool of her dress. She stroked his hair.

From outside she heard the sound of a large group of people. Den was arriving with his entourage, she guessed. She stood up, still holding Alain in her arms. She went out.

Den was marching across the compound at the head of a large squad of men-at-arms. Ragna joined him and walked by his side. A crowd was waiting for them outside the great hall.

They stopped at the door and turned to face the people.

All the important men of the town stood at the front of the crowd. Bishop Wynstan was there, Ragna saw; and she was shocked by his appearance. He was thin and stooped, and his hands were shaking. He looked like an old man. His face as he stared at Ragna was a mask of hatred, but he seemed too weak to do anything about it, and his weakness appeared to fuel his rage.

Den's deputy, Captain Wigbert, clapped his hands loudly.

The crowd went quiet.

Den said: 'We have an announcement.'

42

KING ETHELRED HELD COURT in Winchester Cathedral, with a crowd of dignitaries wrapped in furs against the bite of approaching winter.

To Ragna's delight, he confirmed everything Sheriff Den had proposed.

Garulf protested, his indignant whine echoing off the stone walls of the nave. 'I am the son of Ealdorman Wilwulf and the nephew of Ealdorman Wigelm,' he said. 'Den is merely a sheriff without noble blood.'

The assembled thanes might have been expected to agree with this, for they all wanted their sons to be rulers too; but their reaction was muted.

Ethelred said to Garulf: 'You lost half my army in one foolish battle in Devon.'

Kings have long memories, thought Ragna. She heard a rumble of agreement from the noblemen, who also remembered Garulf's defeat.

'That will never happen again,' Garulf promised.

The king was unmoved. 'It won't, because you'll never lead my army again. Den is ealdorman.'

Garulf at least had the sense to know when his case was hopeless, and he shut up.

It was not just the battle, Ragna reflected. Garulf's family had defied the king's rule again and again for a decade, disobeying orders and refusing to pay fines. It had seemed that they would get away with it indefinitely, but now at last their insurrection had come to an end. There was justice, after all. A pity it took such a long time coming.

Queen Emma, sitting next to the king on a similar cushioned stool, leaned over and murmured in his ear. He nodded and spoke to Ragna. 'I believe your son has been restored to you, Lady Ragna.'

'Yes, Your Majesty.'

He addressed the court. 'Let no one take the Lady Ragna's child from her.'

It was a fait accompli, but she was glad to have royal approval publicly stated. It gave her security for the future. 'Thank you,' she said.

After the court, the new bishop of Winchester gave a banquet. It was attended by the previous bishop, Alphage, who had come from Canterbury. Ragna was keen to speak to him. It was high time Wynstan was removed from his bishopric, and the only person who could dismiss him was the archbishop of Canterbury.

She wondered how she could contrive a meeting, but Alphage solved the problem by approaching her. 'Last time we were here, I believe you did me a good turn,' he said.

'I'm not sure what you mean . . .'

'You discreetly revealed the news of Bishop Wynstan's shameful illness.'

'I tried to keep my role secret, but Wynstan seems to have ferreted out the truth.'

'Well, I'm grateful to you, for you put an end to his bid to become archbishop of Canterbury.'

'I'm very glad to have been of service to you.'

'So now you're living at King's Bridge?' he said, changing the subject.

'It's my base, though I travel a lot.'

'And is everything well at the priory there?'

'Absolutely.' Ragna smiled. 'I passed through nine years ago, and the place was a hamlet called Dreng's Ferry, with about five buildings. Now it's a town, busy and prosperous. Prior Aldred has done that.'

'A fine man. You know it was he who first warned me of Wynstan's scheme to become archbishop.'

Ragna wanted to ask Alphage to dismiss Wynstan, but she had to tread carefully. The archbishop was a man, and all men hated to be told what to do by a woman. In her life she had sometimes forgotten this, and found her wishes frustrated for that reason. Now she said: 'I hope you'll come to Shiring before you return to Canterbury.'

'Any particular reason?'

'The town would be thrilled by a visit from you. And you might want to observe Wynstan.'

'How is his health?'

'Poor, but it's not really for me to give an opinion,' she said with false humility. 'Your own judgement is undoubtedly best.' It was rare for a man to doubt that his judgement was good.

Alphage nodded. 'Very well,' he said. 'I'll visit Shiring.'

ÞÞÞ

GETTING HIM TO visit was only the beginning.

Archbishop Alphage was a monk, so he lodged at Shiring Abbey. This disappointed Ragna, for she had wanted him to stay at the bishop's residence and get a good long close-up look at Wynstan.

Wynstan should have invited Alphage to dine with him. However, Ragna heard that Archdeacon Degbert had delivered a transparently insincere message saying that Wynstan would love to entertain the archbishop but would not ask him for fear of interfering with his monkish devotions. Wynstan was mad only in phases, it seemed; and when he was in his right mind he could be as sly as ever.

Ragna got Sheriff Den to invite the archbishop to dinner at his compound, so that Den could speak about Wynstan; but the result was another disappointment: Alphage declined. He was a genuine ascetic, and he really did prefer to eat stewed eel with beans in the company of other monks while listening to a reading from the life story of St Swithun.

Ragna was afraid that the two might not meet at all, which would scupper her plan. However, it was automatic that the visiting archbishop would celebrate Mass at the cathedral on Sunday, and Wynstan was obliged to attend, so to her relief the enemies were thrown together at last.

The whole town attended. Wynstan had deteriorated even since she had seen him the day after the death of Wigelm. His hair was greying, and he walked with a cane. Unfortunately, that was not enough to get him unseated. Half the bishops Ragna had ever seen were old and grey and unsteady on their feet.

Ragna believed in the Christian faith and thanked God for its civilizing influence, but she did not spend much time thinking about it. However, the Mass always moved her, making her feel that she had a place in Creation that made sense.

Half her mind was on the service and half on Wynstan. She was worried, now, that he might get through the rite without revealing his insanity. He performed the motions mechanically, almost absent-mindedly, but he was not making any mistakes.

She watched the Elevation of the Host with more than usual attention. Jesus had died so that sinners could be forgiven. Ragna had confessed her murder to Aldred, who was a priest as well as a monk. He had compared her to the Old Testament hero Judith, who had cut off the head of the Assyrian general Holofernes. The story proved that even a murderess could be pardoned. Aldred had assigned her a fasting penance and granted absolution.

The service continued with no manifestation of Wynstan's madness. Ragna felt frustrated. She had had some credit with Alphage, but now it seemed she might have spent it in vain.

The priests began the procession to the exit. Suddenly Wynstan stepped to one side and crouched down. Alphage looked at him, mystified. Wynstan lifted the skirt of his priestly robe and defecated on the stone floor.

Alphage's face was a picture of horror.

It only took a few seconds. Wynstan stood up, rearranged his robes, and said: 'That's better.' Then he rejoined the procession.

Everyone stared at what he had left behind.

Ragna gave a sigh of satisfaction. 'Goodbye, Wynstan,' she said.

Þ Þ Þ

RAGNA RODE TO King's Bridge in the company of Archbishop Alphage, who was returning to Canterbury. He was a joy to talk to: intelligent, educated, sincere in his religion yet tolerant of dissent. He even knew the romantic Latin poetry of Alcuin, which she had loved when she was growing up. She now realized that she had got out of the habit of reading poetry. It had been crowded out of her life by violence, childbirth and imprisonment. Perhaps there would soon be a time when she could read poetry again.

Alphage had dismissed Wynstan immediately. Unsure what to do with the mad bishop, he had asked Ragna's advice, and she had recommended locking Wynstan up for a while in the hunting lodge where she had spent a year imprisoned. She had been savagely pleased with the irony.

Riding into King's Bridge felt to Ragna like coming home, which was odd, she thought, for she had spent relatively little of her life here. But somehow she felt safe. Perhaps it was because Aldred ruled the town. He respected law and justice, and did not judge every issue according to his own interests, not even the priory's interests. If only the whole world could be like that.

She noticed a massive hole in the ground on the site of the projected new church. Large stacks of timber and stones stood around. Clearly Aldred was going ahead without Edgar.

She thanked Alphage for his company and turned aside to her own residence, right opposite the building site, while the archbishop rode a little farther to the cluster of buildings that formed the priory.

She had decided not to move into Wilf's house in Shiring. She could live anywhere in the region, and she preferred King's Bridge.

As she approached her home – which was looking more and more like an ealdorman's compound – Astrid gave a happy snort of recognition, and a moment later the children came running out, Ragna's four boys and Cat's two girls. Ragna jumped out of the saddle and hugged them all.

She was filled with a strange emotion that at first she did not recognize. After a moment she realized that she was happy.

She had not felt like this for a long time.

ÞÞÞ

THE TIMBER BUILDING that had once been the minster was now Aldred's house and place of work. He welcomed Archbishop Alphage, who shook his hand warmly and thanked him again for his help in gaining the archbishopric. Aldred said: 'You'll forgive me, my lord archbishop, if I say I did it for God, not for you.'

'Which is even more flattering,' said Alphage with a smile.

He sat down, declined a cup of wine, and helped himself from a bowl of nuts. 'You were so right about Wynstan,' he said. 'He is now quite mad.'

Aldred raised an eyebrow.

Alphage said: 'Wynstan took a shit in Shiring Cathedral during Mass.'

'In front of everyone?'

'All the clergy and several hundred in the congregation.'

'Lord save us!' said Aldred. 'Did he offer any excuse?'

'He just said: "That's better".'

Aldred let out a bark of laughter then apologized. 'I'm sorry, archbishop, but it is almost funny.'

'I've dismissed him. Archdeacon Degbert will deputize for now.'

Aldred frowned. 'I don't have a high opinion of Degbert. He was dean here when this place was a minster.'

'I know, and I never thought well of him. I told him not to hope for promotion to bishop.'

Aldred was relieved. 'Who, then, will take Wynstan's place?'

'You, I hope.'

Aldred was astounded. He had not been expecting that. 'I'm a monk,' he said.

'So am I,' said Alphage.

'But . . . I mean . . . my work is here. I'm the prior.'

'It may be God's will for you to move on.'

Aldred wished he had been given more time to prepare for this conversation. It was a great honour to be made a bishop, and a tremendous opportunity to further God's work. But he could not bear the thought of abandoning King's Bridge. What about the new church? What about the growth of the town? Who would take his place?

He thought about Shiring. Could he realize his dream there? Could he turn Shiring Cathedral into a world-class centre of learning? He would first have to deal with a group of priests who had become idle and corrupt under Wynstan. Perhaps he could dismiss all the priests and replace them with monks, following the example of Elfric, Alphage's predecessor at Canterbury. But the Shiring monks were under the authority of Abbot Hildred, Aldred's ancient enemy. No, a move to Shiring would set his project back years.

'I'm honoured and flattered as well as surprised, my lord archbishop,' he said. 'But I beg to be excused. I can't leave King's Bridge.'

Alphage looked cross. 'That's a great disappointment,' he said. 'You're a man of unusual potential – you might have my job, one day

– but you'll never rise in the Church hierarchy if you remain merely prior of King's Bridge.'

Once again Aldred hesitated. Few clergymen could be indifferent to the prospect that was being held out to him. But he was struck by a new thought. 'My lord,' he said, thinking aloud, 'is it impossible that the seat of the diocese could be moved to King's Bridge?'

Alphage looked startled. Clearly it was a new thought to him too. He spoke tentatively. 'Certainly I have the power to do that. But you don't have a big enough church here.'

'I'm building a new one, much bigger. I'll show you around the site.'

'I noticed it as I rode in. But when will the church be ready?'

'We can start using it long before it's finished. I've already begun work on the crypt. We could be holding services there in five years.'

'Who's in charge of the design?'

'I asked Edgar, but he turned me down. However, I want a Norman master mason. They're the best.'

Alphage looked doubtful. 'In the interim, would you be willing to travel to Shiring for every major festival – Easter, Whitsun, Christmas – say six times a year?'

'Yes.'

'So I could give you a letter promising to make King's Bridge the bishop's seat as soon as you're able to use the new church?'

'Yes.'

Alphage smiled. 'You drive a hard bargain. Very well.'

'Thank you, my lord.'

Aldred felt jubilant. Bishop of King's Bridge! He was only forty-two.

Alphage became thoughtful again. 'I wonder what I am to do with Wynstan.'

'Where is he now?'

'Locked up in Wilwulf's old hunting lodge.'

Aldred frowned. 'It looks bad, a bishop imprisoned.'

'And there's always the danger that Garulf or Degbert might try to break him out.'

Aldred's face cleared. 'Don't worry,' he said. 'I know just the place for him.'

ÞÞÞ

AT THE END of the evening Ragna stood on Edgar's bridge, listening to the ever-present warble of the river, watching a red sun set downstream, remembering the day she had arrived here for the first time, cold and wet and muddy and miserable, and had looked with dismay at the settlement where she had to spend the night. What a change.

A heron stood on the bank of Leper Island, as still as a tombstone, gazing with intense concentration into the water. As Ragna watched the bird, a vessel appeared, coming upstream fast. She squinted into the sun, trying to make it out. It was a boat with four oarsmen and a passenger standing forward. King's Bridge had to be their destination: it was too late to go farther.

The boat approached the beach in front of the alehouse. There was a black dog aboard, Ragna saw, sitting still in the prow, looking ahead, quiet but alert. Ragna recognized something familiar about the passenger, and her heart seemed to thud in her chest. He almost looked like Edgar. She could not tell: the sun was in her eyes. It might have been wishful thinking.

She hurried along the bridge. As she descended the ramp to the shore she entered the long shadow of distant trees, and she was able to see the traveller more clearly. He jumped off the boat, followed by his dog, and bent to tie a rope to a post; and then she knew.

It was him.

In a flash of understanding so sweet that it hurt she recognized that broad-shouldered shape, the confident way he moved, the easy dexterity of those wide hands, the dip of his large head; and she felt so filled up with joy that she could hardly breathe.

She moved towards him, resisting the impulse to break into a mad run. Then she stopped, struck by a terrible thought. Her heart was telling her that her lover had returned and all would be well – but her head said otherwise. She remembered the two King's Bridge monks who had found Edgar in Normandy. The elder, William, had said: 'People in the town where he's living say he will marry the daughter of the master mason and eventually become master himself.' Had he done so? It was possible. And Ragna knew Edgar, knew for certain that he would not forsake a woman once he had married her.

But if he was married, why had he come back?

Now her heart pounded with fear, not joy. She resumed walking towards him. She saw that his cloak was made of a fine wool cloth, dyed an autumnal red, obviously costly. He had continued to prosper in Normandy.

He finished roping the boat and looked up. She was close enough now to see the wonderfully familiar hazel colour of his eyes. She watched his face as intently as the heron had watched the water. At first she saw anxiety, and realized that he had wondered, just as she had, whether their love could have survived three years of separation. Then he read her expression, and understood instantly how she felt; and at last he broke into a smile that lit up his whole face.

In a trice she was in his arms. He hugged her so hard it hurt. She pressed her palms to his cheeks and kissed his mouth passionately, taking in the old familiar smell and taste of him. She held him tightly for a long time, savouring the ecstatic feeling of his body pressed hard against hers.

At last she relaxed her hold to say: 'I love you more than life.'

He said: 'I'm very glad.'

ÞÞÞ

THAT NIGHT THEY made love five times.

Edgar had not known it was possible, for him or anyone. They did it once, then a second time; then they dozed for a while and did it again. In the middle of the night Edgar's mind wandered, and he thought about architecture and King's Bridge and Wynstan and Wigelm; then he remembered that he was with Ragna at last and she was in his arms, and he wanted to make love again, and so did she, so they did it a fourth time.

Then they talked in low voices, not to wake the children. Edgar told Ragna about Clothild, the daughter of the master mason. 'I was unkind to her, though I never meant to be,' he said sadly. 'I should have told her about you right at the start. I was never going to marry her, even if they offered me the job of king. But now and again I was foolish enough to pretend to myself that I might, and I looked at her fondly, and she took that to mean more than it did.' He studied Ragna's face in the firelight. 'Perhaps I shouldn't have told you that.'

'We have to tell each other everything,' she said. 'What made you come home?'

'It was your father. He was so angry about Wigelm setting you aside. He raged at me as if I were responsible. I was just glad you were divorced.'

'Why did it take you so long to get here?'

'My ship was blown off course and I ended up in Dublin. I was afraid the Vikings would kill me for my cloak, but they took me for a wealthy man and tried to sell me slaves.'

She hugged him hard. 'I'm so glad they let you live.'

Edgar noticed that it was getting light outside. 'Aldred will disapprove of us. By his standards we're fornicators.'

'People sleeping in the same room aren't necessarily having sex.'

'No, but in our case neither Aldred nor anyone else in King's Bridge will have the least doubt.'

She giggled. 'Do you think we're that obvious?'

'Yes.'

She became serious again. 'My beloved Edgar, will you marry me?'

He laughed happily. 'Yes! Of course. Let's do it today.'

'I want Ethelred's approval. I don't want to offend the king. I'm really sorry.'

'Sending a message to him, and getting a reply, could take weeks. Are you saying we have to live apart? I can't stand it.'

'No, I don't think so. If we're promised to one another, and everyone knows it, no one will expect us to sleep apart, except for Aldred. He will still disapprove, but I don't think he'll make a fuss.'

'Will the king say yes to your request?'

'I think so, though it would help if you were a minor nobleman.'

'But I'm a builder.'

'You're a wealthy man and a leading citizen, and I could grant you some lands with a compound so that you would be a thane. Thurstan of Lordsborough died recently, you could take his place.'

'Edgar of Lordsborough.'

'Do you like that idea?'

'Not as much as I like you,' he said.

Then they did it for the fifth time.

43

THE CATHEDRAL SITE WAS busy. Most of the men were digging foundations and stacking supplies. The craftsmen, hired by Edgar from England and Normandy and farther away, were building their lodges, makeshift huts in which they could shape timber and stones in all weathers. They would start putting up walls on Lady Day, 25 March, when there was little further danger of overnight frost freezing the mortar.

Edgar had built his tracing floor. Parchment was too expensive for designs, but there was a cheap alternative. He had embedded planks in the ground to form a shallow box about twelve feet by six and filled the box with a bed of mortar. Scratches in the mortar showed white. With a straight-edge, a sharp iron point and a pair of compasses he could draw all the columns and arches he needed. The whiteness faded over time, so new drawings could be made over old, though the scratch marks remained for years.

Edgar had built his own lodge over the tracing floor, just a wide roof on four posts, so that he could continue to work when it rained. He was kneeling there, staring at a window he had drawn, when Ragna appeared and interrupted him. 'A messenger has arrived from King Ethelred,' she said.

Edgar stood up, his heart pounding. 'What does the king say to our marriage?'

Ragna said: 'He says yes.'

ÞÞÞ

ALDRED STOOD WITH Mother Agatha while the lepers were fed their midday meal. Sister Frith gave thanks for the food, then the disabled men and women crowded around the table with their wooden bowls. 'No pushing, no shoving!' Frith cried. 'There is food for everyone. The last gets the same as the first!' They took no notice.

Aldred said: 'How is he?'

Agatha shrugged. 'Filthy, miserable and mad – the same as most of them.'

When Aldred became bishop he had dismissed all of Wynstan's clergy from Shiring Cathedral, including Archdeacon Degbert, who ended up a penniless village priest in Wigleigh. Aldred replaced Wynstan's men with monks from King's Bridge, under the supervision of Brother Godleof. On the way home, Aldred had picked up former bishop Wynstan from his prison at the hunting lodge and brought him back to Leper Island. Now Wynstan stood with the others, waiting for his meal.

Wynstan was dressed in rags and dirty from his face to his bare feet. He was skinny and his shoulders were slumped. He must have felt cold, but he did not show it. The nun filled his bowl with a thick stew of oats and bacon, and he ate it all quickly, using his unclean fingers.

When he had finished he raised his eyes and, with a flash of recognition, he looked at Aldred.

He approached Aldred and Agatha. 'I shouldn't be here,' he said. 'There has been a terrible mistake.'

'No mistake,' Aldred said, not sure how much Wynstan could understand. 'You committed dreadful sins – murder, forgery, fornication, kidnapping. You're here because of your wrongdoing.'

'But I'm the bishop of Shiring. I'm going to become the archbishop of Canterbury. It's all planned!' He looked around wildly. 'Where am I now? How did I get here? I can't remember.'

'I brought you here. And you're not the bishop any longer. I am.'

Wynstan began to cry. 'It's not fair,' he sobbed. 'It's not just.'

'It is, though,' said Aldred. 'It's very just.'

ÞÞÞ

RAGNA AND EDGAR got married at Shiring.

The party was hosted by Ealdorman Den. At this time of year there was little fresh food, so Den got in huge stocks of salt beef and beans and dozens of barrels of ale and cider.

Every important man in the west of England showed up, and the whole town crowded into the compound at the top of the hill. Edgar moved through the throng, welcoming guests, accepting congratulations, greeting people he had not seen for years.

All four of Ragna's children were there. By the end of the day I'll have a wife and four stepsons, he thought. It was strange.

The buzz of talk changed, and he heard sounds of surprise and admiration. He looked towards the source and saw Ragna, and for a moment he could not breathe.

She wore a dress in a rich dark yellow with flared sleeves finished in embroidered braid, and a sleeveless overdress of dark green wool. Her silk headdress was chestnut brown, her favourite colour, the fabric interwoven with threads of gold. Her glorious red-gold hair swept down behind like a waterfall. At that moment Edgar knew she was the most beautiful woman in the world.

She came to Edgar and took his hands in hers. He looked into Ragna's sea-green eyes and felt unable to believe that she was his.

He said: 'I, Edgar of King's Bridge and Lordsborough, take you, Ragna of Cherbourg and Shiring, to be my wife, and I vow to love you and care for you and be true to you for the rest of my days.'

Ragna replied quietly, with a smile. 'I, Ragna, daughter of Count Hubert of Cherbourg, and lord of Shiring Combe and the Vale of Outhen, take you, Edgar of King's Bridge and Lordsborough, to be my husband, and I vow to love you and care for you and be true to you for the rest of my days.'

Aldred, wearing his bishop's robes and a large silver pectoral cross, spoke a blessing in Latin on their marriage.

Next it was normal to kiss. Edgar had thought about this for years and he was not going to rush it. They had kissed before, but now for the first time they would do so as husband and wife, and it would be different, for they had promised to love one another for ever.

He looked at her for a long moment. She sensed what he was feeling – something that happened often – and she waited, smiling. He leaned slowly towards her and brushed her lips with his own. There was a ripple of applause from the crowd.

He put both arms around her and gently pulled her to himself, feeling her breasts against his chest. Still with his eyes open, he pressed his mouth to hers. They both parted their lips and touched tongues hesitantly, exploring as if for the first time, like adolescents. He felt her hips push towards his own. She reached around him with both arms and pulled him harder, and he heard the crowd laugh and shout encouragement.

Edgar felt swamped with more passion than he could bear. He wanted to touch her with every inch of his body, and he could tell that she felt the same. For a moment he forgot about the audience, and kissed her as if they were alone; but that made the watchers increasingly raucous, and at last he broke the kiss.

His gaze did not leave hers. He felt moved almost to weeping. Repeating the last words of the vow, he murmured: 'For the rest of my days.'

He saw tears come to her eyes, and she said: 'And mine, my love, and mine.'

Acknowledgements

THE DARK AGES left few traces. Not much was written down, there were few pictures, and nearly all buildings were made of wood that rotted away a thousand years ago or more. This leaves room for guesswork and disagreement, more so than with the preceding period of the Roman Empire or the subsequent Middle Ages. Consequently, while thanking my historical advisers, I must add that I have not always followed their advice.

That said, I have been greatly helped by John Blair, Dave Greenhalgh, Nicholas Higham, Karen Jolly, Kevin Leahy, Michael Lewis, Henrietta Leyser, Guy Points and Levi Roach.

As usual my researches were assisted by Dan Starer of Research for Writers in New York City.

On my research trips I was grateful for the kind help of: Raymond Armbrister at St Mary's Church, Seaham; Véronique Duboc at Rouen Cathedral; Fanny Garbe and Antoine Verney at the Bayeux Tapestry Museum; Diane James at Holy Trinity Minster Church, Great Paxton; Ellen Marie Naess at the Viking Ship Museum; and Ourdia Siab, Michel Jeanne and Jean-François Campario at Fécamp Abbey.

I particularly enjoyed meeting Jenny Ashby and The English Companions.

My editors were Brian Tart, Cherise Fisher, Jeremy Trevathan, Susan Opie and Phyllis Grann.

Family and friends who commented on drafts of the book included John Clare, Barbara Follett, Marie-Claire Follett, Chris Manners, Charlotte Quelch, Jann Turner and Kim Turner.

← glastonbury
ᚷᛚᚫᛋᛏᚩᚾᛒᚢᚱᚣ

✝

ᛏᚱᛖᚾᚳᚻ trench
ᚹᛁᚷᛚᛖᛁᚷᚻ
Wigleigh

Bathford
ᛒᚫᛏᚻᚠᚩᚱᛞ

▲▲▲▲
ᛏᚠ

dreng's fe
ᛞᚱᛖᚾᚷ·ᛋ·ᚠᛖᚱᚱᚪ·
🏚

shiring ᛋᚻᛁᚱᛁᚾᚷ
Outhenham
ᚩᚢᛏᚻᛖᚾᚻᚪᛗ
▲▲▲

theodberht'
ᛏᚻᛖᚩᛞ

✝ 🏰
← eXeter
ᛖᚪᛖᛏᛖᚱ